THE HALF BROTHER

Lars Saabye Christensen is Norway's leading contemporary writer. He is the author of ten novels as well as short stories and poetry. Christensen has won many prizes, including the Nordic Prize 2002, the Tarjei Vesaas Prize for First Fiction, the Critics Prize and the Booksellers Prize. His writing has been published throughout Europe, in the US and in Pakistan. Lars Saabye Christensen lives in Oslo.

Kenneth Steven is a young Scottish translator, poet, novelist and children's author whose work has been translated into Scottish Gaelic, German, Dutch, Slovenian and Korean. He has been awarded two bursaries by the Scottish Arts Council and is the winner of a Hawthornden Fellowship. He lives in Perthshire.

Lars Saabye Christensen

THE HALF BROTHER

TRANSLATED FROM THE NORWEGIAN BY
Kenneth Steven

𝒱

VINTAGE

Published by Vintage 2004

2 4 6 8 10 9 7 5 3 1

Vintage acknowledges with gratitude a translation grant from
the Nordic Council of Ministers (Nordbok)

First published in 2001 by J.W. Cappelens Forlag, Oslo,
under the title *Halvbroren*

First published in Great Britain in 2003 by
Arcadia Books

Vintage
Random House, 20 Vauxhall Bridge Road,
London SW1V 2SA

Random House Australia (Pty) Limited
20 Alfred Street, Milsons Point, Sydney
New South Wales 2061, Australia

Random House New Zealand Limited
18 Poland Road, Glenfield,
Auckland 10, New Zealand

Random House (Pty) Limited
Endulini, 5A Jubilee Road, Parktown 2193,
South Africa

The Random House Group Limited Reg. No. 954009
www.randomhouse.co.uk

A CIP catalogue record for this book
is available from the British Library

ISBN 0 099 45916 7

Printed and bound in Great Britain by
Cox & Wyman Limited, Reading, Berkshire

TABLE OF CONTENTS

TRANSLATOR'S NOTE

All translation is a compromise; there are inevitable losses in bringing a richly woven literary text from its native tongue. It is not the *thousands* of words that pose the difficulty, it is the single words – the tiny words that have been chosen by the author for their resonance, for their resemblance to other words in the language, their interplay with different elements of the text. And that is of supreme importance in the work of Lars Saabye Christensen, where all the strands of the narrative are drawn together and held, intricately and often imperceptibly.

To add to the fluidity of the reading of the novel, I have translated the names of *certain* Oslo streets. Others have been left in the Norwegian, names that haven't been envisaged as stumbling blocks, so as to preserve the integrity of the whole 'world' of the original.

A word of explanation has to be given concerning the significance of the moment of Fred's naming, as this is something that is lost entirely in the translation of that section. The noun *fred* means peace in Norwegian.

I debated long and hard over the translation of the phenomenon of the 'pole' – the state-run liquor store – and finally left the word as nearly intact as possible. In Norwegian it is used as a rather euphemistic abbreviation, and I wanted a sense of this to be conveyed in English. It is also important that the connection is made between the ordinary 'pole' and Boletta's North Pole (the licensed premises she frequents).

My sincere thanks to Lars himself for his patient co-operation in the completion of this translation, and also to my good friend John Virang in Oslo, whose guidance on the text has proved invaluable on numerous occasions.

Kenneth Steven
2002

Prologue

'Many thanks!'

I stood on tiptoe, stretched out my arm as far as I could and took back my change from Esther – twenty-five öre from one krone. She bent out through the narrow hatch and laid her wrinkled hand in my golden curls and let it rest there for a while. Not that it was the first time either, so I was beginning to get used to it. Fred had long since turned away, his bag of sugar candy stuffed down into his pocket, and I could tell by the way that he was walking he was furious about something or other. Fred was furious and nothing could have made me more ill at ease. He ground his shoes against the pavement and almost seemed to push his way forward, his head low between his tall, sharp shoulders, as if he were struggling against a strong headwind. Yet it was just a still afternoon in May, a Saturday at that, and the skies over Marienlyst were clear and blue and rolled slow as a giant wheel towards the woods behind town. 'Has Fred begun to talk again?' whispered Esther. I nodded. 'What has he said?' 'Nothing.' Esther laughed a little. 'Hurry up after your brother then. So he doesn't eat everything.'

She took her hand from my hair and for a moment smelled it, while I ran on to catch up with Fred – and it's this I remember, this is the muscle of memory – not the old woman's fingers in my curls, but rather my running and running after Fred, my half brother, and it being all but impossible to catch him. I am the *little* little brother and I wonder why he's so furious; I feel the sharpness of my heart in my chest and a warm, raw taste in my mouth because it's possible that I bit my tongue when I ran out into the street. I clench my fist around my change, that one warm coin, and I chase after Fred – that narrow, dark shadow amid all the light about us. The clock over at the NRK building is showing eight minutes past three, and Fred has already sat down on the bench by the bushes. I sprint all I can over Church Road; because it's a Saturday there's almost no traffic. Only a hearse drives past and all of a sudden breaks down right at the crossroads; the driver, who's clad entirely in grey, gets out and hammers and hammers on the bonnet, swearing. And inside the car, in the extended boot behind the seats, there's a white coffin, though it must be empty because nobody gets buried on a Saturday afternoon – the gravediggers are bound to be off, and if there *is* someone lying there it won't matter anyway, for the dead have plenty of time. That's the way I think. I think that way to have something else to think about, and then the grey driver with his black gloves finally gets the car started again and disappears away towards Majorstuen. I inhale the heavy stink of exhaust and petrol, and hurry over the grass, past the tiny pedestrian crossings and traffic lights and pavements which have been constructed there, like a city built for dwarves. And once a year we're brought here to learn the Green Cross Code by tall, uniformed constables with tight, broad belts. It was there, in the Little City, that I stopped growing. Fred's sitting on the bench looking away towards something else altogether. I sit beside him and it's just the two of us now, this Saturday afternoon in May.

Fred sticks a sharp piece of sugar candy in his mouth and sucks it for a long time; his face bulges and I can see the brown spit beginning to trickle from his lips. His eyes are dark, almost black, and they're trembling – his eyes are trembling. I've seen it all before. He's silent. The pigeons waddle soundlessly in the dull grass. And I can't stand it any longer. 'What is it?' I ask. Fred swallows and a shudder passes through his thin throat. 'I don't talk with food in my mouth.' Fred stuffs more sugar candy in between his teeth and slowly crushes it. 'But why are you so mad?' I whisper. Fred finishes all the sugar candy, crumples up the brown bag and chucks it out onto the pavement. A gull swoops down, frightening away the pigeons, scrapes the concrete with a screech and rises towards a lamp-post. Fred brushes back his fringe but it falls down over his forehead again and he leaves it that way. At long last he says something. 'What was it you said to that old dear?' 'To Esther?' 'Who else? Are you on first name terms now, too?' I'm feeling hungry and queasy. I want to lie down in the grass and sleep there, in amongst the pigeons. 'I don't think I remember what I said.' 'Oh, yes you do. If you think about it a bit.' 'Honest, Fred. I don't remember.' 'So why is it I remember, then? When you don't?' 'I don't know, Fred. Is that why you're mad?' Suddenly he puts his hand on my head. I crumple up. His hand is clenched. 'Are you stupid?' he asks. 'No. I don't know, Fred. Be fair. Please.' He lets his fist lie in my curls. 'Please? You're very near the edge, Tiny.' 'Don't talk like that. Please.' He glides his fingers down my face and they smell sweet; it's almost as if he's rubbing me with glue. 'Shall I tell you exactly what you said?' 'Yes. Do that. Say it.' Fred leans down towards me. I can't bear to look him in the eye. 'You said many thanks.'

I was actually relieved. I thought perhaps I'd said something else that was much worse, something I should never have said that had just slipped out, words I didn't even know – pure crap. I coughed. 'Many thanks? Did I say that?' 'Yes. You bloody well said *many thanks*!' Fred shouted the words, even as we sat there on the same bench, close together. *'Many thanks!'* he screeched. I didn't quite get what he was on about. And now I became even more scared. Soon I would have to go to the loo. I held my breath. I wanted so much to do what was right, but I didn't know what I should answer since I didn't know what he meant. *Many thanks*. And I certainly couldn't start crying. Then Fred would have got even madder, or made fun of me, and that was almost the worst thing possible, that he'd make fun of me. I bent over my knees. 'And so?' I whispered. Fred groaned. 'And so? I reckon you're dumb all right.' 'I'm not, Fred.' 'And how d'you know that, then?' I had to think about it. 'Mum says so. That I'm not dumb.' Fred was silent for a moment. I didn't dare look at him. 'And what does she say about me, then?' 'She says the same,' I said quickly. I felt his arm on my shoulder. 'You don't tell your brother fibs,' Fred said, his voice low. 'Even if I am only your half brother?' The light round us blinded me. And it was just as if the sun were full of sound; a high, resounding noise from every side. 'Is that why you're so angry with me, Fred?' 'What d'you mean?' 'Because I'm only your half brother?' Fred pointed at my hand where my change was still lying, a twenty-five öre coin. It was warm and clammy, like a flat sweet someone had sucked for ages before spitting out. 'Whose is that?' Fred asked. 'It's ours.' Fred nodded several times and I felt all warm with joy. 'But you can have it, of course,' I said quickly. I wanted to give him the coin. Fred just sat staring at me. I grew anxious again. 'Why on earth do you say many thanks? When you're getting back money that's ours?' I drew in my breath. 'Just said it.' 'Well think before you do the next time, right?' 'Yes,' I breathed. ''Cos I don't want a brother who makes a clown of himself. Even though you are only my half brother.' 'No,' I whispered. 'I won't do it again.' 'Many thanks is a load of crap. Never say many thanks. Understand?' Fred got up and gobbed a thick, brown clump of spit in a high arc that landed with a crash in the grass in front of us.

I saw a flock of ants scrabbling towards it. 'I'm thirsty,' Fred said. 'Sugar candy makes me bloody thirsty.'

We went over to Esther's again, to the kiosk just by Majorstuen church; the white church where the vicar wouldn't baptize Fred, and later refused to baptize me too, though that was just because of my name. I positioned myself in front of the hatch, on tiptoe, and Fred leaned against the guttering and lifted his head and nodded, as if we had decided on something monumental. Esther came into view, smiled when she saw it was me, and had to feel my curls one more time. Fred stuck his tongue out as far as he could and pretended to vomit. 'And what's it to be then, young sir?' Esther asked. I shook her fingers out of my hair. 'Carton of juice. Red.' She looked at me, rather taken aback. 'Yes, all right. One red carton of juice it is, then. Message received loud and clear.' She produced what I'd asked for. Fred stood there, in the shadows, almost blinded by the fierce glare of reflected light from the church wall on the other side. Fred just kept staring at me. He didn't let me out of his sight. He was seeing everything. He was hearing everything. I lay the coin quickly in Esther's hand and immediately she gave me back five öre. 'You're welcome,' she said. I looked her in the eye. I stood on tiptoe and kept looking at her right in the eye, swallowing several times as the skies rolled still and slow above us, towards the woods, like a giant blue wheel. I pointed at the five öre piece. 'That's ours!' I said loudly. 'Just so you know!' Esther almost tumbled out of the narrow hatch. 'Blimey. What's got into you?' 'Nothing to say thanks for.' And Fred took me by the arm and pulled me up Church Road. I gave him the carton of juice. I didn't want it. He bit a hole in the corner and squeezed it out leaving a red trail behind us. 'Not bad,' he said. 'You're coming on.' I was so happy. I wanted to give him the five öre too. 'Keep it,' he said. I closed my fingers round the brown coin. I could play pitch and toss with it, if anyone wanted to play pitch and toss with me.

'Many thanks,' I said.

Fred sighed deeply and I was afraid he'd get mad again. I could have bitten off my tongue. But instead he put his arm round me while he squeezed the last drop from the carton of juice into the gutter. 'D'you remember what I told you yesterday?' I nod quickly and barely dare breathe. 'No,' I whisper. 'No? Don't you remember?' I do remember. But I don't want to. Nor can I forget. I'd rather that Fred hadn't begun to talk at all. 'No, Fred.' 'Shall I ask one more time?' 'Yes, I do,' I whisper. And Fred smiles. He can't be mad, not when he smiles like that.

'Shall I kill your father for you, Barnum?' he asks.

My name is Barnum.

THE LAST MANUSCRIPT

The Festival

Thirteen hours in Berlin and I was already a wreck. The telephone was ringing. I could hear it. It woke me. But I was somewhere else. I was somewhere nearby. I was unplugged. I wasn't earthed. I had no dialling tone, just a heart that went on beating heavily and out of sync. The telephone kept ringing. I opened my eyes, from a flat, imageless darkness. Now I could see my hand. It wasn't a particularly beautiful sight. It came closer. It felt my face, investigating, as if it had woken up with a stranger in bed – attached to another man's arm. The stubby fingers suddenly made me queasy. I lay there. The phone kept on ringing. I could hear low voices and, now and then, moaning; had someone already answered the telephone for me? But why was it still ringing then? Why was there someone else in my room? Had I not gone to bed alone after all? I turned round. I could see that the sounds were coming from the television. Two men were forcing themselves on a woman. She hardly looked enthusiastic, just indifferent. She had a tattoo on one of her bottom cheeks – a butterfly – and the choice of site was unfortunate. Her thighs were covered with bruises. The men were overweight and pale, and they barely had erections, but that didn't stop them – they grunted loudly as they took her from every possible angle. It looked awkward and lugubrious. The woman's indifference was for a moment replaced by pain; a grimace twisted her face as one of the men slapped his flaccid cock across her mouth and hit her. My hand left my face. A moment later the picture was gone. If I punched in my room number I could watch twelve more hours of pay TV. I didn't want to see any more. I didn't even remember my room number. I lay sideways across the bed, with my suit jacket half off, probably after an attempt to undress and go to bed properly. I obviously hadn't got far before the bulb went in the innermost cubbyhole in the west wing of my head. Yes, one shoe was lying on the window sill. Had I actually stood there admiring the view, or had I been thinking of something else altogether? Possible. Impossible. I had no idea. One of my knees was hurting. I found my hand again. I shoved it towards the bedside table and, as it hung there like some sick, wide-spanned bird above a white rat blinking with one single red eye, the phone stopped ringing. The hand flew back home. The quiet washed back and pulled down the tight zip in my neck, and licked my spine with an iron tongue. I didn't move for a good while. I had to get myself into water. The green bubble of air had to find calm soon in the capsized flesh, in the hollow of the soul. I could remember nothing. The great eraser had rubbed me out, as on so many occasions before. And the erasers I had already used up were not few. I only remembered what I was called, for who can forget such a name as Barnum? Barnum! Who do these parents really think they are, who condemn their sons and daughters to life sentences behind the iron gates of their own names? Can't you just change your name, as someone who didn't know what they were talking about once suggested? But it doesn't help. A name will pursue you with double the shame if you try to get rid of it. Barnum! For half my life I'd lived with that name. I was on the point of liking it. That was the worst of it. All of a sudden I noticed I was holding something in my other hand, a card key, a plain flat piece of plastic with a number of holes in a particular pattern which one could shove into the door's cash dispenser to empty the room's account, so long as it hadn't been overdrawn by previous occupants who'd left behind only nail clippings under the

bed and a hollow in the mattress. I could have been anywhere. A room in Oslo, a room on Røst, a room without
a view. My suitcase was standing on the floor – the old,
silent suitcase, still not opened, and empty anyway, no
applause in it, just a manuscript, some rushed pages. I'd
come and gone. That's me. Come and gone and crawled
back again. But I could still read. Over the chair by the
window the hotel's white dressing gown was draped. And
on it I could see the hotel's name. Kempinski. Kempinski!
Then I heard the city. I could hear Berlin. I could hear the
diggers in the east and the church bells in the west.
Slowly I got up. The day was in full swing. It had started
without me. And now suddenly I remembered something. I had an appointment. The telephone's red eye kept
blinking. There was a message for me. I didn't give a
damn. Who other than Peder could be calling and leaving
messages right now? Of course it would be Peder. He
could wait. Peder was good at waiting. I had taught him
the art. No-one with half a brain had meetings before
breakfast on the first morning in Berlin – except Peder, my
friend, my partner, my agent – he had appointments
before breakfast, because Peder was in charge. It was
twenty-eight minutes past twelve. The numbers were
illuminated square and green beneath the lifeless TV
screen, and became twelve-thirty precisely between two
irregular heartbeats. I dragged off my clothes, opened the
minibar and drank two Jägermeisters. They stayed where
they were. I drank one more, and went out to the bathroom and vomited for safety's sake. I couldn't remember
the last time I'd eaten. The toilet roll seal was unbroken.
I hadn't even been to the loo yet. Then I brushed my
teeth, slung on the dressing gown, stuck my feet in the
hotel's white slippers, and before going out saw that the
telephone's red eye was still staring at me. But Peder
could just wait; that was his job. Peder could waffle on
until the room he sat in was on fire.

  I took the lift down to the swimming pool, borrowed a
pair of trunks, drank a beer and one more Jägermeister,

then managed three lengths before I was knackered. I lay
down by the side of the pool. Classical music wafted from
loudspeakers that I couldn't see – Bach, of course – syn-
thetic versions, untouched by human hand. A few ladies
lay on their backs and floated in tranquillity. They floated
in an American way, their arms like wings, and with sunglasses on, sunglasses they constantly had to shove up
onto their foreheads to see better, to catch a passing
glance. For maybe Robert Downey Jr himself might walk
unevenly along the poolside, or Al Pacino in his platform
shoes, or even my old friend Sean Connery – I'd have
treated him to a proper drink and caught up with his
news. But no one from that level of heaven was in view
and I wasn't much of a pretty sight myself. The ladies
flicked their sunglasses down once more and kept themselves afloat with relaxed, blue arms; they were a company of angels with small, inflated stomachs. Suddenly
this made me feel so placid, so knackered and placid and
almost happy. I floated too. I floated in a Norwegian way,
with my hands at my sides and my fingers working like
shovels to keep my balance, sculling water behind me.
Now I was in water. Then angst gripped me – it always
came abruptly, even though I knew it *would* come, in the
same way as snow. Angst crept into my tranquillity. Had
something happened during the night? Was there someone I had to buy flowers for, say sorry to, ask forgiveness
from, work for nothing for, or whose feet I had to kiss?
No idea. Anything could have happened. I was in the grip
of misgivings. I turned over, making waves under the
American ladies, clambered up the unsteady steps like
some hunchbacked hermaphrodite, and heard a low
ripple of laughter passing over the water. At that moment
Cliff Richard appeared from the changing rooms, the man
himself, wearing a hotel dressing gown and slippers. His
hair lay like a plateau on his head, and his face was hale
and he held it high. He looked like a mummy who'd fled
from the pyramid of the sixties. He'd aged well, in other
words, and the ladies out there showed a bit of interest;

they breathed like friendly porpoises, even though Cliff wasn't necessarily at the top of their wish lists. But for me he was more than good enough. He made me actually forget my fear for a moment; by his sheer proximity he gave me a break, just as he did back then, in that life that is our story, my story and Fred's story, and which I just call *that time*, when I sat in our room, that time, in Church Road, with my ear fastened to the record player listening to 'Livin' Lovin' Doll'. While Fred lay dumb on his bed with wide eyes; he hadn't spoken in twenty-two months, for as long as elephants are pregnant; he hadn't spoken a single word since the Old One died, and everyone had given up trying to get him to speak, whether it was Mum, Boletta, the teacher, the school dentist, Esther from the kiosk, God or anyone else; nobody got a word out of him, least of all me. But when I lifted the pickup to play 'Livin' Lovin' Doll' for the twentieth time, Fred got up from his bed, tore it off, went down into the backyard, chucked the gramophone into the bin and started talking. It took a Cliff to do that. And I wanted to thank him for it. But Sir Cliff Richard just walked past me in a wide arc, sat astride an exercise bike between the mirrors in the corner and pedalled away towards his own reflection, without getting any closer, like a mummy with tennis elbow. And my hand slid over the bar counter and picked up the first thing it came in contact with – gin and tonic – the Real McCoy. Four different clocks showed the time in New York, Buenos Aires, Djakarta and Berlin. I made do with Berlin. Quarter to two. Peder would be sweating now. He'd be making small talk, apologizing, fetching beer and coffee and sandwiches, phoning hotels, searching for me, leaving messages, chasing round to the press centre and nodding to all those he remembered, bowing to all those he didn't remember, and leaving his card with all those who didn't remember him. I could almost hear him saying – *Barnum'll be coming soon, he's probably just taken a roundabout route, you know how it is, as often as not the best ideas come from the most muddled heads, and I've just got the practical imagination to transform them into reality – let's drink to Barnum*! Yes, Peder would definitely be sweating by now and it would do him good. I laughed, laughed loudly at the side of the swimming pool in the Kempinski Hotel, while Cliff Richard raced on his bike with the three mirrors and the gazes of the fat American ladies, and just as suddenly as both angst and laughter had hit home so a shadow enveloped me. What was the matter with me? What twisted delight had carried me off, what sort of black humour possessed me? I froze. For a moment I staggered there on the green marble tiles. I sucked that laughter into me. I called it back. This wasn't the stillness before the storm. This was the stillness that makes cats tremble long before the rain begins to fall.

I showered and wondered for a while if I should go and lie in the solarium. A hint of a tan and a facial before the meeting could be beneficial. But I was in an awkward and restless frame of mind. I got myself a beer instead. The waiter gave me a thin smile along with the bottle. It struck me suddenly how young he was. He wore the hotel uniform with a clumsy dignity, almost defiantly, like a child who's taken his father's suit. I reckoned he was from the former East Germany; it was something about the defiance that made me think that. He'd begun the long climb to the top from the swimming pool at the Kempinski. 'Mr Barnum?' he said in a low voice. He evidently believed that was my surname. He wasn't alone there. I forgave him. 'Yes. That's me.' 'There's a message for you.' He handed me a broad envelope with the hotel logo on it. Peder had found me in the end. Even if I'd hidden behind the fish sheds on the island of Røst he'd have found me. If I was sleeping in a drunken stupor, the odds were it would be Peder who roused me. And if I woke at Coch's Hostel on Bogstad Road, it would be because Peder had hammered on the door. I leaned against the bar. 'What's your name?' I asked. 'Kurt, sir.' I nodded in the direction of the mirrors in the corner. 'D'you see that guy there, Kurt? Cycling away?' 'Yes, sir,

I can see him.' 'Yes, but do you see who it is?' 'Sorry, sir. No.' And I realized, slowly, that I was old now. 'It doesn't matter, Kurt. Just take a Coke over to him. A Diet Coke. And put it on my bill.'

I folded the envelope four times and put it in the pocket of my dressing gown. If Peder wanted to make me sweat too, he would have his wish fulfilled. I took my beer with me into the sauna and found a place for myself on the top ledge. There was someone sitting there whom I half-recognized but couldn't quite place, so I acknowledged her without actually meeting her gaze – just a quick nod – my speciality, my personal gesture to the world. But the others stared right at me, quite brazenly. I just prayed there weren't any fellow countrymen present – scriptwriters from Norwegian Film, journalists from the gossip columns, chatterboxes from magazines, or directors. I immediately regretted this move of mine, this mad detour, because in here everybody was supposed to be naked, and there were both men and women present. And the one with a towel round his waist was an intruder who put all the others in a terrible dilemma. I was the clothed one who made their nakedness immediately visible and unbearable – all the varicose veins, the flat bums, the spare tyres, the sagging breasts, the scars, the rolls of skin, and moles that might be malignant. There was nothing else to be done. I couldn't retreat because that would only have served to reveal my cowardice and brand me a voyeur, and the festival still had three days to run. Reluctantly I folded my towel beside me to show them that I too could be natural, unafraid of revealing my vulnerability. I sat with my legs crossed, stripped in a German sauna, marvelling at the fact that in this rigidly law-abiding and humourless land, men and women were more or less obliged to sit together naked in order to sweat a bit. In ultra-natural Norway, the country that's only just broken free of its glaciers, this type of behaviour would have prompted a constitutional crisis and letters to the editor. But there was a sort of logic in it being

mandatory here. There was just one sauna in the hotel
and this was for the use of both men and women,
unclothed and at the same time. If it had been optional
the whole thing would have been indecent. The war had
to have something to do with it. Everything here had
something to do with the war, and I thought about the
concentration camps – that final shower where men and
women were separated, once and for all, and about the
precision of those mass murderers. There was even a
camp for females, Ravensbruck, and for a moment,
almost excited, it crossed my mind that this could be used
in some way, this leap, this linkage between the Holo-
caust and a chance meeting in the Kempinski sauna
during the film festival in the new Berlin. But as so often
happened lately, the idea fizzled out. The thought faded
away, the spark wasn't trapped in time, and as it flickered
out I sank deeper into self-doubt. What did I really have
to offer? Which stories was I capable of handling? How
much can you steal before you're caught? How much can
you lie before you're believed? Hadn't I always been a
doubter, a run-of-the-mill doubter? Yes, I'd doubted
almost everything, including myself; in fact I wasn't even
sure there was someone who could be described as a 'me'
at all. In periods of gloom I considered myself just a piece
of meat put into a biological system that went under the
name of Barnum. I had doubted everything, apart from
Fred. Fred was indubitable, he was beyond doubt. I
remembered what my father used to say – *It's not what you
see that counts, but rather what you think you see.* I emptied
the bottle and now recognized one of those who was sitting there. It was just as I'd feared – a well-known critic
and old acquaintance whose name I won't mention – we
simply called her the Elk because she always reminded us
of a sunset. She had written in her time that I was 'a Volk-
swagen among Rolls Royces', but I never read that article
because at the time I was out of favour generally. Peder
planned legal action for harassment, something that mercifully never came to pass, but if she wanted to play

games with metaphors she'd come to the wrong man. Now she was looking in my direction and starting to smile, and even though she seemed far less pompous in here than in her columns, looking almost like a slightly over-ripe fruit, I was still keen to avoid returning the smile. Besides, I might have said something I shouldn't. She was my ill omen. What doom did she herald this time? I didn't dare imagine. I smiled. 'To hell with you!' I said. I leant forwards over my knees and coughed violently. It couldn't be true. My tongue had become restive again. The tongue was a banana skin. *Your tongue is a slide,* Fred used to say. It was only me who'd heard. To hell with you. But the Elk looked up in surprise; I coughed my lungs out and was on the point of throwing up, when yet again Cliff Richard came to my rescue. For at that moment he came into the sauna, with a Coke in his hand; he was reminiscent of the cover of 'Livin' Lovin' Doll'; he stood for a second or two by the glass timer in which the sand dropped and gathered. Then Cliff sat down beside me on the uppermost ledge. It was cramped. It would soon be too hot. The needle was at ninety. The Elk had had enough. She sneaked out behind her towel and gave a last quick glance over her shoulder. Was she laughing? Was she laughing at me? Would she have a tale to tell in the bars tonight? Someone threw water over the stone chips so they hissed. The humidity was like boiling fog. I turned towards Cliff. He wasn't sweating. He was quite dry. Every hair was in place. His skin was finely bronzed. Now at last I could finally tell him. 'Thanks,' he said suddenly. 'For the Coke.' 'It's me that should be doing the thanking,' I said. 'Thank *you*.' Cliff lifted the bottle and smiled. 'For what?' 'It was your song that made my brother talk,' I replied. He looked embarrassed for a moment. 'It wasn't my song but the power of God.'

It got too hot. I took my towel and tottered out, dizzy and thirsty, showered again and caught a glimpse of Kurt at the bar. He nodded discreetly and blinked. He was my man now. I took the lift up to my room. The phone still displayed its red light. I lifted the receiver and dropped it again, threw my dressing gown onto the bed, changed into my suit and put a bottle from the minibar in each pocket. That suit had many pockets. I was armed with spirits. Then I drank the final Jägermeister and it remained hanging there like a burning column all the way from throat to innards; I ate a spoonful of toothpaste and put extra insoles in my new Italian shoes. I was all ready for the meeting.

And what could I possibly know about everything that happened in my absence, moves that were beyond my control? I had no idea. I was still unaware, in the grip of misgivings, nor did I want to know. I stood in the slow-sinking lift with mirrors on every side, even the ceiling. I just wanted to *be* in that moment, a man of his own generation who took one second at a time, frozen into the tiniest of all epochs, where there was only room for me. I caught a glimpse of my face in the mirrors and imagined a child who falls, gets up again and only starts howling when he sees the terrified and anxious humans around him – like a delayed pain, the echo of the shock. I had time to gulp some vodka. Then a white-haired porter opened the door and wanted to follow me out with an umbrella. I gave him five marks so he wouldn't. He looked aggrieved at the banknote, and then suddenly it had vanished between the smooth, grey fingers, and it was impossible to tell if I had offended by giving him too much or too little. He resembled a servant from colonial times. He was the one who tied up the loose ends at the Kempinski Hotel. It was he who broke the seals on the toilet rolls. I went out onto the red carpet, which was already worn at the edges. Four black limos with soot-dark windows were parked at the pavement edge. None of them was for me. There's an old saying in this business: *No limo, no deal.* I didn't give a damn. The vodka burned at the back of my tongue. I lit a cigarette. Two television crews, one from CNN and the other from NDR, were waiting for something to happen. A thin film of rain fell over Berlin. The smell of ashes. The furious noise from building sites. Cranes slowly swung round, barely visible beneath the low clouds. God was playing with Meccano. Yet another limo – a long, white locomotive with American streamers – stopped right in front of the hotel, and a woman with the straightest back I had ever seen emerged from it. Nineteen umbrellas were put at her disposal. She laughed, and her laughter was drenched with whisky, thickened by tar and polished with rough sandpaper. She never stopped laughing and started over the red carpet, waving with a thin hand that crept with the elegance of a pickpocket between the raindrops. And there was no one who could walk a red carpet like her. It was Lauren Bacall. It was none other than Lauren Bacall. This was her right here, in flesh and blood, each and every gram of her. She filled her own self to the ends of her fingers, to the lobes of her ears, to her very eyebrows. The umbrellas turned inside out above her as she jutted out her chin. She had just invaded Germany. And I simply stood there, fastened to the electric sight – Lauren Bacall walking slowly and powerfully past me – and I was left standing in the aftermath of her passing. And it's like a back-to-front omen of doom, a mirror-image *déjà vu*; I see it all in front of me, Rosenborg cinema, row 14, seats 18, 19 and 20, *The Big Sleep*, with Vivian sitting in the middle. It's close and clear, I can even feel the new turtleneck that's scratching my neck, and I can hear Lauren Bacall whispering to Humphrey Bogart, with that voice that gives us goose pimples in our mouths and restlessness in the very marrow of our spines – *A lot depends on who's in the saddle.* And Peder and I put our arms round Vivian at the same time; my hand meets Peder's fingers and nobody says a word but Vivian smiles, she smiles to herself, and leans backwards, into our arms. And yet when I turn towards her I see that she's crying.

And now I was standing in the rain in Berlin beside the red carpet, outside the Kempinski Hotel. Something had happened. Someone was still calling out and I couldn't

hear a thing. The lights had gone out, the limos had
driven elsewhere. The same porter took hold of my arm.
'Is everything all right, sir?' 'What?' His face came closer.
Everyone has to bend down to me. 'Sir, is everything all
right?' I nodded. I looked around me. The cranes were
still; God couldn't be bothered with Meccano any more,
or maybe it was just that the clouds had piled across the
sky in the opposite direction and made it look like that.
'Are you sure, sir?' A cigarette was floating in the gutter.
Someone had lost a camera. It lay there and the spool was
winding backwards. 'Would you get me a taxi?' 'But of
course, sir.' He blew a whistle he had at the ready in his
hand. I got out some money, wanting to give it to him, for
he deserved it. But he shook his head and looked away.
'Just keep it, sir.' Quickly I put the money back in my
pocket. 'Many thanks,' I said.

The taxi arrived and the porter opened the door for me.
Inside it smelled of spices or incense. A prayer mat lay
rolled up on the front seat. 'Zoo Palatz,' I said. The driver
turned quickly and smiled. A gold tooth shone in the
middle of his black mouth. 'Shall I stop by the zoo?' I had
to smile myself. 'No, at the Festival Centre. The animals
there are more amusing.'

It took half an hour to get there. It would have taken
five minutes on foot. I swallowed some cognac and
nodded off. In my sleep an image appeared – Fred dragging a coffin over snow in the yard. The driver had to
wake me. We were there. He laughed. Now I was hearing
it. The compassionate laughter. The gold tooth blinded
me. I paid far more than I needed to and perhaps he
believed it was a misunderstanding, that I was a tourist
who couldn't count, or else a tipsy cinema manager in an
over-expensive suit. He wanted to give me some money
back, that honest Berlin Muslim, but I was already out on
the pavement, between ruins and cathedrals, between
monkeys and stars. Someone immediately wanted to sell
me a leather jacket. I shoved them out of the way. It
stopped raining. The cranes continued drawing their slow

circles, and the skies over Berlin were suddenly clear and all but translucent. A chill sun pierced me right in the eyes as a flock of doves rose up as one and cut the light to pieces.

I went into the Festival Centre. Two armed guards checked my accreditation card with its tiny picture, taken the evening before – *Barnum Nilsen, screenwriter*. They stared overlong at me and let me through the security zone, the hallowed portals separating those who belonged from those who didn't. Now I belonged. People were tripping over each other like lunatics, hands crammed with beer, brochures, cassettes, mobiles, posters and business cards. The women were tall and slender, their hair done up, their glasses on strings round their necks and all wearing tight, grey skirts as if they had come straight from the same shop. By and large, the men were fat, short, of my age, and with bloodshot expressions that were intensely strained. You could hardly have told the lot of us apart, and at least one of us would die before the day was done. On a giant screen the trailer for a Japanese gangster film was being shown.

Aesthetic violence was obviously on its way in. To kill slowly was acceptable. Someone handed me a glass of sake. I drank. I was given a refill. I carpet-bombed my liver. Bille August was being interviewed by Australian television. His shirt was as white as ever. They should have asked him about that. *How many white shirts do you have? How often do you change shirts?* Elsewhere Spike Lee stood and gesticulated in front of a camera. And through all of this stormed Peder, the knot in his tie hanging down over his middle and his mouth moving all the time – it looked as if he was hyperventilating or trying hard to passively smoke. It couldn't be that it was Peder who would die in the course of the evening. He came to a halt in front of me, completely breathless. 'Well then,' he said. 'You're here.' 'Most of me.' 'How drunk are you?' 'Five and a half.' Peder leaned closer, his nostrils flaring. 'This looks more like postal surcharge, Barnum.' 'Not a bit of it. I'm in control.' I liked it when Peder used our old sayings. But Peder wasn't laughing. 'Where the hell have you been?' 'In the sauna.' 'The sauna? Do you have any idea how long we've been sitting waiting for you? *Do* you?' Peder shook my arm. He'd lost his equilibrium. 'I've bloody well said so many nice things about you I could bloody well vomit!' He started to drag me in the direction of the Scandinavian section. 'Relax,' I told him. 'I'm here now.' 'Can you not get yourself a mobile phone, damn it! Like other normal people!' 'I don't want a brain tumour, Peder.' 'Then get yourself a pager! I'll bloody well buy you a pager myself!' 'D'you think they work in saunas?' 'They work on the moon!' 'You always find me just the same, Peder.' He suddenly stopped and looked at me hard. 'You know what? The more time goes on the more you become like that bloody nutter brother of yours!' And when Peder said that every fuse inside me detonated and time came at me from all sides. I grabbed hold of his jacket and pressed him up against the wall. 'Never say that again! Never!' Peder looked at me thunderstruck, sake all down his trousers. 'Damn it all, Barnum. I didn't mean it like that.' I think people were starting to stare. I could barely recognize the old rage that was burning inside me. Yet it almost did me good. It was something to build on. 'I couldn't give a shit about what you think! But never compare me to Fred. All right?' Peder tried to smile. 'Fair enough! Let me go, Barnum.' I had to give it a bit of time. Then I let Peder go. He stood completely still by the wall, amazed and embarrassed. The fires of rage inside me began to cool and left in their wake only shame, angst and perplexity. 'I just don't want to be reminded of him,' I murmured. 'I'm sorry,' Peder breathed. 'It was thoughtless of me to say what I did.' 'It's all right. Let's just forget it. Forgive me.' I took out my handkerchief and tried to wipe the Japanese alcohol from his trousers. Peder didn't move. 'Shall we get ourselves to this meeting?' he asked. 'Who's there?' He sighed. 'Two Danes and an Englishman.' 'That's funny. Is it a joke? Two Danes and an

Englishman.' 'They have offices in London and Copenhagen. They had a fair bit to do with *Driving Miss Daisy*. I told you all this yesterday, Barnum.' I'd spilt sake all over his shoes too. I went down on my knees and started polishing them as best I could. Peder began kicking me. 'Pull yourself together!' he hissed. I got up again. 'What do they want, basically?' 'What do they want? What do you think? To meet you, of course. They love *The Viking*.' 'Thanks a lot, Peder. Do we have to be all smarmy now?' 'No. We're going now, Barnum.'

And off we went. The crowds were diminishing all the time. It was typical that the Norwegian stand was situated furthest away in a corner; we still hadn't progressed beyond *The Trials of the Fisherfolk*, that keystone of Norwegian melancholy, and it had pushed us out to the very fringes of Europe and of the Festival. It took a whole expedition to reach Norway. Peder glared at me. 'You bloody well sound like a whole minibar when you walk.' 'It'll be empty again soon, Peder.' I opened the whisky and drank it. Peder gripped my arm. 'We need this, Barnum. It's serious.' '*Miss Daisy*? Wasn't that basically a really crap film?' 'A crap film? D'you know how many nominations it got? These are big boys. Bigger than us.' 'Why have they bothered hanging around for three hours then?' 'I've told you, Barnum. They love *The Viking*.'

They were sitting at a table in an enclosed section within the bar. They were in their early thirties, wore tailor-made suits, with sunglasses in their breast pockets, and had ponytails, earrings, large stomachs and small eyes. They were men of their time. I had already begun to dislike them. Peder breathed deeply and pushed up the knot in his tie. 'You'll be nice, polite and sober, Barnum?' 'And ingenious.' I slapped Peder on the back. It was soaking. And then we went in to meet them. Peder clapped his hands. 'The wanderer has returned! He got mixed up at the zoo! Didn't notice the difference!' They got up. Smiles were polished. Peder had sunk as low as platitudes and it wasn't even three o'clock. One of the Danes, Torben,

leaned over the ashtray where two cigars lay dying. 'Is
Barnum a pseudonym or your real name?' 'It's my real
name. But I use it as a pseudonym.' There was a ripple of
laughter at this and Peder attempted to get us to raise our
glasses, but the Dane had no wish to give up so easily. 'Is
it your Christian name or your surname?' 'Both. Depends
who I'm talking to.' Torben smiled. 'Wasn't Barnum an
American con man? *There's a sucker born every minute.*'
'Wrong,' I said. 'It was a banker who said that. David
Hannum. But it was Barnum who said *Let's get the show on
the road.*' Finally Peder managed to squeeze in a toast. We
clinked glasses and now it was the turn of the other Dane,
Preben, to lean over the table. 'We simply love *The Viking*.
A magnificent script.' 'Many thanks,' I said, and drained
my schnapps glass. 'Just a shame it's never become a
film.' Peder leapt in. 'Let's not get bogged down in technicalities.' 'Oh, but I think we should.' Peder kicked me
under the table. 'We have to look forwards,' he said. 'New
projects. New ideas.' I was on the point of getting up and
couldn't manage it. 'But if you think the script is magnificent, why don't you go ahead and make the film?' Peder
looked down and Torben twisted in his chair as if he was
sitting on a gigantic drawing pin. 'If we'd got Mel Gibson
to play the lead it might have been possible.' The other
Dane, Preben, leaned over towards me. 'Besides, action is
out,' he said. 'Action is old-fashioned.' 'But what about
Vikings in outer space?' I asked. One of the mobiles went
off. They all began fumbling for their own like rather tired
gunfighters. It was Tim, the Englishman, who won. There
was talk of high sums and a couple of equally elevated
names in passing – Harvey Keitel, Jessica Lange. There
was no alternative but to smile at one another and drink.
I managed to get up and go to the loo. I swallowed some
gin, leaned with my forehead against the wall and tried to
work out what I should say. I didn't want to give them
what I had. I was the empty-headed scriptwriter they had
waited for for three hours. The mirror image from the lift
was suddenly vivid before me. It was no pretty picture.

My damaged eyelid hung down heavily. I tried to find a moment to hide myself away in. But I didn't find it. When I got back Peder had exchanged my schnapps for coffee. I ordered a double schnapps. Tim was sitting ready with his time-manager, more hefty than the Bible in the Kempinski Hotel. 'As you know, Barnum, you're high on the list of scriptwriters we want to work with.' Peder grinned from ear to ear. 'Have you any fixed projects?' I asked. 'We would like to hear what you have with you.' 'After you,' I said. 'Then I'll have more of an idea of the lie of the land.' Tim looked slowly from me to the Danes. Peder was sweating profusely again. 'Barnum likes to play ball,' he said quickly. It sounded so meaningless that I couldn't help laughing. Barnum likes to play ball. Peder kicked my leg again. Now we were behaving like some old married couple. Suddenly there was schnapps in front of me. Torben took over. 'OK, Barnum. We're willing to play ball. We're keen to do *The Wild Duck*. As I've said, action is out. The public wants what's familiar, what's close to home. Like the family. Hence *The Wild Duck*.' Peder sat and stared at me continuously. It was extremely exasperating. 'This is something for you, Barnum,' he finally said. 'You'd turn the piece around for film in a couple of months, right, Barnum?' But no one was listening to Peder now. 'Would it be a Norwegian production?' I asked. 'Or Scandinavian?' 'Bigger,' Torben replied, smiling. 'American. Keitel. Lange. Robbins. There's no reason why we shouldn't bring in Max or Gitta. But the dialogue'll be in English. Or else the money won't be there.' 'And we'd have to update a bit,' Preben put in quickly. 'It would be set in our time. *The Wild Duck* of the nineties.' 'What's the point of that?' I asked. 'Of course it would be set in the present,' Peder said. 'We're not interested in costume drama, are we?' Quiet fell for a moment. I discovered another schnapps. Tim whispered something to Preben who then turned to me. 'We were thinking of something along the lines of *Rainman* meets *Autumn Sonata*.' I had to lean closer. 'Excuse me? Who meets

what?' 'We only want to illustrate Ibsen's genius,' said
Torben. 'And fundamentally his timelessness.' 'Timelessness? *Miss Daisy* meets *Death of a Salesman*, so to speak?'
Torben's expression looked a little wilted. There was a
momentary burst of laughter from the others. Peder
couldn't stand it any longer. He tried to salvage the situation. 'Anyone want something to eat?' he asked. Nobody
answered. Peder lit up. He'd given up smoking eight years
ago. Torben clasped his hands and looked at me over his
knuckles. 'And what kind of ball are you playing,
Barnum?' 'Porn films,' I answered. 'Porn films?' 'I sat in
my room this morning watching pay TV. And I realized
just how untalented and awkward these porn films really
are. No dramatic composition. Pathetic characterization.
Appalling casting. Particularly bad dialogue. Repulsive
sets.' Torben was getting impatient. 'You're meaning
erotic films, right?' 'No, no, I'm talking about porn. Hard-
core porn. With strong narrative, interesting characters
and razor-sharp composition. An Aristotelian build-up to
orgasm. Porn for a modern audience. For women as well
as for men and all the rest of us. It's *Nora* meets *Deep
Throat*. It's timeless.'

It was the Englishman who got up first. The Danes followed. They shook hands with Peder. Business cards were
exchanged. 'We'll keep in touch,' Peder said. 'Barnum can
get through a first draft in a couple of months.' 'Remind
him it's Ibsen,' Torben said. 'Not pay TV!' Peder gave a
shout of laughter. 'No worries! I've got Barnum under
control.'

The big boys left. We remained sitting. Peder was taciturn. Peder is the only person I describe in such a way.
When Peder elected to be silent, he truly became taciturn.
Now he was taciturn as never before. I've learned to live
with it. If there's anything in this world I'm able to do it's
to be in the company of taciturn people. All you have to
do is to shut up yourself and see who says something
first. Peder lost. 'Well, that went splendidly,' he said and
looked at me. 'You arrived three hours late and when you

finally did arrive you were quite unapologetic, still drunk as a lord and empty-handed. Quite unbelievable. Cheers, Barnum.' We drank for a bit and then it was my turn to say something. 'D'you think Meryl Streep'll play the duck?' I asked. Peder looked away. 'You're right on the edge, Barnum. Good God. Aristotelian porn!' 'What do you mean by *on the edge*?' 'You know exactly what I mean.' 'No, I don't, as a matter of fact.' Peder turned round sharply to face me. 'I've seen this before, Barnum. I've seen you fall. And I can't be bothered following after you any longer.' I got up. Suddenly I was scared. It was that image from the lift which returned, a whole hive of faces that stung me, one after another. 'Damn it, Peder. I hate the way they talk. *Rainman* meets *Autumn Sonata*. All that shit they come out with. I just loathe it.' 'Yes, yes. I hate it every bit as much as you do. But do you see me putting on airs and graces? That's the way they talk. They all talk like that. *The Graduate* meets *Home Alone* and *Waterfront* meets *Pretty Woman*. One day we'll talk like that too.' Peder put down his schnapps, rested his head in his hands and became taciturn once again. 'I met Lauren Bacall,' I told him. Slowly Peder looked up. 'What are you on about?' I sat down again. I had to be seated to tell him this. 'I saw Lauren Bacall,' I repeated. 'I almost touched her.' Peder moved his chair closer, the edge of a smile just visible. '*Our* Lauren Bacall?' 'Peder, now. Is there any other Lauren Bacall than ours?' 'Of course not. Forgive me. I'm not quite myself.' At that moment I saw three moneybags leaving the place. I took Peder's hand; it was warm and trembling. 'What did she look like?' he breathed. I took my time. 'Like a sphinx,' I replied. 'Like a blue sphinx that has torn loose from a floodlit plinth.' 'Good, Barnum.' 'It was raining and she didn't get wet, Peder.' 'I can see it all before me, Barnum.' I think that for a moment too Peder was transported into dreams. His face became quite childlike, and I could clearly see the goose pimples from the collar of his shirt to his ears, as though they had frozen there that night in row 14 of

Rosenborg cinema, when together we put our arms round
Vivian as Lauren Bacall said with those husky, inflaming
words – *Nothing you can't fix*.

Then it was as if he awoke and had suddenly aged. A
great furrow I'd never noticed before slanted down from
his left eye, in the midst of lines that had long been there,
and that furrow created an imbalance in his face which
threatened to make his head topple right over. Peder and
I were beginning to resemble one another. 'Vivian called,
by the way,' he said. 'I think she's worried about Thomas.'
'Vivian has always been worried.' Peder shook his head
sorrowfully. 'I think we should buy something nice for
Thomas.' I tried to smile. I failed miserably. 'Of course we
should,' I laughed. 'Remember what the big boys said?
It's the family that counts now.' Peder sank into his glass
and was taciturn for a time. 'Everyone thinks you're a
sod,' he breathed at last. I heard him saying the words,
but they didn't get through to me. 'Everyone?' I asked.
Now he was looking at me. 'I can't think of anyone right
at this minute who doesn't think so,' he said. 'Thomas,
too?' Peder turned away. 'Thomas is such a quiet boy,
Barnum. I don't know what he understands.' I lit a cigarette. My mouth was sore. I lay my hand over Peder's fingers. 'Maybe we can buy him something together?
Something really special. How about that?' 'Of course,'
Peder said.

Later on we dragged ourselves over to the festival bar.
It was there the important players hung out. Peder maintained that we had to be visible. That was how he put it.
We had to be on course, in the groove, at the right place
and at the right time. We ate greasy sausages to keep our
balance. We drank X-ray fluid with ice. We became visible. There was plenty of talk concerning Sigrid Undset,
and whether *any* male director was capable of making
Kristin Lavransdatter's film. This was the elite. I didn't
mix – apart from drinks, and I thought about Thomas. I
was a sod. I was going to buy a massive present for him;
I'd buy a whole wall he could write on and a crane from

Berlin. I'd take with me God's Meccano set, so that
Thomas, Vivian's son, could screw the skies back
together again. The voices were coming from all around
now. I drank myself into oblivion. If I closed my eyes all
the sounds were swallowed, as if my optic nerve was
somehow attached to the labyrinth of my ear, but it had
been a long time since I believed the world disappeared
so tantalizingly easily, after nothing more than the closing of my eyes. Ideally I would have wished for the disappearance of both, the sounds *and* the world from which
they rose. But when I opened my eyes the critic from the
sauna was approaching, my ill omen. Already she'd
acquired the festival look – that of a boozy Cyclops. Of
course it was Peder whose back she now stroked. 'Have
you anything to write home about then, boys? Other
than Barnum treats Cliff to Coke in the sauna?' Peder
moved his head horizontally, as if the space was dangerously cramped beneath the ceiling. 'Too early to tell,' he
said. 'But there's no smoke without fire. You can write
that Barnum and Miil are in business.' The Elk was
almost suffocating him with her dress. I was on the point
of ordering snorkels. 'Are you travelling on the Kristin
train? Is Barnum going to translate the script from
Swedish?' Peder pushed away her hand. 'If Kristin
Lavransdatter's going to be champagne,' he said, 'then
we'll be making heavy water.' The Elk sniggered and bent
backwards to catch the last drops in her brandy glass.
'Tell me something else, boys. We've had enough
clapped-out metaphors.' 'Then imagine *The Elk* meets
The Sunset,' I said. She turned slowly towards me and
acted as if she was only now realizing that I had been
standing beside her all along. Of course that wasn't the
case. She'd seen me the whole time. She gave a slow grimace. 'We'll give you the nod when the time comes,'
Peder said quickly. 'An exclusive.' But she just kept looking at me. 'It's a date then. Say hi to Cliff from me,
Barnum.' Suddenly, she leaned down close to my ear. 'To
hell with you.'

And with that she vanished into the thick fog in the direction of the toilets. Peder began to tug at my jacket. 'Did she say Cliff in the sauna? Cliff and Barnum in the sauna?' 'Saunas are mixed here in Germany, Peder. D'you think it has something to do with the war?' 'What are you on about? Were you in the sauna with Cliff?' 'The Elk was there first. It's the only time I've ever seen her naked.' 'I'd prefer to avoid hearing this, Barnum.' 'She was like an overripe pear.' 'What was it she muttered to you?' 'Just my old saying. To hell with you.' Peder rolled his eyes and slumped over once more. 'Don't tempt her to write more crap about you, Barnum. That's the last thing you need.'

When on rare occasions Peder got drunk all of him started sloping downwards – his hair, his wrinkles, his mouth, his fingers and his shoulders. The alcohol hung like a lead weight in his body. All of him slipped towards his own shoes. I could have said to him that we were getting old now, two curious companions who had shared everything in life, and who were now left with only half of the best of it. And with a smile I could have stroked a finger carefully along the deepest furrow in his face.

'The last thing I need,' I told him, 'is for you to tell me what the last thing I need is.'

'The last thing we need is a drink,' said Peder.

He stretched one arm into the air but it collapsed amid ashtrays, used napkins and bottles. Somebody sang in Norwegian at a table where mercifully there wasn't room for more. The credits would soon be rolling. The last drinks appeared. Peder hoisted his glass with both hands. 'Here's to you, Barnum. Basically we don't really have much more to do here in Berlin, eh? Except for buying a gift for Thomas. Or maybe you've forgotten that by now, too?' I looked down and suddenly remembered what I had in my suitcase at the hotel. 'I have a script with me,' I said. Peder quietly put down his drink. 'And you tell me that now? That you bloody well have a script with you?' 'Aren't you pleased, Peder?' 'Pleased? Hell, give me something, Barnum. A hint of some kind. A title.' '*The Night*

Man,' I told him. '*The Night Man*,' Peder said and smiled. 'D'you have to say everything twice?' 'What's it about? Pitch me, Barnum!' I had to smile. That was the way we were talking now. Pitch me. Fill me in. Give me something. 'My family,' I told him. 'What else?' Peder gripped his head with both hands and shook it. 'Why didn't you say something at the meeting? Why the hell didn't you take the script with you to the meeting!' 'Because you woke me up, Peder.' He let go of his head and it slipped onto his shoulders. 'I woke you?' 'Yes, Peder. You wake me and hang up and there are messages for me everywhere. I barely get any peace in the sauna, Peder. I hate it. And you know that.' 'I know, Barnum.' 'I hate being nagged. I've been bossed around and nagged all my life. Everyone's bossed me. I'm basically fed up with it, Peder.' His eyes had become empty and expressionless. 'Are you finished now, Barnum?' 'Don't nag,' I said. Peder came closer and tried to straighten up. He almost held my hand. 'It's not me who's been calling. And I haven't left any messages for you.'

And in the moment he said that I became clear-headed and was frozen to ice; everything around me trembled, horrible and close. Everything I had put off was happening now. I left. Peder tried to make me stay. He failed. I went out into the Berlin night. It was snowing; a glimmer between the lights and the dark. I heard the animals screeching from the zoo. I walked through the ruins and past the restaurants which had already closed, back to the Kempinski Hotel, where the same limousines stood filed like extended hearses in a hopeless queue. And the white-haired old porter opened the heavy door and doffed his hat and smiled indulgently; I took the lift up to my room, opened the door and saw that the maid had been in to make up the room – and I saw too the telephone's red light; I tore off the receiver but heard only a foreign dialling tone. And then I noticed the envelope, the one I'd folded and put in the pocket of my dressing gown – it lay on the desk beside a bowl of fruit and a bottle of red wine there courtesy of the festival. I dropped the receiver and went over to it. I opened the envelope and pulled out a sheet of paper. I sat down on the bed. It was a fax, and at the top I could read where it had come from: Gaustad Hospital, Department of Psychiatry – that morning at 07.41. The writing was my mother's; just two sloping lines of trembling letters. *Dear Barnum. You won't believe it. Fred has come back. Come home as fast as you can. Mother.*

I read the two lines one more time and then slowly got up, almost calmly; my hands as they lifted the paper were quite still, yes, my hands were still, and I glanced over my shoulder, quickly, just as I always do, as if I imagined someone was standing there, in the shadow by the door, watching me.

THE WOMEN

The Drying Loft

It is Thursday 8 May 1945, and Vera, our mother, is standing deep inside the drying loft in Church Road, unpegging the clothes that have become dry and soft up there in the course of the night. There are three pairs of woollen socks that can be put away for good now, two green bathing suits with buttons and neck straps which haven't been used yet, three bras, a white handkerchief, and last but not least the three thin frocks and pale rayon tops which have lain so long in the bedroom cupboard that they have almost faded in the dark. Vera hasn't dared hang the clothes out in the yard; so much has happened in the course of those days and years, why shouldn't someone steal their clothes too, even now at the last moment? And she hurries, she's impatient and can hardly be finished quickly enough, because she's going out to celebrate the peace, the victory; every bit of it she'll celebrate, of life and of spring, together with Boletta and the Old One, and perhaps Rakel will be back home too, now that it's all over. And she laughs quickly as she stretches up to the slack clothes lines which feel rough against her fingers and which can easily sting if she isn't careful. It's Vera, our mother, who stands thus, alone in the drying loft; she laughs and drops the wooden pegs down into the wide pocket of her apron, and carefully places item after item in the woven basket beside her. She is warm and she is thinking of nothing; she's just full to the brim with a great and curious joy, like nothing she has ever known before. Because she feels new now.

There has been war for five years and in the summer she'll be twenty, and it's now, right now, that her life is beginning, if only she could get these clothes down. And she wonders if she should leave the woollen socks up, but decides not to, for it isn't right to be hanging clothes to dry on such a day, not even high up in the drying loft. Vera has to rest a moment, straighten her bent back, and lift her head to breathe in the thrilling scent of the clean clothes, the three frocks. She laughs again. She blows the hair from her forehead. In the corner under the coke shaft there sits a grey dove cooing. She can just hear shouting and music from the streets. Vera stretches up to the clothes line to take down the final piece, her own blue frock, which she hasn't yet had the chance to wear, and at that moment, as she unfastens one of the wooden pegs and holds up the garment with her other hand so that it won't fall onto the dusty floor, she hears footsteps behind her. Slowly they come closer and for a moment Vera imagines it's Rakel who's come back and that she's run through all the corridors to meet her, but she knows it's probably just Boletta who has lost patience and who has come to help her finish, for there's no time to lose – it's peace at last and the war is over. And Vera is about to say something to her mother – *Oh yes, there's only this one frock to go, don't you see how fine it is*? – or perhaps she'll just laugh, laugh with sheer delight, and afterwards they can carry the clothes-basket down all the steps together. But then she realizes it's not her mother, nor is it Rakel, for these steps have another rhythm, another weight, the floorboards give in the wake of their passing, and the dove in the corner suddenly stops cooing. These are the steps of war which keep going, and before Vera can turn round someone has gripped her and held her tightly, and a dry hand has been pressed over her face and she cannot even scream. She senses the harsh stench of unwashed skin, the raw stink of a strange man's mouth, a tongue that rasps her neck. She tries to bite, her teeth sink into the rough skin, but he doesn't let go of his hold. She can't breathe. He lifts her and she kicks for all she's worth; one of her shoes falls off and he forces her down onto her knees and pushes her forwards. She notices that the frock is hanging at an angle on the line by the one peg and she tears it down with her in her fall. He takes his hand away from her mouth and she can breathe, yet now that she's able to scream she doesn't all the same. She sees his hands tearing up her skirt, and it's only this that she sees of him – his hands – one of them missing a finger, and she plunges her nails into this hand, but even then he doesn't make a sound. Nine fingers, that's all he is. He forces her face to the floor and her cheek is chafed by the rough planks. The light is distorted now and the clothes-basket has toppled over; the dove is preening itself. She feels the man's hands about her hips, nine fingers that scrape against her skin, and he tears her open, he pulls her apart. She doesn't hear him; she shoves the frock into her mouth, chews the thin material over and over, and the sun in the loft window shifts with a shudder. He presses himself through her and in the same moment the church bells begin ringing, all the church bells in town ring out at the same time. And the dove suddenly takes off from the corner under the coke shaft and flaps wildly about them; she can feel the wings brushing against her and now it's all too late. She still isn't twenty and in the end it's he who screams.

Afterwards everything is quiet. He lets her go. She could get up, but remains lying nonetheless. He puts his hand on her neck. It smells of urine and vomit. Then he runs. She can feel it, a soundless drumming against her face, her cheek. He crept up on her, and now he's running away through the long attic corridors in Church Road, on 8 May 1945. The dove sits on the window frame. And Vera, our mother, just lies there like that, her cheek against the floor, her frock in her mouth and her hand full of blood, as a beam of sunlight slowly passes over her.

The Flat

Boletta, Vera's mother, was anything but religious – rather quite the opposite – she'd had enough of miracles. But now she opened the door onto the narrow balcony over Gørbitz Street, stood there and drank in that moment to the last drop; the church bells ringing together across town from Majorstuen, Aker and Fagerborg, even the bells of Sagene and Uranienborg audible. The wild, sweet clamour seemed drawn and carried by the light and the wind, and rose in one tremendous sound to deafen once and for all the sharp, white echo of the air-raid sirens. 'Can you close the door! There's a draught!' Boletta turned towards the living room, almost blinded. The dark inside had grown bleaker still. The brown furniture resembled immovable, heavy shadows, bolted fast by the hard ticking of the clock in the entrance hall. She had to shield her eyes for a few seconds. 'Do you really think we want to get colds today? When we've been fine and healthy the whole of the war!' 'There's no need to shout, Mother.'

Boletta closed the door to the balcony and now she could see the Old One over by the bookcases. She was standing there in her ankle-length petticoat and red velvet slippers tearing out books which she proceeded to throw into the fireplace, talking all the while and evidently just to herself. The cacophony of church bells diminished to one single song. Carefully Boletta went closer. 'What are you doing, Mother?'

But the Old One didn't answer, or rather didn't hear her, and for that reason didn't reply. For the Old One was deaf in one ear and the other one didn't function as it should. The damage had happened when Filipstad exploded in December 1943. She had been sitting in the dining-room twisting the dials on the radio back and forth, the radio she had refused to give up on the grounds that she was a Danish citizen and considered it inconceivable not to listen to programmes from Copenhagen. She maintained that the explosions came out of the loudspeaker in varying degrees of intensity, accompanied by an unauthorized jazz band from America, and this was how the anvil in her left ear was put out of action, and the stapes in the other pushed forward. Deep down Boletta was sure that her mother's ears were in perfect working order, but that she had decided it was her prerogative to hear just what she wanted to hear. Now she realized that it was the novels of Knut Hamsun that the Old One was tearing from the shelves and stuffing into the green stove. 'What are you doing?' Boletta shrieked a second time, and grabbed her mother's arm. 'I'm finished with Hamsun!' 'Hamsun? But you love Hamsun!' 'I haven't read him in five years. And he should have been out of this house a long time ago!' The Old One turned to her daughter. She waved *The Crops of the Field* in front of her nose. 'Particularly after what he wrote in the paper!' 'What did he write?'

The Old One laid *The Crops of the Field* in the stove too and fetched the afternoon edition of *Aftenposten* from the previous day. She banged her finger at the front page so hard it almost made a hole in the paper. 'Now I'll tell you word for word what that wretched creature wrote! *We, his close followers, now bow our heads at his death.*' The Old One looked up. 'Could you imagine a worse time to write Hitler's obituary? There shouldn't have been an obituary for him in the first place. Better that we danced on his grave!'

She dropped the paper in the stove and attacked the shelves again with venomous rage. Her long grey hair waved about her; she swore mightily as she threw out each of Hamsun's collected works. And I'd have given anything to see this sight – the Old One, our great granny, removing all trace of the deaf Nobel prizewinner in our living room in Church Road on 8 May 1945. But suddenly she stopped, just as she was about to throw away the last part of the August trilogy, *Yet Life Survives*, and she remained standing with the first edition in her hand as she silently bent towards the bookcase and manoeuvred out something else that had been hidden behind the traitor's novels – an untouched bottle of Malaga from 1936. The Old One lifted the bottle carefully and for a second forgot Hamsun and all his works. Boletta came beside her to see what it was. 'The thing I've been looking for everywhere,' the Old One sighed. 'In the dirty laundry basket. In the fuse cupboard. In the cistern. And it's here, for heaven's sake, right behind the stiff covers of the August books!' She gave the bottle a quick kiss and turned back towards the bookshelves. 'Thank you for your company, Knut. Now we're going our separate ways!'

For safety's sake she took a peek behind Herman Bang and Johannes V. Jensen, just to see if there might be some bottles there too, but there weren't, neither there nor behind the collected works of Ibsen. The Old One was already on her way towards the kitchen. Boletta stopped her. 'Did you hide that in the bookcase?' 'Me? If so I'd have found it an eternity ago and drunk it before Hitler invaded Poland! It must have been you who put it there.' Boletta leaned in against her mother's working ear. 'There aren't other things you've hidden in there, are there?'

But the Old One heard nothing of this and instead began twisting the cork with her crooked and wrinkled fingers, and Boletta had to hold the bottle for her while the Old One twisted and pulled, and they stood there long enough labouring and panting. But all of a sudden the Old One let go of her hold and looked down at herself in horror, as though it was only now she realized she certainly wasn't dressed properly. She took the bottle from Boletta and was almost offended on her account. 'One doesn't drink Malaga from 1936 in one's underclothes! But where on earth is Vera? I wanted my frock right away!'

Boletta spun round towards the oval clock which stood

on the cabinet out in the entrance hall, the magic clock
from the life insurance firm Bien where we always put our
premium on the first Saturday each month. For that
reason, for long enough, I believed that it was money that
made time go. Boletta looked closer. It couldn't be so late.
It wasn't possible. Vera should have been down with the
clothes ages ago. The clock must be fast; perhaps,
improbable though it seemed, it was because of the
stresses of the last twenty-four hours that it had gained
time; when the prisoners in Grini were released and General Rediess shut the door on himself on the first floor at
Skaugum, put his gun as far into his mouth as he could,
and fired. Boletta could just hear the beat of the second
hand's jagged wheel and the coins which still clinked in
the drawer under the clock face.

She looked quietly at her own watch. The clock was
showing the right time. 'I'll go and see what she's doing.'
Boletta turned and gave her mother a hard look. 'Don't
you dare touch that bottle before we come back down.'
The Old One just smiled. 'I can't wait to see King Haakon
again. When do you suppose he'll come?' Boletta bent
towards the other ear. 'Don't even think about opening it!
Not before Vera and I have come down!' The Old One
kissed her daughter on the cheek and shivered. 'I honestly think I'll put the fire on for a bit. The war has made
the walls cold.'

Boletta sighed, threw a shawl over her shoulders,
hurried through the flat and began to climb the steep
staircase.

The Dove

The door into the loft is open. It's so still. Boletta can hear
neither voices nor music from the town and the streets,
nor even the wind which always makes the walls tremble,
as if the whole block is shifting just a little each time it
gusts. 'Vera?' she calls. But no one answers. She goes
along the corridor, past all the storerooms, drawing the
shawls tighter around her. It's draughty, but the wind is
soundless. Bright dust shimmers down from the high
beams under the roof. 'Vera?' she calls again.

Why isn't she answering? Perhaps she's sneaked off to
Masjorstuen. Impossible. Boletta laughs. As if Vera would
sneak off! She's probably just far away in dreamland
again. And today of all days there's no law against dreaming. Today one can forget and tomorrow remember
exactly what one wants. Today one can do anything. Suddenly Boletta freezes. A pram full of logs for the fire lies
tipped over in front of her.

She stops. 'Vera?' Even the doves aren't cooing. The
quiet is twice as intense. The door to our drying loft is
still trembling in its frame. And then she does hear a
sound – a constant chaffing sound, a buzzing, like a
swarm of insects which is coming closer all the time, but
which is impossible to see. It's this sound which she'll
never be able to forget. Boletta shoves the pram to one
side and runs the last part of the way to stop out of breath
in the doorway. That's how she finds her own daughter.
Vera is squatting beside the clothes-basket. In her lap
she's holding the newly washed frock, and she strokes it,
over and over again, humming softly to herself all the
time, as if some distorted tune has stuck fast inside her.
Slowly Boletta goes over to her. Vera doesn't look up. She
stares at her own hands as they smoothe the thin material, faster and ever faster. 'What is it, Vera?'

Vera just turns away, rubs her fingers over the blue frock. Boletta kneels in front of her daughter and presses her hand in Vera's lap to make her stop what she's doing. She was almost becoming annoyed and felt like shaking Vera, but this day of all days was not fit for being cross or for scolding. Instead she tries to laugh. 'The Old One has found a bottle of Malaga behind all the Hamsuns but she won't drink it before she's wearing her frock. Are you coming?' Vera turns slowly towards her mother and smiles. Her lips and whole face are twisted, her left cheek is all swollen. She has a cut on her temple, under her hair. But it's her eyes that are worst. They are huge and clear, and they focus on nothing and nowhere.

Boletta almost screams. 'My dearest love. What on earth has happened?' Vera just hums. She tilts her head to one side and keeps humming. 'Have you fallen? Did you fall on the stairs? My love, say something, Vera!' Vera closes her eyes and smiles. 'Remember to let the dove out,' she says. Then Boletta realizes that the new frock is damp and sticky. She lifts her hand. Her fingers are dark with blood. 'The dove? Which dove?'

But Vera makes no answer. Vera, our mother, has withdrawn into silence and utters not another word for eight months and thirteen days. *Remember to let the dove out*, those are the last words she speaks. Boletta gazes up as the blood drips from her hand. The sun has long gone from the attic window. Instead shadow, like a pillar of dark dust, falls jagged through the room. And on the clothes line right above them the grey bird sits motionless.

Boletta shakes her hand. 'Good Lord! What have you done with all this blood!' Vera leans against her mother who lifts her carefully and carries her through the corridor and down the stairs. Sheer terror has made Boletta, small soul that she is, strong and frantic. One of them is crying, or perhaps they both are, and Vera will not let go of the blood-drenched frock. The pegs spill from her apron pocket with every step that her mother takes, and they lie strewn behind them. But it doesn't bother

Boletta; she can pick them up again when she goes to fetch the clothes-basket which is still in the drying loft. And I remember the bird we found inside the storeroom one night, Fred and I; a hard and dried-up dove, like a mummy with feathers, that time that Fred had bought himself a coffin and wanted to practise dying. But all that's still far away.

The Ring

The Old One stood by the white sideboard in the pantry and poured equal measures – to the last drop – into three wide glasses, for Vera was old enough now to drink Malaga, indeed all those who had survived a world war deserved at least one Malaga. The smell of the dark, flowing flower of 1936 made her dream of Copenhagen's harbours – decks of ships, sails, hawsers and cobbles – it was as if the mere scent of it could conjure up each image from her shadowy memories. The Old One thumped the table and wept a little for sheer joy. This was a sorrowful joy! Underwear notwithstanding, she proposed three toasts – one to him who had been lost in the ice, one that she might never forget him, and one, finally, to peace and to the sun that shone upon it. Oh yes, it was a sorrowful joy! But sorrow was seldom joyful. Life wasn't just top hats and slow waltzes. Life was also about waiting for those who never came back. And she drank that sorrowful joy and emptied her glass, then filled it exactly as before, and only then became aware of scuffling in the kitchen. She put the cork back in the bottle and saw Boletta coming towards her with Vera who had fallen asleep in her arms like a little child. She could look like that too, on first glance. 'Boil some water!' Boletta shouted. 'Get vinegar and bandages!' The Old One lifted her glass and put it down again. 'What on earth has happened?' 'She's bleeding! She'll say nothing!'

Boletta carried her daughter into the bedroom and laid her down on the double bed. The Old One immediately got ready the largest pan with water and hurried after them. Vera lay with her eyes shut and her arms clasped tightly about the blood-stained frock. Her face looked more twisted than before. A blue shadow covered one cheek. Boletta sat by the edge of the bed and didn't know what to do with her own hands. 'I found her like this,' she breathed. 'And she won't speak! Not a single word!' 'Hasn't she said anything at all?' 'The only thing she said was that I should let the dove out.' 'What dove?' 'The dove on the clothes line. There was a dove on it. What do you think she meant?' 'She just meant you should let it out. The dove.'

The Old One sat on the other side of the bed. She passed her hand carefully over Vera's forehead and felt the warmth and dryness of her skin. Then she put two fingers against the girl's thin, pale throat and felt, barely, the rhythm of her heart, slow and even. And the same sound came from far back in her mouth: a low, dark intoning that made her lips vibrate. Boletta could stand it no more. She pressed her hands over her ears. 'She's hummed like that ever since I found her.' 'She isn't humming. She's cooing. Oh, Lord.' The Old One tried to take the frock from Vera but couldn't manage. The girl's hands were white, with three of the nails broken. 'Shall we call the doctor?' Boletta whispered. 'The doctor is bound to be here, there and everywhere today. Do you think it's her monthly?' 'So much blood isn't possible!' The Old One looked at Boletta sharply. 'Oh, don't be so certain of that. We have more than enough blood.'

They heard the water boiling in the kitchen, and while Boletta fetched the pan, the Old One rummaged for vinegar, camphor, cloths, iodine and towels. Carefully they lifted Vera, undid the knot of the apron on her back and softly laid her down once more. They took off her shoes and stockings, and unbuttoned her blouse, but when they once more attempted to wrest the frock from her grasp they found it as impossible as before. They had to use force; they had to pull away finger after finger, and even then they didn't manage it. In the end the Old One took the scissors and cut the whole garment loose from the hem of the skirt right through the bloodied fabric, up to the collar and down the length of both arms. Now and

again Vera opened her eyes almost as if trying to find out
where she was, or to see what it was they were doing
around her. But that lasted only a short while, thereafter
she sank cooing into her own blue shadow. They pulled
up her clothes and saw that her panties were bloody too.
They removed everything and she no longer resisted at
all. Boletta cried the more when she saw her own daughter like this on the huge bed; she was almost see-through
in the dull glow from the chandelier above, and her hands
kept searching for something, her fingers kept twisting
into hard fists, as if they were still holding onto a blue
frock that would never now be worn.

After that they washed Vera with a sponge, pumice and
brush – always using the mildest of soaps. They dried her
then with the softest towels, changed the bedclothes, laid
a greased poultice and a cloth sprinkled in vinegar on her
cheek, and gave her three layers of towels just for safety's
sake. She was given hot tea and they let her wear the Old
One's Chinese nightdress. Vera wasn't humming any
more. Vera slept soundlessly and even her hands finally
let go of their hold and found their rest in silk.

Then the Old One fetched her bottle of Malaga and two
glasses, and sat down with Boletta. 'We'll celebrate peace
indoors,' she whispered. They could still hear the rejoicing from Majorstuen to Jessenløkken, from Tortberg to
Bislet, St Hans' Hill and Blåsen. Now and again someone
would fire off shots and windows were broken. But Vera
never woke from her sleep.

The Old One poured another round. Boletta drained
her glass immediately. 'I should never have let her go up
there alone,' she mumbled. 'What do you mean?' 'I
should have gone with her.' The Old One leaned closer so
that her grey hair fell down over her face. She slowly
pushed it away. 'There weren't any others up there? With
her?' Boletta shook her head. 'With her? What do you
mean?' 'You know perfectly well what I mean!' Boletta
was on the point of shouting, but she stopped herself.
'She was alone,' she said quietly. 'But there could have

been someone there before you arrived?' Boletta glanced at her mother. 'Tomorrow we're going to the hairdresser's,' she suddenly announced. 'All three of us.' The Old One giggled. 'Speak for yourself. The two of you can go to the hairdresser's if you want. But I'm not coming.' Boletta sighed. 'Your hair is far too long. But just go on looking like a tramp. If that's what you really want.' The Old One got worked up now. 'I refuse to be dressed up like a dog's dinner just because it's the end of the war.' 'And you're moulting like a cat!' 'Vera can put up my hair. When King Haakon comes home!'

A thump against the window made them start yet again. The two of them were brittle and jumpy. Someone was standing outside throwing stones at the window. The Old One put down her glass on the bedside table, went over and opened the window a fraction. It was just some boys from the block. They had buttonholes and Norwegian flags in their hands. They were cocky and friendly and invulnerable. They were looking for Vera. But the Old One had already raised a cautionary hand. 'Vera isn't too well,' she told them. 'Besides, you've chosen the wrong window. Unless it's me you want to go out with.'

The boys down below laughed, and then ran on to other windows, other girls. Here and there between the tenements across the road bonfires burned – bonfires of black-out blinds. People came with them in their arms and threw them into the flames; the black smoke rose into the chill skies and stood like pillars to left and to right, and the smell was luscious, almost sweet, filled as it was with the heavy scent of new-flowering lilac. The evening sun made the asphalt glow, as if the whole town had been hammered from soft copper. And along Church Road there marched a battalion of young men in sportswear; they had guns over their shoulders and they were singing. Where had all these people come from? The Old One wondered at it all. And she thought to herself – *war is silent, peace is loud.*

She shut the window and sat down by the bed again. 'This is my second world war,' she sighed. 'And it can be the last.' The Old One knocked three times on the wood of the bedpost. Boletta changed the cloth on Vera's breast and gingerly lifted the nightdress to see if more blood had appeared, but the towels were still white and dry. 'I just don't understand how she hurt herself like this,' the Old One breathed. 'She must have fallen,' Boletta said quickly. 'Yes. You're right in what you say. That she's fallen.' Boletta leaned close and when she spoke her voice was scarcely more than a whisper. 'Do you really think there could have been someone else there?' The Old One drank in the scent of the bottle and then looked away. 'No, for who would it have been? It was you who said she was alone.'

They talked thus, their voices low and anxious, back and forth, our great grandmother and our grandmother, each with their glass of Malaga. And I somehow believe they never quite managed to get rid of the odour of that dark, sweet wine, and that when many years on I was allowed to lie there, either because I'd had a nightmare or else was pretending that I wasn't well, I always breathed as deeply as I could and at once my head began swimming. Malaga was a memory which floated into my blood, and I dreamed tipsy dreams, and I loved those dreams, which washed through me in my tipsy sleep. But for now it was Vera, our mother, who lay there in vinegar and silk, as peace reigned outside. And sometimes I'm gripped by the thought of what would have happened it she *had* spoken then, if she had recounted what had taken place up in the drying loft – the rape? Then our story would have been otherwise. Perhaps it might never have been told at all; instead it would have gone down other roads which we would never, ever learn of. Vera's silence is the beginning of our story, just as all stories must begin with silence.

Boletta moistens her lips with water. 'Little Vera,' she whispers. 'Has someone been bad to you?' But Vera makes no reply, she only turns away and Boletta looks at the Old One instead. 'I just can't comprehend where all that blood has come from,' she breathes. 'Never has she bled like that. Such a tiny body!' The Old One is bent over and holds her empty glass with both hands. 'When I heard that Wilhelm was to go to Greenland, I bled continuously for two days.' Boletta sighs. 'I know, Mother.' The Old One smiles suddenly as if she has been reminded of something she's almost forgotten. 'And then he came to me the night before and stopped the bleeding. He was a sorcerer, Boletta.'

Vera turned slowly in her sleep and they removed the poultice on her cheek. They saw that the swelling had gone down. She almost looked herself again. The Old One gently combed her hair with a wooden comb. 'You're right,' Boletta admitted. 'It was all too much for her. Everything that's happened. She hasn't been able to cope with it.' 'And little Rakel who's gone,' whispered the Old One. 'Imagine how Vera must miss her.' 'Maybe she'll still come back,' Boletta said quietly. 'No. Don't believe that. Don't say that. May we not have any others to wait for here in this house.'

And I still haven't managed to tell you anything of Rakel's story that began before this and is already over. Mum's best friend, the dark Rakel, is dead in a mass grave in Ravensbruck, and no one will ever find or recognize her again, for she is lost in the anonymity of death. She has been wiped out by matter-of-fact executioners, genteel murderers who kiss their wives and children each morning before leaving for the offices of annihilation. Little Rakel, fifteen years of age, from the corner flat on Jonas Rein Street, a threat to the Third Reich. They came for her and her parents in October 1942, but they were magnanimous and generous-hearted, and let her run over the yard in the rain and come up to say goodbye to Mum. 'I'll be back soon,' Rakel told her. 'Don't be afraid, Vera. I'll be back soon.' Two girls, two best friends, in the midst of war: the one our mother, the other her best friend who has to leave. How much do they know? How much does she know? A raindrop runs down Rakel's nose and Vera wipes it away and laughs, and for an instant it's almost an ordinary goodbye. Rakel is wearing a brown coat her mother used to wear, which is far too big for her, and she has grey mittens which she hasn't had a chance to remove. She doesn't have time. They're waiting for her, her parents and the police. She has a long journey ahead of her. The ship is called *Donau*. They hug each other and Vera thinks, as she says the words inside herself, *she'll be back soon, that's what she said, don't be afraid.* 'Be careful,' Rakel whispers. 'Say goodbye from me to Boletta and the Old One.' 'They're out trying to find potatoes,' Vera smiles, and both of them laugh again. But suddenly Rakel lets go of her, takes off the mitten on her right hand, and tugs loose the ring on her middle finger to give to Vera. 'You can borrow it until I come home again.' 'Can I?' But Rakel changes her mind, just as suddenly. 'No. You'll keep it!' 'I don't want to,' Vera replies at once. 'Yes, you will keep it!' 'No,' Vera insists, stubbornly and almost angrily. 'I don't want to keep it.' Rakel takes hold of her hand and pushes the ring into place. 'At least you can look after it for me then!' After that Rakel kisses her on the cheek and starts running back because there's no time to lose; she's off on a long journey and she mustn't be late. And Vera stands in the kitchen wishing Rakel hadn't given her the ring. She hears her quick feet going down the stairs, those small brown shoes taking step after step, and Rakel will never return. I remember something Mum said, and she repeated it often – *It's those footsteps I hear disappearing out of my life.* I made those words my own. And sometimes I like to believe that Rakel is there at the edge of this story, or at the very core of my mother's silence, watching us, sorrowful and merciful.

The Old One put the cork back in the bottle. 'So you think I look like a tramp, do you,' she said. Boletta was packing the ruined clothes in paper and tying the parcel with string to banish it to the back of the cupboard. 'I only

said that all three of us could go to the hairdresser's,' she
sighed. 'You said that I looked like a tramp!' 'Vera and I
can go ourselves. If you don't want to.' 'Oh, go to the hairdresser's then, and tart yourselves up now the war's
over.'

It would soon be night and still the Old One hadn't
managed to get properly dressed. She sat by the bed in
her faded petticoat and red slippers and I would love to
know exactly what she was thinking. Did she feel that yet
another disaster had befallen them? Boletta stood behind
her and lifted the long, grey hair with both hands. 'You
don't look like a tramp. You look like an angry witch.' The
Old One cackled at that for a bit. 'And tomorrow Vera is
bound to be better again. Perhaps she'll go for a walk with
the witch?'

And they tried to comfort themselves with this
thought, that it was Vera's menstrual blood which had
driven itself through her with extraordinary force on that
extraordinary day – 8 May 1945 – and taken her feet from
her up in the drying loft.

'I'll call the doctor all the same,' Boletta whispered.
'He's bound to be busy,' the Old One insisted as she had
before, her voice as low as her daughter's. She crossed
herself three times, very quickly. Boletta let her mother's
hair drop against her hunched back and came round to
face her. 'What was that you did just then?' 'What? What
are you talking about?' 'You know exactly what I'm talking about. Don't make such a face.' 'I'm tired,' the Old
One announced sulkily and tried to get up. Boletta
stopped her. 'You crossed yourself. I saw you.' The Old
One freed her arm. 'Yes, yes. So I crossed myself! An old
witch who crosses herself! Is it of such importance?' 'I
thought you'd given up on God and wouldn't talk to Him
again. No?' The Old One crossed herself again. 'It's a long
while since God and I stopped being on speaking terms.
But now and again I let Him know I'm there. So that He
won't feel lonely. And now I'm tired!'

The Old One went into the dining-room and slept there on the divan, while Boletta lay down with Vera, her arm round her, just as they'd lain many times together during those last five years. Sometimes all three of them had slept together, after they came up from the cellar in the wake of air-raid sirens and explosions. And then it might be that the Old One would read from Wilhelm's letter, as they lay together waiting for night and sleep and peace, and Vera would always cry when the Old One neared the end, that last beautiful sentence which Wilhelm, Boletta's father, had written before he disappeared in the land between ice and snow.

Boletta lay awake a long time. She thought of the Old One, who'd crossed herself, who'd found it right to converse with God with finger language that evening. Boletta trembled, she shook so violently she had to raise both arms so as not to waken Vera. Was Boletta as disturbed by the Old One's sudden piety as Vera had been when Rakel gave her the ring? Oh, when we consider all we do that backfires – our actions which are turned on their heads – the comforting which is transformed into pain, the rewarding that becomes punishment, the prayer that changes to cursing. Still laughter and shouting echo from the streets. Peace. Terboven had dropped the corpse of Rediess into the bunkers at Skaugum and ordered the guard to light the fuse of the enormous explosives' container. It was said that for a second Terboven was filled with regret, not for his deeds but for this final action – the fuse that glistened along the stone floor. He attempted to stop the fuse's burning but didn't succeed (he was too drunk), and no one noticed the massive explosion that made the birds cloud upwards from the surrounding woods. The war was over. For the first time Boletta felt afraid.

She must have slept nonetheless but had no memory of doing so. When she woke, suddenly and exhausted, Vera wasn't there. The space beside her in the bed was empty.

It was already after seven. Boletta had to go to work. It was just an ordinary Wednesday, a Wednesday in May. Someone was talking in the dining-room. Quickly she got herself there. The Old One had gone to sleep with the radio on. *This is the Norwegian Broadcasting Service. The genuine, bona fide broadcasting service.* Boletta turned it off and through the stillness that swam back she could hear something else, the same humming, cooing, except that it was even deeper now, almost like gurgling. The sound was coming from the bathroom and it chilled Boletta to the marrow. She woke the Old One up and brought her out with her into the hallway. The bathroom door was locked. Vera was in there.

Boletta knocked. 'Vera? Would you open the door, Vera?' The humming died away, almost with a sigh. Everything was silent. But now and again they heard water dripping and something rubbing, the same sound Boletta had heard up in the drying loft, only it was stronger now, like a shoe on a doormat. 'Are you coming, Vera? What is it you're doing?' The Old One bent down and looked through the keyhole. She felt a slight blowing, a draught against her eye. 'I can't see anything. The key's in the lock.' All at once Boletta rattled the door handle and shouted, 'Vera! Open this door! Stop this nonsense at once! Are you listening? Open this door!' The Old One had to intervene and calm her down. 'Pull yourself together and don't bring down the whole building!' Boletta let the door handle go and forcing herself not to shout she whispered behind her fingers, 'What are we to do?' 'Stop shouting, first of all. There's nothing I like less.' Boletta gave a laugh. 'Oh, really. Are you hearing so well that it's a nuisance now?' 'That's none of your business.' 'Has the world healed both your ears, eh?' But the Old One had nothing to say to that. Instead she produced a hairpin and stuck it in the keyhole, and twisted and turned it until they heard the big key fall onto the floor inside. At once Boletta tried to push open the door, but it was no less locked than it had been. The Old One looked through the keyhole again. 'Can you see anything now?' the Old One breathed. 'I think she's sitting in the bath. I can see one arm.' Now Boletta herself bent down to have a look through the keyhole. She felt a cold wind against her eye, and always, for as long as I can remember, it was this she blamed, the times when that one eye became red and swollen and started running, as though that eye, alone in her face, was weeping.

Boletta saw it too; Vera's arm, her bare arm over the side of the bath, and her hand, the thin fingers and Rakel's heavy ring. 'We'll get the caretaker! He can break it open!' Boletta was already on her way to the kitchen, but the Old One managed to stop her and hold her back. 'He's probably up to the eyes with other things right now,' she told her. 'But someone has to get that door open!' 'Would you really want that nosy fool to see her like that in there? Naked!' Boletta was crying now. 'But what are we to do?' 'Talk to her. Talk to your daughter!' Boletta took a deep breath and went back to the bathroom door. 'Vera? Will you be finished soon?' But she wouldn't answer. And all at once Boletta became aware of the clock in the hall and the seconds that were ticking away; it was as if the shadow of the clock face itself fell over her. 'I've got to go to work, Vera! I have to get ready or I'll be late!' The Old One caught her arm. 'Work? Today?' 'Even though the war's over don't you imagine people phone each other?' 'No, in all honesty, I think they'll neither think of it nor have the time.' Boletta shoved the Old One to one side. 'Vera, love. D'you know what I thought we could do tomorrow? When I'm off? We could go to the hairdresser's in Adamstuen.' Now it was the Old One who shoved Boletta out of the way. 'The hairdresser's in Adamstuen! What rubbish!' 'Be quiet!' 'Do you really think the hairdresser's will have the time to be open? Not a chance.' 'It was just something to say!' 'Just something to say! You talked about nothing but hairdressers all yesterday!' 'I did not.' 'You said my hair was like a tramp's. I won't forget that!' 'I said you looked like an old witch!'

Then Vera began humming again inside, so low and softly it was all but impossible to hear her. Boletta went to pieces completely and had to be supported by her mother. 'I'm so afraid,' she whispered. 'Just so long as she doesn't harm herself.' 'Harm herself? What are you talking about?' 'I don't know what I'm saying any more!' 'No, that goes for all of us.' The Old One turned to face the door and knocked on it hard, three times. 'It's my turn now, Vera. And if I don't get in right away there's going to be an accident!' But Vera neither answered nor opened the door. She just went on humming and humming. Three more times the Old One knocked on the door as hard as before. 'You don't want your poor grandmother to have to sit on the sink, do you?' They listened, the two of them, they stood with their faces close together, so close they were aware of the other's breath, and suddenly everything fell silent inside once more. Vera stopped humming and there was no sound of water either. It was then the Old One went at the door at full tilt. There wasn't much 'tilt' to draw on, but she ran at the door with her shoulder nonetheless. It did no good and so she tried again, her neck bent, her shoulders lifted, her head down. She was like a bull; the Old One became like a bull – it was as though an inexorable power rose within her, the muscles of grief, and she threw herself against the door so it broke open with a terrific crash. She all but pitched over onto the floor, but Boletta caught her, and together they stood there on the threshold beholding that which made them utterly terrified, terrified and yet at the same time relieved and thankful, for Vera was alive.

She's sitting in the bath, one arm hanging over its curved edge, and in the water, the dark water, a brush is floating – the floor brush from the kitchen. And Vera doesn't notice them, or else she doesn't want to look at them; she stares away somewhere else, just as she did up in the drying loft, and her eyes are far too large for her, they're clear and almost black. The skin on her breasts, her shoulders, her throat, her face – is discoloured and streaked, as if she has tried to wash it away, to scour it from her body. And that thin body is trembling.

Boletta knelt beside the bath. 'My dear, beloved Vera, what have you done?' Water was trickling over the edge of the bath, grey and tepid. Vera made no answer. 'It's over now, Vera. It's over. There's nothing to be afraid of any more.' The Old One sat down on the laundry basket in the corner; she sighed and massaged her shoulder. Boletta gently caressed her daughter's arm. 'Rakel will come home soon, that's for sure. You don't want to be ill then, do you? You'll get pneumonia lying here.' The Old One gave an even deeper sigh. 'Take out the plug,' she said simply. 'That's enough talk.' Vera drew back her arm. Boletta tried to keep hold of it, but it was far too thin and slippery, and it just slid from her fingers. 'Say something!' Boletta shouted. 'Say something to me!'

But Vera remained cocooned in her muteness and the only thing she could do was hum. Her lips were almost blue – they quivered as she kept cooing. The Old One got up and raised her hands towards the ceiling and folded them there, like a clenched fist above her head. 'Pull out the damned plug, for God's sake! Or do I have to do it myself?' Boletta put her hand into the water. And then Vera hit her. She hit her smack in the face with the floor brush and Boletta screamed so shrilly Vera had to cover her ears. And folk in Church Road and Jacob Aall Street, those who have lived long enough to remember those days, say that they can never forget that scream which was talked about for years. It loosened the plaster, shook chandeliers and caused whole slates to fall – indeed it almost made some believe that the war had started up again. It wasn't that the blow itself hurt so greatly; Boletta screamed more out of sheer terror, for she was sure that now they had lost the plot completely, that finally the war had robbed them of whatever sanity they'd ever had. For now Vera was hitting her own mother, she was sitting with a floor brush in the bath hitting her own mother in the face. The Old One had to calm Boletta

forcefully, and when finally she'd managed to do so and
the two of them were kneeling breathless together on the
stone tiles, Vera began scrubbing her neck. She scrubbed
at it with the hard, stiff brush, as if there was some speck
there on her neck, which she hadn't managed to get rid
of. 'I can't take any more,' Boletta sobbed.

And right then the kitchen doorbell rang. For a second,
the briefest moment, Vera stopped scrubbing herself. Perhaps she thought it was Rakel, Rakel finally home and
ringing the kitchen doorbell because she wanted Vera to
come out and join her. Perhaps she did believe that, in the
fleeting blink of an eye between two seconds, but then
she continued scouring, even harder; she bent her head
and her neck vertebrae stood out like a taut bow of glowing coals. 'Who can that be?' Boletta hissed. The Old One
leaned against the side of the bath and let her hand trail
in the water; five twisted and wrinkled fingers in that dark
water, carefully trailing around Vera's body. 'There, there,
child. You're clean enough now.' The doorbell rang again.
The Old One pulled her hand out of the water. 'Who the
devil? Can't we be left in peace! Don't you think so,
Vera?' And Vera turned towards them; it almost looked as
if she wanted to give in, to give herself up to Boletta and
the Old One, but she remained in her cave of silence
nonetheless. The Old One plunged her arm into the water
again and pulled out the plug. 'Now I'm going to throw
someone down the steps,' she said.

Gradually the water began to sink around Vera. Boletta
put a towel over her shoulders without her protesting.
The Old One struggled out to the kitchen and opened the
door. Of course it was none other than Bang, the caretaker for the building who had his own tied flat in the very
bottom corner by the bin sheds. It was Bang – protector
of the flowerbeds, guardian of the laundry, terror of tom-
cats, and commander of law and order. He was forty-two,
a bachelor, a former triple jump champion, and he was
hopeless when it came to conflict. He was standing there
in all his finery – a wide, blue jacket hanging from his

gangly frame, trousers that were too short for him and
with saliva stains on the worn, thin knees. From his top
buttonhole there waved a bow composed of the national
colours of Norway – it was so enormous it almost made
him topple forwards. Bang's face was shining with sweat;
it was as though he had rushed up all the steps to the loft
and down again and round the yard and back, or perhaps
he had just rubbed spit on his forehead too. Inquisitive-
ness was glowing in his eyes, and he smiled with a full set
of teeth as he raised his hat and bowed. 'So, it's the
handyman,' the Old One said. Bang's mouth puckered.
'Has something happened?' he asked. Behind him, on the
next landing, stood the neighbours – the chatty housewives from their kitchen sinks. They were jostling each
other to see better – the Old One still in her petticoat –
and the time already quarter past eight on 9 May. She's
standing there in nothing but her petticoat and with her
hair like a grey avalanche down her hunched shoulders,
this strange creature from Denmark who talks pretty
much as she looks and whom they've never quite got the
measure of, even though she's almost the oldest resident
in the place, living in this flat on the corner of Church
Road and Gørbitz Street, where to that day no man had
been in residence. 'Happened?' the Old One repeated.
'What makes you think something happened?' The caretaker leaned against the door frame. 'I heard a scream.
Everyone here heard a scream.' The neighbours nodded
and took a step forward; yes, they had heard it too, an
appalling scream. The Old One smiled. 'It was only me –
I burned myself on the stove.' And she wanted to shut the
door on them now, but Bang remained standing there
with one shoe a little too far forwards. He looked hard at
her wet arm. 'Are you quite certain that everything's all
right?' 'I am completely certain and thank you so very
much for your concern.' Bang wasn't about to give up so
easily. 'And how's Vera, by the way? Some of the boys said
that she wasn't well.' 'What did you say?' The caretaker
smiled again. 'They said you had said so. That Vera wasn't

well.' The Old One looked down at his shoe; it was mis-shapen and the lace didn't reach through all the holes. 'If you don't move your foot right now, you will be the next one to scream in this neighbourhood.' Bang took a hurried step backwards, but his eyes remained fixed on her all the while. 'I only wanted to ask, ma'am. These are troubled times.' 'I'm aware of that. But house-to-house searches are, I believe, a thing of the past now?'

The Old One attempted to close the door yet again, but the caretaker leaned his frame in and the smile had disappeared now. 'I think you forgot this on the stairs.' He scrabbled in his jacket pockets and at last produced a bunch of pegs. 'Careful with those. Someone might have had a nasty fall. Hope your hand's better soon. And Vera.'

Bang limped up to the housewives who immediately encircled him. The Old One shut the door, put the pegs in a drawer and hurried out to the bathroom. Vera sat in the empty bath, the towel over her shoulders, hugging herself, her head against her bony knees. Boletta gently caressed her back and Vera allowed her to do so. Together they carried Vera into the bedroom again. There they put on her blankets and quilts, silks and creams, and she fell into dreams immediately in the warm light. 'I looked at the towels in the laundry basket,' Boletta whispered. 'She hasn't bled any more.' 'Good. That means we won't have to get the doctor here.' They went out into the dining-room so as not to wake Vera. Still dust glittered over the furniture and along the walls, on lampshades and over paintings. The windows were streaked with soot and dirt. Soon they would have to begin the spring cleaning. 'Who was it who called?' Boletta asked. 'That fool of a handyman.' 'Don't call him a handyman, mother. His name is Bang. He's the caretaker.' The Old One stared out of the window. 'What did you say?' 'His name is Bang!' The Old One laughed. 'That handyman had a whole flag in his buttonhole. And what did he do in the war? Search the attics for Jews?' 'Be quiet!' Boletta snapped. 'Don't tell me to keep quiet! I'll say what I want to.' 'What did he want then?' 'To hand in the pegs. That you dropped on the floor.' 'Did he say anything?' 'What about?' 'Perhaps he'd seen something.' The Old One sat down on the divan and sighed. 'It's only nine in the morning and it's already been a long day. I'm exhausted.' 'Why don't you lie down with Vera then?' 'I'll keep an eye on her, that's for sure. Off you go to your work. And if you happen to see a bottle of Malaga on the way, please bring it home with you.'

The Old One turned round and fell asleep without another word. Boletta went into the bathroom to wash. There was no more hot water so she drenched herself in the perfume she'd been saving up for long enough now. At least she wouldn't smell bad when she arrived late for work at the Telegraph Exchange on the first day after the end of the war.

She peeped in on Vera. She was asleep, and at that moment, in such light, she resembled the child she had been, not so very long ago.

The Old One heard the bang of the door and the quick steps on the stairs. She clasped her hands over her breast and gave up a short prayer, almost shameful, for hadn't God, if He was indeed somewhere in us or between us, in the power of word and thought, enough to sort out as it was?

The Telegraph Exchange

Eighteen women sit beside each other in front of the switchboard on the first floor of the Telegraph Exchange, and the nineteenth still hasn't got there even though it's already nineteen minutes to ten. Seat number eight from the right is not occupied and Boletta hurries through the low, rounded room and just manages to hang up her coat by the director's table before taking her seat, for she has seen Miss Stang. The manageress herself (she is the one who has been here longest), and the one, as a result, who has the stiffest neck and the most frequent headaches, makes a careful note in her logbook, and gives Boletta a hard stare as the newcomer plugs in and affixes earphones and microphone. The other women turn towards her momentarily and give her a resigned smile. Everything's chaotic today anyway. Today the network is in tatters. Today all that can be done is to make the best of it, and there are just these nineteen women and the manageress controlling Norway now. They send signals along power lines across mountains, in cables beneath towns; they weave in to the right apparatus in this flat and that home, so all of a sudden it rings and someone can lift the receiver to hear a voice they thought was lost, the voice of someone they may love who has something precious and beautiful to say. And they connect all these voices to conversations, they bind the country tight with threads of words, in a flood of sound waves, they open the lines to a thrill of electricity, they conduct this language and decide who it is who gets through. A fisherman from Nyksund will talk to his daughter who is a maid in Gabel Street. A woman from Tønsberg wants to be put through to Room 204 at the Bristol. A girl from Hamar is trying to find her fiancé and begs tearfully for the numbers to Victoria Terrace, 19 Möller Street, and each and every hospital across the city. Someone too wants to call Grini, and a teacher from Drammen is searching for a colleague in Vadsø, but Finnmark is closed, Finnmark is still out of touch and it never ends, there's a queue on the lines from Stockholm and Copenhagen and London, they're red hot and the relays are burning and sometimes the lines get crossed and several conversations end up confused on the same line. But it doesn't matter because today everything is chaotic anyway – a true chaos – for peace has broken out and these nineteen women, Boletta number eight from the right, are Norway's shadow cabinet. I saw them once and I remember it with a curious clarity and intensity, because it was the day both the Old One and King Haakon died. I was seven and Mum had fetched me from school and taken me with her to the Exchange to tell Boletta, to tell her that the Old One had died in a traffic accident and that Fred was in Ullevål Hospital, uninjured, but in shock and unable to talk. We went first into the enormous public hall and I saw the painting that all but covered the furthermost wall inside, and then we went up to the first floor, the switchboard, and Mum stood in the doorway and held my hand. We couldn't see Boletta among the women who sat there, all thin and in black they were, and I believed they already knew the Old One was dead, that that was why they were so gloomy and gaunt, but that was impossible since only Mum and I knew that the Old One had been knocked over at the Palace Park, when she went there with Fred to look at the mourning wreath which hung from the balcony on the day of King Haakon's passing – 21 September 1957. But at that moment I imagined there was nothing they didn't know, for after all they heard everything that was being said, and now they were passing it on, that the Old One was dead. They talked and talked into tiny mouthpieces and wore heavy ear muffs that crackled, and as we stood looking for Boletta an even older woman came over to us (she was in black too), and with a completely bent neck as if her head had been screwed on at the wrong angle and couldn't move. And she asked, not in an over-friendly way, what we wanted, and Mum said that we were looking for Jebsen – it was so strange when she said it, her whole name, Boletta Jebsen. Was it perhaps her break now? Then the woman smiled as crookedly as her head was fixed, and told us that Boletta Jebsen didn't work here any longer, at this very switchboard, because she had been moved down to the basement several years ago, and were we not aware of that? Mum went red and all funny, and we went down to the public hall again and she asked me to wait there while she went to fetch Boletta. I stayed there in the high vaulted hall and looked at Alf Rolfsen's fresco. There were only men in the picture, men clearing broad swathes through forests, men heaving cables across mountains and under towns, men erecting telegraph posts. It was a heavy, precise ballet of labour, and these pictures resembled sacred stories, as I remember them now, like the stations of the cross. And after that it was the women who blessed this labour by connecting it – connecting the electric signals in relays and sending them off on their journeys. And perhaps it's just me adding to my own recollection, connecting my writing and pictures to the memory in some great dialogue with myself, but I state it nonetheless – I was seven years old and I believed I was standing in a church. The telegraph building in Tolbu Street became a cathedral, that day the Old One and King Haakon died and Fred was struck dumb, and the thin black-clad women were souls in mourning who called on God through their cords and apparatus. I remember Mum being gone a good while. Then at last she came back, alone, and she still hadn't found Boletta. 'She must be eating,' she whispered. And now we went to the canteen, but she wasn't eating. She was standing behind the counter serving coffee. When we sat together in the taxi to go up to Ullevål Hospital, Boletta said that coincidence knew no limits; the Old One had come to Norway in 1905, the very year King Haakon came, and now they had left this life on the very same day.

'God has to have a sense of humour,' she said, and lit a cigarette. Mum was suddenly enraged and told her to be quiet, but all this is far in the future, and I should realize that myself, that one shouldn't break a narrative like this. How many times have editors scrapped a *flashback*, without even bothering to read it, for flashbacks mean trouble, and *flashforwards* even more. These become the detritus of the editing room, and on the occasions when I have painstakingly researched poetic retrospective reflections, as well as all the anticipated memories, I've been told that what you can't convey in the present tense, in hard currency, is nothing but bullshit and artistic ambition which you can take back home and make short films with.

And instead I cut back to Boletta, to where she's sitting number eight from the right on that first day after the end of the war, threading the electric signals through the country as she thinks of Vera. But there isn't time to think of anything other than the conversations which have to be connected, for everyone in the country is falling over each other to get a word in edgeways and Boletta is in the *present tense*, she is *now*. She is aware of an incipient headache; it creeps along her neck and spreads out towards her forehead like a magnetic wind – and they call the pain *Morse*. For it will attack sooner or later and render many of them sleepless and nerve-racked, and when finally one o'clock comes Boletta can go to the staff room along with half the duty team, but the conversations continue in there – conversations that have to be listened to. Boletta remains silent, thinking about Vera and Vera's blood, and the other women pay no attention for they're used to Boletta's silence – she has never become one of them, one of these telegraph women, all of whom resemble one another despite their different ages. They come from spacious apartments in Thomas Heftye Street, Bygdøy Alley and Park Road; they are perhaps the youngest from a flock of brothers and sisters, and have suddenly found themselves left over. They have spent at

least one summer in France – in Nice or Biarritz – where
they ventured down to the beach, their parasols at the
ready, and the oldest among them are even paler thanks
to the vinegar they rubbed on their skin. They are unmar-
ried, childless, have barely known the touch of a man's
hand, and speak two languages stiltedly. Boletta is a spin-
ster too, but she has a daughter, and this is not only
unusual, it is unheard of. They've never quite got to the
bottom of this scandal and they've long since given up
hope of finding out more than they already know, and
that's almost less than nothing. All they do know is that
Boletta Jebsen lives with her Danish mother, who apparently was a star of the silent film world in her younger
years, and with her daughter Vera, who was born in 1925,
and although these bird-like women from the Exchange
go to church each Sunday, read their Bibles and are otherwise God-fearing in every respect, they don't set much
store by virgin births and miracles of that kind. But now
they're falling over each other to get a word in, of lost
fathers released from Grini and brothers they imagined
were dead but who suddenly emerged from hiding places
in the depths of Nordmarka. Each one has a hero in their
family today, and each has at least one story to tell, but
suddenly they fall silent almost as if someone has
unplugged them, and Boletta realizes they're all looking
in the direction of the door – she turns and Stang is standing there. The manageress, who is by no means a partici-
pant in chitchat at break times, would have preferred the
professional discretion of official silence. She's looking in
Boletta's direction and nods, her head bent. 'Director
Egede wants to talk to you. Now.' Miss Stang returns to
her table before Boletta can ask what this is about, and
none of the others says anything at that moment, but perhaps they're thinking, not without a certain triumph and
schadenfreude, that now the Director's had enough and the
top floor's going to put its foot down – Boletta Jebsen has
come in to work late for the very last time, and there are
plenty of young women of spotless conduct who would

give their eye teeth for positions at the Exchange. Perhaps they do think that way, privately, but to say so openly isn't on, for when put in front of Egede, the man behind the door on the floor above, they will stand together with military precision. Instead they help Boletta to tidy her hair, they lend her a pocket mirror and powder, and she's moved by their thoughtfulness as she's given a word of encouragement for the long journey up to Egede's office. And when she finally knocks on the door she thinks this herself, but with no hint of triumph, *Today I've arrived late for the very last time, and now we're going to be left high and dry*. She hears Egede's order to *Come in* and she barely remembers opening the door and closing it behind her. Egede is sitting in his leather chair behind his enormous desk, and Boletta walks slowly towards him, collects herself and curtsies; she curtsies like a schoolgirl before the headmaster and it angers her – and the anger does her good.

The Director smiles and motions for her to sit down. Boletta remains standing, looking straight at him. Once upon a time he was perhaps a good-looking man. Now he has outgrown his own face, and even a world war has made no impression on the double chins that roll the length of his collar in waves of pale fat and are too heavy for him to raise – his head bobs forward in the space between. He lights his pipe and takes his time. Boletta waits. She holds her hands behind her back and can look anyone in the face now. 'Yes, yes,' Egede says at last. 'It's good that it's over.' Boletta says nothing to this. But it amazes her that he can go round the garden path like this. She doesn't like it. Her rage is in danger of cooling. 'Yes, thank God,' she says, nonetheless, her voice low. Egede puts down his pipe in the ashtray and dries the corners of his mouth. *This is it*, Boletta thinks and clenches her fists behind her back. *Now he's going to tell me that enough is enough*. 'And all is well with your family?' he asks. Boletta doesn't know what to say. She just nods. Egede looks up. 'Your mother is an actress, is she not?' Boletta becomes even more bewildered. 'Yes,' she replies. 'But that was a long time ago.' 'Yes, it must be back in the days of the silent film. In all honesty I miss the silent film.' Egede gets up, and it takes a time for him to leave that deep chair. 'And you yourself have a daughter, is that not so?' 'Yes. I have a daughter.' Boletta feels a spark of anger now. *If his game is to try to embarrass and humiliate me before he gives me the sack then let him just try.* She has nothing to be ashamed of. She'd happily clean out that pipe in the middle of his face. 'And how old is she now?' 'She'll be twenty this summer.' Egede shakes his head and sighs. 'It's sad to see our young ones cast aside by the war. Has she left school now?' Boletta is still more bewildered. She has no idea what he's driving at, and that's perhaps the worst of it. She decides to be polite in her answers, but to say no more than is necessary. 'She has completed secondary school.' 'I see.' Egede goes over to the window. He remains standing there with his back to her, looking out over the city. 'What does your daughter herself think of pursuing?' 'She's very keen to work with photography.' Egede turns to face Boletta and laughs. 'Photography? Has the young lady ambitions to become a photographer?' Boletta swallows, she has to swallow to make any kind of answer at all, and she curses this dressed-up pile of suet for daring to laugh in her face like this. And yet as soon as she begins to speak again she hears the meekness and politeness of her own voice; it's as if she has always too much in her mouth and should be ashamed of herself. 'What she's really thought of is getting a job in a photographer's.' Egede brushes the answers away with his hand as if he's suddenly fed up listening to all this, even though it was he who pursued the matter to begin with. He sits down heavily once more and Boletta doesn't say a word, she is silent and would be glad not to make another sound. 'You've been here many years now,' he says, his tone suddenly friendly again, almost flattering. Boletta lets out her breath and has no idea where all this is going. Egede lights his pipe again and the tobacco smells stale.

Boletta feels the urge to turn away but she remains rooted to the spot. *This is it,* she thinks. Now he's raised her as high as possible and can let her drop like a stone.

'It won't happen again,' she mutters. Egede looks at her. The pipe hangs crooked from his thick lips. 'Happen again? What won't happen again?' 'My arriving late. But this morning all the clocks were wrong.' Egede gives her a long look and then laughs again. He puts the pipe down once and for all and a fit of coughing puts an end to his laughter; when he recovers his voice sufficiently he asks, 'Would you like to move up a couple of floors?' Boletta can hardly believe her own ears and has to lean forward a moment. She is aware that her expression must be completely silly. 'To the fourth floor?' she whispers. 'There's no need to look so frightened.' Boletta takes a step backwards and tries to look sensible. 'You mean to the Exchange office?' 'That's precisely what I mean. We need more operators there. And we need women with experience. As you have. A great deal of experience.' Suddenly Egede looks away, as if he's caught himself saying something improper. Boletta likes seeing him like that. Somehow it gives her the upper hand. She composes herself. She should be pleased, grateful. She can rise to where there are no more headaches. She smiles. 'I only have experience with the main switchboard,' she points out. Egede shrugs his shoulders. 'We run courses. It's easy work. For someone like you.' Egede taps the ash from his pipe. Boletta can see that the mouthpiece is almost completely chewed away. The man has something of his own to struggle with – a conscience. All at once she feels sorry for him. He has a thick black stripe under the nail of the middle finger which he uses to fill his pipe. A white dust like a halo encircles his thin, dry hair whenever now and again he makes a sudden movement. Like now. He gets up quickly, as if he's aware of a change in Boletta's expression and wants to recover the reins. 'So what do you say to my offer, then?' Boletta knows what she wants to say all right, but she bides her time, she wants to savour this as long as possible. When Egede sees her hesitating he sits down again heavily as if forgetting he got up only moments ago, and rests his elbows on the desk. 'Well, well. You can think about it. Of course there's no hurry. But all the posts will have to be filled by the autumn.'

Egede looks down and starts leafing through some papers, and Boletta nods, she doesn't curtsey this time but gives a hint of a bow and moves backwards towards the door. But as she puts her hand to the gilt handle of the Director's office door in the building known in the streets as the Telegraph Palace, but which inside I christened the Telegraph Cathedral, Egede raises his arm and looks once more at Boletta. She lets go her hold and stands there silent while a new anxiety begins to grow in her, that somehow all this has been too good to be true, that life itself had taught her that there's plenty that's too good to be true, and that triumphs are shorter-lived than disappointment. 'There can't be many such photography jobs?' he asks. 'No,' Boletta breathes. Egede gets up and comes over to her. 'If you do accept my generous offer there'll be a position vacant down at the switchboard, is that not so?' 'Yes,' Boletta replies. 'That's true.' 'And then it would be very convenient if your daughter were to take it. You could show her the ropes.' Boletta looks right at him and smiles. 'It's very kind of you. But that isn't going to happen.' Egede's eyes darken bewildered. 'Isn't going to happen? What do you mean?' 'As I said, my daughter has other plans. But thank you all the same.'

Boletta reaches for the door handle once more and at the same moment feels his hand on her shoulder. Slowly she turns and sees his fingers hanging there, almost like a large insect that had crept mistakenly over her. Now she knows. This was where he wanted to go – right there. 'I will let you know tomorrow,' she tells him. 'Oh, there's no hurry. Take your time.' Egede lets his hand fall over her arm and the black nail scratches over her dress, making a low crackling. 'May I go now?' The Director

takes out his watch, opens it and studies the hands for a
long time. Then he snaps it shut and puts it back in his
waistcoat pocket. He looks at Boletta, his expression no
longer dark – just grey and indifferent. 'Pity,' he says.
'Your daughter would have fitted in well here. Since she
won't have considered marrying right away?' Boletta
laughs. She laughs out loud, her hand over her mouth.
She can't believe what he's standing there saying. 'Has
she not? That's not unlikely.' Now it's Egede's turn to
laugh; his chins ripple beneath his face. But suddenly
he's silent and his head almost tips forward, as if all this
has tired him enormously. 'And who do you think will
want to marry an illegitimate child?' he breathes. 'What
did you say?' 'You can go now.' Boletta clenches her fist.
'My daughter is as legitimate as anyone else's!'

Boletta hears the door closing behind her. She crosses
the tiled floor and hears the sound of her own steps, but
almost delayed, as if all her senses are still catching up
with her. Three men appear from the control room and
pay no attention to her. She has to clasp the banister as
she goes down the stairs. She sneaks into the toilet on the
half landing and washes her hands; it stinks of tobacco
and ash, and when she looks at her reflection in the
mirror she's almost astonished that it's her own face she
sees there. She feels the desire to be sick, but drinks some
water instead and waits until her breathing has eased.
She fixes her hair and her skirt, then walks the last bit
down to the switchboard, sits at her place, plugs in, as all
of them look at her. Out of their minds with curiosity,
wondering what in the world happened for her to be so
long with Egede. The manageress herself is on the point
of quizzing her, but Boletta sits there as solid as stone;
she looks neither to the left nor to the right and meets no
one's gaze, and never will she reveal a jot of her conversation with Director Egede. Then she does something
forbidden, but she has nothing more to lose – that's how
she thinks at the moment, that she has nothing more to

lose – she connects to her own telephone number, she
sneaks into the queue, breaks into the ingenious network, and in the silent rooms of the flat in Church Road
the black telephone begins to ring.

The Button

Vera heard the ringing, far away, on the other side of sleep, of war; she heard the telephone that no one answered. She got up slowly, surprised, and went out into the hall and found herself there so suddenly that she couldn't remember the distance, the seconds, from the bed to there, as if she had been cut straight from one room to the other. The telephone continued to ring and inside the dining-room Vera could see the Old One lying with her back to her on the divan, her hair a great grey tangled mane about her shoulders. Did Vera hope that it might be Rakel, her Jewish girlfriend, who was calling? If Rakel had indeed come back home she wouldn't phone, rather she could come chasing over the yard and up the kitchen stairs to throw her arms around Vera, and Vera would tell her everything. Yet maybe she'd had an accident, had broken her leg perhaps, or else something different had happened that meant she had to phone instead, so quickly Vera lifted the receiver of the black contraption. Its numbers operated back to front, so that when you put your finger in the frame of the nine, turned it right round and let go so that the spring would return the dial to its normal setting and break the connection, it was broken just once, not nine times, and in this way only one impulse would be transmitted to the Exchange. So nine corresponds to one, eight to two, seven to three – that was the way the back to front Oslo telephone worked. Just as Vera picked up the receiver, a split second later, as if the threads of time had been severed; there was nothing but the dialling tone – the humming of the network like wind in an electric forest. She was out of reach, out of reach of the conversation, and just as quickly as she had lifted the receiver she replaced it. The silence carried from room to room and left its mark in the light. The Old

One lay still on the divan. Why was she lying there now? Why was Vera wearing the Old One's Chinese night-gown? The clock from Bien struck the half hour. Vera turned abruptly and everything came back to her – the memory opened like a wound. She ran to the bathroom, leaned over the sink and drank from the tap. She didn't have the courage to look in the mirror. She checked care-fully under her nightgown and the towels were dry, she was dry. There was no longer any pain. That amazed her. There should have been pain. She would rather have had some sort of pain to make her forget. She was just thirsty. In the bath there was a wide band of dirt, as if the water had dried to dust along its edges. She opened the cup-board above the sink and caught the smell of Boletta's heavy perfume. It almost made her sick. Maybe Rakel had been calling from abroad, from somewhere very far away, and the connection had been broken – she was bound to call again when she reached another telephone, one that was nearer home, in Denmark or Sweden, where the con-nection was better. For just a moment she felt happy at that thought. She took the comb that was lying on the Old One's shelf, shut the cupboard and looked up in spite of herself – at her face in the mirror. There was a shadow along the length of her cheek, a cut in her forehead. With a bit of powder it would be invisible. What was it possi-ble to see? Something in her eyes? Something in her mouth when she opened it? On her tongue? Had he been there too, in her mouth? Vera couldn't remember. All she could remember was a missing finger and a bird on the clothes line. She went in to the Old One, sat on the divan, carefully lifted her grey hair and began combing it. The clock in the hall chimed twice. The Old One's hair smelled sweet, of earth and foliage. 'Did you think I was asleep?' she whispered. But Vera made no reply. She just kept combing. Her lips were locked. 'I never quite sleep, you know. When I sleep it's just another way of waiting.' The Old One sighed and lifted her head a little. 'I like you combing my hair, Vera. It makes me think of the sea. Of

beaches of sand. It brings back good memories. I'll sort
your hair later. We don't need to go to some hairdresser's,
do we?' The Old One listened but heard only the sound
of Vera's fingers. 'You can talk to me, my love. I won't
hear you anyway. My ear was damaged, you know. In the
terrible explosion of 1943. I don't quite remember which
of my ears it was, but I'm just as deaf in the other one too,
so it makes no difference. So speak to me, if there's anything you want to tell me, my little Vera. I won't hear a
thing.'

But Vera kept silent. The Old One waited. The clock
chimed a single time again out in the hall. Time was going
backwards. 'Well, all right then. If you won't speak to me
then I can speak to you instead. You heard the telephone
ringing all right.' The Old One felt the hesitation; the
comb got caught in a tangle of hair and Vera tried to pull
it through, hard and fast. 'You're not to scalp me, my
sweet. Who do you think it was then? Who was calling?
Boletta? She's not allowed to call from the Exchange. But
it was bound to be her all the same. And then she got cut
off. I can't abide telephones. You always say the wrong
thing when you're speaking on the telephone and can't
look the other person in the eye. Because it's the eyes that
count, you know, not the words. Shouldn't I know that,
Vera, eh? I was silent too in my time, but that was in
films. On the screen I was silent and my eyes did the talking for me. We painted our eyelashes green so they'd
shine. I could have been a great star, Vera. Bigger than
either Greta or Sarah. I could well have done! But one day
my eyes didn't shine any more, even though they were so
made up I was almost blind.'

The Old One fell silent. She now sensed Vera's hands
behind her. 'Well, well, my little hairdresser. Am I done
now or are you just fed up with all my old stories?
Because I certainly am. All that I'm telling you I've heard
before. Far too many times. There's nothing new to add
any longer. But perhaps you would fetch me the bottle of
Malaga? It's behind Johannes V. Jensen now.'

Vera let go of her hair and went in to the bookshelves
in the living room. The Old One sat up. She was more
bent than usual; soon she would be a whole circle. She
had lain down with her red slippers on and both feet had
gone to sleep – yes, her feet were the only part of her that
ever got any sleep. She tried to rub them but couldn't
reach down, despite being already bent. Instead she just
sat and waited for her toes to wake up again. That was
what growing old meant – waiting for your toes to wake
up. The comb lay by the pillow, full of long, grey hair – it
almost resembled a dead animal. Quickly she cleaned the
comb and put the hair behind the divan. She shivered and
pulled the blanket round her. She heard Vera pulling out
The Lost Land and *The Glacier*, and at long last she returned
with the bottle and a glass which she carefully filled and
then gave her. The Old One held the glass up to the light
to see the sun illuminate the brown wine and fall to the
bottom like mahogany dust. After she'd seen that she
slowly drank up and her back grew soft as straw, and her
small, crumpled feet awoke so well they were on the point
of getting up and going of their own accord. 'Sit here with
me for a bit,' the Old One said. 'We have plenty of time
today. Perhaps we could get a photograph taken of us all
together? Once Boletta comes back home?' Vera sat on
the divan and the Old One began to comb her hair. It was
fine and soft and cascaded so smoothly through her fingers. 'Are you looking forward to going to the cinema
again, Vera? Maybe you could take me with you to the
Palace Cinema? Or the Colosseum. I haven't been to the
cinema since sound came. Can you imagine that? The last
film I saw was *Victoria*. With Louise Ulrich as the heroine.
She wasn't bad, but unfortunately she was German. Oh,
no, it was a sad day when they brought in speech. The
eyes disappeared. The eyes and the dance disappeared
and the mouth took over. D'you know what they used the
Palace Cinema for all those years? A potato store! But
there'll be others you'll want to go to the cinema with
rather than a *chaise-longue* like me. Anyway, my feet would

just go to sleep.' The Old One sighed and put her hand on Vera's arm. 'Your knights in shining armour were here yesterday asking for you, by the way. You can pick them off one by one, Vera, slow as you like. There's no hurry. For heaven's sake, don't hurry. Men are basically like forged banknotes who aren't worth the paper they're written on. Apart from Wilhelm, of course. But sometimes it's more exciting to say no than to say yes. Believe me.'

A tremor went through Vera and the Old One had to hold her tight a moment. She laid her cheek against Vera's jutting shoulder and stroked her back, smoothing out the creases in the silk. 'Wilhelm gave me this nightgown just after I met him. Imagine that! Giving me a nightgown before we were married! Is it any wonder that I locked my door every night and put the moon and the stars in the keyhole to be sure no one would find a way in? Not in the least. Shall we read some of his letter this evening, Vera? From the part where they're stuck in the ice.'

Vera bent forwards and her hair parted so that her slim neck curved in a white bow. The Old One drank another glass of Malaga and wondered where she had found this great weight of silence. And what frightened the Old One most was that she recognized this silence, as if it had come as an inheritance and had consumed Vera with even greater intensity. Her silence was loud within her. 'Did you think it was Rakel who wanted to talk to you just now?' the Old One whispered. Vera shut her eyes. 'Because don't believe that, Vera. Waiting without hope only prevents you living yourself. I know that. I've waited so long now that it's too late to give up. I'm still waiting, Vera. And I've used up my nine lives many times over. Those who are silly and sentimental amaze me. But I know better. Hope is a tired and feeble old lady.'

The Old One turned to Vera again and it was then she noticed it, a mark on her neck, a nick in the skin with tiny capillaries of blood extending outwards from it. At the moment she noticed it and was about to raise her hand the kitchen doorbell rang. Vera sat up. Her hair fell back into place. The Old One thumped her fist into the divan. 'If that's the wretched handyman again I'll knot his tie once and for all! Don't be surprised if you hear screams, Vera!'

The Old One went out barefoot into the kitchen and opened the door. And there was the caretaker as before, the same enormous bow hanging from his lapel, except that it was tied askew now, and his breath was so bad it could have stripped the paint off the walls. He leaned forwards in an attempt to execute a bow. The Old One narrowed her eyes and waved him away like a fly. 'What do you want now? Is there a stone missing from the gravel? Is peace giving you a headache?'

Bang stood tall again, but his gaze was fixed somewhere down by the Old One's foot. 'I only wanted to inform you that you have left your clothes-basket up in the loft.' 'And?' 'I also wanted to say that I can fetch it and have no objection to bringing it down to you.' 'But I *do* object, young man. Thank you very much and goodbye.'

The Old One shut the door in his face and waited until she could hear him limping down the steps talking to himself. And when the caretaker talked to himself like that it was generally about the triple jump and records he'd have broken if it hadn't been for injury, envy and fate in general, and he got himself pretty worked up when he talked like that. But the Old One trotted back to Vera and sat down with her again, passed the comb through her dry hair and lifted it so she could see her neck again – so thin it was that the Old One could almost have cried. She tried to laugh. 'Men always go in the same suit regardless. Whether it's a wedding or a funeral, war or peace, they'll have on the same worn suit. Except for Wilhelm. He never wore a suit. Have I told you about the last night he was with me? I'm bound to have, but I'll tell you again all the same. I let him in, even though I'd locked the door beforehand with three different keys and put a whole constellation in the keyhole. He was to leave the next day

with the SS *Antarctic*. I was your age, Vera, and I was
bleeding so heavily right then I thought I'd die, that
there'd be no blood left in my heart. And so he came to
me, Vera, through all the locks, or maybe I'd forgotten to
turn the last key, who knows? And he lay down so quietly
with me and stopped the blood. That was our first and
last time. Our first and last.'

The Old One fell silent and let go of Vera's hair. The
nick on her neck wasn't the result of scratching. It resembled a bite mark, a blue dent in the skin made by teeth.
She felt a sudden chill pass through her. 'What was it that
happened up there in the loft, my child?' she whispered.
'Was someone bad to you?' Vera sank into her lap and
wept silently – that was her only answer – a great wave
that passed through her body until no more tears
remained. And the Old One sensed a rage rising inside
her, a rage that was the other side of sorrow, and that
sorrow she had already had her fill of. Yet it was sorrow
that nourished her, that gave her strength, that powered
her heart. She stroked Vera's cheek and believed that if
someone, if anyone at all really had interfered with her
then she would hunt them to their death. 'There, there,'
she said, her voice lilting and soft. 'There, there. It'll pass.
Everything passes. Even a world war. And now I think I'll
go up to the loft to fetch our things.'

Vera gripped her arm. 'It's all right, little one,' the Old
One told her. 'I'm not afraid of the dark any more. And
that way we can avoid having the handyman round
again.' Vera's hand fell onto her lap. 'D'you want to come
with me? Or can you not be bothered?' Vera remained
where she was, looking into space, her eyes troubled and
trembling. 'All right, then. I'll just go myself. And later
you can borrow Boletta's frock. And don't forget that
photograph we're going to have taken.'

The Old One put on her red slippers, a long coat over
her nightgown, and a broad hat since it was always so
draughty in the loft, even now in May and in the middle
of the day. And when Vera saw her in this rig-out she

suddenly began laughing, she had to cover her mouth
and the Old One laughed too. *Yes, laugh, my child*, she
thought – *laugh at me and fill these rooms with laughter*. The
nightgown hung below her coat and the hat was askew,
but this was hardly the time to worry about it either.
'Should I take my stick with me? Yes, I jolly well will. Oh,
stick! Where have I put you?'

And for safety's sake she took the key to the bathroom
with her too, and she began to struggle up the long staircase. She noticed that the doors were ajar on every level
as she passed, and the eyes were no doubt watching her.
But the Old One couldn't have cared less; nor was she the
type to tiptoe past, rather she banged her stick against the
banister rail so they would know she was coming, and the
doors closed silently again once she had passed.

She was aware of the wind as soon as she reached the
loft – it was as if the whole building was softly whistling.
She went along the corridor, past the store-rooms. The
pram was still on its side with the logs that had fallen
from it; there was a ski strap in national colours and an
empty brown bottle gently rocking. The clothes basket
was standing in the middle of the floor, beneath the loose
lines from which a single grey woollen sock was still
hanging. A dove was sitting right up on the corner roof-
beam. The Old One opened the attic window with a long
pole which lay there for that use and she stamped hard
three times, but the dove didn't move. She waved the
stick at it but it was to no avail, the dove remained where
it was and might have been dead. The Old One muttered
to herself, unpegged the sock and lifted the basket – but
immediately put it down again. Because in the thin layer
of dust on the white floorboards she saw several footprints, and they were bigger than any Vera's small feet
would leave. And then she spotted something else. In
among the clothes in the basket there was a button, a
clear and shining button, and one that didn't belong to
them. She picked it up. A black thread was still fastened
to it. Someone had lost it there. Someone had been there

and a button had been torn from a jacket. The Old One
put it into her coat pocket, hooked the stick over her arm,
carried the basket down to the flat and immediately telephoned Dr Schulz in Bislet. He had been to see them
before, several times now, when Vera was suffering her
various childhood illnesses and screamed both day and
night. Dr Schulz came over from Bislet and generally
advised *fresh air* – fresh air was definitely his best medicine – and he went as far as to call Nordmarka the great
chemist's. One could walk into that wild country summer
and winter and get as much fresh air as one wanted – and
all of it for free. Consequently, it was with real unwilling-
ness that the Old One telephoned him now, but there was
simply no other doctor she could imagine contacting.
When Dr Schulz eventually answered, his voice sounded
slurred and impatient. He could just about guarantee
looking in that evening, as long as he wasn't dispatched
to other locations in the city; the fight was far from over
yet – something each and every citizen should be damn
clear about – with the danger of desperate Germans and
native traitors striking back at any time. There had
already been skirmishes and loss of life – these were the
last twitchings of war, the final writhings of the van-
quished before the *rigor mortis* of defeat. And Dr Schulz
from Bislet couldn't shirk his duty now at this late stage;
he had to be prepared to intervene on behalf of wounded
patriots, he had to be at his post. The Old One sighed and
put down the receiver; she hid the button she had picked
up in her jewellery box in the bedroom and then went in
to see Vera. She was sitting on the divan and hadn't
moved a muscle. The Old One thought that now she
resembled the bird on the roof beam and she tapped three
times on the door frame just to be sure. 'Now we'll get
the frocks ready,' she said, 'and after that we'll play
patience and drink some Malaga.'

Vera slowly followed her into the kitchen and once
there they ironed the frocks and Vera put on the green
one, Boletta's. It was far too big for her, but the Old One

brought it in at the waist by pinning each side and then together they stood in front of the tall mirror in the hall. Vera looked down. Vera looked away. She refused to meet her own gaze. The Old One put her arm round her. 'Look,' she told her, 'you've caught up with me. I've begun to grow down instead. I'll soon be standing with my head in the ground.' And they were still standing like that in their finery in front of the mirror when Boletta arrived home, white and perturbed. She got no further than the door and stared at them amazed – for a moment almost relieved. 'You look lovely, Vera,' she breathed. And Vera lifted the hem of her skirt and hurried back into the dining-room. Boletta watched her go. 'Has she said anything?' 'We have to clean the windows,' the Old One said. 'Before long the sunlight won't get through.' Boletta gripped her mother's arm. 'Has she spoken? Has she said anything?' The Old One looked in the mirror again. 'My time's over,' she grumbled. 'I look like a lonely circus.' Boletta was at breaking point. 'Could you stop talking like a whole circus too?' The Old One sighed. 'Your headache's back. You should have a lie-down instead of shouting.' Boletta closed her eyes and breathed deeply. 'Can you answer my question?' 'Did you bring anything nice with you? I'd love hot chocolate with butter!' Boletta had to support herself against the wall. 'What has she said? Do I need to drag it out of you?' The Old One sighed again, but even more deeply now. 'She hasn't said a word, Boletta. But she's combed my hair, if you hadn't noticed. And there's another thing, I feel we should hoist the flag on the balcony. We seem to be the only ones who don't have a flag flying today.' Boletta wanted to go after Vera. But the Old One stopped her. 'Let Vera have a bit of peace.' Boletta stood there and smoothed her brow. 'Are you sure we shouldn't call the doctor?' 'Be quiet!' the Old One hissed. 'I've called the idiot already.'

And Dr Schulz arrived when they were drinking coffee. And when Dr Schulz was approaching the world was aware of it. He bore his black bag on a perfectly angled arm, his hat was soft and broad-brimmed, and he wore shining black galoshes from 1 September to 17 May, whatever the weather. His face was gaunt and ruddy, and his nose was positioned like an exclamation mark between his forehead and his mouth. From this prominent feature hung that famous drop which had frozen fast when Dr Schulz skied from Mylla during the winter of 1939 – the last time he got fresh air. Now he preferred sitting at home in Bislet trying to wipe it away. This particular evening he required the entire pavement and a portion of the street to get where he was going. He weaved about like a black crab and the youngest of the boys from Jessenløkken followed him over Ullevål Road giving encouraging shouts and ringing their bicycle bells every time he stepped into the ditch. Now and again someone had to venture close enough to get him going in the right direction again, since occasionally he veered off towards Nordmarka instead, as if some gigantic magnet was positioned high up there, drawing him inexorably closer. In other words it was no great secret when Dr Schulz stopped at the corner outside Number 127 and rang the bell. And I've often wondered if everything would have been different if Dr Schulz hadn't drained the day's fifth whisky and soda (to say nothing of the sixth), if his hands had been steady, his head clear and his vision sharp. If so he might have noticed something which would have changed our story and perhaps stopped it altogether. I say this now and I always will – Fred lived vicariously even before he was born. It's thoughts like these which can still keep me sleepless and afraid, for we hang by a thin thread, a thread composed of chance's shadow. I can see him now, that pathetic doctor from Bislet – should I love him or despise I don't rightly know. I see him there leaning against the door so that when Boletta opens it he almost tumbles into the hall. And the whispers go from door to door that the pickled Dr Schulz has come to see the single women in Gørbitz Street, the strange women whom no one can quite fathom. Now it's ringing out at the building's telephone exchange, and down by the bins in the yard the caretaker is connecting the rumours to lengthy tales which I myself can rely on when my time comes.

Boletta gets Dr Schulz into a chair and he gathers himself while they help him remove hat, galoshes and cape. 'What is it that ails the patient?' he asks. The Old One giggles. 'That's what we'd like to know. That's why you're here, if you didn't realize that.' Boletta offers him a cup of coffee. 'She has suffered terrific bleeding,' she tells him quickly. 'I found her up in the loft. Perhaps she fell.' Dr Schulz's hands shake so badly he has to drink from the saucer and his voice is in an equally bad state. 'Well, well. All she needs is some good fresh air. After all these years of being shut in.' The Old One all but flies at him and Boletta has to stand in the way. 'Vera's lying down in the bedroom,' she tells him. 'I think she's had a shock.' Dr Schulz manages to get onto his feet after a struggle and knots and unknots his fingers. 'Well, well, but what does she say herself?' Boletta looks down. 'She'll say nothing. She hasn't spoken since I found her yesterday.' 'Hasn't spoken? Well, well, I'd better take a look at her. And I would prefer to be alone with the patient.'

Dr Schulz takes his black bag, goes in to see Vera and shuts the door behind him. He remains there for nineteen minutes. The Old One and Boletta wait outside and don't hear a sound. But when Dr Schulz re-emerges he seems more sober than in a long while. He sits down in the same chair and is silent.

The Old One can't stand it any longer. 'Would you be so kind as to tell us something? What's wrong with her?' Dr Schulz looks at Boletta instead. 'You are indeed right. She is in a type of shock. Or may I call it psychosis.' Boletta has to sit down herself. 'Psychosis?' 'Or call it a *condition*, if you will. If you feel that sounds more helpful.' The Old One leans forward and waves her fist. 'Would you tell us now what it is that's wrong with her and not bamboozle us with words! And don't dare mention fresh air again!' Dr Schulz wipes a handkerchief over his high forehead. The drop under his nose wobbles. 'She has lost a considerable amount of blood and is very weak. It's likely that she's fallen and suffered concussion. She needs all the rest she can get. I've given her a tranquillizer.' 'But she's never bled like this before,' Boletta quietly tells him. 'These are strange times that we're experiencing,' he answers.

Dr Schulz gets up and they follow him out to the door. While Boletta searches for two banknotes from the drawer under the buffet the Old One draws him to one side. 'What's your opinion of the mark on Vera's neck?' Dr Schulz considers the question a moment. 'The mark on her neck? It's probably just an insect bite. One she's scratched afterwards.' He pulls his cape about his shoulders impatiently. But the Old One won't let him go so easily. 'Did you examine her womanhood?' she asks in a low voice. Dr Schulz snaps his bag shut. 'I beg your pardon?' 'You know perfectly well what I'm talking about! Is she intact?' At that moment Boletta returned with the money. He stuffs the notes quickly into his pocket and just as quickly wipes his nose with one finger, but the drop remains there. 'I can't detect anything wrong with Vera other than that she's suffered severe bleeding and as a natural result has been left weak and anxious. Give her an iron tablet morning and evening.' Boletta grasps his arm. 'But why won't she talk?' she quizzes him.

Dr Schulz searches a long time for the right words. 'The motor function responsible for speech is currently out of operation. This could have been the result of a blood clot. I mean concussion. When the pressure inside her is raised she will talk normally again.' The Old One was becoming impatient again. 'And when *will* this pressure be raised?' 'It could be tomorrow or it might take longer. Time is the great healer.'

Boletta opens the door and Dr Schulz goes out onto the landing. He gives his hat a half turn. 'Well, well, call me again. If she doesn't pick up in the course of the summer.'

He takes a firm hold of the banister and guides himself down the stairs. He chases away with his stick the children who're still hanging about at the bottom, and weaves his way slowly home where not a soul has telephoned to ask him to assist with first aid in the death rattles of the war. The Old One bangs shut the door, locks it and turns to Boletta. 'What did I tell you? He's still an idiot. In the past it was fresh air. Now time's the solution!'

Then they go in to have a look at Vera. She's sleeping and they don't disturb her rest. Afterwards they fetch the little flag they bring out each 17 May and on King Haakon's birthday, and they put it in the empty flower-box on the balcony. It's still not dark. The skies stretch high and taut over the city. There is still a glow at the heart of a bonfire of blackout curtains, and in the middle of Church Road there's a top hat being blown along by the balmy wind from the fiord. And all at once Vera's standing there in the living room. They turn round suddenly to see her and cry out either in terror or sheer joy; perhaps they imagine she'll say something, that she's herself again. But right there and then she raises her camera and takes a picture of them, out there on the narrow balcony in front of that little Norwegian flag. Boletta is in her brown outfit and her broad hips are showing; her mouth is open and one hand is on its way to her face as if she wants to hide. The Old One is in her long yellow frock and her hair is billowing from her head; the right hand has suddenly closed into a fist, except for the thumb and little finger, extended in the sign of the devil. She's all hunched and bent over, yet she looks right at me nonetheless, as I attempt to put the colours into this photograph with my awkward words. Because it was me who developed this picture; I discovered the film once upon a time when I was sorting through Mum's things. It had been forgotten, and I imagine somehow that I can see her too in this picture, the one that she herself took – our mother, as if on that unclear May evening there had been a mirror behind the two women on the balcony in which the shadow of Vera is reflected like a dark sorrow, a pain I have never seen before, in that which I call the slow exposure of memory.

Spring

On the day King Haakon was to come back to Norway the
Old One got up early, put the Danish flag beside the Norwegian one in the flower-box, and hurried into town
before seven to be sure of a good seat in the front row
along Karl Johan, putting the fear of death into any who
dared block her view when *her* monarch drove past.
Boletta was on night shift at the Exchange and still hadn't
come home. That left Vera on her own in the flat when
she woke in the double bed. She threw on some clothes
and didn't bother looking at herself in the mirror. Nor did
she bother sorting her hair. It didn't matter. She borrowed the Old One's slippers and went down the kitchen
stairs and out over the back yard. All was so still. The
windows were open. She stopped outside Rakel's stairway. A white cat padded between the flowers and the
gravel by the bins. She stole up to the third floor. She listened at the door. And suddenly she felt a shock of joy in
her heart for she could hear voices inside. She rang the
bell but no one answered. Then she realized the door was
open. She pushed it and went inside. The kitchen was
empty. The cupboards had been cleared. Not a glass, neither a cup nor a bowl, remained. It had been cleared.
Everything had been cleared out. She could just catch the
scent of the strange dishes Rakel's mother used to pre-
pare, especially on Sundays – with vanilla and spice. Even
scents disappeared; the scents Rakel had lived in were all
but gone. Vera could hear nothing now. Perhaps she'd
been mistaken? She went on deeper into the flat. She
opened the door of Rakel's room. The curtains had been
taken down. Her bed and her desk were gone. A coat
hanger lay on the floor. In the living room an empty
flower pot was standing on the windowsill. But that was
all. The walls were bare. She could catch the light patches

on the wallpaper where paintings had hung. And then she heard someone just the same. Someone came in. She was happy again, both happy and anxious at one and the same time, but mostly happy. She ran through the living room but was brought to an abrupt halt in the entrance hall. Two men in overalls were hauling a piano up the stairs; the sweat poured from them and they swore loudly on every second step – then the man at the back caught sight of Vera. 'Out of the way, girl!' he shouted. Vera glued herself to the doorframe as they bore the piano into the living room and put it down beside the fireplace. The two removal men put the straps of their overalls over their shoulders and one of them lit a cigarette. Now and again they looked over at Vera and smiled. The smaller of the two brushed back his hair and scratched his red fringe. 'Are you going to be the maid for the posh lot that's coming here?' he asked. The other one lit a cigarette himself and fought free of the strap that hung like a noose round his neck. ''Cos your hair needs a good comb, girl! That's a bird's nest you've got on your head!' They both began to laugh. 'You're welcome to borrow my comb,' the red-haired one said.

Vera hurried down the steps. The men gazed at her disappearing form, none the wiser. Outside a lorry was parked and the ground was covered in furniture. The caretaker was standing there in his dark suit talking to a lady with a green feather in her hat wearing pale gloves. Vera had never seen her before. She must have been a good deal over thirty and she was pregnant; her coat was tied tightly over her stomach, and she had her hands on her back and was pushing out her stomach as if she wanted to show the whole neighbourhood just how pregnant she was. Vera just stood and stared at her. In the end the newcomer became uneasy and pointed towards Vera, and the caretaker turned and saw her on the steps. He shook his head and at the same time smiled and started walking towards her. The removal men emerged from the stairway. Vera began to run, she ran round the corner, and as she did so she imagined that Rakel had just moved somewhere else, to another flat, one that was smaller – perhaps in the wake of all that had happened they could no longer afford such a substantial property, nor one that contained a separate room for their daughter. That was what she thought, over and over again – she held on to that thought. She had to go through the cellar to get to the backyard and the kitchen steps again; as she went she thought to herself that everything would be as before. *Everything would be as before* – the words were within her, she could hear them clearly and strongly, but she couldn't utter them, she couldn't even talk aloud to herself, as if it was silence that chose *her* now. She went up to the flat. No one was home yet. She went into the bathroom, undressed, found the scissors in the cupboard and put them into her mouth. She held the scissors in both hands and pressed the blades against her tongue. She closed her eyes, and pain was another language she did not need to speak – it was just a scream that sank deep inside her. She felt the point of the scissors passing through the soft flesh of her tongue and blood flowed into her mouth. She took out a fresh towel and soaked it in blood, then put it into the linen basket. She wiped up the blood on the floor and in the sink, and put another towel in between her legs, went into the bedroom and lay down. Vera smiled. Her tongue no longer felt strange in her face. She had made it part of her. *Now I have enough blood for each and every month.* She heard Boletta coming back. Boletta slammed the door behind her and came heavily through the flat and out onto the balcony. Immediately afterwards she was in the bedroom with Vera. She pretended to be asleep. But she could see her mother nonetheless, as if her eyelashes were see-through. She had a Danish flag in her hand and look pale and at the end of her tether. Silently she went round the side of the bed and picked up the *Telegraph Service Handbook* which was lying on her bedside table. And Vera could hear her reading aloud from it. Boletta sat in the living room and read aloud the rules for sending telegrams and the various rates that applied; she read aloud as if she had to listen to her own words in order to understand them completely. It sounded like wailing and cursing. It was like both prayer and complaint.

Calculating words. For the first word rendered in normal written form the number of letters permitted is fifteen. In code and cryptographic word or words, up to five letters or ciphers are permitted. The ungrammatical creation of compound words is not permitted. The names of individual locations, places, streets and ships may be written as single words and accounted for as such, as long as the total tally of letters does not exceed fifteen. Vera heard each and every word, and Boletta read them over and over again. There was something threatening about the language and the names – it was like the war. *Coded telegrams, express telegrams, radio telegrams.* The only one that sounded beautiful was the *congratulations telegram. Sent to Norwegian, Swedish, Danish and Icelandic stations together with Great Britain and Northern Ireland with a charge of fifty öre levied on attached forms.* Vera dreamed that a message boy in uniform, perhaps a blue uniform – yes, it had to be blue – with shining buttons, would stand at the door with a telegram like that for them. Then it would have to signify good news because otherwise he wouldn't have come, and this telegram, this attached form for fifty öre, would turn all that was bad to good. It could be in the form of a greeting from Rakel who wrote in short sentences (for otherwise it would be too expensive) that she'd be coming home soon. Or it could be that someone had found Wilhelm deep in the ice and cold, and that at last the Old One would have a grave to visit. Or perhaps it would just bear the words – *Everything that has happened has just been a dream.* But it was no message boy that came, it was the Old One, and she slammed the doors too. 'Where's my flag?' she shouted. 'Where's my Danish flag?' Vera noticed what a time Boletta took to close her book and get up. 'I've taken the flag away, Mother. You're showing us up in front of the whole city.' The Old One stamped the floor. 'What rubbish! King Haakon is

Danish!' Now it was Boletta's turn to shout. Vera dragged the quilt over her head and could have laughed aloud. 'King Haakon is Norwegian! That's the end of it!' 'Maybe he's the King of Norway, but he's my Danish prince! Aren't I allowed to have a Danish flag in my own flower-box?' 'I refuse to listen to you when you talk like that.' The Old One snorted. 'It's that wretched book which has put such nonsense into you. Your head's gone completely telegraphic!' Now Boletta stamped too, or maybe they both did as they screamed at each other. 'And you left Vera on her own at home! Have you no sense whatsoever, you old witch!'

After this peace reigned supreme in the living room for a long while. Boletta went to the bathroom; she shuffled over the floor as if she couldn't be bothered lifting her feet. But she ran back. 'Vera's had it!' she cried. The Old One listened. 'What's that you said?' 'You heard me well enough! Vera's had her bleeding!' Boletta held out the bloodied towel. The Old One folded her hands and had to sit down.

'God be praised,' she whispered. 'The King has come back and Vera has menstruated. Now life can go back to normal again.'

The Clock

And I can feel someone's breath on my neck now, I feel their breath, though this still isn't my story – I haven't made my appearance yet. I'm not on the track, out in the warmth – and even when I do get there, out onto the track, I'll no doubt get caught up in reams of detail like the slowcoach I am. A lace that breaks on the way to dancing classes, the vicar I stick my tongue out at, right in front of Majorstuen church, a lemonade bottle I have to get my money back on from Esther in the kiosk – all these things, all this that some will believe is meaningless, missing the point, a roundabout way of saying things simply – but which may be just as much the mysterious passive perspective necessary in all stories, from the stillness somewhere at one side. It's right there I intend to sit and listen to all you others, but you won't be able to see me. And it's in this quiet I hear the Old One saying, over and over again – *Now life can go back to normal again.* Because they believe everything is as it should be. They think that Vera is herself again. She has bled as normal and everything will be as it was before. The red slippers are neatly positioned beside the divan. The Palace flag is hoisted. The moon is hanging from a branch over Aker and once again a day has exactly twenty-four hours. Because for five years of war time has been out of action. War took time prisoner and cut it up, second by second, minute by minute. War is precise. War is from hand to mouth. War is made of moments, of little happenings. But now they can put time together again, wind it up and make it go. The Old One buys more Malaga at the Majorstuen 'pole'. Boletta keeps on reading from the *Telegraph Service Handbook*, until her headache hammers inside her like a woodpecker. And at the Exchange she avoids Director Egede because she still hasn't said whether or not she'll accept the new position.

Vera has a long lie-in every morning. Then, without any sense of joy, she gets up. She drags herself slowly through the flat. She puts on big jumpers and loose jackets even though the weather is becoming warmer and warmer. Some say it's set to be the hottest summer of the century, and there's a reason for that, for this is the summer the people deserve. She barely eats, preferring to feel her own lightness; she would rather grow inwards and get closer to her own shadow. From the kitchen she can see that there are new curtains in Rakel's flat – dark-red – but she still hasn't seen anyone inside. Down in the yard the clothes-lines are crammed with winter garments and sheets; the caretaker walks along the gravel weeding. The stray cat lies in a sunny corner in a circle of fur – until Bang sees it and chases it off with a rake. Even then the cat only stretches sleepily, lifts its tail and sprays a flowerpot before vanishing unhurriedly through the gate onto Jonas Rein Street. The boys out in the yard are polishing their bicycles and repairing the tyres; occasionally they glance up at her window but there's no one there now. Vera sees all of this and fills her silence with all of it, a silence that's beginning to get on Boletta's nerves – she's on the point of shaking a few words out of her daughter. But the Old One whispers – *Those who speak no words, tell no lies*. One night Vera cuts open the wound in her tongue again and feels her mouth fill with blood to overflowing, and she lets her towels absorb this blood. This is her hopeless lie – her hope nonetheless – as hopeless as waiting for Rakel. Time had been taken prisoner. Now time had been set free. Vera stands by the window and sees that the boys are clad in waterproofs and that they've grown in the course of the summer; they're almost unrecognizable and they cycle out through the gate without looking back.

One morning, just before Boletta left for the Exchange to meet Director Egede and finally give him an answer, the doorbell rang. Vera heard the sound in bed and was awake at once. Someone rang their doorbell early in the morning in September 1945. For a second she was sure, quite sure, that it was Rakel, that finally she'd come back. Vera got up, almost paralysed with joy and looked out into the hall. Boletta opened the outer door. But it wasn't Rakel. A bald man was standing there instead, and Vera could just recollect him, but the memory was vague and indistinct, from another time altogether. He wore a light coat and the rain was still dripping from his narrow shoulders; he carried a small square case with two polished clasps on each side, and in his other hand he held a grey hat. And when Vera set eyes on the suitcase she was certain she knew who he was, and for some reason he gave her the creeps – she always shivered when he came to visit. He lifted his case, as if realizing it was that they would recognize first. 'I hope you remember me,' he said. 'Because I certainly remember you as if it was only yesterday I last saw you!' His smile enveloped his whole face and he bowed. Boletta let him in. 'Of course I remember you. Barring the hair, of course.' He quickly drew a hand over his bald head and the smile was reduced to a tight moue. 'I was in Grini,' was all he said.

He let his case drop to the floor. Boletta blushed and hung up his coat. He glanced round quickly; his eyes leapt from wall to wall and door to door as if his gaze alone could record every detail. Vera retreated. 'And everything's just where it was?' he asked. Boletta followed him into the hall. 'Yes, everything here is just where it was.' 'That's good to hear. There are far too many who're all for changes these days. They have to refurnish. And what's the point of that?' Again he let his gaze circle, slowly, right until it rested by the oval clock on the cabinet. It was twelve minutes past ten. 'I'm not quite certain if there's enough money,' Boletta breathed. 'We've rather lost count.' 'And tell me who hasn't? It'll take the rest of the autumn before we're back to normal again.' The man

turned to Boletta. 'I take cream with my coffee. If you
remember?' Boletta clapped her hands. 'But of course I
remember. Cream with your coffee. Can I tempt you with
some sugar too?' 'If you have it. Just three spoonfuls,
thank you.'

All at once the Old One stood at the dining-room door
in her nightgown and slippers. She shaded her eyes as if
there was strong sunlight in the flat. 'Are you talking to
yourself again, Boletta? Or are you trying to get Vera to
answer you?' Boletta hurried over to her. 'Arnesen's here,
Mother. You remember Mr Arnesen, don't you?'

For it was Arnesen, from the insurance company Bien,
who had come that morning. It was with him we had
insured our lives. Almost all those in the block had. He
tended to put in an appearance twice a year, once in
autumn and again in the spring, on exactly the same date,
as long as that didn't turn out to be a Sunday in which
case he would come on the Monday instead. It was a long
while since he last visited – back in September 1941. And
I can remember the oval clock, too, which always kept the
right time. On the last Saturday of each month, Boletta or
Mum would put money in the drawer under the clock-
face, just as if it was a savings box, and it was almost like
a time of prayer. Fred and I would stand with our hands
behind our backs and follow it all, as the coins were slot-
ted into the thin gap and we would hear the sharp ringing as they landed, all depending on how much was there
already. The soundless notes, too, that were folded
together with great concentration to be small enough to
fit. I liked the five kroner note best, with its blue colour
like the sky on a fine summer morning when there's
nothing to dread, and, of course, with the picture of
Nansen's face. I couldn't count to a hundred yet and
those notes were far too large and all but impossible to
get into the drawer. After that Arnesen could come to collect what they called the premium. I thought this was
something we could win, that the money would be transformed into a prize, a gift. But Arnesen never had one

with him. Quite the opposite, he just took the premium and went. In the end he took too much and put the premiums in his own shadowy pocket and lost everything just the same. And for long enough I believed that it was the money we put there which made the clock go. And if we put too much there it would go quicker, and if we forgot altogether time would slow down and soon stop completely. If only it had been like that! I tried it out one Christmas Day. I put two extra five öre coins in and it sounded as if there had been a landslide at the bottom of the clock. It made no difference. I remember Fred once emptying the whole drawer with a hairpin. But time didn't stop. The Old One needed to take a step closer. 'Arnesen? Is it really Arnesen? Well, life really is back to normal again.' He gave a deep bow. 'We insure both highdays and holidays. Life itself has a place on our calendar.' The Old One snorted. 'I think you should leave that in the hands of the Almighty, my good man. Your little briefcase isn't big enough for eternity.' Arnesen drew in his breath and pulled out a handkerchief with the insurance firm's monogram printed on it, as though he was surrendering, and begging for an end to hostilities. But the Old One came closer still and peered at him. 'Tell me, is there nothing left of what you used to have on your head?' 'He's been in Grini,' Boletta hissed. 'Shut up, Mother!'

Then Arnesen brought out the tubular key that only he had and positioned himself with his back to them, like a magician who didn't want to give away the secrets behind his tricks. He glanced over his shoulder and suddenly saw Vera in the shadow of the door. He smiled. Then all of them heard a click and Arnesen brought out the drawer under the clock-face; there was a rushing slide of money and no one could count that faster than Arnesen from Bien. He never needed to use his fingers – he counted with his eyes, his eye was the quickest muscle he had. Finally he put the whole lot in a leather bag with a zip (not unlike a pencil case), and placed it in his briefcase which he then proceeded to lock on both sides with enormous secrecy. All of it was like one great performance.

Boletta went into the kitchen to make coffee. Arnesen straightened up. 'It'll take a bit of time before the arithmetic's all sorted,' he said. 'The war's turned everything topsy-turvy.' The Old One crumpled into one single smile. 'Yes, the cheaper the human life, the dearer the premium. Isn't that it?' Arnesen gave her no answering smile. 'It's rather the case that some things are so precious they can't be valued in kroner and øre, Jebsen.' The Old One threw back her shoulders. 'Talk's cheap!' she said. 'Just you count your coins, that's what you're best at.'

Arnesen was about to answer back but decided against it. Instead he went into the living room, carrying the case that he never took his eyes off. Arnesen was given hospitality wherever he went, almost as if people felt guilty about something or wanted to make a good impression on him. Maybe it was because they thought their lives were in his hands. He walked slowly past the bookshelves, letting his finger run along the leather spines, looking round the room as he did so at the dining-room divan that was made up as a bed, the glass of Malaga, the game of patience. His fingers stopped at a wide gap in the shelf from which only the dust rose. Now Arnesen smiled again. 'He should have been shot,' he said. He sat down in the soft seat with his back towards the balcony. The Old One leaned over the table. 'Who should have been shot?' 'Hamsun. The traitor.' 'You mean the writer?' 'The writer and the traitor.' The Old One leaned back in the sofa. 'I prefer reading Johannes V. Jensen,' she said.

Boletta came back with the coffee tray and a bar of milk chocolate. Arnesen immediately broke off a piece and sucked it, and put four spoonfuls of sugar in his cup. The Old One was on the point of walking out but Boletta restrained her. 'What was it like in Grini?' she asked. Arnesen clamped his eyes shut and swallowed. 'It was worse for my wife. She had to wait with all that fear and uncertainty.' Now Arnesen could see clearly again and he cleared his voice with more chocolate. 'But she came through it. Women can be stronger than you think. That's certainly something the war's shown us.'

He gave a quick glance in the direction of his coffee cup. Boletta poured him some more and the Old One's sigh was even deeper. 'Waiting is a privilege we more than willingly surrender.' But Arnesen wasn't listening any more. His gaze ranged around the whole room again and suddenly he asked, 'Isn't it smaller here?' Boletta put her cup down. 'Smaller than what?' 'Than the flats on the other side of the block?' The Old One secured the last bit of chocolate before Arnesen got his hands on it. 'It's possible they *are* larger,' she admitted. 'But we have more sunlight up here.' 'I wouldn't be certain of that. We ourselves have a south-facing balcony.' Boletta and the Old One leaned forwards. 'We?' Arnesen smiled from ear to ear and his arm sailed through the air like a conductor's. 'I've got the corner flat on Jonas Rein Street. The one where that poor Jewish family lived.'

The Old One got up. Her hair scattered softly over her shoulders. 'Is Arnesen telling us we're neighbours now?' He lifted his cup with two fingers and looked about for more sugar. 'By rights we should have moved in before the summer. But first my wife wanted everything in place. You know what it's like, don't you?' Arnesen found the sugar bowl; he put two more spoonfuls in his coffee, pursed his lips and slowly drank. The Old One remained on her feet. She was shaking. 'No,' she said loudly, 'we don't know what it's like. What is it like?' Without a sound he put down his cup and suddenly his tone was very confidential and quiet. 'A piano, dessertspoons, an ironing board. And a cot. All the things that make a home. My wife is expecting our first child, you see. After all these years.' 'Shall I fetch more sugar?' the Old One asked. Arnesen looked up at her. 'No, thank you. I'm quite full now.'

Boletta had to cling onto the table. 'Are you quite sure they're not coming back?' she breathed. 'Who?' 'The

Steiner family. Rakel. Their daughter.' A shudder passed through Arnesen as though the teaspoon had given him a shock. He dropped it on his plate. Then he leaned back and almost sounded offended. 'But of course. They never came back from down there. Everyone knows that. There isn't even someone to whom we can give insurance money. Unfortunately.'

The Old One looked past Arnesen who sat sunk in his chair with a sad smile, and it was then she saw Vera. Vera was suddenly standing by the bedroom door staring in at them, and as the Old One saw her Vera hid her face in her hands and blood flowed out between her fingers. She collapsed onto the floor and now Boletta and Arnesen had turned too; they saw Vera and the blood that gushed from her mouth. Arnesen upset his coffee cup and the sugar bowl; Boletta reached her daughter in a single bound, and for the second time since the end of the war the Old One had to call for Dr Schultz from Bislet. Arnesen just stood by his chair unable to take his eyes off Vera – her nightgown, the skin that was almost transparent, the blood pumping from her mouth. Now he had something to keep secret on his rounds – but if someone pressed him he could perhaps let slip a word or two, about Vera lying on the floor twisting with spasms as she babbled between mouthfuls of blood. And those who listened to the tale he had to tell (perhaps the caretaker), would at once hunch closer and demand – *But what did she say? Did she mention any names?* Then Arnesen could guard his precious lies and keep quiet until neither he nor his audience could stand it any longer. Many years later I heard this one day when I was coming home from school and took a shortcut through the laundry rooms in the basement. The caretaker was standing there by the mangles telling stories to the women from the block, because he'd made those stories his own now – he'd converted his lies for a new currency. 'The blood was foaming all round her mouth,' he hissed. 'It was a red foam and she was hitting out with clenched fists like a wild animal!' 'But what did she say?'

the others wanted to know. 'Did she mention any names?' But the caretaker couldn't say any more than that.

The Old One put down the receiver. 'Dr Schultz is coming right away,' she said. Boletta was crying and Vera lay quiet in her arms. 'She's got an ulcer from eating so little! I've been saying that the whole time. That she must eat!' The Old One turned towards Arnesen. 'Now we're done with one another for this occasion. Pass on greetings to your wife.' But Arnesen had no wish to go. Arnesen didn't want to miss out on any of this. He tidied up the sugar he'd spilled and put his coffee cup back in its place and dried the cloth with his large handkerchief. He did everything quite slowly and he took his time. He even wanted to help Vera into the bedroom. 'I did my first aid training in the army,' he said. Then the Old One pointed in the direction of the hall and the outer door. 'I see your coat's still hanging there. You can take it on your way out.'

But first Arnesen had to count the money yet again. He had to open the briefcase and check the total, coin by coin and note by note. When the Old One came out of the bedroom and Vera now lay in bed, Boletta weeping and ages late for work, Arnesen was still standing in the hallway, his coat over his arm, twisting his hat like a rat between his hands. 'Is the poor little girl any better?' he murmured. 'Does she often suffer attacks like that?' 'Vera's had pneumonia for several weeks now. I said goodbye.' Arnesen's smile was all but imperceptible. 'Pneumonia? It's possible the firm might want to see a medical certificate before deciding the premium.' The Old One opened the door wide. 'We have already called the doctor. For the third time goodbye and farewell.'

Arnesen bowed, picked up his suitcase and slowly went out towards the stairs where he stood buttoning up his coat. The Old One was about to shut the door but suddenly changed her mind and caught hold of his arm. 'How can you really be so sure the Steiners aren't coming back?' 'Because they're dead! I told you that. D'you not read the papers? And there's no point letting the flat lie empty.' The Old One let go her hold of him and immediately he began rummaging for something in his pockets. It was a cutting, a photograph. 'Look at that,' he told her. 'It's from the journal *Vecko*. That's Mrs Steiner and her daughter Rakel, isn't it?'

The Old One took the picture from him and raised it closer to her eyes. It was them. A huge sorrow and an equally huge anger suffused her. It was Rakel and her mother. Her mother is dying or perhaps already dead – skin and bones, clad in rags, the skin stretched taut over her skull, her eyes far too large and staring towards the camera or God or their executioner. And Rakel is holding her mother's hand – she is all but naked, her shoulders sharp as wishbones. She is clinging to herself, crying, screaming – her mouth an open sore in her young girl's face which is already old, ageless, gone beyond time. Death is closing on her too, a crippled child, and this is what the picture shows – the dying clinging to the dead. Underneath the photograph are written these words – *The dreaded Ravensbruck camp. Eventually the concentration camp became too crowded and some no longer had any prison garb.* That's all. The Old One has to support herself against the wall. 'And you go round with this in your pocket,' she said in a low voice. 'You should be ashamed of yourself.' 'I only saw that it was them,' he mumbled. 'So I cut it out. May I have it back now?' 'No,' the Old One said. 'I'm keeping this picture. For as long as you live in their flat.' Arnesen put on his hat and slunk off. The Old One let him pass. 'I hope one day we'll all sleep soundly again,' she said.

At that moment they heard Dr Schultz down below on the stairs, his footsteps heavy, his hand on the banister. Arnesen glanced at the Old One. 'Thanks, but I myself sleep perfectly. Except when my wife lies awake.' Then he quickly went downstairs and as he passed Dr Schultz, who was thinner than ever but sober that day, he gave

him his card. Dr Schultz stood there a moment, read it
and shook his head. Arnesen had stopped on the landing
below; he stood holding his hat and was smiling again.
'Call whenever it's convenient, Doctor!' 'But it isn't convenient. Unfortunately there's nothing I want to insure.'
Dr Schultz put the card in his pocket and climbed the last
of the stairs to the Old One who was waiting impatiently.
She pulled him inside and banged the door shut behind
them. 'She's in the bedroom. Hurry! There's no need to
take off your shoes!'

Once again Dr Schultz chose to be alone with Vera
while he conducted his examination of her. The Old One
and Boletta waited in the living room. They said nothing.
They listened. It was so still, almost as if Vera's muteness
had filtered into the furnishings themselves – the walls,
the lampshades, the carpets, the pictures – to give everything a darker shade and a deeper smell. There was a
draught from the door onto the balcony, a cold shudder
about their feet. The wind thrashed the leaves from the
trees in Church Road. The first summer after the end of
the war had well and truly disappeared beneath its own
foliage. Denmark beat the Norwegian national squad 2–1
in Copenhagen. The bombs had fallen on Hiroshima and
Nagasaki, and man's shadow had been imprinted on the
earth for ever. And still Dr Schultz remained with Vera.

The Old One got up, impatient. 'I'm freezing! Whatever you say, I'm freezing!' Boletta sat with folded hands.
'I haven't said a thing,' she replied. 'I'm still freezing,'
the Old One told her. 'Has the doctor gone to sleep in
there? I'm going in to see!' Boletta held her back. 'Let
him be.' 'Well, I'll light the stove instead. Tonight I'm
having warm Malaga and Vera'll have some too! With
quinine!' Boletta let her go. 'You do that, Mother. Light
the stove.'

The Old One lit a match, dropped it through the hatch
and opened the damper. Soon they could feel the growing
warmth and the Old One laid her hands on the insecure
surface of the hob and sighed. 'I don't want to be insured

with Arnesen any longer,' she said. 'And that's final.'
'Don't be silly,' Boletta replied. 'Then he'll take the clock
too.' 'That can't be helped. I just cannot abide him!' Now
it was Boletta's turn to sigh. 'You've just become a moan.
That's a fact. A moan!' The Old One stamped her foot. 'I
have not. I'm only saying that I can't abide Arnesen!' 'And
you can't abide Dr Schultz either. You're insolent to the
whole lot of them!' The Old One whispered over her
shoulder, 'But what is that idiot doing? He was sober
when he went in, wasn't he?' Boletta had got herself
worked up now and wouldn't let it go. 'Nor can you bear
the caretaker!' The Old One chuckled by the stove. 'And
what sort of sport was it that fool did when he was
young? The triple jump! That ridiculous creature! And
now you've gone and got your headache again and you
should just give your tongue a break.' 'You like no one any
more!' Boletta shouted. 'That's not true.' 'Then tell me
someone you like. If you can still remember the right
name!' 'With pleasure. I like Johannes V. Jensen!'

The Old One interrupted herself with a little squeak
and brought her warm hands against her breast, almost as
if she'd burnt her fingers on the stove. Boletta got up
quickly. 'What is it, Mother?' The Old One pointed at the
small, sooty stove window where the flames rose tall and
golden. 'We've burnt Hamsun,' she whispered. 'There is
Hamsun burning.'

At the same moment Dr Schultz came out of the bedroom, and he came quietly. He closed the door behind
him, went in to the two women in the living room and
carefully put down his bag. He remains standing like that
for a time, looking down at his galoshes. One of them
hasn't been cleaned, or perhaps it's because he stood in a
puddle on the way over.

At last Dr Schultz looked up. He spoke at length, his
voice low. 'Vera has again lost a good deal of blood.' The
Old One took a step closer, her breathing heavy. 'We
know that. But this time she bled from her mouth!' Dr
Schultz nodded. 'Yes, she's given herself a nasty bite in

the tongue.' Boletta sank down in the sofa and smiled. 'She's bitten herself in the tongue? So it's not a stomach ulcer she has?' 'Oh no. It's anything but a stomach ulcer. Pardon me, but is it particularly warm in here?' Dr Schultz's forehead was shining and he drew one finger inside his crumpled collar to let some air in. The Old One went closer still. 'Yes,' she said. 'It is warm in here. As a matter of fact we're burning the collected works of Hamsun.' 'What did you say?' 'But would you now tell us Vera's condition!'

Dr Schultz turned instead to Boletta. 'There is nothing wrong with Vera,' he told her. 'Except for . . . I mean . . .' He was suddenly quiet and looked down again at his ridiculous galoshes. The Old One was up on her toes. 'Except for what, young man? Speak up, for God's sake!'

Dr Schultz, that young man of close on sixty, drew himself up as best he could. 'How can I put it?' he began slowly and hesitatingly. The Old One was almost on top of him. 'Well, I'll tell you! Quite simply you'll spit it out and not stand there stammering like a knock-kneed cadet!' Dr Schultz drew his hand under his nose where the drop still hung and refused to be wiped away. 'So you both know nothing?'

But now the Old One did something that was talked about for long enough in Church Road and which is talked about perhaps to this day by those who also remember Boletta's screech which caused plaster, slates and loose change to rattle from Fagerborg to Adamstuen. It wouldn't surprise me. But what *does* surprise me is that anyone at all got to hear of it, because I can't imagine that Dr Schultz himself told a soul – quite the opposite, he would rather have kept it quiet or even lied about it. And it certainly wasn't one of us. Besides, Dr Schultz died not long after. When the first snow came in November he decided to embark on the great journey from Mylla once more, and he never returned. Some walkers found him the following spring, way out beyond the ski runs, between Sandungen and Kikut. He was still holding onto his poles, but the single drop under his nose had finally broken off and it lay like a pale pearl in his decayed mouth. In his pockets there wasn't so much as a wallet or a scraper for his skis, just a card from a man who sold life insurance – and as a result the police first thought this was Gotfred Arnesen, the agent from the Bien insurance company, lying there having taken his last stride. There was a good deal of a rumpus over this when the two officers called on his wife to tell her that tragically her husband had been found dead on Nordmarka. It was she who almost died as a result, even though the misunderstanding was cleared up when Gotfred Arnesen arrived home from work at the usual time, impatient to see his little boy who was three months old. After that she was never quite herself again; the groundless message left a scar in her, and she grew afraid of opening the door when the bell rang and always dressed in black. In the end she forbade her husband, Gotfred Arnesen, to leave the flat.

But that's not what I want to relate now – I'm jumping ahead, caught up by my own flashforward. For this is what happened now – the Old One quite simply slapped Dr Schultz, with the flat of her hand she hit him hard across the face. 'Would you tell us what you're hiding!' Dr Schultz bent down and rubbed his finger over his dirty galosh. Then he drew himself up, the drop a pendulum under his nose, his cheek burning. 'Perhaps I too saved a life,' he murmured. 'Today Hippocrates would be proud of me.' 'What on earth are you babbling about?' the Old One roared.

Dr Schultz swallowed and had to clear his throat.

'Vera is pregnant,' he said.

Boletta was already on her way to the bedroom but the Old One stopped her and addressed Dr Schultz again in the gentlest of tones. 'My dear Dr Schultz. Tell us something we *don't* know. We know that Vera is pregnant. What we want to find out is if everything is all right with the child and herself.' The doctor exhaled. 'Everything looks to be perfectly fine.' Boletta could barely speak. 'Has she said anything?' Dr Schultz shook his head. 'Not yet. But give her time. May I ask, by the way, about one thing?' The Old One nodded and had to support Boletta. 'Who is the lucky father-to-be?' 'He died in the events of last May,' the Old One answered quickly. 'They were to be married then.'

Dr Schultz looked away and stroked his finger over his cheek. 'Please forgive my indiscretion. I'm a doctor, not a vicar. Hippocrates is displeased with me. You ought to hit me again.'

The Old One carefully laid her hand on his and gently squeezed it. He took his black bag and left them. They never saw him again. They heard only the youngest of the boys ringing their bicycle bells and laughing as he came out onto the street.

Boletta stared at the Old One who was still holding her arm, and she hardly knew whether to weep or yell. 'Did you know?' she hissed. The Old One shook herself free. 'Were we to let Dr Schultz think we didn't? A lie is quicker told than the truth.'

And then they went in to see Vera. She lay in the bed staring up at the roof, at the angular crystal chandeliers, her eyes shut. Boletta fell on her knees beside her daughter. 'Tell us,' she begged, 'what happened in the drying loft.'

But Vera would say nothing. She maintained her silence. The Old One went to get the bottle of Malaga and had to use both hands to pour the last of it into her glass. 'We have to take good care of this child,' she said softly.

That afternoon the Old One went down to the police station in Majorstuen. She had to wait three quarters of an hour before being admitted to see a young constable positioned behind his typewriter. 'I want to report a rape,' she tells him. The constable looks up and can't hide the smile beneath his fair, thin beard. 'A rape? Have you been raped?' The Old One looms over the raw recruit. 'My granddaughter has been raped, young man! Are you trying to make a monkey out of me?'

The constable blushes and prepares the sheet of paper in his typewriter. 'Not at all, madam. And when did this happen? The rape, I mean.' 'The 8th of May,' the Old Ones replies. The constable raises both hands from the keys and looks at her again. 'The 8th of May? That's almost four months ago.' 'You don't need to tell me that,' the Old One retorts. 'Can you now get going with the investigation!'

And the constable slowly writes down on the sheet of paper the name, address and date, together with the nature of the crime, and he then puts it at the bottom of a whole pile of accumulated reported incidents. The Old One purchases a bottle of Malaga at the 'pole' and makes inquiries about Chinese bark at the chemist's, for when a concoction of this is prepared it soothes sorrow, hangovers and waiting. Never before has Church Road been so steep beneath her feet. She stands for a while down in the yard. She watches the young boys playing pitch and toss by the stairs. Their faces are soft and incomplete, they squat around the money pot – with laughter and quick fists and clinking five øre pieces. Then they become aware of her, almost as if the Old One's gaze is too heavy for their narrow shoulders, and they get up, silent and serious, and turn in her direction. *No*, she thinks, *they're innocent, they haven't grown up enough to commit such a deed; they're still just children in search of their own faces*. The Old One smiles and finds a coin to throw them, and their earnestness breaks into rejoicing and merriment as they stretch their arms into the air and playfully push each other out of the way.

But then Bang the caretaker comes out onto the stairs with a toolbox under his arm. He picks up the coin which has landed on the step right in front of him. The boys fall silent once more. 'What's going on here? Play here in the yard is strictly forbidden!' *No*, the Old One muses, *no, neither was it him, all-powerful as he is in his own simplicity and with a limp that would have given him away as the perpetrator in the blink of an eye.* 'Give them back their money!' she commands him.

And the Old One can't get to sleep that night. She goes in and disturbs Boletta who's also lying awake watching over Vera. She's the only one who's sleeping. 'There were all kinds of folk here over those days,' the Old One murmurs. 'What do you mean?' 'Up in the lofts. All kinds of folk were hiding there through the month of May.' Boletta hid her face in her hands. 'Let's hope it was a soldier,' the Old One goes on, her voice still quieter. 'A Norwegian soldier who couldn't come to terms with the war inside.' 'Oh, Lord,' Boletta moans. 'That we let her go there alone! Oh, Lord.' The Old One sits down on the bed. 'God hasn't been a great help to us yet,' she admits.

Blåsen

One afternoon in January in the new year of 1946, the Old One's sitting up on Blåsen, the highest part of Sten Park, looking out over the silent city. It makes her feel at peace to sit there. This is her place. She can see the fiord lying grey and heavy beneath the cold fog piling over Ekeberg. The Christmas trees are on the balconies with the remains of decorations hanging from their dry, brown branches. The Old One is sorrowful and afraid. Vera has still not said a word and she's carrying a child she can no longer conceal. It's an insanity which is driving them all quietly mad. Boletta lies awake at night and is losing weight, unable to forgive herself for letting Vera go alone to the drying loft. And every day Vera stands in front of the mirror, her head bowed, unable to look at herself. Soon she will have to have two mirrors. Who was it who broke in on her on that day of rejoicing? The Old One doesn't know. She only knows this – he who did this, he who is the father of this child – he had his way, he ripped up and he destroyed, he brought the darkness down over Vera and deserves nothing more than even greater pain and an even greater darkness. But she says it again in her inmost being – *we have to take good care of this child*. Because the Old One knows all about grief. Sorrow is the Old One's strength. That's what sustains her – it's her storm, her fulcrum. She will teach Vera to carry sorrow like triumph, and pain like a bouquet which will burst into flower each night. But at that moment she hears footsteps in the snow and she doesn't need to turn around because she already knows who it will be. And she thinks to herself – *I'm neither sorrowful nor afraid. I'm old and wise*, and who else was there to be that – old and wise and brave – if not her? The Old One smiles as Vera sits down beside her and waits a long while before saying anything; they're both equally quiet and accept one another's silence. 'I'm sure you haven't come here to talk,' the Old One says at last. 'But you can come here to me just the same.' Vera lays her head against her shoulder. The Old One trembles for a moment. She remembers a time they'd been filming for three whole days and eighteen scenes had been done – the film's title was *The Chambermaid and the New Guest*. They had even built a studio on a piece of ground outside Copenhagen, and her eyes were burning after all those hours in the strong light. But she felt good, for this was going to be a success, a sensation – they were sure of it and each one of them felt good, from the person in charge of the clapper-board to the director, from the pianist to the hero. Then they heard a shout from the photographer and all at once he began crying. He had forgotten to put film in his camera. It wasn't possible. It couldn't be. And yet it had happened. All was in vain. Each and every glance and movement forgotten, disappeared, as if it had never been, as if everything which wasn't imprinted on a roll of film was untrue, unreal, nothing. The director got up, just stood where he was, then sat down again and buried his head in his hands. No one dared say a word. And the Old One, who was young then, beautiful and sought after, she was the only one who dared speak. 'We'll just do it again,' she said. But it didn't work. It couldn't be done again. They had to find something else, a new title, a new story. And regardless of what they did they always compared it with that which hadn't been filmed, and they were always dissatisfied. They could never improve on that which wasn't there. *That was the end*, the Old One thinks now, and she shivers again. The best film wasn't just silent, it was invisible too. She'd like to tell Vera about it, but she says something else instead because maybe she's told the same story before and essentially it's a sad one. 'I know what you're thinking, even if you don't say anything, Vera. That's what it means to be deaf. I only hear thoughts and dreams and the beating of hearts.'

The Old One gives a sigh and puts her arm round her and brushes the snow from her hair. 'Someone hurt you, my little Vera. As badly as it's possible to hurt another. But forgive me and forgive Boletta for not having understood your silence.'

They sit thus, Vera and the Old One, their arms round each other at the top of Sten Park with its view over the city, that same city I'll get lost in, even though it lies small and cramped between the hills, and with skies overhead smaller than the lid of a shoebox. 'Have I told you about the Night Man? That's what they called him. The Night Man. He came here with dead horses and buried them here. We're sitting on a hill of buried horses, Vera. But no one knew what he did by day. Some said that he slept with the dead horses. And in the end he disappeared completely.'

Now it's the Old One who has to lean on Vera's shoulder.

'There are too many night men in our family,' she whispers.

They go back home before it becomes too cold to sit there and Vera gets to borrow the Old One's shawl. And when they cross Pilestredet, below Bayern, where the odd-shaped German barracks remain standing and are used as nursery schools, they meet Arnesen and his wife – she as many months pregnant as Vera. She has an expensive fur mantle about her and she measures Vera with a silent smile as Arnesen raises his hat. 'I see that the fortuitous circumstances are no longer to be hidden,' he says. The Old One looks him right in the eye. 'My good man, we have nothing to hide! Goodbye!'

She takes Vera by the arm and pulls her away. Arnesen returns his hat to its lodgings. 'I'm coming to empty the clock soon,' he calls after them. 'And remember that the premium's to be raised. If you keep the child.'

But the Old One walks on, her back straight, holding Vera tight. 'Don't look back,' she breathes. 'That's one joy Arnesen and his equally wretched wife won't have.'

She notices that Vera has grown pale round her mouth; her lips are trembling and on the stairs she grows unsteady as if under a heavy weight – she gasps for breath and in the entrance hall she sinks to the floor with a scream. Boletta's there at once. 'Good Lord,' she whispers. 'Has the cold made her ill?' The Old One is kneeling by Vera. 'No,' she answers. 'Vera is giving birth.'

And how am I to begin to describe that pain, birth's very fury and love – I, the infertile one, standing beyond all this? I settle for this – the sudden contractions in the powerful muscles of the womb have begun. The lowest part of the cervix stretches; a tunnel for the foetus that has lain in this warm cavity, this balloon of water, for thirty-eight weeks. In other words, this is an impatient and inconsiderate foetus who's driving a course through the pelvis, and the pain increases, tearing at the edges of the abdominal wall and the diaphragm, for now is the moment – the child is digging its way out. And Boletta gets hold of a taxi and together with the Old One they carry Vera down and put her in the back seat, and the driver, a young fellow in his uniform and newly cleaned cap, looks at them terrified as the Old One commands – 'To Ullevål Hospital, young man. The maternity unit! Now!'

And he drives up Church Road faster than the law permits, Vera moaning and making noises in her throat, sheets of sweat streaming down her face. Then all at once every sound from her is stilled and she sinks down in the seat. Carefully Boletta raises her skirt and sees the head appearing – a wrinkled, slimy head already drawing breath for a first scream. Then the rest of the baby appears and it's a boy; together with the placenta and a torrent of blood and mucus membrane.

The driver screeches to a halt and the child lies howling on the seat between Vera's thighs – alive and raging – and that's how my brother came to this world, my half brother, born in a taxi at the junction of Church Road and Ullevål Road.

And this is the first thing Vera says; she sits there with fastened eyes and utters these strange words – 'How many fingers has he?' Boletta looks at the Old One who bends down over the roaring child to count the fingers on each hand. 'He's ten fine fingers,' she murmurs.

Vera opens her eyes and smiles. The driver leans against the steering wheel, and he doesn't give a thought to his leather seats covered in blood and afterbirth and fluid; because there is no time for that when a new person has come to the world in his cab. No, instead he works out weeks and months and does all sorts of mental arithmetic to arrive at May, May 1945. 'You can't call that boy anything but Fred,' he says in the end.

Fred used to say that. *I was christened by a taxi driver in the middle of a bloody junction.* And I think he liked saying it, because he always smiled afterwards, just a little; he'd give a quick laugh and brush his hand over his face as if he were blushing, even though it was only me there to hear him.

The Name

Vera's awake. The Old One and Boletta are sitting with her. There's a screen behind them. Vera can see shadows slowly moving on the other side. She can hear low voices and all at once the sound of a baby crying. 'Where is he?' Vera asks. The Old One gently dries her damp forehead. 'They're looking after him,' she says. Vera sits up. 'Is there something wrong? There is something wrong, isn't there? Tell me!' The Old One pushes her softly back onto the pillows. 'Nothing's wrong, my little Vera. He's happy and healthy and has the best lungs of them all. Don't you remember what the taxi driver called him?' Vera glances at her and gives a quick smile. 'Fred,' she breathes. 'And it was Fred who got you talking again,' the Old One reminds her, and turns towards Boletta, who has been silent up to this point, but now stretches out to take her daughter's hand. 'There's something they have to know, Vera.' 'I want to see him, Mum.' 'Yes, you'll soon get to hold him. But they'll ask you something first. Who the father is.' Vera shuts her eyes. Her face twitches. 'I don't know,' she answers. 'Didn't you see him?' The Old One puts a finger to her lips. 'Talk more quietly. There are too many listening ears.' The shadows have stopped at the screen. Vera weeps. 'He came behind me,' she murmurs. 'I only saw his hands.' Boletta leans still closer. 'There were all sorts hiding up in the loft in those days. Did he say anything to you?' Vera shakes her head. 'He didn't speak. He had a missing finger.' Quite suddenly she starts laughing. 'He just had one finger missing,' she repeated. 'Just one finger!' The shadows pause and tremble a moment before moving away from the screen. Boletta has to cover her mouth with her hand and the Old One bends her head. 'Forgive us, Vera. Forgive us.'

And Fred himself lies with the other newborn infants, the first babies of peacetime, in rows to left and to right. These are the golden ones, the beautiful, who will never know war, who will grow up with a prosperity that runs away with itself and eventually becomes too much for them to bear. For a time they will turn their backs on this opulence and seek out nature instead and adopt an affected poverty, only to catch up later with all they left behind in an even greater orgy of eating at the groaning buffet of good living. Fred sleeps fitfully, as if already at two days old he's suffering nightmares, and when he wakes up he screams more piercingly than all the others. He clenches his little fists into red spheres, but still no one has carried him in to his mother's breast – instead he gets warmed-up milk from a bottle. When he cries, for such a time that all the other babies begin to try to outdo him, they take him into another room and lay him down there. And suddenly Fred grows still, becomes soundless, he doesn't shut his eyes but stares instead, as if in that moment he's starting to explore the loneliness he can't escape and which in the end he will choose for himself.

The next time the screen is moved three men approach Vera's bed. Two are doctors but the third is wearing a dark suit and carries a folder under his arm. They position themselves around her. 'I want to see my child,' she whispers. 'Please.' One of the doctors pulls a chair to the bedside and sits down. 'Your mother says you were raped.' Vera turns away, but she can't avoid being seen all the same. 'You don't know who the child's father is,' the other doctor says. *He could be Norwegian. Or German. But you don't know. The child has no father.* They talk together warmly and unhurriedly. The man in the dark suit draws out a sheet of paper. 'The case is shelved. On the grounds of the nature of the evidence. The relationship was not reported until four months following the alleged assault.' The two doctors are silent for a moment. The one who's seated then takes Vera's hand. 'How do you feel now?' he asks. 'I want Fred,' she breathes. 'Can you not bring him?'

The doctor smiles. 'You've already given the boy a name?' Vera nods. 'I want to talk to Dr Schultz,' she says. 'Dr Schultz is not available. He went missing on a skiing trip.' The doctor lets go of her hand and looks up. 'She's suffered deep psychosis and hasn't spoken for nine months.' A nurse pushes the screen to one side and for a second Vera sees Mrs Arnesen sitting up in bed under a window, her back supported by a large pillow, her little one cradled at her breast. And Mr Arnesen suddenly stops, he has a bouquet in one hand and his hat in the other; they both stare at her, and the moment is devoid of sound and movement, until the screen is put back in place and shadows are dispelled by the light. 'Why can't I hold Fred?' Vera weeps. The man in the dark suit has sat down too now. 'You must realize that everything we do is in your best interests. And that means in the best interests of your child too. Because the child must come first, mustn't it?' Vera nods. He puts a sheet of paper beside her glass on the bedside table. 'There are many good homes to be found, both here in the city and across the country. That's perhaps for the best.' 'What do you mean?' Vera murmurs. 'That the boy will be sent to another part of the country. That will be for the best.'

Then the screen is pushed to one side again, but so violently this time that it clatters to the floor. The Old One is standing there. She is aroused but her voice is low. 'The three women in our house have a combined age of 131, and together we will take good care of Vera's boy! Is that understood?' She goes round the bed, snatches up the form on the bedside table and rips it in such small shreds that not a letter remains legible. 'Can the child now meet his mother?'

They bring him that same evening. He lies peacefully at her breast. He waits. Can I put it that way? Can I say that Fred waits, that it's warm and well where he lies, there in the circle of the heart, and that he waits? Yes, this is the way I choose to express it. Fred waits. *He doesn't like me,* she suddenly thinks. And Vera hears the stillness that moves from bed to bed when she carries him out two days later, and she meets the gazes that follow her down the length of the corridor. The silent rumour spreads; doors that open quietly and whisper shut once more. It's snowing and all is still. She keeps to her bed for three weeks until she stops bleeding. Fred waits. The Old One and Boletta are amazed that he doesn't cry any more. They lie awake at night because of his stillness. Each forenoon they can hear the piano playing that comes from the other side of the yard – it sounds like Mozart. And one morning as the snow melts and runs in streams through the streets and drips from the gutters, Vera's out pushing Fred in his pram. He gazes up at her with the dark stillness she's already begun to get used to. When the sun shines on his face he turns away and closes his eyes, and doesn't open them again until the shadows return. Then Vera notices Mrs Arnesen rounding the corner with her pram. The two of them are immediately cautious. They stop just the same. They are proud and don't say a great deal. They look ahead. Vera tries to be friendly. 'You play the piano so beautifully,' she tells her. Mrs Arnesen smiles and spreads the quilt over her little boy. 'He always falls asleep before I finish.' They both laugh. They are two mothers, without apprehension, united – before they are jerked out of this fragile friendship, this fleeting encounter. 'Do I disturb you?' Mrs Arnesen suddenly inquires. Vera turns round. The caretaker's standing by the gate staring at them. He's holding a dead cat. He flings it away and goes into the yard. 'What?' Vera asks. Mrs Arnesen hesitates. 'Does my playing disturb you?' Vera looks up. 'No, I think Fred likes it too. He doesn't cry any more.' Now Mrs Arnesen smiles again. 'You've already a name for him,' she says. 'Yes, it would appear so. What's your boy to be called?' 'He'll have my father-in-law's name. We're christening him next Saturday.'

The following day Vera is seated in the vicar's office in Majorstuen church. The vicar's name is Sunde and he is close to fifty. His forehead resembles a shield. He pushes his glasses into place and looks through some document or other, and takes all the time in the world to do so. The cross behind him is hanging askew. The huge Bible with its black covers seems to suck in all the light to itself and concentrate it in one single dark glowing point in the middle of the table. Finally he looks at her. 'Is it not good to hear that?' he asks. Vera listens – she can't hear a thing. 'What?' she whispers. 'Did you not hear them?' Vera listens again, but isn't able to understand what he means, and chooses not to say anything either. The vicar leans towards her. 'The church bells,' he says. 'Is it not wonderful to hear real church bells after five years of ungodliness?' 'Yes,' Vera murmurs, but doesn't hear them, it's completely silent. The vicar waits a while. He just looks at her. 'You must listen inside,' he tells her in the end. 'Deep inside, Vera. Or is it silent there too?' Vera looks down and the vicar looks through his document once more. It's good to think that one day I'll get the chance to stick my tongue out at him and call him vicar vomit. Vera hears her heartbeat now, heavy echoes that make her fingers tick. 'Who is the father?' the vicar asks suddenly. 'The forms explain what happened,' she replies. 'There's no need to tell me what's written there. I can read that myself.' The vicar gets up and comes round the table. 'Let me ask you something, Vera. Have you done something you regret?' She shakes her head. 'You haven't in any way had intercourse with the enemy?' Vera holds her breath. Then she gets up herself. 'Yes, I have done something I regret.' The vicar waits. He's waiting for more, for her confession, and he waits with a smile. 'I regret that I came here,' says Vera and goes towards the door. The vicar follows her, pale and raging. 'I hear the kid has already got a name,' he says. 'But d'you know what Fred really means?' Vera stops a moment. 'It means the name of my son,' she answers. The vicar's mouth twists to a smile once more. 'It means *powerful*,' he hisses. 'Don't you think that's a mite inappropriate?'

Vera stands outside on Church Road. She can't remember how she got down there. Esther waves from her kiosk. Vera forgets to wave back. She goes homewards.

She stops in the yard. Something smells, something rotten. It's the dead cat. It's still lying there in the bin shed. Vera hurries past. She notices Mrs Arnesen hanging things out to dry: clothes for the baptism, a skirt, a white shirt. The pram stands in the shadow of the tall birch. Everything is green and still. Then two men come in the gate. One is dressed in uniform, the other's wearing a long, dark coat despite the warmth of the day. They go over first to Vera and for a second she thinks they're from Majorstuen police station and that they've found the perpetrator, the man who attacked her. And it frightens Vera as much as it surprises her that she doesn't know at this precise moment, a moment of truth in her eyes, whether she's relieved or made even more afraid. Because now the shadow of evil that came over her from behind, the shadow with just nine fingers, will have a name, and she doesn't know if she wants it like this, that she should hear the shadow's name and see the shadow's face. But it's not Vera they want to talk to, it's Mrs Arnesen they're looking for; there was no one in the flat and so they're seeing now if she's down in the yard. The men are grave, almost dismissive, and Vera immediately imagines they're there with bad news, with some dreaded message, and she turns towards Mrs Arnesen who's standing under the clothes line and is still ignorant of what is about to happen. Vera points. 'That's her,' she says. The two men nod and go towards Mrs Arnesen. Vera sees them shaking hands; Mrs Arnesen looks astonished to begin with, perhaps even expectant. Then she gives a laugh, high-pitched and brittle, more like a shriek, and suddenly her face becomes utterly still, thin and taut like dry grass. And this puzzle, this inconceivable and impossible thing, that her husband, the insurance salesman Gotfred Arnesen, should be found dead far off the beaten track on Nordmarka, between Mylla and Kikut, with only a calling card in the breast pocket of his anorak, which has kept far better than the frail body the same anorak covers, now that the spring and the mild nights have melted the snow which for several months has preserved the human form of the body; this puzzle lowers such a great weight over Mrs Arnesen that she seldom sees the light again. And even then only vague shadows, like fragments of memories from another time, and not even when Mr Arnesen, her husband and the father of her child, comes home hale and hearty from work, as if nothing in the world has happened, and in this way with his sheer proximity clears up the whole phenomenal misunderstanding, almost more akin to comedy than tragedy, can she be herself again. The darkness never quite leaves her. The hours as a temporary widow burn that darkness forever into her consciousness. She can neither be cheered nor healed. It was the skeleton of Dr Schultz that lay in the blue anorak and white plus fours; he had slid into death with another man's card in his pocket. And late that evening everyone in the block can hear Mrs Arnesen sitting down at the piano, but her touch lacks mood and variation; she plays the same tune over and over again in one endless unvarying circle and Fred begins to cry louder than ever. Later it was discovered that Dr Schultz had left various bits and pieces to patients in his will. We got *The Medical Handbook for Norwegian Homes assembled by M. S. Greve, Director of the Royal Infirmary* where under *cynicism* this definition was given – *carelessness; all in all, a danger in relation to personal hygiene. The result of this has the potential to inflict serious injury.*

A SUITCASE OF APPLAUSE

The Wind

The sun is green and runs down the steep mountainside to the women who're waiting on the shore to haul it onboard the boat. More come running down. There's an avalanche of heavy, green sun and Arnold stands on the heights with his scythe; he'll soon be twelve and the scythe is far too big for him – almost twice his size. And he sees that the grass just bends beneath the narrow blade; he can't cut it, no matter how hard he tries, and try hard he does. He just combs the grass which only rises once more once the scythe's passed; he combs the hair of this outcrop's precipitous head which sticks up out of the sea, that looks right out in this world of wind. Arnold thumps the blade against the hillside and it sparks when he hits a stone; he's on the verge of tears but he doesn't cry. Arnold laughs instead and looks up at the huge sky and hears the quick hisses of the other scythes and the green sun which rushes past him; he hears the chittering of the bewildered gulls circling over the fishermen who aren't at their nets today but are dizzy harvesters instead, cutting the grass that grows so thick and richly in this fertile guano ground here on the golden islets which frost and sea have dried and left behind – smouldering leftovers of creation. Arnold leans on his scythe and he doesn't need to stretch up to see. Here he can view everything, even though he's so small in stature; he can see the whole world and the world is bigger than he can imagine. The world stretches further than the eye can see. For the horizon hangs before him, further out than anyone could ever row, and behind him the mountains lie in blue mist, and behind those mountains are towns in which more than a thousand people live and there, there are church spires higher than the mast on the mail boat, and electric light. Arnold sits down, because he can see just as well that way. He doesn't cry but rather he laughs, and he hears too the laughter of the women down on the shore. Aurora, his mother, waves up to him before she has to collect yet another green sun, bound up tightly like a precious gift, while his father stands a bit away, his scythe burning through the grass, cutting it low and quick. He glances over at his son who's already sat down. The others have a rest themselves. The women wash their hands in the water and Arnold thinks the ocean turns green thereafter. Only Aurora keeps standing and Arnold waves to her. Then his father shades his eyes. He takes the scythe from Arnold. 'Do some raking instead,' he tells him. So Arnold fetches a rake from the other boys – they're younger than he and bigger – some aren't more than nine years old and he doesn't even reach their shoulders. And the rake is so heavy in his hands he has to grasp the middle of the shaft, but then he drags along soil too and the teeth stick fast in the soft scalp. He lets go of the rake, gets down on his knees and uses his hands instead. He rakes the grass with his fingers and it's soft and moist to the touch. The other boys stop for a second, they look at each other and laugh. 'What are you going to be when you grow up, Arnold?' they ask, their voices full of mirth. Arnold thinks and then he answers, 'I'll sell wind!' He shouts this a second time because he thinks it's such a blooming good answer. 'I'll sell wind!' The fathers who're standing with their backs to him in a steep row, swinging their scythes in rhythm like some great orchestra, they turn round too, and his father comes over to him again, his face darker now. 'You can bind for us,' he says, and his words are clipped and tight. And Arnold crawls back to the boys and begins to tie old fishing line around the grass, but it slips, he can't get it into place. It's like packing light, and he feels the tears at the back of his throat, and for that reason he begins to laugh instead – he laughs as the grass tumbles about him. And Arnold sits there at the steepest point, where only the birds and the dogs can keep their balance. He curls up into a ball, shuts his eyes, and lets himself fall. No one notices him before it's too late – Arnold, the only son of Evert and Aurora Nilsen, tumbles like a runaway wheel down the slope. Faster and faster he spins, and the women on the shore drop their grass and cry out, and Aurora cries loudest of the lot of them. Evert throws away his scythe and chases after Arnold, but he can't catch up with him – it's too steep and Arnold's wheel is far too fast. He just remains suspended in the air with his arms stuck out, almost as if he's trying to catch hold of the falling light. And it's utterly still on this green islet on the outer edge of Norway, on the edge of the sunset, as Arnold hits a broad stone on the shore, is thrown up into the air and lands in the green bay, head first, and disappears from sight.

And for ever after Arnold always said that it was when he came to rest there on the bottom and rose up in the heavy, soft sand with the Norwegian Sea itself on his small shoulders, that he made up his mind to escape. He had to get away and as quickly as possible. 'I couldn't scythe,' he used to say. 'When I was supposed to collect eggs I let them lie because I felt sorry for the birds. I got seasick on the water. And when I gutted fish I more or less hacked off my fingers too!' Then he would always take the specially made glove from his right hand and show off the sewn-up chunk of flesh which he could only just move, and I shivered and had to look at it more closely. I had to touch it, feel the rough skin, and Arnold wiped away a tear and murmured, 'I was born in the wrong place. Even the colour of my eyes wasn't right!'

And he gazed at us with that dun look which had saved him so often, while slowly putting his glove back on, the glove that had been fitted with five pieces of wood so that the missing fingers wouldn't be noticeable to one and all.

But that early evening in July, when Arnold is transformed into a living wheel spinning wildly down the land's edge and stands now on the bottom, making his dark plans under water, he feels his father's fists grasping his shoulders and hauling him onboard, a humiliated and dripping creature from the deep, a halfling from the ocean floor. And Aurora holds him close and weeps while the other women throw grass onto dry land again to lighten the boat. And his father rows them home, faster than anyone has rowed that stretch of water before; the water rushes in sheets from the oars. He's relieved and raging, he's gloomy and happy in spite of everything, he both praises and curses himself. In short, Evert Nilsen is a deeply troubled man, for he doesn't know what to do with Arnold, how he'll make anything of him, turn him into an able fellow of some sort – and Arnold is the only son that he and Aurora have been blessed with. And Evert Nilsen can't get the thought out of his head – *I've only got half a son*.

Arnold is dried, wrapped and rolled up in woollen blankets and fur rugs. They give him a cup of brandy – Arnold gasps and smiles, and they take this as a good sign. They even light the stove so the July night won't catch them out and creep with its sombre sea cold beneath the door. He gets to lie with Tuss beside him, the retriever everyone says that Arnold resembles, and the dog growls low and puzzled, and licks Arnold's face. Evert and Aurora keep watch over him and whisper low to one another words that no one hears. And for some reason Evert suddenly wants her; she pushes him away but he won't be stopped, and in the end she lets him have his way. He's wild and silent, and doesn't need more than a few seconds; he holds her so hard up against the wall that for a moment she's breathless and all she thinks is – *Dear God, don't let Arnold wake now, keep him in dreamland where he can neither hear nor see a thing*. But afterwards it isn't she who cries but rather Evert Nilsen, the heavy man of few words who just as suddenly has become a stranger. He sinks down on a chair and buries his face in his hands; a wave passes through his bent back and it's Aurora who has to comfort him. She pulls her dress straight, turns slowly towards him, and cautiously puts her hand on his shoulder. She can feel his shaking. He turns away, for he just can't bring himself to look at her. 'It's too late,' Aurora whispers. 'We just have to make do with Arnold.'

Next morning Arnold is stiff as a stick; he can't so much as wiggle a finger and he seems even smaller there where he's lying on the narrow bed, almost as if the sea has shrivelled him up or he's lost precious centimetres in his fall. The dog's gone, they can hear its howling over by the graveyard. And when they bend over their son he just stares right through them with eyes of brown glass. They send for the doctor. He comes after two days. Dr Paulsen from Bodø comes ashore on this island that isn't intended for humanity but rather for mad dogs and birds, a landfall for shipwrecked souls who should abandon it as quickly as possible whenever the opportunity presents itself. Instead they cling to it, hang by their fingertips to this tiniest twig of geography. It's raining and a thin, silent fellow at once opens a torn umbrella over him, but Dr Paulsen's shoulders are wet already, and he's aware that further maladies and complaints will spring up the minute this fragile population claps eyes on him. Then the patients will be queuing up and he'll be forced to harden his heart, because it's not possible for him to cure the incurable. God can take care of the irreparable, but here he is in this forsaken ocean outpost, under half an umbrella, dreaming of office hours in the capital, tables for reservation in restaurants, and warm operating theatres. 'I jolly well hope it's something serious when you drag me all the way over here,' he says in an irritated voice. Evert Nilsen goes out into the rain and grasps the ancient umbrella with both hands. 'We can't get any life into our son,' he mumbles. 'We don't know if he's alive or dead any more.' 'And is there really any great difference out here?' mutters Dr Paulsen, and tramps into the cramped living room, shakes the water from his coat and

demands silence before anyone has said so much as a
word. He turns towards Arnold who's immobile as
before, and lying deep and barely visible in his woollen
blankets. The doctor goes a step closer and screws up his
eyes. 'Well, for God's sake unpack the boy! I haven't
come here to thump the dust out of dirty blankets!'
Aurora bows her head in shame and rolls Arnold out,
right until he's lying naked in front of them all. Evert
turns away – he looks out of the door at the angled rain,
the sea like a white collar round the lighthouse, the dog
leaping about on the shore. The mother weeps at the
sight of her son – the tiny, all but blue, boy in the bed, as
still as it's possible for a living thing to be. For a moment
Dr Paulsen is moved and humane. 'Well, well,' he says,
'we'll just have to see, we'll just have to see.' Then he
opens his leather bag, takes out his medical kit, sits down
on the chair made ready for him and begins painstakingly
to examine Arnold. Faces pass the windows, quickly
glance in and then vanish again. Elendius, the neighbour
who is always the bearer of bad news and who always
looks forward to sharing it, stands there longest, until at
last Evert hounds him away. Dr Paulsen checks his blood
temperature. He carefully presses Arnold's right eye. He
ties a thread tightly round Arnold's left index finger. He
places a pocket mirror over Arnold's pale mouth. Eventually he straightens up and looks at Evert. 'Are there
spirits to be found in this hut of yours?' he asks. And
Evert pours a glass for him there and then, but the doctor
doesn't drink it at that moment. Instead he first places it
on Arnold's chest, bends down and closely scrutinizes
the liquid. After that he drains the glass and asks for
more. Reluctantly Evert pours another measure, but only
a half one this time. And again the doctor places the glass
on Arnold, and puts on his glasses to see better, whatever
it is he's looking at. At long last he lifts the glass and
drinks it. 'Skin-dead!' he pronounces. 'Quite simply the
boy is skin-dead.' Aurora sinks down by the bed wailing.
'Is it dangerous?' 'Is it or isn't it,' Dr Paulsen replies. 'I

wouldn't recommend someone to become skin-dead just like that. But the boy's more alive than dead and actually far from dead.' 'Oh, thank God,' murmurs Aurora. 'Thank you!' The doctor sighs. 'But did you not notice the movement of the liquid? Like the sea. Like a wave on his chest! I'll happily show you again. If there's more in the bottle.' Evert is quiet and hesitant. The bottle's to do both Christmas and New Year. The doctor notices his reticence and his brow tightens. 'Perhaps I'd better stick a hat-pin in the boy to observe if the heart muscle motions can be seen on it?' Evert pours a third glass and the doctor puts it down on Arnold, and everyone bends to see if the liquid remains steady or not. And then they catch sight of a wave rising through the clear water from the very depths of Arnold, a sudden jolt. And when they've seen enough Dr Paulsen drinks up this drop in the ocean. 'His little heart is beating,' he says and gets up. He remains on his feet looking down at Arnold. 'How old is he?' 'Ten,' Evert answers quickly, and when Aurora's about to say something else he repeats loudly, 'He had his tenth birthday this summer!' Dr Paulsen smiles weakly and lets his gaze fall full over Arnold's dumpy body. 'Well, your boy is small all right. But to make up for it he's extremely well-equipped.' The doctor turns towards Evert who nods, and Aurora folds the blanket carefully over Arnold as her face flushes and she looks away.

And Arnold hears all of this. He lies there in his skin-dead state and hears all that is both unheard and full of riddles. He hears his father lying about his age, making him younger than he is, and the doctor's strange voice answering so mysteriously – *extremely well-equipped*. And now the selfsame doctor rubs a cream over his forehead and pronounces, 'The boy is only barely conscious as a result of his time underwater. He requires rest and cleanliness and regular bowel movements. Then he'll come to of his own accord.' Aurora's voice is clipped. 'It is always clean here! And the potty is ever at the ready!' With those words she departs and bangs the door behind her, and the father takes the doctor into his confidence, for neither of them takes the skin-dead Arnold into consideration. 'Does the good doctor think that Aurora and I might be blessed with further children?' Evert asks, and his hands are twitching as he speaks. 'Well, she's certainly got the temperament for it,' the doctor replies, and then adds, 'How old is she?' Evert has to give this some thought. 'We've been married sixteen years now.' It's the doctor's turn to think, long and hard. 'Don't have too high hopes,' he says in the end. And when Dr Paulsen's taken back to the mainland that same night after having left behind both quinine and Glauber's Salt, Arnold is still aware of the pressure of his thumb against his eye, the heavy glass on his chest, the fumes of alcohol that flowed over him, the tight knot round his finger. Neither would he ever forget the sight of his own face in the doctor's clear pocket mirror. 'Skin-dead,' Arnold whispers. 'I'm skin-dead and extremely well-equipped!'

And for ever after Arnold Nilsen said that he really could not have had a better time of it. 'I was a prince there where I lay! No, I was a king. I was made a monarch. No, closer to God one couldn't have come without leaving this world entirely. Those were the best weeks of my childhood. Believe me! I can recommend being skin-dead to all those who want some peace and quiet. It's wonderful. It's like being in a hotel!'

And so Arnold quite simply goes on lying where he is, still skin-dead, when Holst, the teacher, the portly graduate who's an optimist in September and a great danger to himself in June, arrives to impart knowledge and learning to the restless youngsters of Røst for fourteen days. Thereafter he departs exhausted for the mainland once more, well aware that his words and wisdom are forgotten the moment he's out of sight, and he gives them up to the school of life as some call it, where the curriculum is the ocean, the sea stacks and the grass. After a fortnight he's back, paler and more seasick, for such is the ebb and flow between book and physical labour, pointer and fishing line. And the days grow shorter in Holst's head too and he stares exasperated at Arnold's still empty desk. For Arnold lies on at home, suffering and content, and Aurora nurses him, more and more concerned – she barely manages to coax mashed potato and lukewarm fish soup into his mouth. Evert stands in the shadows by the door watching his wretched son, and he's aware that there isn't any change in Aurora either; her waist is as slender as ever, and he wonders in the stillness and yet the anxiety of his heart – *how long can a person remain skin-dead*? It eats away at Evert's patience to have a son who's skin-dead. Either living or dead Arnold would be a sorrow, a cross to bear, but skin-dead he'll soon become quite unbearable. Besides, the talk has started. He encounters the rumours about his own son whichever path he takes. And it's the teacher, Holst, who rows out with those rumours every fourteenth day.

Aurora carefully dries Arnold's lips, kisses his brow and whispers, 'I'll always look after you'. She doesn't look at Evert as she passes him with the washing bowl, cloths, underwear and leftover food. And it's on this October night Evert makes up his mind. He sends for no less than the vicar.

And it's on this night too that Arnold begins to feel bored. He's not just been crowned the skin-dead king, he's also been elevated to the status of the greatest lowliness, for he can listen but not speak. And there was something about his mother's words which terrified him, which filled him with restlessness, with unbearable anxiety. He hears his mother crying out in her room, the dog whimpering at the door, and his father thumping the table. And on the same morning Arnold hears too the heavy sound of oars out on the sound, the cries of the oarsmen as they keep up the rhythm of their rowing, and the hymn that booms through the storm and drowns out the roar of the breakers: *God is God though every land laid waste.*

Arnold just can't help himself. He gets up. He rises from the skin-dead and looks out of the window. He sees the boat rolling in towards the quay, the men rowing in a circle of white sea, and at the stern there stands an almighty form, the vicar himself, his arms outstretched. He resembles a giant cormorant, a black sail, and it's he who's singing *God is God though every man were dead*. Arnold gets shivers down his spine and shouts, 'The fatty's coming! The fatty's coming!' Then his father steps out of the shadow by the door, whirls Arnold round and smacks him full in the face, a thump that burns as hotly in Evert's fist as on Arnold's cheek, for Evert has punched in wicked delight, in grand terror, almost as if another power controlled his arm in that instant. And he looks down benevolently, almost shamefully, at his own son standing ablaze on his bed. 'That's no fatty! That's the vicar, you little bugger!' And his father drags the terrified Aurora with him and chases to the quay to meet the vicar and send him back where he came from as quickly as possible, for Arnold is *compos mentis* and has recovered his speech and is in need of no vicar. 'The boy's up and about!' Evert shouts to them one and all. 'Go home while there's still time!' But the vicar's already standing steady on the quayside and he places his hands on Evert's trembling shoulders. 'Well, well, my good man,' he says. 'If your boy's truly woken up then I'd like to speak to the miracle in person.'

And no one can say no when a vicar invites himself. Before long the whole population is trooping up to Evert and Aurora's house. The men have laid aside their equipment, the women leave their washing lying in the tub and the children are only too happy to come in late to Holst the teacher's first lesson. And the teacher himself, quite out of breath, is the last one to join the long, expectant trail of humanity that has designated an ordinary morning in October a holy day.

Arnold sees them from the window. Arnold sees all the approaching faces; the vicar's red chin shrouded by its black beard, his parent's nervous hands, Elendius' quick smiles, the teacher's thin hair beneath his wet hat. And all the figures are leaning forward, as if someone's pushing them from behind, and Arnold knows there and then that they've caught up with him, that he's been overtaken. He was lost, but at that moment he's found, and it's now that Arnold Nilsen's second life begins.

He lies down, shuts his eyes, and hears the vicar whispering out on the doorstep, and it's both a terrifying comfort and a friendly threat: 'I want to speak with the boy alone.' And when Arnold opens his eyes next the vicar is leaning over him in all his might and says, 'Tell me. Tell me what it was like to be skin-dead.' Arnold doesn't know how to respond and so he decides to say nothing. The broad head waits above him, and Arnold searches for some kind of sign, a hint in the man's face, a clue to follow – anything that might indicate what's right to reveal or withhold. Then a heavy drop falls from the vicar's shining nose onto Arnold's forehead. The vicar lifts an edge of his cloak and wipes the great drop away. 'It was fine to begin with,' Arnold says. 'But in the end it became a bit depressing.' The vicar nodded slowly. 'Yes, I can appreciate that all right. Jesus only endured three days.' Arnold sits up on the bed and the vicar places his hand on his head and Arnold leans forward. 'Look me in the eye,' the vicar says. Arnold looks up as much as he's able and meets the vicar's gaze. 'You are to honour your father and mother,' the vicar says. 'Yes,' Arnold whispers. 'You shall honour the sea that is the dwelling-place of the fish and the heavens where the birds have their home.' 'Yes,' Arnold whispers. 'And you shall honour the truth!' 'And that too,' Arnold says. The vicar has come even closer, he's no more than a whisker away. 'Yes, not least that!' the vicar cries, and Arnold tumbles backwards, but it makes no difference because the vicar follows after. 'And what, pray, is the truth?' he asks. Arnold thinks and thinks. He doesn't know. He's stuck for an answer. 'I don't know whether to laugh or cry,' he says instead. The expression quivers and breaks into a smile. He breathes deeply, draws his hand over his eyes and smiles, and that smile is just like a bow between laughter and tears. 'No,' he says. 'That's exactly what we poor, amazing humans just don't know. Whether to laugh or to cry.' The vicar gets up and stands in the middle of the floor with his back to Arnold. His cloak is like a black pillar about him. Outside there is the sound of anxious voices. Someone knocks on the door. Apart from that everything's still. Then the vicar turns back to face Arnold and is about to say more, but Arnold beats him to it, for he has something on his mind. 'I want to go away,' he says. 'That's the truth.' The vicar listens and smiles a second time. 'You've travelled far, Arnold. But you went in the wrong direction, lad.' 'Thank you,' Arnold whispers. And for a second time he receives the vicar's hand on his head. 'And now it's time to go back to our people,' the vicar says. 'Where we belong.'

The following morning Arnold's there at the schoolroom door, and the whole crowd turns in his direction and someone shouts from the rear bench: 'The fatty's coming!' The laughter tumbles from their faces, and Arnold laughs himself; he laughs and realizes that everyone knows just about everything. Not absolutely everything, for only the vicar knows that – but they know just about everything, and that's more than enough. For everything he says and has said and will say flits from person to person, words he'd prefer to keep to himself; they're like a shoal caught in someone else's nets. And Arnold thinks as he laughs – *It's too small here. It's too cramped*. And Arnold laughs the loudest of the lot. Then the teacher bangs his pointer on his table and gives Arnold a bow in the sudden ensuing silence. 'Welcome back, Arnold Nilsen. Sit down so we don't think you're going to leave us again.' Arnold walks between the rows and finds his place. His desk is just as big as it was before the summer. Perhaps it's even bigger. His feet don't reach the floor. His feet are left hanging in thin air, heavy as lead. Holst the teacher comes towards him. He has his hands behind his back. He's smiling. Perhaps he's smiling because he'll leave for the Lofotens that very evening to rest there for fourteen wonderful days. He stops right in front of Arnold. 'So you're going to sell wind?' the teacher says. And the laughter starts once more. The laughter has been skin-dead too and now it's come back to life. Holst the teacher lets it take its course, until he's had enough. Then he stamps hard and the laughter falls away. 'But tell me, Arnold Nilsen, are you going to sell wind in kilos or litres?' Arnold can't get a word in because Holst is thoroughly enjoying himself and is not about to be stopped. 'I know,' he goes on. 'You'll sell it in tons. Quite simply you'll find the wind in tons and send it all south so that when it's calm on the Oslo Fiord – exactly what it is most of the time – and the sailing boats can't move a milli-metre, they can just open one of Arnold Nilsen's tons of wind and pour it into the sails!' The class roars. They hang over their desks laughing. Holst the teacher looks down on Arnold and shoves his pointer under his chin to force him to look up, and Arnold feels the end of it pressing against his throat, against his Adam's apple, as the laugh-ter keeps pealing about him. 'But how are you going to manage to close your containers before the wind's escaped again, little Arnold?' But now it's Arnold's turn to laugh, and he laughs more than all the others put together. 'I'll just put your fat bum on them first,' he replies. There's utter silence. Holst the teacher drops the pointer. He barely manages to bend down to pick it up, very slowly, and his breathing is more like quick wheez-ing. 'What did you say, Arnold Nilsen?' 'That I'll just put your fat halibut of a bum on the containers first!' Arnold laughs, and that instant the pointer whams down on the bridge of his nose. Arnold just gapes in amazement at Holst who is already on his way back to his table to sit down; thereafter he leafs through the hefty register and dips the nib of his pen in ink. It's at that point Arnold first becomes aware of the pain – it's like an aftershock, delayed, too late and awful – the blood swells behind his forehead and gushes into his mouth, drips onto the floor in great gouts. And Arnold slides down from his seat, gets up in bewilderment and leaves the classroom; behind him the silence is more profound than ever and Holst the teacher lets him go. For he has more than enough to do recording incidents in the register's columns, clearer than the black ink with which he's compiling his account in oblong columns beside appalling test marks, so that future generations will know the barbaric conditions in which he had to work, out here in the very mouth of the sea.

Arnold stops on the doorstep. He glimpses his father down at the quayside. He goes there and his father turns towards him. 'Have you gone and fallen again?' he asks. Arnold carefully shakes his head and more blood comes, he has to tilt his head backwards and look up at the heavy, grey skies. 'No,' he whispers. 'I haven't.' His father takes a step towards him, impatient. 'What's happened then, boy?' 'Holst the teacher caught me with the pointer.' His father bends down. 'You mean he hit you?' Arnold nods, equally carefully, as if everything in his face is loose and could fall to pieces at any moment. His father pulls a rag from his pocket, quickly dips it in water and gives it to his son. Arnold wipes away the blood and starts crying, even though he is determined not to. But it stings, it stings so badly and something inside him has shattered. 'I think your nose is squint now,' his father tells him, and he takes the blood-soaked rag from Arnold, spits on it and rubs off the marks on his chin, and it amazes the boy that those massive hands can be so gentle. 'You're not crying?' his father asks him. 'No,' Arnold replies, and swallows. 'Not now.' 'That's good. You won't die of a crooked nose. Did he really hit you with the pointer?' 'Yes, with the full force of it.' His father ponders a moment. Then he starts walking away from the quayside. 'Where are you going?' Arnold calls after him. 'Don't go.' But his father doesn't turn round. 'To have a chat with Holst the teacher.'

And Arnold hurries after his father with his hand covering his sore and out-of-joint nose. His father doesn't stop until he reaches the classroom door and is looking in on Holst who closes his register with a bang. 'I am Arnold Nilsen's father,' he announces loud and clear. The teacher looks up quickly and uncertainly, his eyes swivel a bit before he glances at the register again and smiles. 'Yes, Evert Nilsen. Naturally I recognize the fathers of my dear pupils.' Holst the teacher got up. 'And your son has learned an important lesson today. For my part I consider the matter of no consequence and will not pursue it any further, either here or in the portals of my superiors.' Evert Nilsen stands there dumb and dark, as if he's forgotten quite why he's there. His broad figure casts a long grey shadow through the room. Arnold waits behind him, hidden. He tugs his father's jacket hard because he knows he can't cope with too many words at one time – they just bewilder and exhaust him. 'And now we must continue our class,' the teacher says, getting up and looking right past Evert Nilsen. 'Arnold, would you be so kind as to sit down at your desk?' But his father holds him back. Then he goes forward to the teacher's table, between the restless pupils who realize already that something's about to happen they'll never forget. Evert Nilsen says nothing. Enough has been said already. Holst the teacher looks at him in amazement. And Evert Nilsen takes the pointer and hits Holst on the forehead; the blow isn't perhaps all that hard, but he folds up all the same, more in astonishment than in pain. He howls and clutches at his face, and Arnold considers that it was his father who first hit him, then Holst the teacher who hit him, and now his father has hit Holst, as if the one action has led to the next with a kind of justice that Arnold can't quite fathom. Evert Nilsen then snaps the pointer and drops the two halves over Holst the teacher who's still kneeling in front of the class. He leaves the classroom and takes Arnold with him, out into the mighty wind where there's room for everyone. 'You'll never go back there,' his father tells him.

The following day Arnold goes out in the boat with his father. Aurora says no to begin with, but Father stands his ground. The boy has to be toughened up. The boy'll survive all right. There's nothing else to consider. It's simple, obvious and fine. That's what it all comes down to. Now Arnold's sitting on the hatch, his blue nose packed into a rough bandage so he has to breathe through his mouth. He sits there gaping while his father rows with a slow, inexorable rhythm, taking them out from land. It's calm, calm indeed for October; the sea lies dark and broody like a black mirror. But as soon as they've passed the breakwater and can see the lighthouse standing like some wide neck in a collar of foam, the breakers start beneath them, lifting the boat in a constant, intolerable motion. The father smiles and looks at his son; he rows and doesn't take his eyes off him. The breakers roll beneath them and nothing is still any longer; there isn't a single thing to hold onto. Not his father either, who smiles, rows, rows them out, further yet, until they can only glimpse the island like a plateau in the very depths of the fog. Arnold shuts his mouth and can barely get breath. He is shut in himself. The breakers fill him with a warm queasiness. He tears off the bandage and chokes back his own scream, chucks the dirty thing onto the water and breathes in quick, blissful gulps of air. His father looks at him and smiles, keeps rowing, for they haven't got there yet. Arnold carefully feels his nose; it's tender and soft and runs jagged down his face. 'You look like a boxer now,' his father says all at once. Arnold looks up at him in surprise. 'A boxer? Do I?' 'The one there was a picture of in the newspaper. Don't you remember?' 'No. Who d'you mean, Father?' 'The one who's actually boxed in America. Otto von Parat.' For a moment Arnold forgets his queasiness and senses instead a wonderfully good feeling. His father has spoken to him. His father's said he looks like a boxer. Arnold punches the air and laughs. It hurts high up in his forehead. He's happy and it hurts. But just as the good pain passes, the sick feeling grows once more, and he notices that his father is sculling back the water as if he's trying to moor the boat on the waves themselves. Then he puts one oar over his thighs and points behind Arnold. 'Pay attention now,' he tells him. 'When the flagpole crosses the beacon and the lighthouse is in line with the breakwater, you're lying right.' Arnold turns and looks, while his father keeps talking, and it's a long while since Evert Nilsen has said so much, and perhaps he's happy too at that moment being there with his son. 'Those are our landmarks, Arnold. The flagpole, the beacon, the lighthouse and the breakwater. It's like a constellation. When everything's confusion and currents, they'll stand firm. Never forget that, Arnold.' And Arnold screws up his eyes and looks, looks at these landmarks which create this strange form, this image which is broken if they move by a single pull of an oar in one direction or the other. And the more Arnold stares at the landmarks, the sicker he becomes, and it dawns on him that out of everything in the whole world he's the only thing that can't manage to stand still. 'What was it you said to the teacher?' his father suddenly asks. Arnold has to think. 'I just said that his bum was bigger than a halibut.' His father laughed loudly. 'Bigger than a halibut! Did you really say that to that great bag of wind!' 'Yes!' Arnold exclaimed. 'Twice! I said it twice!' Arnold looks at his father. They're outside the normal conventions of behaviour. It's just the two of them. They're free, were it not for the waves and the queasiness. His father falls silent again and Arnold sits as still as he can, for he doesn't want to destroy this moment. Then his father asks, 'What was it the vicar said to you?' Arnold has to think again. 'He said I should honour my father and mother.' 'Did the vicar really say that?' 'Yes, that I should honour you and Aurora.' And as he says those words Arnold vomits. He vomits up the contents of his guts right into his father's lap. His father swears and raises his arm as if to lash out, and Arnold has to vomit again; he cries and vomits and through a film of tears he sees that the landmarks have disappeared. Everything slides apart. He's out of rhythm.

He sinks down into the bottom of the boat and closes his eyes. 'Now I don't much look like a boxer,' he whispers.

His father rows back. He's silent the rest of the day. Aurora puts out food on the table. Arnold can't face eating. He goes to bed early. Everything's still rolling. He's brought the breakers home. His bed is a boat. The boat bears Arnold. It bears him out to the landmarks of his dreams.

His father rouses him early the following morning. 'Find the landmarks,' he orders him. When they have passed the breakwater his father changes places with Arnold and gives him the oars. Arnold rows. The waves press against them. Arnold rows and watches. His father doesn't take his eyes off him. The oars lift aside the surface of the water like huge, slippery spoons. Arnold turns and gazes in towards land. But the landmarks aren't where they should be. They've moved round. The beacon has moved in front of the flagpole, the lighthouse has sunk into the sea, and the waves are tearing down the breakwater, stone by stone. The constellation has been thrown to the four winds. Arnold thinks to himself – *My landmarks are here, there and everywhere! Here, there and everywhere are my landmarks! My crooked nose'll point me in the right direction*. His father grasps him by the shoulder. 'Further out!' he cries. And Arnold rows further out. He makes up his mind. He'll do it now. He's an oarsman – Arnold the oarsman! And Arnold rows into the heart of the breakers. He rows through the waves. He rows into the storm. The oars aren't spoons, they're trees. And each tree's crown is the blade of the oar which pushes the sky backwards. But he doesn't find the landmarks. The landmarks aren't there. Nothing at all will stand still. The wind is gnawing at their hills and soon there'll be nothing but dust on the surface of the water, like fly shit on the window sill. His father shouts something but it's impossible to hear a word. His father points but there's nothing to see. Arnold rows through rain and foam. He rows with his mouth open and he gulps the sea and throws it up; the ocean on whose floor he stood and made his most secret plans. His father rips him away from the hatch, takes the oars and rows in once more. Arnold tumbles down between his huge boots. He wets himself. He cries. His father kicks him away. 'Are you off your head, boy?' he shrieks. 'Are you trying to ruin my boat?' Arnold can't say a thing. His father rows, giving long pulls to the oars. His father swears and rows. Arnold gets up and sees to his amazement that the water is dead calm. Aurora is standing right out on the breakwater. She is a patient, black shadow. And Arnold goes onto land for good. He follows his mother up to the house, hearing the laughter of the boys over at the classroom. 'Don't worry,' his mother whispers. 'I'm not a bit worried,' Arnold replies and clenches his teeth. 'Did you go green again?' she asks him. Arnold doesn't answer. He is the land crab encircled by sea. He is the seasick one, born on an island. 'My father,' Aurora says. 'He got seasick too. Every single day he got queasy and vomited.' She laughs, and her laughter is queer, and she takes his hand. Arnold is silent, for he doesn't know if this is meant as a comfort or a threat. No, it's not a threat, but it's poor comfort.

One day Arnold is sitting on the quayside gutting fish. His father's at sea. Arnold raises his knife. The knife is weighty in his hand. Time passes slowly and heavily. The old boys are keeping an eye on him. They mumble together about this half portion of a boy. They tell the stories they've told all down the years. Soon the stories'll be about Arnold. When they turn away, just for a second, perhaps because that lazybones Elendius is approaching to inflict bad news on them, Arnold loses hold of the knife and it slices his finger right to the bone. His finger is left hanging by a thread, a sliver of flesh, yet Arnold doesn't cry out; he's completely silent and just stares at his hand, at the index finger from which blood is pumping in great gouts. He hears the knife landing on the ground and the others getting up, and Elendius screeching so the whole island can hear, 'The Wheel has chopped off his finger! The Wheel has chopped off his finger!'

And it's this Arnold remembers when he comes to with just nine fingers, that they called him the Wheel. Arnold is the Wheel and won't be known as anything else. Everything that powers through the world has wheels – cars, trains, buses – even ships have wheels, and wasn't the ocean itself one great wheel that rolled from coast to coast, and wasn't the earth too a shining blue wheel spinning through the dark of the universe? Because nobody could forget that Arnold had rolled like a human wheel down the steepest slope, and neither did Arnold forget the promise he had made himself, there where he stood on the sea floor with the waves on his shoulders, that he'd get away from this island, whatever the cost. He doesn't know where he'll go, he only knows he has to do this one thing – get away. He is a wheel and he can't stop. The road is his home. That's the way he's been made. And one night he steals out. He leaves a letter for his mother. His father's fishing far out on the fiord. The nights are starting to grow lighter. For several weeks he's been composing this letter, trying to find the right words and put them in the right order. It's short enough, since Arnold Nilsen isn't one to whom the written word comes naturally. This is what his mother will read when she rises early the following morning, startled by the silence of the tiny dwelling. She'll see the piece of paper on the kitchen table. *My dear mother. I've left home. I'll return when the time is right, or never. You'll find the boat on the other side. Good wishes to my father too. Loving greetings, Arnold.*

And Arnold slips out into the bright night. Quickly he goes down to the quay. Tuss follows him, confused and happy. He strokes the dog and then sends it back up to the house again. He's taken a loaf with him, coins he's been saving for two years, and a drop of his father's brandy. He looks about him. He sees everything he's going to leave behind. He lets go the mooring and the night is still and his heart hammers. He cries with joy and sorrow. He has surpassed himself. He is bigger than himself. Soon there won't be room for him. And while he rows with his nine fingers he sings so as not to hear his own crying: *God is God though every man were dead, God is God though every land laid waste*. And the whispers are to be heard yet about this voyage through the roughest and most dangerous of currents – a feat it was indeed, a miracle. Arnold must have had the Almighty Himself in his oars that night, and perhaps the feat cooled his father's rage and grief – his half portion of a son taking on the ocean like a man, thereby transforming himself into a whole legend.

And on the evening of the third day Arnold stands in front of the church on Svolvaer and everything's bigger than he'd imagined it would be. People live on top of each other in houses of stone. The lamp posts are dense as a forest and there's electric light in the shop windows. But it amazes Arnold that it's so quiet, that a town could be so still. Maybe they're already asleep in towns by this time of day, Arnold thinks, so that by night-time they're rested. Because in towns everything's topsy-turvy, the sun goes down when people get up. But then he hears something approaching and indeed it's several things, for the hillside is juddering under him. Arnold turns and sees a whole procession of humanity trailing past on the opposite pavement, both adults and children. There are fishermen and tradesmen, women and men, dogs and cats, and every type of person imaginable, and as if this isn't enough the vicar himself emerges from the church, the heavy door bangs behind him and he lifts the skirts of his robe so as not to trip over, and runs like a woman to join this amazing crowd turning down the main street towards the quayside. Arnold hides behind a lamp post and the vicar doesn't see him. They're on their way to the other side of the quay. There, on the rough ground between the sawmill and the silo, are booths and merry-go-rounds, blazing lights, a plethora of colours, mechanical horses riding round in circles, and a great tent pitched in the midst of it all, fastened to a hook in the heavens which is the moon, and above golden portals Arnold reads – CIRCUS MUNDUS. He observes that everyone has to pay a uniformed gentleman with a neat moustache curled under his nose, and then they stream in, one after another, shouting and fighting and pushing each other over to get in first and find the best possible seats. Arnold's left standing there in the dust, on the outside edge of the old football pitch. Soon he's able to hear the playing of the orchestra, the neighing of horses, the trumpeting of elephants, the firing of guns, laughter and the crack of the whip. Arnold shuffles closer. There's no one on duty now. The uniformed gentleman's gone. Arnold remains for a moment beneath the ornamental portals looking about him one final time. A placard hangs on a post close by. Here one may find the famous snake-man, Der Rote Teufel. Here there are sword-swallowers and lion-tamers, grotesque human freaks and beauty queens. Not least, here is the world's tallest man, Paturson, the legendary Icelander. Arnold takes a deep breath and slips inside. He steals between booths and tents. The horses circle riderless on the shining merry-go-round. Is it not perhaps this he's dreamed of and longed for? Hasn't it been here he yearned to come to; wasn't getting away all about this very place? He stops outside the tent where there's a sign with the words: *Mundus vult decipi*. What amazing sounds. This is a language for haddock and halibut a thousand metres down. He lifts the flap to one side but before Arnold has seen a thing a hand pulls him out and drags him roughly round. The gentleman with the uniform and the moustache is staring down at him. 'And where are you planning on going?' The man speaks Norwegian. He bends down closer. 'I'm looking for my parents,' Arnold answers quickly. 'Well, well, have you wandered off from your parents, then?' Arnold smiles. He's no longer afraid. Lying is that easy. The words are put into his mouth and transformed into truth. 'Yes,' Arnold whispers, 'I've wandered off from my parents.' But these words, that are both the truth and a lie, have unwanted consequences for Arnold. The man in uniform actually lifts him bodily into the air. 'My name is Mundus,' he says. 'And no one will lose their nearest and dearest if Mundus can help it.' With that he carries Arnold right into the big top. Der Rote Teufel is in the process of sticking his head between his legs as he hangs beneath the dome from a trapeze, and everyone is gazing in his direction. He folds himself up and peers out from between his own thighs, and now he's only holding on with one hand, and the onlookers gasp and hardly dare look. The drummer gives a drum roll that goes on and on. Then suddenly there's a rustling sound from on high and there's unease on the trapeze. It's Der Rote Teufel's gold-embroidered hosiery that's ripped in the most unfortunate of places. For a moment the bulk of the audience think this is part of the performance, but then they realize this is a scandal of the highest order and that Der Rote Teufel hasn't been given his name by accident, for an unmistakable smell fills the tent, and the poor snake-man is lowered at top speed with his white bottom cheeks like a shameful moon above his burning, tightly clenched face. A great hissing breaks out on the benches at the back; the men get up and chuck balls of paper and earth in the direction of the Teufel and it's now that Arnold Nilsen makes his début. Mundus realizes that the show is about to go to pieces and so he carries Arnold out into the middle of the big top and holds him up. Silence falls all round and the cocky, exuberant fishermen sit down in the end and Mundus seizes the initiative. 'Ladies and gentlemen!' he shouts. 'This little gentleman I have in my arms is missing his parents! Would his mother and father make themselves known, and reunite themselves with him in our presence before the world's tallest man rises in our midst?'

Everything becomes completely still once more. Arnold takes in the faces which all but encircle him. They stare, they gape. The closest among the audience stretch forward and all but touch him. The vicar makes to get up but in the end remains seated, sorrowful and uncertain. And perhaps there are some who for a time believe that this is part of the act too, for the laughter begins and then spreads, and in the end the big top is full of laughter – people applauding and stamping their feet. Only the vicar remains quiet; he keeps looking at Arnold and doesn't know whether to laugh or to cry. Mundus gives a deep bow, circles the ring as the public continues clapping, and in the end he carries Arnold backstage, puts him down and hurries out once more. It's almost pitch dark. Only one pale light shines over a mirror. Arnold doesn't move. He can hear fanfares and drum rolls coming from the ring. Then he hears something else. He hears heavy footsteps; the ground beneath him shakes and the chair he's sitting on starts trembling. It isn't an elephant approaching. It's a human being and Arnold has to brace himself because he realizes it's none other than the world's tallest man. And the world's tallest man has to walk with his head bowed. His face is long and sorrowful. His nose casts a shadow over everything. He wears a black suit and his tie is longer than the moonlight reflected over the ocean. He's accompanied by a lady with a short dress that sticks right out and a shiny cap on her head. She's probably quite normal but only reaches up to his belt, and barely even that. He stops by the heavy golden curtain. He bends even lower and the lady lets go of his enormous hand. The music subsides. Everything falls silent, only the quick pattering of the drum is left and the full power of Mundus' voice: 'Ladies and gentlemen! Please welcome the man declared the world's tallest man at the Copenhagen medical congress, the Icelander Paturson from Akureyri! He's two metres seventy-three centimetres tall, and that without shoes on his feet!' Paturson stretches up and goes out. Some people shriek and some laugh, others gasp in astonishment. But most are just silent, for they've never seen anything so huge before. Then the lady with the funny cap notices Arnold. 'Who are you?' 'Arnold,' says Arnold. She smiles, twists her head, and comes closer. 'And what are you doing here, Arnold?' 'Waiting for Mundus,' Arnold replies. The lady peeks through the gap in the curtain and quickly waves Arnold over. He jumps from his chair and goes over to her. Arnold feels the lady putting something into his hand. It's a sweet. He puts it into his mouth before anyone can take it from him again, and sucks on it for a long while. Inside the sweet is something still softer that melts round his tongue and which almost dizzies him from head to foot. She gives him another bit. 'I'm the Chocolate Girl,' she whispers, and kisses him quickly on the cheek. 'Look, Arnold.' And Arnold sees Paturson standing there in the ring with his back to them. Mundus is measuring him with a silver tape and has to get up on a ladder to record the final centimetres. Then he shows the measuring tape to those at the front so that they can see with their own eyes Paturson's exact height – two metres and seventy-three centimetres! Everyone claps and Mundus stands by Paturson once more, takes his right hand that's as big as a spade, and begins working free a ring from his index finger. 'Is he married?' Arnold asks. The Chocolate Girl just shakes her head and laughs. 'Be quiet,' she tells him. Mundus has got the ring off and he shows it to the crowd. Then he produces a real silver two kroner coin and draws it through the ring so that everyone can see that the ring is wide enough to let the coin pass. It's almost beyond belief and the crowd is wild with exultation, but Mundus has kept the best for last. He gets two blushing girls from the front row to come out with him into the ring. Once there they're allowed to touch Paturson so that no one will be in any doubt that he's genuine flesh and blood. They then get to sit on each of his arms, as if they were up in the branches of a great tree, and now it's Paturson's turn to blush rather than the girls' – his cheeks blaze and shyly he buries his head as the girls swing about and laugh and wave the whole way home. A couple of the blokes at the back want to come down and arm-wrestle the bashful giant, but that's going too far for Mundus. Someone could get badly injured. Instead he lets a table covered in an embroidered cloth be brought in. He draws this off like a conjurer to reveal Paturson's supper which consists of nothing less than a dozen soft-boiled eggs, fourteen rolls, a pork chop, three kilos of potatoes, eighteen prunes and two litres of milk. All this the Icelander partakes of before the wide eyes of the audience. And as Paturson eats Mundus goes closer to the crowd and folds his hands. 'Ladies and gentlemen,' he says. 'Our Icelandic friend comes from the impoverished house of a fisherman in Akureyri, and as you have seen, his size causes him great tribulation. He yearns to return and fish with his family as before. But neither clothes nor normal fishing gear are feasible. Even his shoelaces have to be ordered from abroad. For this reason we have produced some cards which he will now go round with and sell. The more cards you buy, the bigger the clothes and fishing equipment he can obtain. Please give generously!' And the world's tallest man dries his mouth with a cloth and quietly goes from row to row with his colour cards. But few are willing to buy them since they've already had to pay fifty öre to get in, and the only one to put two coins in Paturson's fist is the vicar. The show is over. The orchestra strikes up. Paturson withdraws and the Chocolate Girl takes his hand once more. Mundus storms out backstage. He's seething with anger. 'Where's that damned Teufel?' he shrieks. 'I'll give him Teufel!' Mundus rushes out but comes straight back to look down darkly on Arnold. 'And you're still here?' Arnold nods. He can't deny it. He's afraid Mundus will throw him out, but instead the man sighs heavily and painfully, lights a cigar and sits down exhausted. 'This is a wretched circus,' he says. 'The acrobats fart so their outfits rip and no one'll buy the cards I've printed.' 'The vicar did,' Arnold whispers. 'Oh, yes. The vicar obliged and I'm left with 348 cards! Is there anybody around here except heartless, tight-fisted wretches?' Mundus exhales smoke from beneath his moustache and waves it away with his hand.

Arnold reflects for a moment. 'It's perhaps not so wise to give him all that food first,' he ventures. Mundus looks at him again. 'What do you mean?' 'They won't feel sorry for him once he's eaten so much,' Arnold mumbles. Mundus gets up. He chucks his cigar out of the door and smiles. 'What's your name, boy?' he asks. 'My name's Arnold.' And at that moment the Chocolate Girl comes in. She's holding the still-lit cigar in her hand and looking astonished at Mundus, who in turn is pointing at Arnold. 'Arnold's right!' he exclaims. 'Why in the world did no one ever say that Paturson shouldn't eat for king and country right in front of a peckish audience the moment before he sells his cards!' He turns towards the Chocolate Girl. 'Did you get him to bed?' The Chocolate Girl nods and has a drag of the cigar. Mundus grabs it from her and chucks it out once more. 'Find somewhere for Arnold to sleep,' he orders her.

And the Chocolate Girl takes Arnold's hand and leads him out of the tent, and they walk along the muddy path that runs between the stalls. 'I think you've found the elephant's hair,' she murmurs. Arnold doesn't quite follow. 'Has an elephant hair?' 'Yes,' the Chocolate Girl replies. 'But only on its tail.' She gives him a quick kiss on the lips and Arnold feels dizzy again. 'You can sleep with Paturson. But I'm just in the next wagon. If you need anything.'

She stops outside one of the wagons, carefully opens the door and lets Arnold in. This is where Paturson is sleeping. He's sleeping deeply. Two beds have been pushed together to give him sufficient space. Arnold's to lie beside him on the floor. The Chocolate Girl gives him a blanket. 'I'm in the wagon right beside this one,' she whispers. 'If you need anything.' She hurries out. Arnold remains standing in the poor light for a time, just looking at the world's tallest man. His face is huge and lonely on the white pillow. He has three quilts, but even they aren't sufficient. His socks are torn and his toes stick out in all directions. They're bigger than Arnold's thighs and resemble bouquets of flesh with the crooked yellow toenails as petals. Then Arnold catches sight of Paturson's jacket hanging from a nail behind the bed. He hauls it down and tries it on. The buttons reach right down to his shoes, and the arms are so long that he has trouble finding his hands again. He could go on a long journey into that jacket. Paturson turns round in bed. Arnold holds his breath. It takes some time for the tallest man in the world to turn round. It's almost as if the globe itself trembles on its axis for a moment. Arnold climbs out of the jacket, hangs it up again and then feels something in one of the pockets. It's the silver measuring tape. He turns towards the bed. Paturson is still sleeping soundlessly. And Arnold begins at his longest toe and rolls out the shining tape right to Paterson's topmost hair. Arnold looks at the figure. He must have made a mistake and he measures again, this time the other way round, from his head and down to his feet, just to make certain. But he arrives at exactly the same measurement. Paturson isn't two metres seventy-three centimetres, he's two metres four centimetres. Arnold puts the measuring tape back in his pocket. He's surprised but not really disappointed. There's something he's gradually understanding, something which hasn't yet become clear but which is beginning to make sense; a shadow in his head, a lie.

Arnold steals over to the wagon where the Chocolate Girl's sleeping. He wakens her. 'I need something,' Arnold tells her. She sits up smiling. 'What is it, Arnold?' she asks. 'Paturson isn't two metres seventy-three centimetres.' The Chocolate Girl's smile vanishes. 'What was that you said, Arnold?' 'He's only two metres four. I've measured him!' The Chocolate Girl takes hold of Arnold and lays one finger hard on his lips. 'Paturson is two metres four centimetres in length when he's lying down,' she tells him. 'And when he stands up he's two metres seventy-three! Mundus decides how tall Paturson is. D'you understand?' But the wheels in Arnold's head are turning rather slowly now and not getting very far. 'How old are you?' the Chocolate Girl asks instead. And suddenly Arnold notices that she's almost naked. 'Sixteen,' he answers quickly. She laughs. 'Sixteen? And how old are you when you're lying down?' The Chocolate Girl pulls Arnold down beside her and puts her arms round him. Arnold grows in her arms and she explains just about everything to him.

Now he knows what the elephant's hair is.

Next morning Arnold presents himself in Mundus' own wagon, the biggest of all the circus vehicles, with its own staircase, curtains and chimney; Mundus himself is sitting up eating breakfast in a four-poster bed. He's wearing a burgundy dressing gown and his moustache is behind a protective leather cover under his nose. He wipes egg yolk from the corners of his mouth with the end of a white napkin. 'Where are you from?' Mundus asks. 'Nowhere in particular,' Arnold answers. Mundus looks at him. 'Nowhere in particular? Everyone comes from somewhere, Arnold.' 'Not me.' 'Then perhaps you're a little angel who's landed among us?' Arnold says nothing. Why not, though? He could well be an angel. Mundus gives a sigh, puts his breakfast tray to one side and reaches for a cigar. 'We don't want the police on our backs now, do we?' 'The vicar knows who I am,' Arnold says, 'I've told him everything.'

At that moment he hears heavy footsteps outside. He turns towards the window and sees Paturson going past with the Chocolate Girl who throws a large tarpaulin over him once they're in the vicinity of the ornate portals. Mundus gets up from his bed and stands beside Arnold. 'We don't want anyone in the town to see him for free,' he says, and lights his cigar with a long match. Arnold watches the world's tallest man going for a walk under a tarpaulin and the sight affects him. 'Have you heard of Barnum?' Mundus suddenly asks him. Arnold shakes his head and can barely see Mundus for the smoke. 'Barnum was king of America, Arnold. He was mightier than Alexander the Great and Napoleon put together!' Arnold steps closer. 'Bigger than Paturson too?' Mundus laughs, coughing. 'Yes, bigger than Paturson! Because Barnum made the world his circus! The earth was his big top and heaven itself the tent he pitched above us!' Mundus was moved by his own tale. 'Barnum wanted to make people happy,' he breathed. 'He wanted to make them laugh, tremble, gasp and dance! And could one individual possess any nobler ambition?' The Chocolate Girl comes back with Paturson. She gives Arnold a wave. Mundus lays a hand on his shoulder. 'Do you know what *Mundus vult decipi* means?' he asks. Arnold smiles. He knows almost everything now. 'The world will be taken in,' he replies. Mundus is stunned. 'Ah, but can you tell me what *Ergo Decipiatur* means?' 'Thus it is deceived,' Arnold tells him. Mundus has to put down his cigar. 'All right, can you tell me lastly what's bigger than Paturson from Iceland?' Arnold thinks about it. 'God?' he suggests. Mundus shakes his head. 'Oh, no, God's four centimetres smaller than Paturson.' 'Barnum?' Arnold suggests. Mundus bends right down to his level. 'Imagination, Arnold! Imagination is the greatest thing there is! It's not what you see that counts first and foremost. It's what you *think* you see! Always remember that.' Mundus sits down on the bed, but doesn't take his eyes off Arnold. 'Turn round,' he tells him. Arnold turns round and stands with his back to Mundus. 'Right round!' Mundus thunders. Arnold turns the whole way round and now Mundus has put on a pair of spectacles. 'Well, well, my small friend. So tell me what you can do!' 'I can be a wheel,' Arnold replies, and he circles over the floor and gets up again. Mundus isn't impressed. 'We've enough wheels, Arnold.' 'I've only got nine fingers,' Arnold says, and holds both hands in the air. Mundus shrugs his shoulders and couldn't care less. 'I have worse monsters than you to rely on.' 'I can be skin-dead,' Arnold suggests. 'Being skin-dead's far too old a trick. The public are fed up with that one.' 'I'm well-equipped,' Arnold finally whispers. 'Well-equipped? Who told you that?' Arnold looks down. 'The doctor himself. And the Chocolate Girl,' he quickly puts in. Mundus dismisses this with a wave of the hand. 'Leave me in peace,' he says. 'Mundus has to think.'

Dutifully Arnold goes out. He looks about him. It's still morning and he notices that everyone has their place to go to. He sees that all of them are performing their own tasks and working together. The animal-tamers, the carpenters, the musicians, the clowns, the cooks and the acrobats are working away – rehearsing and preparing for the evening performance. And Arnold realized that he has to find his niche, his place among them, in the sweat and the song.

But then he notices something else. It's the Chocolate Girl. She's standing with her back to him stretching up to the clothes line extended between two wagons. She's hanging up Der Rote Teufel's costume with its gold embroidery, and it gleams brightly in the sun. Arnold's about to go over to her when Der Rote Teufel himself appears. He puts his arm round the Chocolate Girl and kisses her neck. She protests, but rather weakly, and begins to laugh instead. Der Rote Teufel kisses her all the more and pulls her into the shadows by the tent. Arnold hears the laughter disappearing in more laughter. Arnold shrinks. Arnold becomes smaller still. The elephants are bald. His happiness has run out. And he considers that laughter's ways are inscrutable – laughter is always unique and never the same twice itself. And he decides that he'll compile a list of different kinds of laughter. At the top of that list will be his mother's – his mother's careful laughter as she stood outside in the wind, as if the salty wind was tickling her. But he doesn't know who should be second on the list, for it occurs to him that he never heard his father laugh.

Arnold sneaks over to the clothes line. Der Rote Teufel's costume has been mended; it has a large leather patch on the back. Arnold holds his breath. Quickly he raises his hand, pulls a thread loose, and unravels it.

That evening Mundus stands in the centre of the big top beside a broad, black silk curtain, and there is absolute silence in the tent, for everyone knows that now he will display his renowned chamber of horrors. His voice is quiet, but everyone can hear him all the same. 'I would now ask children, those of a delicate disposition, those who are with child, seasick, with a tendency to hypochondria or a fear of the dark to leave the big top forthwith, and instead to keep up their strength in the company of the charming and bounteous Chocolate Girl at the Wheel of Fortune!' There was disquiet in the audience; mothers put their arms round their little ones, fathers put their arms round mothers, and even the hardiest sea salts on the back row are seized by the gravity of the moment. But everyone remains sitting where they are, just a bit closer in to their neighbours, and a deep sigh passes through the place as the light sinks to a shadowy blue and the orchestra saws silence from their instruments. Arnold stands behind the big top and sees everything. And later he subtracts things and he adds things; he exaggerates and he misses out, he's clearsighted and he smudges things, he makes an amalgam of all of them – Mundus, Der Rote Teufel, Arnardo, the dwarfs, the world's tallest man, the Chocolate Girl, the elephants, the sky and the sawdust. For this is Arnold Nilsen's first circus and it's here his lies begin. But this is true, this is what happens now – Mundus has laid his hand on the silk curtain out there and he says in a dark, controlled voice: 'Ladies and gentlemen. I will now reveal to you God's misunderstandings. And if there should happen still to be any among you who are not able to look with their own eyes at creation's rejects, I may be of assistance with smelling salts and other preparations.' Mundus then extends a brown bottle, and proceeds to unscrew the lid and let those in the front row get a whiff of the contents. Then he puts the bottle back in his pocket and waits a few more seconds, in silence, as if for a moment he's considering sparing the onlookers the mad horror of the sights he's about to reveal. The wind brushes against the tent and the heavy silk curtain in the big top trembles. A woman shrieks, but her nearest and dearest take her hand. Mundus gives a bow and at last he draws the curtain quickly to one side. An Egyptian mummy grins at the crowd with 5,000-year-old teeth. The skeleton of a bloodthirsty Viking rises from his grave and slowly swings a rusty sword through the air. The front row gasps and reels backwards to meet the bench behind. Mundus conjures up calm once more. For this is only the start. He raises both hands. 'History speaks sorrowfully to us through these dead witnesses,' he murmurs. 'Do not forget them in your prayers tonight.' He falls silent and lets the corpses speak for themselves a little longer. Then he draws closer to the onlookers, for he senses a certain impatience – perhaps some have even seen these apparitions before. 'You will now behold,' he says, his voice lower still, 'you will now behold God's condemned creation, the abandoned riddle of the angels or the devil's own twisted mischief. Ladies and gentlemen, please welcome Adrian Jefficheff from the Caucasus, our terrifying and tongueless relative, the monster caught between monkey and man – the missing link! Don't annoy him!' A new set is revealed and the crowd screams. And Adrian Jefficheff from the Caucasus stands there stuffed and unwavering, looking emptily at the still shrieking crowd, for his face is covered in thick hair, a dark fur that all but hides his eyes and mouth. His hands are just as hairy and his nails long and black, and when Mundus unbuttons his shirt everyone can see that Jefficheff is a mass of hair from throat to waistband. 'Is he related to the former vicar?' the shout goes up from the back. 'He had tons of hair on his chest too!' The tent is filled with a liberating thunder of laughter, a moment's delicious release of tension. Mundus swears under his breath and quickly bundles Jefficheff from the Caucasus away again, and then conjures a chair from the darkness. Someone's sitting there, hidden beneath a red blanket, only one bare thigh just visible. The tipsy fishermen fall silent and mothers put their hands over their sons' wide eyes. 'May I present,' Mundus says, 'may I present Miss Donkey-head, born in New Orleans, and of all things christened Grace – voted the world's ugliest woman in 1911! When you look at her you will thank the Good Lord each morning and each evening, and I daresay each noontime too, that you don't have to wear such a face!' Mundus pulls away the blanket and the inebriated fishermen don't just fall silent they also become stone-cold sober, for a worse-looking dame they haven't seen on the surface of the earth – she's uglier than the inside of a cat-fish's mouth. The women in the big top emit shrieks of terror and cast themselves on their men folk who want, but can't manage, to take their eyes off Miss Donkey-head, christened Grace, from New Orleans. Her face is like raw meat. Her cheeks are like great bags and push down her massive, leaking nose so that it encompasses her entire face. It looks as though she's actually in the process of eating her own nose, and her eyes are sunk deep and close in her head between folds of dark-red skin. The atmosphere is at breaking point. Arnold feels it there where he's standing looking into the tent – it's as if a string is being drawn more and more tightly, and the whole assembly is fastened to it. But Mundus doesn't let it go yet – no, he keeps it up, he goes on tightening and squeezing the string, and uniting the audience in delicious pain. He produces a scalpel and raises it as the light intensifies, and says in the deepest of voices, 'Shall we leave it at that or shall we reveal the very heart of this poor woman's composition?' He doesn't wait for a response. He makes a cut with the scalpel from her belly up between her breasts, folds the skin to one side, shoves in his hand and brings out a foetus with two heads, four arms, four feet and two necks, all in one shrivelled knot of flesh. At this point five ladies and one gentleman faint and Arnold has to turn away himself, for it's just like out on the water – he feels the swell inside, he's in the middle of a wave and *becomes* the very wave that's making him sick. He thinks he can hear the approach of Paturson's heavy tread; perhaps that's what the cause of the swell is. Arnold tries to keep himself together but he loses the battle and sinks down on the filthy floor and vomits his guts up. All the chocolate he consumed in the course of the night comes up, but suddenly he feels someone lifting him. It's the seamstress and she says something but he doesn't get the words – her mouth is full of needles and she looks like a sea urchin. She washes his face and round his mouth with hard hands; she takes his old clothes off and puts new ones on him, and she does something with his lips. The horrors have gone and finally he can hear what she's saying. 'Now it's your turn, Arnold.' 'My turn?' he breathes. The seamstress puts a mirror with a long crack down it in front of him, and Arnold sees that he's dressed like a girl, with a dress, stockings and slim white shoes, and on his lips he has something dark-red and solid. On his head they've put a stiff wig that scratches his forehead. Arnold doesn't recognize himself. He's struck by a strange thought. *I can't go any further*, he thinks. *I couldn't go any further*. And right behind the distorted mirror is Der Rote Teufel laughing, throwing back his red forelocks and pouting. But there isn't a chance for Arnold to see any more, for suddenly everyone's scurrying about and they shove him in the direction of the curtain and on into the big top where Mundus immediately gathers him and a breathless sigh passes through the crowd. 'Don't say a word,' Mundus hisses. 'For the time being you're Paturson's dumb daughter!' Then Mundus straightens up, folds his hands and takes in his audience. 'My dear ladies and gentlemen. A wondrous thing has happened. Paturson's handicapped daughter has sailed across the ocean to be reunited with him again! She has but nine fingers and no voice with which to speak, but all the bigger then the heart that beats within her!' Only now does Arnold see Paturson right beside them, and the gaze of the world's tallest man ranges in hunger and bewilderment. Mundus takes hold of Paturson's hand, whispers something to him, and when Paturson bends right down to enfold Arnold, the audience's sigh melts into tears. Paturson says something which Arnold alone hears and which he doesn't understand; they're just heavy sounds in his ear, but he doesn't forget them all the same – never will he forget them, those words which Paturson speaks to him and which he doesn't understand. *I spread the dust of stories and let it blossom in the mouths of all as bouquets of the most beautiful lies.* Instead Arnold curtsies; Arnold curtsies like a grateful, disabled daughter and shows off the missing finger, and sniffs become sobbing as Mundus himself wipes away a tear from his smile. 'Sell cards and shut up!' he hisses. And Arnold gets the whole pile and goes from seat to seat, from lap to lap, and everyone buys them. For Arnold looks so shabby and dejected that they've never felt more sympathy for anyone in their lives before. He sells each and every card; they have a colour picture of Paturson on them and a wiggly signature from the medical congress in Copenhagen from the occasion of the measuring of the giant (the figure being recorded in centimetres, feet, inches and ells). Arnold is laden down with coins which he carries back to Mundus who wipes away yet another tear. Paturson embraces Arnold once more, still as bewildered and hungry, as the audience applauds father and daughter, themselves and their own generosity, and God's grace. And the orchestra plays a fanfare for Arnold and Arnold alone; he bows – no, he curtsies, because that's what daughters do. He curtsies and this is Arnold Nilsen's first masquerade, as daughter to the world's tallest man, and he curtsies once more, in triumph and amazement. And finally it's Der Rote Teufel's turn. He climbs up onto the trapeze and throws himself out in dizzying spins – for he will avenge himself, rub out the previous day's blunder and consign it to history by surpassing himself. He will have his revenge and daring is his weapon. Der Rote Teufel (who is in reality Halvorsen and comes from Halden), has made up his mind to be a bird that night. Halvorsen is an eagle flying in the light. But when he folds himself up and peers out between his legs way up there it's not the hammer of hearts he hears, neither is it a breathless hush – rather it's the sound of laughter. The crowd is laughing. Halvorsen can't comprehend it. They're laughing and for an instant he imagines he must have been hearing things. But no, there's nothing wrong with his hearing. Even Mundus is bewildered. Something isn't right. This isn't the funny number. This is the back-breaking acrobat who arouses fear, awe and ultimately that blessed sigh of relief which renders us all equally immortal for one heedless moment. Halvorsen is a bird who scorns and defies death and plays with it. That evening he will conquer death itself and create eternal life. But the audience is laughing. And Arnold realizes at once what they're laughing at. They're waiting for Halvorsen's costume to tear again. That's what they're looking forward to. For the story of the devil's torn bottom has gone the rounds. That's why they're laughing. And Arnold prays silently, *Forgive me, Lord, forgive me*, and can feel the thread from the gold-embroidered costume between his fingers. Halvorsen crosses his feet above his head and hangs there doubled up, on the edge of the impossible, and the public just laughs. And it's this laughter which bewilders Halvorsen and which for a moment makes him careless. It's enough. It's more than enough. For in death there's no such thing as overtime. Der Rote Teufel loses his hold and falls, and in that moment the laughter vanishes, but too late. He falls through the big top like a broken bird and lands on his back. A hair from the elephant's tail is of no use now. Not even a whole elephant can bring Halvorsen back. His name's been wiped from the list of performers. His number is hereafter cancelled. He's dead. And Arnold hides behind Paturson, the world's tallest man. 'It wasn't my fault,' he says. But Paturson doesn't understand what he means. 'It wasn't my fault,' Arnold says again. 'He fell before his costume ripped.'

   That same evening they begin to pack up. They can't stay. One accident always brings others in its wake. That's fate. It's like an infection and they're infected. They have to get away. They have to be out on the road and leave the accident behind them. Everything in the tent is moved. Electricians dismantle the lights. Carpenters fold up the tiers of seats and bring down the curtain. The Chocolate Girl weeps and is busy herself. And finally the big top is lowered – the great tent itself – and the sun, which has barely set, rises already across the blue fiord. Mundus has been taking medication all night to keep awake and his eyes are red and transparent, like balls of coloured glass. Death is a bad advert for any circus. He's spoken to the police and the doctor, and has sent a telegram to Halvorsen's family in Halden. Now he comes over to Arnold who rid himself of the girl's costume ages ago. 'Help the men with the tent,' he says, impatient and restless. Arnold takes up position beside the men in charge of the big top. The workers are standing in a circle lowering the huge canvas which descends like a balloon – all of them have their own special positions and duties. They shout to one another and there's almost no interval between their cries so it sounds like they're singing. 'What should I do?' Arnold asks. The man in charge looks down at him. 'You can fetch Halvorsen's shoe,' he says, pointing. Arnold sees that one of the Der Rote Teufel's shoes, more like a thin slipper than anything else, is still lying out there. He's about to chase off for it, but the man stops him. 'Take this.' He gives Arnold a knife, and Arnold grasps it as he hurries off to fetch Halvorsen's acrobatic shoe, though he doesn't quite know why he should have a knife to accomplish this. But he notices that all the others are carrying knives too and so he doesn't question it; that much he's learned, not to ask needless questions. Instead he thinks to himself – *That's all that's left of Der Rote Teufel – one lonely shoe.* But when he reaches down to pick it up, something else happens. He hears the men giving a roar, and it's just as if a great gust of wind upends him, and he's pressed against the ground. For there's been one accident already, and accidents seldom come in ones. Two ropes have given and the whole circus tent topples down on Arnold's head. And those who're standing round about that morning, on the outside, can see the canvas moving – a tiny, shifting bulge – and perhaps some of them think it's a cat that's wandered in there, but it's Arnold Nilsen. He scrabbles about on all fours in a strange transparent darkness; he can't get out of that darkness under the heavy, damp canvas – it's as if it has solidified above him. The voices on the outside sound annoyed now; the man in charge of the tent gives orders and Mundus is shouting his name, but they can't help him now. And Arnold knows what he'll do with the knife; he grips it in both hands and digs it into the ground with all his might so dirt flies up into his eyes. He realizes he's lying the wrong way round and he raises the knife towards the clouds that scud above him. Soon he won't be able to breathe and he rips the canvas with the blade of the knife. He cuts himself free, he hacks his way out, he rises and sticks his head up through the gash he's made and into the light, into the sun, and the men lift him up into this world where he belongs.

Later that day they take the ferry over Vestfjorden to Bodø. Arnold stands on deck beside the lifeboats, watching the hills sink in blue wind. Right out there, where sky and sea become one, he glimpses the islands he hails from and which now he has left – they lie like fullstops made of stone between the waves. Arnold smiles. He isn't seasick. He feels strong. He raises his four-fingered hand and waves. Then he goes inside to join the others in the cafeteria. No one says anything. They have enough to brood on without talking. Halvorsen's body has been stored in the refrigeration chamber below the cabins, but he won't ever make it back to Halden because the weather's getting warmer, the ice is melting, and soon he'll start to decompose.

Arnold sits at Mundus' table. He has on his lap a large suitcase with string round it. 'What's in there?' Arnold asks. Mundus turns and looks at him with bloodshot eyes. 'You'd really like to know, wouldn't you, Arnold?'

And Arnold regrets having asked. But Mundus puts his hand on the lid and leans closer to Arnold. 'In this,' he whispers, 'in this I've packed all the applause. You're welcome to take care of it for me.'

At Bodø the circus goes ashore. They bury Der Rote Teufel in the graveyard closest to the sea, in a narrow strip of land between the gate and the stone wall. So narrow is the grave that he has to fold himself up into his final, furthest jump. Arnold never sees the Chocolate Girl again. Once more he vanishes from our sight. He's stood on the ocean floor. He has been skin-dead. He's lain beneath the circus tent. Now at last he's reached his dark mainland. He carries with him a suitcase of applause and he disappears round the corner.

The Laughter

Incidentally I found something Dad had written when we had to sort out his things, after what we called the accident. He got a discus right in the head and died. I didn't perhaps quite understand then what it meant, what he'd written, on a leaf of paper he must have torn out of a Bible, one night when he was lying sleepless in a cheap hotel somewhere out in the wide world. The leaf of paper was in the pocket of the pale linen suit that had grown far too small for him ages before. I kept it. I have it still. His handwriting is childish; he uses only capital letters and I imagine he was writing extremely slowly, at the same speed as his thoughts gathered and flowed out in blue ink. Or perhaps his writing was like that because he was missing a finger and didn't have a proper grip of the pen. It's a sort of list, a list of different kinds of laughter. *Aurora's laughter: shy. Father's laughter: silent. Holst the teacher's laughter: evil. The vicar's laughter: sorrowful. Doctor Paulsen's laughter: drunken. Mundus' laughter: black. The public's laughter: malicious.* Through the last word, *malicious*, he's put a stroke, as if he regretted using it, and instead he's written *helpless*. At the bottom he's added something – probably a long time afterwards, perhaps when he found this list again in his pocket much later after he'd forgotten all about it, one summer day when he was sitting on a bench in a park in some strange city. And then he was struck by a new thought, a question to which he has no answer but which is important for him to record. And his handwriting looks even worse now, and for that reason I reckon it must have been after he damaged the rest of his hand, and that meant he had to manoeuvre the pen with just half a thumb. And the clumsy letters scratch out over the thin, porous paper: *Is there such a thing as compassionate laughter?*

Mum used to say to us – *I took him because he made me laugh*. And the next time Arnold Nilsen appears in our story, from out of his dark mainland, he's driving down Church Road in a polished yellow Buick Roadmaster Cabriolet. It's the spring of 1949 and almost May; the sun is shining from the renowned skies over Marienlyst and there's barely a shadow to be seen. Everyone who's out that afternoon stops in their tracks and stares at the car, except for Vera. They stare at this car with its hood and red leather seats as it slowly glides past, for no one has seen a car like it in these parts before. Mrs Arnesen stands right in the middle of the crossroads while her spoiled son pulls at her arm and wants to run after the car; the vicar hesitates for a moment at the sight by the church steps, and Bang the caretaker who's sweeping the pavement for Liberation Day drops his brush in sheer consternation. Even Esther leans out of her little window, squinting in the fierce sunlight, and she can see the small man behind the wheel who has to sit on a fat pillow to be sufficiently high. She can see his black hair like a shining helmet about his head, and the crooked nose in that broad face. He's dressed in a striped suit and is wearing white gloves, his summer gloves, and he looks like a foreigner who's got lost. But Vera, our mother, won't be distracted. She's carrying heavy bags, having been shopping at Butter Petersen's, and it would take more than an open-top American car to disconcert her. She walks slowly and with her eyes cast down, looking at the dust and at her own steps – it's a habit she's got into. She meets no one's gaze, for the looks she gets are unpleasant and patronizing; or else people turn away and let her pass by in the sudden silence between smiles. She knows what they're thinking. Like the vicar the whole lot of them think that she collaborated with the enemy, since she could never account for the father of her illegitimate child. There are even those who maintain that they saw her by the Underground and in the Bygdøy woods during the war, committing unmentionable acts with Germans. Then the Old One sits up when she hears something like this, and her heart within her is cold as she says to the person, 'Now you are completely mistaken. But I understand that you were at both places!' And it isn't true that time is the great healer. Time freezes wounds to open scars. In time it's only Esther in her kiosk who will greet her at all. 'What a silly fool,' she says, shaking her head. 'I blooming well reckon he's sitting on a pillow to make himself more visible!' Vera puts down her shopping nets. 'Who?' 'Did you say who? Did you not see the car?' Esther points and Vera sees the open car that has parked on the corner of Suhm Street and the dark, shining head that's just sticking up over the back of the seat – it almost looks comical. Esther pulls Vera to her side. 'He's most likely driving illegally,' she whispers. 'If he isn't a travelling salesman, that is.' 'And now he must be out of petrol,' Vera replies, her voice just as quiet. 'Serves him right!' Esther exclaims. 'If he thinks he can walk into Fagerborg and soften us up with his pomade and flash car! But if he's selling nylon stockings he's welcome to stay!' The two of them laugh and Esther screws up a bag of sweets and gives it to Vera. 'How's Fred?' she asks. Vera sighs. 'At least he's stopped crying.'

And Arnold Nilsen sees in the mirror that the young lady puts a little brown bag in her coat pocket, picks up her shopping nets and slowly walks along the pavement towards the crossroads where he's parked. She's looking down, he thinks. She's looking down on her old shoes and thick stockings. Her bent neck is white and thin. He shivers and quickly wipes the sweat from his forehead, twists a lock of hair with his fingers and then leans over the passenger seat as she passes. 'May I help the young lady with her over-heavy burden?' Arnold Nilsen asks. But Vera doesn't reply. She just goes on, past the crossroads, and Bang follows her with his eyes without saying anything. And Arnold Nilsen hasn't run out of petrol. Now he cruises along the edge of the pavement and catches up with her again. 'Would you at least be so kind as to look in my direction?' he asks. But Vera is resolute and doesn't give in; she looks down, she walks straight ahead and she will soon be home. Then Arnold Nilsen puts the whole of his weight on the horn and the noise is like a fanfare and a foghorn. Vera goes to pieces completely and drops one of the nets; Arnold Nilsen's out of the car before she has managed to reach down for it and he catches it up himself. He keeps hold of the net and gives a deep bow. 'I saw you right back at Majorstuen. And I simply couldn't take my eyes off you. May I offer you a lift?' Vera is both bewildered and angry, but more bewildered – she hasn't heard the like of this, and she's aware that everyone in Church Road can see them, and that those who can't will get to hear of it all before long from the caretaker who's leaning on his brush and smiling, knowing that soon he'll be able to add new chapters to his rumours. 'I live here,' Vera mutters. 'Well, I was there for the last little bit,' Arnold Nilsen laughs, and he catches up the other net and follows her round the corner. Vera stops by the door. 'Thank you very much,' she says, and wants her shopping nets back, but Arnold Nilsen isn't going to stop there. He gives another deep bow and goes with her up to the first floor, and when they get there Vera stands in the doorway. 'Thank you very much,' she says a second time, amazed at herself, and the little man with the shining black hair puts down the shopping nets on the mat, takes the glove from his left hand but extends his right one instead, the glove still covering it. 'A war wound prevents me from showing my bare arm,' he breathes. 'My name is Arnold Nilsen.' Vera takes his hand. The glove is thin and smooth, and she realizes there's something hard in it, something that isn't pliable – stiff, square fingers – and she shudders. 'I apologize for my intrusion,' he continues, 'but you were simply too beautiful to drive past.' Vera turns crimson and drops his dead hand. She hears someone coming up the stairs. It's Boletta and Fred. They stop on the landing below and the moment Fred sets eyes on Arnold Nilsen he cries, he howls more than ever before. There's such a capacity for wailing in the skinny boy that no one knows where it comes from, but those who remember it have never forgotten the time when Vera screamed, and it's possible that the child she bore heard that scream and decided to mimic its mother. Fred howls and in the end Boletta has to put a hand over his mouth. He bites it and now it's Boletta's turn to swear, and just as suddenly there's quiet again. Boletta hides her arm behind her back and Fred stands there with darkness in his eyes and tight-pursed lips, and a droplet of blood runs down his chin. The door behind Vera opens wide and the Old One sticks out her wild head of hair. 'What in the name of heaven is going on here?' Vera turns towards Arnold Nilsen. 'This is my grandmother,' she tells him. 'And down there's my son, Fred, with his grandmother.' And Arnold Nilsen bows to one and all and has to gather his thoughts for a moment. He has to compose himself, win some time, as he puts on his glove again and looks right at Vera. 'It has been a great joy to meet your family. If I am not mistaken there are three mothers, two grandmothers, one great-grandmother, two daughters and one son standing here, all from the same family!' Vera meets his gaze and for a second she has to think too. Then she gives a laugh, and Boletta and the Old One look at each other, as surprised as the other, because they can barely remember when Vera last laughed, and Arnold Nilsen kisses her hand and starts going down the steps. He stops in front of Fred who's standing there dark and with his jaw set. Boletta holds him close. Fred struggles. 'Did you see the car out there?' Arnold Nilsen asks. Fred is silent. 'It has a hood you can put up when it's raining.' Still Fred doesn't say a word. 'That car starts fast as an aeroplane and has driven all the way from America.' Fred draws his hand over his chin and wipes the blood away. 'You can come for a drive with me, if your mother lets you,' Arnold Nilsen says, continuing down the steps. They hear the door banging and shortly afterwards the car starting. Then Boletta chases up to Vera. 'Who was that?' she hisses. The Old

One's question is the same. 'Who in heaven's name was that creation?' 'He just helped me to carry my things,' Vera tells them. 'His name's Arnold Nilsen.' She turns towards Fred who hasn't moved on the landing. 'Can I, Mum?'

Arnold Nilsen is back two days later. He has flowers with him which he leaves outside the door. He doesn't ring the bell. He lets the bouquet stand and speak for itself. It's the Old One who finds it there when she comes back from the 'pole' with enough Malaga to celebrate four years of freedom. She lifts the bouquet and counts twenty-one wood anemones, and takes them all in with her. 'Who can these be for?' she asks. Vera turns crimson once more (she can still blush), and tries to take the flowers, but the Old One won't let her come close. 'There's no card here. They could just as well be for me. Or maybe they're for Boletta.' 'Stop fooling around,' Vera says, getting angry. 'Give me them!' But the Old One refuses to allow this rare opportunity for some merriment to pass her by. 'Boletta!' she calls. 'Have you a secret admirer who leaves anemones at the front door?' Boletta shakes her head and Vera chases round the Old One to get hold of the bouquet, and tears it from her at last with a sudden fury that brings silence over them all once more. Vera puts the flowers in a blue vase which she then places on the windowsill. She remains standing there looking out. Boletta gets her telegraph illness again and lies down. The Old One tests her Malaga just to see if it's worth drinking. It is, and she goes over with her glass to Vera. 'It is your turn to wait now?' she murmurs. 'I'm not waiting for anyone,' Vera says firmly. 'That's for the best.' The Old One kisses her cheek. 'The flowers look rather battered and bruised,' she observes. 'But at least he picked them himself.'

I once asked Esther, after Mum and I had taken over the little kiosk in the entry near the church, and she herself had been given a double room at the Prince August Memorial in Storgata, about what exactly happened that day Arnold Nilsen came up in his car from Majorstuen. 'Happened?' Esther repeated. 'Did anything happen?' 'Yes, you might well say it did. He met Mum.' Esther looked at me in a sudden moment of clarity. 'Love is a chance thing, isn't it,' she said. I smiled. 'Is it?' She shrugged her shoulders and I saw her sink back into her own darkness once more. 'Your father was a no good man,' she whispered. 'Even if he did have dashed nylon stockings with him.'

When Arnold Nilsen next appears in Church Road, on Liberation Day itself, he has a flat packet in his suit pocket and this time he doesn't leave it outside the door – instead he rings the bell confidently and hopes that his poor flowers have paved his way back to the door. It's the Old One who opens it. 'Well, well,' she says, and lets him in. Arnold Nilsen gives a bow. 'It's perhaps going too far intruding at this juncture. But nevertheless I'll be bold and ask if your granddaughter is at home?' 'Everyone is at home,' the Old One replies. Arnold Nilsen turns, and the doors are open between the various rooms, and at the far end of the dining-room he sees Boletta and Vera and Fred sitting at the set table, where the candlelight is barely visible against the sunlight falling through the tall windows, almost making the panes tremble. They look up at Arnold Nilsen and a tremor passes through him at the sight of Vera and her son and her mother, and the white anemones that he himself picked. He has to cover his eyes, and he cries, or else the sun and the piercingly white cloth blinds his sight. And so the Old One follows after him in and Arnold Nilsen is given a seat at their table.

There's quiet for a time. Fred upsets his glass and is about to cry again. Boletta puts her napkin over the spill and Vera goes to get a cloth from the kitchen. Then the Old One asks, 'What is it that actually brings you here?' Arnold Nilsen is taken aback for a moment, stunned into embarrassed silence. 'I'm here because you let me in,' he says in the end. The Old One furrows her brow, taken aback by his answer. Boletta looks at him. 'Why don't you take off your gloves?' Arnold Nilsen sighs. 'Because I wouldn't want you to lose your appetites. My right hand exploded like a shooting star thanks to a German mine in Finnmark.' 'Let's see,' Fred says. But at that moment Vera returns and wipes the floor where the juice has spilt, and the Old One loses her patience. 'We won't do the spring cleaning right now! We do have guests!' Vera finally sits herself once more and breathes so heavily she all but blows out the candles. 'Thank you for the flowers,' she says. 'They were just standing there doing nothing and I picked them,' Arnold Nilsen tells her. The Old One turns to Boletta. 'He talks like a novel we once threw in the stove,' she whispers, but loud enough for everyone to hear. Vera bows her head and is on the point of upsetting her glass too, but Arnold Nilsen gives a big laugh. 'You're absolutely right,' he admits. 'As a matter of fact I speak three languages fluently. Norwegian, American and Røstish.' 'Røstish?' Arnold Nilsen takes his time. 'If you were to translate the wind to human speech and put music to it and colour to that, then you'd be as close as you could be to my mother tongue.' He falls into deep and melancholic reverie. 'I was born on a full stop called Röst right out on the edge of the ocean,' he says in a low voice, with no music in the words. Then he remembers that he has brought things with him. He gets out the packet from his pocket and places it on the tablecloth, in front of Vera. 'A present to the women in the family,' he says, and slowly looks at each one in turn. Carefully Vera takes off the paper and even the Old One leans closer, and they become silent and lowly when they see the contents. 'What is it?' Fred asks. It's three pairs of nylon stockings, from Denmark. Vera holds them up; they're soft and lovely to the touch. 'Thank you so much,' she whispers and can't say any more. She looks at Arnold Nilsen who's sunning himself in this great, childish gratitude. Boletta wants to feel them too, while the Old One pours a glass of Malaga that she pushes over the table. 'But what is it that you live off?' she inquires. 'You can't live on wood anemones and nylon stockings and nothing else?' 'I live off life,' Arnold Nilsen answers. The Old One is no more satisfied with this response. 'You live off life?' she echoes. 'And does it yield much?' Arnold Nilsen looks down at the brimful glass in front of him. 'Thank you, but I'm driving today too.' He leaves his glass where it is and turns towards Fred who isn't crying but who rather meets his gaze with black stubbornness. 'Have you asked your mother, by the way?' Fred nods. Arnold Nilsen places his damaged hand on his shoulder. 'And did you get permission?'

And they drove up towards Frognerseter. Arnold Nilsen sits on his pillow and carefully follows the various instruments on the dashboard, since it is not permitted to drive any more than 25 kilometres from one's home, and today his home is Church Road, and he intends to be an upright citizen. But twenty-five kilometres is a long enough journey that day – it's a fairy tale, a circumnavigation of the globe – and Vera and Fred sit in the back seat, the hood down, and they are in wind, light, speed. Arnold Nilsen stops at the famous view and hurries round with ceremony to open the door for Vera, and they sit together on the bench there, while Fred remains in the back seat. A long while passes without a word being spoken. Instead they gaze down over the town beneath them, lying under a haze of sunlight. 'Things are getting better now,' Arnold Nilsen asserts, and moves closer to Vera. At first she moves away, but he comes closer once more, and she lets him do so until eventually they're huddled together. And he regrets that he didn't sit on the other side because then he could have taken the glove from his healthy hand and perhaps stroked her hair. 'Thank you,' Arnold Nilsen says. 'Because soon it wouldn't have been possible to move any further along the bench.' And Vera laughs, she lets herself go, and I like to think that this laughter was a kind of falling in love, or a release. That laughter bound her to this little man who came from a full stop on the ocean, and the laughter drowned out everything else, it cancelled out the darkness inside her. She could laugh, and perhaps it was this very laughter that Arnold Nilsen had been searching all those years – a compassionate laughter.

Then Fred stands in front of them. 'Let me see your hand,' he demands. Arnold Nilsen shifts away from Vera a little and looks at the thin, obstinate boy. And so carefully and extremely slowly he takes off the glove. He has filled out the fingers inside with little pieces of wood so that they still extend, as though he's loosened the whole of his hand and laid it in his lap; and the end of his arm is nothing more than a knobbled clump of grey flesh, sewn together with rough stitches, and half a thumb without a nail, a useless lump. Vera has to hide her eyes. Fred leans closer still and wants to touch the mutilated hand, but before he goes that far Vera gets up, quickly and impatiently, and pulls him forcefully with her back to the car. Arnold Nilsen puts on his glove again as fast as he can and goes after them. 'I apologize unreservedly for my thoughtlessness,' he whispers, and bows his head. 'I don't want him to have nightmares,' Vera says quickly. 'It was my fault.' 'Absolutely not,' Arnold Nilsen protests. 'It was me and none other that let the sorrowful remains of my hand be seen. How may I make things better?' Vera makes no reply. She just looks at him instead and smiles. And this smile gives him the courage to ask her something, as Fred settles in the front seat. 'I don't see any man in the house,' he says. 'And you saw correctly,' Vera tells him. 'Does the boy not have a father?' Vera turns away. Fred holds the steering wheel and makes noises more like an animal than an engine. 'Forgive me once more,' Arnold Nilsen pleads.

They drive down to the city again. It's clouding over. The shadows chase over them. Vera's cold. Fred's in the front seat staring at the speedometer. And then they meet another car, a black Chevrolet Fleetline Deluxe; they pass slowly and brake. Arnold Nilsen gets out, and the other driver, a tall, young man with fair hair and a cravat, gets out too. They say hello, and the two of them circle their cars and praise the respective models. They trace the shining chrome plating, they open the bonnets and need say no more. They just nod, intuitively, and stand in that brotherhood of American horsepower, and Arnold Nilsen suddenly senses a great, deep feeling of belonging that he can't remember having felt since that time he entered Mundus' tent. He notices that there's also a beautiful woman sitting in the Chevrolet; she gives him a tired but happy smile through the open side window – she's pregnant and has barely enough room in the seat. Then they drive on, each in the other direction, and they'll never meet again, though they'll continue to live in the same city, living their lives there, their broken and ruined lives, for they will both meet with terrible accidents. The young strangers in the Chevrolet will encounter theirs just round the next corner, while Arnold Nilsen will have to wait many years before being met, as one says, by that which some call fate, but which might just as well be called mathematics. Or as I later tell Peder, when I present my reflection of what I experience in a complete dramatic work – it was nothing other than the symmetry of the triple jump.

It starts raining the minute Arnold Nilsen sits down behind the wheel again. That suits him fine. Now he can perform a miracle with impunity. He makes a swinging gesture with the stiff glove in order to get their attention, and with the other hand he depresses a button on the dashboard. Slowly the hood closes over them. Fred holds his breath. Vera claps her hands. Arnold Nilsen is pleased with his show and with his audience. 'Now we can drive home dry,' he says, and changes gear. Vera quickly turns round and catches the red brake lights of the other car reflecting on the wet surface and disappearing into the rain behind them. 'Drive carefully,' she whispers. 'The road's slippery.'

And Arnold Nilsen carefully drives home. The Old One and Boletta are at the window when he parks by the corner. They see Fred emerging from the front seat and banging the door behind him, while the two others remain sitting where they are. 'Now he's asking if they can meet tomorrow,' the Old One says. Boletta turns towards her. 'D'you think it's serious?' The Old One sighs. 'She doesn't have the choice she once did. And neither does he.' 'Oh, be quiet!' Boletta says to her. Arnold Nilsen lights a cigarette with the electric lighter. 'I hope I haven't scared you off with my half hand,' he murmurs. Vera shakes her head. Arnold Nilsen waits until he's finished his cigarette before saying any more. The tobacco's dry and burns his throat. 'I'll happily go for another drive tomorrow,' he tells her. 'Me too,' Vera says at once. 'I'm afraid I can't ask you back to my place. I'm still staying at a rather wretched hostel.' Vera leans forward between the seats. 'Hostel?' Arnold Nilsen looks out. Fred's pressing his nose against the window. The rain's pouring down. 'Coch's Hostel. Until I find a place for myself. But empty properties aren't exactly growing on trees just now.' Arnold Nilsen sighs. 'I've searched the whole city and followed up every single advert since I came back from America. Even the hotels don't have room for me! But in New York I stayed at the Astoria! Have you heard of the Astoria?' 'No,' Vera says. 'There they take your suitcase right to the door and the suites have four rooms each in them!' He thumps his healthy hand down on the steering wheel. 'At Coch's three of us share the same room! One of them drinks every night and keeps us two others awake.' He falls silent and looks down at his hand in shame. Vera sits in silence, pondering. 'I'll have a talk with Mother,' she says at last. Arnold Nilsen looks up and turns towards her. 'What was that you said?' 'I'll talk to the Old One too,' she adds. He smiles. His face breaks into a wide smile; he forgets himself completely and lays his bad hand on her arm. 'Just as well I'm so small,' he says. 'I can lie on a pillow in the windowsill!'

In June Arnold Nilsen moves into Church Road. It causes a stir – a Buick on the corner and a man in the women's flat. At first he sleeps on a narrow mattress in the entrance hall. He gets up at seven, has his coffee, goes down to his car and returns home at half past five. They don't quite know what it is he does and he doesn't enlighten them himself. 'Now he's off to live off life,' the Old One echoes and shakes her head, but deep inside she can't help liking him all the same. He's never in the way. He's clean and tidy. He isn't a noisy sleeper. He puts his money in the housekeeping tin each week. He takes the rubbish out. And on Sundays he takes them on drives, out to Nesodden and the fiord, or in the other direction towards the woods and lakes. Fred sits in the front and there's plenty of room for the women in the back. They have coffee and Danish pastries with them, and wherever they go people stop and gaze at the slender Buick, and Arnold Nilsen waves to one and all. And in the evenings he makes Vera laugh. Boletta has carried out her secret research at the Exchange. He hasn't lied about anything either. He does come from Røst in the Lofotens; his father was a fisherman and the family has never had a telephone. He's promoted to the dining-room in July and gets to sleep on the divan there. The Old One and Boletta bicker in the maid's room while Fred sleeps with his mother. One night Arnold Nilsen is wakened by the boy standing and staring at him. He could have been there long enough. The thin shadow in the darkness is straight and determined. He says nothing. That's perhaps the worst thing. Arnold Nilsen sits up. 'What is it you want?' he asks him. Fred doesn't reply. Arnold Nilsen becomes nervous. 'You don't need to be afraid,' he whispers. And yet he realizes at once that Fred is anything but fearful. Had he been afraid he wouldn't be standing like that in the darkness by the divan. On the contrary he's angry, threatening. Arnold Nilsen searches for words; he who can talk most people round has now to search feverishly for the right sentence – to address a boy who's barely five years old. His voice is quieter still. 'I won't take your mother from you, Fred.' He stretches out the arm without a hand. Fred doesn't move. He just stands, staring silent and sullen, and then goes soundlessly back to his mother's bedroom.

Arnold Nilsen doesn't sleep a wink the rest of the night. And when his alarm clock goes off he doesn't get up, he just lies there. Then he hears something beyond the door – an anxious noise – they're talking quickly and quietly, as if they can't quite make up their minds, and in the end Vera looks in on him. 'Are you ill?' she inquires. Arnold Nilsen has to turn his face to the wall so she won't see he's on the verge of tears, because someone cares about him, someone wonders how he is, and he's almost overcome by such concern. 'I'll stay off work today,' he whispers.

Vera quietly shuts the door and passes the message on. Arnold Nilsen is quite well. He's just going to stay off work that day. They don't quite know what it is he's going to stay off from. He just remains lying there on the divan and stays off work. Boletta goes to the Exchange. Fred goes down into the yard. The Old One and Vera wash sheets. 'If it's life he lives off, it must be life he's staying away from,' the Old One says. Vera hushes her. 'Don't tell me to be quiet! I'm only quoting his own words. Has he said anything to you?' The Old One pulls at the sheet so violently that Vera loses her balance and has to be supported by her grandmother. 'Said anything?' 'Yes, about what he does. What he has done. What he's thought of doing. It can't just be poems he whispers in that little ear of yours!' Vera sits down on the edge of the bath. 'I don't ask him. And he doesn't ask me.' The Old One sighs and lays the cloth in her lap. 'We just have to hope he isn't another night man.'

Arnold Nilsen's breakfast is waiting for him when he comes into the kitchen. The flat is silent. He's alone. It's the first time he's been alone there. He takes his coffee cup with him over to the window and looks down into the yard. Vera and the Old One are hanging the washing out to dry – great white sheets that they stretch and throw over the clothes lines, and then attach with pegs they have in bags round their waists. All this Arnold Nilsen observes. It's an ordinary morning in the summer of 1950; soon the sun will fill the whole of the yard. Some boys are repairing their bicycles over by the gate; the lame caretaker is standing facing away, filling a bucket with water, and behind everything is the sound of someone playing a simple tune on the piano, over and over again. Vera and the Old One laugh as a stray gust of wind blows in and billows up the sheet they're holding and all but carries them off. Arnold Nilsen sees all this. He is a witness this morning. A witness to this humanity – a bucket that has to be filled, a bicycle repaired, sheets dried in the sun. His first anxiety has passed. Instead he is filled with wonderment, and that too is a sort of anxiety – he is filled with wonderment at all this which is becoming his. He is a man on the far edge of his youth – soon it will be gone – he's almost thirty and the world is growing smaller and smaller about him. This is his world and he is a witness to it. He must forget everything that has been and begin remembering anew. Then he notices that Fred's sitting in the only corner where shadow remains. He's sitting there staring. He tears this morning to pieces. Vera calls him. Fred doesn't move. She calls again. But Fred remains sitting there, in his dark corner, and when it gradually begins to fill with light he covers his eyes.

Then the doorbell rings. Arnold Nilsen puts down his cup and hesitates. He doesn't officially live here. His name still isn't on the door. The bell rings again. He looks down into the yard where the Old One's squatting down and hugging Fred. Arnold Nilsen goes out into the hall and opens the door. It's Arnesen. He pretends to be surprised. 'Are none of the ladies home?' he asks. 'They're down in the yard hanging out the washing. I can get them if you want.' But Arnesen just waves his hand and is past him in a flash. 'I know the way.' He puts down his little case on the floor in front of the clock, takes out the key to it and then turns towards Arnold Nilsen. 'They say it's you who's the owner of the new car.' Arnold Nilsen nods. Arnesen smiles. 'And what sort of horsepower does an engine like that have?' '150.' '150? My word. So it can drive faster than the law actually permits?' Arnold Nilsen laughs. 'A fast car can go slowly too,' he says. 'True enough. As long as one doesn't give in to temptation. And each and every one of us has the power to do that. When no one's looking, I mean.' Arnold Nilsen says nothing to this. Now it's Arnesen's turn to laugh. 'Well, here I am standing talking on the job without actually introducing myself. I'm Mr Arnesen, the insurance agent.' He proffers his hand, clasps the stiff glove, and lets go of it immediately. A shudder passes through him. 'An accident?' he enquires. 'The war,' Arnold Nilsen replies. Arnesen smiles, turns away, pulls out the drawer under the clock and collects the money in a leather bag which he then places in his case. Arnold Nilsen observes the speed and flexibility of the man's fingers; he's seen it before, but he knows that no one's ever quick enough, that there's always someone who'll catch you out, sooner or later. You make a mistake and drop everything on the floor; you tremble a tiny bit and blow off your arm. 'Is it your wife who plays the piano?' he asks. Arnesen pushes the drawer into place and looks at him. He isn't smiling any more. 'Does it disturb you?' 'Not in the least.' 'But you think that she should practise something else?' 'That hadn't crossed my mind.' 'If you live here long enough it will cross your mind.' Arnold Nilsen produces a banknote from his jacket pocket and drops it into the case. 'Now I'm insured too,' he says. Arnesen snaps shut the lid. 'Yes, you might need to be.'

Arnesen retreats with a bow, but doesn't offer his hand this time; he's felt the artificial fingers once. Arnold Nilsen remains standing by the oval clock – it's six minutes past nine. Then he hears the others in the kitchen. He goes to meet them. 'Arnesen's been to collect the premium,' he tells them. The Old One looks round. 'Yes, I felt it had grown cold here,' she murmurs.

Fred chases out into the hall, climbs onto a chair and shakes the clock. There's almost no sound, only Fred

laughing, almost screaming, as he shakes and shakes the
clock, until in the end the Old One has to tear him away
and re-position the hands. Arnold Nilsen produces
another note and gives it to Fred. 'You can have that to
put in the drawer.' Fred stares at the curled blue paper. 'I
want money,' he says. Arnold Nilsen laughs and instead
fishes out a coin which he bites into hard before giving to
Fred. 'You'll hear when this hits the bottom all right!' For
a long time Fred rubs the coin against his thigh and then
drops it in his pocket. 'You have to put it in the clock,'
Vera tells him. 'So nothing will happen to us.' Fred shakes
his head and wants to get away. Vera holds him back. 'At
least you can say thank you. Say thank you very much,
Fred!' 'It doesn't matter,' Arnold Nilsen assures her. But
Vera has made up her mind that Fred will do as he's told.
'Say many thanks!' she shouts. 'Or else give the money
back!' Fred's mouth is clamped shut and his hand knotted deep in his pocket; he twists away. 'Say many thanks!'
Vera shouts and refuses to let him go. At that point the
Old One comes between them. 'Let him be,' she says, and
puts some money into the clock for all of them.

   That evening Boletta and Vera bring in the dry washing.
The sun is shining low from the other end and has lifted
the light from the yard. They carry the basket down to the
mangle in the basement, put the first sheet between the
rollers and have to join forces to turn the handle. When
the next one has been put through and smoothed out
Boletta asks, 'Has something happened to Fred?' Vera
rests against the handle. 'I can't talk to him. He won't
listen to me any more.' Boletta folds the sheet and places
it in the basket. 'He's just a bit confused,' she says. 'And
then it's easy to become angry.' Vera's close to tears. She
covers her mouth. 'Perhaps it's best if Arnold leaves,' she
murmurs. Boletta smiles. 'Oh, it wasn't exactly that I was
thinking of.' She puts her arm round her daughter. 'Fred
isn't used to hearing you laugh.'

   At that moment they hear someone coming along the
passage and they know at once who it is. One shoe drags

continually, delayed and out of step, scraping along the stone floor. He stops in the doorway. It's the caretaker, Bang. He lets his gaze rest on the pile of sheets. 'You can never have enough sheets,' he says, and that's all he ventures for a time. Boletta turns away and sprinkles some water on the final sheet to go through the mangle. The caretaker focuses his attention on Vera. 'Would you like some help to crank the handle?' Vera shakes her head. 'No, thanks.' He smiles and goes closer. 'There are obviously more to lay the table for these days.' Vera turns the handle with all her might and the sheet disappears between the rollers. 'It must be a comfort indeed to have a man in the house at last,' Bang continues slowly. Suddenly Boletta whirls round once more and the two of them stand almost eyeball to eyeball. 'Now just you take your foot with you and get lost!' she tells him. The caretaker limps backwards, speechless and hurt, and hurries away through the basement. Boletta and Vera look at one another, hold their breath as long as they can, and finally burst out laughing. 'That was just like listening to the Old One!' Vera said, laughing still. Boletta has to be supported by her and can hardly speak. 'Oh, dear,' she gasps. 'Have I really begun to be like my mother!'

When they go back again with the sheets the Old One's already gone to bed. She says she feels washed out and dizzy; she wants to see Dr Sand, Dr Schultz' successor and his complete opposite – a confirmed teetotaller who uses mouth pads and cortisone. She has pain behind her forehead. She feels strange right down her arms. 'You've infected me with your headache and your bruised elbows!' she accuses Boletta, and wants to be left in peace. They leave the patient be and next morning the Old One's up before the others, orders a taxi, and won't be dissuaded by Boletta and Vera who hear her telephoning and come to her aid. She doesn't want anyone's company and most certainly doesn't want to be driven in Arnold Nilsen's car. No, she'll manage the last bit alone, just as elephants step aside to die with dignity without troubling the rest of the herd. 'You're making a fuss,' Boletta giggles at her. 'There's nothing wrong with you!' But the Old One gives her an angry look, goes down to the taxi and seats herself in the back. She asks the driver to take her round the corner of Jacob Aall Street and stop there. 'That's a hundred metres,' he says. 'And I'm paying,' the Old One replies. And I would love to say that it was the same taxi driver as on the night when Fred was born, but it wasn't. Things don't happen like that, but had it been the case the narrative might perhaps have turned and taken another direction, or the reader would believe it was a lie, an invention, and therefore doubted the rest of our story too, and probably given up on it for good to look out more reliable accounts. All the same I wish it had been the same driver because I'd love to have heard the conversation between the Old One and him. Perhaps she'd have invited him back later that day for a cup of tea or coffee; they could have told each other about the intervening time since they stopped at the junction of Church Road and Ullevål Road and a very bloody child came to the world in his back seat. Afterwards he could have greeted Fred, the boy he himself had christened, for hadn't they kept the first name that had been spoken in that holy taxi? Yes, this indeed is Fred. But the driver's someone else, an older man who continually draws his fingers over his untidy and not entirely clean moustache. 'Are we waiting for someone?' he enquires. 'That is something you needn't concern yourself with yet,' the Old One replies. She's keeping an eye on the Buick parked on the other corner. There still hasn't been any sign of Arnold Nilsen. For a moment she's worried. Perhaps he's taken the day off again? The meter in the taxi keeps clicking. Then at last he appears, gets behind the wheel, and swings out into Church Road. 'Now you will please follow that car,' the Old One tells the driver, while she herself sinks as low as possible in the seat so there isn't the faintest risk of being spotted.

Arnold Nilsen drives through Majorstuen and down Bogstad Road. It's spitting rain and he's driving with the hood up. A few souls are waiting outside the 'pole' with their hands in their trouser pockets and with their heads bowed. The pigeons on the Valkyrie take off like a shoal of fish and alight on their chosen cornices. A baker brings out loaves to his delivery van and the fresh crusts steam with heat. The city is awake and sleepless in the mild rain. And Arnold Nilsen just drives on unsuspecting through yet another morning. He parks in a back yard in Grønne Street, and walks the last part of the way over to Coch's Hostel. The Old One has stopped the taxi at Park Road and from there she can observe him ringing the bell and gaining admittance. She waits. She has time enough. The meter reaches an unheard of sum. She has sufficient to pay. The driver moves his finger back and forth beneath his nose. But it's patience she doesn't have enough of. She pays and hurries over the street to the lugubrious doorway. This is Arnold Nilsen's emergency exit and his back door, she thinks to herself. His smokescreen. Or else he has someone else with whom he amuses himself, that little stain of a man. Whatever the reason he's going to suffer for it. The Old One rings the bell of Coch's Hostel. Eventually the door opens a little, and a fat woman with heavy eyelids peers out. 'I'm here to see Arnold Nilsen,' the Old One tells her. The woman looks embarrassed. 'Don't know him.' She's about to shut the door again but the Old One has no intention of leaving Coch's Hostel with her mission unaccomplished. She puts her shoe in the door, grabs hold of the woman's ear and twists it. 'You shouldn't lie to elderly ladies,' she hisses. 'Take me to Nilsen's room!' The Old One's admitted. They climb a steep staircase to something that resembles a reception lobby, with a counter that has ashtrays and old newspapers on it, and a board from which hang two keys. The place smells of tobacco and mouldering mattresses. Three men sit in a windowless room playing cards and drinking beer. They glance at the Old One, uncertainly, before hunching over their bottles once more. 'You'll find him in 502,' the fat woman says, massaging her ear. 'But why didn't you say that to begin with?' the Old One says brightly. 'Because our guests demand complete privacy,' the woman replies, raising her eyebrows. The three men titter from their room. 'Yes, I can believe that,' the Old One says. 'But now it's going to be anything but complete for Arnold Nilsen!' With that she proceeds up to the fourth floor and comes to a long, narrow corridor with tall windows on one side and doors on the other. Outside one door there's a pair of shoes. Slowly the Old One goes down to the end of the corridor where she finds Room 502. At first she listens and hears extraordinary gusts of wind coming from inside the room, gusts that rise and fall in strength. She peers through the keyhole and sees clouds scudding past. Then the Old One stands tall and hammers on the door. 'I'm not to be disturbed!' Arnold Nilsen shouts. 'How many times have I to make that clear!' 'One more time!' the Old One shouts back. There's silence in Room 502, total silence. Then Arnold Nilsen opens the door and looks out at her, pale and dishevelled. 'Well, you'd better come in.' The Old One walks past him and stops. The bed is made up. A whole assortment of tools are lying on the floor. Various designs are folded out on a table by the window, the curtains of which are drawn. The shade has been removed from the standard light and the bulb sends golden light in every direction. No one else is there. But in the centre of the room there's a tall stand with a propeller on it that almost resembles a crooked star and a ladder leads up to the top of it. Arnold Nilsen shuts the door. 'You're looking at my windmill,' he whispers. The Old One turns towards him. 'A windmill? Have you been keeping a windmill hidden in Coch's Hostel?' He puts the shade back on the lamp and stands by the window. 'It's taking time to finish it,' he says, 'with only one hand'. The Old One circles the windmill and doesn't know whether to be disappointed or relieved. As a result she feels bewildered and in the end sits down on the bed. 'Are you making it yourself?' she asks. Immediately Arnold Nilsen shows her the drawings, but all this geometry is meaningless to her and she pushes him away. 'You don't understand wind down here in the south,' he tells her, 'because you don't really know what wind is! You think it's windy when it blows a bit in Frogner Park. Oh, no!' he climbs up a few steps on the ladder, pushes the wheel into motion, and the same sounds are to be heard, of gusts of wind, and the Old One has to lean backwards so as not to be hit in the head. Arnold Nilsen laughs. 'The wind is like a mine, a mine under the skies! There one can find the purest, most flowing gold that's to be found.' Suddenly he grows serious and comes down the ladder again. 'You aren't sick,' he murmurs. 'You followed me.' 'Of course!' the Old One responded. 'I wanted to know what sort of man you really were!' 'You thought I had someone else apart from Vera, was that it?' The Old One says nothing. Arnold Nilsen sits down beside her. 'And so you found me here with a windmill instead! What sort of man do you think I am now?' The Old One gets up and goes over to the window. 'Have you heard of the elephants in the mountain country of Deccan?' she asks him. Arnold Nilsen shakes his head. 'It's at the very top of India. The train runs there between the various borders and has to cross a great plain where the elephant herds range. On one occasion a young elephant was driven over by the train. Are you paying attention, Arnold Nilsen?' He nods, and the sweat glistens on his forehead. 'Yes. I'm hearing everything you say and more.' 'Good! Because when the train was on its return journey, the mother of that elephant was standing on exactly the same spot, waiting. She attacked a train engine and twenty-five carriages. Because she was determined to avenge the death of her young one. She was determined to derail a whole train.' The Old One sits with him once more. 'Who do you think won, Arnold Nilsen?' she asks. He doesn't answer her immediately. And when he does it's to ask another question. 'Perhaps that's why a hair from an elephant's tail is lucky,' he whispers. For a long while the Old One sits in silence. 'I don't know what sort of man you are, Arnold Nilsen. I only know that you're to be careful with Vera and Fred. They are very fragile, both of them. Is that understood?'

Arnold Nilsen moves into Vera's bedroom in August, and he hangs all his suits right at the back of the cupboard behind her dresses. He lies down silently beside her in the double bed. He stares up at the ceiling. He smiles. Perhaps he thinks that now, finally, the green sun has risen high enough and is shining on him. He breathes deeply, moved and wondering, and senses a sweet and heavy taste in his mouth. 'I think I can taste Malaga in here,' he murmurs. And Arnold Nilsen turns over to Vera and she lets him come.

They got married in September, in the Majorstuen church. Vera said she would prefer the ceremony to be somewhere else since the same vicar as before was employed there. Arnold Nilsen peacefully replied, 'If the wretch wouldn't baptize Fred he can hardly refuse to let us go to the altar! If he did I'd haul him and his congregation up before the King, the cabinet and I don't know who!' It rained that Saturday. The Old One, Boletta, Fred, Bang the caretaker, Arnesen and three bleary-eyed men from Coch's Hostel were there. The vicar read the liturgy quickly and sulkily, and stared with revulsion at Vera's white dress. And Vera resolutely met his gaze, smiling, but when Arnold Nilsen slipped the ring she had promised to look after for Rakel onto her finger, she bowed her head (to the vicar's great satisfaction), and wept. And she knew then there's no such thing as pure joy, and it's perhaps for that very reason that we laugh.

I was born in March. I came to the world with my feet first and I caused my mother great pain.

BARNUM

Baptism

'Barnum?' The vicar put down his pen and looked at Mum, who was sitting on the other side of the desk with me on her lap. 'Barnum?' he repeated. Mum didn't answer. She glanced instead at my father who was slowly turning his hat with his fingers. 'That's right,' he said. 'You heard correctly. We are decided on that. The boy's to be called Barnum.' Perhaps I screamed at that point. Mum had to comfort me. Mum sang there in the vestry. He took up his pen once more, impatient, and wrote something on a sheet of paper. 'Is Barnum really a name?' Dad sighed gently at his ignorance. 'Barnum is as good a name as any,' he responded. The vicar smiled. 'You're from northern Norway, Arnold Nilsen?' Dad nodded. 'From Røst, Mr Sunde. Where Norway puts the full stop.' I stopped crying and Mum stopped singing. The vicar got up. 'You're perhaps rather more liberal when it comes to the giving of names up there. But down here we have our limits.' Dad gave a laugh. 'Barnum is no northern Norwegian invention, my dear reverend.' The vicar pulled out a book from the shelves behind him. He leafed through it on the hunt for something. Mum gave Dad a kick and nodded in the direction of the door. Dad shook his head. The vicar sat down and laid the book on the table. 'Is that the Bible you're consulting?' The vicar didn't reply. He read aloud. 'It is expressly forbidden to confer a name which might become a burden to the one

who is to bear it.' I started to cry. Mum rocked me and
began humming. The vicar closed the book and looked
up, his jowls taut. 'The law pertaining to the giving of
names from 9 February 1923.' The hat stopped turning in
Dad's hands. 'But is it not the case that the name is sham-
ing no one?' he inquired. The vicar had no answer to this.
Instead he said, 'I would ask you to find another name for
the poor child.' Mum had already got up and was going
towards the door. 'He is no poor child!' she said. 'And
now we're going!' Dad remained a moment longer. 'This
is not the first time the vicar has taken a spite at my children,' he whispered. The vicar smiled. 'Your children? Are
you the father of both?' Dad put on his hat. His breath
choked him and he could have cursed his crooked nose.
'There are other vicars,' he hissed. 'But only one God and
one law,' the vicar retorted. Dad banged the door after
him as they left, but out in the corridor Mum began to
lose her nerve. 'Could we not call him something else?'
she wept. Dad wouldn't hear of it. 'He's going to be called
Barnum, damn it!' Now I started crying again. And Dad
tore open the door of the vestry and leaned his head and
hat in. 'We had a neighbour at home by the name of
Elendius,' he shouted, 'it would have suited you better!'

Dad never slept that night. He sat up brooding. He
walked back and forth in the living room and kept the rest
of us awake too. On several occasions he thumped the
table with his fist and muttered loudly to himself. Then
there was quiet for a long while. By the time breakfast
was ready he was standing in the kitchen, exhausted, but
resolved, and preferred not to sit down. 'I left a note for
my parents,' he said. 'That I'd return when the time was
right. Or not at all. Now it's time.' The spoonful of porridge which Mum was trying to coax into my mouth
stopped in mid-air. She looked up. Boletta put down her
teacup and the Old One had to hold Fred to keep him still.
'What do you mean?' Mum asked. Dad took a deep
breath. 'The boy's going to be baptized on Røst!' he
answered.

Dad disappeared for a couple of days. There were things that had to be sorted first. On the morning of the third day he came back in a tailored black suit, a pale coat, and shining shoes, with his hair – equally shiny – cut and sweeping over his brow. He kissed Mum and waved a whole bunch of tickets. 'Pack your case and get ready!' We left that evening on the night train to Trondheim. Boletta, the Old One and Fred came with us to the station. Mum cried in the departure hall. Fred was given a bar of milk chocolate by Dad and the first thing he did was to throw it down onto the tracks. Oh, if only they'd just called me Arne, Arnold junior or Wilhelm the second! But no, my name was to be Barnum and we had to travel to Røst to have it inscribed in the parish records. A conductor carried the case to the sleeping car. Then the train gave a lurch and Mum leaned out of the window to wave while Dad held me in his arms. And I can still catch the scent which I'm able to reconstruct, piece by piece, like some chemist in the laboratory of memory. Hair oil mixed with sweet perfume over rough cheeks; the powerful whiff of tobacco from the gloves, and the hint of sweat from the tight shirt collar. All this rises into a higher unity, into the bitter-scented formality of the platform – leaving. I slept and could have no knowledge of all this. I was still beyond memory. I slept with my mother in the lower bunk and Dad unscrewed the top of a hip flask and poured brandy into the tooth glass. He gave it to Mum who could only face smelling it. Dad drank the lot instead and breathed out. 'Now the boy will get his rightful name,' he said. 'And I will pick up all the loose threads.' He poured a second glass and emptied that too. 'Cheers, my dear. Let's make this our delayed honeymoon too.' Mum took his mutilated hand and whispered, since I was still sleeping and mustn't wake up. 'Do they know we're coming?' Dad suddenly felt pain in his missing fingers. 'They?' 'Your parents, Arnold.' 'I don't even know if they're still alive,' he whispered. And he sank down on the floor and kept like that, on his knees, and leaned close to my mother's breast. 'I'm afraid, Vera. I'm so afraid.'

It's raining in Trondheim. Mum carries me from the train. A conductor comes with a pram and I'm laid down in it. Dad has put his fear behind him. He gives the conductor some money and claps him on the shoulder. 'I'll happily carry the suitcase with the other goods,' the conductor says, and quickly puts the money in his cap. 'Good idea.' Dad pushes him away, and then exchanges the empty hip flask for an umbrella with a man waiting for the café to open. 'What sort of goods?' Mum asks. 'Oh, just a little gift,' Dad laughs, and puts up the black umbrella over us, and thus I'm wheeled through the broad streets to the quayside. There lies the waiting vessel. Mum turns pale. Now it's her turn to be afraid. 'We can't be sailing in that tub, can we?' she murmurs. But Dad hasn't time to reply at that moment, for a wooden crate at least four metres square with strong rope round it is being winched onboard; it sways in the wind and is on the point of tumbling from the ropes that hold it. 'Careful, damn it!' he roars. And eventually the crate is safely lowered onto the deck; the whole boat rolls still more and the passengers standing along the rail applaud and Dad gives a deep bow, as if he has personally lifted the precious cargo with his one and a half hands.

The captain himself shows us to our cabin. It's low and narrow and the waves wash over the porthole. Dad pulls him to one side. 'How long will we be berthed in Svolvaer?' 'An hour,' the captain replies. 'Excellent,' Dad says. And the captain proceeds to invite the Nilsen family to dinner at his table that evening at six o'clock. But Mum is as sick as a dog before we've even left the Trondheim fiord and rounded Fossenlandet, the bow finally pointing north. Dad stands on deck, in the lee of the great wooden crate on which his name is written in red paint. He stands there under the black umbrella. The angst he has left behind him creeps back once more. He could go on land at the next port of call and vanish. He's done it before. But no, it's too late now. He has been through his winter darkness. He knows that. Now he's visible. Now it's June. They're heading for the sun. They're sailing out of the rain and into the sun. All of a sudden he begins laughing and throws the umbrella overboard; it flaps away like a wounded cormorant and vanishes in the waves. For who's ever come back to Røst with a gentleman's umbrella in their hand – only a nutter or a ghost who didn't know that the only umbrella that's survived the wind on Røst had spokes made of halibut bones and had stretched over it the skin of four catfish. Dad puts his ear to the crate and thinks he can hear a weak whistling from within. Afterwards he goes back down to the cabin. Mum's lying on the narrow berth. The sweat's pouring from her. 'We're dining at the captain's table at six,' he tells her. Mum vomits. And as she does so, so do I, as if I'm still a part of her. We vomit together and Dad has a busy time of things. He finds a female cabin steward who changes the sheet, mops the floor and puts two buckets by the bed. Mum is exhausted and drained. She just manages to hold me. 'Come up,' Dad says. 'It's the walls that are making you seasick.' 'Be quiet,' Mum whispers. 'You have to look at the waves to be able to stand them,' he tells her. Mum groans. 'Why didn't we drive instead?' Dad becomes uneasy and has to wipe the sweat from his own brow. 'Because there wasn't enough petrol, and anyway, the car's at the garage just now,' he tells her. 'And besides, they haven't tarmacked over the Moskenes whirlpool yet.' Mum manages a watery smile. 'That was three answers, Arnold. And now I know you're telling me tales.' Dad gives a laugh. 'And now I know that you're going to be better soon!' He gets up and looks down on Mum and me. Perhaps he notices now that I'll come to resemble him in time, except for my eyes, which are blue. And it's a moment of joy and unease, triumph and grief. 'I'll ask the captain to send the food down,' he whispers. 'No, you go up to join them,' Mum tells him. 'Please.' And he does as she requests. Arnold Nilsen sits at the captain's table. He

eats halibut steaks with a buttery sauce and drinks a
bottle of beer. He talks loudly and in American to some
tourists, and proposes a toast to those about him. 'What's
your business up here in the north?' the captain enquires.
'I'm having my son christened,' Dad tells him. The captain lights a cigarette and looks at his gloves. 'Then it's
perhaps a church that you have with you in that crate?'
Dad smiles. 'Yes, you could well say that.' But he doesn't
disclose any more. He doesn't intend rewarding his
curiosity with more answers. One truth is enough for that
day. He loves being secretive, a well-hidden riddle speaking several languages. He keeps his mouth shut. They
have coffee. The table begins to roll. The plates slide to
the edge of the table. A bottle tumbles. The lamps flicker.
The captain is dissatisfied with the conversation. 'Would
your wife not dine with us?' he enquires. 'She's unfortunately not able to cope with the swell,' Dad tells him.
That was one more truth, he realizes at that moment.
And often two truths can be too many, if they follow each
other with too brief a gap. Either he should have told a lie,
been rude or just kept quiet. Because at once the captain
becomes considerate. 'There's a doctor onboard who
might take a look at the young mother,' he says. 'Oh,
that's really not necessary,' Dad pleads. But the captain is
already clapping his hands. 'Dr Paulsen!' he shouts. And
an ancient, thin fellow with a worn collar, a crack in one
of his spectacle lenses and only two buttons on his waistcoat, slowly turns where he's sitting at the table in the
corner. He pushes back his chair, and it's almost as if he
arises from another place in another time altogether and
looks back through the hours and years that lie in the
darkness. His mouth trembles. 'Who?' he mumbles. The
captain gives a wave. 'Come here, doctor!' Dad hunches
over his coffee cup. He has no idea why and he curses
himself for it, but his fear grips him again; he can't escape
it – it's quicker than he is. It's this he dreaded. It's this
he's looked forward to – recognition. But not like this, not
in this manner, in such a miserable way. He wants it to be

triumphant; unrivalled wonderment. And Dr Paulsen comes towards them unsteadily over the sloping floor. He stops. The captain draws him closer. 'We have a young woman onboard who's seasick and she's got a young child, my dear doctor. What would your advice be in this particular instance?' All at once the old doctor starts laughing. It's quite inappropriate. It's a drunken laughter that doesn't know what it's laughing at and in the end just laughs at itself. Arnold Nilsen ventures to look up. 'So you think it's funny that my wife is so ill?' The doctor coughs and dries his wet mouth with the sleeve of his jacket. 'Gentlemen, no one has died yet of seasickness. It's only a sign of human discomfort. Before one grows used to the movements of the ship.' Arnold Nilsen becomes over-confident. 'A hat pin in the heart might help,' he says. Dr Paulsen jumps, takes off his glasses, looks at Arnold, puts them on once more. 'On the contrary I would recommend some hard, dry bread and half a glass of wine.' He bows and returns to his table. Arnold Nilsen, my father, gives a laugh, for he's survived – he hasn't been recognized yet. 'Is that the ship's doctor himself who came over?' he asks. The captain shakes his head. 'No, Dr Paulsen is himself ill,' he whispers. 'He's coming back after having been examined in Trondheim. Sadly he's dying.' And Dr Paulsen stops there among all the tables and looks again at Arnold Nilsen, as if he can see something too through the broken lens of his spectacles – a shadow, a loosened knot of time. 'There's no doubt your wife will be fine,' he says. 'But for safety's sake I'd like to take a look at the child.' Dad brings his coffee cup down with a bang. 'The boy's fine! He's in need of no doctor!' The captain comes round the table. 'It's best if you do as the doctor says. The swell's set to get worse.' Together they go down to the cabin. Mum sits up in bed at once, taken aback and enraged when she sees the strange man. Dad has some dry slices of bread and a splash of red wine with him. He hurries over to her. 'The ship's own doctor has agreed to see if Barnum has come to any harm because of the choppy seas,' he explains. Mum draws a hand through her stiff, tangled hair and covers her shoulders. 'There's nothing wrong with him,' she murmurs. But Dr Paulsen is already leaning over the pram where I'm lying. He folds the blanket to one side. He presses his finger against my stomach, releases the pressure and just stands there like that looking down on me, silent. Mum grows anxious. Dad's about to say something. But all of a sudden Dr Paulsen starts crying. He stands hunched over the pram, sobbing. And Dad takes the old man by the shoulder and pushes him out, and when he returns Mum's sitting on the edge of the bed with me in her arms, her cheeks pale. 'Why was he crying?' she whispered. 'The doctor wasn't sober,' Dad replies. 'He wanted to make his sincere apologies.' 'Did you know him?' Dad dips the hard bread in the wine and gives it to her. 'No,' he says. And Mum chews and chews until she has to be sick again. Afterwards Dad holds her. 'I was seasick every day of my childhood,' he says. 'It hardened my stomach and made me humble.' He wipes a tear from the corner of his eye. 'The doctor said, by the way, that he's seldom seen a finer child.' Mum falls silent. The waves resound against the ship's hull. The vessel sails further north one night and night itself slips away and lets in the light. We barely sleep. 'The Arctic Circle is a boundary inside the head,' Dad whispers. 'Can you feel us crossing it?' But Mum feels nothing except an overwhelming exhaustion and a deep sense of dislocation. Her brain is drained of blood and I am outside latitude's measurement; I am my own ruler, still nameless and on the way to my own baptism. Dad goes up on deck again when the vessel leaves Bodø. Dr Paulsen's standing down at the quayside, bent and trembling. He raises his hand. Then he turns for the last time and is swallowed up by the town's light. It's early morning, and sunny. The fiord is shining; it breathes, a slow, broad wave that propels itself. He sees the mountains rising on the other side, in blue mist, as if they have broken free and are hovering somewhere between heaven and sea. He saw the very same sight before when he first journeyed into the mainland. He has to keep hold of himself. He's in the process of losing his grip, of falling. It's too late to turn now. The relief he had experienced for a time has turned to indifference and is like a kind of tipsiness. The captain hails him from the bridge. 'How are your wife and child?' 'They're toughening up!' Dad calls back. The captain laughs and goes into the wheelhouse. The wall of the Lofoten Islands looms closer. The gulls hang in a screeching cloud round the vessel. And at Svolvaer Dad hurries ashore. After an hour he still hasn't returned. The ship's bell is rung for the third time. The captain's uneasy. The quayside is jam-packed, and the crowd is bemused by the vessel's delay. It's already a quarter of an hour late. A couple of boys who can run like hares are sent off to search for Arnold Nilsen, the short fellow with the shiny, black sweep of hair over his brow, and his pale coat and gloves. They have no luck; he's not to be found at any of the pubs, at the hotel or the quays for the fishing vessels. A half hour has now passed. The captain gives the order for the gangway to be drawn up and the moorings to be released. He swears. Is he to be burdened with an abandoned, seasick woman and a babe in arms for the rest of the passage, or should he send them ashore too? He swears again and then suddenly there's a movement over by the sheds. The crowd moves aside to make room. The voices quieten. The shouts die down. Hats and caps are raised aloft. Arnold Nilsen's come at last. And not alone. Arnold Nilsen has with him the old vicar. He no longer resembles a black sail in the storm. He's nothing more than a frail flower in the sunlight, barely managing to keep up with Arnold Nilsen who has to stop and haul him on. The gangway's lowered once more and the captain himself helps the old vicar onboard and gets him to the nearest seat. He turns towards Arnold Nilsen. 'Is your wife that ill?' he asks, and smiles. Arnold smiles himself and his reply is enigmatic. 'If I have a church with me

then I have to have a vicar too,' he says. With those words
he goes down to the cabin to fetch Mum who carries me
up with her into the light. 'Say hello to my old friend,' he
tells her. 'He's the best vicar in these parts and in the rest
of the land for that matter!' Mum looks shyly at the little
man who rises from his seat and slowly extends his hand
to touch mine. I could swear that I felt a shock, a shock
that passed through my mother too, and she curtsies; she
holds me tight in her arms and curtsies for this old soul
who has all but no voice left, just clear eyes full of energy
and a cross about his neck. 'I have sung too much,' he
whispers. 'I tried to drown out the storm.' 'And did you
manage?' Mum asks him. 'No,' he replies. And this is the
bow, the bow between crying and laughter, curved in that
old man's smile when he says as he does, 'It would be a
joy to baptize your child'.

   After that they stand on deck as the vessel sails under
the steep wall of the Lofotens. Mum stands tall and
strong as I sleep, exhausted by wind and electricity. Not
even when the boat cuts into the Moskenes whirlpool
does she waver. She has toughened. Instead it's Dad's
turn to weaken. He sees the lighthouse. He sees Nykene.
He teaches Mum the many names of the birds in order to
forget his own fear in that moment. He sees the white
stacks that are the cormorants' landmarks. He's getting
closer. He's been away for eighteen years. He has no idea
what awaits him out there. When the vessel comes in to
that flat island which the storms and the salt have worn
down to nothing out there on the edge of the world,
there's barely standing room left on the cramped quayside. The rumours have travelled more swiftly than the
ship. The waves have rolled in their reports. The wind has
sent its telegrams. Arnold Nilsen holds Mum close.
'What is it I'm smelling?' she murmurs. And Dad is glad
she asks because it gives him time to get his land legs, to
feel his roots again. 'Dried cod, my dear. The perfume of
the nets.' Mum sees the fish hanging everywhere from
wooden frames, as though in some great, strange garden

a new fruit is drying on its deformed trees. Afterwards Mum said that she never could get rid of that smell again; it caught hold in her hair and skin and under her nails and in her clothes. It came with them when they left again, and it could make her sick at any time, while on other occasions it made her dream, wild and silent. But now the waiting crowd below are growing impatient. Isn't Arnold Nilsen going ashore? Has he only come to show his face before turning again and making fools of them all? And then someone suddenly shouts, 'The Wheel's come home! The Wheel's come home!' And now they're all shouting. Shouting for the Wheel. They can see that height-wise he hasn't achieved much, but as far as breadth is concerned he's certainly caught up pretty well. Arnold Nilsen closes his eyes; he swallows, swallows the piercing wind, the acrid wind – he takes Mum by the hand and goes with her down the gangway. And I wake up. I become aware of the same smell. Ever since I've never been able to eat fish. I cry. Mum comforts me. Dad is greeting people; he shakes hands with some and the faces stream past. It's just as much the city girl they stare at; the young city girl with the thin shoes and wailing child. Dad stops, looks about him. 'Aurora and Evert,' he murmurs. 'Where are Aurora and Evert?' But no one has time to answer because now the mighty crate has to be lowered onto the quay – Arnold Nilsen doesn't only have wife and child with him, he's also a crate the size of a boathouse. 'Are you not going to open it?' the most inquisitive among them ask (and that means the vast majority). Arnold Nilsen laughs. 'It's not Christmas yet,' he says. And he pulls Mum with him; he wants to go over to his house. He's put this off for eighteen years and he wants to go home, he wants to see his parents, Aurora and Evert – it has to be done. Then an old, smiling man stands before him blocking his way and Arnold knows who it is – it's his neighbour, the one they called Elendius. He'd been given the name because it was always he who came bearing news of shipwrecks, unusable saws, illnesses, sheep that had got stuck on outcrops, delayed mail and hurricanes. He hasn't grown any older, Arnold thinks, he's always been this old. 'Don't you know?' Elendius asks, and takes off his cap. Arnold Nilsen realizes what Elendius is going to say but he shakes his head nonetheless; he doesn't know yet. 'Aurora and Evert are dead.'

And so Dad, the half son, has to go to the graveyard first, in order to come all the way home. He walks between Mum and the old vicar; pushing the pram in which I'm lying in front of him along the narrow gravel track over the island, past the lighthouse. Behind us come all those who refuse to let Arnold Nilsen out of their sight, and Elendius is first among the last. The church warden comes running from the storehouse for the funeral biers and shows them to the right grave which can barely be described as a proper tomb at all – just a crooked, white wooden cross stuck in dry soil in the weeds beside the dyke. Two names are scratched into the plank – Evert and Aurora Nilsen. Dad sinks to his knees, pulls off his gloves and clasps his hands. The old vicar kneels too, and even he, who hasn't missed much in his time, starts when he sees Arnold's mutilated hand. 'Death and baptism,' the vicar whispers. 'You have come in sorrow and joy.' Dad doesn't hear him. He just stares at the two names, written in the same writing. He gets up again. 'Did they die at the same time?' he asks. At once Elendius is beside him. 'Aurora departed in the winter of '46,' he tells him. 'Evert followed her at Pentecost. Once the ground was soft enough to take them.' Arnold Nilsen nods. 'Yes, we follow those we love,' he says, and begins to cry. Elendius looks down at all the missing fingers on my father's hand. 'No one could find you to tell you,' Elendius says. Dad turns instead to face the church warden, one of the boys he cut grass alongside and he, perhaps, who laughed loudest of the lot when the scythe grew too heavy and the slope too steep. 'I want a proper memorial to my parents,' Dad said loudly so all could hear, as he pulled on the glove with the false fingers. 'I want a mausoleum built of nothing less than the biggest stones to be found here, and I want it to be filled with sand from the sea and their names to be inscribed in marble!' The church warden nods. Everyone nods. Because that's the way it's to be. At last the Wheel is to honour his father and mother. The wind gusts between the crosses. Flowers are torn loose and hang like restless bouquets over graves. 'It won't come cheap, a mausoleum like that,' the warden says. 'Yes, and make it even dearer than that!' Dad cries. 'And send the bill to Arnold Nilsen, Oslo!' People are beginning to drift from the graveyard in ones and twos, slowly and with heavy steps, for they're keen to hear where Arnold Nilsen has planned to stay. Perhaps he's thinking of moving into the Fisherman's Mission with the vicar to make his confession, or perhaps it's a caravan with windows and a garden he has in his intriguing crate on the quay? Then Elendius, at long last and for the first time, wants to be the bearer of good news. 'You are welcome to stay with me!' he shouts as loud as he can. And none of the others want to be outdone. Arnold Nilsen and his family can stay with all of them. Arnold Nilsen takes Mum's hand, moved, downhearted and yet uplifted. 'No, dear friends. We will stay with ourselves!' Silence falls about Arnold Nilsen and people look down, shake their heads and go their own ways.

It's Saturday. It'll soon be night and night is without darkness and full of wind. The following day I'm to be baptized in the new church by the old vicar. My name's to be Barnum. Dad points out the road back; he's taken that same way so many times before he could walk it in his sleep, even though telegraph poles have appeared now that might bamboozle him. It's just a case of following the smell of the dry, skinny fish which will be collected from the drying lofts and sent south before the Midsummer bonfires are lit – although the smell will stay just the same, like the pain of his lost fingers that never quite disappears. At the mill they take the path along the length of the sound. Arnold Nilsen's chest tightens. It's a path that's been seldom used in the past. They leave the pram by the lopsided gate and Mum carries me. She loses the heel of her right shoe but doesn't say a word. There's not an ounce of shelter to be found from the wind. Dad toils on with the suitcase. 'Should have made a suitcase with wheels,' he says. Mum doesn't hear him. She hears only the wind and the sound of swift birds swooping on them and swinging away so close she can hear the tips of their wings in front of her face. She steps in a hole and loses her other heel too. She feels the urge to cry, to turn round – but she does neither. For where else is she to go on an island like this? She has to follow Arnold Nilsen home. And now he stops. Over on a low mound there stands a house. No, it's the remains of a house and perhaps even that's overstating it – it's the memory of a house. They go closer. The grass has grown tall and wild. The window panes are shattered. The door bangs in the wind. There's a jawbone on the doorstep. Arnold Nilsen puts down the case and hesitates a moment. *The dog*, he thinks. *Tuss*. They go in. Mum has to bend her head. She looks about her. The kettle's on the stove. A clock has tumbled down from the wall. Arnold hangs it in place on the hook his father hammered into the driftwood they found on the beach. The hands of the clock slip and hang vertically down behind the dull glass; at the back of the figure 6 there's a fly. He rights a chair. He picks up some fragments of glass he doesn't know what to do with. There's sheep dung in the corners. 'We're not going to sleep here?' Mum whispers. 'It'll be fine,' Dad says. 'It'll be fine.' With that he goes out, finds the scythe at the back of the house, sharpens it, and begins to cut the grass. Mum stands in the doorway with me in her arms, looking at this man, Arnold Nilsen, cutting the grass, cutting it for all he's worth in his dark suit and leather gloves. He scythes like one possessed, and the tool is still huge and unwieldy in his grasp, but he refuses to acknowledge defeat. And Mum lets him go on, even though he's ruining the clothes he'll wear in church, and perhaps she thinks that she doesn't really know him, that she knows nothing about him at all. Yet it's not he who is a stranger that evening; she is. And Arnold Nilsen slices through the grass; he breathes heavily, he cries and laughs. And when that rugged bit of ground lies flat and new-mown, he fetches the dry remains of the fishing nets from the shed to bind up the dry grass – and the green sun has turned golden.

By the time he comes in it's already night. He has with him a bucket of water from the barrel, but it's salty too. The rain here's salty. The wind's salty. I'm asleep on the hard bench. I have a strong heart. They lie down on his parents' bed. There's barely room for them both. Mum lies awake. She points in the direction of a door she's been curious about, a tall door in the outer wall of the wind trap beside the doorstep. 'What's that used for?' she asks. Dad smiles. 'That's the coffin door, Vera. They could carry the coffins right out and not dishonour the dead by turning them on their sides.' They're silent for a time. Perhaps it's me they're listening to. 'I would like to have met Aurora and Evert,' Mum whispers. Dad takes her hand in his. 'They would no doubt have wondered how I managed to get hold of you.' Mum smiles too. 'And I'd just have said that you made me laugh,' she replies. All of a sudden Dad gasps for breath and crushes her hand with his artificial fingers, so strongly that it hurts. She cries out but he pays no attention. He gasps. 'There's something I have to tell you, Vera.' He almost shouts and lets go of his hold at the same time. But he doesn't say any more. 'What is it, Arnold?' She waits. He's silent. She thinks he's just being precious. She turns towards him, amused, and sees him lying there paralysed beside her, the sweat pouring from his face and running in black rivers from his hair. He has saliva about his mouth – froth, white foam – and his eyes are like brown glass, and broken at the bottom. Mum screams again. 'What is it, Arnold?' And then it's as if he wakes up, recovers his breath, and the darkness falls from him. He can see – he sees her, shocked. 'Nothing,' he whispers. 'It's nothing.' He has no idea how long he's been out, perhaps only a second. He gets up and has to go outside, alone, to get some air. He sits down on the doorstep and picks up the grey, smooth jawbone of the dog, smells it and throws it away. After a while Mum gets up herself. She stops behind him. He waits. Perhaps he's talked in his sleep, said too much and revealed everything. He waits and in that moment knows that all could be lost. 'What was it you wanted to tell me?' she asks him at last. He sighs. Only that – a sigh of relief. 'You have to be rested for tomorrow,' he murmurs. She hides her face in her hands. It's shining brightly from everywhere around, even the sea. 'It's impossible to sleep on nights like this,' she says. 'It's just a case of closing your eyes, Vera.' She doesn't take her hands away. 'The light's too strong.' With that she goes in all the same, perhaps because she's heard me waking. Arnold Nilsen remains sitting there. He looks at the wind. It's never the same wind. The wind is a wide river that flows through his world. The boat lies down beside its shed, turned over on its side and decaying like some dead, rotting animal. He's still trembling; there's an echo yet in his body. It'll soon be gone. There has to be a bottle somewhere in the house, a mouthful of brandy left over for Christmas. Arnold Nilsen gets up. He stands in front of the coffin door. Not that way, he thinks. No, not that way now. He goes round and quietly comes in by the kitchen. He pulls out a drawer and finds cutlery, plates, cups and tools heaped together – it must have been Evert who couldn't keep everything in order after Aurora departed. And everything is covered in dust and salt that wears away all colour, just as the island itself is being consumed until the day the sea rolls over it. But then Arnold Nilsen finds something he wasn't looking for. Under the sheets in the bottom drawer, together with the message he left for his mother on a page he'd torn out of his arithmetic book, there's a card. He lifts it up. It's the hand-coloured picture of Paturson, the world's tallest man. And on the reverse side he's written a message to his good friend, Arnold, in May 1945. He writes that the Chocolate Girl is dead. A fresh tremor passes through Arnold. The card has been sent from Akureyri on Iceland, and has travelled to numerous addresses both in Norway and abroad before in the end coming to rest here, with his parents, on Røst. Arnold Nilsen secretes it in the old black suitcase, in a corner of the lining, and this card is the only thing he takes with him when we leave.

It's morning. It doesn't show. Day and night are seamless. Time has no edges. Mum has had some rest just the same – he's let her sleep, with me at her side. He goes out. He observes that boats are approaching from the other islands in the vicinity; it's like a whole armada – even the men employed on Skomvaer and their families are making the journey here this Sunday. Arnold Nilsen smiles. He's on top of things once more. His hands aren't shaking. No one's going to sit at home when the Wheel and his fine wife from the city are going to have their child baptized in the new church. The boats toss in the wind. The waves are white about the lighthouse and they break over the jetty. Arnold Nilsen laughs. The wind is appropriate and there's more than enough of it. He washes his face in the salty water, shaves, and wakes Mum and myself with a kiss. 'The pews in our church are hard,' he says. 'Take a cushion with you.'

And not a seat remains. People are standing against the walls too, impatient in their shining Sunday best. And there aren't enough hymn-books either this Sunday, and when they sing *God is God though every land laid waste*, they sing it faster than they've ever done before. The organist attempts to keep up with them for a while but in the course of the second verse just gives up. They want to be over and done with it as quickly as possible so they can get to the matter in hand – namely what the Wheel's little boy's to be called. And that can't be anything too insignificant when he's made his way back after all these years in foreign parts, with the circus and then in silence, to let his

boy be baptized by the retired vicar. But more than anything they want to be done with the sermon, the singing
and the offering so they can find out what's inside Arnold
Nilsen's crate, the mysterious crate that's still standing
on the jetty. Then at last Mum brings me forward, Dad
hurries out behind, and I'm the only one to be baptized
that day. Some of the congregation get up on the benches
at the back to get a better view. A hymn-book falls to the
floor. The church warden pours some water into the font.
Then a complete hush falls. And the old vicar is almost
like a black sail once more in his robes and his collar, but
he's a sail without wind, lashed tight to the mast. For his
voice is just as low when he dips his fingers in the water,
the water that's salty too, and lets it fall in drops over my
head, and reads my right name so softly that not even
Mum can hear him. There's disquiet in the congregation.
There's muttering. Shoes scrape against the floor. And
finally, as the old vicar's drying my head with a rough
towel, someone gives a shout and it turns out to be
Elendius: 'What the devil is it he's saying the boy's to be
called?' Arnold Nilsen turns in their direction and the
faces are the same – the men with their hair combed back
from their white brows, the women's jutting chins and
wary smiles, the children's big eyes. These Sunday faces
are the same faces he's seen in every big top he's been in,
and he knows that if he can't love these faces then he
can't love any others, and least of all himself. Arnold
Nilsen stretches his arms aloft. 'The boy's name is
Barnum!' he shouts. 'And now you're all invited to the
festivities!' I have been recorded. I have been accounted
for. The church bells ring and thus begins my life as
Barnum; the party continues on the ground floor of the
Fisherman's Mission. Arnold Nilsen has ordered a mausoleum for his parents. Now he has no wish to be any less
generous to the living, and tucks into every dish and
every sandwich of the island population, who don't ask
for anything twice themselves. And in the medical report
of 1950 from Røst penned by the local doctor Emil Moe,

one may read that sobriety was encouragingly good on the island that year, basically because no one had the money to buy brandy. The exception was one Sunday in the month of June when wetting-the-head-of-the-baby festivities degenerated into a protracted bout of drinking, though mercifully the only damage was one sprained hand, some grazes and two broken dentures. Nonetheless the extent of the alcohol intake could be measured by the all too frequent visits to the district nurse to obtain the last rations of American orange juice. But the women swarm round Vera; the youngest girls want to hold me and are allowed to do so, while Dad stands with the men folk who're unbuttoning their stiff collars that itch in the heat and keeping an eye on the bottles being brought in. And Elendius has positioned himself between the two groups so that he's able to hear what's said in both places and doesn't miss a single word. The glasses are filled and the men drink. 'You've done well indeed, Arnold Nilsen,' says the lighthouse keeper. Arnold Nilsen looks down modestly. 'I certainly can't complain,' he whispers, and pours out more drink, for the glasses look so terribly small in those huge hands. 'But what have you done?' the church warden asks. Arnold Nilsen smiles. 'I have done so much that there would barely be enough time to tell the half of it,' he answers. The men are very much satisfied with their brandy, but less so with the reply. 'We've plenty of time,' the scrap merchant informs him. Arnold Nilsen remembers them even more vividly now, from the slopes when they scythed the grass and from the classroom – he remembers their names and their laughter. 'Soon you'll get to see something of what I've done,' he says placidly. The men feel satisfied with this because perhaps at last they'll get to see what's in the crate on the quayside. Another toast is proposed. Arnold Nilsen turns in Elendius' direction and observes to his irritation that he's creeping closer to the women. 'Can't you take your brandy any more?' he shouts. Elendius pads over and Arnold Nilsen gives the inquisitive old chap an empty glass. 'I'll just give you a half since your hand's shaking so much,' he tells him. Elendius smiles. 'It's rather you who's the unsteady one. You've even fewer fingers than you had before.' Elendius drains his glass and holds it out for more. Arnold Nilsen puts down the bottle. 'Don't remind me of the accidents that have befallen me on a day like this,' he replies in a low voice. Elendius is still waiting with his empty glass. 'I remember all right that it was no accident when you lost your first finger.' 'I lost the rest of my hand in the war,' Arnold murmurs and fills Elendius' glass to the brim to make him shut up. But the brandy only makes him more talkative. 'Yes, the war was certainly an accident for most of us,' he sighs. 'By the way, why did you not bring your other son here with you?' Arnold Nilsen closes his eyes. Everyone knows just about everything here. He listens to the wind. He grows anxious. Is he to lie? He listens to the wind in the flags – it's there in abundance and he'll show them all right. Amicably he puts his arm around Elendius. 'He is my wife's first son,' Arnold tells him. 'And he's being looked after fine and well by my dear mother-in-law.' 'Was your wife married before?' Elendius quizzes him. Arnold Nilsen shakes his head. 'But let me tell you this, Elendius. My mother-in-law isn't just anybody at all. She is no less than the director of the Telegraph Exchange down in Oslo and the one who makes it possible for you lot to telephone and talk your heads off to each other.' He laughs at his own pronouncements, and now the men have got rid of their jackets and are starting to go over in the direction of the women. Vera gets up and puts me in the pram. I'm tired of the girls who can't resist fingering my curls that are already growing like a fine halo from ear to ear. 'I didn't realize that such distinguished women worked in the city,' Elendius says. Arnold Nilsen almost feels sorry for him. 'So you see how little you know, Elendius.' But Elendius won't give up yet. Brandy has breathed life into his curiosity – already his head is a dictionary of gossip. 'Then perhaps your father-in-law has an even more exalted position?' he asks. Vera turns in their direction and Arnold Nilsen doesn't have time to reply. She beats him to it with her honesty. 'I don't have a father,' she says, loud enough for everyone to hear her. For a few seconds there's utter stillness. The glasses are empty again. Arnold Nilsen fills them and breaks the silence. 'I am the only man in the family,' he laughs. Elendius hunches over his glass. 'Well, well, you've just got it all, haven't you, Arnold?' he says. At that moment Dad must have seen red. He lets fly with a clenched fist and the blow meets Elendius' temple – but it isn't Elendius' wretched head that breaks, it's Arnold Nilsen's artificial fingers inside his glove. And before Elendius falls to the floor Arnold Nilsen catches hold of him, as if the blow had never been struck, as if his arm had taken it back – and the women don't even have time to shriek. 'Oh, and Vera's grand-mother is a famous Danish actress,' Arnold Nilsen says, and pulls his glove on more tightly still. 'But perhaps you don't know about her?' No one answers and everyone's stunned and silent. Arnold Nilsen gives a deep sigh. 'Well, that doesn't surprise me. She was an international star in the days of the silent film, unsurpassed on the silver screen, her face speaking every tongue.' He fills Elendius' glass to the brim, puts his arm round his shoul-der and looks about him. 'She was married to the renowned Danish explorer and saver of many a life Wil-helm Jebsen. You do know of him?' The men glance at one another and nod, just to be on the safe side. After a time the church warden clears his throat. 'Yes, what was it now that he discovered?' Arnold Nilsen lets go of his hold on Elendius. 'I won't exactly say that it was he who discovered Greenland, but he was sent into the ice floes to find Andre. But he was lost himself and never returned from the silence of the glaciers.' Arnold Nilsen puts his arm round Mum and gives her a long kiss. After that he goes outside for a breather, and standing beside the flag-pole, puts his fingers back together. A little later the old vicar needs some air and sits down beside him. 'It isn't easy for someone to come back,' he says quietly. 'No,' Arnold agrees. 'Either one comes back too early. Or else too late.' The old vicar nods. 'But it's better than not at all,' he whispers. They sit together in stillness for a time. The celebrations continue inside. Two women have gone to fetch their respective cakes. Young boys rush after them begging to be allowed to share a bit. Quite suddenly the flags hang still. Yet just as suddenly the wind lifts them once more. 'You have been a good man, both to myself and to others,' Arnold Nilsen tells him. 'I've neither been better nor worse than anyone else,' the old vicar mumbles. 'But I know that you've been one of the better ones. You bought one of Paturson's cards and you didn't hold me back when I wanted to leave here. And you've baptized my son.' The old vicar looks down. 'It isn't always the case that good things come from the good,' he mumbles. Arnold Nilsen doesn't want to think about that. Instead he says, 'Now, I want to ask you another favour.' The old vicar nods and waits. Arnold Nilsen closes his eyes. 'I ask you to forgive me,' he whispers. 'But what for?' Arnold Nilsen turns away and doesn't answer him. The old vicar sighs. 'Are you thinking of when you left your parents?' he enquires. Arnold Nilsen shakes his head. 'I'm simply asking for forgiveness. For all my wrong-doing.' The old vicar moves closer to Arnold. 'I have to know what deeds God is to forgive you for. He keeps a strict account.' Arnold Nilsen is annoyed, almost enraged, over this particularity. He cries out, 'In that case I ask rather if God can forgive everything?' The old vicar takes Arnold's hand in his own, feels the loose fingers inside his glove, and for a second shivers. 'Yes,' he whispers. 'God can forgive everything.' Arnold Nilsen retracts his hand. 'Thank you. That was all I wanted to know.' At that moment Vera comes out onto the stairs with the pram and looks up at them. Behind her stands a scowling Elendius. Arnold waves and starts down in their direction. But the old vicar holds him back. 'But God would want us to ask forgiveness of our fellow men first,' he whispers. Then Arnold continues over to Mum who's waiting for him. He stops in front of her, drunk with the wind, the brandy, my name and all the words of the old vicar. 'What is it?' Mum asks, and stretches out her hand. Dad hesitates; he feels her fingers stroking his shirt and he hesitates, breathes deeply and turns instead towards Elendius. 'Forgive me for hitting you,' he says. 'My hand didn't know what it was doing.'

Elendius looks the other way and rubs his forehead. 'Just as well your fingers were made of sawdust or else you might have had a life on your conscience,' he mutters. But Arnold Nilsen laughs it off. 'Go and get the strongest men you can find,' he demands. 'I want the crate taken to Veddöya.' Elendius forgets he's almost been finished off; he hurries away to find the right team, and soon the lot of them are standing down on the quayside watching the selfsame crate being taken onboard the post boat and transported over the sound to the steep, green rock whose wall juts up from the surf. And the islanders follow in their wake; there hasn't been such activity in these waters since the winter fishing of 1915. But Arnold Nilsen grows anxious there where he's standing at the bow. The wind is losing its strength. The wind is lessening. He's able to light a cigarette without having to shield the flame. Finally they all go ashore and five men carry the crate to the highest plateau, and they don't put it down before the sun is hanging in cobwebs of cloud and light above the horizon. The grass is wet and thick. The birds dive from their rock ledges, white and shrieking. The women remain standing down on the shore with the old vicar, watching their delicately balanced men with anxiety. But Mum carries me up to the top; she climbs with me in her arms and even Elendius looks on her with new eyes – this city girl used to her pavements and banister rails. And Arnold Nilsen is filled with a wonderful, passionate pride; he feels moved to tears, tears of joy, but he doesn't cry – he laughs instead. The wind is on his side once more. The wind has just teased him a bit, played

with the one who stood here once upon a time and swore
he'd sell the wind that's now blowing full in his face. And
so they get there. The men have a drink. It's time. Arnold
Nilsen approaches the crate, revelling in every second,
when he sees the women down on the shore waving to
him (the same women, except for Aurora), as if all the
dark years in between disappear in one benevolent,
redeeming moment. Then he frees one side of the crate
and drags out a creation none of them has seen the like of
before. It resembles a scaffold with wings, a scarecrow
with wheels on top. The men edge closer. They're silent.
They stare. Arnold Nilsen turns in their direction. Still no
one says a word. Mum sits in the background, on the
grass, and no longer worries about spoiling her dress.
She's silent too, and she rocks me in her arms. I'm awake
and dizzy – everything there is too huge for my eyes – and
I've often wondered if this sight of Dad right out on the
green plateau beside his fragile secret laid its imprint on
the skin of my memory as an image I'd later develop. For
that's always the way I see him, my father, on top of Veddøya, there where he stands waiting for a rejoicing that
never comes. Instead it's Elendius who seizes the initiative. 'What kind of creation is this you've dragged the
whole way up here?' he demands. Dad looks at each of
them, one by one. 'It's a windmill,' he says. But when he
gazes out once more, towards the horizon and the sun
which has fallen in a column all the way down, it's neither
an optical illusion nor a mirage he sees, nor is it the
brandy that plays havoc with his reason. The sea lies still.
Even the birds fall in disbelief. For the first time in as long
as anyone can remember it's utterly windless on Røst.
Arnold Nilsen waits. It has to change. But it doesn't. The
wheel on Arnold Nilsen's lopsided windmill stands still.
In the end the men climb down once more. Only Mum
remains; Mum and myself. She sits with Dad, on the edge
of Veddøya, in front of the windless windmill. They see
the boats being pushed out and the men rowing their
women home in the light and empty night. They sit there

like that without saying another word. They wait for the wind. But it doesn't come. Mum leans her head against Arnold's shoulder, and I imagine she's happy in that moment – she is in another world and I am dreaming on her lap.

The Name of Silence

I'll tell the story of a strange day. I was woken by the Old One crying. I lay for a time listening. She cried softly and protractedly and what frightened me most was that I'd never heard her crying before. I got up. I packed my school-bag. I had begun at school. Now Mum was crying too. I could hear them in the living room. They were crying together and trying to comfort each other. The school-bag was almost new and full of timetables I'd got at the booksellers in Bogstad Road. I actually only needed one timetable, but it felt good to have lots. Then I could make up my own timetable, and in the first period write *dream* so I could sleep longer. Perhaps Fred had done something bad and that was why they were crying? I went out to the bathroom. He was standing there in front of the mirror combing his hair. He glanced at my bag. 'Thinking of going to school, Barnum?' He stuck the shining comb in his back pocket. 'Don't need to go to school when the king's dead,' he said. 'Is the king dead?' Fred sighed. 'He died at four thirty-five during the night.' I smiled. I could have laughed out loud; I was so relieved – it was only the king who had died and that was the reason they were crying. I was about to run in to see them but Fred held me back. 'Not so smart to go around laughing today, Barnum.' I thought about this as I walked the long way between bathroom and living room, that it was wicked of me to start laughing when the king was dead, and that I must be a bad person. And I went as slowly as I could so that the smile would be wiped from my face, except that somehow it had stuck on my mouth, my lips had locked, and I had to think of something else instead. I had to think that it was Dad who was dead, that he had crashed on a bend, or been hit by a train and crushed beneath eighteen wheels, and it was me who now had to tell Mum because she still didn't know he was dead. But he had managed to whisper her name, and half of mine, before finally giving up the ghost. I was on the verge of tears by the time I came to a halt in the doorway. The Old One sat on the sofa beside Mum, sobbing behind a handkerchief. Boletta was standing beside the balcony; she wore a black dress and was quite pale. She was holding her coffee with both hands. *Aftenposten* lay on the table with just one headline – *The King is Dead*. I couldn't speak. My cheeks were streaming. Mum got up, smiling regardless, and enfolded me in her arms. 'There, there, my boy. There, there.' I laid my head against her tummy and cried. 'You don't need to go to school today,' she said. 'When the king dies everyone stays off.' 'Not me,' I heard Boletta say. But then it was the Old One's turn to speak. 'Come here,' she whispered. Mum let me go and I went over to the sofa. The Old One dried my face with her handkerchief and it tasted sweet, as if it had been dipped in sugar. Perhaps that was how tears should really be, like juice, not bitter and hard like mine. On her lap was a picture of King Haakon which she'd shown me so many times I could memorize it perfectly. It was from when he returned home after the war and drove through the city in the open A1, at precisely seventeen minutes past one, and passed the Lotus Perfumery in Torg Street beneath a billowing canopy of flags. The Old One's visible on the left amid a rejoicing throng waving for their king, and drops have fallen onto the picture, black drops that have gradually rubbed out this moment of celebration. 'Now you're my little king,' the Old One said and kissed me on the forehead.

I went to school nonetheless. I went with Boletta as far as Majorstuen. Autumn was just beginning. Bang the caretaker stood in a dark suit sweeping leaves from the pavement. It was raining on the little city. The flags hung at half-mast. Esther had tied a black ribbon round the window of her kiosk and she cried in there among the weeklies. The cars drove slowly and the trams waited for everybody. Boletta kept hold of my hand right to the point where we had to go our separate ways. 'Today there won't be many people calling each other,' I said. Boletta wiped away a tear – a real tear, not like mine which I'd just made myself. 'The world isn't always the way we would like it to be,' she whispered.

At school the grown-ups cried too. All the teachers were crying. They tried not to, but they couldn't manage, and in the end they just gave up. It was quite a sight. I thought that nothing could be the same after we'd seen them crying. Some of the girls stood in a huddle by the fountain supporting each other. I envied them because they could cry. They were good. I wasn't. I was bad. I had never seen the playground so quiet before. Nobody laughed. No one threw chestnuts at me. No one called my name. It was a fine morning. It should have been like that every day. It was just the way I wanted the world to be – slow, quiet, and with no jagged edges. I would much rather have heard crying than laughter. The bell didn't even ring. Instead we were led down into the gymnasium which was set out with chairs; the wall bars decorated with branches and flowers. *Just imagine it could look like this every time we had gym*, I thought. *Think if the king could die every night*. First Class 7 sang 'Between Buttress and Bluff', and when finally we sat down I found I wasn't with my own class but was sitting beside a girl I didn't know at all. She had a mole on her cheek that shone. I couldn't take my eyes off it. She moved to an empty seat right at the front and whispered something to a girl who turned round and stared. I thought I needed the loo. Then the head teacher made a long speech of which I remember very little bar the first sentence – *During the occupation we wrote Haakon the Seventh's name in the snow*. For I'd discovered that Aslak, Preben and Hamster were sitting right behind me (they were in Fred's class). They couldn't do anything to me there. The king was dead. But when the head teacher asked everyone to stand for a minute's silence, Preben whispered, 'Isn't your half brother here?' I didn't reply. Hamster leant forwards. 'Didn't he have the guts to come today?' Still I didn't answer. The minute wasn't up yet. Aslak breathed right in my ear. 'The king isn't everyone's king,' he whispered. When the minute had passed the head teacher summoned Aslak to the lectern. I thought he was going to be given a telling off. In fact Aslak was to read a poem. He had been the pupil of the year the previous term, had won the woodwork prize and had come second in the athletics tournament, right behind Preben. The pupil of the year doesn't get told off. The pupil of the year reads Nordahl Grieg in a command- ing voice. *Toil's tired and heavy furrows, in his face are all his own. Yet the pain there is for others. Thus the face of peace must be.* Aslak gave a deep bow and after we had sung the national anthem we all went to our classrooms. Once there Knuckles told us to take out our jotters and draw the king. She herself sat behind her desk and it looked as if her face was framed by the blackboard. But I couldn't get out of my head what Aslak had whispered in my ear, even though it was the shining mole of the girl who'd moved that I'd never forget. I put up my hand. Everyone looked at me. Knuckles gave a nod. 'Was the king every- one's king?' I asked. Knuckles' smile was sad as she answered. 'He was indeed, Barnum. King Haakon was king of the small, the great, the high and the low.' That wasn't what I had wanted to hear. I wanted to know if he was king of the halves and the wholes as well. But now suddenly everyone had their hands up, and particularly Mouse in the back row who had both arms in the air – the keenest one in the whole class. Knuckles pointed at him. 'There'll still be the game against Sweden even though the king's dead?' Mouse asked. Knuckles got up, walked between the desks, stopped at Mouse's desk and twisted his ear round three times. 'When the king has died we do not think of football,' Knuckles said. 'Our thoughts should be pure and honourable.' She let go of her hold and Mouse's ear unwound once more like a propeller, and he all but fell off his chair. After that no one had any more questions. Knuckles wrote in capitals on the blackboard –

ALL FOR NORWAY. I bent over my jotter and drew a tall man with a crown and a red mantle. Underneath I wrote *King Barnum*. Then the door opened. It was the head teacher. We stood at our desks. The head teacher whispered something to Knuckles and both of them turned in my direction. I thought Knuckles was a fine name. I wondered if men could be called Knuckles too. She came over to my desk and I had to go with them. The head teacher went first. And down at the bottom of the corridor, between the pegs, Mum was waiting. She's like a black paper cut out, seen from far away at the bottom of the corridor and in her sombre attire. She was standing quite still. I started running. I was the only one running today. At last I stopped in front of her and she crouched down, held my hands and looked straight at me. She had been crying. The skin of her cheeks was streaked. She smelled of perfume strongly and sharply – as if she had tried to sweeten her tears. 'There's been an accident,' Mum whispered. I closed my eyes. Mum laid her cheek against mine. 'The Old One is dead, Barnum.' Knuckles put my schoolbag onto my back. I followed Mum out into the playground. It was empty. We were alone there. The drinking fountain was shut off. And right at that moment the cannons on Akershus boomed twenty-one times, and all the church bells in the land rang together. The Old One was dead.

We went down to the Exchange to tell Boletta what had happened. Mum was silent the whole way there. She needed time. And I didn't dare ask anything else. Perhaps it was best not to know. I knew that the Old One was dead. That was enough. It was my fault. If I hadn't had all those thoughts about Dad being dead the Old One would still be alive. I couldn't cry now either. It was just as if my tears had frozen inside me and couldn't get out. I held Mum's hand when we finally stood together in the enormous hall in Tolbu Street. Everyone spoke in low voices. 'Hush,' Mum said. But I hadn't said a thing. We had to climb a wide staircase. Inside another room sat a whole squad of women with apparatus in their ears, pressing buttons in tables full of wires. We couldn't see Boletta there. A few of them glanced at us before turning away again just as quickly. I got a headache. My tears were flakes of ice whirling round in my head. Mum spoke with a woman who sat at a table leafing through some great tome. When she came back she was surprised. 'Boletta must be eating,' she whispered. We had to descend the same staircase again. In the end we found Boletta in the canteen in the basement. She was standing behind the counter serving coffee. She had a white apron on. When she first realized we were there she looked another way and acted all embarrassed, as if she'd been caught red-handed stealing money from the drawer under the clock. But soon she appeared angry instead, and I thought that she must already know the news that the Old One was dead, since here everything was heard, and I thought that maybe she was angry with the Old One for being dead. 'What are you doing here?' Mum asked her in a low voice. Boletta started moving abruptly and roughly. 'What am I doing here? What are you doing here?' Now Mum had to say what she'd come to say, but she didn't give in all the same. 'Why are you not up at the switchboard?' 'Because I'm down here,' Boletta replied tersely, and spilled some coffee. Mum was bewildered and beside herself. 'But you're employed as an operator, not a waitress?' Boletta took hold of Mum's arm. 'I couldn't operate the switch-board any longer! I began to lose my hearing in my right ear! Satisfied?' But Mum was anything but satisfied. She was irritated and it was just as if she was talking in her sleep. 'And so they sent you down here?' Boletta sighed. 'Yes, I'm down here now. At the bottom of the building.' Mum just shook her head. 'How long has this being going on?' 'For twelve years.' 'Twelve years!' Mum exclaimed. Boletta looked down. 'Yes, I've been working here since the end of the war.' I couldn't understand that they could talk like this on that day of all days – talk about everything other than that which had happened. 'And not a word have you spoken to us about this,' Mum hissed. Boletta laid out a series of cups. 'I have kept my fall to myself,' she said. I took Mum's hand. 'Aren't you going to tell her?' I asked. Boletta laid her hand on my head. 'It's the king who's dead, Barnum.' Mum drew in her breath. 'The Old One is dead too, Boletta.' Boletta didn't start crying. She just dropped the coffee cups onto the floor. They broke, one after the other. Then she tore off her apron and threw it onto the counter. After that we took a taxi up to Ullevål Hospital. We passed through endless corridors that smelled horrible before we finally found Fred. He was sitting on a bed in a room without windows. He stared at us and his eyes were shining brightly, like two spoons. Mum rushed over to him. Fred turned away. Boletta held me back. We stood together in the doorway and watched Mum trying to hug Fred – but he didn't want to be touched, he pushed her away. Not long after that a doctor arrived and whispered something to Mum, just as the head teacher had to Knuckles. And I had to wait with Fred while Mum and Boletta disappeared with the doctor. I remember Boletta saying something about the Old One having been sent to the basement too, and Mum snapped at her to be quiet. I sat down beside Fred. We sat like that for a long while. The bed was hard and too tall and most likely uncomfortable to lie on. There was a drop of blood on Fred's jacket, at the bottom of one sleeve. Had Fred been injured too? 'Are you bleeding?' I asked him. He didn't answer. An ambulance approached outside. A nurse chased past. There was a picture on the grey wall – of someone pulling a net up from the sea. 'Why is the Old One dead?' I whispered. But Fred was as silent as before. Fred had begun his long silence. His eyes were the reverse sides of spoons and he stared straight ahead, at the door or at nothing. I wanted to hold his hand. He clenched his fist and buried it in his pocket. I didn't want to sit there any longer. I jumped down to the floor. Fred didn't try to stop me. I went out into the corridor again and tried to find Mum and Boletta. The corridors were like the ones in school, except that here there were no pegs to hang coats on. First I ran down some stairs. I heard sounds coming from a room. I peeped in and saw a man crying behind a bouquet. I crept on and came to more stairs, went down those too. It grew colder. I was freezing. I wished Fred had kept me from going. I had to be in the basement now, for there were no more stairs. I couldn't go any further down. I continued through the corridor. Long pipes shone in the ceiling. An old man in a white jacket was wheeling a bed in the opposite direction. He hesitated for a second, but let me go on. The bed was covered in a white sheet and someone lay beneath it. One foot was sticking out. I came to a corner. There were some letters on a wall which I couldn't understand. Perhaps it was another language. I could speak another language, but only the sounds. Dad had taught me them – *Mundus vult decipi*. Now I was lost. Perhaps I would never find my way above ground again. I wanted to cry, properly now – the ice melted behind my forehead and flowed towards my eyes. Then I sensed it – another smell, a hint of sweetness – Mum's perfume. I ran in that direction, the direction of Mum's perfume, Mum's smell; and it grew stronger and stronger, as if she was leading me the last part of the way, until at length I came to a standstill outside a wide door that wasn't shut. I looked in. Mum and Boletta were standing there, one on each side of a table with shining sides and wheels, and the doctor was leaning against a cupboard right under a light which cast a strong, black shadow over both my shoes. Mum looked up and saw me. I went in to them. The Old One was completely naked. I dared only look at her face. She had a pronounced dent in her forehead. I raised my arm and laid one finger on her lips, and her lips were cold and soft and my fingers sank down into her mouth.

It had happened in Wergeland Road, at the corner of the park. The Old One had waited to go to the Palace to see the guardsmen hoist the mighty royal banner to half-mast from the balcony. She had wanted to say farewell to her Danish prince, her companion. The driver of the lorry (who was on his way to the docks with pallets), said in his evidence that the Old One suddenly swerved out into the crossing and that he hadn't a hope of braking in time. Witnesses of the accident (the man selling papers in his shop, and a whole host of customers who were in there to read the latest news) could confirm this, and they added that it was a miracle the driver had managed to avoid hitting the boy who had run out into the street too. The Old One had been thrown against the bonnet and flung several metres through the air. But no one could say precisely what had happened in the moment the Old One let go of Fred's hand and tumbled out into the street. And he tripped, got a bang on the head, or basically just went off into his own heavy world of dreams that black morning. I've often thought of it subsequently, of what really transpired in those seconds prior to the accident, before the Old One lost her balance at the corner of Palace Park and landed in front of the lorry. No charges were made against the driver since the police considered the pedestrian had acted 'extremely irresponsibly'. When the ambulance arrived the Old One was already dead, and Fred was sitting speechless on the edge of the pavement with his comb in his hand, and no one got another word out of him for the next twenty-two months.

The church bells rang out between twelve and one each and every day before the Old One's funeral. On the radio there was nothing but ponderous music; the flags hung at half mast, and even the national team played with black armbands, and managed a score of 2–2 against the Swedes, having been blessed by the bishop. Mum and Boletta didn't have time to cry any more. There was so much that had to be sorted: notices, wreaths, hymns, sandwiches, cakes and papers. I realized that death was tiring, at least for those who were left behind. And they tried to get hold of Dad who was off on his travels, but they found no sign of him, neither did he get in touch. They pay no attention to the fact that Fred still hadn't said a single word. I did. For each evening when we went to bed he lay there dumb with the same frozen eyes open all night long.

Dad arrived in the middle of the committal. When the Majorstuen vicar had spoken in tongues and we who were there (those always present at our funerals, and they didn't number so very many) had sung as well as we were able, the door at our backs was flung open loudly and there he stood, hat in one hand and white flowers in the other. 'The queen is dead! Long live the queen!' Dad cried. Then he walked down the aisle, laid the bouquet on the coffin, gave a deep bow, sat down beside Mum who had flushed to her roots, kissed her, and pointed to the vicar. 'Now you can go on,' Dad said. I turned towards Fred. Fred was staring at his shoes. Boletta was hiding behind a handkerchief. The vicar stepped down and took Dad's gloved hand. 'You are obviously a man who always comes too late, Nilsen,' he whispered. Dad stared at him hatefully and smiled at the same time. 'And he who comes too late should not blame himself for it!' The vicar dropped his hand and hurried over to the coffin on which he scattered some earth. I felt angry. I wished that Fred had stopped him. Fred did nothing. He didn't move. His hands lay in a white knot on the Bible in his lap. I was on the point of getting up; I wanted to kick the vicar and tear the spade away from him, but Dad laid his arm over my shoulders and afterwards we drove down to Majorstuen in the Buick. Mum was beside herself. 'Where have you been?' she shrieked. Dad shifted the pillow he always had on his seat and glanced over the steering wheel and got the low sun right in his eyes. 'Where have I been? Have I not been working?' 'For two weeks!' I managed to catch sight of the grey smoke rising from the tall chimney of the crematorium and thought that it was thus the Old One would come to heaven. Dad laughed. 'It took a bit longer than I planned,' he said. 'The speed limits are put down at a time of national mourning.' 'At least you could have telephoned!' 'I came as quickly as I could,' Dad murmured. 'As soon as I read the notice I drove here!' Now Mum laughed too, but her laughter was dark. 'And crashed your way into the service like a clown!' Dad took a deep breath and his hands slid round the steering wheel in their tight gloves. 'Oh, I believe the Old One was well used to waiting. Or are you in the vicar's camp today?' 'Be quiet!' Boletta exclaimed and held her ears. 'I have a headache!' Mum turned round towards us, for Boletta was sitting between Fred and myself in the back seat. 'A headache? Really? You who've been serving coffee since the war?' Then Boletta started to cry and Mum couldn't take any more either; it was all too much for her, she was sobbing, and Dad swung in to the kerb and stopped. 'There, there,' he said. 'Today everyone can cry themselves out to make plenty of room for laughter. But would you be so kind as to tell me where we're going?' We were going to the upper floor of Larsen's. And I can remember that Fred and I each sat on a chair by the wall in a brown room; at the far end in the corner there was a black piano with two candles on it, and the grown-ups sipped from tiny glasses and ate equally tiny sandwiches. Arnesen and his wife were there, Bang the caretaker didn't miss the opportunity to be part of things either, and Esther had sweets for everyone from her kiosk. That was the lot and there were plenty of empty chairs. This was my first funeral and for the first time I wondered if the Old One had been lonely during her life. 'Why are they all talking so quietly?' I asked. Fred didn't answer. Then Dad got up and silence fell around him. 'I am glad I got to the Old One's funeral,' he said. 'She chose a grand time to die. The whole nation's clad in black, the royal families across Europe are in mourning, and the Akershus cannons are thundering. And it has been earned. The Old One was loved. I dare say that she was also, now and again, feared. Already she is sorely missed!' Dad drank from his tiny glass and kept standing by his seat. Fred shifted his feet on the floor. Dad smiled, refilled his glass and kept on his feet; he drew out this pause, further and further, until no one had a clue what was going to happen next. The silence became intolerable and Boletta was on the point of tearing the cloth from the table. Then

Dad seized the initiative once more. 'But what I will say is that I consider it disgraceful that the Old One let herself get knocked down by a wretched lorry! She could at the very least have gone in front of a Chevrolet or a Mercedes! Cheers!' The silence lasted one more second and then we laughed – every one of us except Fred. Because that was the thing about Dad, that he could make people laugh; sorrow somehow didn't affect him, it ran off him like water off a duck's back, and perhaps it was for that reason no one could quite help liking Arnold Nilsen, the man with the stuffed fingers in his glove. Mum put both arms round him and laughed and they kissed; I felt a warmth and a goodness inside as I saw them, and from that time onwards there was no more whispering. 'Dad'll sort things,' I said aloud to Fred. But Fred just stared at his shoes and spent ages tying his laces. Mum let go of Dad and he came over to us with two halves of bread with egg on them. I was hungry. Fred didn't want one. Dad looked down at him. 'How could this happen then?' he asked. Fred sat there, silent; his bent neck trembled. 'What?' I asked, my mouth stuffed full of egg. Dad sighed. 'That the Old One was run over, Barnum.' He ate the other piece of bread himself. 'Didn't you take good care of her, Fred?' Fred looked up sharply, and I wondered if he was going to say something since he opened his mouth; a thread of saliva hung between his lips. But at that moment Mrs Arnesen began playing the piano at the other end of the room; the only tune she knew and the one she had played every day all those years since the time when, because of a crazy misunderstanding, she'd been made a widow for two and a quarter hours. Gotfred Arnesen, the insurance broker, who came home that day to find his wife a widow, hid his head in discomfort and shame, and would have dissuaded her from playing there and then, but Dad turned round and held him back. 'Oh, yes, now is the time of reckoning,' Dad said. Arnesen grew nervous. 'What do you mean?' Dad smiled. 'The money under the clock that we've saved, Mr Arnesen.

Our life insurance.' The broker shoved away Dad's hand. 'This is most certainly not the right time for such talk,' he hissed. Dad's smile was wider still. 'The right time? Well, we can certainly wait till your wife's finished.' That took time and the piano on the upper floor of Larsen's wasn't in particularly good tune. We sat there with bowed heads. And when she did finally hit the last chord on the keys she did so with such violence that she managed to blow out the flames of the candles on each side of the table. And silence fell once more because no one knew what to say or do, and Mrs Arnesen herself just sat on as if she'd been glued to the piano seat, there between the smoke from the black wicks, until Dad finally raised his arms aloft. 'Bravo!' he cried. 'Bravo! I envy you for each and every one of your ten fine fingers!' Now we could all applaud, while Arnesen offered his thanks and followed his wife out. After that I fell asleep and Dad carried me home. I think I dreamed that the Old One stood and waved from the Palace balcony; it was raining and she had almost no clothes on, and it was as if all colour ran from her. When I woke up the church bells had stopped ring-ing, Dad went to fetch the Buick from outside the upper floor of Larsen's, and Fred was asleep with his eyes open. I stole over to his bed, across the white line, and woke him up. 'What have you dreamed?' I whispered. But Fred made no answer, not yet – it would be a long time before he replied, and when he finally did I would no longer remember what the question had been. I went in to join Boletta and Mum instead. I tried to sense whether the world had changed now that the Old One was dead, and I hoped it had because I couldn't bear it if you died and everything just went on as before as if you hadn't been noticed. I stopped by the bedroom. Mum and Boletta were tidying, they were tidying the Old One's things. I almost felt relieved. The world had changed after all and things could never be the same again, at least not in our flat in Church Road. 'Now there'll be more room,' I said. Mum turned sharply, tight-lipped, but Boletta dropped what she had in her hands – a long, thin dress with a flower in the middle – held me, and smiled between her wrinkles. 'That's quite right, Barnum. That's why we humans die. To make more room.' 'Is it?' Boletta sat down on the bed. 'Yes, it is indeed,' she said. 'Because otherwise there wouldn't have been room for anyone in the end and what would we have done then?' Boletta's face was still and leaden for a time. I was disappointed – death had to mean more than this, more than cleaning and a game of musical chairs. Were things such that we got thrown out of the world when it began to get too cramped? Was death just a grumpy janitor who chased us out of the playground? Boletta got up again. 'And now I've moved forward in the queue,' she said. 'Next time it'll be my turn.' Mum stamped her foot. 'I forbid you to talk like that!' she hissed. Boletta laughed. 'I'll talk exactly as I please, just as long as I mean what I say!' She picked up the dress from the floor; the long, narrow dress with its flower – she held it up in front of her and danced across the floor humming a tune I didn't know. Then Mum turned too, smiled, and joined in the humming of that slow song which sounded so strange and sad but familiar nonetheless. Soon I could whistle it too and I became aware of the sweet scent of Malaga which was everywhere. I breathed deeply and whistled, dizzy and bewildered and happy. That day after the Old One's funeral. All at once Mum stopped. Boletta fell silent too. I was the only one whistling. 'Fred,' Mum whispered. I turned round. It was as if my mouth withered away. It was Fred. He was wearing the clothes he'd had on the previous day; the black suit that was far too broad for him and the white shirt. I thought that at last he was going to say something. Then he just turned away and went. Mum sprang after him. Boletta held me back. Shortly afterwards we heard the door slamming. Mum came back and went on nonchalantly clearing through drawers, cases, boxes – everywhere the Old One had had her things. 'Did he say anything?' Boletta asked. Mum just shook her head without looking at her. Boletta sighed and opened yet another cupboard. The sound of clothes hangers clashing together was something I couldn't stand – I had to cover my ears. I don't know why, but I just couldn't bear it; the clashing hangers as Boletta sorted through the thin dresses. Since that time I've never been able to stand that sound either; whenever I'm staying in a hotel I put my clothes over a chair instead, or else throw them on the floor or lay them on the bed. Because as soon as I hear the noise of clothes hangers in a cramped wardrobe I feel again the touch of the Old One's soft, cold lips against my fingers, as if I have disturbed a great silence. I ran over to the window. Fred disappeared between the blocks on the other side of the road without turning round a single time. It had rained during the night. The pavements were glistening. The leaves were thick in the gutters. The pale light hung trembling like a veil in the air. Where did I stand in the queue? Certainly I was behind Fred in the long line, and in front of him were Mum, Dad and Boletta and we never stood still; the whole time we got closer and one of us would perhaps be wrenched out of the queue before our time. And behind us the unenlightened pushed and shoved because they imagined it was all about getting there as quickly as possible . . . I couldn't bear to think about it any longer. 'Shall I help?' I asked. Mum leant against the bed post and nodded. I got to clear the bedside table. I didn't like the dentures in their glass of water, as if teeth were all that were left of the Old One – the inside of a mouth, a smile. The potty on the floor was empty, mercifully. But when I lifted the Bible she also had lying on her bedside table for safety's sake, something fell out – a picture, probably a cutting from a magazine or a newspaper, since it was thin and curled at the edges. Slowly I read what was written underneath. *The dreaded Ravensbrück camp. Eventually the concentration camp became too crowded and some no longer even had any prison garb*. An emaciated girl, almost transparent, a shadow – was sitting beside a woman who must be dead.

'What is it, Barnum?' Mum came over to me. And when I gave her the picture she sank down onto the bed and her hands shook. Boletta had to see it too and she quickly hid her face in her hands. 'Why did she never show it to me?' Mum whispered. Boletta sat down beside her. 'Because there are many different ways of caring,' she said, her voice equally low. Mum bowed her head and wept. 'I always knew. But still I didn't know for sure until now.' Boletta put her arm round her. Mum dropped the picture and I picked it up again. I saw the dead in the arms of the dying – their visages and over-large eyes staring at me. The dark girl who wouldn't take her gaze away – perhaps she was only seconds from her own death. Perhaps he who took her picture was her executioner too; perhaps he was holding a sword or a pistol in one hand and the camera in the other. I knew many nights would elapse before I got any sleep again. A fearful thought struck me that I would never sleep properly again while these faces stared at me from every vantage point in the darkness. And if I shut my eyes they would be there just the same – those faces – for I'd seen them. 'Who is she?' I asked, and could barely hear the sound of my own voice. Boletta took my hand. 'It's Mum's best friend,' she said quietly. It sounded so strange. 'Did Mum have a best friend?' 'Of course, Barnum. She was called Rakel. She was extremely pretty and she lived over the way.' I looked at the cutting again. I didn't want to, but couldn't help it. I was somehow sucked into that chill picture – the dead in the arms of the dying, an ordinary girl from one of the neighbouring flats, a best friend staring at her own executioner. 'Why did they do that to her?' I whispered. Boletta considered this a long while. Mum went on clearing the Old One's things – her slippers, her scent bottles, her jewellery, her glasses – and everything she did she did slowly, as if she was doing it all in her sleep and was tidying up in a dream where she would never quite be done. 'Because people are wicked too,' Boletta said. I didn't understand but nor did I ask any more. *It's these steps I hear*

disappearing out of my life. It's Mum's song. Now she
turned round abruptly, almost smiling, holding out something she'd found in the jewellery box. There was a
rhythm to her thoughts. It was a button, a shining button
from which there still hung a black thread. She gave the
button to Boletta but she had no idea either. They sat
there quite still, staring at the button that was bigger than
the top of a lemonade bottle. 'Can I have it?' I asked.
Mum looked up. She was pale, her cheeks sunk deep into
her face, and for just a moment I thought she resembled
the girl in the picture – her best friend, Rakel. I turned
away. I didn't want to see any more. 'Of course you can,
sweetheart,' Boletta said. 'Since you've done so well at
tidying.' She gave me the button. It was heavy and cold
between my fingers. 'Thank you,' I whispered. I went in
to our bedroom. I put the button in my pencil case. I tried
to do my homework. The drawing of the king was still not
finished. But I couldn't pull myself together. The only
thing I did was to cross out what I'd written underneath
the thin, crooked figure – *King Barnum*. These too were
things the Old One had left behind – a picture of Mum's
best friend and a shining button with a black thread. I
started crying. It was all I could do. I cried until Dad came
home and we were to eat dinner. Fred's place was empty.
Mum was silent and barely touched her food. We ate
fishballs in white sauce. Dad mashed his potatoes with
his fork and for a long time was as silent as Mum. Boletta
drank beer and apart from that it was a dismal mealtime.
Eventually Dad said, 'I've been speaking to Arnesen.' No
one responded to this. Dad grew impatient and spilled
some food on the cloth. 'Do you perhaps want to know
what I spoke to Arnesen about?' Boletta stretched over
the table. 'What did you speak to Arnesen about?' she
asked. Dad dried his mouth with his napkin. 'The life
insurance money. We will receive a payment of no more
than a miserable 2,000 kroner.' Boletta pushed away her
plate of fishballs. 'Have you begun working out what the
Old One's worth already, Arnold Nilsen?' Dad got up and

all but overturned his chair. 'Have you become so high
and mighty, Boletta? I just think the Old One was worth
more than a measly few thousand kroner.' 'Sit down,'
Mum said suddenly. Dad did sit down. Silence fell once
more. I could hear the sound of the fishballs as they slid
round the slippery plates. 'Our premium has been too
small,' Dad whispered. 'We've always paid what was
expected of us,' Mum said. Dad shook his head and
turned to me. 'Perhaps someone's been tempted by the
money under the clock,' he said. I looked down. I'd
spilled food on the cloth too. 'Not me,' I whispered. 'No,
but have you perhaps noticed Fred being a little light-
fingered with the money in the drawer?' Boletta banged
the table. She thumped it so hard the glasses overturned.
Mum shrieked and Dad's face became white as his
napkin. And I was actually relieved because perhaps now
I wouldn't have to answer. 'You're not always to blame
Fred,' Boletta said. Dad twisted round on his chair. 'I'm
not blaming anyone. I'm only trying to find out what's
happened.' Boletta smiled. 'Perhaps it's Arnesen who's
cheated us?' she said. For several minutes Dad was pensive. Then he laid his hand on Boletta's small fingers. 'At
least we could have done with that money,' he said. 'Now
that you're not working at the Exchange.' 'I have my pension,' Boletta said. 'And you're welcome to borrow money
if you need it.' Dad got up slowly and left the table, without so much as uttering a single word. Mum groaned.
'You didn't have to say that,' she breathed. Boletta rested
her head in her hands. 'Arnold Nilsen is a storeman from
head to foot. I can't abide all this money talk!' Now Mum
left the table too. I remained where I was. The fishballs
had gone cold. The white sauce was congealing round the
fork. 'Don't listen to all we grown-ups say,' Boletta said.
'All right then.' Boletta chuckled. 'But you have to listen
to me when I tell you that you're not always to listen to
all we say.' Boletta had had two glasses of beer. Maybe
that was the reason she was talking like this. 'All right,' I
said. Boletta brought her chair a bit closer. 'Has Fred said

anything to you?' 'No. About what?' 'I'd so like to know what they were talking about before the Old One died, Barnum.' 'He hasn't said anything,' I whispered. I helped to clear the table. Afterwards I dried while Boletta washed and then I waited for Fred. He came in after I'd gone to sleep. All of a sudden he was sitting there on his bed. I could just make him out in the dark. It was his eyes I could see most clearly. I didn't dare put on the light. 'What were you talking to the Old One about?' I asked him. The eyes disappeared. He didn't reply. I got my pencil case from my school-bag and carefully laid the heavy button in his hand. The eyes became visible once more. 'It's the Old One's button,' I whispered. Fred put on the light. He stared at the button and closed his hand. 'You can have it if you want,' I told him. I thought he was going to say something but then he just dropped the button on the floor. I had to crawl under the bed to find it and Fred switched off the light. He continued his long silence. No one paid any attention to it at first apart from me, because Fred had never been particularly talkative to begin with, in fact quite the opposite. He spoke little, and reluctantly. He wasn't someone with words on his side. Words were topsy-turvy inside him and letters often came out in the wrong order. Fred wrote the world's shortest compositions – that was if he handed them in to begin with. He got the lowest mark in Norwegian without fail and once he got nothing at all. At break-time he stood facing the wall. No one ever went over to him, though I could see myself that the girls took secret peeks at him and went past arm in arm with hopeful smiles. I so much wanted to be proud of Fred. One day someone had written the word *bastard* on the shed wall. The janitor took about two hours to wash it off and there was a good deal of a rumpus, but nobody got caught. The following Monday, Aslak came to school with sunglasses on although it was raining. One eye was dark blue and hung in a fat bulge beneath his forehead. Aslak said he'd bumped into a door and got the lock in his eye. There

weren't many who believed the tale (except for the teachers). Still Fred stood silent by the wall. I went over to him.
He didn't turn round. Aslak, Hamster and Preben sat on
the railing behind the tram stop following everything.
'Shall we go home?' I asked. We went home. I walked on
one pavement. Fred walked on the other. Esther leant out
of her kiosk and stuck some sugar candy wrapped in
crackling sandwich paper deep in my pocket. 'Share it
with your brother,' she told me, and drew her hand
through my curls. But Fred had disappeared ages ago;
Fred never waited, he was off round the corner or away
behind the church – I don't know, he could vanish in an
inkling, before I'd so much as had a suck of sugar candy I
was left standing there all on my own. It was as though
the only thing that remained of him was a slim shadow on
the pavement, a shadow that Bang the caretaker would
have to sweep up with his brush and carry off to the dust-
bins. Fred usually didn't come home until after I'd gone
to bed. Sometimes Boletta came in later still. She took her
time finding the way between bathroom and bedroom,
and the following day she'd have a headache and Mum
would be testy and on her guard. 'Have you been at the
North Pole again?' she'd whisper, her mouth straight as a
ruler. She said it like that, *have you been at the North Pole
again*, and I became equally perturbed each time she
did. For I had a vision of Boletta struggling through ice
and wind and cold, and perhaps not making it; and I
didn't understand what she wanted with the North Pole
anyway – was she searching for something there? 'Why
does Boletta go to the North Pole?' I asked Fred that same
evening. But Fred didn't say anything. It began to snow
one Friday in the middle of November. I lay and listened
to the growing silence. Then it was suddenly broken. Mrs
Arnesen was playing the piano – but it was a new tune,
and not only that, she played a whole series of pieces. It
was like a complete concert, and afterwards everyone
around the yard opened their windows and applauded;
even Bang the caretaker straightened his back, leaned on

his snow shovel and clapped. And the following Sunday
we saw Gotfred Arnesen going for a walk down Church
Road with his wife; they were off to church and she wore
a great shining fur, which made all the heads turn (particularly those of the Fagerborg ladies). They shook their
heads – amazed, suspicious and envious – and there was
talk and plenty in private about that fur in the days that
followed. A goodly number of men had to work out just
what a fur like that would cost if one were to pay for it in
instalments over a couple of years. 'What do you want for
Christmas?' Dad asked. 'A fur coat,' Mum answered. Dad
got up and went towards the door, trying to clench the fist
of his damaged hand. 'I think our dear Arnesen must be
in sore need of forgiveness when he goes to church and
it's eighteen below!' Mum wasn't going to let that pass.
'That was why his wife was wearing the fur,' she said.
'Because it was cold!' 'But it's warm enough in church!'
Dad protested. Mum sighed. 'You're just envious.' Dad
roared with laughter. 'D'you really think I'd march
around in a wild animal with buttons like that?' Now it
was Mum's turn to laugh. 'You're envious of Arnesen
who can afford to give his wife gifts!' Dad thumped his
damaged fist against the door. 'At the cost of our insurance money!' He was gone for two days. Mum turned to
Fred. He was sitting by the stove with his hands on his lap.
'What do *you* want?' she inquired. But Fred said nothing.
Mum asked a second time. And Fred maintained his
silence. 'If you don't want anything you don't need to get
anything,' Mum told him. 'Let the boy be,' Boletta murmured, and went to the North Pole. Mum hid her face in
her hands and cried. My stomach hurt. My throat burned.
I put my hand on her back. It was as warm as the stove.
'Could we read the letter?' I asked warily. Mum nodded.
'On you go, Barnum.' I fetched the letter from the cabinet
and sat on the sofa under the lamp. I read, slowly and
carefully, for the words were heavy, even though I almost
knew them off by heart. And while I read Fred stared at
me; and there was something in his expression, in the

way he looked – a darkness that grew and grew in his eyes, his smile. It was just as if he had changed in the course of those sentences, so that I all but lost the place in my great-grandfather's letter from Greenland. *It was decided that we should take back with us a musk ox, and on the same day we anchored we found a flock grazing on arctic willow, all but the only vegetation to be found. The captain and myself and five men went ashore to attempt to capture a calf. There was indeed a calf in their midst, but it was such that we could not come into close proximity. The creatures saw us – there were fifteen or sixteen in all – and they gathered themselves into a tight circle with their young in the centre and began snorting and pawing the ground like wild bulls. We were forced to return onboard, our mission unfulfilled, to the great amusement of the others on the ship. However, two bull calves were later taken (of which the one was dead), but it was at the expense of the lives of twenty-two adult beasts, since two flocks had to be shot to obtain them.* All at once Fred laughed, and it was the first sound he'd emitted since the death of the Old One. Yet it was only when the class teacher phoned after Christmas that Mum realized Fred wasn't just introverted and strange but that he'd actually stopped talking altogether. 'I must insist that you attend a parents' evening next Wednesday,' the class teacher eventually said. Mum had to sit down. 'Has he done something wrong?' she breathed. There was silence for a time at the other end. 'You've perhaps not noticed then?' the teacher finally asked. 'Noticed what?' 'That your son hasn't spoken a word for three months and fourteen days.' Mum hung up and went straight into the bedroom. 'What is this nonsense!' she demanded. Fred was lying on his bed. He didn't move. I was doing my homework. At least trying to do it. I'd got a ruler for Christmas with centimetres on one side and inches on the other. It wasn't the same length when I turned it over. With this ruler I was drawing lines to resemble streets and crossroads because the class was shortly to have a visit from a constable who would give us instruction in traffic safety. 'Now you're to talk to me,

Fred!' Mum shrieked. She shouted the words. Fred still didn't answer. There was utter stillness. Mum sat down on the bed. Fred stared at the ceiling. 'You can talk to me, Fred,' she whispered. That didn't help either. Mum began crying; she shook him so violently that it actually forced him to get up. But then he did something strange. He put his arms round her and kissed her brow. Then he went. She just sat there, thunderstruck, feeling the spot in the middle of her forehead where Fred had kissed her. It almost looked as if she were trying to rub away a mark. Slowly she turned towards me. 'Has he said anything to you, Barnum?' I shook my head. 'You're not telling fibs, Barnum?' 'No, Mum, I don't tell lies.' She put her arms round me and felt heavy. 'You couldn't lie, could you, Barnum?' she said. 'Now you said Barnum three times in a row,' I said. Mum gave a bit of a laugh, but not anything to write home about. Next day it was Dad's turn. He sat in the living room waiting for Fred. 'Come here,' he said. Fred went straight to our room. And I wondered if he hadn't heard – perhaps that was what was wrong with him, that his ears had stopped working. A bit later Dad stood at the door. 'I hear you've lost your voice,' he said. Fred didn't bother turning round. He just kept on staring at the ceiling. Dad went closer. 'It's best you find it before it's gone for good,' he told him. And I saw in my mind's eye Fred's voice lying somewhere, in a gutter perhaps, or down a drain – calling on him. But Dad refused to give up. 'If you're pretending to be skin-dead you're doing a bad job,' he told him. After he'd said that there was silence for at least three minutes, until Dad cracked. 'Speak to me!' he screamed, and stamped the floor so hard that the lines in my jotter wobbled and broke. 'Let the boy be,' said Boletta. But no one would let Fred be. Everyone wanted to get him to talk. They didn't manage. Fred's silence just grew outwards – it infected us, as Mum's silence had once driven Boletta and the Old One to distraction in the days when she was expecting Fred. Now he had inherited it. Now it was his. In the end it exceeded Mum's. As Easter

approached and Fred still hadn't said a word, and not a
sound had escaped his lips either at school, at home or in
his sleep – he was sent to a specialist in muteness at the
Royal Infirmary. There they attached wires to his head to
measure the pressure in his brain. The muteness specialist reckoned that Fred had probably received a blow to the
head when the Old One was run over; perhaps he'd fallen
or else been hit by the vehicle itself, something which
could have resulted in bleeding which impacted on the
part responsible for speech, thereby depriving him of the
ability to speak. But in all the reports on the accident it
had been concluded that Fred was not in the vicinity of
the car at the time the accident took place. And it was this
that was so strange, that all of a sudden the Old One had
been out in the middle of the street while Fred was still
standing crying on the pavement. The specialist measured the pressure once more and affixed still more wires
and electrodes. Fred lay on a wooden platform looking
like a Martian. Boletta just sneered at all this science.
'Fred was so frightened when the Old One died he just
lost his voice,' she declared. 'It's as simple as that. He'll
talk again in the fullness of time.' But at least Fred's
muteness was given a name. The specialist described it as
aphasia. And on the same day that Fred's at the Royal
Infirmary getting electricity in his head a constable comes
to our class to instruct us in traffic safety. We had written
take time to trust traffic in brightly coloured letters on the
board to please him. The constable has with him road
signs that he explains to us, because without these we're
in trouble. We learn too how he directs the traffic at a
crossroads and are taught that a bicycle has to have two
brakes, a bell and a light. These are things we have to
have, but gears, a bicycle kit and a baggage stand are
useful too. The following period we all go up to
Marienlyst, to the little city with its streets, pavements,
pedestrian crossings and traffic lights – just the same as
in any real city – except that here everything's much
smaller, as if they've been out in the rain and shrunk. We

eat our packed lunches and Esther waves to me from her kiosk, and for a time the rest of the class are envious because I know a lady in a kiosk full of sugar candy, ice cream and magazines. But that passes soon enough and then it's down to serious business. Now we have to put into practice what we learned the previous period. We're made to stand in a long line and the constable passes us one by one until finally he stops in front of me, smiles, and puts a hand on my shoulder. And I have to go over with him to the little crossroads. Maybe he's heard about the accident involving the Old One and it's for that reason he chooses me. I know that you have to look right and left twice when you're crossing the street. That was what the Old One forgot. A red light represents danger, amber signals that the lights are changing, and green means that it's safe. None of us is so busy that we can't wait for green. That day the constable could have asked me any question he liked. 'You might almost have lived here,' he says instead. He laughs and gives me a pat on the back. I look at him. I have no wish to live here. 'Why?' I ask him. The constable bends down. 'Why?' 'Yes, why?' He straightens up once more. Knuckles stands impatiently on the pedestrian crossing. The rest of the class take a step forward. 'Because here everything's so small that it's just big enough for you,' the constable replies. That's how he says it, that here everything's just big enough for me – and he laughs. Everyone laughs. I stand in the middle of the mirth and the constable pats my curls. 'But can you tell me what important things we have to remember when we're crossing the street?' I don't say anything. I notice how the others in the class are watching me. And I realize that in the wake of this nothing can be as it was. From now on I'm small. I'm the only inhabitant of the little city. My shortness, my lack of stature, has suddenly become visible. The constable has pointed me out. I can feel the weight of all I don't possess. 'Answer the constable, Barnum!' Knuckles shouts. But instead I walk away over the grass, away from the constable, Knuckles and the class, away from the little city – and no one stops me. That's perhaps the worst of it. I'm allowed to go. I don't turn round. There's no one at home when I get there. I measure my height against the doorframe and draw a line with a pen where I reach to. I climb up on a stool and look at myself in the mirror. Not a lot of mirror's required. And a pocket mirror goes a long way. And perhaps this is the first time I've really seen myself. I don't want to see any more. I go back to my room, close the curtains, put out the light, creep under my quilt and shut my eyes. And isn't it the case that everything falls together – all this that's life itself – events that have nothing to do with each other but which are connected nonetheless in a strange order composed of coincidence, death and luck? As if the lorry which knocked down the Old One caused a chain reaction through time, beginning with Fred's muteness, the picture of Mum's best friend in the concentration camp, the shining button, the constable's fearful words – and then continued with the Buick Dad lost, the course of special nutrition in the countryside, and Cliff Richard and the gramophone. Events I still know nothing about but which will soon take place and which I can't alter, because I know nothing. And basically everything started with King Haakon the Seventh's passing. This is my film. And there are no living pictures. Just points, joined together, like a calendar you can leaf through at speed seeing the rain turn to snow. It's at this point I change rolls – Fred comes home from the Royal Infirmary with aphasia, but despite the fact that his muteness has been given a name and address, he doesn't start talking again because of that. He just turns round in the doorway and goes out again – no one knows where – but I reckon it's to Wester Gravlund, to the Old One's grave. Later that evening Mum stands by my bedside. 'Where's the button?' she asks me. But I don't answer. I don't want to be any worse than Fred. I want my aphasia too. Mum bends down. 'Barnum?' I clench my teeth. It hurts my mouth. 'Are you asleep?' she whispers. I let her believe that I am. She steals out once more. I'm silent the rest of the night. Next morning I say nothing either. At school I'm equally quiet. During the first period Knuckles says I have to move desks. She points to the one nearest her table. 'The smallest has to sit at the front, Barnum. So I can see you.' I pack my bag and set out on the long journey between the rows. I'm already what I'm to become – the smallest. I hear the new names for me whispered so softly yet just audible – midge, pygmy, dwarf – it's not the last time it'll happen and there'll be other names too, as if I didn't have enough with my own name. I sit down at the new desk. Miss Knuckles smiles. She's so close I can smell her. She doesn't smell good. Here I'll sit still for the rest of my life while everyone else grows at my back, taller and taller, casting their shadows over me. 'Now you're sitting fine, Barnum.' I say nothing. I go home dumb. My teeth hurt. I eat dinner without saying a word. I'm on the verge of bursting into tears. And when I finally go to bed, more silent than ever, and the light's switched off, I open my mouth with a deep groan and draw in my breath, as if I've been underwater since the day before. But a suspicion has crept into me. No one's noticed that I've stopped talking. My silence is going by unnoticed. My aphasia is achieving nothing, neither good nor ill. I might just as well be dead. I manage to keep it up for two days. I'm sitting in the living room. Mum's standing at the open door to the balcony, smoking a cigarette. 'My pencil case,' I say. She turns towards me slowly and blows a ring of smoke that I break with my finger before disappearing in thin air. 'What did you say, Barnum?' 'The button's in my pencil case,' I whisper, and stick my finger in my mouth. Mum goes out onto the balcony and waves. I follow after her. Down on the street Dad's standing polishing the Buick. Soon enough he'll be able to see his own reflection in the hubcaps. The sky is shining on the bonnet. It's spring, the month of May, a fine time – for the herbarium and for maps and plans. Mum stubs out her cigarette in the flowerpot and puts her arms round me. 'Wouldn't you like to

go on a long drive in the summer?' she asks. 'Where to?'
'Where? You tell me, Barnum.' I didn't want to decide on
my own. 'Fred and I can decide,' I tell her. Mum smiles.
'That's fine. You and Fred make up your minds.' I change
mine at once. 'Greenland.' Mum lets me go and lights
another cigarette. 'There isn't a road to Greenland,
Barnum. Think of somewhere else.' 'Denmark perhaps?'
Now it's Mum's turn to ponder. And Dad leans over the
shining car down below and shouts, 'Are you coming,
Barnum?' At that moment Fred crosses the road and I
look up at Mum. 'Hurry,' she says. And I can see the happiness in her face; for the first time in a long while – since
the death of the Old One. I hurry down and Fred's already
sitting in the back. I go in the front, beside Dad, who
twists his hands round the wheel and glances in the
mirror. 'Where d'you want to drive to, Fred?' Fred does-
n't reply. He sits in the corner of the back seat, his arms
folded. Dad waits, but it does no good. He turns in my
direction instead and suddenly starts laughing. Then he
goes out, fetches something from the boot, and when he
returns he has a large cushion with him, even bigger than
the one he uses himself. 'Here you are, Barnum. You want
to see something yourself, don't you?' He puts the cushion underneath me but it doesn't make me any bigger. I
get smaller; I'm not raised higher, instead I sink down
into the red leather seat and Dad gives me a pat on the
head. 'Can you see fine now, Barnum?' I nod. All I do see
is the edge of the dashboard and a sky that's blue with
fuzzy white stripes. Dad drives down to Majorstuen and
turns right there, rolls back the hood, keeps a hold of his
hat, and continues up towards Holmonkollen and the
woods. People on the pavements turn round after we pass
and Dad delights in it each and every time. The breeze is
warm and strong in my face. I have to close my eyes. I
can see almost everything now. The sun fills every corner.
An insect hits the windscreen and gets stuck there.
Dad wipes it away. But one wing remains. A car appears
behind us. It's a taxi. Dad changes gear and by the next

bend it's gone. 'That was that,' he says content. The road becomes steeper. We're alone. Soon we can see the ski-jump tower and the blue lake below the jump. Dad brakes a second and turns round. 'You've driven here before, Fred. D'you remember?' Fred says nothing. Dad sighs, but it's a good sigh. 'That was a fine drive, even though it began raining.' He muses a bit. 'That was when Mum fell for me, Barnum.' 'Even though it began raining?' I ask. He laughs. 'Then it was just a case of putting up the hood and driving on indoors. Isn't that right, Fred?' But Fred is still just silent. All sound has been turned off inside him. The taxi comes to view again, moving slowly. 'I think someone's following us,' I murmur. 'Now you're fanta-sizing on a grand scale, Barnum,' Dad tells me. He glances quickly in the mirror and drives on; we don't stop before we've reached the final bend. Once there he rolls the car forward to the edge and it's just as if we've parked on a cloud, and beneath us are the fiord, the city and the woods. Dad gets out and rubs away the sticky mark on the windscreen. 'Have a look in the glove compartment,' he says. I open the glove compartment. There's a bottle of cola lying in there. Carefully I take it out. Dad has a bottle opener too, and takes off the top, has a long drink himself first before handing the bottle on to Fred. But Fred doesn't want any. He's sitting in the corner of the back seat, his arms folded, and his hair has been blown back into a high wave. Dad gives the bottle to me instead; I take a gulp and thereafter we're quiet for a long while, and the blue, smooth skies slide away, driven by a mild breeze that makes the treetops tremble like torches. Dad lights a cigarette and leans back against the headrest. 'Now we're having a fine time of it all right, boys. Don't you agree?' I'm the only one who answers. 'Yes,' I tell him. Dad lays a hand on my shoulder. 'It's good when we men get a bit of time alone, Barnum. Because we'll never quite understand women.' 'How much?' I ask. 'How much what, Barnum?' 'How much can we understand,

Dad?' He drinks slowly from the bottle of cola and then gives it back to me. 'Two per cent,' he says. 'And barely even that.' Fred clambers out and goes over to a tree to relieve himself. Dad goes on smoking. 'Hasn't he spoken to you either?' he whispers. 'No, Dad.' I draw in the strong, blue smoke and feel a little dizzy. It's good. Dad's silent himself for a time. He presses the cigarette down in the ashtray between us. When he looks over to Fred who's still peeing behind the tree, I swipe the cigarette end. 'How's it going at school?' Dad asks. 'I'm the smallest in the class.' 'That doesn't matter, does it?' 'I wish I could be a bit bigger.' Dad gives a laugh. 'I was the smallest too, Barnum. And look what's become of me!' I didn't quite know how to respond to that, whether it was meant as a comfort or a threat. 'I see,' I whisper. We sit on our respective cushions. Dad's stomach has just enough room behind the wheel. His thigh is soft and pushes against my knee. 'Once upon a time I knew the world's tallest man,' he tells me. 'And he was none the happier for his height, Barnum. Quite the opposite.' 'How tall was he?' Dad smiles. 'There was much debate about that. But he was so tall that he couldn't reach down to his own shoes, Barnum.' I laugh. That must have been something, not being able to reach down to your own shoes. Dad's face is covered by shadow. He closes his eyes and puts on his sunglasses. And then he says something he'll repeat time and again in the few years that lie between him and his own death. 'It's not what you see that matters most, Barnum,' he says, 'but what you think that you see.' Fred finally finishes and sits once more in the corner of the back seat. It's just as if a breath of cold air comes with him, as if his silence freezes our teeth. 'We're sitting here talking about life,' Dad tells him. 'What would you like to say about that, Fred?' But he gets no answer. Nor is there any point in waiting for one. Fred is switched off. Dad sighs again, but it's a heavy sigh this time. 'Aphasia,' he says. 'Does it hurt or do you not really notice it?'

Immediately afterwards he laughs. Fred doesn't. There's still not a sound from him and Dad gives up. 'Once upon a time I rowed alone over the Moskenes whirlpool,' he says instead. 'And the currents there are the most powerful of them all. It's like rowing in the devil's eye.' Now I'm silent myself. 'But I got across all the same, boys. And that's what counts. Getting there.' 'Where?' I ask delicately. Dad lets go of the wheel. 'Here, for example. You're my harbour.'

It's then the two men appear. They come out of the wood. They stop for a moment, look around them, or else at each other, and then continue in our direction. They're wearing dark clothes and they keep in step with each other. I just manage to catch a glimpse of Dad as he's about to turn the ignition key, but it's too late. He lets go, pulls the cushion from beneath me and puts it instead on his own seat, draws himself up and turns towards the two men – one cushion taller than normal. 'A lovely day,' he says in a loud voice. 'Arnold Nilsen?' 'Yes, the name sounds familiar.' The other man opens the door. 'We want to have a chat with you,' he says. Dad just sits there. It's as if he's keeping himself together by clinging to the steering wheel. His face becomes devoid of expression. And so he goes off with them and they disappear between the trees. I don't know what's going to happen. Only that it can't be any good because I'd seen Dad's face. I'm afraid in a different way. Now Fred *has* to say something. 'Say something,' I hiss. But he doesn't. Isn't he afraid? I turn round. I can't notice any change, except that there's a hint of a smile there. His lips curl round his mouth. I grow even more afraid. Whatever happens I mustn't make a mess in my trousers or start crying. If I pulled up the handbrake between the seats now the car would roll out and perhaps it wouldn't stop before it landed with its front wheels in the Oslo Fiord. I clasp the lever; it's warm to the touch and I can feel it trembling between my fingers. Now I can break all the traffic rules. I get goose bumps down both arms. Suddenly Fred thumps me in the back of the head. I feel so happy. I let go my hand and want to thank him. But there isn't time for that. Dad's coming back with the two others. He stops by the open door and looks down at us. His trousers are filthy. He's lost his hat. His hair is in a mess. He tries to laugh, but all he can do is make the attempt. 'Think you're going to have to get out of the car, boys,' he says. I go and stand beside him. Fred doesn't move from the back seat. 'Get out of the car,' Dad says again. Is Fred going to begin talking again now? Is it at this moment he'll say something to make the men flee, to make us laugh, and to make everything be the way it was before? That's what I hope. It's this liberating moment I'm always waiting for. But it never comes. Fred is no less silent. He's just dawdling. Dad bends inside the door. 'Please,' he whispers. Fred shrugs his shoulders, as if all this is beginning to bore him, and finally gets out of the car. The two men shove Dad out of the way and get in. The one who hasn't got behind the wheel chucks the cushions out and roars with laughter. Then they drive off. They drive off in Dad's Buick and disappear round the bend. We're left standing there. It's incomprehensible. It's that scorching smell of sun and petrol. Dad goes back into the wood to find his hat. It's dented. 'The cushions,' he whispers. I pick them up. We start down towards the city. None of us says a word. Dad leads the way; his breathing is heavy and his neck is wet – he's a black square in the hot light. I walk in the middle. I carry the cushions. And it's as I walk, a heavy cushion in each hand, that I decide to stop eating. There's nothing else for it. Why didn't I think of it before? It's so simple. If I don't eat then I'll get taller. Instead of growing outwards (just as Dad might have done with the years, pressed down by his own weight), I'll stretch, thin and weightless – hunger will raise me aloft. Dad wants to go into a place called the Bakkekro. He buys a beer for himself there. But before he drinks it he disappears out to the loo. Fred and I sit at a table by the window. A decoration of faded flowers is between us on the table. I'm sitting on the cushions. Soon I won't need them any more. When Dad comes back he's combed his hair, straightened his hat, polished his shoes and cleaned his trousers. He looks more like himself again, and yet not quite. There's a shadow under his eyes he can't get rid of. 'Do you boys want a sandwich?' he asks. 'No, thank you,' I reply. I've already begun not eating. I imagine I can almost feel myself growing. Dad drinks off the dark beer in one gulp and puts down the glass carefully once more, as if the smallest sound could destroy everything, or else the little that still remains that hasn't been destroyed a long time ago. Dad looks at me. 'We're not going to say anything about this to Mum,' he whispers. I shake my head many times. Dad nods and turns abruptly to Fred. 'And if you start talking again now then you've chosen the wrong time to do so! Keep up your aphasia!' Then we go home. Mum's waiting for us. 'What a long time you've been,' she says. Dad takes the cushions from me, goes straight into the living room and lies down on the divan. Mum watches him go, amazed. Fred changes his shoes and goes off again. I'm the one left standing there. 'Was it a good trip?' she asks. 'Oh, yes, Mum.' I have to think so hard so as not to say anything silly, something I shouldn't. I mustn't say too much. 'Where did you drive to?' 'To the same place where you fell for Dad, Mum.' For a second she's taken aback and has to stop and think herself. Then she comes closer. 'The button wasn't in your pencil case, Barnum.' She turns towards Dad who's lying on the divan with the cushions pillowing his head and with the news-paper over his face. The pages flutter. 'What d'you want with the button?' I enquire. 'Wash your hands,' she tells me. She hurries out to the kitchen because there's a smell of burning. I go into our room and get out my pencil case. She's right. The button isn't there. Either I've lost it at school or else I know who's taken it. And a long while will pass and a good number of years skip by before that button shows up again, like a little wheel that's rolled through our lives. 'The food's getting cold!' Mum shouts.

Dad's wasting time in the living room. I'm wasting time in my room. I stand against the doorframe and lay my hand flat on my head, but my height's just the same, even if I add my curls. But then I've only just begun to starve myself, and saying no thanks to one simple sandwich at the Bakkekro can't be expected to add any great degree of height. More food than that is going to have to be refused. Mum gets impatient and shouts even more loudly. We sit down at the kitchen table. It's fishballs again. Both Fred's and Boletta's places are empty. Mum pours water into our glasses. 'Where have you parked the car?' she asks. Dad chews slowly – no, he just breaks the fishballs between his teeth. 'Boletta's back at the North Pole, is she?' he asks. Mum doesn't reply. Dad fills his mouth with more fishballs. 'Do you really think she should be there at her age?' Mum's brow grows rigid. 'I asked you where you'd parked the car,' she says again. And it strikes me that neither of them answers the questions they've been asked, and reply instead by asking something else. I've never seen Dad like this before. He doesn't even manage to laugh it off. His eyes are restive the whole time. 'It's at the garage,' he mumbles. Mum leans across the table. 'What did you say?' 'It's at the garage, damn it!' Now he's doing anything but mumbling. He shouts. Mum crumples slightly. 'The garage? Did you break down?' Dad glances at me, as if he's stuck. 'The handbrake was making a noise,' I say. Mum shrugs her shoulders and passes the dish round. I pass it on. 'Are you not eating, Barnum?' 'We had a sandwich at the Bakkekro,' Dad says. 'Just beside the garage.' There's quiet for a time. It's as if peace has descended on us once more. But it doesn't last long. 'Was the handbrake making a noise?' she asks. Dad can't take any more. 'Since when have you been so knowledge-able about cars?' he asked testily. 'I never said I was.' 'Well, shut up, then!' Mum puts down her knife and fork and just stares at him. His neck becomes a bow from which his head hangs low. 'I shouldn't have said that,' he whispers. 'No, you shouldn't,' Mum says, and goes off into her bedroom and locks the door behind her. She doesn't open it again until the following morning. Dad's taken the whole night to work out what to say. 'I've sold the car,' he tells her. Mum looks at him. Dad looks at me. Boletta gets up from the divan. Fred comes out from the bathroom. 'Sold the car?' Mum breathes. Dads nods. Mum can't believe her ears. 'I thought we were going on a long drive this summer,' she says. Dad looks down. 'Perhaps next summer, dear.' Mum slams the door and opens it again just as quickly. 'Next summer? When I've promised Barnum we'd go this summer!' Dad turns to look at me. 'It doesn't matter,' I whisper. Dad gives a smile, his mouth heavy. 'There you are,' he says. 'But why did you sell the car?' Boletta asks him. Dad takes a deep breath. 'Because we needed the money.' Mum stamps the floor and becomes enraged. 'That's a lie!' she shrieks. 'You're lying through your teeth!' Dad doesn't know where to look or what to say. Instead he pretends to be deeply offended and that makes Mum all the angrier. I go between them. 'It's not what you see that matters most,' I say, 'but rather what you think that you see.' Dad lays his smooth, stiff hand in gratitude on my shoulder, but Mum just shakes her head and is mad for at least a month more. She goes out loudly to the kitchen and makes up a packed lunch for me, which I chuck in the nearest bin as soon as I know no one's watching. In fact no one paid particular attention to the fact that I'd stopped eating, any more than they had noticed my muteness. But I held out longer. I starved in silence. Now I had my own aphasia, the aphasia of the stomach and the intestine. And I set to work on it with a will. If I got sweets from Esther I'd hide the bag under a stone behind the broadcasting centre. At the school canteen I affected to eat a sandwich with caviar spread and some carrots, but I went to the loo afterwards and vomited the whole lot up again. At home I just passed the pots and dishes on and no one said a thing. I was invisible. Hunger made me see-through and hollow. Each evening I'd measure my height against the doorframe but still couldn't notice any change. My mark remained the same. My curly shortness remained rock solid. Growing is a slow process. And fortunately everyone had other things to think about. Mum was still livid because of the whole business about the car and Dad did his level best to make her happy again – he bought flowers, was home each evening, cleaned the windows, said she was more lovely than ever – but it was all to no avail. Mum's rage couldn't just be interrupted; it had to run its course until nothing more remained. Boletta drank her beer at the North Pole and Fred was just taken up with his own silence. One evening I felt he looked at me with new eyes all the same and I thought that perhaps he was going to say something – but no. I'd lost several kilos. I wanted to trade them in for centimetres, but I was still waiting. To start with I became lethargic. I managed to get up all right in the mornings. Everything was focused on not eating. Hunger was my one thought. I had to go to the toilet a lot too. Something had to give soon. There was nothing to come out. It was like a piece of addition – it kept on increasing. Except that I still hadn't got any taller. But I didn't give up. I've never not eaten so much. I became a small shadow in the spring sunlight. No one saw my starvation right until the moment I collapsed in Knuckle's arms in Religious Education on the last Friday before the summer holidays and was borne down to the school doctor. I came to on a mattress there. Hunger was a strange song in my head. The doctor took in my thin, stubby body with large, worried eyes. 'How long is it since you last ate?' he asked. 'A long time,' I whispered. The school doctor shook his head. 'But why not?' That I couldn't answer. I couldn't tell him the real reason. He wouldn't have believed me. 'Don't know,' I replied quietly. The doctor laid a finger on my wrist and counted out loud. 'Do you get food at home?' he asked when the counting was done. It was now I gave the wrong answer. I knew it as soon as the words were out. The lie was born in my mouth, and that lie would lay its own trail of

consequences in its wake. 'Not much,' I answered. The
school doctor glanced at the nurse who stood by the door
with her arms folded. She phoned Mum right away. I was
weighed and was allowed to get dressed again. Mum
came within the hour. First she had to have a long talk
with the school doctor and the head teacher. I was waiting on the mattress. The nurse kept an eye on me. Did she
really think I was going to run away? Not a chance – she
could be more than certain of that. I hadn't the strength.
I barely managed to lift my hand to scratch my nose. 'So
you don't get fed at home then,' she said. I wanted to
say something, that that wasn't true, that our table was
positively groaning with food – fishballs, chops, stew,
cauliflower soup and pickled gherkins. But then Mum
appeared from the office – hunched, red-faced, bowed
with shame. Not only did she have a son with aphasia but
she had another son who was both short and malnour-
ished. But suddenly she straightened up and blew back
the hair from her brow and her eyes became clear and
strong. 'What did we have for dinner yesterday, Barnum?'
'Leftovers,' I whispered. Then she took my hand and
went out with me. But by the time we got to the park she
couldn't take any more; she sat down on a bench and
began crying. 'How could you say that? That you didn't
get fed?' 'I didn't mean to,' I murmured. Mum wrung her
hands. 'What is it I've done wrong?' she sobbed. I went
closer. 'You haven't done anything wrong, Mum.' She
looked up and it was just as if she first noticed at that
moment how thin I'd grown. She hugged me, felt my ribs
like the frame of an abacus under my shirt and cried the
more. 'What are we to do with you, Barnum?' She'd find
out soon enough. A letter came to Mum and Dad from the
school doctor. I was to be sent to a farm for twelve days
to be fattened up. Now it was Dad's turn to become livid.
He thumped the table and refused point blank, but they
had no choice. I'll say no more at this stage; I'll just say
Weir Mitchel's Remedy, and that it was Mum who took
me to the train. I had with me a rucksack with clothes,

toothpaste and a ruler; and I was met at Dal station by the farmer himself, and driven in a lorry to the farm by Lake Hurdal. I could see the lake in the evening from my room. Fish floated there in the moonlight. The farmer had a wife with large hands. There were two other boys there too. I was thinner than they were. When I came home I was a butterball. But before school started up again I was myself once more, neither taller nor smaller, neither more nor less – I was Barnum once and for all, as if nothing had happened, as if Weir Mitchel's Remedy in Hurdal had been but a dream. I was called in to see the school doctor and he examined everything from my bum to my back teeth and pronounced that I'd improved, that the Remedy had been a success; the fat was plentifully distributed over my body and the intestinal pistons were working so well they were a joy to behold. 'Was it fun to be on the farm?' the school doctor asked. I couldn't answer. I just nodded. Mum and Dad could breathe a sigh of relief; Esther could put her hand in my curls and the rest of the class could laugh at me because the girls had grown too in the course of the summer. They'd spurted up, way beyond me; I remained alone in the lowlands, out in the cold. And I stood still; I had to look up to everybody else and there was no one I could look down on. I would have given anything to be able to tell Fred all that happened on the farm. I could have told him that it hadn't been fun at all. But I couldn't do that either. He was still more than silent. His silence laid waste streets and cities. Perhaps there was a similar remedy for the dumb? That was a thought that appealed to me. I could see it in my mind's eye – a farm in the country (or in a park), where the dumb sat together in the shade under the trees and had to talk to each other. One word on the first day, four the next, and by the time the twelfth and final day had come they'd be able to speak an entire sentence. I christened it Barnum's Remedy. But there was no remedy for Fred.

It began to rain in September. Dad had been away the whole weekend. On Monday he came home. He didn't

even waste any time taking off his coat and his muddy
shoes. He went straight into the living room and put a
huge cardboard box on the table. He was going to bring a
smile from Mum once and for all. 'Look!' he cried. We
gathered round the cardboard box. All of a sudden Dad
started taking his time. He dried both gloves carefully
with his handkerchief, combed his hair, put a cigarette in
his mouth and looked about for some matches. 'You can't
wait now, can you?' he said. But he didn't get the
response he was hoping for. We weren't pawing the
ground with expectation, driven mad by the waiting. We
didn't leap on the box and rip it to shreds. We were a
pathetic and ungrateful audience. Perhaps we were just
tired out by all that had transpired since the deaths of
King Haakon and the Old One – an interval of only a few
hours between them. It had been too much for us; soon
we wouldn't be able to take any more, the show had gone
on too long and our senses had gone to sleep. We'd hit
rock bottom. Dad was bewildered for a second; he took
the cigarette from his mouth and instead put it back in his
case, as if he wanted to rewind time and begin everything
again from the start. That didn't help either and he was
sorely disappointed in us; he became offended and had to
improvise. He jolly well took the box out again. Perhaps
he'd make a new entrance, come in a different way, without his coat and wet shoes – and there was almost something comforting about this, that there was a possibility
of doing things over again in a better way. 'Where are you
going?' Mum asked. Dad stopped, turned round slowly,
and pretended to act all surprised. 'Oh, I didn't know you
were here.' Mum smiled. 'We're here, Arnold.' We *were*
there – Boletta, Mum and myself, even Fred. Dad looked
at each of us in turn as if he were seeing us for the first
time. 'I thought I would just take out the rubbish,' he said
sulkily. Mum had to coax him now. 'Don't be silly. Let's
see what you've got there.' Dad hesitated a moment
longer before returning with the cardboard box. He had
the upper hand now and knew it; finally he had us right

in the palm of his hand. 'Well, well,' he sighed. 'As if my little presents could be of any remote interest to you.' With that he tore the string in two, pushed the lid to one side, took a deep breath, and our eyes became saucers as Dad lifted out a gramophone, a real Radionette gramophone with two speeds, 45 and 33, and automatic pick-up. We went closer. We trembled with wonder. Dad found his cigarette and lit it, and appeared satisfied with the performance, despite everything. 'But we don't have any records to play,' Boletta said. As if Dad hadn't thought of that. This was the moment he'd been waiting for. He gave a crooked smile and blew smoke from the upper corner of his mouth. 'That's why I'm bringing this house the new star shining with such brightness in the skies of the music world.' Suddenly he was holding a gold single between his gloves and I wasn't able to see where he'd produced it from. Now it was we who sighed, all of us except Fred. Dad whispered, 'And his name is Cliff Richard.' Dad laid the record down carefully on the gramophone, depressed a button, the pick-up glided into place of its own accord, and the needle landed on the grooves. There was whistling and crackling and to begin with there were some dark, heavy noises and the voice that started singing was so deep the whole thing sounded pretty much like King Haakon's funeral backwards. Dad began fussing, stuck his cigarette in Boletta's mouth and twisted a knob three times. The speed increased and the needle leapt forwards a couple of grooves, but in the end we could hear it, pure and clear and close as if he had been standing in our own living room – Cliff Richard singing 'Livin' Lovin' Doll'. As soon as the record was played the needle was lifted back to the beginning. We could hear it long after we went to bed. Mum and Dad danced in the living room and Cliff Richard sang. Thereafter there was loud noise from the bedroom. The same thing happened the following evening. Cliff Richard sang 'Livin' Lovin' Doll', Mum and Dad danced in the living room, and for the remainder of the night they were equally loud in bed.

Fred stayed out until after they'd calmed down. Boletta
fled to the North Pole. Once I lay there at home, the
pillow over my face, listening to those long drawn-out
concerts each and every evening – Cliff Richard, 'Livin'
Lovin' Doll' and the strange rumpus that always came in
its wake. Mum and Dad had found each other again and
both of them had found Cliff Richard. All through the
autumn it went on like that. I should have been happy. Yet
I couldn't be. The Old One was dead, Fred was mute, and
I didn't grow any taller. The doorframe never moved. And
for that reason for long enough I sensed a sinking of the
heart, a tinge of sadness that quickly changed to shame
and panic, whenever I happened to hear Cliff Richard in a
lift or a bar. That dry yet smooth voice – a voice without
any defect, beautiful and invisible. Right until I saw him
with my very own eyes by the swimming pool in the
Kempinski Hotel in Berlin; then it was as if the curse was
lifted, the sinking of the heart dissolved at the actual sight
of Cliff, just as Fred himself broke his own protracted
silence in the end. Because one evening there wasn't a
sound in the living room, neither was there any noise
thereafter. I lay awake and heard nothing. The following
morning Mum came into the room. She had the gramophone with her. 'Here you are,' she said. I wanted to ask
what had happened, but I didn't. She just put the gramophone on the table and went back out again. Dad disappeared for several days. Boletta had a headache. Fred
came home, as mute as ever. It started snowing. We were
living in a silent film. There weren't even subtitles
between the scenes. The snow kept falling. And there
came a point when I couldn't take any more. It was a completely ordinary evening. Spring had come. I heard the
bicycle bells chasing down Church Road. The room was
filled with stillness and sunlight. I stood by the doorframe
and measured my height. I hadn't got any taller. I had to
have sound. I had to hear something. I pressed in the
button on the gramophone. The pick-up lifted. It
descended towards the grooves. I blew the dust from the

needle. Never had it been stiller in my head. And that second, or immediately thereafter, in that second's end, Cliff Richard started singing, yet again and for the very last time in our house, 'Livin' Lovin' Doll'. Then Fred got up, broke off the pick-up, hurled the record at the wall and stared right at me. The silence was redoubled. 'Shall I kill your father for you?' he demanded. Fred had spoken. It was the first thing he said. I was so happy. I laughed out loud. 'What did you say?' I asked him. Fred came closer. 'Shall I kill your father for you, Barnum?' I stopped laughing. Fred took the whole contraption with him, went down into the yard and chucked it in the bin. I think Bang the caretaker rescued it, since he always tended to sift the bins before they were emptied, but he obviously never knew how to get it working again. I ran into the living room. Mum was sitting sleeping by the open balcony door. 'Fred's talked,' I whispered. She woke gradually, raised her head and rubbed the sleep from her eyes. 'What did you say, Barnum?' 'Fred's talked!' Mum got up quickly. 'Has he?' 'Yes, Mum. Fred's talking!' 'But what did he say?' she asked. I fell silent. Mum grabbed my arm and shook me. 'What did he say, Barnum?' I looked down. 'That he doesn't like Cliff Richard,' I said.

The Obituary

One morning Mum screamed. We were sitting in the kitchen eating breakfast. Fred had been talking again for a good while, though he was saying nothing then. In fact it was Dad who was the quietest. He missed the gramophone. And not least he missed the Buick. The rest of us weren't particularly talkative either. We missed the Old One. Sometimes I thought to myself that perhaps it wouldn't do any harm if we were all to lose our voices at the same time, to be inflicted with aphasia, since there was so much we couldn't talk about anyway. Then it was that Mum shrieked. And she came tearing out towards us, her hair a crow's-nest and her nightie all to one side, and in her hand she was waving *Aftenposten* like a flag. 'We're in the paper!' she cried. 'We're in the paper!' Never had I seen her so worked up – nor did I ever see her like that again either. She swept breakfast things to the four winds and threw the paper down on the table. There we could see it with our own eyes. It was about the Old One. It was her obituary, two years too late. Mum sat down with us, already crying. Boletta, who generally couldn't see clearly before the arrival of the afternoon edition of the paper, leaned over the table, pale and shaken. 'Read,' she whispered. And Mum lifted the paper and read aloud, in her grandmother's voice, and this is how I remember those crooked, soft words in her mouth.

THE INVISIBLE STAR

The beautiful Ellen Jebsen has relinquished her human role and left the ever-changing scenes of the times in which we live. Those of us who knew her now feel a deep sorrow in our hearts, a sorrow that may only be assuaged when we follow into darkness in her wake. She was born in Køge in 1880. Her father was a highly respected saddler and upholsterer, but it was her mother she took after, early on in life when she learnt to love the art of storytelling, when in the evening she listened to her tales as the scent of baked apples on the stove filled the living room with an aroma that opened the pores of her imagination.

But it wasn't before she met her beloved Wilhelm, then a young and gifted mariner, that her life took its first abrupt change of direction – the first of many. They met when the Jebsen family was on an excursion to Copenhagen, on the skating rink at the Sø Pavilion, and he wasn't about to let go of this magnificent girl. There is no blame to be put on her parents, even now at this juncture in the closing chapter of her story, for their refusal to look with favour on this alliance, and indeed their attempts to do all in their power to prevent it. I do not mention this to cast any doubt on their own renown – not in the least; I include it solely to illustrate the sheer strength of the young ones' love. Yet as the great poet wrote: It is the truest love that leads to the greatest misfortune. They never married. In June, 1900, Wilhelm left with the SS *Antarctic* which was sailing from Copenhagen to Greenland to carry back a musk ox for the zoological gardens. He never returned. Wilhelm vanished up there in the ice. He never came back to the ship in the wake of a hunting expedition when he and the second gunner were searching for musk oxen on the other side of the fiord. His tracks disappeared beside a fissure in the ice and his body was never recovered. May he rest in peace. But she who awaited his return was still in Køge. She waited in vain. And in the same year she gave birth to their daughter who was christened Boletta. I will not dwell on this which was unheard

of in its time, save to establish that she broke with
her family and moved to Copenhagen, where she
was to be found thereafter in the ticket-office in the
first cinema in Denmark. This was at Vimmelskaftet,
in the pioneer days of the silent film, when films had
titles like *Susanna in the Bath* and *An Emigrant's Story
or the Vanished Bag of Money*. And many there were,
from gentlemen to one-time servants, who would
rather have turned their eyes on Ellen Jebsen than
on the mystical women of the screen. And one of
those who could not take his eyes off her was the
legendary Ole Olsen, the juggler and cinema manager. He came upon Ellen Jebsen in the ticket-office
at Vimmelskaftet and he knew that her face had been
made for the silent film. For after her beloved, the
father of her daughter, vanished in the blue ice, her
beauty had deepened – tragedy itself was sculpted in
Ellen Jebsen's face and love's very features were visible in her expression. She spoke to him without
words. And right away Ole Olsen offered her a place
in what he called his actors' stable, and that same
summer she and little Boletta went out to the Visby
allotments where the studio consisted of a rickety
shack which would later become Nordic Films. A
magnificent epoch began! We attacked comedies and
dramas alike with gusto, and little did we realize the
future we were setting in motion, in those days
when Visby was bigger than Hollywood. Here the
early Storm-P was rapidly developing; here were real
Chinese, wild lions, trees painted with palm leaves,
murder and romance. And in the midst of this creative anarchy Ellen Jebsen stood like a pillar of sorrowful beauty. She could have been an Asta Nielson,
yes, she could have become a Garbo. It is, therefore,
a double calamity and disgrace that our generation is
unable to see her. The films from the Visby days have
been lost and later she was cut out entirely. Ellen
Jebsen's moment in the electric theatre was rubbed

out. She was the forerunner left in the shadows by those who came in her wake.

And soon she left us. Two separate events coupled with deep longing led her north, to Norway, in 1905. The Danish prince, Carl, was to be crowned king. In addition she had been offered a role in the first Norwegian film drama, *The Trials of the Fisherfolk*. In this way she would also be closer to her beloved, the one she waited on with constancy – for thus was her heart, faithful to the end and always defiant, no matter what. But when life swings dramatically one may never be certain what will happen round the corner. Ellen Jebsen's role in *The Trials of the Fisherfolk* was cut out either on economic grounds or else for erroneous artistic reasons. Only three characters played in the drama – the parents and their son – who in the course of the action drown in the Frognerkilen Baths, used to represent the turbulent and perilous ocean. Let it be said at once that this passing over was not only a personal disappointment to Ellen Jebsen, but a tragedy for Norwegian film *per se*, which barely made it onto its feet after this wretched start. The film would have gained an added timbre and moved audiences profoundly had she starred in the supporting role as the drowned son's lover. For is not this the primary objective of film, to move its viewers, transport them to laughter and tears, pain and pleasure? Ellen Jebsen put her career on one side after all this and was given an appointment at the Telegraph Exchange where her daughter Boletta also came to be employed. Ellen Jebsen lived in Oslo until her death on the selfsame day that King Haakon, her prince, passed away himself. There was a predestined quality to her life which surpassed her own art and which met the unexpected head-on.

I write this two years after her death (having only now become aware of it), certain that it is never too late to remember and honour an extraordinary life.

We lost Ellen Jebsen. Would that these simple words, written in sorrow and gratitude, might hold her intact and raise her to those skies where her star belongs.

> Respectfully,
> Fleming Brant,
> Bellagio, Italy

After Mum had finished reading and put the paper down we cried too. The words from the newspaper grew in us; the words that had come long after it was all over – just as the letter from Greenland first reached its destination long after the sender had vanished, lost in the ice. In the end Mum sighed. 'It's a shame the Old One never read this.' Dad got up abruptly. 'Who the hell is Fleming Brant?' Mum looked at Boletta, who was paler than ever, but she just shook her head and lowered her gaze so we no longer saw her eyes. 'I have no idea,' she murmured. Fred opened his mouth. 'Where's Bellagio?' he asked in a low voice. 'Italy,' I told him, quick as a flash. Fred stretched across the table and hit me on the temple. 'D'you think I can't read or what, Tiny?' Mum interrupted the dispute before I started crying. 'No arguments now, boys.' She got a pair of scissors from the drawer in the kitchen and carefully cut out the obituary, and I can remember too, clearly and sharply, as if I'd never left the table at all that morning but was sitting there yet – the sound of the slow, blunt scissors cutting the paper. Mum has to clip hard, twice each time, to get a grip, and the remainder of the obituaries are chucked in the bin, crackling like flames. Black columns of names they are, like credits in a film that no one has ever seen. We don't go to school that day. Mum writes sick notes for us. The two of us clearly have tummy upsets. I laugh aloud and am told to be quiet. We go to the graveyard instead. All those whom we meet down Church Road greet us in a different manner now; they nod and keep turning round long after we've passed them by. They've read *Aftensposten* and

know which star we come from. It's been there in black
and white beside the other obituaries and can't be denied.
Esther opens her kiosk window and waves with fingerless
gloves. 'Congratulations!' she shouts. Mum waves back.
'Thank you very much!' But when we come to a halt by
the Old One's grave Fred's vanished. He slipped away
among the trees at the back of Frogner Park. I just saw his
back. Mum calls him. Fred doesn't hear us. The headstone, with its famous name – ELLEN JEBSEN 1880–1957 –
is standing crookedly in the ground. Dad attempts to
straighten it; he puts his shoulder to the dark stone and
shoves, and I stand behind him and push, but we can't
manage it. The ground has frozen about it. Water has
frozen in the earth. The dead are freezing in their beds of
ice. But Dad still won't give up; he's taken a dislike to this
stone. He's going to get it back where it should be. Mum
wants to stop him, but Dad's determination has turned to
ice too, his stubbornness has frozen solid. He puts everything he has into shifting this obstinate pillar, standing
there lopsided and blasphemous. He swears, and Mum
covers her ears, Boletta grips my hand – but the stone is
stronger, it's the stone that pushes him backwards. It
knocks him down and overpowers him completely, for all
at once he's blue in the face, lying sprawling on the Old
One's grave. Mum falls to her knees and cries his name.
He scrabbles on the grass. Then he lies utterly still, his
chin against the ground, as if he's fallen asleep there at
the foot of the crooked headstone. Boletta runs over to
the chapel to get help. My feet are freezing. I can hear the
sound of an organ. Mum shakes Dad. Then he sits up
slowly, looks at me surprised, brushes the earth from his
coat and turns towards Mum. 'Don't be angry,' he murmurs. Mum holds him and cries. 'I'm not angry. Why
should I be angry?' She laughs instead. Dad closes his
eyes once more and rests in her arms. They sit together
like this on the Old One's grave until Boletta comes
running back. 'The church warden's calling an ambulance!' she cries. Dad pushes Mum away and looks at
Boletta who's stopped breathless in a cloud of frost. 'An

ambulance?' he repeats. 'Are you sick, Boletta?' Mum strokes his cheek. 'You've maybe taken a turn, Arnold. You should go to hospital.' Dad wants to get back up but his legs won't support him. He tumbles over and swears worse than ever. 'I'm going to no hospital! D'you hear me?' He tries to get up again but it's just as if a mighty hand is keeping him down. 'Help me, damn it!' he shrieks. 'Help me!' Eventually we get him into a vertical position. He can barely stand unsupported. We can hear the sound of the approaching siren. Dad presses his hat down on his head. 'Farewell,' he says. Mum tears at his coat. But he's not to be stopped. He walks incredibly slowly, as if each and every step demands enormous concentration. The ambulance backs in through the gates and two men in white coats hurry over towards us. Mum points to Dad who's tottering away between the graves. They chase after him. But Dad has no intention of giving himself up. He waves the doctor away and for a time it looks as if they might take him away by force. But in the end they give up and let him be, while Mum stands there covered in shame, apologizing into the ground. Boletta reckoned the Old One would have refused to be pushed like that. The stone was meant to stand just as it was, an irregularity in Wester Gravlund's serried ranks of stones, a crooked reminder of her greatness. But the following spring, once the sun had washed winter away from under our feet, the gravestone stood straight once more – a black, stone ruler – as if the Old One had moved one final time in her sleep and turned her pillow.

But I lay awake that evening. Mum sat up waiting for Dad; restlessly she paced back and forth, stopping by the window, sitting on the sofa, unable to keep still. Boletta put the obituary in the same drawer as the letter from Greenland. For a while I thought Mum's false sick note was going to be true after all. My stomach was unsteady; it listed and was on the point of being upset. Suddenly something hit me on the forehead. It was a hard ball of

silver paper. Fred had thrown it. When Fred threw something it generally hit its target. He stank of tobacco, I
could smell it from where I was lying awake. 'Was he
dying?' Fred asked. 'It looked like it,' I whispered back.
'How did he look?' Fred demanded. 'He was blue in the
face,' I told him, my voice low. 'How blue?' 'What do you
mean?' Fred chucked a second ball of silver paper at me.
'Was he dark blue or light blue, Barnum?' I had to think
hard. 'He was dark blue, Fred.' Fred tittered in the dark.
'Did he say anything?' 'Yes,' I whispered. Fred stopped
tittering and grew impatient. 'Do I have to beat everything out of you, Barnum?' 'Don't be angry,' I told him.
Fred groaned. 'I'm not angry. Just tell me what he said.'
'That was what he said, Fred. Don't be angry.' He lay
quiet a long while. 'What did Mum say?' he asked eventually. 'That she wasn't angry.' 'Bloody hell,' Fred murmured. And just then Dad came home. He crept carefully
along the side of the wall. He wasn't stooped and he
didn't make any less of himself than there was. That was
him to a T, knocked flat one minute and up on his feet the
next – the blows he took just glanced off him. The fact
that he'd lain prostrate on the Old One's grave, blue in
the face, was quite forgotten – swept away by triumph
and loud talk. I ran in to the living room. There he was
down on his knees unfolding an enormous map on the
floor. I stood between Mum and Boletta. It was Europe
and Europe was almost as big as our carpet. Dad thumped
his fist into the map with a bang. 'There!' he exclaimed.
'There's Bellagio!' We bent closer. Bellagio lay at the top
of Italy by a narrow, blue lake called Como. 'It's far away,'
I whispered. Dad glanced at me. 'Far? It's no further than
to Røst, my boy.' Dad shook his head and laid his other
hand on Røst. 'Europe's no bigger than what I can blow
my nose with on this map!' 'Be quiet,' Mum said and
laughed. Dad did anything but keep quiet. He was warming up. He was sunning himself now. 'But if you were to
add America then we could begin to talk about distance.'

'Where's Greenland?' We turned towards Fred. He was
leaning against the wall, his face sulky. Dad smiled.
'That's a good question, Fred. Because Greenland isn't on
this map. But if you look under the sofa you might find
Greenland there.' Fred didn't move a muscle. 'I thought
you were dead,' he said. It grew so still. And Fred went
back to bed before anyone could say anything. Dad
laughed, but too late, as if his face and his laughter somehow didn't go together. I scrabbled under the sofa and
searched for Greenland, but didn't find anything except
an old dusty sweet and a used cork with a strong, sweet
smell. Dad had to drag me out again. 'Look,' he said. 'You
can drive through Europe with this car!' He gave me a box
of matches. I looked at it for a long time. 'It's not a car,' I
whispered. 'Oh, yes, Barnum, it is a car.' 'It's a matchbox,'
I said. Dad breathed heavily. 'No,' he said, his voice just a
shade sharper. 'If you look at it really closely you'll see
that it's a car. It's actually a Buick Roadmaster Cabriolet!'
I had a really good look. 'Now I can see it,' I whispered.
Dad laid his hand on my shoulder. 'But if you want to go
by boat instead, there's nothing to stop it being a ship
too.' He took a match from the box and stuck it through
the lid. 'D'you see? Now you could sail, for instance, all
the way up the coast to Røst.' 'I'd rather go by car.' 'No
problem, Barnum. Just as long as you remember to drive
on the left-hand side of the road in Sweden.' Dad lit a cigarette with the mast and the matchbox became a car
again, a Buick, with room for the whole lot of us. I lay
down on the map and began the journey south from Oslo.
But before going the length of Svinesund I felt carsick and
collapsed over Skagerak. I have no recollection of Mum
carrying me off to bed. It's all I can do not to be sick. The
bends were too sharp. The speed was too great. The
moon behind the window's a golden steering wheel. I've
parked. Night is a garage. Fred is sleeping fitfully. And
each time you close your eyes you jump. Each and every
blink is a clip from the film of your life. In my sleep I join
together the pieces of film; I splice time, not in a long

dissolve but a sudden cut. I am the demigod who throws away everything that isn't in the script. And when Dad wakes us up again the room's full of light, it's summer, and it's Mum's birthday.

The Divine Comedy

And we slip in to Mum. Dad leads the way; he's holding a candle but the flame is barely visible in the sunlight filling our rooms. Boletta has made buns (at least she claims she has, though I reckon she bought them the day before in Majorstuen, and has just reheated them and put an extra raisin on top for decoration). Fred and I each have a present for Mum. We stop by the door and sing Happy Birthday. Dad drowns out the rest of us. His dressing-gown cord has loosened. We sing a second verse. But Mum just remains in bed with her back to us and doesn't even turn round. We fall silent ourselves. Dad grows impatient. 'Vera?' he whispers. 'Happy Birthday!' That doesn't do any good either. It's as if Mum's asleep or else she simply doesn't want to hear us. Boletta becomes restive. 'I think we should leave her alone,' she says. Fred's pale and he's holding his flat gift in both hands. Dad protests. 'Alone? It's her birthday, for heaven's sake!' He blows out the candle flame with his voice and in that moment Mum finally turns round. She's thin and her face is grey and I can barely recognize her at all. Her hair's all tangled, as if she'd never seen the inside of a hairdresser's in her whole life. She takes us in with huge, dry eyes. Perhaps she doesn't know who we are? Perhaps she thinks we're strangers who've just broken in? I've never felt so afraid. I want to cry but don't dare; I just let out one gulp and Fred thumps me in the leg. Dad moves closer still to the bed. Boletta catches his arm but he shakes her off. He can't understand this. He's worried and hurt. 'Are you ill, Vera?' And Mum sits up in bed. 'How old am I today?' she asks. Dad stops. He attempts a laugh. 'Well, have you forgotten that too?' he says. 'How old am I?' she repeats. I'm about to answer myself but Fred thumps me even harder in the leg. Instead Dad tells her. 'Today, my dear, you're no less than, and not a single hour more than, thirty-five years of age.' Mum lies back down and is just a shadow on the bed. 'And what have I got out of my life?' she asks. She answers her own question. 'Nothing!' she says, and thumps her fist into the mattress. 'Nothing!' I don't want her to talk like this. How will we ever go on if Mum is unhappy and just gives up? Is she angry with us? What have we done? I clench my teeth until I feel it in my jaws. Boletta puts down the plate of buns and coffee. 'Well, well,' she whispers. Dad stands paralysed by the bed and attempts a smile. 'Nothing? You're exaggerating just a mite there.' Mum looks at him and there's a rage in her expression I've never seen before. 'Well, tell me then, Arnold Nilsen! Tell me what I've got out of my life?' Dad thinks a bit. 'First and foremost you've two wonderful sons,' he replies. Mum starts crying. Then Fred goes forward and puts his present on the quilt. 'Happy Birthday, Mum,' he says in a loud voice. Mum hesitates and opens it with slow hands. It's a breadboard. Fred's made it himself in woodwork. At the top he's burnt in: TO MUM FROM FRED; the letters are crooked and brown and still smell scorched, but not one of them's out of place. Mum barely looks at it. 'Thanks,' she says, her voice low. Disappointment's writ large in Fred's face – it's branded on him – he swallows and tries to disguise it but doesn't succeed. Dad pats his shoulder. Fred seethes and twists away. Then it's my turn. I give my present to Mum. She opens it, equally slowly, as if everything's a labour to her. It's a napkin ring. 'Thanks,' she mumbles, without so much as looking at me. And she puts both the breadboard and the napkin ring straight into the drawer of her bedside table and hides under the quilt once more. Dad's worried. 'Now you just need some bread and a napkin,' he says. There's silence from the bed. 'Now that you have a board and a ring, I mean.' He laughs loudly. He's the only one who does. Mum looks at him, with the narrowest eyes in Fagerborg. 'If all you have to offer me is your fake laughter then you can get out!'

Dad just stands there. He feels wounded. Deeply wounded. But he remains where he is. He tightens the cord of his dressing gown. Boletta's gone for the Malaga and pours a generous measure, but Mum can't be bothered with that either. Boletta drinks it herself and I breathe in the hot, sweet scent which in a moment of giddiness makes me forget that it's Mum's birthday at all, and that she's unhappy and doesn't care for the presents we've made. 'It's not my laughter I'm giving you,' Dad says, his voice trembling. 'What is it then?' Mum asks, and doesn't even look at him. Boletta pours more Malaga into the glass. But Mum still won't have any. I turn to Fred. His fists are clenched. Dad goes even closer to the bed. 'It's not my laughter I'm giving you,' he repeats. 'It's your own. Because I make you laugh.' 'Not any more,' Mum whispers. Dad shakes his head a long while over those words. 'Shouldn't I, who's carried a suitcase full of applause through Europe, manage to make Vera Nilsen in Church Road laugh?' Mum sighs and waves him away with a small hand, all the fingers hanging down. I know now. She's tired of us. She wants to be rid of us. It hurts right down to my tummy. It burns somewhere under my heart. And then Dad does what he always does best. Perhaps he's waited for just this moment to chance everything on his last card. He goes towards the door, stooped and silent. Then all at once he stops and spins round again. He stands tall and snaps his fingers, as if all of a sudden he's remembered something he forgot to mention. He turns the situation round. He turns all the wrongness of the moment inside out and wins the public over to his side. He makes it unbearable to endure. He magics laughter from melancholy. Oh, I wish Dad had said it in the first place! 'If I can't get you to laugh any more, perhaps you might care to join me on a trip to Italy instead?' There's complete silence in the bedroom. We stare at him. He bobs up and down in his worn-out slippers and finds half a cigar in his dressing gown that he sticks in his mouth. Even Mum's restless and soon won't be able to stop herself turning round in bed. 'What are you talking about?' Boletta demands. 'I'm talking about magnificent Italy,' Dad replies. Boletta gives a loud snort and has some more Malaga. But slowly Mum gets up. 'Italy?' she whispers. And this is Dad's triumph. He's put colour in Mum's cheeks. He's breathed into her hair. He's won her over again. He gives a glance over his shoulder and looks at me, as if we've achieved this conquest together on the morning of her thirty-fifth birthday in August 1960 – with a breadboard, a napkin ring and an Italian dream. Dad puts the cigar back in his pocket and sits down on the bed. He's filled with peace now. He has us in the palm of his hand. We are all tied to the same string and he stretches it; he tightens and stretches it till it's on the point of snapping, till Mum raises her hand to tear the rest from him physically. But he gets in just before her. 'Once upon a time you came north with me to the island farthest out in the ocean to have Barnum baptized. And now I want to take you even farther south.' Mum's silent once more. She has question marks in both eyes. It's Dad's turn to sigh, not heavily, but good-naturedly and indulgently. 'Might it not be an idea to visit Fleming Brant, the Old One's necrophilic friend in Bellagio?' he suggests. Boletta stamps her foot. 'He wrote her obituary, Arnold Nilsen! That was all!' Dad just laughs. 'Ah, what's the difference! What d'you say, Mum? Are you coming?' 'We can't afford it,' she whispers. Dad just shrugs his shoulders, enjoying every minute of this now. 'Maybe we can,' he replies. And he produces a packet from his dressing gown, as if he's performing a magic trick, and when he folds the brown paper on top to one side we see that it's money – stacks of banknotes – and we huddle up, holding our breath. I grab Fred's hand and he doesn't let go. 'Italian lire,' Dad whispers. Boletta snorts all the louder. 'It's not worth more than an øre piece!' she exclaims. Dad doesn't pay the least attention to her. His attention is focused on Mum who lifts one of the thin notes and lets it fall equally fast – worried, mistrusting, and back to her former state. 'Where have these come from?' she demands. Dad realizes that he's in danger of losing ground, that he has to keep up the momentum. He has to dispel this anxiety, remove the doubt. He has his answer ready. 'This is the final settlement for the Buick, at long last, my love.' He says this and kisses her cheek. She lets him do it. Boletta all but comes between them. 'And how are you planning on getting to Italy? Are we going on foot?' Dad glances up at her and his face is etched with patience. And now he manages to crown it all. He surpasses himself. He's on first name terms with God Himself that day. 'I rather thought we might drive there,' he replies. And he points to the window. We run over and tear back the curtains. And down in the street there's just one solitary car. It's not exactly a Buick Roadmaster Cabriolet. It's a black box with wheels. It's a Volvo Duett. And Dad has bought himself new gloves for driving, made of black leather. He puts his arms round Mum. 'Happy birthday, darling,' he says.

That same evening she asks in a low voice, 'How did you get hold of that car?' I lie in bed listening. I hear Dad clearing his throat and beginning to pace the floor. 'I'll make a long story short,' he begins. 'Yes, you do that!' Now it's Boletta's turn to be loud. 'Be quiet,' Mum says to her. 'A friend owed me a favour,' Dad murmurs. 'Which friend?' Mum demands. Dad lets out a peal of laughter. 'I have many friends,' he replies.

I can't sleep that night. Joy renders me sleepless. We're going on a summer holiday. We're going abroad. I've been given an Italian coin by Dad to practise with. I say the word in to myself – *lire, lire*. It's so light in my hand and worth less than an øre. And this weightless coin reminds me of Mum's dark depression that morning; it's the shadow over my joy that night. What can I buy with a coin like this? What'll I do with it then? I drop the coin onto the floor and don't even hear it landing. 'Why was Mum so sad?' I ask carefully. But Fred isn't there and there's no one to answer me.

We left two days later. Dad drove, Mum was the navigator and Fred and I sat in the back with Boletta between us. She was awkward and demanded so much room that we had to press our cheeks against the windows. It wasn't much after four when we drove down Jacob Aall Street and out of the silent and abandoned city, where not even the paperboys were up. Our black box was stuffed with suitcases, bags, flasks, petrol cans, sleeping-bags and suntan lotion; we drove past the fiord that resembled polished linoleum, because Mum did at least manage to find the road to Moss. But just before Moss she got carsick; Dad had to park at the side of the road while she knelt in the ditch and vomited for quite a while. Perhaps it was because the Volvo Duett had worse suspension than a toboggan. In the meantime Dad felt that it was becoming a strain having to look at the map while driving at sixty kilometres an hour. 'What's the point of this!' Boletta exclaimed, and was equally reluctant. 'The point?' Dad repeated. We were waiting outside the car. Everything was beautiful that morning, except for Mum. She was still down on her knees. Boletta pointed at her. 'Don't you see that you get ill travelling like this?' Dad lit a cigarette. 'Yes, travelling's strange when you're used to a sedentary existence,' he admitted. Boletta went up to him. 'Shut up!' she shouted. Dad just laughed. 'I well remember she got seasick on land as well.' But Boletta wasn't about to give in. 'It's a sacrilege to disturb the dead,' she hissed. Dad gave a start. 'Dead? Is Fleming Brant dead?' Boletta was uncharacteristically aggressive. 'I know nothing about that, Arnold Nilsen. But the Old One is dead and we are not going to disturb her.' Mum got up from the ditch and took a deep breath. 'Let's go on,' she said. Dad clapped his hands, hesitated a second, then finally pointed at me. 'From now on you're my navigator, Barnum.'

I changed places with Mum. I was the navigator. I sat beside Dad. He had to have three cushions to see over the steering wheel. I got to borrow Fred's sleeping-bag to sit on. I had a wonderful view. I laid the map of Europe in my

lap and followed the red lines with my finger. We were off
again. There had been a time when I'd thought we could
just trundle our way to Italy (it was downhill all the way,
after all); that it was simply a question of crossing
Majorstuen when the lights changed to green and that
was it. Now I knew better. It's both up and down and
there's no short cut. A navigator needs to know that.
'How far is it to Helsingborg?' Dad asked. 'It's 565 kilometres from Oslo to Helsingborg,' I told him. 'But we've
already driven forty-two miles.' 'In that case we'll make
the ferry before dinner time,' Dad said with satisfaction.
'And the ferry to Helsingør takes twenty-five minutes,' I
informed him. 'Good, Barnum!' Dad slapped my thigh.
'And how far is it to the moon, you jerk?' Fred demanded.
Even Boletta laughed. We wound down our windows and
ate dry buns. We were the only ones on the road. A train
passed over the empty fields. People waved from the last
carriage. We waved back. The sun rose and emptied its
light over everything, and the air was clear and mild. If
God had seen us then He might have thought the car we
sat in was just a matchbox blown over the world He'd
sent out into space.

We got petrol at Svinesund and bought Villa mineral
water and Kit Kat bars in the little kiosk. Mum and
Boletta joined the queue for the ladies' and Dad had to
produce a whole bundle of papers for those on duty at the
border. Then we were let through. We were abroad. I
didn't notice any difference, except that we had to drive
on the left. There wasn't so much as a bump where
Norway became Sweden, and the sky looked exactly the
same. 'How far is it to Helsingborg, my *pojke*?' Dad asked
me. Perhaps that was what happened when you went
abroad. You immediately started speaking Swedish. And
when we crossed into Italy, would we be able to speak
Italian too? I did every calculation I could on the map.
'425 kilometres, Dad,' I was still speaking Norwegian, as
far as I could tell at any rate. 'But how far is it to Göteborg?' he wanted to know now. I did my adding and sub-

tracting of the miniscule figures written alongside the various roads on the maps. Soon I wouldn't be able to see any more. My eyes were carsick and I shouldn't have eaten that bar of chocolate. 'Eleven miles,' I murmured. 'In that case we can eat in Göteborg, right?' My stomach was a spinning drum. I kept swallowing and swallowing. Borders and roads and towns and lakes floated together into one nameless zone. Perhaps I couldn't cope with driving on the left? Dad glanced at me. 'How are you doing, Barnum?' he inquired. 'I'm sorry,' I told him. Now I was talking Swedish too. And then I was sick. I vomited all over the map, the dashboard, the steering wheel and the windscreen. I broke in two. Dad screeched to a halt, Mum shrieked, Fred laughed, Boletta went on sleeping and a bus roared past blaring its horn. I fell down into the ditch at the side of the road and got rid of what remained in my stomach. My mouth, my nose and my eyes were all running. Every orifice was in action. And ever since, I've got carsick even thinking of figures or glancing at a map. I failed geography miserably and have never managed to pass my driving test. My time as a navigator was over – three kilometres into Sweden. Mum hung up the map to dry. Boletta got out some clean clothes for me. Dad washed the car and Fred shinned up a tree and wouldn't come down again. But when I came to once more he was sitting in the front with Dad and I was lying in a bundle between Mum and Boletta. I could smell the sea. I got up. We could look across to Denmark. We were an hour in the queue. After that we drove on-board the ferry. We climbed to the upper deck because you don't get seasick if you can see the horizon. In the middle of Øresund Dad began talking Danish. 'D'you want some ale, Boletta?' he asked. But Boletta didn't bother replying. She just turned away and went off into the saloon. She was becoming more and more difficult the further south we went. She didn't want to go to Køge and see the house where the Old One had been born, nor did she want to go to the zoo and see the musk oxen that were direct descendants of the beasts that had been finally brought back to the King's city by the SS *Antarctic* in December 1900. 'It's wrong to disturb the dead,' she said again.

It was already late evening by the time we trundled onto land once more in Helsingør. Dark was falling over Denmark. Fred had to use a pocket torch to see the map. We ate fried plaice at a roadside inn. Finally Dad was able to drink his ale. Mum asked if there were any rooms available – there weren't, but if we had a tent we'd be welcome to put it up in the garden. We didn't and slept instead in the car. Once we'd stowed our luggage on the roof-rack and put down all the seats, there was just about sufficient room for the lot of us. Fred preferred to sleep outside. Boletta talked in her sleep. I didn't understand what she was saying. Perhaps it was her night language, a tongue only she could comprehend? Mum gently told her to be quiet. Dad breathed heavily through his nose; it was a wind instrument. I edged open the door and crept out to join Fred. He was awake too. I sat down beside him. The sky was bigger here than in Norway, probably because Denmark was so flat. A Danish insect hummed by and left the stillness even more pronounced. 'Why's Boletta so strange?' I whispered. 'Boletta isn't strange,' Fred replied. 'What is it then?' 'She's old, Barnum.' I loved it when Fred talked to me like this. I leaned my head against his shoulder. 'Are you looking forward to it?' I asked. 'To what?' 'Italy, of course.' Fred was silent for a bit. 'Wish we'd gone to Greenland instead,' he said. At that moment we heard a strange sound, a whirring in the dark, a wave that beat against us without getting us wet. Fred got up and started walking, in the opposite direction from the car. I went after him. We got closer. We went into the wave and stopped. A great wheel was rolling through the night and yet stood still too; or perhaps it was a bird that couldn't get off the ground. It was a windmill. And a memory was reawakened within me, there where we waited in the depths of the Danish night – a memory that was invisible and heavy, outside my consciousness and inexplicable to me, and therefore not fixed in my mind. It was more like a scar, an imprint – put there in dreams – and something first interpreted only when I returned to Røst, years later, like a refugee, and found the sorrowful remains of Dad's invention on the heights of Veddøya.

We reached Flensburg the following day and were waved across the border by two men in tight-fitting uniforms. Boletta was our navigator now, and she'd folded Europe away and put it in the glove compartment a long time ago. I think what she wanted more than anything was for Dad to go the wrong way. I wanted him to speak German to us but instead he was silent and sullen. He wanted to get on and he swung down onto the autobahn. It went to Hamburg, where we were to stay the night. I saw nothing except the speedometer needle rising towards a hundred. The Volvo Duett shook. We had to hold tight. But we were still overtaken the whole time. Low sports cars chased past us and it was just as if we were standing still. We were the slowest. Dad pushed our speed up to 110. It made no difference. His new gloves were slippery on the steering wheel. He was sweating. Everyone else was just driving faster. I grew sad. How could we be last when we'd never driven so fast before? And Dad told us about those drivers who become *speed blind*, who think they're standing still and get out of the car while driving sixty at least. Ever since I've always thought that Fred wasn't dyslexic – *word* blind – but rather *speed* blind; he left language too quickly. Then everyone had to slow down anyway since a bit further on blue lights were flashing; something had happened, an accident. Perhaps it was a word-blind driver who'd mis-read a sign. I caught a glimpse of a crashed car and the accident's detritus – an arm, blood on the tarmac, clothes, a kneeling woman, a stretcher, a dead dog and a crumpled pram – before Mum put her hands over my eyes and held me tight. She held me like that all the way to Hamburg where we got lost at a roundabout, and it was then Dad first began talking, and it was Norwegian he spoke. All of a sudden a guy ran out onto the road in front of us waving his arms and pointing at something, and we thought we had a puncture, that that was what he was trying to tell us. Dad swung up onto the pavement and wound down his window. The stranger bent down and looked in, beaming. He had a scar in the corner of his mouth which was like an extension of his smile. 'Norway?' he said, his accent rather broken. Dad nodded. 'Norway?' he said again. 'Yes,' Dad said. 'We're from Norway. What do you want?' The German stuck his arm through the window to shake hands with each of us. 'I was in Norway during the war,' he explained. 'A magnificent fatherland!' Dad stared at him, incredulous. Boletta pushed his hand away as if it was unclean and infected. Mum put her arm round Fred and me. The smiling German with the scar on his face was moved. He wiped away a tear. 'I hope I can come back to Norway one day,' he whispered. Then Dad snapped. He took off his glove and exposed his mutilated fist; it was as if he clenched that fist with all its missing fingers and shook it right under the German's jaw. But then all at once he changed his mind. Perhaps he remembered we'd got lost at a Hamburg roundabout and that it was late in the evening and we'd still nowhere to stay because none of us was keen to spend another night in the boot of a Volvo Duett. Instead the injured fist relaxed in friendship and the man took the lump of flesh in both hands and wept. 'We're just two injured soldiers, you and I,' he whispered. Dad was greatly moved. 'Could you recommend a hotel round here?' he inquired, and quickly drew back his arm. 'Only the best is good enough for you,' the German said, and pointed in the opposite direction. 'On the right hand side of the lower lake you'll find Vier Jahrzieten.' Dad wound up his window so it closed with a thud and spun the car away from the pavement. I turned and saw the German soldier, the polite loser, still standing at the roundabout with his hat raised in salute. 'Oh, yes, you really won that war, Arnold Nilsen,' Boletta said. 'Couldn't you just have knocked him down?' Dad didn't reply. He leaned pale and sullen against the steering wheel and pulled on the glove with the artificial fingers. Someone tooted their horn behind us. There were cars everywhere. We just flowed with the traffic down into Hamburg, as in a river on wheels, and there, beside a small lake surrounded by a thin belt of trees, lay the hotel, Vier Jahrzieten. Dad stopped in front of the broad steps. A doorman stood in attendance on the red carpet. 'It looks dear,' Mum breathed. Dad just smiled, brushed back his hair, polished his shoes with his handkerchief, lit a cigarette and went up the steps – quickly giving some money to the little doorman. Up at the top another employee opened a golden door to admit him. We waited. Time went by. 'Can't we just turn and drive home?' Boletta whispered. Mum was annoyed and leaned forward between the seats. 'You are not going to ruin this holiday for me!' Boletta turned round and said for the last time, 'You shouldn't disturb the dead.' Just then the doorman pressed his face against the windscreen to take a look at us. He resembled a clown with his shining lips and white cheeks. Boletta raised her fist and he retreated, bowing, to the red carpet. 'Perhaps the rooms have showers,' Mum murmured. We sat in silence then, just waiting. We could see guests in the foyer slowly walking back and forth with glasses and cigarettes and sparkling jewels. Eventually Dad returned. He shoved the doorman to one side, tumbled into the car behind the wheel and drove off. He was angry about something or other. His hands were shaking so badly he could barely manage to steer. 'There were no vacant rooms,' he mumbled. Mum attempted a smile. 'No vacant rooms?' Dad breathed heavily. 'And just be thankful there weren't!' he shouted. 'That wretched youth hostel of a place only had five stars anyway.' Boletta glanced at him. 'Five stars? Isn't that a lot?' Dad roared with laughter. 'I've stayed in hotels with ten stars and that's twice as many as five!' Boletta laughed herself. 'Perhaps we weren't good enough for Vier Jahrzeiten,' she suggested. Dad fell silent and had to stop at the corner. He was in a black mood again. Mum dried the sweat from his brow and could have wrung the handkerchief out afterwards. 'What do we do now?' she asked carefully. Dad produced a map of Hamburg from his pocket. In the middle of the creased paper there was a cross. 'In their great charity they recommended a hotel in Grosse Freiheit,' he replied. 'Grosse Freiheit?' Mum repeated. 'It's a well-known street here, love. We have to look out for an elephant.' We drove on – not down, but in – to the loudness and the light which quickly engulfed us, all the way till we reached the inner chambers of the city's godless heart. It was a heart that beat madly and unevenly, a wonderful systole that made the car's bonnet shudder; and finally we came to a halt in a blood clot in a narrow street where the windows were all red. I glanced out. I saw women with naked thighs, sailors drinking beer, shadows that resembled dogs in dark alleyways, men with high heels and doormen enticing people to come inside. Mum put her hands over my eyes again, hard this time, so I could barely breathe. 'An elephant?' she murmured. Dad pointed. 'There!' he exclaimed. Mum let go her hold and down a lane we saw a sign with an elephant on it. Its trunk hung in a circle which shone in several colours. Dad drove the last part of the way there and parked in front of the entrance. The place was called the Indra Club. There was no red carpet, no doorman and no stars. 'Have you taken us to the circus?' Boletta asked. Dad said nothing. He sat thinking for a bit. Then, all of a sudden, he'd made up his mind. He wanted us all to come with him and to bring our luggage there and then. Fred and I took our cases through the door of the Indra Club. We came to a cloakroom. Behind the counter a man with a shaved head stood looking at us in amazement. And at last Dad talked in German. He spoke at length and he spoke fluently, and I haven't the slightest idea what it was he said. But the bald man listened intently, pointed to the ceiling and mentioned something which sounded like a figure. Dad turned to us with satisfaction. 'I've just got us

a room on the first floor!' he announced. We were led
through a smoky place where a handful of guests sat at
round tables drinking from wide glasses with handles.
They looked at us as we passed, and smiling, shook their
heads – foam on their mouths. On a stage right back
against the wall there was a set of drums and three ampli-
fiers. A black electric guitar lay on the floor. Then we went
up a steep, angled staircase and arrived at what was to
pass for our room for the night. Mum stood there staring.
There wasn't even a washbasin. The double bed sagged in
the middle and it had obviously been a fair time since the
sheet was changed. On the window sill there was a light
with a red lampshade full of flies. On the pillow was half
a roll of toilet paper. Even Dad himself had to take a deep
breath. 'We'll just have to make the best of it,' he said.
Boletta sat down on the one and only chair. 'But not with
the best of them now,' she murmured. Fred rolled out the
sleeping-bags. Mum crept out into the corridor to find a
shower. She came back almost immediately, even paler
than before. 'What is it?' Dad asked. Mum had already
begun gathering up her things. 'Are we really going to
spend the night in a brothel?' she shouted. Dad blinked.
'A brothel?' Mum was seething. 'Oh, yes! A brothel!
There are women in these rooms!' Dad tried to put his
arms round her but his attempt failed – not even laughter
was a help now. 'I'm not staying here one second longer!'
she hissed. And with that we left the room, our bill and
the Indra Club hastily and soundlessly. Mum had her
hand on my neck and whispered the whole time, 'Look
straight ahead, Barnum. Look straight ahead!' We
reached the bottom of the stairs and discovered a rear exit
on the ground floor. And just as we sneaked out I caught
sight of five boys in tight trousers and lilac jackets jumping onto the stage, picking up their guitars and drumsticks. I stood still for a moment. I wanted to hear this.
The tallest of them leaned towards the microphone,
twisted his mouth, counted in English – *one, two, one two
three four* – and was about to begin singing. I saw his lips

shaping into a yell. I saw the chords on the guitars, the drumsticks falling heavily towards the drums, the pointed black shoes about to begin keeping time. And right at that moment, before they started, before the five boys began – in a strange and heavy silence as in the seconds between lightning and thunder – Mum pulled me away and the door closed behind us. We ran to the front, chucked suitcases and bags in the boot, flung ourselves into the car, and Dad drove off as fast as he could between the neon lights and the stars. And the last I managed to glimpse of Hamburg was a gaudy poster on a brick wall – *The Beatles. England. Liverpool.*

We reached Bellagio the following evening and stopped at a sharp bend before the town. We got out of the car. Only Boletta sat where she was, her arms folded. The sun went down behind the green hills and all the steep roofs shone like dark, angled mirrors. It was just like the sea sinking too from blue to black. The air was full of still, hot wind. A row of narrow, pointed trees hung like dark knives on a hill above the graveyard, impaled on the sky. Dad, who'd been singing opera ever since Austria so as not to nod off at the wheel, and who could barely stand on his feet, drew us close. Thus we stood together in the humming dark of Lombardy. We had got there. 'What do we do now?' Mum murmured.

First of all we found the police station. It was beside the market-place. We parked there. Three officers came out right away and peered in curiosity at our number plate. Dad wound down the window and greeted them. Dad spoke Italian. It was unbelievable that there was room for so many languages in the one mouth. They spoke at length. Mum followed it all with pride and continually put her finger to her lips as if she were afraid we might disturb him. But we were dumb with wonder. Even Boletta had to raise an eyebrow. And I like to think this was Dad's finest hour, the high point of his shady career, when he spoke in Italian with the officers at Bellagio market-place. Already a crowd of people had gathered round the car. Perhaps they'd never seen a Volvo Duett in Italy before. Dad wound up his window again, the conversation over. 'They knew who Fleming Brant was all right,' he said, and tantalizingly revealed no more for a time. Boletta shut her eyes and Mum had to drag it out of him. 'So tell us then,' she begged. Dad smiled. 'They call him the Red Dog.' 'The Red Dog?' 'Why?' 'Don't ask me,' Dad replied. 'But he works at the Villa Serbelloni.'

A flock of thin, golden boys ran ahead of us to show us the way. The Villa Serbelloni was a hotel. It lay right out on a spit of land which extended deep into Lake Como, and it resembled a castle with its arches, pillars and terraces. This had to be a place for those with nothing less than blue blood. The boys didn't dare go any further and they disappeared in the shadows under the palms. Dad slowed gradually and finally stopped the car by the tennis-court which lay deserted in the floodlights that made the red gravel glow. We got out of the car. Our eyes were like saucers. Never had we seen anything like this before. A man in dress coat and tails was coming quickly to meet us. Dad asked for Fleming Brant. And as soon as Dad had mentioned the name Fleming Brant we were treated like kings and queens. A veritable army of doormen arrived to take our luggage. A chauffeur in grey uniform parked the Volvo in the garage on the other side of the hotel and we were all but carried up the wide steps. 'I said we were related to him,' Dad whispered. The ceiling above the reception was so high I got dizzy and Fred had to keep me upright. Boletta wanted to leave, but Mum kept hold of her. Dad put a pile of banknotes on the table. The receptionist smiled and got down a huge key from a board. Then the head waiter appeared too. He bowed and showed us into the dining-room. Guests looked up from their dinners. Waiters wheeled trolleys groaning with cakes and strange fruit. A man sat on his own right in at the corner. It was a long way away. Boletta wanted to go back but Mum wouldn't let her. The man was extremely old. He wore white gloves and dark glasses. He read from a book as he drank coffee from a tiny green cup. The skin of his face was rough and ruddy, as if he'd sat for too long in the sun, and his hair was white and thin. It was Fleming Brant. He didn't notice us until we'd reached his table. He laid down his book, Dante's *Divina Commedia*, and got up, amazed, reeling as he did because he recognized us, or saw the Old One again in us. And I couldn't see all that this brief meeting constituted; I only knew that this moment was bigger than itself, that here time came together. But this I did see – Fleming Brant's sorrowful serenity, a dark joy, as he slowly took off his glasses and lowered his pained gaze. It was Mum who offered her hand in greeting. 'We've come to thank you,' she said. 'Thank me?' But Fleming Brant wasn't looking at Mum. He was looking rather at Boletta. 'For the beautiful words that you wrote about my mother, Ellen Jebsen.' Fleming Brant just stood in silence in front of Boletta, and Boletta herself was lost for words. Slowly he turned towards Mum again. 'Sit down,' he whispered. He spoke slowly. Waiters were there in the blink of an eye with more chairs. A trolley of fruit and cakes was brought over and bottles of wine and glasses put on the table. We sat down. I thought that it had to be Fleming Brant who owned the hotel – maybe he had the lake and the whole town into the bargain. He picked up the book he'd been reading. 'It was my dream that one day Ellen Jebsen would play the part of Beatrice in Dante's *Comedy*,' he said. 'Is it funny?' I asked. Fleming Brant thought for a moment. 'Yes, it is. What's your name?' 'Barnum,' I replied. Fleming Brant put on his sunglasses again. 'I'm very moved,' he said, his voice low. Dad extended his hand. 'And I'm Arnold Nilsen!' They shook hands – one black and one white glove – and Fleming Brant withdrew his hand first and apologized for doing so. 'I have this rash,' he exclaimed. 'Eczema. I got it from the films.' 'Yes, they called you the Red Dog,' Dad laughed. There was silence for a few seconds. Fleming Brant looked down. 'I couldn't tolerate the light and the chemicals. I gradually fell to pieces.' Mum looked at him. 'Were you an actor yourself?' she asked. Fleming Brant shook his head and smiled, but it was a sad smile. 'I cut the films,' he replied.

Later on we went up to the room. It was larger than the flat in Church Road. There was a four-poster bed, bath, shower and veranda. Mum was such a long time in the bath that in the end we had to check on her. She lay there laughing in a cloud of foam. Dad sat down on the side of the bath. Mum put her wet naked arm about him. We had got there. We had found Fleming Brant. Soon we would turn round once more. Then Fred spoke and he hadn't said anything the entire evening. 'Where's Boletta?' Mum fell silent. Dad rolled up his sleeve, took off the glove from his good hand and plunged it into the foam. 'Not here,' he said. But Mum wasn't amused. She got up quickly and I looked the other way. Fred was standing over by the window. I went to join him. And down there on the terrace was Boletta, together with Fleming Brant; they were the only ones there, the other tables were deserted and the lights along the balcony rail cast blue shadows beyond them. A waiter came out with a blanket and Fleming Brant laid it over Boletta's shoulders. I thought, without knowing it, that now she'd disturbed the dead just the same. 'I can't believe he's anything but an exceptionally rich man,' Dad said.

I see Fleming Brant the following morning. I'm out on the veranda before the others are awake. He's standing down on the beach. His face is withering away. The skin is flaking. He supports himself against a rake. Then the first guests arrive – both men and women – hand in hand. Silently they go out into the water and start swimming. And Fleming Brant rakes away their tracks in the sand, laboriously, from the steps and down to the edge where the first waves are lapping. And when the guests come out of the water again and hurry towards the terrace and breakfast, it's Fleming Brant who has to rake away their prints, so the sand can be smooth and even for the new guests coming.

   And this is my memory – of windmills in the night, the band I never heard, and the cutter of films who rakes away footprints in the sand – so carefully and efficiently that nothing shows. And when I go down shortly onto the same beach the cutter of films will follow me too and rake over my tracks in the cool, light sand that falls away beneath my feet.

Barnum's Ruler

I'm not saying how tall I am. It's recorded in the school doctor's notes. It's marked on the door frame in our room. It's entered in my passport. But my eyes are blue, not brown. I only inherited Dad's stature. I didn't grow any taller. Right to that day when the constable cursed me in the little city in front of the whole class I wasn't particularly different. Except for my curls which old ladies in kiosks and on trams yearned to touch. But after that I somehow lagged behind. I came to a standstill, while the others rose about me – rose and rose like some forest gone to seed. I was left down there in among the moss and the pine needles, a prisoner for ever of my own wretched centimetres. And considering that growth is greatest in the early years and reduces thereafter until one grows less than a fraction of a centimetre by the time one reaches thirty and starts shrinking thereafter, my prospects were pretty bleak. It's of little comfort to learn that the heart keeps growing to the very last. Of no comfort to me either that I'd certainly have been above the minimum height required to enlist in the Roman army round about 200 BC. That was one metre fifty-one. Even the girls shot past me – with their long legs and straight necks I was hardly worth a second glance. When they did occasionally look at me, they looked down, right down – and I think they enjoyed that, looking down on me, because it meant I had to look up to them. What else were they to use their new-found height for if not to look down? I've been called Tom Thumb, toadstool, titch, dwarf, pygmy, midge, pipe cleaner and semicolon – as if my real name wasn't enough to be lumbered with. There was no choice about it. I remember one time I was on my way home from school. It was in October. It was raining;

of course it had to be raining. Fortunately I escaped
having to wear wellingtons because they more or less
went up to my groin. I refused to be seen dead with an
umbrella or a sou'wester. I just had a short yellow raincoat and simply got wet. I didn't care. I felt those curls
that I hated so much, but couldn't rid myself of nonetheless, being plastered flat over my head as hair should lie.
I liked the rain. I've always liked it. Sun's a drag. Sun
hounds you. With rain you can rest among the drops. I
pottered through Urra Park. I tended to stop at the church
and lean over the railing to look down on the tram as it
passed by. Now and again someone standing at the back
would wave up to me. I'd wave down to them. It felt good
to look down, to look down on somebody and wave to
them at the same time. That day there wasn't a single passenger at the back of the tram. I waved just the same and
thought about everything you do that no one ever sees.
And when you shut your eyes, how could you really and
truly be sure that everything didn't disappear for that
time and reappear when you opened them again? Was
that how God had created the world, by blinking twice?
What if God were to get tired and close His eyes again,
once and for all, or if He got fed up and fell asleep? I stood
leaning against the railing in the rain, lost in my own
thoughts. If God had decided everything already, what
was the point then? It made no difference what you did
because everything would happen as it had to anyway. By
the way, Fred had started at a new school right in the city.
Perhaps God had a hand in all that too. The teachers said
that Fred was stupid and had to go into a special class at
the boys' school in Stener Street. Class F it was – yes,
Class F; designed for boys who for one reason or another
had fallen behind in primary school. Some said that the
boys there were so thick they couldn't have managed to
find their way to the girls' school in Osterhaus Street,
even if you were to supply them with map and compass
and follow them half the way there. You could say plenty
about Fred, but stupid was one thing he wasn't, and God

ought to have known that all right. Yet there was something about his letters he couldn't quite manage. Of course he could talk fine and well, but on paper everything went to pieces. He would write his name as *Ferd* and everyone laughed their heads off at this to begin with. Once he wrote *Branum* on a present for me. I thought it sounded all right. *To Branum.* I had no objection to being called that. And it was the best present I've ever been given – a real typewriter. But soon enough the sniggering melted away and no one laughed any more, barring me, and when Fred kept writing *Ferd* and was reading Ibsen's *Peer Gnyt* the teacher gave him a clip on the ear you could have heard over by the bins on the far side, and everyone put their hands to their heads as if to ease a soreness they could feel themselves. The school had decided that Fred was sufficiently stupid and now he was down in the slums in Stener Street together with the city's morons – all branded backward, hopeless and impossible. I gobbed down on the cobbles and then heard someone approaching between the raindrops, long before the gob landed. I opened my eyes and turned round. I knew it. It was the gang from the seventh grade – Aslak, Preben and Hamster. They were smiling nastily, with toothy smiles and I couldn't stop thinking that if I hadn't shut my eyes this would never have happened.

Then the sound was turned up – the whine of the tram at the sharp bend behind the school, the trees rustling in the rain, the tyres on the wet tarmac like long sighs through the city, and the gob landing with a crack in Holte Street. 'Where're you going, eh?' 'Home,' I whispered. 'Home? Sure of that, eh?' I nodded. 'Quite sure, huh?' I nodded again. 'Maybe we'll come with you, shall we?'

All at once the church bells began ringing – for some reason or other they suddenly started ringing. Maybe somebody had forgotten their own funeral in all the rain. The birds scattered from the rooftops. I froze like a tulip. Aslak, Preben and Hamster came closer and bent down towards me; they sniffed at my face like mad dogs. I had to close my eyes again and just wait for them to bite, bite like bitches, or for the end of the world and for everything to disappear. That would be best. 'Just what I told you. His face smells of fanny.' Slowly I opened my eyes. The bells had stopped. They held their noses and backed away. 'Old fanny. That's what he stinks of. Bloody hell.' Aslak quickly bent towards me again – all but banged my forehead – then backed off once more. 'Sure it's not cock he smells of. I reckon it's boy fanny and cock too.' 'Yeah, it must be both. His face smells of fanny and cock.'

They stood there staring at me. The railing was hurting my back. After a while they looked at each other instead and whispered together. That was worse. Now they weren't going to leave it at that. Aslak laughed. 'What have you got in your school-bag, eh, Fanny? Pipe cleaners or knickers for your face, huh?' There wasn't a lot of point in answering them. They pulled my bag off me, opened it and emptied everything over the railing – my pencil case, my geography jotter, my eraser, half a packet of sandwiches with sausage, my home economic books and my ruler. Everything floated through the rain and landed on the cobblestones in Holte Street between the shining tramlines. Then they put my bag on my back again and took it in turns to pat me on the head. 'Weren't you on your way home, Peg?' I started walking. Peg was a new name. They followed me. They didn't say a word. That was almost the worst of it. They just followed me and I could do nothing but keep walking, over Bøgstad Road, past Rosenborg cinema where the old film was being removed from the advertising boards – *Days of Wine and Roses* – and the new film hadn't yet been displayed. It was right between the two screenings; the guy from the ticket booth was carrying a pile of dog-eared photos of Jack Lemmon and Lee Remick with him into his booth. It was the interval and I walked on in my own darkness – Aslak, Preben and Hamster hard on my heels – and a raindrop ran inside my shirt and clung there like a stamp at the bottom of my back. Do I not remember that? Do I not remember how many paces there are from Uranienborg church to Sten Park on an afternoon in October, when it's raining and you're being followed and your brother has started at another school on the wrong side of town? It's 634 steps. I missed Fred. None of this would have happened if he hadn't made such a mess of his letters and written his name wrong. And then he did come. Fred came out of the toilets down at the bottom of the hill. He had a cigarette in one hand and with the other he was pulling up the zip of his trousers. Wet and thin he stood there in his suede jacket which had turned dark in the rain. I heard the steps at my back come to a standstill. Fred put the cigarette in his mouth and inhaled deeply; the glowing end came close to his lips before he spat it out and it burned on in the wet. He didn't say a word. He just looked at me. No one said a thing. I was standing in the middle. Then he looked up, just a little, and stared over my shoulder, past me, for perhaps just a second. Not more than a second, but time somehow stretched in that moment, like a heavy drop beneath a leaking tap. Anything could happen now and I just stood there, between Fred and the gang from the seventh grade. Then I heard them turning and leaving, for few could bear Fred's gaze for any length of time – there was a dark calm in his eyes which was unendurable. And Aslak, Preben and Hamster slunk along by the wall on the other side of the road – dogs that they were – and Aslak turned when they were away a bit and clenched his fist and said something, but that was all. 'Dogs!' I shouted after them. But it's strange to think that when I came to reading obituaries – since that was where I could find out about old acquaintances – I felt a great sadness the morning when I found Preben's full name there. He was just 41, and I felt a real sinking inside me, a profound sadness, even though he'd been a pest and a bully. Aslak had written his obituary. He praised Preben's sense of justice, his loyalty, and above all, his disarming capacity for humour. He'd made a name for himself in the travel industry with so-called adventure expeditions, and died needlessly after diving from a rock face at the end of the Oslo Fiord. Condolences were offered to his wife Pernille and to their daughter. Aslak himself was a legal consultant in the same company (which went bust in the wake of Preben's death), while Hamster had gone off on an adventure expedition inside his own head and got lost on it. He never quite came back after that last shock. I saw him occasionally in town. He begged for money for food. I tended to cross the road to the other side. 'Dogs!' I shouted one more time. 'If you knew!'

Fred stood on the cigarette end in the wet grass and came closer. 'Everything all right, Barnum?' 'Oh, yes. Did you know they were following me, Fred?' 'I was just going for a piss. Lucky for you, Tiny.' I swallowed. There was such a tightness in my throat. 'They emptied my bag,' I whispered. 'Could have been worse,' Fred replied and was obviously beginning to get bored. I held his arm. 'They said my face smelled of fanny.' 'Your face smelled of fanny? Nothing to cry about either. All right?' I nodded. 'You're not crying, Barnum?' I shook my head. 'Because if you are I won't bother standing here with you.' 'I'm not crying, Fred.' 'Good, Barnum.' He pulled back his arm. 'What would you have done if they'd beaten me up?' I asked him. 'I'm not telling you, Barnum. ''Cos then you wouldn't sleep at night.' I laughed loudly and Fred turned and lit another cigarette. I thought he was pissed off at me because I'd laughed, and I wanted to make things all right again by saying something he might like. 'Then they'd certainly smell of fanny in the face,' I said, 'after what you'd do to them. If you did it, I mean.' Fred shrugged his shoulders. He wasn't actually pissed off at all – he'd just turned round to get his cigarette lit because of the breeze. 'Where did they empty your bag?' 'By the church,' I replied. Fred looked at me again. 'And wipe that grin off your face before I do it for you. You look bloody stupid.' I drew the back of my hand quickly over my face.

Fred blew smoke in my face and groaned. Now he was on the point of snapping – I could see it in his eyes – the dark calm was beginning to run, like oil on water, and I had to say something I knew would please him. 'Shall we read the letter tonight?' I asked carefully. Fred looked away. 'I'd read it aloud,' I said, my voice even quieter. Then he laid his hand on my shoulder and it was such a surprise that I almost jumped for joy. But I don't think he heard what I said; he just came back with me to Holte Street and helped me pick up the sorrowful remains of the contents of my bag. My geography jotter had fallen apart – page after page was floating away in the rain. – Turkey, Egypt, America and the polar regions. Parts of the world were drifting in different directions; I found the pages of my test on Greenland which I'd got an A for. The handwriting had been all but washed away, but I could remember what I'd written. *Icebergs can be as high as a hundred metres. But those parts of them underwater are nine times as big.* The gulls had begun fighting over my half packet of sandwiches. My pencil case had been driven over by trams at least three times. My ruler was broken and I might as well write my home economics exercise all over again. 'I reckon I'll empty my bag one of these days,' Fred said, and began walking home while I ran. Fred was always a bit ahead of me and I had to run on my flat feet to have any hope of keeping up with him at all. 'How's the new school?' I asked. 'Damn good. All the idiots in one place.' 'But you're not one of them.' He stopped right outside Rosenborg cinema by the glass cases where new pictures of stars would soon be displayed. He stared at me but said nothing. I got scared again. 'What film d'you think's coming, Fred?' 'One you wouldn't get in to see,' Fred replied. The guy from the ticket booth was standing in the foyer looking out of the doors. Perhaps he wanted to see if it was still raining because all at once he put up an umbrella and the pile of pictures he had under his arm tumbled to the floor. 'Who am I one of?' Fred asked. 'What did you say?' Fred bent close. 'Who am I one of?' I didn't know what to say. It was in his eyes again, that utter darkness. 'I can help you with your letters,' I whispered. Fred shoved me against the glass cases so they jangled. Now he shouted. 'I'm not one of anybody's! Understand? Huh?' He took one finger the length of my brow and down my cheek. 'Your face bloody well stinks of fanny.' Then he crossed the pavement at an angle, as if to trick the rain, and just then the cinema attendant came out. 'For God's sake,' he said. 'Are you trying to ruin my cinema?' 'No,' I whispered. I wanted to go but he wouldn't let me. 'Are you all right?' he enquired. 'Yes, thank you.' He bent down. 'D'you want a sandwich?' 'No, thanks.' But he was kind enough to push me into the foyer where the linoleum was so smooth and slippery that I all but fell down the steps. He took my arm and went on, with me in tow, until we came to a cramped room behind the cinema itself, and there stood an enormous machine protruding from a hole in the wall, while on the floor were stacks of round boxes with English titles on them. *Days of War and Roses*. It was warm there and didn't smell very nice. Then it became apparent that the man wasn't just responsible for selling tickets, he was the projectionist as well. It was he who showed the film – without him the screen would just have hung in blackness like a broad and heavy curtain over a window in the dark of night. 'This is where I live,' he said. He opened his packet of sandwiches. 'What d'you want? Cheese or salami?' I wasn't hungry. Old ladies wanted more than anything to feel my curls while old men wanted to feed me. It was all rather tiresome. 'Salami,' I replied. I got a sandwich. I had to eat it. We ate together. 'Did he beat you up?' the projectionist enquired. I shook my head. We kept eating. All at once I saw the cinema as a ship, a ship bound for America, crossing the ocean. And the projectionist stood down in the projection room and it was he who made the propeller revolve and the stars light up. And as that thought struck me something else came to me – I could scarcely believe it was my own thought – it was as if someone else had had it first and I'd just adopted it. I thought that silent films were sailing ships on the same ocean and that the wind was the unmanned projection room. 'Are there many who bother you?' he asked. I wasn't quite following. 'What?' He asked me again. 'Are there many who bother you because you're so small?' I didn't say anything. He meant it well. I realized that. That's what I always say. Most people mean well and they're the worst. I could have answered – *Yes, you bother me particularly*. I said nothing. I just looked down. He put his hand on my knee. 'In the old days cinema projectionists couldn't be more than five feet tall,' he said. 'Otherwise they wouldn't have had enough space in the projection room. That would have been a job for you!' 'Yes,' I murmured. 'Yes.' He followed me out again. I ran after Fred but he'd been gone for ages. At Norabakk I tried to reach five feet, but if my feet were going to be used, it wasn't much to boast about. So I wondered if one foot was measured with or without a shoe on, and then all those who had size 48 shoes would come to a completely different result. I stopped at Church Road. The trees were still and black. Esther was fastening all her weeklies with clips to a line in the little kiosk window, as if she was hanging them there to dry. She waved to me and held out something that looked like a bit of sugar candy, something I'd maybe get if I first let her put her wrinkled hand in my curls. But my curls had been washed out, like the different parts of the world in my geography jotter, and I just stood there pretending I hadn't seen her. She tilted her head to one side and looked sad; she used to do that after I stopped saying thank you very much, at the same time putting the whole bit of sugar candy into her mouth. And the sound of her teeth crunching the dark brown crystallized sugar make me quake. I put my hands over my ears. Where was Fred? A hearse drove slowly down the other side of the street, and only one car with a grey cross on its roof followed, equally slowly, and I was filled with a strange yet vivid sensation that I'd seen this before, that something was being re-enacted. Not just as I remembered it but a version of it – the hearse, the driver, the white coffin in back, and the small pale curtains over the car windows. It gripped me so powerfully that I had to lean against the black tree where I'd stopped, because at the same time I thought that perhaps I hadn't seen it before but that it reminded me instead of something I'd see again soon. Inside the car was a man laughing. He leaned against the steering wheel and laughed. Perhaps I was mistaken. Perhaps he was crying. Perhaps laughter resembled crying when one couldn't hear it. Then they had passed by. I clasped my hand to my face and sniffed my fingers. *Fanny in my face?*

Mum had made stew, but I wasn't particularly hungry and nor was she. Boletta had been away since she disappeared the evening before, complete with black gloves and veil. Then everyone knew where Boletta was off to. She had gone to the North Pole to cool her heart in beer. She just had to, whenever it came over her like that. It was Mum who used to put it that way. *Now it's come over her again.* Fred hadn't returned either and Dad was away on his travels. He seldom said anything himself. We just knew that he sold things and sometimes put in an appearance with what profit he'd made. Those occasions tended to be short in duration. I picked at my food. Mum picked at hers. We sat there in the kitchen, each with our plate, silent, picking at our dinner. It had already got dark outside. The Virginia creeper rustled against the window. The clock in the hall ticked. Silence was Mum's gift. She could have won the women's world championship in silence if such a discipline had existed, while Fred would have won the men's. I reckon it was those silences, which could often last for several weeks at a stretch, that made Dad even more restless. He'd made Mum laugh, but that was all. Suddenly she took a handful of stew and flung it against the wall. It sounded similar to the noise of a lorry driving over a hedgehog. Afterwards she sat staring into thin air – neither at me, nor at the bits of meat trickling towards the floor and making a pattern that reminded me of a photograph I'd seen of a Russian officer shot to pieces at a street corner in Budapest, except that this was in colour. I had actually been thinking of asking Mum something, something I'd been turning over in my mind for ages, but I decided to let it be. Mum had had enough and I just let her sit there staring, her expression blacker than a gentleman's umbrella. I went to the bathroom and washed my face. I used soap and scouring powder and then rinsed my face with iodine, and when I looked at myself in the mirror I resembled an orange someone had tried to peel wearing gloves. I slunk into the bedroom and crept under the quilt. *Fanny in my face*. The ticking clock. The wet tarmac down Church Road. Mum trotting back and forth through the flat, stopping by the phone, going on into the living room, returning to the phone, lifting the receiver and slamming it back down again. I listened. I was the little listener with fanny in his face. No one phoned. Who was she waiting for most of all – Fred, Dad or Boletta? Or was it someone else entirely? Did she still hope Rakel would come back? I didn't know. I listened to Mum's steps growing heavier and heavier. To her silence, which would soon be intolerable even to herself. She opened the door sharply and looked in. 'Have you gone to bed already?' Now I could ask my question, but having got the chance at last I asked about something entirely different instead. 'What sort of car was it Fred was born in, Mum?' She sighed and leaned against the door frame. 'A taxi, Barnum.' 'Yes, but what sort of taxi?' There was the hint of a smile on her lips. 'Oh, I don't remember that. I had other things to think of.' She fell silent once more, as if she'd secretly kissed the Singer sewing machine. Her shoulder reached to where the last measurement had been recorded. It had been there a long time. Fred's mark was many notches higher. 'Why don't I get any taller?' I asked. Mum removed the stitches from her lips. 'You don't think you've stopped growing yet, do you, Barnum?' I looked down. 'Yes, I think so.'

Mum quietly closed the door and I opened my school-bag and took out the broken ruler. I tried to glue it back together. But although the pieces fitted, there was something missing all the same, where the edges of the fractures met – the dust of millimetres and the dust of fractions. The ruler had become less than itself – it no longer reached to its own twenty centimetres. And I thought of the metre that lay in Paris in a vault of lead – the metre of metres, the mother of all metres, neither any greater nor any less, but filling its own length with its maker's precision. I stretched out in bed as far as I could and decided that from now on I'd have my own measurement – Barnum's ruler. I liked the sweet smell of the glue.

Someone came in. It wasn't Boletta. I saw her in my mind's eye. Boletta sitting among the brown tables at the North Pole drinking beer from big glasses with rough men telling stories that make her forget. While the beer brands somewhere inside her head and seals the memory that froze in her at the sight of Vera her daughter and our mother, in the drying loft that day in May 1945. I've seen all this. I've seen it through the golden windows of the North Pole as one of the men slowly pulled off Boletta's black gloves.

It was Fred who came in. He was laughing. Mum shouted at him. Fred just laughed. Then she wept and something fell to the floor and shattered. I didn't wait to hear. I was asleep. I was asleep in my own ruler. Soon Fred went to bed himself. His breathing was quick. Mum was crying in another room. The sounds of the sweeping brush. How far into sleep is it possible to go before it's too late to turn back? 'Boletta's dancing,' Fred whispered. 'Boletta's dancing now at the North Pole.' I woke up. 'Do we have to go and get her?' Fred didn't reply. And suddenly I couldn't remember what I'd asked. *Who can lift granny's veil?* Had I asked that? *Who's Fred's dad?* I heard Mum putting on outer garments and then the sound of her quick steps as she went downstairs. She was going to get Boletta. It was night now. I looked over at Fred. He hadn't taken off his shoes as he wanted to be ready to nip off at any given moment. 'Now I know,' I whispered. 'What?' 'You're one of us.' 'Shut up!' I did shut up. The room smelled of Karlsen's glue – so did my fingers. I grew dizzy. I had an urge to stand over by the window sill. Fred's shoes shone in the dark. If the house caught on fire he could run straight out. 'Shall we read the letter?' I asked him. Fred said nothing. I think he turned away. I didn't need to light the lamp. I knew it off by heart. I could recite it by rote. I breathed deeply. *I send to all of you at home the warmest greetings, from here in the land of the midnight sun, together with a brief account of how our expedition has progressed thus far, since I imagine that it will be of interest to you to hear something of what we occupy ourselves with up here in the land of ice and snow*. The land of ice and snow. I couldn't help it. I got shivers down my spine every time; I got a lump in my throat and felt that gentle tug of crying – but they were good tears, it was a warm grief. 'Can you hear, Fred?' I murmured. There wasn't a sound from his bed. I shut my eyes and saw it all before me, the ship in the land of ice and snow. *First the vessel herself. She is of wood, built sturdily indeed, and encrusted with ice.* 'Shut up,' Fred said. *She was constructed to be a whaler and her original name was* North Cape. 'Shut up, you tit!' 'I'm reading slowly because it's in Danish,' I whispered. Something banged against the wall right above my head. It was a shoe. Fred's shadow moved about against the wall. A second shoe all but hit me. 'D'you know why they said your face smelled of fanny?' 'No, Fred.' 'Shall I tell you?' 'No, Fred.' 'Because you only reach up to the girls' fannies, that's why. Are you completely thick, or what?'

Fred's shadow stopped moving. I put his shoes on the floor. I didn't sleep any more that night. I dreamed of Tom Thumb instead, the American midget who never grew to be more than 89 centimetres in height and weighted at most 24 kilos; he was exhibited all over America in the nineteenth century, and then came to Europe and met Queen Victoria and got lost in her skirts. When he ate

dinner there were never jugs of water on the table in case
he drowned in them. It was said of Tom Thumb that God
had put a veto on his future when he was just two, and
that that was why he didn't grow any more. That's what
I dreamed. Maybe God was angry or had got fed up after
a while. At one time in the Middle Ages Jewish rabbis had
tried to prove that the average height at the time of creation had been about 50 metres, and that subsequently it
had just gone down and down. In 1718 the Frenchman
Henrion picked up on this by creating a mathematical
table showing how humankind had shrunk through time.
According to his calculations Adam had been at least 40
metres tall while Eve had been about 38. But the decline
had already started. Noah measured just 33.5 metres,
Abraham was no taller than 9, Moses a mere 4.22, Her-
cules just 3, and Alexander the Great only 1.92. But God
must have then begun to grow anxious, and at this point
he sent Jesus into the world to put a stop to all this, and
Jesus himself grew no taller than 1.62, something that
could be shown by the marks on the Cross.

I dream that God has forgotten me.

And I woke up, not having slept. Both of Fred's shoes
were gone. I got up and stood against the door frame. I
wanted to see if I'd grown during the course of the night,
but I'd stopped, stopped for good, and in the time that's
followed I've concentrated rather on maintaining what
height I have and not folding up like Boletta when she
comes home from the North Pole, her back curved like the
moon over Majorstuen church in October. I began to take
extra good care of my curls; they lifted me – yes, my hair
lifted me – and I was the first in Fagerborg to have an Afro,
and a blond Afro at that. It seemed natural – I resembled
a white poodle – but I didn't have it long. In winter I wore
an enormous bearskin hat, like one of the great Russian
dissidents – I found it among the Old One's effects. I've
even tried to starve myself taller, and I haven't turned a
blind eye to cork heels and double soles. When affecting
poverty became the latest fashion I could employ thick-

soled boots all year round, not to mention platform shoes. That was perhaps my greatest hour (not that I want to anticipate events, they'll be revealed in good time), but simply so as to stitch my life together into one impossible but necessary picture – fanny and platform shoes. And really it's funny that I should have felt particularly taller in those lonely years – the time of my elephantiasis – when the rest of them were wearing platform shoes. I was still precisely the same number of centimetres smaller than them. But I'd somehow risen above the lowest height. I had my head above water and I was mostly alone, since those I knew and loved had gone abroad. I took detours and went by the back streets on my wobbly, glittering shoes. All the greater the come-down when platform shoes were chucked on the dunghill of derision, thrown at the back of the cupboard and kept hidden for fancy dress parties or Salvation Army collections. I was the last in Oslo to wear platform shoes and if I think about it, this was my real high point, that glorious moment between two fashions when I took power and stood up on my platforms while the rest were in the process of-climbing back down into their old sandals. But it couldn't last. I abdicated. I fell. The king of platform shoes was deposed and I dreamed instead that God would wake one morning and find sixty centimetres he'd forgotten to give humanity and pronounce – *Thirty of these belong to Barnum's ruler*. Dad thumped me on the back once when he was in a good mood and said that it wasn't height that counted when nature had equipped us as well as she had. That was what the doctor from the mainland had maintained after his meticulous examination of the Nilsen body. *Just ask your Mother*, he said. I didn't. But I did wonder for a while if it might be possible to amputate a bit of extra skeleton. I had read in an *Allers* journal that it was possible in America. They'd lengthened a Norwegian-American from Fargo by six centimetres by bolting a joint between his kneecaps and his hips. But he was never much of a walker afterwards and had to sit down most of the time, so what was the point? As it happens he died of a heart attack – he bent down to tie his laces and died on the spot, according to the next issue of *Allers*. How Fred laughed at me when the mood took him! Once he carried me on his shoulders down the whole length of Church Road and Majorstuen to the Colosseum cinema. And I let him do it. But all of a sudden he put me down and said, 'Shall we change places, Barnum?' I was immediately frightened because I didn't know *what* he wanted to change, and before I was able to ask he'd gone. If someone wanted to be really funny they'd say that I barely reached up to my own head. Then they'd laugh themselves silly. Or they'd say that my face smelled of fanny. I seldom laughed. As a matter of fact I once met James Bond, but he couldn't help me either. It was actually Sean Connery I saw, in the tobacconist's on Frogner Road, the place where I went to buy *Cocktail*, which everyone knew lay under the counter together with *Weekend Sex* and *Pin-up*. But of course I couldn't buy it anywhere near Fagerborg – I had to go as far away as possible. I waited for something like an hour out on the pavement before even daring to go in. I thought I was alone, but there was James Bond himself, and he looked a bit bedraggled too. He had thin, almost carrot-coloured hair which he probably hadn't brushed for at least three months. He'd just bought a cigar which he was trying to light. I was about to go straight out again because I thought I was seeing things and my head felt queer. But it was him, Sean Connery himself, in that shop on Frogner Road, Oslo, Norway, Europe, the world, the universe. And the lady behind the counter, who probably hadn't recognized him, leaned over the chocolate display and asked what I wanted. I couldn't take my eyes off James Bond. At long last he'd got his cigar lit. He smiled at me. He had bad teeth into the bargain. The lady asked me again. I couldn't get out a single word. I just remember feeling such disappointment that James Bond was so shabby. He made to put a hand on my curls. Then I ran – I ran the whole way home. After we'd gone to bed that evening I told Fred. 'I saw James Bond today,' I whispered. Fred turned round. 'You been to the cinema?' 'No, I saw him on Frogner Road.' There was irritation in Fred's voice. 'You saw James Bond in Frogner Road?' I nodded. 'He had thin hair and bad teeth,' I told him. Fred was silent a good while. 'You did not see James Bond in Frogner Road,' he said in the end. 'Yes, I did! In the tobacconist's!' 'What were you doing there?' I looked down. 'Buying *Cocktail*,' I murmured. Fred laughed and rolled over. 'Good night, Barnum. Don't make a noise while you're at it.' 'It's true,' I told him. 'What's true?' 'That James Bond was there. Or Sean Connery.' Fred sat up again and he was really mad. 'Just shut up, will you, you dwarf!' 'I did see him!' I shouted. 'I saw James Bond!' Fred came a foot closer and thumped me full in the face. I fell back on the pillow and just lay there. As the blood pumped from my face in great gouts it came to me that no one believed me when I told the truth, but everyone did when I lied. And once I'm in full flight I'll trot out Humphrey Bogart, Toulouse Lautrec, James Cagney – and Edvard Grieg, who was so small that he had to sit on Beethoven's complete works to play the piano. And Mickey Rooney, last but not least Mickey Rooney, that unkempt little midge, who was still married five times to some of the world's most beautiful women. We have the same blood, I explain, we're the little guys and we're nearest the gutter! Then Peder puts his hand on my shoulder to calm me down, as the women glance at one another speechless and the men make a get-away to the veranda. 'Don't bring Grieg into it next time,' Peder whispers. And sometimes, when from time to time I lean against a door frame as I'm waiting for someone, or am bored or nervous, without being conscious of it I lay my hand flat on my head and spin round to see if I've grown. But there'll be no mark on that particular door frame, no notch with which to compare, and I close the door instead and go back where I was going. How long does a dream take? Who can say the alphabet backwards in their sleep? I'm cutting my life, our lives, into pieces. I've broken into the editing suite with my silver scissors and afterwards glue the pieces back together with my small hands, but in a different order. And forgive me if I have to lie, for a lie is just what one adds to make the broken edges that constitute the narrative's ruler fit back together. And I state here that what I narrate always ends up being shorter than what's actually been experienced. So I go back to that morning I was standing in the doorway, my face still tender, to see whether or not the night had borne any fruit. Fred's shoes were gone. Everything was still. The first words of my great-grandfather's letter lay soundless in my mouth. *Loving greetings I send you.* And this is not a flashback – just you standing in a room you vaguely recognize. You can just hear someone crying behind you, and when you turn you see a child and that child is you.

I peered into the living room. Boletta was asleep on the divan and the curtains were drawn. She emitted a small sound each time she inhaled. Her black gloves had fallen to the floor. I didn't want to wake her. I tiptoed over, lifted her veil as carefully as I could, and kissed her brow. As I was about to go back to my room I saw Mum standing there. 'That was nice of you, Barnum,' she said. She was wearing a blue apron tied round her waist so I could see just how thin she really was. She was holding a grey cloth in her hand – it smelled sour and was full of the remains of the stew and other meat. I suddenly felt sick. I remember one particular Sunday when Dad grumbled about the beef – it was either overdone or underdone – and at that Mum chucked a similar cloth into the frying pan and dished it up to him with gravy and all. But worst of all was that Dad ate it – I don't know how on earth he managed – but he cut it into small bits and no one ever saw a sign of that cloth again. *Mum is like Røst,* Dad used to say. *No meteorologist in the world can predict what kind of weather she'll have in the morning.* 'She's asleep,' I said quietly. Mum's smile was tired. 'She probably won't waken until it's passed.' That was the way it was. Whatever it was that *came* over Boletta had to *go* over her too. I'd like to have known what it was, the thing that came over her. 'It'll soon be time for you to begin dancing classes,' Mum said all of a sudden. 'Oh, no.' 'Oh, no? Of course you will. You won't regret it either!' She dropped the smelly cloth on the floor, held me in my pyjamas and spun me round the living room – past the sofa, taking an abrupt turn at the stove, almost toppling one of the lamps and laughing out loud. She smelled of washing-up liquid and perfume, and I could feel her sharp bones beneath her apron. I tried to tear myself loose but then she peered more closely at my face and immediately became aware of something strange. 'What have you done to yourself?' she demanded. 'Done to myself? Nothing.' 'But you're all red and swollen.' 'I have to go to school,' I whined. 'With that face?' She put her finger on my cheek to feel. 'You've not got mumps? No, you've had mumps. Thank the Lord. Let's see if you've a rash, Barnum.' I turned round. 'I'm not ill, I just washed myself.' Mum laughed. 'Yes, I'll say. Well and truly. Did you use chlorine?' 'No, soap, scouring powder and iodine. My face smelled of fanny.' Mum let go of my pyjamas and her lip trembled as if she'd been shaken by an unexpected blow. 'What did you say, Barnum?' And at that moment Dad came home. I saw him behind Mum – he came into the hall, pushed the door closed with his elbow – and in that instant, that second when he thought he was unobserved that Friday morning in October, as he put down his shiny briefcase, hung his hat on a hook between the bracket lamps, put his umbrella on the stand, got out of his raincoat, took off his shoes with a sigh, ripped off his stocking suspender to scratch one white leg, and leaned against the wall – all in one fluid movement, without pause, I could see that his neck was bent and his back round, and his suit jacket was tight almost to the point of bursting. I could see the hand-kerchief in his breast pocket with his initials on – A.N. – the drops of sweat on his brow and the hand that slowly drew the handkerchief (not all that clean any longer) to mop it over the wide brow of his forehead. But the sweat seems to cling like mould – he rubs and rubs at it, bewildered and enraged. He thumps his fist against his forehead as if that can make a difference, and now Mum turns round herself, but she hasn't seen anything of what I've witnessed, of Dad's homecoming. I cough, and Dad straightens up sharply, the handkerchief still in his hand, and he smiles. That selfsame second he smiles, flings wide his arms and like that comes towards us, as if the moment when he stood leaning against the wall thumping his fist against his forehead was nothing more than an illusion, a mirage. 'I didn't think you were coming home until tomorrow,' Mum said. 'Neither did I. So I came now!' Dad folded away his handkerchief so I didn't see where it disappeared to, laughed, and kissed Mum on both cheeks. Dad had grown even fatter. He got fatter every time he went away. The skin hung over his collar like whipped cream over a brimming cup. He'd stopped using a belt and just had braces now. Even his knees were fat. Soon he'd be as broad as he was tall. Finally he let go of Mum, turned towards me and winked. 'What's happened to your face, Barnum? Has Fred tried to spell it?' He laughed again, loudly this time. Mum flinched. 'He's just got a cold,' she said hurriedly. 'That's why he's not at school.'

But Dad had noticed Boletta now. She lay hunched on the divan and it still hadn't passed, whatever it was that had come over her. 'I see,' Dad chuckled. '*Lit de parade*.' Mum took his arm. 'Be quiet. Don't talk like that.' 'What did that mean?' I asked. Dad had to use his handkerchief for his forehead again. '*Lit de parade*. Quite simply it's French and means hangover. Shall we put a glass of brandy on her chest and see if she's still alive?' Mum tugged hard at his jacket – it was all crumpled down the back and the middle button had loosened and was about to come off. 'Why are you home early?' Mum demanded again. Dad breathed deeply. He raised his damaged hand.

He tried to smile. 'D'you want me to go again?' he asked.
Mum gave a sigh. 'I just wondered, Arnold.' Suddenly
Dad lost his head completely. He couldn't take any more.
'Shall I tell you why I'm home early?' he all but shouted.
Mum nodded and tried to quiet him down. But it was too
late. 'Because the car broke down! It couldn't cope with
the drive to Italy!' Dad sat down. 'Is it a write-off?' Mum
asked carefully. 'It's at Kløfta scrapyard! I got two kroner
and fifty øre for it!' Dad got to his feet again. 'You can at
least say for a certainty that we made a loss on that
damned journey,' he murmured. 'Because there wasn't
exactly much to get out of Fleming Brant.' Mum's eyes
narrowed. 'So that was why you were so keen to go there.
To see if he had money?' Dad realized he'd said too much,
but it was impossible to stop now. 'Yes, damn it! He could
have been the king of Bellagio, for all we knew!' There
was utter quiet. Dad held his handkerchief like a faded
white flag in his hand. He had to say something more
now. He mopped his neck, and somewhere away in
among all the fat and sweat there was a smile. Some
people used to say that I'd inherited Dad's smile too and
that I ought to be grateful for it. And although it was
becoming harder and harder to detect Dad's smile I could
see that it was one that served its purpose, because it
made us expectant. It made Mum gentle and lenient and
it made him handsome and irresistible, as if that one
smile raised him from the heaviness of his own body and
elevated him above the banal distractions of everyday life.
He became again the boy who wanted to sell the wind.
'Guess what I was thinking about when I sat alone on the
train in that wretched compartment,' he said. It was
impossible to say because Dad's ideas ranged so far and
wide that they rarely reached fruition but rather got
blown away in bad company. He folded his arms. He only
just managed to do so. Now he was waiting for a drum
roll and fanfares. He was waiting for himself. 'Tell us,
Dad! Tell us what you were thinking!' 'Easy, Barnum.
Take it easy. All in good time.' He kept standing as he did

a bit longer. Mum took my hand. Then at last he went out into the hall and fetched his little briefcase. This he carefully placed on the living-room table and we took up position beside him, one on each side, to see what he had. Dad rubbed his gloves together. 'Apart from thinking of you, something I do all the time, I have to tell you that I was thinking too of the Olympics! I felt Olympian and thought of the games in Tokyo – and reckoned it's time to get into shape! And I decided there and then to start a new life. For that reason I stopped at Bislet Stadium and did a little deal with the steward there. He got a signed Jens Book-Jensen gramophone record. And I, ladies and gentlemen, got nothing less than this.'

Dad opened the briefcase, but stood bent over it so we couldn't see what was inside. Then he lifted a round disc that was a little higher in the middle and resembled a solidified cowpat he might almost have lifted from a field in Østfold. He held it out in front of us. We didn't say a word. Mum looked away. Dad's eyes roamed frantically. 'Well, say something, for heaven's sake!' he exclaimed. 'What is it?' Mum asked, her voice low. And now Dad laughed aloud for the third time since arriving home that morning. 'My dear, beloved, ignorant wife! What would you have ever done without me to bring knowledge and love into this house? Tell your mother what it is that I'm holding in my hands, Barnum!' 'A discus,' I whispered. 'Well done, Barnum! Nothing less than a discus!' Mum let out her breath. 'A discus? Is that all you have with you?' Dad's wide brow had an angled furrow down it, like a ditch for his sweat. But the smile was there yet, somehow fixed in place. Everything Dad did took a long time – his body was slower than his brain – and as a result he could still smile when he was mad, or, on the other hand, he could give a clip round the ear when he was in a good mood. He looked at Mum a long while. 'All?' he laughed. 'The discus is civilized humanity's medal! This is the first thing that human beings threw without intending to kill!' With that he tore off his jacket, laid the discus flat in his bad hand, bent his knees and began to swing round on the carpet. 'Tamara Press!' he groaned. 'Tamara Press!' Mum hid her face in her hands and shrieked behind them – I had to sit down because otherwise I wouldn't have managed to keep on my feet. I just laughed and laughed because Dad resembled a deranged elephant on one leg looking for its trunk. Then Boletta woke up. She got up off the divan, drew back her veil and pointed at Dad. 'What is that man doing?' 'Dad's throwing the discus!' I shouted. 'Nothing is to be thrown in my house! Do you hear me?' Dad gradually stopped spinning, he went slower and slower until in the end he just stood facing one way, swaying, as the sweat ran from his ear lobes, as if his head was leaking. 'You're right, my little Boletta. The discus is for outside. We'll wait for the spring instead.' He put the discus in a drawer in the cabinet. And then he put his arms round us – he even managed to get Boletta onto her feet – and he drew us all close. 'It's good to come back home to you,' Dad said. 'My God, it's good to come home to you all!'

So we stood like that, huddled close, our family, on a Friday in October. It was then Dad whispered to me and only I heard him: 'Spread rumours and sow doubt, Barnum.' 'Why?' I asked. 'Because no one'll believe you anyway,' he replied. He laughed. 'And besides, the truth's boring, Barnum.' And just at that moment I saw, in the shadows between the door and the cabinet, Fred's gaze, Fred's eyes. How long had he been standing there? I had no idea. Perhaps he'd been there the whole time. Now Fred was smiling. He smiled and I wanted to hold out my hand to him. But he just shook his head, closed his eyes, and leaned into the dark. And I thought to myself – *Now we don't exist. Now we've gone too*.

The Mole

I toyed with those thoughts. They were what I toyed with most. I had no one else to play with. I toyed with thoughts of catastrophes, accidents, illness, death and all sorts of other irreparable damage. Then it felt good. It was a comfort to know that everything could have been worse, so much worse. If our flat were to catch fire on Christmas Day, for example, with all the presents burned, and if I alone survived among the charred remains of Mum, Fred and Boletta, and had to be on a ventilator for at least three months while eighteen doctors fought to keep what remained of me alive, then everything would have a different complexion. Oh, yes. Then those who'd bullied me would be smitten with guilt and come crawling for forgiveness, and I, compassionate in the midst of my agony, would grant it. And the papers would be full of articles about my fate – books would be written about me, films made, paintings commissioned and operas composed. And at the end of the day this was all I dreamed of – that everything would be different, different to what it was. I saw myself going round with my burned face swathed in bandages, lonely and exalted. That was what I dreamed. For the thoughts I toyed with became dreams, and I dreamed only when I was awake and never during the night (I didn't dare to then). But I went on dreaming on my own for hours, right until I had to sit down somewhere – on a stone perhaps at the top of Sten Park – and cry, for so overwhelming were these dreams that they drove me to a strange madness. I cried, I sobbed – I was possessed by the violent dramatic intensity of my own day-dreams. I was inside my own violence. I was at the heart of my own dreams. I dreamed that I fell ill, that death was close and that this sickness was incurable, desperately slow and agonizing. Then it was that they came to me, all those yearning forgiveness and wanting my friendship. But soon it would be too late, for I was dying and the last thing I'd do was raise my hand in blessing to all those standing by my side. But I didn't get any further in my dreams, my thoughts. That annoyed me. I couldn't imagine myself dead – well, yes, I could imagine it all right, but it gave me no joy, none whatsoever. The dreams of me dead in a lonely coffin in the Western Crematorium or Majorstuen church were always too short – I couldn't hold onto them and they ended of their own accord. They ran out into the sand before they really were anything to speak of at all. The dream of my own death was always a failure. It was just as if I couldn't quite believe in it. It was better to dream about suffering and accidents that I survived screaming, that brought everyone flocking round me with amazement and compassion. I dreamed that it's me and not Fred who's sitting on the edge of the pavement when the Old One's knocked down and killed. Except that I don't sit there uninjured, I try in vain to save her life, thus putting my own in jeopardy. And her death only makes my fate the worse, because I try as valiantly as any human can yet she still dies. And I collapse into the gutter, one leg broken and the blood pouring from a deep gash in my forehead, so the front part of my brain is visible like a small scone. I dream that it's me their hearts go out to and that I get the glory – yes, the glory, because I've risked my own life for another's and I'm a noble and true soul. I mulled it over in my mind – can a thought be evil? Even if it's just in one's head? Can a dream be equally evil? If it remains in one's innermost thoughts, in silence, undisturbed and never released into the world? That was how my thoughts went. And one day my dream became real. I was to lift my thoughts up from their darkness. I was to free my dream into reality, which was too small, even for myself.

She was in the same year as myself, in the other class. I had had my eye on her for ages. She stood by the bike

sheds, always on her own and with her face turned away.
I got it into my head that she was lonely, as lonely as I
was. I circled her, but she didn't come any closer. What
was it I imagined? That Barnum was going to get a girlfriend? Yes. It was unprecedented, but that was what I
imagined, that I'd get a girlfriend, and that it would be the
girl who stood on her own facing away over by the sheds.
She had short, fair hair and a mole on her left cheek, just
below her eye. And I liked that mole particularly because
it rendered her imperfect and attainable. It gave me hope
and courage – yes, it was this that ultimately drew me
to her. The mole was her mark, just as my height was
mine – my shortfall of centimetres – visible to one and all.

I began following her when she went home from
school. I kept my distance. She didn't see me. I ran from
corner to corner. She was always on her own. Her bag
seemed far too heavy. Now and again she had to stop to
rest. I would have loved to help her – I could have carried
her bag, it would have been the easiest thing in the world
to do. But I never did. I just stood there looking at her,
from the shadows of some entrance she didn't know
about and where the smell of dinners being cooked
drifted from under doorways and through keyholes. They
came down and filled me with a heavy, grey queasiness
that made me vomit under mail-boxes overflowing with
delayed postcards of ships and beaches. It was September.
When I got up again she was gone. Her name was Tale. I
knew from before where she lived. I ran there, to Nobel
Street, and saw the curtains being drawn in a room on the
second floor.

For quite a while I just stood there watching. But nothing happened. She didn't come out again. And so I
wended my way home again, dreaming that I had fallen
from a plane somewhere over the middle of Africa and
was the only survivor. There I was taken care of by a tribe
nobody had previously heard of, and I lived with them for
three years. There was just one fly in the ointment with
this dream. What was I actually doing in a plane over

Africa? I had to know or else the dream was somehow null and void. In the end I got it. I'd won an essay competition at school and was now off to Madagascar where pupils from the world over would assemble to compose new essays. But on the way there my plane falls from the skies; by a miracle I survive and am cared for by a tribe of natives who've never seen a white man before, and I live with them for three years. Back home in Norway, once all hope has faded, a memorial service is held for me in Majorstuen church and it's so full there's a queue all the way down to the 'pole'. Everybody's there – my class, the teachers, the whole school, Esther from the kiosk – not to mention the members of the royal family who've found their way to Majorstuen church (because I was going to represent Norway, after all, at the essay-writing competition on Madagascar when the plane came down). The vicar is overcome by grief and guilt and declares that thereafter all those bearing the name Barnum will do so with pride, and Barnum becomes the most popular name for boys in the years which follow. Fred gives the eulogy – he's written the text himself and not a letter's out of place. He's missed me so much that he's no longer dyslexic; he can see properly, and clearly at that. He remembers me as his faithful and lonely half brother (though in his eyes I was complete – yes, a more complete brother couldn't have been found in the world). And beside Mum, Dad and Boletta is Tale, crying bitterly, for there is not even a coffin beside which she can kneel or leave flowers. But now they can jolly well just get on with it while I'm left lying in a straw hut in the middle of Africa, and I see the medicine man who's about a hundred years old bending over me, a bolt through his nose. He just shakes his head and says something in a language I don't understand. I'm left lying like this for long weeks and months, with only rainwater to drink and boiled monkey kidneys to eat. But one day I get to taste a soup the medicine man has concocted from plants that grow underground and which for that reason are rare and difficult to find. And this soup, which is thick and blue and stinks of warm cat's piss, works wonders with me. My wounds heal, my memory comes back – but not just that, I grow. I can feel it there where I'm lying, that it's further and further down to my feet, and when I finally do get up I'm taller than everyone else. But I can't be absolutely certain because perhaps it's just that the natives are even smaller, perhaps it's just an illusion. Then I'm found by a missionary who has with him a suitcase full of Bibles he gives away to the tribe, and a green board on which he sticks felt figures representing Jesus and His story. I ask how tall he is. *God wanted me to be one metre seventy-four,* the missionary replies. Then I know it's true, because I'm taller than he is – the poor missionary only reaches up as far as my shoulder. I must be at least one metre eighty. And when he packs away his flannel-graph and all the figures, I travel with him through the jungle. And on the day I land at Fornebu airport, three months later, there are thousands waiting in the arrival area and out on the runway too, with flags and great banners proclaiming *Welcome Home, Barnum*! And at the very front is Tale with her mole, but I walk right past her and the crowds gasp when they see me – one metre eighty tall and all but unrecognizable. But inside I'm the same Barnum as ever – just good old Barnum – with a heart of gold. The photographers fight for pictures and I walk right past Tale who tries in vain to hold onto me. But I tear myself away and run over to Fred instead and he throws his arms about me. He's been inconsolable since he gave his eulogy and more dyslexic than ever, and he cries his eyes out on my shoulder.

I had to rest beside the fountain in Golden Lion Street. I was exhausted. The water had been turned off and only chestnuts and leaves floated at the bottom of the pool. But I was my own fountain. I sobbed on my own shoulder. And my dream dissolved in tears that fell heavily onto the slippery tarmac, amid scattering slaters. I could go no further; the dream stopped at the point where Fred threw his arms round me. I didn't care about the next instalment. It was too slow and boring. I couldn't be bothered dreaming it. And the best part of the dream had really been the memorial service, with me lying in the heart of Africa and the rest of the world in Majorstuen church, at the funeral with no coffin. I cried a little again. Then someone bent down, close against my face. 'Here you are all sorry for yourself,' a voice said. And someone dried my tears with a handkerchief that smelled of fish cakes and cough mixture. 'And why is a lovely little boy like you so sad then?' I opened my eyes and looked right into an ancient mouth. The lipstick had rubbed off onto her front teeth so they resembled pale-red shells, and her tongue was as wrinkled as a snail. I leaned back. 'Have you fallen and hurt yourself?' I shook my head. She was so close now that I thought she was going to lick me with her snail, and I couldn't lean back any further or I'd have fallen backwards into the pool. 'My brother's dead,' I told her. She stopped and her eyes almost seemed to swell up. 'Is your brother dead?' 'Yes,' I sobbed, and drew the back of my hand across my cheek. She put her hand on my head and her voice became all soft; her old tongue spilled over. 'Is it a long time since he died?' 'Yesterday.' 'Did your brother die only yesterday?' 'Yes, just yesterday. He'll be buried the day after tomorrow.' And I felt gripped by this, even more strongly than by the dream of Africa, when I said that Fred had died – when I said it aloud and didn't just think it. And the woman who heard my words thought they were true. It was as if it really had happened; I believed it myself and listened intently to every word that my mouth spoke. 'He drowned,' I said. 'In Gaustad brook. I tried to save him but...' I began to cry in earnest. I couldn't speak. The lady cried too and dried my face once more. 'You are a special little boy,' she murmured. And then she gave me five whole kroner, ruffled my curls with her hand, put away her handkerchief and went away through the golden leaves. Then something strange happened. When I was about to say thanks, many thanks,

other words came out of my mouth instead. 'Snail fanny!'
I screamed. The old lady stopped for a second, turned,
and her face fell to pieces there under the black trees. I
ran hell for leather as far as the fire station and I couldn't
have cared less if it had gone on fire itself at that moment.
The whole town could burn down, and the Palace catch
fire – with the king himself in flames on the balcony. But
the engines stood soundlessly there in the station, the
helmets all on their hooks. The sirens were somewhere
else. The burning was just inside my own head – a bonfire in my throat – and no fireman in the world could put
those flames out. I raced against myself and didn't stop
before I'd reached Bøgstad Road. I stood outside the perfumery, on the corner where the tramlines turn, and I
could see my face in the mirror behind the window. There
was no smoke coming out of my ears, nor were my curls
singed. I was more or less as before, my cheeks just a
shade red and my eyes a bit too big, as if they'd seen too
much. But I had a five kroner piece in my hand. I went
into the shop. There were ladies everywhere and all of
them turned at the same moment and the smiles broke
out on their poker faces – as if the sight of me had aroused
them from deep dreams at the bottom of a sea of scents.
Yes, those scents were like the wet leaves that pile up
beneath trees, and I don't quite know why, but all of a
sudden I saw in my mind's eye hedgehogs sleeping buried
in a heap of dead leaves. Someone's going to put their
hand on my head in a minute, I thought, and I wasn't
even finished thinking this when the assistant in her light
blue dress put her fingers in my hair, ruffled my curls and
gave a laugh. 'Snail fanny,' I said, and bit my tongue. But
she bent down and smiled the more, and the ladies
laughed in chorus. 'Have you ever seen such a nice boy!'
And probably they hadn't, since all of them wanted to
touch my head, one after the other. And when this was
finally over the assistant asked me what it was I wanted –
cologne, perhaps, for my mother, or maybe a steel comb?
'I want a ring,' I whispered. The assistant bent down to

me. 'What was that you said, little fellow?' 'I said a ring,' I repeated. 'With a letter on it.' Now she smiled knowingly and pushed me deeper into the shop and pulled out a little drawer full of rings. 'Which letter would you like then?' I would have liked the whole alphabet, just to be on the safe side, but I didn't have the money for that much. If I'd begun at A, I wouldn't have got further than E, and I didn't know anyone with those letters who merited a ring from me, except for Esther from the kiosk. 'T' I said quickly. She got out a ring with a T on it. 'What's your girlfriend's name then? Turid?' I shook my head. 'Tone, then?' she suggested. 'No,' I said. Now she was almost on her knees in front of me. 'She's called Trine!' And then I said something I was rather pleased with. 'T for Tongue-tied,' I told her. 'T for Tongue-tied.' The assistant put her hand in my hair once more and got up. 'You are a clever little lad.' *Snail fanny*, I thought, so my skull burst – but not a sound was emitted from my thoughts. T for Tongue-tied. I wouldn't forget that.

The ring was wrapped in cotton wool and silver paper; I put the five kroner piece on the counter and was given three kroner sixty öre in change. If all went according to plan I would ask Tale out with that money; we could go to the Student café and order raspberry milk shakes, or else to Esther's and buy sugar candy and liquorice which we could take with us up to Sten Park where we could eat in peace and quiet. No, we could go right the way to Gaustad brook and sit there by the edge on a blanket, because no one would find us there. I didn't say many thanks this time. I just thought it – *many thanks*, I thought – and carefully bore my present home. Mum and Boletta had already had dinner and Mum asked where I'd been. 'Nowhere,' I told her. 'And I'm not hungry.' I went into my room and put the present at the very bottom of my pencil case – under the eraser, the pencil sharpener and the ruler. Suddenly Fred was behind me. 'What are you doing?' he asked. I hunched over the pencil case. 'Nothing,' I whispered. 'Nothing?' Fred laughed. I wished he wouldn't. 'It's the truth,' I told him. Fred put his hands on my shoulders. 'There's no such thing as nothing. You're fibbing.' 'Please,' I begged him. 'I'm not.' But Fred wasn't about to be lenient. He stretched out, ripped the pencil case from me and unzipped it – as if he'd known the ring was there all along. He held out the shining little parcel in his fingers. 'What's this then, Barnum? Nothing?' I looked down. 'A ring,' I whispered. Fred smiled. He sat down on the bed and unwrapped it. I was close to tears. But I didn't cry. If only he'd known what I'd been dreaming, that it was he who gave the eulogy by an empty grave in the wake of my disappearance. 'T,' Fred said. 'Who's that?' 'A girl in the other class.' 'And you're going to give the ring to her?' I nodded. Fred was quiet a while. I didn't say a word myself. I just wondered what he'd do now, whether he'd throw the ring down the toilet, or perhaps even break off the letter. But he did none of those things. Instead he wrapped up the ring once more, so it was just as it had been, and gave it back to me. 'Good, Barnum,' he said. I still didn't dare say a thing. I pushed the little parcel carefully down into my pencil case. Fred went to the window and stood there, facing away. It was already dark outside. The bus made a slow slushing noise as it passed and the street lights shuddered in the wind. 'D'you like her a lot?' Fred asked, his voice low. I froze. 'Yes,' I whispered. 'What is it you like best about her?' 'She's got a mole on her face,' I replied. Fred turned back towards me. 'Can I give you a bit of advice, Barnum?' 'Yes,' I said. He came closer. 'Don't tell her it's the mole you like best.' He put his hand through my curls – I think it was the first time he'd ever done so. Then he went, without so much as saying another word.

That night I dreamed something new, even though I was sleeping. I'd travelled far. I'd gone deep into the cold and the dark to find Wilhelm, my great-grandfather, and I'd travelled alone. I went on for several days, or maybe it was months – time there couldn't be measured in hours and minutes – without finding a thing. Then it was that I

stumbled over a box; it was lying beside a stone and I had
to chip it free. I remember that box perfectly. It was black
and had two shining, rusted locks on each side of the
dented lid. I got it opened and inside there lay a dusty
bottle of Malaga, three tins of sardines and four kilos of
shoe polish. I sat down by the stone – had a gulp of the
sherry, ate the sardines, drank the king's health, and polished my shoes. Then I fell asleep and when I woke up
again I was surrounded by polar bears. I shot two of them
with a rifle I suddenly found I had in my hands and thereafter the others made themselves scarce. I continued on
my way but saw no other sign of life. My shoes were
heavy and kept getting stuck in the snow. Soon enough I
died. It was strange. I died and yet the dream carried on
nonetheless. I sank down into the ice and lay there, in the
jaws of the cold, in a coffin of soundless ice. After the
same number of years had elapsed since Wilhelm himself
vanished in Greenland's ice and snow (or perhaps it was
just a week, since time couldn't be relied upon in the
same way), someone found me. They cut out the block of
ice in which I was encased and took me back to Norway.
Once there I was exhibited in the music pavilion on Karl
Johan – Barnum in a chunk of ice – well-preserved in my
cold, transparent coffin. But then the sun comes out and
the ice begins to melt – to drip and run – the onlookers
cheer and as soon as I wake up I decay, and am left clutch-
ing the pencil case with the ring.

Each break time it rained and Tale stood on her own by
the sheds, I waited by the drinking fountain. She didn't
see me. The mole resembled a dark drop of rain that had
come to a standstill on her cheek. The last period was
gym. I sat in the changing rooms listening to the others
running about in circles in the gym hall. Then there was
quiet and the Goat appeared in the doorway. I had to
think of my dream, because it was just as if the Goat had
melted too and was in the process of rotting. His massive
muscles ran down his body like shining waves of fat.
When he showered with us he needed the water from

three different units, and even then his feet didn't get wet. 'Aren't you changing?' he demanded. 'I'm not all that well,' I murmured. 'What's wrong with you today, then?' 'I've got a cold,' I replied, my voice even fainter. 'I forgot to close the window last night and my bed got soaked with rain.' The Goat gave a deep sigh. 'All right then. But don't leave till the bell goes.' He went back to the other boys and blew his whistle. I heard apparatus being pushed over the floor and some of them swinging from wall bar to wall bar. I sat on the bench between the raincoats. Changing rooms are lonely places. They're all alike. They have the same smell. The same story. Changing rooms are places where pain and sorrow remain like lost property that no one comes back to collect. You take conquests out with you into the playground and the streets. The defeats you leave behind. One of the showers was dripping. If I counted up to five hundred drops the bell would ring. I counted to four hundred and thirty. Then I couldn't wait any longer. I'd had an idea and I didn't have much time. I ran all the way down to Plesner's at Grensen, where Mum tended to buy me extra soles and cork heels. It was the only shop in town that had skeletons in the windows. I went in and the woman behind the counter, who was more like a nurse in her white coat and clogs, recognized me right away. But this time I didn't want anything to raise my diminutive stature. I asked her for a sling. 'A sling?' she repeated. 'Yes,' I told her. 'My brother's sprained his arm.' 'Really. And how did he manage that?' He was doing cartwheels in the living room and it was too small.' She looked at me for some time. Then she disappeared into the back premises and came back with a clothes hanger with a selection of slings. There should really have been a sling with letters too – a huge B, B for Broken and B for Barnum. But that was probably asking too much. I was in such a good mood. Now I'd elevate my dream from the dark; imagining would become fact and I'd become real. I chose a green sling. Then the injury would appear all the more serious.

But I changed my mind because the green sling was almost the same colour as the jumper I was wearing underneath. So I took the white one instead – white was the colour of illness, white was suffering like snow and ice, white was a colour everyone could see. I paid three kroner and ten ore which left me with fifty öre. That wasn't much to write home about – it was barely enough for two iced drink packets. But we could sit in her room instead and I could put my arm round her, the one that wasn't injured. The lady in Plesner's wanted to wrap the sling but I just picked it up and hurried out. I went into the nearest entryway and tried to knot the sling correctly. But first I had to be sure which arm it was that was broken. I hadn't thought of that. I had to laugh at myself. I'd planned everything in minute detail but forgotten the question of the arm. I chose the right one. That looked worse. After a struggle I managed to make a knot; I hung the sling round my neck and straightened my left arm. Now my arm had been broken, and in the most dramatic of ways. I groaned. I went down to Karl Johan. I walked slowly and often had to rest, the pain was so bad. People were going back and forth, hunched from the rain under black umbrellas. They didn't see me. That annoyed me. They could surely have noticed me and felt sorry for me, and perhaps asked if I wanted help crossing the road or carried my school-bag for a bit. I would have said no, but it would have been nice to be asked all the same. The benches at the Studenterlund were being hoisted onto a lorry and driven away. It was nothing less than autumn. The trees shook loose their leaves. I went a roundabout way since I had to practise wearing the sling. I stopped in the City Chambers Square. A train came from the Western Station pulling goods wagons in its wake – twenty-three of them at least – and after the last one had passed I could look right over to Akers Mek. At that very moment an enormous ship slid from the dock; a tall, black hull floated soundlessly through the rain and down into the dark water. And it was so beautiful because that was how my dreams were now too; I would send them to sea, I would sail.

I went straight to Nobel Street. The curtains on the second floor were drawn. It was twenty past three. She had to be home from school. I took the ring from my bag, put it in my pocket, hid my bag under the stairs, went up two floors and rang the bell. For a time nothing happened. Then her mother opened the door. She looked down at me. 'Hallo,' she said. 'Is Tale at home?' I asked. 'Indeed she is,' her mother replied and just stood there. I didn't know what else to say. Instead I leaned against the door frame, closed my eyes and gave a little whimper. 'What's your name?' Tale's mother asked. 'Barnum,' I whispered. 'Barnum?' 'Yes, would you say to Tale that Barnum's asking for her?' She leaned a little closer. 'What have you done to your arm, Barnum?' I opened my eyes. 'Broken it,' I groaned. She let me into the hall and asked me to wait there. She had a worried expression. The furrows gathered her face into one knot in the middle. She disappeared into the flat. I waited. It smelled of soap and boric acid, like the waiting room of the school doctor's. I noticed a piano in the living room, its lid down. There were no flowers there. A pair of glasses lay on a chest of drawers, staring at the wall. I reckoned Tale's mother would come back to get me. But instead Tale herself appeared in the hall. She stared at me in amazement. The mole was shining beneath her eye. I had to find a chair against which to support myself. I whimpered. I was on the verge of falling. 'Barnum,' she said, nothing more. I hadn't heard her speak before. Her voice was dry and low. I straightened up. Her mother was standing at the far end of the living room. Then she disappeared. 'Yes,' I whispered. And I realized that perhaps Tale wouldn't know who I was because she'd never seen me – it was just me who'd seen her. And if she did know who I was then it was because she'd heard the rumour of that hopeless retard of a midge in the other class. Rumour of the school's smallest pupil, the smallest boy in the city – the one who only reached up as far as the girls' fannies, and who was greeted by laughter everywhere he went. I began losing my nerve. 'I'm in the other class,' I told her. 'I know that. But what are you doing here?' She appeared more impatient now than surprised. There was a ring of mud round my shoes. My arm hurt. 'I've broken my arm,' I said. It didn't make much impression on her. She didn't put her hand gently on the sling and ask where it hurt. She didn't kiss my cheek to comfort me and ease the pain. 'How did you know where I lived?' she asked instead. 'Did you follow me home?' 'Yes,' I admitted. There was quiet a moment. And very slowly a smile appeared on her lips, the tiniest smile – it was as if her lips were too small for a full smile. But it was enough for me, that little smile was more than enough. 'How did you break your arm?' she asked. I had to close my eyes again. 'In gym,' I told her, and regretted the answer as soon as I'd given it. This lie could fray at the edges and unravel completely, but it was too late to change my mind now. 'I jumped over the horse and landed wrong,' I went on. 'The bones came right out of my elbow.' Someone on the landing was fiddling with the lock, and Tale turned towards the door which was then opened, and her father came in. 'I can't see,' he said. 'I've forgotten my specs. Where are they?' At once Tale's mother was there to give him his glasses which had been lying on the chest of drawers, staring at the wall. He gave a sigh of relief, drew Tale close and kissed her brow. 'How are you, my sweet?' he murmured, and she slipped from his hold. 'This is Barnum,' Tale's mother said quickly, and he turned in my direction and blinked. 'Barnum? Well, hello, Barnum. Have you hurt your arm?' But I didn't have time to reply. 'He broke it jumping over the gym horse,' Tale said. 'Oh, dear, let me have a feel.' 'No!' I exclaimed. Tale's father laughed. 'Calm down, lad. I'm a doctor.' He started rolling up the sling. 'But why isn't it in plaster?' he asked. I turned towards Tale. 'I like your mole,' I said loudly. Tale's father dropped my arm. Tale tried to keep smiling but her lips couldn't manage and her mouth puckered like mud. Suddenly I thought she looked ugly, she and her mole. 'I think you should go now,' her mother said. I only remember standing in the street once more. I had my bag on my back and the ring in my pocket. It had all been in vain. I didn't even dare look up at the window on the second floor. I was finished. Barnum's story was over. I might as well go and lie down. It was still raining. I went through Frogner Park. I tore off the sling and gave it to a drunk sitting shivering under a bush. People could feel sorry for him instead. When I got home I just went to my room and lay down. Shortly afterwards Mum appeared at the door. 'I'm ill,' I whispered. 'Leave me.' 'Ill? What is it, Barnum?' 'I'm just ill. It's infectious. I can't go to school tomorrow.' Mum sighed. 'Nor do you need to. It's the first day of the holidays.' She sighed again as she closed the door, and I realized that Boletta was at the North Pole again drinking beer.

I stayed lying where I was. The time for dreams was over. I had dreamed my final dream. I pulled the quilt over me and wept. I was at sea and I sank in deep water. The hull wouldn't hold. It fell to pieces and I went to the very bottom. To think I could have said what I did about the mole! To think I could have pretended my arm was broken! Why hadn't I pretended I was mute instead? Then I could simply have given her the ring without saying a word, and the ring with its single letter would have spoken its own clear language! Now I hadn't given it to her at all and everything was too late.

Mum came in with supper. I didn't touch a thing. She took my temperature and went again. Later on Fred came in. He went to bed and lay for a while listening. I didn't say a thing. I could smell tobacco and beer. 'Can't you be bothered telling your brother?' he murmured. 'Or are you just a half brother?' 'What, Fred?' He groaned. 'How it went with the ring, of course.' I thought a bit. 'I didn't give it to her,' I told him, my voice low. Fred sat up in bed. 'You didn't have the guts, you mean? You chickened out, like a bloody wimp?' 'No!' I all but shouted. 'I was in her home!' Fred sank back down on his pillows again and stared up at the ceiling a long while. 'You said something about her mole, didn't you?' I crept as far under the quilt as I could. 'Yes,' I whispered. I could hear the sound of singing down in the street. It was Boletta. She was singing hits everyone had grown sick and tired of ages ago. Mum began bustling about and rushed down to get her before there were complaints and the caretaker was roused. Then the night went quiet, except for my heart. 'I told you you shouldn't say anything about the mole,' Fred whispered. 'D'you not listen to me any longer?' 'Yes, Fred. I do listen to you.' 'Think of all you could have mentioned, Barnum. Her eyes, her mouth, her ears. That's what girls like to hear.' 'Her nose too?' I asked cautiously. 'Yes, her nose too. And her neck, her hands, her feet. But wait a bit as far as her bum and her tits are concerned, Barnum. Till the coast is clear.' 'I'll wait,' I whispered. I could see Fred shaking his head in the dark. 'Is she nice-looking?' he asked. 'Yes,' I told him. 'I've never seen anyone nicer.' 'And you manage to mention her mole instead. You'll have to put things right, Barnum. Otherwise you've messed up big time.'

I think Fred went to sleep. That was the best conversation we'd ever had. I had the urge to go over to his bed and lie down beside him. Mercifully I didn't. I lay where I was thinking about everything I could put right. It was something to draw comfort from. I saw before me the ship that had slid out from the Akers Mek dock and sank in the black water. But it still wasn't too late. The ship could be raised and brought back to its dock; it could be welded together and made sea-worthy once more. That was how my thinking went. My bed was my dock. And there I lay for the remainder of the autumn holidays, while others in my class picked potatoes on farms belonging to cousins in Nittedal, or raked leaves beside white country cabins on the fiords. I wondered what Tale was doing and then the mercury in Mum's thermometer rose so dangerously high that she was on the point of phoning for a taxi to take me to the surgery. But I survived. And when Monday came I declared myself fit and well, got up and went to school with the ring in my pocket.

I didn't see her at break time. But I did see something else. The girls from her class stood crying by the sheds. Next period I couldn't concentrate. Something was wrong. Knuckles was even paler than usual and asked what I, for one, had done in the potato holidays. Laughter spread through the class, and Mouse managed to say: *They thought Barnum was a Kerr's Pink*, before he got the pointer on his neck like a whip and had swallowed half his tongue, as dust snowed over the sudden silence. Nor was she there at lunchtime either. The sheds were quiet now. Not even the other girls were there. Preben was standing with Hamster and Arnold beside the drinking fountain, staring at me. The janitor had turned off the water. I went the long way round the first year classroom and ran in the back entrance, past the school canteen and up to the third floor. All was utterly still. It was lunchtime. Someone had dropped a sausage sandwich and just left it lying there. The pegs stuck out emptily from the walls like a row of shining question marks. The ring was in my pocket. Something was very wrong. Slowly I walked the length of the corridor. The door to her classroom was open. I stopped and cautiously peered in. The girls sat quiet, their heads bowed, in a circle round a desk on which a white candle was burning. Someone was crying, soundlessly. On the blackboard in large letters were the words – *Tale, we miss you*. I retreated. I hid under the pegs. Then Knuckles came round the corner and I ran straight into her. Her hand came down heavily on my shoulder. 'And what are you doing in here?' she demanded. But for one reason or another she didn't seem angry. I decided to tell the truth. I had nothing else to lose. 'I just wanted to give Tale something,' I whispered. She lifted her hand and it grazed my cheek. Her fingers were cold. She crouched down. 'Tale isn't here any more,' she said, her voice low. 'Has she changed schools?' I asked. Knuckles twisted her hands till the nails cracked, and it was absolutely true – she stank of old medicines as if her face was a one-time chemist's. 'Tale is dead,' she murmured. *Tale is dead*, I said inside myself. *Is dead. Dead*. 'That can't be right,' I said. Knuckles gave the tiniest of smiles and held my hand. I wished she would let it go. 'Tale died over the holidays, Barnum.' I pulled back my hand. 'How, though?' 'She had a terrible disease. Cancer.' Knuckles leant closer still, whispered. 'Her mole. It was malignant.' 'I have to go,' I said. 'The bell will be going soon.' I went back down the corridor. I ran my finger along the pegs. And I thought to myself – *Now Tale can't tell on me. Now I'm safe. Now she can't tell anyone I came round with my arm in a sling and lied*. And I thought at the same time that this was the wickedest thing I'd ever thought. 'What was it you were going to give her?' Knuckles asked. I stopped and turned round. She was standing outside the classroom and some of the girls peered out, pale and silent. I picked up the piece of bread at my feet and slowly ate it. And what I said now was really even more wicked than what had gone through my head. 'Nothing,' I said. Then I ran down the staircase to the loos, fell on my knees and vomited up everything inside. After that I dropped the ring into the toilet bowl and pulled the chain. But I regretted it as soon as I'd done it. Fortunately the toilet was pretty blocked and had been so for a long time. I stuck my hand down as far as I could into the brown water, searched with my fingers through soft lumps and paper, and in the end found it. I dried the ring as best I could on my jacket and slipped it back into my pocket. T for Tale. T for Tongue-tied.

The bell rang. I went home. There was no one there. I got the key to the loft and sneaked up there. I was a bad person. I knew it. I was a bad person – that was the only sizeable thing about me, my badness. I stood up there in the drying loft among the low-slung clothes lines. Drops of water fell from the window. The wind made the puddle

on the floor tremble. My thoughts were ranged in a circle
of blackness at the back of my eyes. How could she die
when her father was a doctor? And the only thing I could
see was her mole; it spread over the whole of her face and
grew until it covered her entire body. Then I became
calmer. Then I felt cold and empty. I went back to the coke
shaft and hid the ring there, under the rusted hatch
beside it. Then I found something else. Under a piece of
sacking there was a bottle. Eau-de-vie was written on the
label and it was half full. I uncorked it and drank. My
teeth hissed with fire. But afterwards laughter rose up in
my head. It was a kind of laughter I liked. I drank some
more and put the bottle back under the sacking. The
laughter was so good in my head. I climbed the ladder to
the attic window and opened it as wide as I could. I was
barely able to hold it. I looked out over the city. Everything was moving. Nothing would stand still. The weath-
ervanes took off and became a distorted flock over the
fiord. But when I looked away towards the graveyard to
the west, the dark trees stood like swords under a grey
sky. And a procession of black-clad people bore a white
coffin between the stones and stopped at a place where
the ground was exposed like a newly-picked scab. I tore
off my jacket, stuck my right arm over the edge, left it
there, drew in my breath and let the window drop. I was
aware of it crashing and in the same instant the laughter
in my head was snuffed out. I lost my footing, but
remained hanging from the window, before bringing
shards of glass with me and tumbling down the ladder,
rolling round the clothes lines and meeting the floor –
elbow first.

    With half an eye I could see Boletta. She was crouching
over by the coke shaft raking about under the sacking.
Then she found the bottle that was lying there. She drank.
I wasn't dreaming. It was real. I'd been out for a long
time. I don't know how long, it was just time. But in the
shattered attic window darkness was already sinking
between the fragments of glass. Blood was pouring from

my arm which lay crookedly at my side. The skin had been torn in one long strip and something white and shining glittered at the very heart of the wound. I fell into a faint again. And then Boletta turned round. She screamed and I heard the bottle falling from her hands, and the scream that followed was closer. So it was that Boletta carried me down the staircase, and the whole time she did so she talked – to herself, to everyone, to God. 'I'm going to burn down that loft. Yes, I am. I'm going to burn that loft to the ground!'

I woke in a bed at the surgery. Mum was sitting beside me and she ran her hand through my hair. I think she'd been crying. My right arm had been stitched. Thereafter I was wheeled through to another room where it was put in plaster. I tried to raise my arm but couldn't manage. 'How did we get here?' I asked. Mum smiled and kissed my brow. 'We took a taxi, Barnum. Don't you remember?' I shook my head. 'No, I don't. Blast it,' I said. But I got a taxi home the following morning, my arm in a sling, a white sling. And slowly my memory came back. Everything I'd wanted to forget became clear. Now I didn't have to pretend. I had become the one I was. Mum and Boletta had to help me up the steps. I drank some cocoa, swallowed a round pill, laughed a little and went to sleep. The next time I came to Fred was standing at the window, his hands in his pockets. 'Hi, Tiny,' he said. 'Hurt yourself, huh?' Then Mum came in and I had to go back to school. I tried to protest. But it wasn't working now. She helped me with the sling and fastened it at my shoulder with a safety pin. Boletta had made a packed lunch with eggs and herring, but I was hollow and full. And so I wandered out, in that which I'll call my second life – my life after Tale – along the path of the low and all but white autumn sun, the length of Church Road. Esther leaned out of her kiosk and gave me a bag of sugar candy. I didn't have to buy a ticket on the tram. A lady got up and gave me her seat. The conductor supported me going down the steps. It was just as I'd wanted it to be – this was what I'd dreamed of. But now it didn't give me any pleasure, nor did it give me any sorrow to rejoice in – just an even greater emptiness.

I was the only one in the playground. The bell had gone. Slowly I went up the steps. I heard the echo of my own footsteps long afterwards, and once or twice I could hear the echo *before* I put my foot down. Then I stopped outside the classroom. It was utterly still. It was horrible. My arm hung heavy in the sling. I knocked. The stillness lasted a little longer. Then I heard Knuckles' voice. 'Come in!' I opened the door. All the boys were standing beside their desks staring at me, and on the blackboard, in huge letters, were written the words – *We've missed you, Barnum*! I wanted more than anything to go back out, but Knuckles led me over to her table and there was a cake the girls in the other class had made. I had to eat the first piece, and it had a thick, grey glaze on top and solid-baked raisins; I ate as Knuckles took off my school-bag and helped me to my seat. *We've missed you, Barnum*. I chewed and chewed and couldn't get the cake down, and when there was nothing left on the plate Knuckles hung up a colour drawing representing the inner parts of an arm and pointed at me. 'Now you can tell us what happened, Barnum.' But I had nothing to say. I had a mouth full of cake and lies. Knuckles just smiled and pointed to the drawing. 'All right then, Barnum,' she said. 'But our arms are the most vital work tools we possess. When we stand tall the tip of our middle finger will reach to about the middle of our thigh. But our right arm is generally half a centimetre longer than our left since that's the one we use most frequently.' All of a sudden she interrupted herself. 'And what are you laughing at now?' she demanded, very loudly, because everyone in the class, except me, was hanging red-faced over their desks laughing. And I was almost happy, because now things were as they were before. Knuckles came down from her table, her pointer in the air. I swallowed the last of the cake, and suddenly Knuckles turned round to face me instead, and lowered

the pointer. 'Did you say something, Barnum?' I hadn't
said a thing, nothing I'd heard myself. And I was afraid I'd
let slip some unheard words, *Knuckles' fanny*, and now
everyone was looking at me and I had to say something. I
asked a question, for surely a question can't be a lie?
'Would you sign my plaster?' I asked. Knuckles hesitated
a moment, as if greatly perplexed. Then she fetched her
fountain pen and wrote her name slowly on the plaster in
small, wobbly letters – *Miss K Haraldsen, M.A.* Then the
bell rang.

And during break time the whole class queued up to
sign my arm. The girls from the other class came too –
yes, soon enough the whole school had written their sig-
natures. In the end it was Preben's turn and the other
boys stood in a noisy huddle, because in a playground
everyone knows everything – all that's said gets passed
on. There are no secrets here, and here the rumours fly.
'D'you know why your right arm is longer?' Preben asked.
And he answered his own question. 'Because that's
the one you wank with.' He signed his name beside
Knuckles'. 'So now your left arm'll become just as long,'
he said, and joined the others in one big circle of laughter. They laughed and laughed. I began to laugh myself.
'Not if you do it for me,' I said. There was utter stillness.
They gawped. They shuffled forwards. Everyone in the
playground stared at us. But they couldn't beat me up
now. They knew it. I knew it. I'd just asked for a complete
and utter hammering at some point in the future.

When I got home Fred was still standing by the
window, hands in his pockets. I sat down on my bed.
'Hasn't Dad come home yet?' I asked. Fred turned to me.
'Who?' 'Dad,' I repeated. 'Is he working away?' 'Who are
you talking about, Barnum?' The blackness was back in
his eyes, that blackness that danced at the heart of his
eyes. 'Arnold,' I whispered. 'Arnold Nilsen, you mean.
That fat idiot with the greasy hair? The one who occasionally puts in an appearance, eats our food and shags
Mum?' I turned away, nodding. Fred looked out of the

window again. He shrugged his shoulders and lowered
his head. 'No idea.' I dug out the bag of sugar candy and
put it on the table. Fred just stood there. 'Help yourself,'
I said cautiously. The seconds ticked by. Then he said,
'Many thanks.' I didn't know if it would be so smart to
laugh, though I wanted to. But Fred didn't touch the
sweets and so I didn't, I didn't laugh. 'Many thanks,' he
said again. 'Help yourself,' I repeated. The brown bag just
lay there on the table. 'Would you help me if someone
were to beat me up, Fred?' He shrugged his shoulders
again. 'Not if you deserved it. Getting the beating. Now
he's coming, as a matter of fact.' 'Who?' 'Who? The fat
idiot who eats our food and shags Mum.' I was near to
tears. 'Don't talk like that, Fred.' 'Get free sugar candy off
Esther, huh?' But before I could answer Dad came in the
door, picked me off the ground and just about broke the
plaster. 'You stupid boy!' he shouted. 'Were you playing
at circuses up there, or what?' He put me down and
turned abruptly towards Fred. 'Was it you who took
Barnum up to the loft?' Fred just went on staring out of
the window. 'Look at me when I'm talking to you,' Dad
said, and put his good hand on his shoulder. A shudder
passed through Fred. 'Move your fingers,' he said. 'Now.'
Dad hesitated a second, then let his hand drop and he
turned back to me. 'I was just looking out over the city,' I
said. 'From the attic window. Then I fell. Fred wasn't
there at all.' Dad smiled, wiped his face with his handkerchief and ran his fingers over all the names on my plaster. 'Well, I never. You've plenty of friends, Barnum! More
than I've ever had!' Fred laughed quietly over by the
window. Dad got out five fountain pens from his jacket
and finally decided on the fattest of them. He took off the
top and wrote round the whole elbow. *Get better soon.
Greetings, Dad.* 'Where have you been?' I asked. Dad put
the top back on the pen and put it back into his breast
pocket. 'Where have I been? I've been working, Barnum.
How else would there be food to put on the table?' Fred
laughed once more. Dad's fist clenched, but the fingers

relaxed again just as quickly. 'Well, now I'm going to surprise Mum too!' he said, clapping his hands, and he went towards the door. 'Have you nothing with you?' I asked. He stopped abruptly and the great, shining face seemed to fall to pieces before the smile was hoisted into place once more. 'Have anything with me? But I had to get rid of everything I was carrying and come home to you, Barnum!' Then he vanished and left in his wake a sweet smell of perfume, hair oil and fruit pastilles. We were silent a good while. 'Perhaps he's been sitting the whole time drinking beer at Valka's,' Fred said in the end. 'He's certainly fatter in the face.' Fred sat down on his own bed and looked tired. 'Won't you write on my arm too?' I asked. 'Why?' ''Cos everyone else has.' 'Everyone? Let's see.' He came over to join me and began going through the names. That took its time. I waited. 'Can't see Cliff Richard's name here,' he said. He looked up. I didn't know whether to laugh or cry. I never did know when Fred looked at me like that. 'No,' I whispered. 'And what about King Olav? Has he written something, huh?' 'I meant everyone at school, Fred.' He bent over the plaster again and this time studied it an even longer time. Then he let go of my arm. 'T hasn't written here either,' he said. I couldn't believe something could hurt so much. It was so sore it almost made me happy. Fred lifted his gaze and maybe became aware of the change in my expression, for the dark in his eyes ran out, as it were, like oil. 'She's dead,' I whispered. Fred considered this. 'If anyone wants to beat you up, just thump them in the face with your plaster. Right? Right, Barnum?' I nodded. I was almost calm. Now I could dare to nag. 'Come on, write something,' I said. 'Please.' And Fred went for his pen. It was so strange to see it in his hand – it was as though it didn't belong there between his fingers. He could hold just about anything else without blinking an eyelid – knives, screwdrivers, hammers, saws, tennis-balls, stones, combs, javelins, whatever – but now his hand was trembling. He sat down beside me again, bent over, and began writing in the last possible space on the plaster. It took him so long. I laid my hand cautiously on his neck. It was warm and wasn't still. I could hear his breath and the heart that beat behind the thin shirt. Then he shook my hand away. And the darkness floated back into his eyes. He had written *Ferd*. 'It doesn't matter,' I told him quietly. 'To hell with you,' said Fred. 'It doesn't matter,' I repeated. He stroked his pen over the disordered letters until the nib broke on the plaster and the ink flooded the length of my whole arm and covered names in blue splotches that grew like shadows in some terrifying pattern. Fred got up and threw the ruined pen against the wall. 'I bet you did it on purpose!' he shouted. 'Did what?' I breathed. 'Broke your arm. You did it on purpose so everyone would feel sorry for you. Damn it to hell! You're a shit!' 'Yes,' I said. Fred was suddenly silent. He looked down on me, almost bemused. 'What did you say?' 'Yes,' I told him. 'I did it on purpose.' He suddenly began boxing my ears. I tumbled over on the bed. Then he let his hand rest still and soft against my cheek. 'How can I possibly look after you when you do things like that, Barnum?' Quickly he hid his hand in his pocket and was about to say something else, but couldn't get the words out. Instead he grabbed the bag of sugar candy and tore open the door. Mum was standing there between Dad and Boletta holding a huge cake on a plate. He pushed them out of the way and we didn't see him again until Monday – it was still just Friday.

But a long time later, after the plaster had been removed and my arm was left grey and thin and sewed up with a seam of crooked blue, and I'd begun at dancing classes and had met Peder and Vivian, Fred wanted me to go with him to Wester Gravlund. I didn't have any particular desire – graveyards held no appeal for me, they left me gaunt and sleepless. But Fred had already nicked two tulips from Bang's flower bed, and now he wanted me to join him because there was something he wanted to tell me, so I had no choice. I got to borrow his suede jacket into the bargain, and I wished someone would see me wearing it – Vivian, for instance. We met nobody. I thought first of all we were going to the Old One's grave but when we got there, to that beautiful and awful grave-yard (it was May and the trees were groaning under the weight of their own verdure), he went right to the far end, to the rough, disordered corner at the bottom of the side street of the dead. He laid the flowers by a slender wooden cross standing crookedly in the ground. Even I had to bend to read the name. K SCHULZ 1885 – 1945. 'Who's that?' I asked him. 'My doctor,' said Fred. I looked at the grave again. I didn't feel good. I wanted to go home. 'Sit down,' Fred said. We sat in the thin, golden grass. 'The finest rot first,' he said. I sat there, completely still. 'What?' 'The finest rot first,' he repeated, and it was almost as though he was smiling. He leaned backwards and I did the same. We looked up at the heavens slowly moving in the light. 'K saved my life,' Fred said. I almost didn't dare breathe. 'But how?' I whispered. 'By rights I shouldn't have been born,' he said. I lay completely still beside Fred in the rigid grass of Wester Gravlund. The wind passed through the trees. The sun flowed through. An ant crept the length of a blade; a plane appeared out of the sky. I tried to imagine Fred not being there, that I was alone, that it was just me – a single child. But I couldn't manage it. My dreams were dry, as if they too had been encased in plaster, and hung now just as thin and impo-tent from sleep's restless old body. A world without Fred was impossible to imagine, even though I'd wished often enough I could have been rid of him for good. 'What?' I said. 'I shouldn't have been born,' Fred repeated. I wanted him to go on, but rather hoped that he'd stay quiet. 'I was forced into Mum,' he said quietly. 'I should have been removed. Scraped out and chucked away. But Mum didn't say anything before it was too late and Dr Schulz was so drunk that he didn't find out I was there.' 'How do you know that?' I whispered. Fred smiled. 'I've listened. In the backyard. In the loft. There are stories everywhere, Barnum. But no one can say who my father is. The one who took Mum. The one who broke his way into her and destroyed her.' Fred was talking so strangely. I'd never heard him talk like this before. It was just as though he'd taught himself a new language or invented it himself. He tore off a blade of grass, stuck it in his mouth, and turned towards me. 'The best thing would be if he was dead, right? Right, Barnum?'

We lay like that a while longer without saying a thing. I was freezing. I wished Fred hadn't told me all this. There was so much I didn't want to hear. Then he got up, brushed the earth and grass from his shirt, and stood for a moment looking down at the two tulips and the wretched grave which no one visited and which soon would have grown over entirely. And I remember thinking to myself – *Can a person vanish without a trace?* 'Soon there won't be space for any more,' I said. 'Space for who?' 'Dead people.' Fred shrugged his shoulders. 'One more, at any rate,' was all he said. He lit a cigarette and began walking faster. I tried to keep up with him but couldn't manage. He left me at Wester Gravlund – that dark, thin form vanished behind the trees at Frogner Park, and I was left standing breathless on the narrow gravel path in the dissolving cloud of tobacco, between tall marble gravestones and bulging bouquets of flowers. And I thought one other thing, even though soon there wouldn't be any more room left in my head. *The dead are different too.* Then I saw it. It was Tale's grave. Her name was written on the black stone, the date of her birth and her death. *Our priceless one* – those were the words inscribed there. *Priceless and already lost.* And suddenly I realized that Fred had led me here to Tale's grave – he'd just gone some roundabout way first. And I felt such a warmth for him – yes, I really loved him at that moment, fully and sincerely, and I cried real tears for him, my half brother. I went back to Dr K Schulz and took one of the tulips and put it beside Tale's gravestone. I wondered for a while if I should fetch the ring but I let it be. It could lie where it was. And afterwards I forgot all about it, I even forgot myself because I had so much else to remember. But when Vivian was expecting Thomas and had moved into the attic in Church Road (which had been renovated and made into flats when money began to flow over this city), I sat there one evening under the angled skylight window drinking. I did so without any pleasure, just deliberately and stubbornly to accelerate oblivion, and then I came on something, namely that ring. It must have been somewhere in the wall by then, plastered in, and there was a certain joy in remembering it, that ring with the letter T, the first letter of the name of the girl who never received it, the ring that had been bought for her. The snow was falling against the sloping window. And I considered, as I drank up and drank myself down – we do not disappear without trace. We leave a wake that never quite disappears, a gash in time that we so laboriously leave behind us.

The North Pole

Fred woke me. 'We're going to the North Pole,' he whispered. I was awake right away. 'Now?' Fred nodded. 'Boletta's dancing, Barnum. Get going.' Fred had already dressed, had on a jumper, a windproof jacket, heavy boots, two pairs of trousers, a hat, a scarf and gloves. I put on the same garb, except for the type of boots. We were going to the North Pole. I couldn't take any chances. It was the middle of the night. Fred had even packed a rucksack in which he'd put oatcakes, cigarettes, a torch, coffee, a flask and some matches. We let Mum sleep. She slept beside Dad who breathed heavily through his nose, a quivering dark exhalation of sound that made the curtains tremble and the room shudder. It was like a whale that had come up for air. We sneaked down to the yard. The toboggan was standing there all ready. Fred secured the rucksack with some string. And so we pulled the sledge out through the gate and began the severe climb up Church Road.

It was so still. The snow was lit by its own brightness, or perhaps it was the moon that caused the ploughed edges to shine, as it hung there over the city like some frozen clock-face. At first it wasn't cold at all. I was almost incredulous. Maybe I'd put on too many layers? Long underwear with ski pants over them could be too much, and not a good idea either. But when we came to the crossroads, where Fred had been born in a taxi, my mouth was filled with a chill that spread like an iron fist through my face, and which knotted the skin to one tight point between my eyes. Fred went at the front and pulled. I stayed at the back and pushed. Our route followed the fence beside the hospital, where blue lamps were lit in the lower windows. Now I no longer heard the silence. I heard the runners of the sledge making a noise against the hard-packed snow and my boots squeaking at every step – soon I wouldn't be able so much as to wiggle a single toe. Fred turned round. 'Everything fine,' I shouted. We struggled on and all but went the wrong way at the school gardens, where one apple hung like a red droplet at the very end of a dark branch. We almost went east and then we'd have landed up in the pack ice round Torshov and perhaps never come home alive at all. Fred changed course. We had the moon at our backs. We passed Northern Gravlund; many had gone here before us and had had to pay with their lives. The gravestones cast long shadows in the night. *Don't give up*, the whisper came from every grave. *Don't give up!* I pushed. Fred pulled. He turned once more. 'The soles of your boots are squeaking something awful,' he said. 'It frightens the polar bears,' I whispered. 'Shut it,' he said. We had to go over an open crossroads; the wind stung from every point of the compass, and pieces of snow broke from the ploughed edges and were whirled in waves through the air. We were on the verge of slipping down to the foul waters by Alexander Kielland Square, and when we eventually got over to the other side we had snow in just about every orifice. We had to find somewhere to rest. We found shelter on the steps at the back of the church. There we could sit in the lee of the wind. We were at Sagene. It was still a long way to the North Pole. And between Sagene and the North Pole there were steep descents, deep gorges and rivers that tore the ice with ease with their fierce rapids and high waterfalls. My eyes bled tears but I said nothing. Fred lit a cigarette and I got a drag too. A cloud covered the moon. The dark became more intense. We were alone at Sagene, right beside the Arctic Circle. 'D'you remember André that great-granddad writes about?' Fred asked. 'Yes, the one they were looking for?' Fred gave me a biscuit. 'D'you know what he had with him on his expedition?' I didn't know. The only thing I did know was that he had a balloon with him that unfortunately came down on the way. 'Twenty kilos of shoe polish,' Fred said. 'Twenty kilos?' 'That's what I said, Barnum.' 'But why did he have twenty kilos of shoe polish with him?' Fred sighed. I shouldn't have asked. I should have known myself. Perhaps he wanted to grease the polar bears. Perhaps he wanted to leave a trail of black shoe polish in his wake in order to find the way back. Fred pointed at my unyielding boots. 'André had twenty kilos of shoe polish with him so he wouldn't get sore feet,' he said. 'Rather smart,' I whispered. 'Each morning and each evening he used it to soften his boots, Barnum. There's no point having the best equipment in the world if your shoes don't last.' 'But it didn't help all the same,' I murmured. 'Twenty kilos of shoe polish.' Fred was quiet for a bit. The moon broke through the cloud and for a second it was just as if the sun were shining down on us. We were blinded by the moon at Sagene that night, before the darkness restored our sight once more. 'No, it didn't help,' Fred said. 'No matter how much shoe polish you take you can never be sure.' I ate another biscuit and had a gulp of coffee from the thermos. 'Did anyone find him at all?' I asked. Fred nodded and started packing up the rucksack. 'Forty years later, Barnum. In a heap of stones on an island. There were just a couple of bones left. He'd been eaten by some creature or other.' I was freezing. More than anything I wanted to turn round now, go back the same way we'd come (if indeed it was still the same way, because maybe the snow had blown over it now). Perhaps our tracks were gone and we couldn't follow the moon either since it was somewhere else, its empty slice of light no longer to be relied upon. I stayed sitting where I was. The steps were cold. 'D'you think great-granddad got eaten too?' I asked, my voice so low I could scarcely hear it myself. Fred looked at me. 'He disappeared in the ice. And he's there yet. Still in one piece.' 'Still in one piece?' Fred secured the rucksack to the sledge. 'A glacier is like one huge freezer, Barnum. Everything keeps in it.' I could see it all before me and had to shut my eyes –

great-granddad deep in the ice, where time makes no impression, the same age as when he vanished and died. Perhaps he's stretching out one hand that's frozen solid and which no one managed to catch hold of. 'But what if the ice melts?' I ask. 'It doesn't melt.' 'But *if* it melts, Fred?' 'Just shut up, Barnum.' Fred began dragging the sledge on northwards. I ran in his wake. My boots squeaked. We had to cross the river with poles as flakes of ice drove past us in sudden merciless gusts. And then the string round the rucksack broke. We might have lost our provisions there, midway between Sagene and the North Pole, had it not been for Fred who lay down and caught hold of one of the ends before everything disappeared for good in the dark whirlpools near Møllene. We crept up onto a snowdrift and found a bench right down by the final, decisive slope. Fred swore and dragged the rucksack onto his back instead. 'What did they do when they had to go to the toilet?' I asked. Fred gave me a dismal look. 'You don't need to shit right now, do you, Barnum?' I shook my head emphatically. 'I just wondered,' I said. Fred pulled his hat down over his head. 'They had to shit where they stood,' he said. 'Did they really just shit where they were standing?' 'What did you imagine? That they had their own toilet with them?' I didn't quite know what I'd thought, but it was something I constantly had to consider, how astronauts, mountaineers, divers, fakirs and polar explorers actually went to the toilet. 'Nansen too?' I enquired. 'Nansen? What about Nansen?' 'Did he shit where he stood too?' The bit of Fred beneath the hat started looking a little weary. I shouldn't have asked. I should rather have saved my strength. The wind was getting up. The night was one raging, white circle. 'Nansen just had to shit where he stood,' Fred said. 'Roald Amundsen had to shit where he stood too. And the shit turned to ice before it hit the ground, so they had to be quick, Barnum. Bloody quick.' 'Did they?' 'They did indeed, Barnum. If not the whole lot might have frozen solid in their bums.' 'Oh, bloody hell,'

I said. 'Yes, you might well say that. And that's why they shaved their bums too.' 'Nansen?' I whispered. 'Have you got hair on your bum, Barnum?' I didn't answer. I'd basically never looked for it. I was glad I didn't have to go to the toilet. It was ages since Fred and I had had such a fine talk together, and it was even longer since we'd said so much at one given time. And now he said even more, as he got up and hunched his shoulders against the wind. 'They found more among André's remains than just bones,' he said. I got up too and had to cling to Fred so as not to fall over. 'What?' 'A watch. One of those old-fashioned watches with a lid. And inside his watch there was a picture of his girlfriend and a lock of her hair.' 'Did it work?' I whispered. 'Did it work? Are you off your head, Barnum? Who would there have been to wind it?' Fred shook the rucksack into place and we struggled onwards – that last slope in the land of ice and snow. I pushed, Fred pulled, and there at the top, at the innermost point of the endless plateau, golden light shone from high windows, and behind them I could glimpse people raising their arms as if all the time waving to one another. This was the North Pole then. Others had got here before us. 'They've beaten us to it!' I exclaimed. 'We've lost!' 'Now you really are going to shut up, Barnum.' Fred drew the sledge closer. I ran after him. 'Why do they call it the North Pole?' I asked him. He didn't answer. He stopped on the pavement by the sharp bend of the roundabout so that we were standing in the shadows between the moon and the street light. We stared at the golden windows. I saw people in there laughing and talking, but I could hear nothing. It was all silent, with their faces resembling red lamps, brightly lit and soundless. These men were sluggish and they could barely manage to stand up. The women in their midst wore white aprons and black dresses, and they went back and forth with heaving trays of foaming glasses and many empty ones, too. Then Boletta was there. She walked between the tables. They scrabbled to touch her but never succeeded. The men wanted to pull her down, but she pushed them away. Boletta laughed. Boletta clambered up onto a table and perhaps there was music there too, because Boletta danced on the table while the men clapped, and the faster she danced the slower everything seemed to go in my eyes. 'Boletta's having fun all right,' I whispered. Fred said nothing. And Boletta danced until she hadn't the strength for more, and sank into arms that were stretched out to catch her, a billowing bed of willing hands. And she was given a seat and a glass was put in front of her. All of a sudden I didn't want to see any more. 'Shall we go?' I asked. But Fred held me back. And it was too late anyway. We'd already been seen. The faces inside were turned towards us. The moon had shifted and we stood now in its cold glow, visible to those who still could see. And since that time I've never been able to forget the scene played out in there, silent and swiftly-moving – as if the window had been a screen and Fred and I were standing outside in the cold watching a film. And perhaps there was a thread from Boletta's life that was fixed here – a fine, thin thread that trembled when she danced on the table, and which was cut, which broke, that day the North Pole was finally closed forever. But for now a man in a white jacket came out of the doorway. 'What are you doing here?' he demanded. 'Waiting for Boletta,' Fred told him. 'So we can take her home,' I added. The white jacket vanished once more and soon enough Boletta appeared, supported by two men who could have done with some support themselves. One of them was wearing a kind of uniform – he looked like the conductor of an orchestra who'd lost all his instruments. The sweat froze immediately to thin flakes on their wide brows. 'We never get to take Boletta home!' the unsteady conductor exclaimed, and cackled with laughter. The other fellow didn't want to be outdone by the first and roared with mirth. 'Boletta is the North Pole's last virgin! No man has got closer to her than Father Christmas to his wife!' Fred took a step in their direction and his eyes had got back their blackness. 'Let my grandmother go,' he said. The sweat broke. The men became sober and meek. 'Shall we call a taxi?' the first one asked. 'We have the sledge,' Fred told them. They let Boletta go. She sank into our arms and we got her down onto the sledge. She was heavy and sleepy. Fred put his windproof jacket round her and she got my scarf to sit on. The two men wanted to help keep her warm too and began dragging off their coats. Fred just looked at them. 'She has enough.' The men put their coats on again. And on the other side of the window the rest of the customers and waitresses sat staring out at us. Now it was happening here, just as in the earliest cinemas when the screen was hung in the middle of the hall and soaked in oil, so that it became transparent, and people could watch the film from both sides. The other man, the one wearing the uniform, bent closer and laid his hand on Fred's shoulder. Fred shook it off. 'Boletta is our angel,' whispered the man. 'Take good care of her.' That we did. We secured her fast with string and then we pulled her home. Fred and I pulled together and Boletta sat on the sledge and slept. We pulled her safe and sound through the storm. We found the way. It was quite a night. There should have been fanfares and flags, grandstands and flaming torches! Oh, to have been seen now, with Boletta tied securely to our sledge, on the way home from the North Pole. And that did happen. Because as Fred guided Boletta, who was walking beside the banister in her sleep, and as I was opening the door as quietly as humanly possible with such frozen fingers I was barely able to hold a key horizontal, Mum was suddenly there instead, pale and out of breath. And behind her in the hallway Dad turned round, the telephone in his hand and his dressing gown the wrong way round, and our welcome lasted no longer than the time it took for Dad to bang the receiver down on its cradle. Mum pulled me close against her own dressing gown. 'Where have you been?' she murmured. 'Just to the North Pole,' I replied. And it was only now she saw Fred pushing Boletta up the last steps. Dad whistled loudly and Mum dragged her into the flat and all but banged the door in Fred's face. But he dodged it at the last moment, and the snow turned to sleet and began pouring from our hair and clothes. Finally Dad put down the phone. 'Well, I don't need to call the police after all then,' he said. 'Be quiet,' Mum told him. She went nearer Boletta, who had woken up. She stood there melting. 'Have you no shame?' Mum hissed. Boletta said nothing. Mum didn't stop. 'At your age! Have you no shame?' Boletta bent her head, but in truth I think it was mostly because it was too heavy to hold up for so long at one stretch. 'Well, well,' said Dad. Mum turned on him. 'Don't say well, well to me!' she shrieked. 'Well, well,' Dad said. 'Soon we'll have awakened the whole of Church Road.' He put his arms round Mum and the air somehow went out of her. This was the life she had to accept. This was the way things had become. Dad's nose was more crooked than usual – it pointed away from his face. 'Now I think we'll send the polar explorers to bed before there's a flood in here,' he murmured. Then Boletta lifted her head and looked about her amazed, as if she'd discovered us all at the same time. 'Greenland is a country particularly suitable for walking in,' she told us. And didn't we laugh! We laughed. Dad laughed through his whole nose, like a blocked clarinet in the night. We had to hold our ears. We laughed and held our ears. Even Mum laughed. She couldn't help it, and what would she have done otherwise – weep? Mum laughed instead. And Fred, even Fred himself laughed; he leaned against the wall and laughed his head off. He laughed, and it struck me as I looked at his thin, wet face split with laughter, that I couldn't recall having seen him laugh before, and that thought frightened me as much as it cheered me. And I thought too that I would make my own list of different sorts of laughter, just as Dad (who was laughing loudest of us all) had done once upon a time. And the list would have looked something like this: *Mum's laughter – albatross; Dad's laughter – cuckoo; Boletta's laughter – pigeon; Fred's*

laughter – cormorant; Barnum's laughter – auk. 'But what is it
we're laughing about?' Boletta suddenly asked. And when
she spoke those words things fell so strangely silent.

I had a cold for two weeks. Fred had frostbite on both
ear lobes. Boletta had a hangover for seven days. But early
the following morning she came right into our room all
the same, banged the door and threw a slipper at each of
us. 'Where's the letter?' she hissed. Fred brushed away
the slipper and sat up in bed. 'In my bag,' he mumbled.
And his battered school-bag with its torn zip was sitting
under his chair. Boletta whipped it up and spilled the contents over the floor. There was a good deal there: four
stones, a knife, three packets of sandwiches, a broken
pencil, a screwdriver, a Mercedes badge, an empty bottle
of Coke, some matches, a packet of Hobby cigarettes,
rolling paper, a cycle chain, two manhole covers, a
condom, an essay jotter – and last but not least the envelope appeared, and Boletta pulled out the letter to make
sure it was there. It was. She turned towards Fred who
was sitting there in bed with his head bent and his ears
crimson. 'Why did you take this to school?' 'To write an
essay,' he said quietly. 'I'm sorry, Granny.' Fred said sorry,
and I even think he blushed. Fred blushed and said *sorry,
Granny*. Boletta came closer. 'Well, Fred. Get to the point!
I have a headache!' Fred searched for the right words.
They were difficult to find. They were higgledy-piggledy
in his throat, they tumbled down his gullet, they got
stuck at his larynx. 'I wrote about the letter,' he murmured at last. Boletta waited. It looked as if he was going
over it in his mind. 'What did you have to do?' she asked
him. 'To write about a hero.' Fred spoke still more quietly.
Now Boletta was smiling and she patted his cheek. Fred
turned away. His ears were burning. 'But what did you get
for the essay?' she enquired. 'An A,' Fred said quickly. 'An
A? Well, and it deserved nothing less!' Boletta went
towards the door. She stopped there. 'Never take this
letter out of the house, Fred! Nor you, Barnum! Is that
understood? Never!' 'Yes,' I said. 'Yes,' Fred whispered.

Boletta kept standing there and then she said something we didn't understand but never forgot either. 'Because everything we come from is contained here,' she said, and waved the envelope in the air. Afterwards we lay in silence a good long while. I was sweating. Fred was burning. 'Did you really get an A?' I asked him. 'F,' said Fred. 'Is that what you got?' F was less than nothing. F was the other side of failure. F wasn't a letter, it was a death sentence. Fred stared up at the ceiling. It looked as if the pillow might catch fire. 'I didn't even manage to copy it out,' he whispered. He turned and faced the wall instead. I'd never got an F. F was about the only thing I hadn't ever had. I think I had a temperature. 'I could write your essays for you,' I said. 'Shut it,' Fred said. All at once he sat up again and began pulling on his shirt. 'I can write your essays if you look after me,' I whispered. Fred peered out of the collar. 'I can't look after you when I'm at that bloody school for the retarded!' I sat up now too. 'Why are you actually there?' Fred loomed against me as he pulled his shirt into place. 'Don't you know, or are you just pretending?' 'Yes,' I whispered. He grabbed my shoulder and pushed me backwards. 'Then say it, you thick-head!' 'You say it,' I whispered. 'Because I was born in a bloody taxi!' And Fred blushed once more, pulled on the rest of his clothes and went to the door. 'Can't be arsed talking to you any more,' he said. Fred just went. I think it was a Sunday. The stillness was almost complete and I had a blocked nose. Outside our tracks had long since been covered over. A bird caused the snow to scatter from a wire. I tidied Fred's things. I put everything back as it had been in his bag. But I had a quick glance at his essay jotter. There was nothing in it. The pages were empty. I shut my eyes. Then I tiptoed into Boletta. She lay on the divan with a chunk of ice on her brow, and as the ice melted the water ran like brooks through the furrows that spread down over her face. The letter, in which everything we came from is contained, lay under her hands. I prised it loose. I read. *We were to walk across a peninsula to*

map a fiord that lay on the far side that was covered with ice; for
that reason we could not travel there with the ship. We had five
to six Danish miles to walk, and the same distance back, but
Greenland is not a country that is particularly suitable for walking in. Boletta opened her eyes. It looked as if she were
crying. The furrows were too small all the same and the
water flooded over her cheeks. 'Why is it called Greenland when there's only ice there?' I asked. 'Because the
first people who reached it found a beautiful flower called
convallaria, Barnum.' I put the letter back in her hand.
'But why is it called the North Pole?' Boletta smiled.
'Because the beer's so cold there.'

Dancing School

It was actually Boletta who enrolled me in dancing school.
She came into our room in early September, a Wednesday
it was, just the vestiges of summer remaining hanging
from the Church Road trees, and diminishing all the time.
Soon there wouldn't be anything left to warm except bare
branches. I was doing my homework – nutrition – and
taking great pains to do it well. I wrote so slowly in my
workbook that Fred himself could have read it if he tried.
Where does digestion begin? In the mouth. Fred himself was
out; he was out wandering as Mum used to say with a sigh.
Fred's wandering again this evening, she'd say, and then I'd
see Fred's shadow, restless and thin and moving sideways
through streets and parks, past doorways and over
bridges. Boletta sat down on the edge of the bed and put
her fingers on my knees. 'Tomorrow you're beginning at
Svae's in Drammen Road.' I dropped everything I was
holding – my pencil, pen, rubber, drawing pins, marbles
and blotting paper – and turned towards her. 'Svae's?' I
whispered. 'The dancing school?' Boletta laughed and
leant closer. 'There's nothing to be so frightened of,' she
said. 'You're not joining the army.' But I'd heard stories of
Drammen Road, of the top floor of the Merchant Building,
about Svae, who was almost two metres tall and thin as a
fiddle. Svae who forced the boys to dance with her, and not
only that, to straighten their backs once and for all by putting an LP of Eddie Calvert between herself and the unfortunate boy, and heaven help the one who was all slack and
slumped over, and let the record fall to the floor. That
wasn't what I dreaded. I was well enough used to old
women. It was the girls who frightened me, the pretty
girls and the other boys. 'Must I, Granny?' Boletta shook
her head as if she couldn't believe her own ears. 'You

haven't really thought of going through life unable to dance? Huh? The rumba. The cha-cha-cha. The tango! Think of the tango, Barnum! Think what you might miss out on!' I thought about things for a goodly time, but not about the tango, the cha-cha-cha or the rumba. I thought about everything I'd like to miss out on, and that one misses out on most things in life, and it was poor comfort but a comfort nonetheless. 'Why hasn't Fred gone to dancing school?' I asked. Boletta looked up at the ceiling and sighed. The skin on her throat had slackened and hung like a small, wrinkled pancake between her chin and her breast, lying quite flat beneath the flowery summer dress she was still wearing. But soon enough autumn would take this from her too and pack summer up once and for all. 'It's different with Fred,' she said. 'How?' 'Fred wasn't born to dance. Tomorrow at six o'clock, Barnum.' Boletta was about to go, but I held her back and her arm was hard and difficult to grasp. 'What is it, Barnum?' Sun filled the whole window with almost crimson light, and this was perhaps the finest moment in our room, my room and Fred's, when the last flicker of light edged over the hill, down between the blocks and right in our window. It didn't last long, barely a few seconds, but it was worth stopping to observe. Then the shadows slid about us. 'Isn't it difficult to learn the steps?' I asked. 'The steps?' Boletta laughed again, and I got her breath full in my face. Was that how it smelled to be old, like opening a door to a room you haven't been in for ages? There was probably a lot of dust in Boletta's corners now. I took a step backwards, as if I'd already started dancing, and don't think she noticed. 'It's not the steps that count,' she said. 'It's the *leading*.' 'Leading?' 'Yes, *leading*, Barnum! Quite simply to take hold of the woman, in a friendly and firm way, and lead her. Women love a man who can lead properly. But now and again you have to slacken your hold a bit so the women think it's really them who're leading. You'll get the hang of it after a bit without a doubt.' 'Will I?' 'Yes, Barnum. When you've got it into you. And your hands have to be dry and firm. You can borrow some talcum powder from me. Can you imagine a slack, sweaty hand over your back and hips and somewhere else besides?' I shuddered violently and looked down. 'D'you think anyone'll dance with me, Granny?' She laid one finger under my chin and very slowly lifted my head. 'And why shouldn't they, Barnum? Why shouldn't women be queuing up to dance with you?' My face grew all heavy but Boletta held it up. There was a thin, sweet scent from her eyes or her hair; it must have been from her hair which was tied in a grey knot at her neck, and it was the only smell of Boletta I liked – it was like pudding. 'Because I'm smaller than them,' I whispered. She let me go and I looked out of the window. The street lights cast small shadows. I could feel her fingers yet, like dents in my skin. 'What sort of talk is this? D'you think women really worry about that? A few centimetres of height? Just you hold them firmly, Barnum, and *lead* them exactly where you want to go. And there was one more thing I wanted to say.' It had begun to get windy – I couldn't see it, I could just hear it – the rustling of the trees and the wood that released its darkness too over the city. 'What?' I whispered. Boletta lifted my face once more. 'Never look down. Look them in the eyes, Barnum. Otherwise you'll never get anywhere.' And I looked her in the eyes; she smiled and gave my brow a quick kiss. 'Six o'clock tomorrow at Svae's! Don't forget! And clean your nails before you go!'

Boletta took a few lopsided steps over the floor, gave a twirl, and disappeared in a gale of laughter, as if the laughter itself had asked her for a dance. Perhaps that was the way one went out the doors of the North Pole, but certainly not those of Svae's dancing school. If anyone asked me for a dance it would be Grief; Grief would twist my face and cover me with its rough hair. I put away my nutrition books for good that day. *How often is one to chew one's food? 26 times. One is to chew one's food 26 times or else one risks contracting stomach catarrh, constipation, infection of the gullet, swollen gums, bad teeth, hernia, or becoming a hunchback.* I skipped supper and went to bed before ten, even though I wasn't especially tired and I actually loathed that

slow moment before you fell asleep, when you just lie
there and time stretches like an elastic band, like round
brackets, like a blue balloon. Right until it bursts – a dull
noise behind the brow, a crackling in the eyes, like a light
bulb fizzling out and being broken by the dark. My
thoughts went on working, long after the light had gone.
I had too much energy in my head. *Look them in the eyes,*
Boletta had said. In that case I either had to use stilts or
else lean so far backwards that I'd break my neck. Who
would dance with a midget like me? I felt my hand. It was
clammy, almost wet; who would want a sponge like that
round them? I would have to hang it up to dry; chop it off
and peg up the whole hand on a clothes line among
underpants, shoelaces and black stockings. And as I lay
there in the narrow bed thinking the worst, and wishing
I was out wandering instead like Fred (because someone
wandering wouldn't have time to think too much, they'd
have enough just concentrating on wandering), I heard
the sewing machine whirring in the living room – Mum's
old Singer machine – and that was always something. I
liked the sound of it, it almost made me feel calm; it
sewed together the tears in the darkness, and stitched my
eyelids silently and gently to my cheeks and night was
made secure. And so I slept and dreamed that I was going
through the world carrying a sewing-machine – it was one
of the good dreams – and I was the one who repaired the
world. I slept stitch by stitch on a long, blue table and
woke abruptly when Fred came home, or did he wake me
on purpose? Whichever it was I was brought out of sleep.
Fred was sitting on the bed pulling off his shoes without
untying the laces as he usually did, and the main light was
on. 'Mum's taking up my trousers,' he said. I pulled the
quilt tighter round me. 'Is she?' 'Yes, Barnum. Last year's
grey trousers. She's taking them up half a metre at the
very least.' I didn't move. I just heard the shining scissors
in my head, the pair that cuts the hems in pieces, that
tears the world. Fred laughed and lay down in bed with
his clothes on. 'The biggest taking-up operation I've ever

seen, Barnum. Reckon it has to be more or less a world record. The world record for legs.'

I thought about my homework for the following day. *Where does digestion begin? In the mouth. On the tongue. In the fingers that lift the food from the plate; in the hand that carries the food to its destination.* I thought of Tale, the girl I never got to dance with, she who never got to dance with anyone. 'Are you asleep, Barnum?' 'No,' I murmured. 'So say something, then.' I lay still a long while. In the end I asked: 'Where have you been?' 'Nowhere.' Fred said nothing for a time himself. I think he was lying there laughing. I didn't dare look. I didn't dare put the light out. 'Are you going to begin at dancing school, Barnum?' 'Don't know,' I whispered. 'Maybe.' 'Don't you know? Don't be stupid.' 'Boletta's enrolled me.' Fred laughed all the more. It was a laughter that went inwards. It emptied space of air. 'You could borrow my plus fours instead, Barnum. Wouldn't that be fine, eh? Dancing pumps and plus fours. Take some sticks with you too.' 'Don't talk like that, Fred.' 'And if the girls try to take the piss out of you, just say they're my plus fours. Those are my brother's trousers, you can say. Right?' 'Please, Fred.' He was silent a moment. 'Are you crying, Barnum?' 'I'm not crying.' 'Yes, you are. I can hear you. You're crying, Barnum.' 'I'm not,' I told him. Fred sat up in bed. 'You cry about everything. You're a sissy, Barnum.' 'I'm not crying!' I shouted. 'I'm not crying!' Fred took a deep breath. He got up. 'Perhaps you could answer me on one thing, Barnum. If you really don't want to begin at dancing school, why don't you just say no?' I didn't reply. Fred went over to the door and put the light out, but just at the moment he stood there with his fingers on the switch, he turned towards me and slowly shook his head. He looked sad – not angry, just sad. 'No bloody idea why I keep picking you up.' That was how he put it. He used precisely those words – *picking you up* – as if I were a stamp, an autograph, a car badge or a bottle top. He lay down once more and shortly afterwards I could hear that he was asleep. But I just lay there thinking. I thought about those trousers, and I pictured Fred's trousers with the world's mightiest turn-up, and the blazer that was too long, and me in all these clothes with the patent leather shoes on my feet and my golden curls on top – Barnum from Fagerborg. The picture was blindingly clear in my head, and there were girls there too – girls from Skillebekk and Skarpsno and Bygdøy – girls who would most likely peer open-mouthed, before becoming all well-brought up and wicked and concealing their laughter. Before hiding their smiles and their sneers behind little hands covered with rings, and huddling together and talking just low enough for me to hear them – *look at that Tiny Tim over there, he's hardly worth picking up, you'd have to be down on your knees to get to know him.* That's probably the way they'd have talked and thereafter turned away completely as if I was nothing more than thin air it wasn't worth mixing their perfume with. And I'd most likely have to dance with Svae instead, an LP against my stomach, and as we danced the stitches in the turn-up would come undone and the folds would roll down over my shoes and onto the floor. And all the couples would stop in the middle of the waltz and stare at me crawling towards the door with my trouser legs trailing behind, as I shouted out that they weren't my trousers at all but Fred's, my half brother's, the illiterate thick-head – *they're his trousers and it's his fault.* And as I thought all this, all at the same time, in one furious picture that flashed past my eyes between two black frames, the stitch in my stomach that I got now and again came back, and I sank down and couldn't keep it in. *Explain how food is continually pressed on. The intestines have muscles that are drawn together and expanded. In this way the food is pressed through.* My bum was doing its homework. It flowed out of me. I closed my eyes in the dark. It was running. If I'd had the choice at that moment I'd rather have been dead. My pyjamas were sticking to my thighs. It felt warm and soft. It was impossible. Fred woke up. I could feel his eyes. I lay as still as I could. How long was it possible to lie like this? How many sewing machines

were there in the world? And were there just as many
pairs of scissors? Fred's shadow grew restive. 'What have
you done now, Barnum?' 'Nothing.' 'Nothing? Have you
done nothing?' 'Cross my heart, Fred. Aren't you going to
sleep?' If I just lay like that long enough it would pass; it
was all just a question of time – the one who holds out
longest wins or bores himself to death. And it was almost
a comfort to know that I could lie like that and let time
pass; the seconds would work for me like the old clock. If
I lay like this till I was dead I could pull out a drawer of
toilet paper and the minutes would wipe up after me.
That was settled. I wouldn't get up again. I'd lie here and
this bed would be my grave. Fred lit the lamp and looked
at me. 'It can't be,' he said. 'What, Fred?' 'It can't be,' he
said again. It was dropping onto the floor too, watery
brown drops. I was a drain, a gutter – I was a toilet that
someone had forgotten to flush. I surrendered because
how else could I give myself up? 'Help me,' I whispered.
'Help me, Fred.' Fred stood for a bit holding his nose with
both hands. Then he opened the window and came over
to my bed. He stood there for a bit looking down at me.
'What are we going to do about this then, Barnum?' I just
shook my head, because everything inside me had gone to
pieces. 'I don't know. Help me, Fred.' And he thought a
good while. Not even the cool air from the dark outside
lessened the stink. 'Shall I give Mum a shout?' 'I'd rather
you didn't,' I whispered. 'Shall I get your father?' Fred
laughed before I'd time to answer. 'No, damn it, he's not
at home. Where is your father, Barnum? The one with the
hairstyle.' 'Don't know,' I answered, my voice as low as
his. 'Working perhaps.' 'Of course. He's working. But
where's my father? Shall I give my father a call too?'
'Don't know,' I whispered. 'Don't know what?' 'Where
your father is.' Fred smiled. 'Wrong, Barnum. You don't
know who my father is. How can I call him then?' I said
nothing. Fred bent over me. 'We'll tidy up after you then,'
he said at last. 'How d'you mean tidy?' I asked cautiously.
Fred gave a deep sigh and went backwards, towards the
window. 'Get rid of the shit and change the bedclothes.

Perhaps I'll chuck you away too.' 'Don't you think Mum'd notice?' 'If I chucked you away? She'd thank me, Barnum.' 'Don't talk like that, Fred.' 'You're so small no one would notice the difference anyway. If I chucked you away. I'd just say you fell down a drain and were gone.' I think I started crying again. Fred came closer. 'Have you any better ideas?' he asked. But I hadn't. I got up, slowly and stiffly. Brown mush ran from my pyjamas. Fred stared at me. This was something he wouldn't forget. Then he went. He closed the door soundlessly. No one could be as silent as Fred. I stood there by my bed. Perhaps he wouldn't come back. That would be just like him, to let me stand there in my own shit. I was freezing. I didn't cry. He came back. He had with him a fresh set of bed linen and an enormous piece of brown paper. I'd stopped asking questions. There was nothing else I wanted to know. He could do exactly what he wanted. He pulled off the quilt cover and the sheet, folded them up and put everything in the paper. Then he turned to me. 'Take off your pyjamas.' I took them off. I stood there naked. I was pretty much freezing. Fred considered me. 'Can I ask you something, Barnum?' I nodded. 'What's it really like being so bloody small?' I looked down. My skin was covered in goose pimples. My behind itched and burned. And then I answered in a way I didn't expect myself. 'It's quite lonely,' I said. Fred looked up and met my gaze – not for long, just a second, less than a second even. But he met my gaze nevertheless, suddenly, as if he was just as stunned as myself, and perhaps he recognized something of himself, perhaps he saw the shadow of blackness in my eyes too, since we were brothers after all. 'Shall we dance, Barnum?' Fred laid his hand on my shoulder. I sank rather. Then he laughed quietly, almost soundlessly, right close to my face, and let me go as quickly as he'd held me. He tied a piece of string round the bundle, took it up under his arm and was off once more. I think I heard his quick steps going down the kitchen stairs. I sneaked out to the bathroom as quietly as I could and showered. The brown water rose in the drain; all at once I felt sick and afraid. I tried to press it, the brown water, and finally it diminished, ran away through the pipes, in the city's dark sewers, and out into the fiord by the Fred Olsen docks, where the eels lie shining fat in the stinking mire on the bottom. I listened. Everyone was asleep. There was no sound except that of the escaping water. I took out the talcum powder from the cupboard above the sink. I doused myself in talcum – a dry snowstorm of it – and squirted a little cologne on my tummy and thighs and throat. No one heard a thing. I was standing in the middle of a great, deep sleep. I could do whatever I wanted in the middle of the others' sleep. Perhaps I was just someone the sleepers dreamed of? I turned to face the mirror and saw my face, pale and only just visible, my curls hanging like punctured spirals round my head. I was real, for a dream can't be reflected – no one's managed that yet. I didn't find any clean pyjamas, but in the next drawer I discovered Mum's knickers. I put on a pair of them instead. They were far too big, even though Mum herself was pretty petite; I could pull them right up to my chest and they felt soft and fine – I almost didn't feel them on me at all. Like that I tiptoed back to our bedroom, in Mum's knickers and covered in talcum powder and cologne. Once there I changed the bed and lay down once more. I wondered if I could manage to be ill the following day. There were only a few hours to go. It was just beginning to get light. I could, for instance, cut off a finger with Fred's knife. I would be in good company in the family. Dad only had five fingers in all since what remained in the way of a thumb on his right hand could hardly be counted, it was more a lump of grizzled flesh. I could just cut off my little finger. I didn't have so much use for it anyway. When I considered it I realized it was pretty much surplus to requirement. I couldn't think of a single thing I couldn't do without. What had become of Fred? I got up again and went over to the open window. I stood there, in Mum's knickers, and felt strange, weird, as if I'd changed bodies. And I felt a dragging in my stomach, though this was a different kind of pull, quivering and dark. I had to lean against the window frame. Was Fred down in the laundry with the sheet and quilt cover? If I stood there long enough I'd get chilled. With a bit of luck I could contract pneumonia too. I wondered what it was human beings dreamed of. Was there someone who dreamed of me? Fred was probably away at the bins chucking everything there. I shut the window, put on Fred's dressing gown which smelled of moths and sweat and dragged over the floor. I was like a boxer who'd been put in the wrong weight category. I was a fly in the heavy-weight's dressing gown. And then I sneaked through to the living room. I tried to sneak like Fred, for Fred roamed and sneaked. Mum's sewing machine was up on the dining-table. Fred's old trousers were hanging over the back of the chair. They'd been taken up. They resembled shorts, grey shorts with a crease. I put my little finger under the needle. If I got the machine going now I could stitch them up and ruin them. Then Mum was there. I hadn't heard her. I hid my hand behind my back. Mum smiled and held her nightie tight about her. 'Are you excited?' she asked.

I looked the other way. 'Could you not get to sleep?' 'Had to go to the loo.' 'You don't have to dread this, Barnum.' 'I'm not dreading it. Just a bit excited.' 'Of course you are. D'you want to try the trousers now?'

I shook my head. I thought I saw Fred's shadow behind Mum, at the end of the corridor. Someone moved on the floor below – perhaps we'd soon have wakened the whole street, I thought. Perhaps my heart, banging in my chest, would waken the whole city and the rest of the world too. 'Tomorrow we'll buy you new shoes,' Mum said. 'You can't start dancing classes without new shoes, now can you?' 'Can't I just borrow Fred's?' 'They're just a bit big for you. Even if you have extra socks.' Mum suddenly took a step towards me and her eyes narrowed. 'Have you been using perfume again, Barnum?' I wrapped the dressing gown still more tightly round me. 'A little,' I whispered.

She gave a deep sigh and breathed out. 'How often do I have to tell you? You're not to use perfume. What would the girls think if they smelled perfume on you?' That I couldn't answer, for somehow I couldn't think that far. I couldn't even imagine them coming close enough to know what I smelled like, and if they did get that close they'd have to bend right down. No, it was impossible, it was almost like thinking of space – then the thought just dissolved in a measureless blue wind. And when the thought travelled so far that it no longer existed, it lost hold and fell slowly towards the inside of my scalp without ever landing. 'Dad uses perfume,' I breathed. 'He uses aftershave,' Mum said quickly. 'And Fred doesn't like you borrowing his dressing gown.' 'Sorry,' I said. 'Are you cold?' 'Not especially.' Mum drew her hand fast through my curls. I twisted away and she just laughed. 'Go and lie down again, Barnum. But wash your face first.' I ran out to the bathroom, stuck my head under the tap and got into bed, after hanging Fred's dressing gown back in the cupboard. I heard Mum going from room to room, as if looking for something she'd forgotten about ages ago and couldn't remember where she'd left it, or perhaps she was just walking off a restlessness that left her sleepless and irritable, and which no sewing machine in all the world could mend. Then her steps finally stopped and instead I heard something different – Fred's laughter – he was lying in bed already and was laughing quietly. I hadn't noticed him before and I didn't quite know what I liked least, Mum's pacing or Fred's laughter, when he laughed as he did now. 'What is it?' I murmured. 'Nothing.' 'What did you do with my pyjamas and the bedding?' 'No need for you to worry about that, Barnum. That's taken care of.' All at once he stopped laughing and sat up in bed. 'D'you hear me?' 'Yes, Fred.' 'You say yes to beginning at dancing school even though you don't really want to. Is that right?' 'Yes,' I breathed. 'Then there's only one thing for it, Barnum.' I sat up myself. 'What's that, Fred? Tell me, Fred.' 'Get yourself thrown out. As quick as possible.' 'How do I do that? Get thrown out, I mean.' Fred hid his

face in his hands for a time, almost as if he was sitting
there crying or had pain somewhere, the kind of headache
Boletta tended to get when it was thundery and she'd been
drinking beer at the North Pole the night before. I didn't
want Fred to get dangerous again. I tried to think about
my homework instead. *How often should we purge our
bowels? At least once a day. What should we do to avoid slow
bowel movements? Take exercise, eat brown bread, fruit and vege-
tables, and keep placid and clean*. 'But how would I get
thrown out?' I asked again. Fred looked up. 'First you see
what everyone else is doing. Then you do the exact opposite. Quite easy, really.' Fred had said enough and lay down
once more and turned away. I heard the paper boy coming
up the street – his great bunch of keys, the whining wheels
of his blue trolley – the trolley that was most likely full of
bad news. *Quite easy, really*. If the others were to take one
step forwards, I'd take one step backwards, or maybe two,
just to be on the safe side. When the boys were to bow, I
could curtsey. I almost grew happy just thinking about it –
it was like a joy in the dark – as if a burden had suddenly
been lifted from my shoulders, and the whole weight of
outer space released in my head. It was as if I'd been set
free. I could do whatever I wanted. Fred was smart. While
everyone else changed their shoes in the changing room
I'd go straight onto the parquet floor with boots covered
in mud, creepy crawlies, wet leaves and dog shit. The
record-player needle would jump the grooves as the trumpet of Eddie Calvert was burnt down in a black memory
with a hole in the middle. But when I thought of shoes, my
stomach began to slide again, just a little, and I curled up
inside Mum's knickers and did everything possible to
think of nothing whatsoever. Was it possible to become
thought-less, to douse each and every thought that glowed
inside, one by one, just as lights die out in a town at night,
to end up with nothing more than profound peace and
long silence? The paper boy ran up the steps. I didn't hear
him running back down. Fred was snoring, far away, and
when I was wakened by the rain on the window he had

gone. I saw before me a big day, perhaps one of the biggest
in my life. Mum opened the door a little. 'Hurry, Barnum,
or you'll be late.'

I laughed quietly to myself. That was something else I
could do. That was the least of it. I could come too late to
dancing school. There were no limits to what one could
do, and as I was thinking about all this (because it wasn't
possible to become thoughtless after all), I realized there
were just as many wrong things that could be done in the
world as right things, perhaps even more. Because when
you first begin to work out all the wrong things you could
do you somehow become more inventive; the possibili-
ties start presenting themselves. And I was in such fine
form that morning that I managed to do a sum without
being sick, and this was it. If you multiply all the right
things you could do by about three then you get the
number of all the wrong things you have on offer. I wrote
this piece of arithmetic on the back of my nutrition book
so as not to forget it, and I called it *Barnum's Formula*.
Then the door was opened properly and Mum looked in
again. I hid behind my bag. 'Well, what are you up to?'
'Reading though my homework, of course. What else?'
'That's fine. Just get a move on. And remember to put on
clean stockings.'

Mum vanished once more and the threads of my stomach began entangling themselves to one giant knot. I had
to concentrate on something else so as not to think of pan-
creatic juices, mucous membrane and intestinal fluids.
Instead I concentrated hard on my head, on all the wires
in my head which bound my thoughts together, just as at
the Telegraph Exchange where Boletta used to work. I
thought of the cerebrum, the cerebellum, the brain stem,
the spinal cord, and finally of what I liked best of all, the
extended marrow. Perhaps it could extend even further –
yes, one night it could increase down my back and so push
me upwards. But then I got dizzy and had to sit for a
minute on the bed, because it's tiring thinking about your
own thoughts. It would be like everyone at the Exchange

calling their own numbers and in the end getting the world's greatest engaged tone, or just hearing their own voices calling round and round. And out of all this a picture came into my mind, suddenly developed on the membrane of spun thought, as if it was this I'd really been thinking the whole time – of the American Walther, who spun six times round the world and landed with a sigh, two minutes later, after travelling 256,000 kilometres, west of the Midway Islands. And perhaps he thought as he floated out there in his cramped capsule, and saw the earth growing smaller like a blue coin in a dark well, that now he was the only one in the world who wasn't at home.

But when Mum knocked on the door for the third time and was on her way in, I put my foot down and made up my mind. I would begin to practise now, practise doing the opposite. For that reason I didn't put on clean stockings, I wore dirty ones instead. I went to the bathroom and washed my face and armpits, but didn't bother brushing my teeth. I was on my way. Fred should have seen me now. Now we were dancing to a different tune. Now we were dancing to a different tune all right, I said, and stood on tiptoe in front of the mirror and saw my curls springing up from my head like soft feathers, as if I were pulling myself up by the hair. Yes, indeed!

Mum was waiting for me in the kitchen. She had an impatient expression but her mouth was smiling – there was a kind of collision in her face so her skin was covered in skid marks. I sat down at the little table against the wall. Boletta was reading *Aftenposten* – she came to view every time she turned a page. I don't know if they saw any difference. That didn't matter because *I* felt it, the difference, inside myself, even though everything on the outside was just about the same. I wasn't the same person I'd been the day before. Fred's words had made me a new man. I was converted! 'No, thanks,' I said, as Mum pushed the dark, sweet blackcurrant jam in my direction, and she rolled her eyes, impatiently rolled her eyes and pushed it away again. But she rolled them all the more when I cut a piece of Danish cheese that had been on the go since about the time of the Old One's death, and which smelled so foul it should have had a kitchen to itself. Fred said once when he was in a good mood (don't quite know *why* he was in a good mood), that I could take the Old One's cheese for a walk in Sten Park, but I'd have to take it on a lead so it wouldn't run away. I laughed for half a week after he'd said that. Now I took a huge bit, my brainstem trembled and my guts were on the point of short-circuiting. Because after this I'd probably smell so awful that they wouldn't let me into the Merchant Building on Drammen Road at all, perhaps I'd even be hunted out of the city and the country altogether. That would have been a joy to me. I chewed and chewed, and it was as if all the cheese in Denmark grew under the roof of my mouth, and my epiglottis hung down like a pendulum of black pudding and pitched about in spit. It got harder and harder; everything became slow and heavy – Mum's expression, Boletta's fingers turning the pages of the newspaper, the rain running down the window. And I tried to remember my homework as I sat there and wondered when things would start to go backwards. *Why should we not drink with food in our mouths? Because then the food does not get sufficiently mixed with saliva. Why ought we not to talk or laugh with food in our mouths? Because then the food goes up our noses or down the wrong way.* I had nothing to laugh about and nothing to say. I was reduced to silence by cheese. Boletta dropped her paper and looked at Mum. 'Has Barnum finally begun to like Old Danish?' I nodded several times, even though it was Mum she was addressing, and in Mum's face there was still the same collision – her expression didn't trust me but her mouth kept on smiling. Boletta turned towards me. 'Girls like men to have strong smells. Strong smells and confident looks. But don't overdo it, Barnum.' Mum laughed. 'And if he doesn't get a move on I'll have to write a note to Miss Haraldsen to say he was late because of Danish cheese!' 'Her name's Knuckles,' I said.

But that was something Mum wouldn't have to do. There was nothing in the nutrition book about not walking with food in your mouth, or even running. I got my bag and was out in Church Road before anyone could reach the window and chuck my waterproof after me. Esther was opening her kiosk and had her hands full of weeklies, but she managed to wave all the same, and everyone waved to Esther. So I didn't wave back, I just stuck a clenched fist in each pocket and walked on, my back hunched and my mouth stuffed full of cheese, towards Majorstuen. I was an inverted pelican with enough food in my beak to last the rest of the year, and I considered that if things continued like this I might be thrown out of the world too. Not just dancing school and the country, but the rest of the world into the bargain, and in that way most of my problems would be solved at one fell swoop. But before I'd properly thought this through I was dazzled by the white wall of the church. I all but had to shield my eyes, blinded amid the raindrops, and I stopped by the church and unloaded all the cheese into the drain, and stuck my tongue out as far as I could into the rain to rinse it. Then I saw there was someone watching me, a man on the steps leading up to the wide door – he stood under his umbrella staring at me. His face was white behind the rain; his fingers too – he smiled with all his teeth and round his neck he had a collar, a white collar. It almost blended with his soft chin, and all of a sudden it struck me that everything about this individual on the third step of Majorstuen church was either black or white – his face, his umbrella, his hands, his collar, his teeth. It was the vicar who would baptize neither Fred nor myself. 'What a witty little fellow,' he said, and took a step down as if to see better. 'And what's your name?' The clock above him, on the high chalk-white wall, where the Virginia creeper extended like thin, glowing wires, was already showing eight-thirty. Soon I would be late. The vicar leaned over the railing. Now his voice was louder, though I'd heard him clearly enough before.

'You dare to stand there and stick your tongue out at me?'
The umbrella began to shake in his hand; it wouldn't have
taken much for it to be turned inside out and become a
black bowl in which he could collect the rain. He smiled
no longer. His teeth were hidden behind narrow lips. 'You
really dare stand there and stick your tongue out at me!'
He folded up the umbrella and was already wet when he
pointed at me with it. Now he was shouting in the rain.
'Can you see to get rid of that tongue of yours?' But I
couldn't get it back in my mouth. Only still more of it
appeared. I hadn't known my tongue was so long. I could
even see my own tongue and it was a weird sight which
I'd happily have been spared. 'My name's Barnum,' I said,
as clearly as possible with my tongue in the way.
'Barnum! D'you remember?' The vicar had to clutch the
railing. 'Yes, indeed, do you really think I could forget
you? You and your wretched brother!' I smiled all I could
and took a step closer. 'To hell with you,' I said, and ran
until I could run no further in the direction of the
Valkyrie, and didn't get my tongue back in my mouth
before I'd reached Vestkanttorg. Once there I had to rest
on a bench. I'd stuck my tongue out at the vicar! I'd stuck
my tongue out – every millimetre of it – at the vicar of
Majorstuen church himself! I'd sworn at him! To hell with
you, vicar! Fred should have seen me now. He wouldn't
have believed his own eyes. But it was true, each and
every word of it, and he'd hear it straight from the horse's
mouth. And there really was no point coming in to school
late after this. Soon it would be impossible to be any more
converted than I already was. God himself must be watching me now. So I ran the last bit of the way too and just
made registration as the bell rang. And at the very same
moment there was a flash of lightning; I didn't manage to
count to more than four when the answering thunder
rolled over the playground and made the steeples tremble. I began to feel worried. Perhaps I'd trodden on God's
toes? Perhaps God was offended? The girls shrieked and
the boys laughed, and suddenly my enemies were right

behind me. I can't be bothered naming them now, but it was the same mob as before; I heard one of them say something when the next thunderclap came. 'Beginning to get kind of dangerous here. Reckon we need a lightning conductor.' And then one of the others said something – it was just as if they'd rehearsed their sentences or written them down for the occasion. And I knew what they were going to say; I could have said it for them. But I counted in my head instead – the seconds before the thunder – and I got to just three this time. 'Perhaps we could use Barnum? As a lightning conductor, I mean.' And even though I was standing with my back to them I could somehow picture them as they nodded to each other and laughed, as if they'd hit on the best idea since they used me as a sledge on Bondebakken. I let them do their nodding and laughing, and then they hoisted me up, bag and all, and like that we proceeded to entrance B, as it flickered and banged about me. God was angry and I was electric. My curls extended like rigid corkscrews, and about then the Goat came and tried to drown God out with his whistle. But it didn't work particularly well, and instead he up-ended us. The thunder was a bit further away now (I could count to nine), and my hair slumped on my head and lay there as normal. It must have been similar to having a perm and all of a sudden I had the urge to say something. *God's a rotten hairdresser* was what I wanted to shout aloud, but I said something else instead. 'It was my idea,' I said. The Goat bent down, his eyebrows joined over the roof of his nose like a black hedge on his face, as he gripped Aslak, Preben and Hamster as best he could, and the whole school stood ringed around us smelling blood. 'What was that you said, Barnum?' 'That it was my idea. That they should carry me.' After a short but rather intense period of reflection the Goat let them go, shook the rain from his eyebrows and looked at me more closely still. 'Lightning isn't a plaything, Barnum! We should have respect for the forces of nature! Now, into your classrooms *immediately*!' 'Many thanks,' I said. I gave a deep bow and hurried up the stairs, and for the remainder of that day sat as still as I could at my desk, at the front of the middle row. Except in gym, when I was allowed to do my own exercise routine. The Goat was good that way, he'd basically given up on me and I even got out of changing. But I'd perhaps do the odd cartwheel, so slowly that I didn't need to shower afterwards, because I didn't go into the showers any more. That's all I'll say. Not after the time they grabbed my legs, pulled them apart like a chicken's, and did various things with the soap. But really there was no one who bothered me that much any more. And I could just as well be a lightning conductor and get carried about on their shoulders if that was the way it was to be. But there were occasions when someone or other had a go – when I was going to have a drink from the fountain, for instance – and had to stand on tiptoe at the side to reach the jet of water. Then it was that the clever clogs saw their chance to do something tough at my expense: to chuck water on my trousers, take me to the run-off channel and give me a soaking or call me names they'd recently taught themselves – midget, mitten, monkey, door handle. The blows glanced off me. I didn't care. I rose above it all – yes, I rose above it. Might they choke slowly and painfully on their own laughable laughter and then sink in their bottomless tears with millstones round their necks and their feet in concrete shoes. But the worst thing was when some of the girls took up my cause and said that it was horrid and couldn't they perhaps be a little more grown-up and not so dreadfully childish as to tease Barnum because he was a bit on the small side. Because it was a shame for Barnum, wasn't it, that when height was being distributed across the globe, he'd been short-changed as far as centimetres went? Then I could hate for several weeks at a time – yes, whole months I could keep hating, and that hate was like an engine inside me, a great dynamo that grated on the deck of my dreams and made a black light shine inside me, a reversed sun that shone darkness instead. And I imagine that the Old One's grief must have been akin to this, a wheel for her longing. Then I grew; I became bigger than myself in this hatred and I almost understood what Fred meant when he said he was evil, evil at the very core. I never drank water from the fountain again either. And in the course of the day I was to start dancing classes God calmed down and I was converted; the thunder rolled away over another town, the clouds parted and the skies showed their best side, became blue as they could be. God's calm didn't last long, however. God was impatient. The last lesson of the day was nutrition with Miss Knuckles – she'd actually earned her nickname long before our time – having had with her one time a genuine thigh bone which she proceeded to show her pupils. And rumour had it that it was her own father's thigh bone that she'd hidden away as a last reminder of him – pretty gruesome really when you thought about it – and some even maintained that she'd done away with her father with poison just to get hold of that particular thigh bone. There weren't very many who liked going too near Miss Knuckles; she smelled of various types of medicine and was absent from school at regular intervals. She'd apparently got too little sun and insufficient nourishment when she was growing up, and suffered from the English illness – perhaps that was why she'd killed her father and stolen his thigh bone. And when Knuckles was off for more than two days we got a supply teacher. This was the third day she'd been absent. I was already worried. The supply teacher hurried into the classroom in full flight as if she were looking forward to getting started. She seemed full of vigour, said *Sit down*, and as we did so she smiled from ear to ear and that made me really worried, because I knew that little good ever comes from smiles like that. At least you know where you are with the nasty ones. The nice ones can think up all manner of things. She told us what her name was and wrote it up on the board too, but I forgot what it was ages ago, and I'm not sure if I ever remembered it at all. I think I'd call her the

Leech. The Leech was filling in for Knuckles. That was
how it was. She went up and down the rows telling us
about hygiene in past centuries (as if that had anything to
do with us), and that one's sight was improved by eating
bilberries. And that wasn't all; she talked about hot and
cold water, tooth decay, school breakfasts, calcium, flat
feet, being hunchbacked and having bad posture. And
although I didn't dare turn round I could see that Hansen
and Mouse had already loaded their rulers with ammuni-
tion in the form of scrunched-up paper and bits of goat's
cheese. But then the Leech swept back to the table, con-
sulted the nutrition book, shaded her eyes and gazed out
over the class. She pointed at Mouse. 'What's your name
then?' She was the type who had to ask what everyone
was called before they got to say anything. My stomach
grew heavy, heavy as a sack of wet sand. 'Halvor,' Mouse
replied. 'Well, Halvor, can you tell me what the spleen is?'
Mouse thought about this for a while. 'An American
skater,' he said. The Leech was a bit despondent at this
response, but tried to laugh and pointed at Hansen
instead. I realized something. If everyone gave the wrong
answer then I could answer correctly. I hadn't forgotten
what Fred had said. 'And what is your name?' 'Hans,' said
Hansen. 'But you're welcome to call me Hansen.' 'That's
fine. Can you tell me where the spleen is?' Hansen pretended to think about this for several minutes but actually he didn't. He was asleep. Hansen had never thought
about anything, but he took his time all the same – no one
could draw out time like Hansen – once he'd managed to
make it last an entire period. The Leech began to get
impatient and her smile trembled on her lips like waves.
'What do you say then, Hans?' Hansen regained consciousness and the Leech went forward as if she were in
the presence of a genius at work. 'The spleen is', Hansen
said slowly, 'the spleen is a tune played by Finn Eriksen
on the request show.' The Leech, our supply teacher,
retreated behind the table and then of course her gaze fell
on me – who else? I knew what was coming now. 'And

what's your name?' Her voice changed when she addressed me, it slanted somehow in her mouth. The class was completely quiet. They were enjoying themselves. This was the best we could get apart from the final period before the summer holidays. 'Barnum,' I said. 'What did you say?' 'Barnum,' I repeated. The blood began pumping through the Leech's face. 'When I'm here as your supply teacher you're to use your proper names. Now tell me what your name is before I get cross.' 'My name is Barnum,' I said. The Leech pulled out a drawer, got out the register, banged it down on the table and buried her face in its pages. Then suddenly her expression became gentle from the forehead down; she looked at me intently and spoke even more softly than before. That's what I say – the nice ones are nasty, the nice ones never give up. 'Barnum? Can you, Barnum, tell us where the spleen might be in our bodies, Barnum?' It was almost a record. A supply teacher we had the year before in wood-work managed to use the word Barnum five times in the same sentence when he presented me with a plane. I didn't react. 'The spleen', I said, 'helps to clean the blood. And it's also where we get a stitch'. The Leech clapped her hands. She could have restrained herself there. 'That's quite, quite right, Barnum. Can you come up here, Barnum?' I kept my seat. 'Why?' I whispered. 'Because you're so clever, Barnum.' 'I can't,' I said. 'I've got a stitch.' But the Leech just laughed and wrote the word spleen on the board. 'Barnum! Now you come up here, Barnum.' I slid from my seat and went up to the table. The Leech looked at me and I could see that she wanted to put her hand in my curls. But she didn't. She put her hand on my back instead. I had a feeling that everything was going to go wrong. I was no longer converted. I was inside out. I ought to break a pointer now, throw a piece of chalk or overturn an inkstand. Fred would have said amen to that. But I just stood there. Everyone in the class leaned over their desks and stared, some of them open-mouthed, as if the worst possible thing had happened. I was getting dizzy. God had a plan and I was part of it. 'Where is the spleen?' the Leech asked. 'On the left,' I whispered. 'Just beside the diaphragm.' The Leech's hand extended once more and this time it was for my head. She couldn't resist the temptation. She couldn't restrain herself after all. 'Yes, that's absolutely correct, Barnum! The spleen is right beside the diaphragm. Can you show us, Barnum?' I hunched over. 'What?' 'Show us where the spleen is, Barnum?' 'Under the diaphragm,' I repeated. 'Yes, Barnum, we heard that. But show us.' I pointed to the left. 'There,' I breathed. But the Leech was determined to get her way. She took hold of my jumper and began pulling at it. 'Show us properly now, Barnum.' And I gave in. I pulled up my jumper and my shirt. And as I did so a gasp went up from the whole class, and even the Leech grew unsteady and had to clutch the table. I peered down at my spleen. There were Mum's knickers. Mum's fine, light pink knickers. They stretched over my hips, the lace like a crooked belt. I let my shirt and jumper fall. But it was too late. Everyone had seen that I was wearing Mum's big knickers under my trousers, and no one would ever forget where the spleen was. Then the bell rang. Slowly I went back to my desk while the others streamed out. I took my time. If only sufficient time might elapse, then this would pass. Slowly and surely it would pass, be forgotten – laid to one side and rendered invisible. Time was the giant eraser that rubbed over my life. That was my only comfort. It was a poor one at that. I was the last to leave. The Leech was still wiping the blackboard. The sponge was dry and hard. She turned to look at me, sorrowful and bemused – it was her turn to be different now, converted. The letters fell in white dust over her fingers. She said nothing. 'Goodbye,' I murmured.

When I came out into the playground the whole class was standing there waiting at the tramlines. I turned on my heel and hurried over towards the other exit. And there was Mum standing there. As if things weren't bad enough, Mum was standing there waving. I could hear the laughter already round every corner in town, along every street, over fences and doorways. I could hear the laughter in the gutters, the drains and the sewers. I went right past her. She came after me. 'Hi, Barnum, it's me!' Did I not know? Would the rest of the school not soon know that Barnum's mum was waiting for Barnum and that Barnum was wearing her knickers? Mum laughed. 'We're going to buy new shoes for you,' she said, and put her hand on my shoulder as we scuffed through the leaves at the back of the church. I crumpled. 'Do we have to?' I whispered. 'Of course we have to. You're not planning on standing on the girls' toes, are you?' Mum laughed again and was obviously in a good mood. And that was probably because Dad was standing at the Valkyrie waiting for us. He was wearing a long, light brown overcoat which he could just button at the middle. 'Feel,' he said. I put my hand on his arm. 'Further up,' he whispered. I moved my hand to his elbow. 'Further in,' he whispered. I moved my fingers over to his elbow. 'Further in,' he whispered. I moved my fingers over towards the top button, but couldn't reach any further. 'A bit down,' he whispered. I did as he told me and then I felt it bulging; the inner pocket bulged and Dad grinned. 'Camel hair,' he said, and produced his fat wallet. 'And now we're going to buy dancing pumps!' And off we went, mé in the middle, like a real family, to the Valkyrie shoe shop. And I'll be brief, as brief as I can. Buying shoes for me, not just any old shoes but shoes for dancing, wasn't easy. The thing is that I was born feet first. They had to go inside Mum with great forceps and press my arms to my sides so my head would have sufficient room and not get caught up in the umbilical cord. Hence my *pes valgus*. I might have ended up with *pes varus* and ought to be grateful as a consequence, but *pes valgus* is no laughing matter either. The soles of our feet are moulded to each and every piece of ground we walk on. That's why we can be heard when we walk. We can't escape our feet. Dad led the way into the Valkyrie shoe shop. 'Shoes for this gentleman!' he shouted, so everyone in the shop heard him. The assistant was there in an instant and had eyes only for Dad's fat wallet, while I had to sit on a chair and take off my old shoes. Mum held her hand under her nose and kept shaking her head. My stockings were crumpled about my toes and the sweat steamed off them in a thick cloud. But Dad just laughed and slipped the assistant five kroner as an advance. I had to try on nineteen pairs of shoes. I had to walk nineteen times past a mirror standing at an angle on the floor. I had to take nineteen dance steps. But it was all to no avail. The shoes were either too tight, too big, too small or too wide. I thought of André who had 45 kilos of shoe polish in the balloon that came down just the same. Soon enough everyone in the Valkyrie shoe shop, both customers and employees, were taken in by my feet. Yes, there were even people outside watching flat-footed Barnum through the window – his feet were the focal point of the district. The assistant was sweating and breathing deeply. Dad slipped him another five kroner. Then he introduced himself, giving his full name and said: 'It's not the foot that has to fit the shoe. It's the shoe that has to fit the foot. Here's to the awkward foot!' Then we had to go with him to the storeroom behind the shop. There were shoes stacked to the ceiling there. I'd never seen so many shoes. Regardless of how far you were to walk you couldn't have worn out all those pairs of shoes in one lifetime. The assistant climbed a ladder and came down with a pair of black shoes which he proceeded to put on my feet with the greatest ceremony, and he didn't even need to use a shoehorn – they slipped on like soft, spacious gloves. 'This pair belonged to Oscar Mathisen,' he whispered. 'He wore them at the banquet after becoming world champion in 1916. But cheap they most certainly aren't.' Mum glanced at Dad. Dad glanced at me. 'Do they fit you all right?' he asked. 'Like a glove,' I told him. Dad smiled and went off with the assistant to a corner where they agreed a price, and when finally we stood outside the Valkyrie shoe shop, in the rain which had stopped and which swam now in the tramlines, with Oscar Mathisen's own shoes in a box and me thinking the worst was over apart from dancing school itself (and that was to be my crowning glory), Dad waved his arm in the air and shouted. 'And now to Plesner's!' We took a taxi there. I got to sit in the front and while I sat there and heard Dad whispering to Mum, and heard too the laughter that reverberated through him in waves when he was in that kind of mood, I fell to thinking of Tale. And I felt utterly hollow inside, and this emptiness, this inner hollowness, slowly but surely filled me with more and more worry. And sure enough, the same woman stood behind the counter at Plesner's, and when she saw me she took hold of my hand. 'And how is your brother?' she enquired. 'Absolutely fine,' I told her quickly. 'I'm so glad to hear it!' She straightened up and took hold of Mum's hand instead. 'What a nice boy,' she said. And I realized that sooner or later lies come back for you – both lies and dreams come back and meet you at the door disguised as care, comfort and truth – for the world isn't big enough to hide a lie in. Lies go on stilts. Dreams go raging in sleep. Mum looked at me oddly. I looked oddly at Dad and fortunately he'd already found the most expensive insoles (handmade, cut and polished, like gemstones for the feet), and we could go home. We took a taxi this time too and I sat in the front as before. 'Are you hungry?' Dad said. 'No,' I answered. 'Are you full then?' 'No, I'm not full either.' He unbuttoned his coat. 'Good,' he said. 'Your weight should be perfectly balanced when you dance. Have I told you about Halvorsen from Halden?' 'Yes. Der Rote Teufel.' 'Precisely. He wasn't perfectly balanced and fell and smashed himself to bits.' 'Now you're just scaring Barnum,' Mum told him. Dad only laughed. 'Am I scaring you, Barnum?' 'No,' I replied. Dad leant forward between the front seats and all but distracted the driver's attention. 'Dancing's like being on the trapeze, Barnum. You're throwing yourself from embrace to embrace. And it's not about falling down among beautiful ladies and breaking your neck.' Mum gave a sigh and Dad leaned back and put his arms round her. 'Today you're beginning at the second most important school in life,' he said. 'What's the most important one?' I asked. 'That's the school of life, Barnum. And ordinary schools come third. Struggle, dancing and maths. That's the right order for us humans.'

I got to shower till there was no more hot water, put the knickers back in the cupboard, smeared deodorant over half my body, and when I stood in front of the hall mirror in Fred's old trousers and blazer, and Oscar Mathisen's shoes (and really it was quite awesome that a world champion skater had worn such tiny shoes), Mum came and stood behind me and began combing my hair, slowly and almost lazily. We looked at each other in the mirror. I heard Dad, who was sleeping on the divan in the dining-room, snoring like a wheel. Boletta had gone to the North Pole and drank my health there with dark ale, and Fred was out wandering among the street lights. Mum smiled in that worried way of hers. 'You look good, Barnum.' 'Do I?' 'As fine as you could be.' 'Yes, as fine as could be,' I repeated, and it struck me that it was a lonely sounding sentence – *as fine as could be*. I couldn't be any finer – I'd reached my full height and that was lower than most others. Mum popped the comb in my pocket and leant close to my ear. 'What did you say about Fred at Plesner's, Barnum?' 'Nothing.' 'Yes, you did. The lady asked how he was.' I pondered. I thought about Fred's command, that I converted, that I became a different person. I lied, but it could have been the truth. 'I just said that he was born in a bloody taxi. But that it's nothing to damn well feel sorry about.' Mum let go of me. Fred would have liked that. I'd soon be in fine form again. 'What are you saying?' Mum whispered. 'That he was baptized by a taxi driver. D'you not think I know that? And that that's why he's so thick in the head.' Mum hit me, with the flat of her hand she slapped my cheek and just as quickly she stroked her fingers carefully along the edge of my collar. It was as though the two actions were one and the same – the blow and the sign of endearment, the latter a continuation of the former. And I saw that the clock behind her had stopped, for it was a long time since anyone had put money in the drawer and the hands hung at five-thirty, like two thin, dead wings. Dad got up slowly from the dining-room divan; the fat poked out between his shirt buttons and he only barely managed to sit, for his stomach was in the way whichever way he turned. He raised his arm and waved as if he were going onboard ship in the Bergen fiord to peel potatoes the whole way to America and would be gone there for good. Had it only been that way. 'Good luck, Barnum,' he said. 'Say hi to the girls from me.' *No, damn it to hell, you fat arse*, I shouted soundlessly. Then Mum kissed me on the cheek she had just slapped and sent me off. And as I was going down Church Road I wondered just how slowly you could actually walk before stopping completely. When starlight that gave out about eight million years ago still hadn't reached us then surely I could take a few weeks to get to dancing classes. I thought I saw Fred in the shadows of the church steps, a glow between his lips and the shining darkness in his eyes. I stopped and raised my hand (didn't know if he could see me or not), but perhaps he just sat there smiling, because it wasn't impossible he'd already heard the rumours about all the things I'd done in the course of that day in my converted state. I'd even irritated God. I was so encouraged by this thinking that I actually ran so as not to arrive too late to be thrown out of dancing school. But as I was going to cross Riddevold Square I was suddenly dragged into the bushes behind Welhaven and pressed down into the leaves – above me stood Preben, Aslak and Hamster. 'Just wanted to see what you've on under your trousers, midge!' I hit out in every direction, but to no avail. They just laughed the more. 'Shame your brother isn't here now, eh?' 'Not going to give your brother a shout, then? Or has someone shut him up?' They pulled off Fred's trousers. They were disappointed all right.

There were no frilly knickers, just white Y-fronts. 'Been home to change your fanny pants, have you?' Hamster enquired. 'I dunno what you're talking about,' I said. They began to kick me a bit, but without any real enthusiasm, just a few taps in the tummy. And this was really the best thing that could have happened, because now I could say that everyone who thought I wore knickers had been seeing things, bewitched by the Leech, the supply teacher. Perhaps they'd beat me sufficiently senseless that I'd have to go to the surgery instead, unable to dance for the foreseeable future. 'Many thanks, fanny faces,' I told them, and buttoned up my trousers. Preben, Aslak and Hamster glanced at each other, shook their heads, buried me in leaves and disappeared over in the direction of Urra Park. I lay there thinking a bit. The world was a strange place. One thing brought the next with it, but none of the events was connected. *Explain the difference between a voluntary muscle and an involuntary muscle. Voluntary muscles: those connected to bones. Involuntary muscles: those which function beyond our control.* So the heart had to be an involuntary muscle while the hands and feet were voluntary, although they could do unplanned things too. I got up from my damp grave, emptied my pockets of leaves and creepy-crawlies, and went straight to Svae's dancing school. The air in the lift was so heavy with perfume and hair oil that it barely managed to rise from one floor to the next. I stood with my back to the mirror and held my breath. In the changing room there were duffel coats hanging to left and to right. Someone had even brought galoshes. I could hear a dry voice in another room but couldn't make out the words. I changed and sneaked in. But no one can sneak in unobserved on the first evening of dancing school. Svae was standing beside a table with a gramophone on it, and stopped talking the moment she set eyes on me, and that was at once. It wasn't a violin she looked like, but a flagpole with a black cloth round it. The boys were sitting on hard chairs along one wall like prisoners going to the gallows, and the girls sat along the other wall – lonely, made-up faces, like oil paintings reflected in the mirror behind them. And none of them looked at each other because everyone was looking at me. 'Well, then,' Svae said. 'Finally we have the tail-end Charlie. And what is your name?' There wasn't one familiar face to be seen. I bowed. 'Nilsen,' I said loudly. And a ripple of laughter spread from chair to chair which stopped just as quickly the moment Svae raised her arm. 'Sit down,' she commanded. 'And let that be the last time you come late, Nilsen.' I almost began to like her. She hadn't asked what my Christian name was. She called me Nilsen. 'Will do, Svae,' I said, and sat down on the unoccupied chair nearest the exit. Svae took a deep breath and stood at the centre of the floor in our midst. It was clear that she was going to talk to us, and she was welcome to do so as long as she pleased. 'In cultured society,' she began, 'dance is an expression of celebration, an atmosphere of joyfulness. It is a form of social interaction – one that youth in particular gathers to perform. Dance enlightens the soul, strengthens the body and gives the dancer good balance, magnificent posture and strong mastery of the limbs.' Svae slowly passed the girls as the boys sat with slumped heads; no one dared look up, because anyone who started laughing now would be history, that was crystal clear. I wondered if I should laugh out loud and get it over and done with once and for all, but before I got that far Svae spun round abruptly, her finger in the air like a bent hook from which she could hang our corpses, as if she'd already heard the laughter before it left its owner's mouth. She spoke extremely loudly. 'But in dancing's alluring essence there also lie perils! Therefore you are to remember the following: a ball begins with tranquil forms of dance and in the same way finishes with them. Always allow an hour to pass after the consumption of food before commencing to dance. In the wake of an exerting dance one ought to walk about a little until the heart has calmed and the skin is restored to its normal state. And if one is warm after dancing one should not stand by an open window or expose oneself otherwise to draught, but rather cover the shoulders, especially if the garment one is wearing is low-cut.' Now she turned to face the girls once more and measured up their dresses. Some tried to conceal their exposed shoulders, suddenly thin and transparent like small, sharp wings. I would never have believed that dancing was associated with such great dangers. Boletta had said nothing about all this. But Svae wasn't done yet. 'It's best to wear dresses of a light material that are not too tight-fitting at the neck, but neither is it without risk – I repeat without risk – to wear dresses cut low to the degree which is now, sadly, all too common.' Svae said nothing for a few seconds and let the words sink in. They did sink in; the girls were shaking, and she took up position in the middle of the parquet floor. 'Let me also say, and stress most particularly, that the longer one continues dancing into the night, the more the pleasure of it diminishes. There comes a point, a critical point, beyond which dance becomes its absolute opposite and may expose one to injury.' Most were on the verge of a nervous breakdown now. Svae clapped her hands. It was like two stone tables being brought together. 'But you know all this from before! Now the boys may, in an orderly and dignified fashion, find themselves partners and we can begin with simple positions and holds. Proceed!' Now battle was to commence. This was the moment of truth and in that dreadful moment there was utter stillness. The girls stared at the floor; the boys sat on the edges of their seats, frozen solid in angst and sweat, in the sudden cold of dreams. The world waited. I gathered all my thoughts, all my strength, for the final, decisive, converted action. And then the boys got up and stormed over the floor. Some had picked out the same girls, and those ones – the prettiest and the finest – delighted in every second of the battle. They smiled when there were attempts at scuffling in front of their chairs, but Svae intervened mercilessly before it got too serious. There were more girls than boys, and those who were left sitting lonely and abandoned – the less attractive ones, the ugly, the fat, the chubby and the thick ones – they bowed their heads the more, in shame and despair, and pulled their dresses the tighter about them. As if that could help – but no, nothing could help them now – they were open sores, they were dead wallflowers, the first to fall in the dancing school's bloody battle. And I recognized it all.

Then I spotted a guy who was slowly making his way between the couples towards one of the girls who was left over. He came over as pretty purposeful the way he was walking, but at the same time lazy, not bothering to lift his feet at all. His blazer was crumpled and his hair was parted in the middle. And the girl he was making for straightened up, and I observed that she was actually attractive, in a kind of fragile and confused way. Or maybe that's just the way I see her now, now that the memories have been refined – pictures refined in distance's fluid. I can still see the pretty, misunderstood wallflowers raising their eyes, and see the two of us stopping in front of her, and me going forward. But it wasn't the girl I ran over to and asked to dance. Instead I asked the boy who was about to bow to her, and this slow, heavy boy turned towards me in disbelief and just blinked. 'What?' he whispered. 'Would you like to dance?' I repeated, and put my arm round him and led him out onto the dance floor. 'Let me go,' he shouted. But I didn't. I held onto him and took some steps. 'Let me go, you horrible little dwarf!' he screamed. The girl by the wall had got up. And suddenly there was complete silence again and everyone stared at us. Then I crowned all my converted acts – with my masterpiece of difference. I stretched up and kissed him on the cheek. He hit me in the eye. And at the same moment I felt Svae's hook at my neck and her voice like a nail in my ear. 'Get out! Get off my dance floor and never show your face here again!'

That's how I met Peder. That's how I met Vivian. That's how we met each other.

The Tree

I remember another night. Fred was sitting on the edge of the bed. I could just glimpse his face like a shadow above his knees. 'I've been with the Old One,' he said. I lay completely still. Fred stared at me in the darkness. There was something different about his voice. He could have been someone else, someone who'd broken in, a stranger come to scare me. 'I've been with the Old One,' he repeated. Fred leaned forward and rocked back and forth. 'The Old One?' I breathed. 'Have you been to the graveyard?' Fred shook his head. A lock of hair fell down over his brow and he almost laughed – I caught a glimpse of his mouth – a dark rift – perhaps a car drove by right then and circled the walls with light. 'I got to talk to her,' he said. Slowly I sat up in bed. 'You talked to her?' Fred nodded and pushed back the stray lock of hair. 'I told her I was alive. That I didn't die too.' I couldn't say anything. All of a sudden Fred put his hand on my foot. 'That made her very happy, Barnum. She'd thought I'd been knocked down too. She said that she forgave me.' Once I'd got used to the darkness I saw that his face was completely pale and that he was thinner than ever. But he was smiling nonetheless and I'd never seen him smile like this before – it was the same smile clowns paint on their faces before they go into the big top. I laughed. 'Don't kid around, Fred.' The smile melted from his face. He bent closer. I thought he was going to bite me. 'I was to pass on greetings to you too, Barnum.' 'From who, Fred?' 'Aren't you listening? From the Old One, of course. She said you shouldn't be so sad because you're so small.' Slowly I lay back in bed. Fred kept sitting like a hunched shadow over me. 'When did you meet her?' I murmured. 'Are you crazy, Barnum?' 'I just wondered where you met her, Fred.' He smiled again and his face became all soft. 'In heaven. Where else?' Fred finally crept over to his bed and lay down. He didn't say anything for a long while. But I couldn't sleep all the same. 'Just think if she'd never found out what happened,' he whispered. 'Just think about that.' I didn't know what to say. I saw the Old One before me as she'd lain on the table in the hospital basement, with her hands folded over her stomach and looking quite peaceful, except for her eyelids which were big as shells. Did our thoughts keep on going after we were dead? Did the riddles live on after us? 'Why did she say she forgave you?' I breathed. Fred sat up in bed. 'Can you keep a secret, Barnum?' 'Yes,' I said. 'Yes, Fred.' He lay back down again. 'Then this is our secret.'

I've always kept it.

But as I walked along Drammen Road that evening of conversion and heard the slow waltz from the top floor of the Merchant Building I'd happily have shouted it out loud to anyone in the world: the tram conductor sitting smoking on the running board, the taxi driver leaning out of his window with eyes closed, the piano teacher coming round the corner with a bag crammed full of sheet music. I'd have told them in a loud voice that Fred, my half brother, had been in heaven and spoken to the Old One. If only everything could be undone, if only it were possible to go back in time at a single stroke and turn what was twisted the right way round once more – because all of a sudden I was in doubt and my doubt was profound, like a tear in my thoughts. I couldn't even so much as remember how I'd got back onto the street again, if I'd taken the lift or taken the stairs. My triumph was cracked like ice. I'd managed to get thrown out of dancing school. But at what price? What would the consequences be? Because you couldn't do anything without there being consequences. There was always something else, always something that came along afterwards as in a tortured dream. I knew it. My eyes were stinging, both of them stung – it was like looking through misshapen glass in pouring rain. I had to lean against a lamp post. If anyone had seen me now they might have taken me for a dog, a rare breed, but a dog nonetheless that snarled for no reason and in the end gnawed at its own tail. Perhaps I'd be thrown out of school too, expelled for being the impossible human I was, and sent to Bastøy and locked in a basement cupboard where I'd get a hammering four times a day. Or perhaps laughter would pursue me the rest of my days like a shadow; I'd never again be able to show my face anywhere without laughter breaking out, meeting me with scorn and derision. *You're a nutcase!*, they'd all shout wherever I went. I was doomed. It was Fred's fault because it was his idea to do everything differently. It was Boletta's fault for signing me up for dancing classes. It was Mum's fault for waiting for me outside school. It was Dad's fault for buying me Oscar Mathisen's shoes, and it was the assistant's fault for selling them to him. It was the Leech's fault for pulling up my shirt and revealing Mum's knickers. It was the vicar's fault for having made me swear at him in the first place. It was Preben and Aslak and Hamster's fault for not beating me up good and proper behind Welhaven. They were all evil. I hated the lot of them. Words poured through me. There should have been a toilet there for words. I could have pissed them against the lamp post. I could have shat them into the gutter.

Then I hear someone running along the pavement. I began to run too. Perhaps it was someone coming to get me. But the figure running behind me wasn't running particularly quickly, because I ran even faster and he didn't manage to catch me, and if he didn't catch me then he'd have to be running pretty slowly. 'Stop!' he shouted. I took a chance on it and stopped, because I was running in the wrong direction anyway; if I continued the way I was going I'd soon come out in enemy territory behind Munkedam Road, and those who held sway there made Preben, Hamster and Aslak look like bunny rabbits. I was standing under the mighty red beech tree in Hydro Park, in a rain of red leaves. I turned round. A chubby shadow careened the leaves panting loudly. It was the guy I'd asked to dance and then kissed on the cheek. He stopped in front of me. I wondered if he'd bash my other eye there and then, but for the time being getting his breath back was all that occupied his attention. Then he looked up. I think that he was smiling, but it was pretty dark where we were standing and perhaps I was completely mistaken. 'I got thrown out too,' he said. 'Really? Why?' 'For calling you a horrible dwarf.' I was on the point of getting worried again. But all at once he started laughing. 'Only kidding. I said that if I couldn't dance with you then I wasn't going to dance with anyone.' He came closer. 'Sorry for hitting your eye, by the way. Did it hurt?' 'Not particularly,' I told him. 'I didn't realize just how ingenious you'd been.' 'Ingenious?' I breathed. 'Smartest way of getting kicked out of dancing classes I've ever heard of.' His face clouded with anxiety for a moment and his brow crumpled like paper. 'That was the idea, right?' 'Of course,' I said. 'What else?' His face relaxed once more, and he stretched out his hand. 'What's your name? Apart from Nilsen?' 'Barnum,' I said quietly. 'Barnum? Cool, I'm Peder.' And we shook hands, under the red beech, as the wind rustled through the red leaves in which we were standing. I don't know how long we stood there like that, but I swear that I saw the moon rising obliquely over the city and positioning itself in the skies like an orange in a deep black dish. Finally Peder let go of my hand. I stuck mine quickly in my pocket. 'Where d'you live?' he asked me. 'The top of Church Road,' I replied. 'Fine. Then we can walk a bit of the way together.'

We went along Bygdøy Alley. I picked up a chestnut but threw it away at once. I was hardly there to collect chestnuts. I felt so happy and bewildered, bewildered and happy, scared and happy. I was perhaps in the process of making a friend. We didn't say anything for a while. Peder whistled a tune from the requests' programme: I knew it too. I began to whistle it with him. But when we were crossing Nils Juel Street we broke down and all but laughed our heads off, and no one yet has managed to whistle while they laugh. I had to thump Peder eight times on the back with the flat of my hand before he recovered. 'What do we do now?' he coughed. I swallowed my laughter. 'What d'you mean?' 'What are you going to say to your parents? That you got sent home from dancing school because you kissed me?' He laughed loudly again till he almost collapsed on the pavement. My mouth went completely dry. I hadn't thought of this. 'D'you think Svae'll telephone our parents?' Peder stood up and shrugged his shoulders. 'Maybe. Maybe not.' He turned round and stared over at the other pavement. 'Look,' he whispered, and pointed with his finger. It was a girl. It was the girl from dancing school, the prettiest of the wallflowers. 'Hi!' Peder called. She stopped where she was between two trees and peered over at us. Peder looked at his watch, took my arm and led me across the road. She was standing still, leaning against the moonlight. She was wearing a red raincoat that almost shone. I think she was cold. She blew on her hands as if she were holding a giant fledgling in front of her face. 'Were you thrown out too, or what?' Peder inquired. She let her arms drop. 'No one wanted to dance with me,' she said. 'I couldn't be bothered staying.' Those were her exact words. *No one wanted to dance with me*. Peder glanced at me, as if we'd agreed on something, and smiled as he looked at her once more. 'Really? Nobody? What d'you think I was doing when this cuckoo came and ruined everything?' He pulled me closer. I bowed. She lifted her hands again and smiled a fraction behind them. 'D'you really think I'd have danced with either of you two?' she asked. Peder was silent a moment. Then he shrugged his shoulders. 'Maybe. Maybe not. What d'you reckon, Barnum?' I shrugged my shoulders too. 'Maybe. Maybe not,' I said, easy as that. She came a step nearer me now. 'What was it you were called?' she asked. I stretched out my hand and she took it. 'Barnum,' I said loudly. She held onto my hand a little longer, or else I kept holding hers. 'And my name's Peder,' said Peder, equally loudly, and we shook hands all round. In the end it was her turn. 'I'm Vivian,' she said. 'Perhaps I will dance with you after all.'

And we continued up Bygdøy Alley – Peder, Vivian and me – and Vivian walked in the middle between us. I don't know what it was but it was just as if we'd always been walking there, the three of us, under the chestnut trees in the damp darkness. And we knew nothing about each other, nothing other than that our first evening at Svae's dancing school had also been our last. 'I know,' Peder said all of a sudden. 'We bank on Svae not calling and just pretend that we're still going to classes. All right?' We stopped and Peder picked up a chestnut and put it in his pocket. 'All right? Then we can meet up each Thursday evening anyway and just do something different!'

And that was what happened. Each and every Thursday that autumn we met up under the red beech in Hydro Park in our dancing clothes. We stood hidden behind the trunk and watched the others going into the Merchant Building. We mocked them. They looked pretty laughable. The boys resembled penguins. The girls peahens. And afterwards we did this or that – went to the cinema if we could afford it (and generally it was Peder who had the money), stood in the tunnel at Skøyen and huddled up close whenever the train went over, had one milkshake between the three of us at Studenten, or sat in Peder's room and listened to the radio. But that evening we just walked home together. When we got to the top of Bygdøy Alley Vivian went through the entrance adjacent to Frogner church, she left us without saying a word but turned round there in the dark, raised her hand and put one finger to her lips, and then was gone. Peder looked at me. 'Bloody hell. To live that close to a church. Is that sad or what?' 'Perhaps her dad's a vicar,' I suggested. We strolled on, towards Frogner Park. 'To wake each Sunday with church bells right over your bed,' said Peder. 'That's really cool.' 'Yes,' I said. 'To wake with your head in the bells.' Peder laughed. 'Her dad has to be a vicar. I reckon we have to save her.' I didn't quite get what Peder meant, but I agreed with him. 'Guess, then,' I said. 'All right, what does your dad do?' Peder asked. I had to think. 'A bit of this, a bit of that,' I breathed. 'A bit of this and that? My dad's a bit of everything.'

Peder stopped outside a house with a fence all round it and yellow lights in every window. This was where he lived, in his own house with a garden and flagpole. There was a sign on the gate reading *Beware of the Dog*. 'Do you have a dog?' I asked, and in doing so felt rather stupid. 'It died a couple of years ago,' Peder said, 'but we hung on to the sign'. Then a car swung up the street, the hubs of its wheels rattling and the exhaust all but falling off – a stream of sparks trailing after it. I think it was a Vauxhall, and it drove right into the garage beside Peder's house and parked there with a crash. A man with a gigantic hat and a flat bag under his arm clambered out and wiped the exhaust from his face. 'That was a close shave,' he groaned. 'I think we need the garage.' 'Hi, Dad,' Peder said. It was Peder's father. He stopped and smiled down to us. 'Well, and how was dancing school?' Peder shrugged his shoulders. 'I reckon it bored us to death.' His dad laughed and turned towards me. 'I can under- stand that all right. What the hell's the point of the fox- trot? You might as well learn to fence instead. And who's this?' 'This is Barnum,' said Peder. 'Good evening, Barnum. You'll join us for supper? If you're not scared of the dog?' I bowed and thanked him, but declined. It had basically been too much for me. I had to go home and rest. I had to store this evening, save it and not use all of it up at one go. But before I went I grasped Peder's arm as if to keep him from going, even though he was standing there quite still. 'You can come to us for dinner tomor- row,' I said quickly. His father patted my shoulder. 'Great idea, Barnum. Right, Peder? Because your mother and I are actually away.' Peder looked at me and smiled.

'When'll I come?' he asked. 'Five,' I whispered and ran off; it was the first time anyone had invited me to supper and the first time I'd ever invited a friend to dinner. The triumph of it – the shining prize of friendship – to have a friend coming home to dinner. I rejoiced along the whole of Church Road – I was a world champion in a world champion's shoes. I was a friend, I was someone's friend, and I almost couldn't wait to share the news. Because I couldn't carry all of this myself – my shoulders were too narrow, my heart too small. But when I did get home I found no one there; Mum had gone to the North Pole to fetch Boletta and Dad had gone again. He tended to be like that; there was forever something to be sorted and he couldn't sit still. He came in, raged a bit, played either the prince or the pauper, dropped a dirty shirt or two and a few banknotes and was off again. And I reckoned that maybe it was for the best to be alone at that moment, because I was carrying a lie with me too, and that was as great as the truth. My tongue wasn't smooth enough yet. I didn't dare tell Mum and Boletta that I'd given up, been thrown out – because they'd most likely paid Svae up-front and would never get the money back. I put my shoes on the shelf in the hall. I hung the blazer on its hook and took off my tie. I had a glass of milk in the kitchen and went into the bathroom to look in the mirror. My left eye was a bit rusty round the edges. It didn't matter. I could have cried for joy. Yes, this was a time for being alone; I'd suck at this joy as if it were a piece of sugar candy. But when I went into our room I found I wasn't alone after all. Fred was lying on my bed with his arms behind his neck, staring up at the ceiling. 'Hi, Tiny,' he said. I sat down on his bed. I wasn't afraid. I had something to tell him. 'I managed it,' I whispered. 'I know,' Fred said. 'Do you?' I asked, my voice quieter still. He turned a degree or two in my direction. 'What's the old bag at the dancing school called?' 'Svae,' I told him. 'That's right. She called here.' I crumpled. 'She called here?' Fred sighed and stared at the ceiling again. 'Where else?' My tongue expanded in my mouth, dry as an eraser. 'Did she talk to Mum?' 'No.

She talked to me. Lucky, huh? That I was the only one home.' Fred was silent a bit. I couldn't bear it. 'What did Svae say, Fred?' He shut his eyes. 'This bed is far too big for you, Barnum. If we cut it in half we'd have more room, right?' 'Fine then,' I whispered. 'What did you say to Svae?' Fred smiled. 'She said you'd done immoral things, Barnum.' 'Immoral things?' 'You need to tell us more, Barnum.' I looked away. My nutrition book was lying on the desk. Perhaps Fred had been leafing though it. Perhaps he'd seen Barnum's Formula. 'I kissed a girl,' I said. 'You kissed a girl?' 'Yes, Fred.' 'You managed to reach up?' 'She was sitting down,' I told him. Now it was my turn to shut my eyes. I heard Fred getting up from the bed. 'I said that I was your father,' Fred whispered. 'And that I'd punish you.' He started laughing. I didn't dare open my eyes yet. He sat down beside me. 'I should have been your father,' he said. 'Instead of that shit who says he is.' He put his arm round my shoulder. 'At any rate I managed to get thrown out,' I breathed. Fred gave me a pat on the back and waited a long time to say any more. I wish he hadn't said anything at all but had just patted my back instead. I could have sat the whole night like that. 'How am I going to punish you, Barnum?' 'Punish me? Don't fool about, Fred.' He withdrew his hand and scraped his nails over my skin. 'Fool about? I promised Svae I'd punish you.' He went over to the window and stood there. 'Mum said they bought you Oscar Mathisen's shoes.' 'Yes,' I whispered. 'Did they fit you?' 'They fitted pretty well actually.' Fred laughed. His whole back shook. 'D'you know what happened to Oscar Mathisen?' 'He became world champion in skating.' 'I mean after he became world champion.' 'No idea. Did something happen?' 'First he shot his wife. And then he shot himself. The world champion.' Fred turned round abruptly to face me. 'Now I know what punishment you'll get.' 'What?' 'You won't lie to me any longer, Barnum.' 'I haven't lied to you, Fred.' He smiled and shook his head. 'See. You're doing it again.'

The Parcel

When I woke up I was lying in my own bed. Fred had gone and Mum was standing bent over my face, impatient. 'How did it go?' she asked. 'At the dancing class?' I sat up and remembered everything all at one go. 'Peder's coming to dinner,' I said. 'Who?' 'Peder!' Mum sat down on the edge of the bed. 'Who is Peder?' And I never thought I'd speak the words I could now. 'He's my new friend,' I whispered. Mum smiled in a strange kind of way and was about to draw her fingers through my hair, but stopped herself. 'Did you meet him yesterday?' 'Yes, we came home together.' Mum sat there silent for a moment, the same smile on her lips. 'And so you asked him for dinner?' 'Yes. Friends do that.' Mum hesitated a moment, then got up and clapped her hands. 'Then we have to get going and set the table!' She strode out and I lay back in bed. I heard her calling Boletta. 'Come and help me, you old bag of bones! We've got guests coming to dinner!' And I lay there listening to the muted noise of saucepans and frying pans, the banging of cupboard doors and dropped lids, and the vacuum cleaner and the iron. And I began to get nervous; everything I looked forward to I was nervous about as well. And I thought (or perhaps I think this now), just as with rain, that which then was just a feeling, a doubt – that nothing is complete and totally whole – everything has a crack in it, be it joy, good fortune, beauty. There's fracture in everything, something missing. Except in the completeness – and the uselessness – of that which is imperfect.

Mum opened the door. She looked bewildered. 'Good Lord! Aren't you going to school today?' I whispered under the quilt. 'I think I'd prefer to stay at home.' Mum brushed away the hair from her brow. She was wearing rubber gloves and a big, white apron. 'Are you ill?' 'No, but you can say that I am.' Boletta appeared behind Mum and peered forwards with red eyes and wrinkled mouth. 'Let Barnum stay at home. You can say in the note he's got fever.' 'I don't like lying,' Mum said. Boletta sat down on the bed and put her hand on my brow. 'Oh, it isn't a lie, my dear little Vera. Barnum's been at dancing school and temperatures rise there! And anyway, he's got a swollen eye. He's been looking too much at the girls!' I was up already. 'I can do the shopping!' I all but shouted. Mum pointed at me. 'You'll at least stay indoors. You can tidy your room and not get in the way.' She disappeared in the direction of the kitchen. Boletta hesitated a moment. 'Your Mum's just so pleased', she murmured, 'that you've got a friend coming. But it isn't easy for her to show it.' She drew her hand over my neck where there were still traces of Fred's nails. 'How was it yesterday at dancing school?' she asked, her voice no louder. 'Yes, fine.' Boletta laughed, but mostly to herself. 'You don't need to say anything. I'm only a foolish old woman who wants to know what's going by her.' I looked at her. 'You're not that foolish, Boletta,' I told her. 'Thank you, Barnum. You've put my mind at rest.'

She hurried off in Mum's wake and I began tidying. I made up the beds. I put all my books in my schoolbag, put my pencils in their case, hid my insoles in the bottom drawer, blew the dust from M. S. Greve's *Medical Dictionary for Norwegian Homes*, and opened the window and sneezed a few times. It was sunny outside. The sunlight cast thin shadows. Time passed. It stood still and passed at one and the same time. Not even time was whole. Boletta was already coming up Church Road. She had the trolley piled with purchases – she could barely pull it behind her. I closed the window and began to feel nervous. I tidied Fred's things too. I hid his knife, cigarettes and all his keys under his pillow. I put his pointed brown shoes in the cupboard, and I scraped the old bits of chewing-gum from the edge of the bed and threw them away. I knew I shouldn't do all this. I knew I shouldn't touch his stuff. He'd drawn a line down the floor. I had to have permission to cross it. Fred didn't need that. He went wherever he chose to. I hoped he wouldn't come home for dinner. And yet I wished he would too, I wished he would sit with us – as a big brother. He could just sit there and not say anything – yes, preferably be like that, silent and mysterious, a proper big brother. But if Dad managed to get home then it would be for the best if Fred stayed away – one of them would be enough. I heard Mum laying the table: the white cloth, the tall glasses, the napkin rings, the Chinese dinner service, the silver cutlery. Now the great past was being laid on the table, that which never became the future. I ran out to her. 'Can't we just eat in the kitchen?' 'The kitchen! Now you've certainly got a temperature.' 'Please, Mum! Can't we just have a normal dinner?' She turned away from me; she was holding a plate in her hands and for a moment I didn't know if she was going to throw it to the floor or put it neatly where it was meant to go. 'What d'you mean, Barnum?' 'That that's the point! That everything'll be like it always is.' Mum gave me a long look. 'I don't think you really mean that,' she said. Then she set the plate down slowly and carefully on the cloth.

Dad came at a quarter to five as if he worked normal office hours and we were a normal family. He stopped in the hall, heavy and stooped – perhaps he'd walked the whole way from Majorstuen again, or further still. He could barely reach down to his own shoes. But then he straightened up again, his eyes darted this way and that, and he sniffed. He looked at me bemused as I stood waiting beside the clock, not for him but for Peder. And slowly he lifted his gaze from the shining buttons of my blazer to the set table in the dining-room, where the candles were already lit and fluttered in the draught from the corners of the windows. His face grew; a smile that hadn't been there stretched it out and caused his eyes to disappear in their skin. 'Well, I never,' he breathed. 'Have you seen the like of that? Well, I never.' Mum carried a dish of potatoes past us and quickly turned to look at him. 'Barnum has a visitor coming,' she said. 'Get yourself ready.' Dad's face tumbled somewhat, like a bonfire; his eyes reappeared. Perhaps he'd thought all this had been done for his benefit – an act of appreciation, a surprise medal. Smells drifted from the kitchen the like of which we'd never known – spices and vanilla and meat – there were recipes in foreign tongues and Boletta sang ballads over the stove. Dad rediscovered his smile and turned to look at me. 'A visitor? Have you met a girl already, Barnum?' 'His name's Peder,' I said. Dad went over to the cabinet and mixed himself a whisky and soda in the heaviest of the glasses. He drank it slowly and swallowed three times. 'Now I've got myself ready,' he said.

Five o'clock came. Peder hadn't. Mum put a towel over the potatoes. Boletta kept the various pots warm. Dad got himself a second whisky and soda, and his head tilted. He looked down at my feet. 'Not wearing the new shoes?' he asked. 'No, thanks.' 'Did they not fit after all?' 'I don't like walking about in a dead man's shoes.' I just said it like that, as if the words came from somewhere else. *I don't like walking about in a dead man's shoes.* Dad's gaze would settle nowhere for a time, until he emptied his glass and stamped his foot. 'Let's get round the table!' he exclaimed. We sat down. Dad stuffed his napkin between his top shirt buttons and was about to help himself. Mum laid her hand on his arm. 'We'll wait,' she said gently. Dad let his hands drop onto his lap; he looked round and his eyes settled on me. 'What's the boy's name, then?' he enquired. 'Peder,' I told him. 'Peder what?' I thought to myself – *but he isn't coming. He just said it to be nice, that he'd come to dinner, because his father was standing there listening. Perhaps he felt sorry for me too, that I was a moron, he isn't coming, he's tricked me. I'd been thrown out of dancing school in a dead man's shoes and I was alone.* 'Peder,' I repeated. 'Peder.' Boletta leant over the table. 'He'll come all right,' she said. 'He'll come.' And right at that moment Fred appeared. He stood over by the door looking in at us. He shook back his hair and came closer. He was smiling but his lips were thin. 'Who's dead?' he asked, and sat down on the empty chair. 'That place is taken,' Dad said. 'And nobody's dead.' 'Yes, now it's taken. And you're dead.' Fred filled his plate and began eating. 'No need to wait for me,' he said, and passed the dish to Boletta who just shook her head. 'Barnum has a friend coming,' Mum said quickly. 'A friend? Barnum?' Fred looked at me. Mum put her hand over his. 'I didn't expect you to be here, Fred.' Dad laughed. 'No, indeed, who can expect that?' he said. 'Fred being here.' Boletta had already set an extra place at the table between Mum and myself, and she pushed a chair into the gap. Fred stared at Dad. 'And who can expect you to be here, huh? You thick-head.' Dad's hand shook. 'I am here. And you shouldn't talk with food in your mouth anyway.' Fred chewed for a good while and turned to me. I hoped Peder wouldn't come. I hoped he'd just said he would to be nice – I hoped he wouldn't come. 'What's happened to him then?' Fred asked. 'Your friend, I mean?' 'He'll come all right,' Boletta said, and poured herself a glass of wine. Dad took the bottle from her and poured a full glass for himself too. 'Perhaps the tram's late,' I whispered. 'Yes, it must be,' Mum said. 'He'll be here soon, you'll see.' Fred laughed. Dad said cheers. 'Out there in the big wide world you can reckon on waiting exactly a quarter of an hour. And now it's precisely quarter past five!' He piled his plate high and was on the point of taking his first bite when the bell rang. There was utter silence in the room; even Fred was still and seemed to freeze solid over the table-cloth. Again the doorbell rang. I all but overturned my chair and ran out into the hall and opened the door. It was Peder. He came in. He seemed pretty out of breath. 'The top of Church Road,' he panted. 'Bloody hell.' 'It's pretty steep,' I said. 'And you didn't tell me what number it was.' Peder laughed. I laughed too. 'How did you find your way then?' 'Just asked where Barnum Nilsen lived,' Peder said. We turned towards the living room. There sat my family. They smiled. Dad had put his helping back in the serving dish, and even Fred was smiling. They looked happy there between the candlesticks and the glasses, as if they were nothing other than happy. And this is how I saw them for the first time: Dad, already in the process of getting up from the chair that's higher than the others, quickly brushing his hand over his smooth hair before making room for Peder, our guest. Boletta, moving the wine bottle to see better, a grey-haired and smiling grandmother at the heart of the family circle. Mum, in the process of getting up herself, looking suddenly younger than the average mother, blushing and holding out her hands as if she's going to put her arms round Peder and embrace him. And Fred who keeps on eating, a pretty omnipotent big brother who doesn't allow himself to be disturbed. This could go all right. 'Blimey,' said Peder.

He greeted Dad first and Dad didn't let go of his hand so easily. 'Peder Miil,' Peder said, and bowed. 'Miil? Is that with one i or two, Peder?' 'Two,' Peder told him. Then he went round the table and shook hands with everyone – yes, even Fred – and finally we all sat down. 'Thanks for inviting me,' Peder said. Mum and Boletta exchanged glances. They hadn't seen the like of this. 'But you came too late,' Fred said. 'That doesn't matter,' Mum laughed, and Boletta passed the serving dishes to Peder and Dad poured his glass to the brim with squash. 'Guests always come in time,' Dad said. 'That's what we used to say in America. So why can't we say it here too!' Peder nodded and helped himself. 'Bet Barnum forgot to say where he lived,' Fred said. Peder pushed the serving dish in his direction. 'Unfortunately the tram was late,' he said. Fred looked him up and down. 'Barnum's never actually had friends round,' he said. 'You're the first.' Peder turned to me. 'So I've come late but in good time.' Everyone laughed, except Fred, and perhaps myself. There was quiet for a time. We ate. Everything was just as it should have been. We should have just sat there eating our boiled pork, smiling to one another and taking small sips

of our drinks, giving each other kindly glances and perhaps making remarks about the weather, if indeed anything had to be said at all. This could go all right. 'What
does your Dad do?' Dad asked. 'Stamps,' Peder answered.
There was quiet once more. Dad took out a toothpick and
fiddled about with it in his mouth. 'Stamps,' he finally
said. 'Yes, he sells stamps. Once he's bought them.' 'Can
you live off that?' Fred asked him. 'Last year he sold a
stamp from Mauritius for 21,734 kroner,' Peder replied.
Dad waved his toothpick about in front of Fred like a
shrivelled pointer. 'It's called philately. If you didn't know
before. Philately!' Dad put the toothpick in his shirt
pocket and helped himself to seconds. 'I notice you're
looking at my missing hand, Peder,' he said all at once.
And only now did I observe that he wasn't wearing his
glove; we'd got used to the grey colour of the flesh
wound. 'I didn't mean to,' Peder whispered. Dad raised
his hand. 'That doesn't matter. But it's a long story, Peder.
These precious fingers were lost when I was clearing
mines in Finnmark after the war.' Fred yawned. 'The
German, you know,' Dad went on, 'is a precise fighter. But
a cunning one too. This particular mine was suddenly
lying awkwardly. And I got in its way. Now you know just
about everything about my right hand, Peder.' 'Have you
been to America too?' Peder inquired. Dad was in his element. He'd happily have got up now and made a speech.
He made do with laying down his knife and fork on the
cloth. 'Have I been to America? America's my second
home, Peder. And I dare say I'm more known over there
than I am here.' I wished we could leave the table soon. I
passed the serving dish to Boletta. 'But how did you get
on at Svae's yesterday, boys?' she asked. Peder gave me a
quick glance. 'Yes, fine,' I said. 'She mostly just talked,'
Peder said. Boletta put down her knife and fork. 'Talked?
You don't talk at dancing school. You dance!' 'She said we
should change our underwear if we were sweaty after
dancing,' Peder said. How we laughed! Even Fred
laughed. Dad had to get up and go round the table. He

laughed and laughed. This could go all right. Dad finally sat down again. 'In America we danced for several nights at a stretch,' he said. 'I'll tell you we were sweaty then!' 'Yes, Arnold,' Mum said hurriedly, but Dad wasn't about to stop there. 'And those who kept going longest were the winners. There was hardly time to think about sweaty underwear!' Fred was staring at me the whole while. 'What's the old bag at the dancing school called?' he demanded. 'Watch your mouth,' Dad told him. 'Watch yourself,' Fred retorted. 'Svae,' I breathed. Fred turned to me. 'She phoned here yesterday.' Peder looked down. I looked nowhere at all. I closed my eyes. It was dark in there. 'Called here?' Mum said. 'But why?' Fred mashed a potato with his fork and took his time. 'She just wanted to say that they're beginning at five-thirty next Thursday. Not at six.'

I opened my eyes again. Fred smiled and right then the bell rang. Worry spread over his face that only I could see. He looked at me. 'Have you made even more friends, Barnum?' I shook my head. The bell rang again, long and hard. Mum hurried out and opened the door. It was Bang the caretaker. He went right past her holding a parcel in his hands, as far away from himself as humanly possible. 'Now I've had enough!' he shouted, and threw the parcel on the table in our midst. 'I got that in the post today!' Mum came running after him. Dad got up abruptly and his chair overturned. 'What on earth is this?' 'Open it and see!' Bang all but shrieked, quite beside himself. I recognized the parcel. Dad folded back the wrapping and retreated. There lay my pyjamas. They stank something rotten. Mum hid her face in her hands. 'Oh, God,' she groaned. Boletta went with her glass into the kitchen. Peder sat there frozen. I looked at Fred. What had he done? 'What kind of disgusting behaviour is this? What kind of behaviour?' Bang stamped on the floor with his lame foot. 'Whose pyjamas are these?' Dad asked, his voice strangely gentle. 'Mine,' I breathed. He boxed my ears. Mum screamed. I nearly fell off my chair. Then he rushed round the table, stopped behind Fred and put his mutilated hand on his shoulder. 'And what have you to say to all this, Fred?' 'Nothing.' 'Nothing? You had noth-ing to do with this revolting business?' 'Nothing,' Fred said again. 'Barnum shat himself and I chucked his pyja-mas in the bin.' Dad bored his stubby thumb into the flesh of his neck. 'And then the pyjamas went up to the caretaker's all by themselves?' 'How should I know?' Fred said. 'Can somebody move that shit, by the way? I'm still eating.' Bang turned the parcel round and there was his name and address, written in large and clumsy letters. 'You can't get out of it, you little guttersnipe! You couldn't even manage to write my name properly!' Bang hammered so hard on the parcel with his finger that his nail all but went through the paper. *Bnag* was what was written there. Fred had written *Bnag*; *Bnag* the caretaker. It was more or less the same as signing the entire parcel with his own name and address, and leaving his finger-prints there into the bargain. And I saw him bowing his head, his cheeks flaming, raging. Dad hit him with his good hand – once, twice, three times – until Mum threw herself on him and made him stop. But Dad just shoved her away. 'Apologize!' he hissed. 'Apologize this instant, you idiot!' Fred just sat there. Something was running from his face. I don't know what it was – tears, blood, saliva. Then he got up; he got up slowly, and he smiled. It's the most horrible smile I've ever seen. He stood right in front of Bang the caretaker. 'Sorry. Thought it was you who washed the pyjamas round here, Bnag.' Dad made to hit him again, but Fred caught his hand, held it a few sec-onds and looked all round, that same smile on his lips, and his eyes running over with oil. Things began to get dangerous. Then he let go and went off into our room. None of us said a thing, nor were we particularly hungry. My pyjamas lay like some stinking dessert in the centre of the table. Mum was shaking so badly she had to sit down. Dad put his arm round the caretaker and led him over to a corner where he produced his cigars and let him take his pick. I suddenly wondered what Fred would say when he saw that I'd interfered with his things and tidied up. But not a sound was to be heard from our room.

Then Mum got up abruptly, rolled up the parcel, stuffed it into the stove and lit it. I walked a bit of the way home with Peder. He didn't say a syllable the length of Church Road. Everything was ruined now. Everything was worse than ever. I turned red with shame at the mere thought of it – my own pyjamas the subject of derision on the dining-table. The following day I'd murder all those who knew about it. I'd have to kill Peder too. I walked three steps behind him. This was the end. I could have howled. When we reached Majorstuen he stopped, turned round to me and smiled. 'Perhaps you can have dinner with us next time,' Peder said.

Nude

There was a naked man standing in Peder's living room. He was standing completely still, his arms folded, and it looked as if he were thinking intently about something, or else about nothing at all. His skin was smooth and golden, his muscles well defined and taut over his tall, thin body – and I didn't dare take in any more than that. He was naked and standing in Peder's living room. My first thought was that it must be his brother, but Peder hadn't a brother, and besides, this fellow was at least thirty years old, so that idea was ruled out. 'Quiet,' Peder whispered, and took hold of my arm before I'd so much as said a word. We stood in the hall behind a stand stuffed with scarves, coats and hats. 'Mum's working,' he said, his voice even lower than before. And now I could see her too. She sat in a deep chair by the window, over which the curtain was closed, drawing on a sheet of paper. Now and again she looked up, squinted and held the pencil in front of her, as if she were measuring the height under the ceiling. Then she bent over the paper once more. Now I observed that it was no ordinary chair she was sitting in either. There were wheels on it. It was a wheelchair. The naked man still hadn't moved a muscle. I held my breath too. He might as well have been dead, dead and magnificent and standing tall. Peder all but leant inside my ear. 'I think Mum's got a crush on him,' he breathed. 'She's been working for three months on just his face.' He gave a small laugh and now it was her turn to look at us. 'Hi, boys!' she exclaimed, stuck the pencil in her mouth, and came over the floor in her chair. She extended her hand and I took it. She had a big blanket round her that almost buried her completely. But I remember her great, beautiful head of hair – it was auburn, it glowed and shone, as if she always wore a soft crown. 'You must be Barnum,' she said. I nodded. 'And you had forgotten that Barnum was to be having dinner with us today,' Peder said, and took the pencil from her mouth. 'That I hadn't,' she laughed. 'We'll have food on the table all right. Look here, Barnum.' She showed me her drawing. 'It isn't finished, but what d'you reckon?' I liked the fine, quick strokes. If you closed one eye and just looked at it with the other it suddenly became quite different, as if the lines went the opposite way and represented something else entirely. But I could see what she'd drawn all the same. The face wasn't quite right, but the rest was unmistakable. Peder sighed. 'Don't plague Barnum,' he said. His mother sighed too. 'I'm not plaguing Barnum. I just want to know what he thinks of it, Peder.' 'I think it's finished,' I told her. She looked up at me in surprise (the wheelchair was pretty low to the ground). 'Finished! But I've barely begun!' 'I think it's finished all the same,' I breathed. Peder's mum stared at her own drawing and just kept shaking her head, and I was afraid I'd made a fool of myself or offended in some way. 'I'm sorry,' I said. She looked at me again. 'I think in actual fact you're right, Barnum. Perhaps it is done after all.' She turned in the direction of the naked man who was standing there as still as before. 'That's us finished, Alain. But say hello to Barnum before you go.' The man called Alain broke as it were from the floor, as if he'd frozen solid there and was suddenly brought to life again by her command. Slowly he came over to me and clasped my hand lightly, no more than the slightest touch. I gave a deep bow but straightened up quickly. It was the first time I'd shaken hands with a naked man. Peder looked away and whistled and pulled me through the living room and up the stairs to the first floor. That took its time since we had to find our way between unfinished canvases and piles of books, cases, newspapers and clothes lines. But Peder's room was different. I kept standing by the door. I considered that you haven't become a real friend until you've seen the other person's room, but Peder hadn't seen my room yet, and besides, it wasn't just mine either since it was every bit as much Fred's; our room was divided by a line you couldn't get rid of. Peder fell on the bed, groaning. 'Bloody hell! Well done for saying that drawing was finished! Otherwise it would never have been.' There was a huge map on the wall above his desk, and beside the map four clocks showing different times. The first was at quarter to five. But the time on the second was already quarter to eight. 'Which one's wrong?' I asked. Peder laughed. 'Neither of them, you tit! Sit down, damn it!' I lay down beside him on the bed. It was wide enough. Peder pointed to the clocks. 'The first one's the time at Frogner. The second's the time in Rio de Janeiro. The third is New York and the fourth Tokyo.' 'Pretty smart,' I told him. 'Yes,' Peder agreed. 'Because if anyone calls from New York I know exactly what time it is.' 'And do they call from New York?' I asked him. 'Never,' Peder admitted, and laughed again. 'Good to know all the same,' I said. We lay there a while not saying anything. It was strange to think about. It was strange to think that time was different, that someone's already going home from school – in Rio de Janeiro, for instance – while others are behind and have barely begun their first class, in Tokyo, perhaps. Some of us are late while others have time to play with. It was really quite unfair. But what happened if you travelled from Frogner to New York? Did you suddenly become eight hours older or younger? It was unfathomable. And if you went round the earth and came back home once more, could you begin all over again, had time gone far enough backwards that most things hadn't been done yet so you could do them again but in a different way? Or else just decide not to do them at all if you regretted what you'd originally done? 'Sleeping?' Peder enquired. 'Just thinking,' I murmured. 'About what?' 'Time.' 'Time's only something we've invented,' Peder said. 'Just like money.' We heard steps down in the garden and hurried over to the window. It was the naked man, Alain, leaving. Mercifully he wasn't naked now. He was wearing a long coat and a huge scarf wrapped at least eight times round his neck. He turned once he was out in the street and waved; he raised his arm a little and brought his fingers together. But it wasn't us he was waving to. 'What's wrong with your mother?' I asked. Peder didn't say anything before the man called Alain had disappeared, and I regretted having asked because I didn't want to say anything wrong. I didn't want to spoil anything – that was the last thing I wanted – because I'd gained admittance to Peder's room. 'Is there anything wrong with her?' I swallowed. 'She's in a wheelchair,' I breathed. Peder shrugged his shoulders. 'Maybe she just likes sitting.' 'Yes, of course,' I said. Peder's shoulders relaxed again. I was on the point of asking something else but let it pass. Instead we stood there in silence by the window. Time passed in Tokyo, Rio de Janeiro and New York. At Frogner it didn't. It was just as if we too had become models, while motionless someone drew us. But we didn't know who was drawing us, nor did we know when the drawing would be finished. Finally Peder said something. 'D'you know how many willies Gustav Vigeland carved?' he asked me. 'Willies?' 'Yes, willies.' 'No,' I said. 'One hundred and twenty-one.' 'How d'you know that?' 'Because I've counted them. And there's 122 if you count the statue of the Monolith.' 'And 123 if you count the guy in the living room.' 'Yeah, bloody hell. There's just one thing worse than living beside Frogner Park.' 'What's that?' 'Living beside a church. Like Vivian does. Think of the noise on Sundays, huh?' 'Or Christmas Day,' I said. 'Must be terrible.' Peder looked at me. 'Some people say her Mum has a secret door from her bedroom into the church.' 'Who says that?' Peder shrugged again. 'Just people. It's probably crap.' Then his dad arrived home. We heard him long before we saw him. The rusty Vauxhall made more noise than an exploding train and the last undisturbed birds flew up from the hedge at the bottom of the garden when he was still just at the roundabout in Solli Square. About half an hour later he backed into the garage (though backing's a bit of

an exaggeration). It was more a case of the car jumping
into the garage, as if the driver didn't quite know how to
use the pedals and used them like a bicycle's instead, or
maybe it was because there was a problem with the
engine, but most likely it was a bit of both. 'It took Dad
three years and five months to get his licence,' Peder said.
'Two hundred and eight hours of driving lessons. It cost
just over what the car cost.' There was a nasty bang from
the garage. Immediately afterwards Peder's dad emerged
with his briefcase under his arm and his hat in his hand.
He looked up at us as if nothing had happened. Peder
opened the window. 'Hi!' his dad called. 'Is that the dancing bears up there?' 'And how often were you stopped by
the police today?' Peder shouted back. His Dad just
laughed and pointed at me instead. 'Barnum! D'you like
deep-fried black pudding and raw onions?' I didn't
manage to reply but he noticed that my jaw dropped. 'Nor
me, Barnum!' And then he vanished and we ran downstairs to find the living room table already set, and it certainly didn't smell like black pudding and onions, but
something I'd probably never tasted before but which
smelled good all the same. And Peder's mum came in
with a large dish and soon afterwards Peder's dad came in
too; he bent down to the wheelchair and gave her a long
kiss. After that we could sit down. And I kept thinking
that only a short time ago there'd been a naked man
standing here, and here we were eating dinner in the
same room. I had to help myself first and Peder's dad
watched me closely. 'Don't be scared to eat,' he said.
'Don't plague Barnum,' Peder sighed. 'I'm not plaguing
Barnum. I'm just saying that there's plenty more where
that came from.' I put an all but transparent slice of meat
on my plate and passed the dish to Peder, and immediately realized I ought to have passed it to his mum
instead, just in the same way that you get up for the
elderly and the infirm on trams. Now I was about to spoil
everything yet again and get put out and told never to
come back, the thing I dreaded more than anything. But

it was too late now and Peder took a double portion right away, and poured gravy over it until there was no more room left on the plate. He turned to me, armed with knife, fork and napkin. I hadn't been thrown out after all. 'Duck,' he said. 'Straight from Frogner Park.' 'Be quiet!' his mum laughed, and threw her napkin ring at him as his dad rescued the remainder of what was in the dish. But Peder wasn't done yet. 'Oh, yes. Mum goes on duck hunts in her wheelchair. First of all she feeds them. Then she wrings their necks. Right, Barnum?' 'Don't listen to him,' his mother exclaimed and sloshed apple juice into my glass. 'Oh, yes,' his father continued. 'Mother gets all our food from Frogner Park. Fish from the pond and swans from the fountain!' 'I do not!' 'And rabbits in winter. Did you know there were rabbits in Frogner Park?' 'Don't listen to them!' Peder's mother laughed. 'Before she used to hunt with a dog. It pulled the wheelchair just like a sledge.' And that's the way the talk went until they tired of it. Peder ate about twice as much as we did put together and in the same amount of time. And before the dessert was brought out a gradual silence fell; satisfied and sleepy it was. We looked at each other and smiled. I almost couldn't fathom how happy I felt. Here I was sitting in Peder's living room eating dinner. I had been in his room. I had lain beside him on his bed. This was somewhere Fred could never come. This was mine and mine alone. Peder's father ran his fingers through his wife's great mass of shining hair. 'Did you get anything drawn today?' he asked quietly. She nodded and rested his hand on her lap. 'Barnum says it's finished,' she said. He turned in my direction, taken aback. 'D'you know about these things, Barnum?' Peder got up and spoke before I could answer, and it was perhaps for the best. 'When Barnum says something's finished, it's finished. Can we finish this debate?' We nodded and Peder carried the plates out to the kitchen and was there a fair time. I had the urge to go after him but kept my seat, for no one had said I could go and I didn't want to be cheeky and make them think I was badly brought up and ungrateful. I wanted them to like me, like me in every way. Peder's father lit his pipe and a cloud of smoke rose over the table. 'Barnum,' he said. 'Yes,' I replied. 'Barnum,' he repeated. 'Yes,' I said, and thought that now it was he who was in the process of spoiling everything, if he too made comments about my name and made fun of it, as most people had a habit of doing. 'Barnum,' he said for the third time. 'I had a stamp with Barnum on it. An extremely rare American stamp.' At that moment Peder returned with dessert. 'And Mum caught these on the dog exercising ground,' he said, and put the bowl down on the table. 'Poodle ears in cream!' It was actually peaches and cream, but I could barely manage to eat because I was still thinking about the stamp, the Barnum stamp. I had my own stamp, Barnum's stamp; if ever I became wealthy enough I'd trace each and every one of them, buy them, and send cards to all those who'd mocked my name. Especially the vicar – he'd get a whole pile from me, all complete with my stamp and *Greetings from Barnum*. He'd have no time for anything else except picking up my cards. 'Come on now, Barnum, have plenty to eat,' Peder's mother insisted. 'Before Peder's had it all.' I helped myself to another poodle ear and Peder's dad lit his pipe again and it clouded over once more. 'Today an old lady came into the shop,' he said. 'She wanted to sell a stamp. I asked her how much she'd thought of getting for it. She answered that she'd imagined about fifty kroner. Her stamp was worth at least 800.' Another match was required to get the pipe lit, and I could barely see Peder's father behind the fog. Peder began to grow impatient. 'That means you made 750,' he said. But his dad shook his head. 'I couldn't do that. Deceive the old lady, I mean.' Peder was on the point of getting to his feet, but he'd probably eaten too much and didn't quite make it. 'Deceive!' he exclaimed. 'But she was the one who named her price!' 'Yes, but she knew nothing about stamps, Peder.' 'What did you give her then?' he murmured. 'I gave her precisely what I thought it was worth. Eight hundred kroner.' Peder buried his head in his hands and groaned. 'I reckon I'll sell it on to a Swedish collector for close on 900,' his dad said, and turned to his wife. 'That'll make a profit of a hundred.' She put her hand over his. 'You're far too nice,' she told him. 'He's far too stupid!' Peder roared. His father put down his pipe and looked at me with a strange smile. 'I'm neither nice nor stupid, Barnum. I'm just honest.'

Peder came with me a bit of the way home. He needed some air. And his mother wanted to come with us too. He wheeled her over Church Road and took the path beside the empty swimming pool, its diving board resembling a white cloud against the black sky where the moon had risen full, in the midst of a shifting ring of cold. Soon the snow would begin. Peder put his scarf round his mother. All at once I came out with something strange. 'You suit snow,' I told her. She leant backwards and looked up at me. 'Thank you,' she said. 'That was a beautiful thing to say, Barnum.' I was glad I hadn't had to explain what I'd meant. I didn't entirely know myself. It was just something I suddenly could see, that she'd suit snow. That red hair of hers. Copper and snow. 'Thank you,' she said again. And Peder put his hand on my shoulder.

Then I went alone along Church Road. I walked slowly so that the evening would last as long as possible. At Esther's kiosk I fancied I caught sight of Fred vanishing into a side entrance. I stopped and held my breath. But it was just the moon playing tricks on me. I kept staring there nonetheless, hidden behind the tree on the corner, until the danger was over. The bark felt cold and rough against my cheek. I wasn't afraid.

By the time I got home Mum had already gone to bed. Dad was off on his travels, for his suitcase and coat were gone. Fred wasn't in our room – he was out wandering – and Boletta was back at the North Pole again. I opened the door onto the balcony and looked at the moon. It had never been so huge, in the midst of its mantle of cold and wind. It was the same moon they could see from Røst and from Greenland, and perhaps from Rio de Janeiro too, if they looked for it hard enough. Boletta had spoken about moon sickness once, that dreams become powerful as steel when there's a full moon. For moonlight is a flame that welds together reality and all our imaginings. During the war no one suffered from moon sickness because everyone had black-out curtains and wasn't allowed to go out at night – that was how we won. Maybe that was what came over Boletta, when she had to go to the North Pole – moon sickness. And it didn't pass until the sun pushed out the moon and melted the fibres in the metal of the dark. I shut the door, closed the curtains and tip-toed in to Mum. I lay down in the bed beside her, even though I knew I shouldn't any more. For a long while she lay there, quite still, turned away from me. 'What is it, Barnum?' 'I'm so happy,' I whispered. She turned round. 'You're happy?' 'Yes,' I said. 'I've been with Peder.' 'Then I'm happy too, Barnum. Very happy.' I closed my eyes. 'D'you think Fred will be too?' I asked. Mum closed her eyes too. 'There's too much anger in Fred, Barnum. Too much anger. Now let's try to sleep, shall we?'

But I couldn't sleep. I lay awake. I let the day remain in me. I breathed deeply and then I sensed a taste that ling-ered in the room yet, the taste of dark wine, and it became a wave in my blood and an undertow in my head. I laughed and Mum told me to hush, but I laughed myself down into sleep, and that's how I close this remem-brance, this light picture of night – bathed in the moon and in Malaga.

The Labyrinth

Peder once asked me what my first memory of Fred really was. Where was I to begin? What image was I to choose from among the pile of memories I kept hidden in a darkness I seldom dared go into? And didn't those images slide over into each other anyway? Didn't the space between them, the years that separated them, get rubbed away when I looked back, so that the images were no longer clear and individual? For memories are always impure, joined together in another order – doubly exposed, impossible to separate, part of a different kind of logic and a confused chronology which is the hallmark of memory. Like the boy's footsteps in the labyrinth in *The Shining* which we saw together a long time later at Saga. At first I wasn't allowed in and had to show my identity card to prove my age. And Peder who was still easily scared (but only in respect of films, whereas I was scared of everything else), grabbed my hand every time the two murdered twins showed up in the bloodbath. He could well have asked what Fred's first memory of *me* was. What did Fred think when he leaned over the pram and saw the tiny, quiet boy lying in there and stretching up small, squat fists at him? Was this our first memory, our shared image, when he shook the pram to make me sleep or to scare me? Was that where we began? Peder raised his glass and drank to my health. 'You don't remember,' he said. I drank. 'I hate the word *really*. You know I hate the word *really*.' 'All right,' Peder said. 'I'll not use it any more. What's your first memory of Fred?' And I think to myself – not what others have told me which I've added to my own memory and now relate to others, as if I'd been there when those things happened, before my time and beyond it. In the back seat of the taxi where he was born, or in the gutter at the corner of Wergeland Road when the Old One was killed. No, that's not what I remember first, my earliest memory of Fred is this – six nylon stockings, the smell of Malaga, and Boletta reading aloud in a peaceful voice from our great-grandfather's letter *Onboard the SS* Antarctic, *17–8–1900*. And how *fragile* the paper it's written on has grown with all the fingers that have carefully leafed through the pages, and how worn are the edges of the envelope from which they gingerly remove the letter. But each time it's done with equal solemnity – each time it's like the first time. Now and again Boletta's voice quavers and then we can hear the glasses being refilled and the crumbs falling from the dry pieces of cake, as the three women take a short break. For Fred and I are sitting under the table in the dining-room. I can count six individual knees, two of them with holes in them (those are Mum's), and the Old One has kicked off her slippers and her big toe is poking out of the thin stocking of one foot, and Boletta keeps the rhythm with one of her own feet as she reads. There isn't much room for Fred but I'm sitting comfortably, leaning against his back, and I can feel his warmth. We're sitting as still as possible, not wanting to miss a word, and finally Boletta continues. *We had a very fine passage north; we passed the uninhabited island of Jan Mayen and lay there at anchor two days while the scientists went ashore. Even before the time we had travelled so far north the sun was high in the heavens at midnight. A short time after leaving this landfall we entered the ice; we fought our way in but it became stronger and stronger until, after two days, we were forced to turn back and remain free of it. We pushed further in a northerly direction through more or less solid ice; at times when the weather was fine or we could not proceed we dropped anchor by an iceberg to take a series of temperature readings, that is to say we investigated the ocean's temperature at different depths, as well as taking soundings. We have equipment on board for taking soundings to depths of 4,000 fathoms.* 'Good Lord,' the Old One murmurs. 'That they dared. Sixteen hundred fathoms!' 'Be quiet!' Fred tells her loudly. There's silence for a moment. And suddenly Boletta reads, loudly and clearly: *I have no need to fear this coming to the attention of any gossips from the press, for I will not have so much as a word of it in the papers*! Then the cloth is lifted and Mum's face comes to view; she looks at us in amazement but I reckon she just puts it on, and that they've probably known we were there all along. 'Guess who's hiding under the table?' she breathes. And now the Old One and Boletta have to have a look too – it's almost as if their heads are hanging upside down and I rejoice at the sight. But Fred's as serious as ever. 'More,' he demands. 'More.' Mum gives a sigh. 'No, that's enough now. It's not good for the boy.' Is it me she's meaning or Fred? Is it really not good for us or is it that she doesn't want us to sit under the table? At any rate not another word was read that evening. Boletta put the letter back in its envelope and tied a piece of blue ribbon round it so none of the pages would fall out, and then it was laid in the bottom drawer of the cabinet. We crawled out from our hiding place under the table behind the cloth. But it wasn't over all the same because the Old One got carried away; it was as if the memories were to the left and to the right of her, impelling her on. She picked me up onto her knee and I saw Fred's expression in the moment the Old One put her arms round me and I laid my head against her breast. I saw the envy in his eyes and something else too – disdain. I can find no other words for what I saw except envy and disdain, but he didn't go, he kept on sitting on the floor in the corner because we knew what was going to happen now. Boletta put out all the lights, drew the curtains and lit candles instead. Mum cooked slices of apple in the kitchen, and soon enough the aroma mingled with the dark and the Old One sighed contentedly. 'Now it's twilight time again,' she murmured. 'What do you want me to tell you?' 'About the letter,' I whispered. 'About the letter!' 'Don't nag,' Fred said from the corner. And when the Old One told a story she always began it from a different place, as if she wanted to come in sideways, as it were. She went the long way round, tested our patience, whetted our appetite; she told us about the little town of Koge where she was born and which Hans Christian Andersen himself has portrayed. She told us about the backbone of the dried cod from which they made cups, sugar-bowls and cream jugs, and part of the cod's head that could be glued onto small boxes in which they could keep secret things. I ate hot slices of apple and dozed; the dark and the Old One's procrastination made me sleepy. And yet suddenly she was there, unexpectedly, on the narrative's plank, ready for the big jump. 'And then it happened that a young seaman fell for me,' she said. I woke up. 'He fell for you?' I asked. Fred growled. The Old One chuckled. 'And I fell for him, Barnum. We fell for each other so heavily that the echo of it reached all the way to Copenhagen and reverberated over the whole country.' 'No more exaggerating,' Boletta ordered her. The Old One took a sip of Malaga. 'Denmark is small enough for such things to be heard,' she said. 'Go on,' I whispered. And the Old One did continue. 'That was the time when I was the Young One, when the world was still in the last century. But our happiness together was to be short-lived. In June of 1900 he joined the crew of the ship *Antarctic* which was bound for Greenland. And he, whose name was Wilhelm and is your great-grandfather, never returned to me but remained up there in the vast northern ice.' The Old One fell silent. I could hear her heart beating inside her dress; it thudded slow and heavy and made her hands tremble. I was close to tears. 'Don't stop now,' I whispered. The Old One drew her fingers through my curls. 'Perhaps it's now the story really begins, Barnum? For one year later, after little Boletta had been born, I was visited by a gentleman sent by the ship's owners and he brought with him a letter they had discovered in Wilhelm's wind-proof coat the day he disappeared. The very same letter that's lying there in the drawer.' The Old One had to have a rest. She ate some of the warm apple. We waited. Far off Mrs Arnesen played the piano, the same tune as always. 'Go on,' I whispered. 'Go on!' 'Don't nag,' Fred said. And the Old One did continue. 'When I read the letter it was just as if my Wilhelm was speaking to me. He was lost, but he spoke to me just the same. It was so strange. I could hear his voice in those words, in the dry ink, in the writing which he had taken such pains over there in the cold. All the same I couldn't help thinking that if he'd put on the wind-proof coat he'd perhaps have still been alive.' Boletta sighed. 'Then the letter might have been lost too,' she said. We thought about that for a moment. Fred got up, but sat back down again right away. It was the overwhelming smell of cooked apple in the dark. It held us fast. There was peel in my mouth, sweet and hard. The Old One wiped her nose. 'And after that I went into the film world,' she breathed. 'For they said I was the most attractive girl in Denmark.' I looked up at her. She was like one single wrinkle above me; her face resembled a great big raisin. 'What does attractive mean?' I asked. 'Beautiful,' the Old One breathed. I looked at her more closely still. 'They lied to you then,' I said. The Old One laughed and pushed me into bed. Fred was rather fed up because he had to go to bed at the same time, but for one reason or another he didn't protest. We lay awake in the dark. 'You should never have said that,' he told me. I grew frightened. I'd done something Fred didn't like. 'What?' 'That they lied.' 'I didn't mean it, Fred.' 'You said it. Don't say it again.' I thumped my head down on the pillow and cried. 'Shall I read to you?' I murmured. Fred threw a slice of apple onto the floor. 'Read what, Tiny?' I thought for a moment. 'If I go and get the letter I can read the rest to you.' Fred lay silent himself for a time. 'No one's allowed to touch the letter,' he said at last. 'Only Boletta and the Old One. And Mum.' He fell silent once more. I had nothing to say either. 'Anyway, you can't read,' he said. I sat up in bed. 'Yes, I can.' 'No.' 'Yes, I can read.' 'No,' Fred insisted. 'You're too small.' I lay back down again. I was close to tears. 'A b c,' I breathed. 'What are you saying?' 'A b c d e

f g,' I said. Now it was Fred's turn to get up. 'What the
hell are you doing?' he shouted. 'H i j k l m n o p,' I said
as fast as I possibly could. 'I'm reading! Q r s t!' Fred leapt
out of bed and came at me, and I had no idea what was in
his mind, I only saw his one hand clenched and I slid
under the quilt, hoping he wouldn't find me in the dark.
But all of a sudden he stopped, right in front of the
window. He stopped and stood there. After a time I dared
peek out. I saw he was holding a pencil in both hands; he
bent down and drew a line along the whole length of the
floor between us. And each time Mum washed that line
away Fred drew a new one, until in the end she gave up
and let it remain there, a line that divided the room in
two. And is it that night or another one on which Dad,
Arnold Nilsen, comes home with a washing machine? It
could be that one. It's that night. That's why Fred doesn't
go and lie down again. He just stands there listening.
There's a terrific noise on the stairs. Dad's carrying a
washing machine on his back and is rousing the entire
neighbourhood. That's of no consequence. He can make
as much noise as he likes because he's coming home with
a washing machine. Mum can't believe her own eyes and
has to clutch Boletta's hand who's already holding onto
the Old One. Dad's panting like an elk and is beet-red in
the face – he's got strength enough to smile nonetheless.
'Here I come,' he breathes. 'Make way!' And he carries
the washing machine right into the bathroom and drops
it there while he sits down in the bath, wipes away the
sweat and lets his thumping pulse calm once more. Mum
fetches a beer for him; it's the middle of the night and it's
still all quite unbelievable. He drinks the contents of the
bottle in one single gulp and we just stand there staring
at him. 'Now the time's over when you'll have to tire
yourselves out with tub-thumping!' he finally says, and
looks at Mum, the Old One and Boletta in turn. 'Because
now I've brought the future home with me!' He rises
from the bath like a sun god. 'How did you get it?' Mum
whispers. Dad's expression grows impatient; there's a

strain at the corner of his eye, a shadow over his smile. But the night is too good to get worked up. Instead he puts his arms round Mum and kisses her so hard she has to push him back forcibly. 'That's the least of our worries,' Dad says and laughs. Then he gets going twisting things and attaching things, and his swearing is worse than ever because he has to do everything with just the one hand. Mum puts her arms round me and keeps Fred's ears out of hearing, while the Old One just sighs and shakes her head at all this future there's room for in one small bathroom. But Dad can rise in triumph one more time. A button on the lid finally lights up and he flourishes his good hand and points at it. 'When you touch this electric dial you set in motion nothing less than washing, spinning and emptying, in the aforementioned order. Apart from that, may I mention in passing that the machine has an element that may be regulated, an automatic pump, a pulser on one side and a rustproof steel door.' There's silence for a good while. We're struck dumb. We're struck dumb with wonder and Dad basks in every second of it. He has us in the palm of his hand. He magics forth a packet of Blenda. 'What are you standing here gawping for?' he exclaims. 'Go and dig out the dirtiest things you can find!' But what were we to bring? Should we start with the curtains, bedlinen, socks, cloths, trousers or all our hankies? We just stand there, huddled together in the bathroom; not even Fred moves a muscle, and Dad has a fair old laugh at all this confusion and paralysis of action. It's the indulgent laughter – patient and good-hearted on a generous night. 'Then I'll have to ask someone to bring the best they have,' he murmurs. Mum vanishes for a second and reappears with her nylon stockings. Boletta's about to protest but Dad nullifies the objection with yet another smile. 'Woollens, silks and delicate fabrics are washed in lukewarm water for one minute,' he says, his voice low. Then he drops the stockings into the machine, one after the other, bangs the lid shut, pours some powder into a little drawer, turns on the tap and holds his fingers over the dial. We have to edge forwards. He twists the dial. Sure enough we hear a noise, a low humming that gradually grows in intensity; the machine begins to tremble and then to shake, a roaring engine on the spot on which it's resting. Mum's white as a sheet, Boletta can't bring herself to look, and the Old One just keeps sighing because this isn't the future but rather the onset of total insanity. Dad becomes a mite anxious (his smile is hanging by a very fine thread), and he flattens himself over the machine to keep it still. On no account must it topple over; these are powers far greater than ourselves – a machine like this can power a ferry from Svolvaer to Bergen and come back home before getting as far as rinsing. I stand behind Fred who's just crying with laughter; Dad's on the point of thumping him, but just as suddenly the machine goes quiet again. Steam rises from the lid then dies away; Dad looks with satisfaction at his wrist-watch and counts the last seconds before the minute's up. Then he opens the lid, lifts out the three pairs of stockings, and drapes them over his injured hand. They're shining, and not just that, I swear even the tears on the knees are repaired; they're whole and clean and smell sweet – they're as good as new. Yes, they're better by far than when they were new, and Boletta and the Old One put on these resurrected stockings and have to go for a walk in their newly-cleaned legs. Dad takes Fred and me to one side. 'Now you see how it's done,' he breathes. 'And not one of us'll forget this night.' With that he pulls off his shirt and chucks it into the machine, and he wants our pyjamas too, but then Mum comes back and sends us off to bed. But we don't fall asleep; we lie there listening to the song of the washing machine, and when everything is still once more we sneak back into the bathroom where Dad's white shirts are hanging to dry, and we crouch down there. Fred takes his fingers over the little metal logo just under the dial and I sit beside him, as close as I dare. His face is serious; he clenches his teeth and slowly moves his fingers from letter to letter.

'W-A-S-H-I-N-G-M-A-C-H-I-N-E,' he spells out just as slowly; he says each letter aloud. But it's not *washing machine* that's inscribed there, it's *Evalet*. Fred turns to me and smiles. I smile too. But I say nothing because it's so seldom he looks at me like that, smiling; he's sort of proud and embarrassed at one and the same time. I don't tell him that it's *Evalet* that's on the washing machine, and not *washing machine*. And we sit there on the cold bathroom floor, under Dad's shirts, and Fred takes his fingers over the letters again and again. '*Washing machine*,' he whispers.

And I think of the small name tags Mum sewed into our clothes so no one would take them by mistake in gym, at the Frogner baths, at dancing classes or at the dentist's. Mum was almost possessed with the notion after we got the sewing machine. All our clothes carried our names: shirts, jumpers, socks, the suede jacket, our plus fours, hats, gloves – even our underpants were equipped with tags. Fred Nilsen, Barnum Nilsen. Our clothes would never get lost. But it's now, when everything that happened long ago is long behind us, that I think of the labyrinth, the boy in the *The Shining* fleeing between the tall, snow-covered hedges and Peder grabs my hand at Saga even though we're both thirty years old. But we're easily scared, each in our own way. And right inside our ears, where the hearing nerve lies, there's also a labyrinth. It's filled with a clear, rather thick liquid – the acoustic water – and it resembles the type of snail you can find beside water in the summer and use as bait. There ought to be a labyrinth in the eye too, right in at its heart, but the eye's just composed of tears and muscle. And I see Fred slowly moving his finger through the dust under the living-room table, along the letter, past the nylon stockings, over the line in our room and out to the washing machine. And he whispers as he tries to spell that day's writing. 'You should never have said that, Barnum.' I grow so afraid. 'What? What should I never have said?' 'That they lied to the Old One,' Fred says.

The Coffin

Fred came home with a coffin. It was night-time. I was
sleeping but not deeply. I woke with the noise of him
down in the yard; he was pulling something heavy over
the snow, and a moment later he called my name, in that
low way. I got up as quietly as I could, filled with anxiety
for what he might have gone and done now. I opened the
window and looked out. And there was Fred on his way
past the clothes lines which were hanging heavy with
slushy snow and all but trailing on the ground. He was
dragging a sledge and on it was a coffin, a white coffin. He
stopped by the kitchen entrance and looked up at the
window where I was standing freezing. His breath drifted
like a grey cloud round his face. 'Are you coming to help
or what?'

Quickly I got dressed and padded through the flat. The
others were asleep. There was a draught from the keyhole
when I peered through it. I couldn't see Mum behind
Dad who was lying on his stomach, for all the world
like a dead whale. If he'd lain on top of her she'd have
expired on the spot. I heard the sound of the sharp,
whining sound emitted from his crooked, blocked nose. It
couldn't be right, that Fred had a coffin with him. I must
have been seeing things. But most of what had to do with
Fred was true. I was most tempted to lie down again and
pretend it was just another dream the following morning.
Instead I went into the dining-room and folded the quilt
more adequately over Boletta so she wouldn't catch a
chill. While Dad was growing larger and larger, so Boletta
shrank and shrank. If things continued like this and she
lived long enough, then in the end there'd be nothing left
of her whatsoever. That would be some way to die. Her
face was reminiscent of the head of a mummy which I'd
seen a picture of in *National Geographic* magazine; it had

lain for about 2,000 years under a pyramid. Carefully I put my hand on her brow, but I'd stopped kissing her now because she smelled of cod-liver oil. Her forehead was as crumpled as a walnut, and she was smiling in her sleep. Of course I'd been seeing things. Fred couldn't have got hold of a coffin. And so I ran down the kitchen stairs. Fred was pretty impatient by the time I got there. He'd lit a cigarette. His fingers were yellow. 'Did you have to take a bath first, or what?' I just stared at the sledge. I hadn't been seeing things. It was a coffin that was lying there. 'What is that?' I asked in a low voice. Fred pressed a finger hard against my temple. 'What d'you reckon?' 'Is it a coffin?' 'No, Barnum, it's a bobsleigh. A one-man bobsleigh. I'm going into training for the Olympics. Have you gone soft or what, Barnum?' 'But where did you get hold of it, Fred?' 'Don't you lose too much sleep over that.'

He took his finger from my temple and gave me a draw instead. It was one of those strong, unfiltered cigarettes which the Old One had left behind; it was as dry as hay and probably rolled about the time King Haakon first set foot on Norwegian soil. I coughed violently. Fred twisted the remainder of it out of my mouth and chucked it into the snow. It didn't burn out even there. He thumped me on the back. 'What d'you say, Barnum? Shall we wake the whole place or not?'

I swallowed tobacco and looked up. Above us all the windows were black. Inside, most lay sleeping, ignorant of what was going on about them. And I contemplated the fact that for about half our lives or maybe even more (since many sleep for most of Sunday), we know nothing at all. For half our lives we're in our beds, dead to the world, and the rest of the time we spend *making* our beds. I'd forgotten to shut our window. I'd get chilled during the night. I'd vanish that night. Fred shoved me in the direction of the sledge. 'Come on, then! Are you a complete cretin or what?'

I saw the cigarette burn out like an eye where it was and sink to nothing. We each took hold of an end of the coffin

and carried it up the kitchen steps. We had to have a
breather on each landing and we kept silent so as not to
wake a soul. I was at the top and Fred below, and up in the
loft the cold came dry and sharp and scraped against our
faces, for the heaters were either switched off or broken –
almost no one used their drying loft any longer. The wind
caused the walls to rattle. It was as if everything was
moving, like on the sea, and I was part of it. I was swaying. The light in the ceiling was broken, but Fred had
thought of that too. He had a pocket torch with him and
he stuck it in his mouth so he could carry the coffin at the
same time as lighting the way. I'd never have thought of
that. But then neither would I have come home with a
coffin in the middle of the night. Someone had left behind
a pair of underwear on a slack clothes line; the pants had
turned completely yellow and stretched towards the floor
as if they fancied jumping down and running off for good.
Then the light flashed elsewhere – cobwebs, a rusty key,
an empty brandy bottle, an old newspaper lying on the
floor turning over its own pages. We carried the coffin
through to the innermost chamber and carefully laid it
down. The moon was shining through the attic window.
A black dust rose up from the sacks of coke along the
wall. I'd been here before, but suddenly it all seemed such
a long time ago, and it felt as if everything was different
now. I wasn't going to break my arm. We just had a coffin
with us. Mum didn't like us coming up here. Fred spat out
the torch and pointed its beam straight at my eyes. I had
to shield them. 'That wasn't so heavy,' I whispered. Fred
laughed. 'Did you think there was someone in it?'

    I didn't reply. All at once Fred chucked the torch over
to me – a yellow arc through the darkness – and I just
managed to catch it. I shone it towards the door, because
perhaps someone we hadn't seen was standing there. I
wanted to empty the darkness and fill it with light. I
wanted to see. 'This was where Mum dried the clothes,'
Fred said. Then I spotted it, the dead bird; it was lying
right under the moon in the window. There was scarcely

anything left of it, just the bones of one wing which had become part of the black dust and almost resembled a footprint. I went closer. Now I could see an eye too, a puckered sphere, akin to a raisin. Fred took my arm and drew me back. 'Shine the torch for me,' he breathed.

I had to hold it with both hands and shone it in the direction of the coffin. Fred lifted off the lid. It was red inside, lined with something resembling silk that lay in folds along the sides. There was a pillow there too; it almost looked as if it would be good to lie in there. Suddenly my back felt freezing; a shiver of cold avalanched from my neck down. Fred turned to me and smiled. 'Stylish,' he said.

Then he took off his jacket and lay down in the coffin. He folded his hands on his chest and lay there deathly still, his eyes wide open. I felt he grew paler, and thinner too; it was as if his cheeks were hollowed out and his face collapsed inwards. I clutched the torch and held it as steady as I could – and perhaps it was just the pale light and the dull glow of the moon which made him look like that, made him look dead. The colours ran from his eyes too and still he hadn't moved a muscle. 'Stop fooling about, Fred,' I breathed.

There was a draught from the attic window. There was frost and ice round the rim. I could hear the snow; big chunks that broke off and toppled down the roof. I wondered what time it was, how much time had passed – but I didn't have the guts to look at my watch. The moon disappeared. Soon my shadow became one with the darkness.

'Fred? Please, Fred.' But he just lay there with his hands folded and his fixed expression that was somehow empty, as if everything he'd ever seen somehow didn't exist any longer. It was as if neither I existed nor the torch in my hands nor the light that met him. Somehow I didn't know him at all; it was as though a stranger lay there dead in the coffin.

Then finally he spoke, quietly and without looking at me. 'Now put on the lid, Barnum.' I staggered backwards.

'No,' I told him. 'Do it. Put on the lid.' 'But why, Fred? Please don't make me.' 'Do as I say, Barnum. Put on the lid. Then go and lie down and keep your mouth shut.' I went a step closer again. 'Are you going to stay here?' I whispered. 'That was the general idea, yes.' 'But what'll I say if anyone asks about you?' 'Told you. You keep your mouth shut. Put the lid on, damn it.' 'I don't want to, Fred.' 'Then d'you fancy lying here yourself, Barnum? Huh?' 'No, Fred.' 'No problem fixing you up with a kid's coffin. 'Cos that's all you'd need.'

I put the torch on the floor and lifted the lid. I think I cried a bit, but I shut my eyes so he wouldn't notice. I hated him. He could just stay there in his coffin. I'd fasten the lid so he'd never get out again. I wouldn't tell a soul where he'd gone and hidden. He'd starve to death after he parched with thirst, but first he'd suffocate. It was one and the same to me, so long as he died and no one found him before it was too late. And who would think of looking for him here? I fiddled with the lid to get it into place, and bent down to retrieve the torch. At that moment I heard two noises; the first was Fred's laughter (he was laughing inside the coffin), and the second was a weak crackling sound. Before I got up the torch went out in my hand and the dark swallowed me as Fred kept on laughing. And it's this I remember – the laughter and the darkness – in that order, but as time passed and I recollected that night in the drying loft, the laughter and the darkness merged into one. They were no longer two separate events that followed each other – Fred's laughter and the torch going out – they were simultaneous and inseparable, and for that reason it's impossible for me to hear someone laugh without feeling the weight of an equally powerful darkness growing in my shaking hands.

I dropped the torch. It hit the floor with a bang. There was quiet from within the coffin now too. 'What was that, Barnum?' 'The light's gone,' I breathed. 'Same here,' Fred said, and I think he thumped his fist against the lid. 'Now go, Barnum! I don't need you any more!'

I found the door. I crept along the wall. I thought I
heard the sound of wings – of a bird and of beating wings
in the darkness. Perhaps it was a bat, perhaps it was just
Fred's laughter. Then I was out onto the staircase; light
showed from below and I chased towards it. Everyone
was sleeping. I lay down with my clothes on. I didn't
sleep. I lay awake while others slept. If only it could just
be morning as fast as possible; if only the new could come
with its gleaming eraser and rub out the writing of the
night. Fred who couldn't so much as *spell* the word *coffin*.
I padded into the living room, took out the drawer in the
cabinet and brought out Wilhelm's letter. *The ship's company consists of First Lieutenant G. Amdrup, second gunner
Jacobsen, Nielsen the blacksmith, first mate Loth, Hartz – a qual-
ified botanist and geologist, Dr Deichman – the ship's doctor and
naturalist, together with Madsen – an assistant from the zoological gardens whose task it is to capture a musk ox and bring
it back to Copenhagen.* If I could have chosen I'd have been
the second gunner, or maybe Madsen, who was to find the
musk ox. But perhaps none of them came back, perhaps
they remained there too *in the land of ice and snow*, in the
great white silence that fastened them down into everlasting death.

Boletta was looking at me; those small eyes scratched
at my spine. I put the letter back where it belonged,
pushed shut the drawer and turned in her direction. She
lay there smiling. She said something strange. 'How old
have you actually become?' she asked. I told her my age,
even though she knew it herself without a shadow of
doubt. Boletta smiled with all her wrinkles. 'In seven
years you'll be just as old as my father.' I had to go nearer
her. 'What did you say, Granny?' 'I never met him. And
had I met him now I'd be three times as old as him. An
old hag like me meeting her young, handsome father. Just
think of that.' 'Have you taken a long time to work that
out?' I breathed. Boletta took my hand. 'Each day and
every day I work it out, Barnum. It keeps me alert.' She let
my fingers drop and I went towards the door. I heard her

sitting up. Perhaps even now she'd add a new day to her reckoning. 'How's your new friend?' Boletta asked. I turned round. 'Peder? Fine. I'm meeting him this evening. I mean tomorrow. Or today.' Boletta smiled once more, but this time the smile was sad; her mouth was nothing more than a fold in her wizened face. 'You have to look after Fred,' she whispered. 'Me? I can't look after Fred,' I told her. 'Yes, you have to look after Fred too, Barnum. Now you've friends of your own.' 'He doesn't need me,' I exclaimed. 'Yes, it's now he does need you. Because it isn't easy for Fred to find friends.'

I ran into my room. I was almost angry. But I didn't dare go up to the loft again. I sat at the window till the first light began showing in a narrow strip along the sky, midway between the pale moon and the city. Fred didn't come down. I left before the others had got up, before breakfast – not even Esther had opened her kiosk yet, and she'd have to clear at least a ton of snow before she did. I cleared most of it for her with a shovel I came across in the entryway below, so at least one person could be happy that day. Because I was both full of dread and anticipation. That was just the way it was. I looked forward to the arrival of the snow, but I dreaded the snowballs. I looked forward to meeting Peder and I dreaded what might happen. The thing I'd feared, as a suspicion, a feeling, was suddenly written in tablets of stone in my mind – that pleasures must be paid for with dread, that laughter is the voice of darkness. Fred was at the very core of my being, but how could I, little Barnum, look after him? It was Fred who had to look after me.

The first thing I got when I came into the playground was a snowball in the face. It wasn't especially hard but what it lacked in solidity it made up for in wetness; it kind of melted on impact and ran down the inside of my shirt. My teeth just chattered and I laughed. And there isn't much more to tell, except that at break time it was my turn to throw. I aimed at the open school kitchen window. It was rather a good aim. I could hear the crashing pots and frying pans. The following period the head teacher came round to discover who the guilty party was. I put my hand up without the slightest hesitation and had to wait behind for three quarters of an hour. Basically I had no problem with that. In addition I had to write thirty times in my best writing – *I must not throw snowballs*. When I had done that I started a new sheet. On this I wrote – *You must not lie in your coffin before you are dead* – nineteen times. Then my three quarters of an hour were up and I could go home. There was no one standing in the park waiting to wash my face in the great snowploughed mounds behind the church. That was the good thing about having to wait behind. But I didn't go home all the same. I went down to the corner of Bygdøy Alley and Drammen Road instead, and stood under the tree there waiting for Peder. There were still some leaves left on the branches. Winter had come too abruptly. Autumn hadn't had time to finish properly. When I leant my head backwards and looked up into the great crown of the branches, the leaves resembled red water lilies floating in a white pond falling down over me. I stood like that for at least an hour. Then I felt someone shaking my jacket. It was Peder. 'You look like the son of the bloody Abominable Snowman!' he exclaimed. He kept brushing away at my clothes. 'Have you been standing here long?' 'A while,' I admitted. 'I got the time wrong.' Peder leant against the trunk of the tree. 'Snow is the most ridiculous thing I know,' he said. 'Why?' 'Why? Give me one good reason we should have snow.' I thought about it. 'You can go skiing,' I suggested. Peder looked at me with something akin to disgust. 'Skiing? Do you ski a lot, Barnum?' 'No, not particularly,' I admitted hastily. 'No, you can see that. I'll tell you something. About a thousand millimetres of precipitation descend on Oslo each year and I have to clear about forty of them. Otherwise Mum couldn't get out.' Peder produced an umbrella he had secreted under his duffel coat and he put it up over us. We stood there for a bit not saying anything, sheltered from the falling snow. 'What did you mean by that?' I asked. 'D'you think Mum can clear snow by herself? And Dad can't be bothered. But at least I get a weekly wage doing it. That's the only good thing I can say about snow. That I make some money out of it. I insist on a tenner a millimetre.' 'You said you could see I wasn't a skier,' I breathed. 'What did you mean by that?' Peder laughed. 'D'you think I look like a cross-country skier, huh?' I shook my head. 'Not in the least,' I admitted. 'Well, nor do you!' We both laughed. Neither of us would be particularly efficient at it – we weren't made for it. That was crystal clear. We'd be better off going in other directions. Then I thought of something. 'Perhaps I know a good reason after all,' I said. 'And what's that then?' 'Your mother can paint it. The snow, I mean.' Peder groaned. 'Mum said that too. I think she likes you. There's just one thing I keep wondering about.' Peder stood still, absolutely silent, under the black umbrella. 'What?' I asked. 'It must be possible to paint snow without having to clear it.'

We didn't say too much after Peder said that. It was enough to consider. We stood there behind the red tree so no one would see us. It was the first time I'd waited for somebody along with someone else. The class would begin in fifteen minutes and the first pupils had gone already into the Merchant Building, as if they believed they'd get asked to dance just because they were early. 'She's not coming,' I said in the end. 'Of course she is,' Peder said calmly. 'D'you want a bet on that?' 'How much then?' 'What have you got?' 'Two kroner twenty.' 'All right, then that's what we'll bet.' 'Deal,' said I. Peder thumped my back. 'And you've just lost two kroner and twenty øre!' Because Vivian was coming down Bygdøy Alley, running through the snow, a great red hat on her head. She jumped over the pavement edge and plashed her way over to us. Her face was wet and she quickly drew her hand over her brow and joined us under the umbrella. It began to get a bit crowded there. We were breathing on each other. 'Barnum didn't think you'd come,' Peder said. Vivian looked at me. 'I came all right,' she said. 'Perhaps Barnum's used to being disappointed,' Peder went on, not letting up. 'Perhaps,' Vivian said, and took off her hat. 'Have you said anything at home?' I asked, so as to change the subject. She shook her head and droplets showered from her hair in a shining circle. 'What they don't know won't hurt them,' Peder said. 'In other words, ignorance is bliss.' Now the rest of the class was coming with their dark clothes and bags with over-narrow shoes in them; they looked as if they were going to a funeral at the very least, or were on their way to the slaughterhouse where they'd imminently be thumped on the skulls and hung up on hooks from the roof till tender, while Svae played *Oh Heiderröslein* over and over before flaying the lot of them with a nail file. It wasn't just a sad procession; it looked rather a pathetic one too. We laughed. We pointed at them and laughed. Now it was our turn. We laughed at them. We were so superior. We were together. It was us against them, us against the crowd, and we had supremacy. And perhaps it was the first time, just then, under the black umbrella there behind the red tree, that I felt this sense of belonging that's beyond one's own family – yes, that's outside your own self. This belonging which eliminates the anxiety in your innermost being and which gives you a place on which to stand. I felt that, strongly and clearly, that evening with Peder and Vivian. Then there was just the snow and all the steps imprinted in it between the street lights on Drammen Road, and we could hear the music from the windows on the upper floor – the beat – and the steps spreading out over the parquet floor we had left once and for all.

We didn't say anything for a bit. We just looked at each other and smiled. There was nothing to worry about. If we wanted we could climb up to the top of the tree and sit there for the rest of the evening. Peder folded up the umbrella. It had stopped snowing. 'We'll go to Dad's place,' he said, and started off. We followed him. He was

walking down in the direction of Vika. It wasn't wise
going particularly much further. The streets hadn't been
ploughed and the snow was all brown. But I wasn't worried. We were together. It wouldn't take much for Vivian
to reach for my hand, and no one had ever held my hand
except for close family members. At least Peder stopped
outside a shop in Huitfeldt Street. Above the window,
which was covered in a metal grill, there were words
in large letters – MIIL'S STAMPS – BOUGHT AND SOLD.
Peder produced a great bunch of keys and unlocked the
door. We went in and he closed it behind us. There was
no one there. Peder lit a lamp in the ceiling which shone
sharp and white. I'd never seen so many stamps. There
was a glass case full of old letters. The place smelled of
glue and tobacco, and something else that I couldn't
diagnose – maybe a particular type of steam used for lifting stamps from letters without them falling apart.
'Smells of rubber,' Peder said. 'You get used to it eventually.' Vivian looked about her inquisitively. 'Can you really
live from selling stamps?' she asked. 'Of course,' I said. 'A
stamp from Mauritius costs 21,734 kroner.' Peder smiled
and pushed us through to the back premises. There was a
sofa and fridge there, and a desk on which strange, shining instruments were lying – magnifying glasses, lenses
and microscopes. It was more like an operating table.
Peder got out some beer and some Coke from the fridge
and opened both bottles with a pair of tweezers. Then he
mixed the two in a glass, took a gulp himself and passed
it on to us. It tasted sweet and sour at one and the same
time. A humming began in one of my ears. We sat down
on the sofa, with Vivian in the middle. 'Are you allowed
to be here?' she asked. Peder splashed more beer into the
Coke. 'Dad says I've got to take over the whole dump
anyway. I'm the one who counts the cost!' Peder laughed
loudly and produced a stamp lying right at the back of a
drawer which first had to be unlocked using two keys. He
sat down with us once more. 'What I like most about
stamps is that the ones that have things wrong with them

are of most value.' He showed us the stamp he'd sought out and we took turns holding it. It was Swedish, yellow, and looked as if it had been sent a good while back. 'A three shilling stamp from 1855,' Peder whispered. 'Should really have been green. The King of Romania bought one for £5,000 in 1938. Just because it was yellow and not green.' Peder put the stamp back in its drawer and turned back to us. But it was Vivian he was staring at. 'I'm fat,' he said. 'And Barnum's tiny. What's wrong with you then, Vivian?' I almost didn't dare breathe. There was quiet for so long I thought Peder had ruined everything. But then she did say something after all, and she looked up and smiled. 'I was born in an accident,' she said.

I thought about that the whole way home, about what she'd said about being born in an accident. I thought so much about it that I forgot what I was going to say myself. Were we worth more because there was something wrong with us? Mum was already standing in the hall, and in the living room Dad was sitting drowsily in a chair. Boletta wasn't to be seen anywhere so she probably had her usual affliction and was at the North Pole. 'Were you kept behind again?' Mum demanded, and her mouth was trembling. 'Yes,' I admitted. 'Well, it's at least good you don't deny it because the head teacher rang to tell us! How could you?' Dad got up from his chair and that was easier said than done. 'Well, well,' he said. 'So you threw a snowball through a window, Barnum.' 'Yes,' I breathed. 'That sounds promising indeed. Once the spring comes we'll get going with the discus, and the great thing about the discus is that it gives you a better grip on the girls too!' 'Be quiet!' Mum shrieked. Dad just laughed and began sitting down once more. Mum tugged at my jacket. 'And you've been to dancing in these clothes!' I looked away. 'We were only doing the cha-cha-cha,' I said. Mum sighed heavily and her hands flew in all directions. 'And where's Fred? Have you seen him?' 'He's lying in a coffin in the drying loft.' Mum's arms dropped. Dad remained on his feet, suddenly awake and white-faced. 'What did you say?' he asked. 'Nothing.' My throat was quite parched. My tongue was stuck to the roof of my mouth. Slowly Dad came closer. 'Nothing? You said nothing?' 'I don't remember what I said,' I whispered. Dad stopped in front of me, his whole body shaking. 'You said that Fred was lying in a coffin in the drying loft.' I looked down. 'Yes, I suppose I did.'

No one would have believed Dad could have taken stairs so fast. Mum hurried in his wake, and barely managed to keep up with him, and I came last. I had to know what had happened. This is what I see: Dad's come to a halt inside the drying loft, right under the attic window. The coffin's lying on the floor. Mum's face is buried in her hands and she screams without emitting a single sound. But the strange thing is that Dad doesn't look at the coffin first but rather at the drying lines, the pegs, the remains of the dead bird, the empty coke sacks – and he breathes so heavily he redistributes the dust in the room. He stands there like that staring at everything about him as if he's forgotten the reason he went there in the first place, forgotten himself entirely. Then Fred himself raises the lid of the coffin and sits up. It almost looks comical. He sits there gasping for breath, pale and thin among all the silk folds. He stares at me. I stand in the shadows behind Mum, whose face is still hidden behind her hands. 'Don't hurt him,' she murmurs. And Dad turns towards her, almost sorrowful and apologetic. Then the strangest thing happens. He bends down and puts his arms round Fred, holds him close and pats his back. Even Mum has to look now because Dad doesn't beat the living daylights out of Fred, he hugs him instead – and I catch a glimpse of Fred's expression over Dad's shoulder, bewildered and horrified. And one of them is crying – not Fred, but rather Dad, Arnold Nilsen.

I ran downstairs again and went to bed. The others came a bit later, their voices low and unhurried. I put my hands over my ears just the same. I didn't want to know what they were saying. But I couldn't hear Fred. Perhaps

I'd get a hammering from him because I'd told them where he was, and most likely I'd get a double helping because Dad hadn't thumped him. That would have been the best thing ultimately, if Fred *had* got his usual hammering and that had been that. I was dreading this already and couldn't sleep. I was as bewildered and horrified as Fred. He came in when everyone had gone to bed. He sat down by my bed. I didn't say a word. Then I couldn't wait any longer. 'I'm sorry,' I whispered. Still Fred didn't say anything. A great stillness held his shadow aloft. He had something in his hands. I couldn't see what it was. Finally he was going to say something. He breathed out. 'I think I'm evil,' Fred said. I wished he hadn't said anything after all. 'You aren't evil,' I murmured. Fred leant closer. 'How do you know?' I had to think about that. A beating would have been better. 'You've never done anything evil,' I told him in the end. 'Haven't I?' Fred had done a fair amount; he'd posted my pyjamas to the caretaker, he'd not spoken for all but two years, he'd lain in a coffin in the drying loft, and that wasn't the half of it. But if there was a God wouldn't he turn a blind eye to all those things? Would he really make a tally of them? 'You've never done anything truly evil,' I said to him. Fred looked away. 'Not yet,' he breathed. Now I was whispering myself. 'Not yet? Are you planning to, Fred?' A car drove down Church Road and the glow from its headlights swept through the room. Then I saw what it was he was holding in his hands. It was the discus. He didn't answer. He just kept sitting like that, the discus in his lap, stroking his fingers over its surface. 'A junior discus,' he whispered. 'One and a half kilos.' That was all he said. He lay down to sleep. He left the discus on the window sill. I took it back into the living room. It was certainly heavy. I was glad it wasn't a senior discus. What was in Fred's mind? I felt anxious. I took the letter back with me, lit the small lamp above my head, and read aloud. I don't know if Fred heard me or if he'd already gone to sleep. But I read it nonetheless, the whole letter, from beginning to end. Right to the final sentence, the most beautiful thing I knew, and I managed to read it without crying once. It was the last time we read it.

There were no coffins reported missing in Oslo round that time. Dad took off the gilt handles, removed all the silk, and chopped it up for kindling which he used for the stove in December, when it began to get cold and the balcony door was letting in the draught. It burned pretty well. But I didn't particularly like sitting in the warmth it gave off; it made me sweat and feel chilled at one and the same time, so I tended to go out when Dad lit the wood of the coffin Fred had lain in. And late on one such evening, after everyone has become somewhat strange with the fierce and feverish heat of the stove, and even Dad himself has gone out to cool down, Boletta tears open the door to our room and stands there shaking a single finger, scarcely able to speak. I had no idea she could get so angry; I'd never seen her like this. The gentle Boletta was like a bird with her feathers all ruffled. 'Where is the letter?' she breathes. It's Fred she's staring at because he's at home too; he lies in bed and simply shrugs his shoulders. 'No idea. Have you, Barnum?' Boletta turns to me. 'Isn't it in the drawer?' I ask her. 'No, it's not in the drawer!' 'Maybe you took it to the North Pole?' I suggest. Boletta lifts her tiny hand into the air. 'Are you trying to make a fool of me, Barnum?' 'No, Granny. But I put it back in the cabinet after I read it last.' Boletta turns the guns on Fred once more. 'If you've taken that letter, you've brought dishonour on the living and the dead! Do you hear me?' Fred gets up. 'I haven't touched it!' he shouts. 'I haven't bloody well touched the letter! Why do I always get the blame for everything?'

Mum's there too now. She has to support Boletta. Thereafter they ransack the whole flat, but they never do find the letter. 'You've gone and lost it yourself,' Mum tells her. Boletta doesn't know what to believe and as a result will believe almost anything. Bewildered and miserable she lies down on the divan. I sit down beside her and try to comfort her. 'It's not so bad,' I tell her. 'I know it off by heart. Boletta opens her eyes. 'Off by heart?' she breathes. I nod and wipe away beads of sweat from her brow. And then I begin reading the letter to her – with neither the paper nor the words in front of me I read the letter in its entirety. But when I'm done, after I've spoken the final words and neither added nor removed anything, not so much as a comma, Boletta takes my hand and slowly sits up and whispers, 'It's not the same, Barnum. No, it's not the same.'

I said no more. And so we sat there like that on the dining-room divan that December as the stove sent out its rays of heat, and since that time I've never been able to think of the letter, written in the land of the midnight sun amid ice and snow, without remembering the coffin.

The Accident

Vivian was born in an accident. It happened on 8 May 1949. Aleksander and Annie, who will become her parents, are driving a Chevrolet Fleetline Deluxe, a gift from his father on their wedding the previous autumn. They're driving up towards Frognerseter. They're young and at the start of their lives together; she will give birth in a couple of months and he has one year of his law studies at Oslo University left – he's considered the sharpest of the class. She was crowned princess in the school-leaving festivities the year before. They're the kind of couple that others admire and envy; the shining stars amid the paler ones around. Their joy is inevitable – they know nothing *besides*, that day, than the joy of being. They are on their way into the future and the future is on their side. It's the sun that counts. The blue skies. The green trees. They stop at the Holmenkollen slope. Aleksander Wie winds down his window and points to the top of the ski jump and the ground below; this man who knows the letter of the law becomes poetic and attentive to every detail. It's love. It's her. It's both the moment and the future. 'It's you and I who're standing in that tower now, Annie,' he tells her. She puts her hand over his. 'We're the ones standing in the tower,' he says again. 'We're setting out and we aren't afraid.' 'No,' Annie laughs. 'We'll fly higher than any of the rest.' 'Yes, Aleksander!' And he bends down to her lap; she leans back in the seat that's like a bed, and Aleksander listens, he listens to the child inside her and he thinks he can hear two hearts pounding – Annie's and the baby's. He lies like that a long while, listening. She runs her hand through his hair. 'You're beautiful,' he whispers. 'Have I told you that before?' Annie laughs. 'You told me this morning.' 'And now I'm telling you again. You're beautiful – both of you.' He kisses her.

He puts up the seat and becomes the pragmatic lawyer once more, the one who will protect her. 'You must sit properly. The child could be harmed. You must be careful.'

They drive on. Aleksander closes the passenger-seat window. He doesn't want it to be draughty for her. He accelerates for a moment, goes a bit over the limit on the last hill, and feels this power that is gentle and manageable; but slows down at once as they swing round towards the woods. There's another car coming towards them. He can scarcely believe his eyes. 'My word,' he exclaims. 'A Buick!' And the cars each stop on their respective sides of the road. Aleksander opens his door. Annie quickly grasps his hand. 'Where are you going?' she asks. 'Where am I going? I have to take a look at his car.' 'Don't be long.' He sits back down in his seat again. 'You're not feeling bad?' She shakes her head. 'Just a bit cold.' 'Cold?' 'I don't know. I got so cold.' 'We're driving home,' he tells her. She laughs. 'Hurry up. It'll pass.' 'Sure?' 'Quite sure. I'm better already.' Aleksander quickly kisses her cheek and hurries across the road. The other driver – a short, dark-haired man wearing light gloves – is already standing beside the open coupé, and he lights a cigarette. Aleksander thinks to himself at once that he looks like an upstart out on the road to show off; maybe an ordinary guy from a whaler who's made too much money. There's a boy in the front who looks sullen and bad-tempered; a thin, pale woman sits behind him and is smiling shyly, as though she knows this isn't the right car for them, that it's out of their league. A strange lot they are altogether, but Aleksander greets the small, idiotic fellow who's speaking a different, northern dialect and trying to disguise the fact by speaking slowly and in capital letters. They go round their cars and boast about them a bit. 'Is that your wife?' the stranger enquires. Aleksander nods. 'Yes, it is indeed.' 'She's most beautiful.' Aleksander's embarrassed by the intrusiveness of the comment. A shadow sweeps over them and draws the

light with it. The clouds are increasing. He stops and
quickly goes back to the Chevrolet, gets inside. 'We're
going home,' he announces. But Annie wants to go on.
'No, not yet. I want to go right up to the top of the tower.'
Aleksander laughs and feels this joy that knows neither
blemish nor flaw. She's with him. She'll follow him. She
wants to follow him to the very top. 'All right then! In that
case we can avoid driving after that charlatan!' He fastens
his seatbelt and at that moment the rain starts. He puts
on the windscreen wipers and drives on towards the next
sharp bend. Annie turns and notices that the woman in
the other car has turned round too – just for a second –
then they're out of sight of each other. And it's on the far
side of this bend that the accident happens. Perhaps Aleksander Wie was driving too fast, perhaps the road was
slippery on account of the warm rain, perhaps some creature or other suddenly came out of the wood and startled
him. Whatever the reason, he loses control of the nearly
two-ton Chevrolet – it all happens before he has time to
react, before he can manage to straighten up. Forces loom
against him, the car swerves to one side, plunges down a
steep slope and crashes into a tree. Annie is slung against
the windscreen which shatters over her face. There's
utter stillness. Only the rain keeps falling. Only a bird
flutters upwards from a branch. Aleksander sits pinned
between the seat and the wheel, all but completely
unharmed – but for a cut in the forehead. He frees himself and turns towards Annie. He can see nothing but
blood; her face is a mass of blood – a piece of glass has cut
her face diagonally and divided it in two. Her neck, her
chest – everything is blood, everything is shattered.
'Annie,' he murmurs. 'Annie.' And he doesn't hear his
own voice but rather something else – not a sound but
rather a movement, and he looks down to the floor by her
feet and sees a bundle. A bundle of flesh and blood, a
human being, still attached to Annie, who suddenly bel-
lows and gurgles, and presses her hands against her
ruined face. The glass breaks between her fingers and she

roars and roars; Aleksander tries to bend down to the new-born baby – a girl – they've already decided the baby will be called Vivian if it's a girl.

It was a girl and Vivian turns towards us. 'Come on then,' she says. Peder looks at me and nods; he's pale and almost appears thin there where he's standing. And we follow in Vivian's wake through the dark and silent flat, cheek by jowl with Frogner church. It's the first time we've been there, at Vivian's, and it took long enough for her to dare to invite us. 'Quiet,' Peder breathes. 'What did you say?' I ask him, my own voice as muted as his. 'Quiet,' he repeats. We go into her room and soundlessly she shuts the door. It's as if no one sleeps there at all. Everything is neat and tidy. Everything appears untouched: her bag, her books, a jumper, a pair of slippers side by side. And it strikes me that this room is almost completely empty; there's nothing there, nothing – no record player, no radio, no magazines. *Maybe this is the way girls' rooms are*, I think to myself, *tidy*. But I realize that Peder's noticed it too, and we crash down on the grey sofa while Vivian sits on a stool, for there's nothing else to sit on there except the stool. We're silent for a bit, as if the stillness of the flat is infectious. Peder has to break the silence first. 'Cool,' he says finally. Vivian looks up. 'Cool? What d'you mean?' 'Our place is stuffed with crap. Here there's nothing.' There's a ghost of a smile on Vivian's lips. 'Full of crap?' she repeats. 'But at Barnum's it's even worse.' He looks at me and laughs, and I realize Peder's talking for the sake of it, and he doesn't quite know what to say and so is babbling like this. I feel freezing cold. Peder's freezing too. His neck is covered in goose pimples. 'Full of crap,' I quickly put in. Vivian shakes her head, realizing we're just talking crap, and we know that she knows, and no one says any more for a long while, and this time I'm the one to break the silence, and what I come out with's pretty stupid. 'Did you tell your parents you'd given up dancing classes?' I ask her. Vivian shrugs her shoulders in exactly the same way Peder does, and it makes me rather worried.

'It's all the same to them,' she says simply. It's then my
eyes alight on a picture on the wall behind her, and I just
sit there gazing at it because I can't take my eyes off it, as
Peder goes on spouting crap. It's a photograph of a lady –
black and white – and definitely fairly old; she's holding a
cigarette in her fingers and the smoke is rising in a faint
spiral in front of her face. Her mouth is thin and wide;
there's something hard and cold – almost hostile – about
her face. Yet at the same time there's also something
about it that's inviting and alluring, as if it's you and you
alone she wants to join in something you've probably
never done before and which you'll probably never have
the chance to do again. *Marble and marzipan*, I think to
myself. The words just tumble from nowhere. Marble and
marzipan. 'If I could choose,' Peder was saying, 'I'd rather
have had nothing at all than a lot of crap.' 'But here there's
actually a lot of both,' Vivian says, smiling. 'Both nothing
and crap.' Peder's sweating now and unfortunately turns
to look at me. 'And what have you to say to that, Barnum?'
'Marble and marzipan,' I reply. And both of them start
laughing; both Peder and Vivian laugh, and it's as if the
sound of laughter doesn't belong there, but I laugh
myself. We lean in towards each other and laugh – marble
and marzipan. It's us three – we say things no one else
could comprehend beside ourselves. And then someone
knocks on the wall and a more sudden silence I've never
heard before. We sit up as if we've been caught in the very
act, and arrested for committing some heinous crime. We
were laughing. We don't laugh any more. 'It's Lauren
Bacall,' Vivian whispers. 'Who knocked on the wall?' 'No,
you nutter. The one you're staring at.' Vivian turns
towards the photograph, the only thing on any of the
walls. Peder looks at it too. 'Who is she?' I ask. 'An
actress,' Vivian replies. 'My great-grandmother was an
actress too,' I tell them in passing. Vivian looks at me
again, and I feel she does so with new eyes, that all of a
sudden she sees me in a new light. 'Was she?' I nod. 'Yes,
she was.' 'In films or on the stage?' 'Films.' 'Must have

been the silent films then,' Peder says, and laughs again, as someone opens the door suddenly and soundlessly. It's Vivian's father. His hair is completely grey – that's the first thing I notice, that and his slender nose. He looks in at us. Peder gets up at once. I get up too. Vivian remains where she is. Her back is curved like a cat's. Her father nods. He smiles momentarily; his lips tremble.

We went. Vivian stood at the window, raised her hand, and we did likewise. She raised her hand and held it like that until we were out of sight. 'Bloody hell,' Peder said. 'Pretty freezing cold there.' 'And silent.' 'You're not wrong there, damn it. Silent and freezing.' The tram passed us; the faces behind the windows pale, almost yellow, and suddenly I thought that every one of them looked like Vivian. 'What was the name of the woman in the picture?' I asked. 'Lauren Bacall,' Peder said. 'Some people say she looks like Vivian's mother. Or the other way round.' 'And does she?' 'Not any more.' Peder stopped and gripped my arm. 'She sits in her bedroom in the dark with no face.' 'What? She has no face?' 'It was gone after the accident. They tried to stitch it back. Didn't do much good.' Peder let go of my arm and walked on. I ran after him. Another tram went by with the same faces in yellow shadow. 'She hasn't been out since it happened,' Peder said. Now it was my turn to hold him back. 'But how d'you know?' I demanded. 'Vivian told me.' I swallowed. My throat grew suddenly tight, for a terrifying thought had entered my head. I looked away. It was as if the edge of the pavement was a line I was balancing on. 'Are you and Vivian together? I mean are Vivian and you together?' 'Maybe. Maybe not,' he replied. The darkness in my head intensified and I couldn't say any more, because I thought that if he and Vivian were indeed an item then I was surplus to requirement – Barnum the midget was left over yet again and might as well go home and lie down. 'I see,' I breathed. Peder turned and burst out laughing. 'I'm not together with Vivian,' he said. '*We* are together with Vivian, Barnum. Don't you get that?'

Discus and Death

Dad woke us early that Sunday. 'And here you lie snoring while the sun's shining bright!' he exclaimed. I opened my eyes slowly, even though I'd been awake for ages. Dad stood at the door wearing a yellow tracksuit that was just a fraction on the tight side. I could smell coffee. Mum was whistling in the kitchen. Boletta toddled past, hands on her back. The curtains couldn't keep the light out. That was something. Dad breathed heavily and clapped his hands; it sounded strange, amputated applause. And the only other thing I could hear was that great silence which belongs only to Sundays, because the church bells hadn't started yet. 'Well, come on then, boys! I've flipping well hired Bislet till one o'clock!' 'Coming,' Fred said. I felt happy and nervous. He swung his legs down onto the floor and glanced at me. 'Are you just going to lie there?' Dad clapped his hands together once more. 'That's the way, Fred! Get Barnum up and about!' 'Coming,' Fred said, and smiled. 'We're coming.'

We put on shorts and singlets, because it was already warm, and when I joined Fred in the bathroom he didn't even get annoyed with me for coming in while he was there, though he usually did. He slowly pulled the comb back through his hair, but as soon as he'd done that the hair fell back into place. I liked looking at that black fringe which somehow defied him – it wanted to lie flat – and I laughed. Fred turned abruptly and I stopped laughing. But nothing happened. He just glanced at me, he didn't stare (then anything could happen). He just glanced at me. I felt relaxed again, almost happy. Then he opened the cupboard and rummaged through all the containers and perfumes and deodorants that were there, and finally got out the oil, Dad's hair oil. He unscrewed the top, bent over the basin and emptied half the contents over his

head. It rained hair oil. He rubbed it in, put the comb into
the front of his fringe, and swept it back once more. And
it stayed. It stayed like that as if it had been glued onto his
scalp – a wall of hair. Fred looked in the mirror, smiled
and wiped his face. I suddenly felt sick because Dad used
to stink of sweat too when he came home with a surplus
of hair oil running in thick stripes down his cheeks and
flowing over his collar. Fred put the bottle back and
turned to me again. There was something in his eyes –
that darkness that had always been there, or maybe it was
just the fringe that cast a shadow. 'What is it?' I asked
him. Fred didn't move. 'What is it?' I repeated. Fred put
both hands onto my head and rubbed the last of the hair
oil into my curls. 'Are you ready?' he whispered. I didn't
understand. 'Ready? Yes.' 'Good, Barnum.'

We went into the kitchen and made quite an impression on Boletta and Mum – singlets and shorts and hair
full of hair oil. We must have been quite a sight that
Sunday at the end of May, still so early that the world
about us was quite still, still and green through the Virginia creeper growing about the windows like curtains of
sewn leaves. Dad banged down his coffee cup and
laughed so his tracksuit slid up over his stomach to
reveal his belly button; it resembled a crater on a previously unknown planet composed of flesh. Boletta got up,
shut her eyes and clasped her hands together when this
rocking planet came into view. 'We dress up for the banquet, boys!' he exclaimed. 'Not for the competition!'
'Banquet?' I repeated. Dad shook his head for a good
while. 'Has anyone ever heard of a proper athletics event
without a banquet?' He got his belly button back into
place again and looked all round. 'Not me,' he said.
'That's why I've done nothing less than book a table
for five at the Grand this evening. If Boletta isn't off
to the North Pole, that is.' 'They've beer at the Grand
too,' Mum said, and smiled knowingly to us; and that
was good, because when she could laugh at Boletta's
beer then she was in good form – gentle and

generous-hearted, happy even. As if she could relax, rest for a little in the ease of the moment. I could barely remember when I'd last seen her like that; it must have been the last time Peder came to visit. Boletta opened her eyes again but stayed on her feet. 'Not as cold, though,' she quickly established. Dad looked up at her and his expression was kindly and gentle. 'As compensation it's served by highly-educated waiters. Sit down and join us, dear Boletta.' 'Only if you keep your stomach where it should be under that abominable outfit!' 'I give you my word,' Dad laughed. Boletta sat down reluctantly, as far away from Dad as possible, which wasn't all that far considering our kitchen wasn't large and Dad took up most of the room. And he hadn't left anything to chance that day. 'Breakfast is the first part of the throw!' he insisted. He had actually been to Bang the caretaker to ransack him for information because he was a former triple jump champion, and he could reveal that Audun Boysen himself had had two pieces of bread with liver pâté, three carrageen tablets, and a teaspoon of cod-liver oil before important events. It was vital that one supplied the body with precisely the right nutritional elements without rendering oneself bloated. It didn't taste particularly good. It was like eating gym kit. But Fred just swallowed everything that had to do with seaweed without wincing once. And I noticed that Mum was thunderstruck, thunderstruck by Fred's passivity, but this turned into suspicion and a shadow came over her once more. 'Isn't Audun Boysen a runner?' I asked. Dad looked at me. 'But of course. He's one of the best runners in the world, Barnum.' 'But he doesn't throw the discus,' I said. Dad shook his head once more at all this lack of awareness, and pushed the last carrageen tablets in my direction. 'Whether we throw the discus, run, do the triple jump, are clowns in the big top, or acrobats on the trapeze, we get the same strength from the same source, Barnum!' He was quiet and his breath became laboured in his crooked nose. He looked down and his eyes overflowed –

possessed by memories, by the moment, by the magnitude of the occasion. I swallowed the tablets. 'From where?' I whispered. 'From the heart,' Dad replied, his voice as quiet as my own. And he looked at us as he wiped away his tears. 'The elephant's hair,' he breathed. 'The rarest thing of all. And that I found here.' He put his arm round Mum and hugged her close. Fred grew restless. 'Aren't we going soon?' he asked. Dad got up that instant. 'We've already gone! Because now my head's Olympic!' He followed Fred out into the hall. I looked at Mum. 'Aren't you coming with us?' She smiled again, but it was a different smile – nervous and fleeting, like a breeze passing over her face. 'Today the men will be left in peace,' she said, and filled a flask with fruit juice. 'And besides, we have to stay at home and get the banquet ready,' Boletta murmured. 'And that takes time for elderly ladies.'

Fred and Dad were calling. They were shouting to me. 'Hurry up now,' Mum said quietly, so only I could hear. 'Hurry now.' Boletta lit a cigarette. I ran out to join them. Dad pointed at my feet. 'Are you going to throw the discus in slippers, Barnum?' Fred was standing at the door. He was wearing white tennis shoes. They were shining. The laces on each foot were like flowers. Now I noticed that Dad was holding something behind his back which I couldn't see. 'Or would you like to compete in your dancing shoes?' I shook my head. Dad laughed and revealed what he'd been hiding. Another pair of tennis shoes, as new and white as the first. I sat on the floor and put them on, and I still recall the grooved soles, the shining metal rings round the holes for the laces, and the soft rubber at the heels. And when I got up it was like standing on air. Dad put a hand on my shoulder and a hand on Fred's and pulled us close – two half brothers in white shoes. 'I once had a friend,' Dad said. 'This was in the old days. When I was in the circus. We called him Der Rote Teufel. He slipped on the trapeze and died. And why? He'd put on the wrong shoes, boys.' Dad sighed. 'One day you'll

understand what I mean. But not for a long time yet.' Dad
had on his black shoes; black shoes and a yellow tracksuit. 'Come on,' he said. It was me who got to carry the
discus. It was lying in a bag with handles. Fred carried the
rucksack. And armed thus we set off for Bislet, that morning, the last Sunday in May. Mum and Boletta waved from
the window. We waved back, all except for me because I
was carrying the discus. Dad turned and smiled. 'Heavy,
Barnum?' 'No,' I told him. 'Only one and a half kilos.'
Fred laughed quietly at my back. 'Exactly,' Dad said. 'A
junior discus! To be big one has to start small! Come on
now!' It was the green of the trees. It was the light in the
streets. It was the stillness of the city. And all at once the
doves from the roofs took off together, the second before
the church bells began ringing. Dad turned round again.
'Shall we go to church or shall we go to Bislet?' It was
Fred who replied, from just behind me. 'Bislet.' We
laughed, one after the other. We laughed together and
went to Bislet – Dad at the front, Fred at the back and me
in the middle carrying the discus in a bag with handles.
And the dark-clad people we passed on the road were
carrying hymn books and umbrellas, and Dad, with his
tight yellow tracksuit and pale gloves, bowed and greeted
them and let them pass on the steep rise by the toilets.
And then we were there. The noise of the church bells
quietened and died. The birds returned as one to their
roofs. Dad had a key to the gate on the north side. He
unlocked it. He went in. I followed and behind me came
Fred, and I heard the heavy iron gate bang shut. We had
to walk through a corridor. Dad went so slowly. A newspaper lay against the wall. The wind played with its pages.
An ice-cream stick. A beer bottle top. All of a sudden I felt
freezing. It was as if we were going further and further
into a cold darkness. I wanted to turn round. But I kept
going. And when we came out on the far side, the three
of us stopped, all but blinded. The empty stands, the thin
grass and the sky above. We had a whole stadium to ourselves, and it was just as if all the light had collected here,

in one great concrete hollow. Our voices echoed, but no one had said anything yet, not before Dad put his arms round us and I felt a tremor go through Fred; a violent jolt that caused Dad's damaged hand to shudder over my back as he said, 'Paradise!' The word chased away round the outer 400-metre track, and returned the same moment it had been uttered except more slowly now, as if someone was standing behind the stands imitating it: *Paradise! Paradise!* Soon enough stillness fell once more. We followed Dad over the gravel. He stopped at a circle of dry ground. He pointed. 'Here,' he said. 'Here's where it happens.' I gave him the box with the discus. He put it down in the grass beside the circle we were to stand in. Then he brought out a measuring tape from the little rucksack, a silver measuring tape. He was sweating already. He wiped his face with his good hand and smiled. 'D'you see this?' he asked. He let the measuring tape extend to its full length before us. We nodded. 'Can you read the last number for me, Fred?' Fred blinked and bent closer. 'Three metres,' he said. Dad turned the tape round the other way. 'And can you read the last number for me now, Barnum?' I shaded my eyes. 'Two metres.' Dad smiled and slowly wound up the measuring tape again as he looked at us. '*Mundus vult decipi*,' he whispered. 'D'you know what that means, by any chance?' He answered his own question. 'The world will be taken in.' '*Ergo decipatur*,' Fred said. Dad dropped the tape and turned to face him, thunderstruck. 'Did you say something, Fred?' '*Ergo decipatur*,' he repeated. Dad couldn't hide his amazement, his sheer amazement and joy. He had to go nearer Fred to believe his own ears. 'Well done, Fred. *Ergo decipatur*. But today we won't deceive the world, will we?' Now it was Fred's turn to do the smiling. 'No,' he said. Dad's face grew serious once more. 'And don't try to pretend you're worse than Barnum! Is that quite clear?' Fred nodded. 'Wouldn't even occur to me,' he said. Dad hesitated a moment, utterly incredulous, and looked at me instead. 'Because today we're going to achieve the same length,

boys! And may the best man win!' Dad opened the box
and lifted up the discus. He held it out like a crown; he'd
polished it and it was shining. We each got to hold it, the
junior discus: one and a half kilos, first worked in wood
and then finished in a smooth ring of metal with brass
plates set in the sides. Dad pulled off the glove on his
good hand and spread his fingers. 'Unfortunately I'll be
forced to demonstrate the subtleties of the throw with my
left hand, since my right was lost to a German grenade.
But let's do some warming-up first!' Dad found a bar of
chocolate and the flask of coffee in the bag. He sat down
heavily in the grass while Fred and I sauntered over to the
gravel and began warming up. I ran. Fred came right
behind me. But he didn't run. And it occurs to me now
that I never saw Fred run; it was as if it was beneath his
dignity to move in such a manner. Or maybe he considered it too much of an admission to run, because not even
when he was knocked down by the Vika Indians did he
run, even though he had the chance to get away. But it
would have been an admission of fear – to run admitted
your eagerness, your haste, your impatience, your humiliation. Fred once said to me, 'Only slaves run, Barnum.' I
ran. Fred walked. I think he laughed, gave a low chuckle,
as he passed me in the outside lane, in the shadows, with
long and soundless strides. I increased my pace and just
managed to keep up with him, and when we got back we
were told the warm up would continue with a dozen body
rolls, in both directions. We lay on our backs in the grass
and rolled. Dad counted each one and laughed. 'The
clowns had to warm up too!' he called out. 'The clowns
and the animal tamers and the chocolate girls!' Dad fell
silent and broody and lit a cigarette. I lay in the grass
beside Fred and exhaled. 'Remember what I promised
you?' he whispered. 'What?' Fred didn't reply. Finally we
had to wheel our arms twenty-four times. Dad got up and
threw his cigarette behind the winning post. 'Well done,
lads! You're like windmills!' Then we were sufficiently
warm. Dad waved us closer. He held the discus in his left

hand, his good hand. 'Are you paying close attention now?' We nodded. Dad spoke quietly, as if he were sharing a secret with us, and the stands were crammed with people desperate to hear us too. No one else was there. Just Fred, Dad and myself. 'The flat of the discus is laid against the inner part of the hand and against the wrist itself. Thus. Are you watching, Barnum?' 'Yes, Dad.' 'Because the discus is no joke.' Suddenly he pulled the glove from his right hand. The bulging lump of flesh hung from the end of his arm; only the remains of the sewn-together thumb minus its nail gave some suggestion of the digits that once had been there. I couldn't bring myself to look. Dad laid the discus in his mutilated hand and at once dropped it in the grass. Fred picked it up for him. Dad's voice was quieter still. 'I just demonstrated to you, with the help of my bad hand, how important it is to have a proper grip when you're holding the discus. And would you open your eyes, Barnum? So we don't have another accident.' I opened my eyes. Fred was smiling. Dad stood in the centre of the circle. He'd put on his glove and was holding the discus in his left hand again. 'Just imagine I'm a mirror you're practising in front of,' he said. He spun round twice and stopped abruptly. And it amazed me that this fat, ponderous man could be so graceful, almost like a dancer. And I saw that Fred was impressed himself. Dad was bewildered. 'What is it, boys?' We didn't say anything. What could we say – that he resembled a dancer in his yellow tracksuit in the centre of the circle? Yes, maybe we could have told him, but we didn't; we just stood there, silently impressed, and looked at him. Fred's mouth narrowed and the dark in his eyes was back. What had he promised me? All at once Dad grew impatient. He spoke loudly. 'With your hand spread you grip the rim with your fingertips. And use your thumb as a support. Thus. Let your arm hang loose and watch that your hold on the discus is good and secure.' Dad quickly pirouetted round once more, and extended his arm without releasing the discus. 'The most

important thing now is to throw the discus out in the perfect path. The discus should slice through the air and
rotate on its own axis. And don't just chuck it! D'you hear
me? No chucking!' We'd heard. The discus wasn't to be
chucked. Dad lowered his voice again. 'And how do you
achieve this? Well, you flick the discus with a quick
underarm twist to the left and sharply propel it outwards
with the index finger.' He demonstrated what he meant,
but still didn't release the discus. 'The most important
thing continues to be that your hand is steady and that
you have the correct stance,' he breathed. 'If the rhythm
is wrong, it's of no consequence how strong you are. Can
I ask that attention is paid to my feet?' We looked down.
'This ring, boys, this unassuming and undramatic circle
on the ground, is the discus athlete's big top. From here
he hurls out his jubilation to the spectators. Watch carefully now!' He made some quick movements, bent down,
swung round, and the discus disappeared from his hand
and landed some distance out on the track. 'D'you see?
The power of leg, body and arm should combine in one
single twisting movement forward and upward, so you
gain maximum power in your throw! Yes, yes, go and get
the discus, Fred.' And Fred did. Fred obeyed. Fred fetched
the discus and brought it back. 'Are we not going to measure the throws?' I enquired. 'We'll practise first. After
that we can start measuring.' Fred gave the discus to Dad.
Dad handed it on to me. 'What's your throwing arm like
today, Barnum?' 'A bit weak,' I said. Dad felt it and
smiled. 'No excuses now. It's fine. You can begin.'

Clouds piled over Bislet and dropped their long shadows. Soon the sun shone once more. It was warmer than
everywhere else down there on the floor of the stadium;
like a great bath filled to the brim with dry light. The air
was still. The heat hung over the length of the hollow.

I fancied I saw someone over by the changing rooms;
there was a movement in the heat – perhaps just an ice-
cream wrapper or a bird. I took my place in the circle. I
tried to do as Dad had. My feet apart. My throwing arm as

far back as possible. My feet at the edge of the circle. Dad
followed everything like a hawk. Fred moved out of the
way. I spun round and let go of the discus. It was a
pathetic throw. The discus tottered through the air and
landed right in front of Dad. He shook his head. 'Flick,'
he said. 'You forgot the flick, Barnum. That's why the
discus flew like a bird with one wing. Your turn, Fred.'
And Fred took up position in the circle, laid the discus flat
in his right hand, bent down, supple and swift, and before
Dad had properly taken in what he was doing, he slung
out the discus and turned towards him before it had even
landed. 'Follow the throw with your eyes, Fred! You can
tell from the discus what mistakes you've made.' There
was the ghost of a smile on Fred's lips. 'Did I make any
mistakes?' Dad was startled. 'You're not world champion
yet, Fred. I feel that your approach wasn't sufficiently
controlled, for one thing. But otherwise it was fine.'

I ran out and got the discus. Dad went for the measuring tape again and a pad to record the results. 'Now we
can get serious,' he said. 'And for the throw to be counted,
the discus has to fall within the delineated ninety-degree
sector. Have you got that?' I'm not absolutely certain I did
understand, but I nodded anyway. It was so warm. The
sweat was pouring from us. I had to wipe my hands in the
dry grass. Dad breathed heavily through his crooked nose
and looked at Fred again. 'And follow the discus with your
eyes. The throw isn't over until the discus has landed.'
Fred nodded too. Dad showed us a shining kroner piece.
'Heads,' I said. Fred smiled. 'Tails.' Dad flicked it up into
the air, caught it, clasped his fingers and then slowly
opened his hand. 'Barnum begins,' he said. 'And remember that in this sport height has no say whatsoever. Inside
the circle we're all equals.' He looked at me. 'All right,' I
breathed. Dad smiled and patted us on the back, one after
the other. 'Good luck, boys. May the best man win!'

So Dad went out into the throwing sector and took
with him the measuring tape and his pencil and pad. He
stood there waiting. He shaded his eyes. Even where I

was I could hear his nasal breathing; he was a locomotive. Fred stood still behind me. My arm was pale and thin and smooth. I threw. I threw for all I was worth. The discus swerved low over the grass and fell sharply to the ground. Dad ran over to the spot, stuck a marker in the ground and measured the distance from the circle. Slowly he noted the figure in his pad. 'Eleven and a half!' he said. 'A long way to go yet. Your turn, Fred!'

And Fred stands in the circle. Dad goes out onto the grass once more. He positions himself to our left, almost out by the running track. We have it in our backs. 'Are you ready, Barnum?' Fred whispers. I don't know what he means, nor does he wait for a reply. Dad waves. Fred doubles up, supple and swift as before; his arm extends like wire, the flick of finger and discus carries on, twists through the light towards Dad who's standing in the heart of the sunlight in his yellow tracksuit, the measuring tape in his hand. The stillness deepens. Fred follows the discus with his eyes. The throw isn't over yet. The throw has only just begun. The throw has its own momentum now; liberated, torn loose and yet at the same time planned – its path has been written in the air long before, directed by the flick of Fred's finger. Perhaps the throw began with the one who made the discus in the first place, or the one who thought of it, thought of the discus' form and weight to begin with. I follow the discus with my eyes. It's still rising. It reaches its height and rests a moment in the light. Then it falls. It travels so fast. I don't see it before it's happened. Dad has to shade his eyes. Perhaps he thinks in that sudden second that the sun is no longer green but black now. And at that moment the discus hits him. It hits him right in the head, at the crown of his brow, and he loses the tape, sinks into the grass and lies there. The pigeons flap away from the changing rooms. Fred turns. His mouth is trembling. I want to run past him. He holds me back. 'Stay here,' he whispers. I'm standing in the circle now. And Fred goes over to Dad. I see him kneeling beside him and lifting his head. He puts his ear to his mouth. Is he saying anything? Is Dad speaking to Fred? I can't bear it any longer. I break out of the circle. I run over to them. I come to a standstill behind Fred, behind his hunched form. 'What's he saying?' I breathe. Fred lets go of his head. 'Saying?' Fred repeats. 'D'you really think he's saying anything?' He moves to one side and sits there in the grass, his arms round his knees, rocking back and forth, rocking. Maybe he sat just like that when the Old One died too, rocking. I see Dad. His skull is shattered. His forehead has been forced down into his face. He resembles nothing and no one. The human in him is gone. I don't cry. 'What have you done, Fred?' He doesn't reply. I ask him again. 'What have you done, Fred? What have you done?' And Fred looks up at me. It's his eyes I see, and the darkness in them that grows and grows. But that's not what I remember. I remember him suddenly smiling. 'Maybe he's just skin-dead,' he said.

The table at the Grand was unoccupied that evening. There was no banquet. Dad had booked a table by the window so everyone could see us there having our three-course meal as they went past on Karl Johan, with more knives and forks than we could use and a white tablecloth that reached to the floor. And maybe someone we knew would pass by and stop in their tracks, impressed and envious, and we could raise our innumerable glasses standing all round the gilt-edged plates and drink the health of the hungry soul out there, pressing their face in vain against the window. But our table was unoccupied. The banquet was cancelled. Dad had been cancelled. And when we came back from Ullevål Hospital, where Dad lay on a stretcher in the basement, with no need to put a glass of brandy on his chest or stick a hairpin in his heart, the telephone rang. Mum tore the receiver off its cradle as if she believed someone might tell her it had all been a misunderstanding, a terrible dream, a late April Fool. I saw her suddenly going red. 'I'm so sorry,' she murmured. 'Unfortunately we've been prevented from coming.' She listened for a moment and held the receiver with both hands. Boletta, Fred and I stared at her, scarcely daring to breathe. In the end she said, 'Yes, I quite understand. But my husband died today.' And it was only then when she'd spoken the words, said to the headwaiter at the Grand that Dad was dead, that she started crying. She dropped the receiver and we could hear the headwaiter at the Grand down in the restaurant on Karl Johan passing on his condolences, and it was then the doorbell rang too. Boletta put the phone down while the gracious head-waiter continued offering his deepest sympathies. A sudden quiet fell. Mum put her arms round both Fred and me and drew us close. The bell rang again. Boletta went out into the hall. It was Boletta who took charge now. She had kept her calm. Her hands didn't so much as tremble. She opened the door. It was the caretaker, Bang. He leaned forward and bowed. 'Terrible,' he breathed. 'A ter-rible accident. But worst of all for Fred.' Bang slowly turned in our direction. Fred took a step backwards, into Mum's shadow. 'And what do you mean by that?' Boletta enquired. Bang looked down. 'Am I not right in thinking it was Fred's throw?' 'Let me tell you something,' Boletta said loudly. 'It was worst for every one of us! But worst of all for Arnold Nilsen! What is it you want?' Bang bowed his head once more. 'First and foremost I would like to offer my condolences. On behalf of all of us in the build-ing.' Boletta nodded. 'Thank you, that's very kind. But we must have some peace now.' The caretaker kept standing in the doorway. 'A terrible accident,' he said again. 'Yes, we know, Bang. We comfort ourselves with the knowl-edge that he died instantaneously.' Boletta was about to close the door but Bang was too quick for her. He was suddenly in the hall and he was holding our little ruck-sack. 'I thought you'd want to keep these,' he breathed. 'What?' Boletta demanded impatiently. 'His things. They were obviously left behind at Bislet.' And he brought out the measuring tape, the pencil, and the pad on which my pathetic score of eleven and a half metres was recorded.

Now Boletta's patience had run out; she tore the rucksack out of his hands, but it was too weighty and fell on the floor with a hollow thud that reverberated under our feet. The caretaker bent down and lifted the discus. Boletta backed away and wouldn't touch it. Mum moaned and hugged me all the tighter, and I realized that Bang, whom the Old One had called the handyman, had been there all the time, hidden beside the changing rooms. He'd seen everything, but what had he seen? He'd seen nothing but an accident, a dangerous throw; he'd seen a man in a yellow tracksuit standing in the wrong place in the geometry of chance. And Bang hadn't come forward from his secret lair. He'd remained where he was, kept hidden and watched, but now he couldn't wait any longer – the vain voyeur couldn't bear to stand in the shadows. And it terrified me as much as it took me aback that this was the strongest and fiercest and clearest I'd felt hitherto that day – I hated Bang the caretaker. 'Where shall I put it?' he asked. Boletta raised both arms and Bang ducked, as if he thought she was going to strike him. 'Just keep the wretched thing!' she shouted. Bang shook his head. 'I don't throw the discus,' he whispered. 'I'm a triple jumper.' I began to cry. Fred kicked the wall. Boletta shoved Bang against the wall. 'Look at what your good deeds have managed to achieve! Just get out of here!' Then Fred suddenly went over to the caretaker and stopped right in front of him; he shrank even further into his corner. He bowed his head. 'Thanks,' Fred said. 'What?' Bang looked about him in confusion. 'Thanks,' Fred said a second time, and took the discus from him. The caretaker bowed and limped backwards down the steps. The door was slammed behind him. Fred stood there in the entrance with the discus in his hands. Mum let go of me and said something strange. Her face was all swollen beneath her eyes and she pointed at Fred and said, 'Get that bad omen out of this house!' And as soon as she'd spoken the words she realized they carried too much weight; they were thrown forward without any spin, they went straight through the air and hit Fred like an electric shock. I could see the jolt in his neck and a pain I'd never observed before – and that pain spread into a smile. He just looked at her and she hid her face in terror in her hands. Boletta immediately put her arm round him. 'She didn't mean it like that, you know.' And she took the discus from him and went through to the kitchen with it, the rest of us following in her wake. She flung it out of the window, right down into the yard where it landed with a crash in the gravel between Bang's flowerbeds. Then she turned to us. 'Now we've got rid of it at last! That bad omen!' The lights were coming on in flats round about. Faces started appearing. It was night already. Dad was dead. Where were his gloves? And his yellow tracksuit? Mum tried to smile but couldn't manage. She took Fred's hand. Fred was shaking, as if he were suddenly freezing cold or was going to cry. 'I'm sorry,' he whispered. Fred had said he was sorry. Boletta carefully put her arm round him once more. He was made of glass. Fred could go to pieces now. He could fall to the floor and shatter. Mum hesitated for a second. Then she ran her hand through his hair. I'd never seen her do that before. 'My beloved boy. It wasn't your fault.' Boletta was enraged, and Mum hadn't even finished. 'Fault!' she exclaimed. 'This was nobody's fault! If anyone's to be blamed at all then it's God!' 'Be quiet,' Mum murmured. But Boletta spoke more loudly still. 'God would do well to listen to me right now! Because today he ought to be ashamed of himself!' Mum drew in her breath and continued to run her hand through Fred's hair that was still full of oil. 'Dad always got in the way, you know. He couldn't stand still. He was a wheel.' Boletta stamped the floor and agreed. 'Yes, Arnold Nilsen was a wheel.' Fred looked at me and smiled. 'He got in the way,' I whispered. 'He got in Fred's way all the time.' Mum sighed and had to sit at the kitchen table. 'Would you both like to be with me tonight?' she asked. I shook my head and laid my hand on Fred's shoulder. 'I'll look after Fred,' I told her.

Everything I clip out, rub away, forget and leave remains. Fred getting up. The birds in a grey swarm over the changing rooms. Dad lying in the thin Bislet grass. Fred moving slowly towards the doorway, without turning round, and I am left standing alone, for Dad isn't there, Dad is gone. His shattered skull. The discus that still hasn't come to rest. The blood along the metal edge. I scream. No one hears me. Then the sirens, the ambulance, the stretcher. Fred sitting in the stand. A policeman talking to us and writing with a ballpoint pen in a black book, asking us to speak slowly. We tell him that Dad got in the way. Dad got in the way and the discus hit him.

I didn't sleep. I thought about how the following day, when I got to school, everyone would know about the accident. Perhaps it would be in the paper with a picture of Bislet Stadium. Perhaps someone would have got hold of pictures of Dad too, and of Fred and myself; the headline would fill almost the whole of the front page – *The Discus of Death*. And everyone would feel sorry for me; I'd not be asked questions about my homework. No one would tease me – quite the opposite, they'd all be so nice and helpful, and talk quietly when I was in the vicinity because I'd lost my father in a tragic and grisly accident, and had seen him die beside me. 'God in hell,' I suddenly said out loud. I had to. The words came without my being able to stop them; my raging alphabet. 'Discus fanny,' I shouted. 'Cock thrower!' I clenched my teeth. My mouth was bleeding. Fred lay quite still. But he wasn't sleeping. And I could hear Mum and Boletta out there. They'd begun cleaning already. They couldn't sleep either. They were sorting Dad's things – and was it out of love or remorse they went through his clutter, on that same night on which he lay dead in that cold room in the basement of Ullevål Hospital? 'D'you hear that?' Fred whispered. 'Yes, Mum and Boletta are cleaning.' 'No, not that. Listen really hard, Barnum.' I listened all I could, but didn't hear anything else. My mouth was warm and heavy. 'Dad's not breathing,' Fred whispered. 'He's not breathing through his nose any more.' Now I heard it too. Dad's heavy breathing was gone. Fred sat up. Then he crossed over the floor, lay down in my bed and put his arms round me. That's how we lay, not saying a word. Soon enough Mum and Boletta were silent themselves. Maybe I'd slept for a moment. I don't know. Fred was still holding me. 'How d'you think we'll be punished?' he asked. I didn't answer. Fred didn't say any more. I wanted to cry again. My eyes were as warm as my mouth. How would we be punished? After a while I got up. Fred let me go. I went out into the hall. There were Dad's things. The measuring tape was lying on the cabinet beside the oval clock that was empty both of money and of time. I remember Peder once saying, long after his father had died in the garage, in the front seat of the Vauxhall (and Oscar Miil must have spent a long time getting everything ready – his bills were paid, his subscriptions cancelled and his underwear washed), 'I'll never forgive him'. That's what Peder said. Had Arnold Nilsen, the Wheel, been ready? No, how could he have been, because who expects to die on a Sunday morning at Bislet in a bit of friendly competition? No one. His life was still unfinished. I looked into the bedroom. Mum and Boletta were sleeping with their clothes on. They'd barely had the strength to kick off their shoes. Dad's suits were hanging over the chair; a whole pile of suits of every shade – black, grey, blue, even green. And on top lay his white linen suit, on a lacquered hanger from Ferner Jacobsen. Maybe he'd even wanted to wear that particular suit to the banquet at the Grand, even though it would most likely have been too tight for him. Maybe I could wear it to the funeral. I lifted the white and crumpled suit carefully from its hanger. I had to try the jacket, and it was then I found the list, the list of different kinds of laughter, written on a page he'd torn out of a Bible. It was lying in his pocket. I just saw the source of the words first – the Revelation of Saint John. *For I testify unto every man that heareth the words of the prophecy of this book. If any man shall add unto these things,*

God shall add unto him the plagues that are written in this book.
And if any man shall take away from the words of this prophecy,
God shall take away his part out of the book of life, and out of
the holy city, and from the things which are written in this book.
And on the other side Dad had written down this strange
list, where finally there was written in crooked childish
letters – *Is there a compassionate laughter?* And perhaps that
night I could add – Dad's laughter.

Funeral

There weren't many at Dad's funeral. It was a Saturday
and it was raining. We sat in the front pew. Esther from
the kiosk was there. So was the caretaker, Bang, who'd
found an unoccupied seat away over by the pillars,
together with Arnesen and his wife, Mrs Arnesen, the
manic pianist. She was wearing an enormous fur, even
though it was now June. There really weren't any others
there when the bells began to ring, except for a few
ancient ladies we didn't know but who tended to turn up
for funerals to practise before their own turn came. No
one from the far north appeared either. Most of them
were dead too. Dad's coffin was black. I sat between Fred
and Boletta. Mum held Fred's hand. It was raining that
day. I looked down. There were dark pools round my
shoes, my shining dancing shoes. A caterpillar wriggled
along the sole of my right shoe and out across the floor
towards the flowers that were lying there. It made its way
there, over the silk ribbon tied round the stalks of the
flowers, from friends in the building. I couldn't take my
eyes off it, that caterpillar there in the Western Crematorium; and maybe I gave a laugh, because Boletta nudged
me hard in the ribs. The vicar had to shake hands with us.
It was a completely different vicar, who came across as
just as nervous as ourselves. For in his brief will, Dad had
written in tablets of stone that the Majorstuen vicar,
who'd refused to baptize both Fred and myself, should
under no circumstances have anything whatsoever to do
with the Nilsen family, whether it concerned marriage,
communion, baptism, confirmation or burial. Perhaps
Dad had been ready just the same, ready for death,
because he'd written his will, his last wish list, his testi-
mony – the words from the Bible and the laughter. The
vicar dropped my hand and patted my cheek. His fingers

were dry. Then he went up into the pulpit. I couldn't see the caterpillar any more. The vicar spoke about Dad. I looked for the caterpillar. But it was gone. And when I turned round, because perhaps it had crawled down the aisle, I saw Peder and Vivian sitting quietly in the rear pew. Peder raised one hand a fraction and slowly shook his head. Vivian waved too and I think she blushed. I felt so happy. My friends were there. Dad had died and my friends had come to the funeral, and it didn't matter they were late. I wanted to run down to them. Boletta held me back. The vicar said that Dad had been a generous person. He'd brought with him a broader horizon from his islands on the edge of the world in the north. Mum wept. I closed my eyes. Fred leaned towards his knees. Boletta got out a handkerchief. Then the vicar said something strange. He talked about the cormorants, the black birds out there on the coast that shit on the stacks and the buttresses to find their way back – white road signs of shit. I opened my eyes. The vicar smiled, but then remembered himself, and turned instead towards the coffin in which Dad lay. He had stood on the ocean floor. He had been skin-dead. He'd lain under the big top. Now there was no way back. I dreaded singing. The vicar had said his piece. The organist began playing. I looked through the little order of service booklet where Dad's name was inscribed in flowing curves, together with his dates and the hymns we were to sing. 'God is God.' We coughed. We waited. Shoes scraped between pews. The raindrops we'd brought in with us. The umbrellas that slid down beside the pews. The painful sorrow. The thin voices. *God is God though every man*. The vicar tried to rouse our enthusiasm, but his own voice didn't carry very far either – it was as dry and flat as paper. *God is God though every man*. We were a pretty feeble choir. I thought I could hear Peder belting it out, and he was hardly choirboy of the year. I wanted to laugh again. But there was another voice that overpowered our own – a dark and powerful and strange voice which suddenly lifted the whole crematorium, and carried the psalm, loud and proud. *God is God though every man were dead*. I turned round; Mum and Boletta too – even Fred had to look, and the vicar himself stared in silence towards the door. And there, midway between the shadow and the light, the stained glass and the rain, stood an old thin figure, clad in a long black coat. He held a hat in his hands, and his hair was white, as white as the beard that tumbled over his mouth and buried it. So it seemed as if the hymn he sang rose out of his whole self; he lifted it in his hands and sang with his entire frame. *God is God though every land laid waste*. We let him finish it alone to the very last verse; he was a whole male choir in himself. I never heard silence akin to that which fell thereafter. Just the rain on the roof. Just the almost imperceptible rustling of the flowers and the dust falling from the petals. Just the last sighs of the organ pipes. And the next thing I remember, after Dad's coffin had sunk down into the floor forever, was our standing on the steps outside the crematorium, and a little queue of people forming to offer their condolences. That strange and foreign-sounding word which is so good to have when we don't know what to say. *Our condolences* – the words we can mumble, whisper or sob; *our condolences* – like a formula, the polite language of sorrow, when we have no other language to take refuge in other than noise or silence, for constraint is always stronger than sorrow. *Our condolences*, said Arnesen; *our condolences*, the caretaker said once more; *my condolences*, whispered Esther from the kiosk; *our condolences*, said the old ladies we didn't know and who cried more than anyone else. Fred went over to the fence by the railway line and lit a cigarette. It had stopped raining. Fred dropped his match on the ground and didn't take his eyes off us. It was Peder and Vivian's turn in the queue and they shook hands with Mum, awkward as at Svae's classes in their dark and unfamiliar garments, and turned to me instead and took my hand too. 'My condolences,' Peder said. 'Thank you,' I said. 'My condolences,' Vivian said. 'I'm grateful,' I said. But the one we were all waiting for was the tall, thin man with the moustache, the singer, the one nobody recognized. He came forward, gave a deep bow, stood tall and looked straight at Mum. 'No one may cheat death, Mrs Nilsen. Death is the great director.' It was odd, his voice was different now and bore no resemblance to the voice that had sung. This voice was frail, and seemed to break at every second word – it was a voice on crutches. But his gaze was utterly confident when he finally stood tall; his eyes were bolted fast in his drawn face, and his beard hung like a hedge beneath his nose. He gripped Boletta's hand too. 'I have had many names, but Arnold Nilsen knew me best as Mundus.' First of all the old priest had sung that hymn to rouse Dad from the dead, then Dad himself sang it as he rowed over Moskenes, and now Mundus the circus master had sung it at Dad's funeral, once he was dead for real. *God is God*. And just at that moment we heard a violent bang from down in the parking place, and before I had any idea of the cause, Peder had hid his face in his hands and begun groaning like a dog. Of course it was his father. He clambered out of the ramshackle Vauxhall and ran up in our direction, a bouquet under his arm, but slowed his pace by and by, until he came to a standstill in front of Mum and could draw breath. 'My sincere apologies,' he said. 'That ridiculous vehicle packed in at Solli Square and I didn't manage to pick up Peder and Vivian in time.' Peder closed his eyes and gazed heavenwards. Vivian was about to laugh herself silly. Fred came closer. Peder's dad gave his flowers to Mum and suddenly became formal. 'I am Peder Miil's father. Your husband made a strong impression on me.' Mum looked at him in amazement. And she smiled. She smiled to one and all, and it struck me that I had no memory of seeing her thus – *happy* – that's the word I have to use to describe her at that moment, happy on the steps of the Western Crematorium. I had to search her face to be sure I was seeing right, that it wasn't a grimace rather than a smile, a mask. But I hadn't imagined it, this was her genuine expression, and I don't quite know why but I felt ashamed of her. Suddenly Fred went over to Vivian. 'D'you have a light?' he asked. Vivian quickly shook her head and moved away. That was what I should have paid attention to; it was this I should have been watching and been aware of right at that moment; Vivian shaking her head and backing off, and Fred taking another step towards her, a caterpillar held between two fingers, before stopping, going off in the other direction, past the station and over the tramlines. Instead I look at Mum. She was standing between Peder's dad and the man who called himself Mundus. She raised her hand and spoke. 'It would be an honour,' she said in a strong voice, 'if you would join us at the Grand to remember my late husband.'

We took two taxis to Karl Johan, since Peder's dad left the Vauxhall behind, not wanting to risk it breaking down again. And he's probably the only one ever to have been fined and had his car towed away from the Western Crematorium car-park, as if the deceased had driven to their own funeral and left their car there for eternity. And so finally we got to the Grand and were given the largest window table there was; and those who went by outside that afternoon, that first Saturday in June, might have imagined we were celebrating something – a particular anniversary or whatever – as the clouds parted and the sun shone on the dark, wet street. They might have imagined we were having a party at the Grand, and I was aware of such a feeling of loneliness and bewilderment, there where I was sitting between Peder and Vivian. For we don't know any more about one another than that which we can see; we stand with a magnifying glass in the middle of the Milky Way. And what we see isn't real either; we know absolutely nothing, we are divided and alone, we stand outside, we are but impatient onlookers, and we know less still about our own selves. Waiters came thick and fast with cake and coffee and liqueurs, and the gracious headwaiter buzzed about us. Boletta had chilled bottled beer, the caretaker ate with two forks,

Arnesen smoked cigars, Mundus wiped his beard with
the whole of his napkin and poured his liqueur into his
coffee, Peder's dad polished his glasses, Esther had one
more liqueur, and Fred wasn't there. And Mum, she was
in such a bustle, so out of it, on the edge either of a nervous breakdown or the greatest joy – and suddenly I understood and felt a sense of peace, for we weren't totally
lonely after all. This was her one and only chance to hold
a party for Arnold Nilsen, the last party and perhaps the
best – and Mum was at the very heart of it, undisturbed
and unchallenged. The wake had been transformed into a
banquet at that window table in the Grand. Peder leant
towards me. 'What happened to Fred?' His dad told him
to be quiet because the man called Mundus had got to his
feet and was going to say something, make a speech. And
it was as though stillness fell over the whole dining-room
and everyone wanted to listen to the words of this
strange, thin man. This is what he said. 'My thanks for
the kind welcome extended to me here today. I hope that
Arnold Nilsen felt something of the same when he came
to me so many years ago. He came to me like a little
angel.' Mum began crying once more and Mundus laid his
hand gently on her shoulder. 'I bring greetings from all
those in the circus – the world's tallest man, the Chocolate Girl, the seamstresses, the clowns and the musicians –
from one and all I pass on greetings to Arnold Nilsen,
even though the majority died a long while ago and my
circus is dead and nothing more than a dusty memory
blown to the four winds.' Suddenly he chuckled quietly at
his own words. Black – that was how Dad had described
his laughter. I listened. Dad was right, it *was* black – his
laughter shone like black marble. And all at once Mundus
turned to me. 'You're like your father,' he said. I bowed
my head. I didn't want to be like Dad. I didn't want to
resemble anyone, least of all him. 'What's your name?' I
looked up once more. 'Barnum,' I breathed. Mundus
smiled a long while. 'Yes, Barnum. Could indeed your
name have been anything else.' He wiped a tear from both

eyes and when he'd done that he shifted his gaze to Peder. 'And you are Barnum's brother?' Peder all but laughed aloud, and just managed to hold himself in check. 'No, I'm just Peder. Peder Miil. Barnum's friend.' Mundus looked at Mum once more. 'Hadn't Arnold Nilsen two sons?' he asked. There was utter stillness round the table. There wasn't a sound in the whole place. The headwaiter stood frozen to stone in the middle of the floor, a bill in his hand; the waiters had stopped in their tracks with trays and menus. And it seemed as if it was only now that Mum felt Fred's absence; her face fell, in the way that silk and leaves do, and she stared at me. 'Where is Fred?' 'Roaming,' I whispered. Mundus remained standing. Disquiet had come into our midst that couldn't be hidden. He broke the silence that had settled once more. 'Arnold Nilsen used to carry my luggage, my most precious suitcase. I lost sight of him. But I never forgot him.' Mundus bowed and left the table. We first thought he was going to the bathroom, or fetching something from the cloakroom. But immediately afterwards we saw him going past outside on Karl Johan, the man who called himself Mundus. And he didn't turn round; he crossed over the street and disappeared from sight. None of us heard from him again, and later we sometimes thought he was just someone we'd dreamed up who didn't exist at all, that he was somebody we'd just told each other about. 'Blimey,' Peder whispers. And the headwaiter comes to our table with the bill. The magic's gone. It's a wake and not a banquet. We're in the wrong place. There we are on show in our awkward grief. People outside on the pavement look in at us and laugh, point at us and laugh. Mum gets up, pale and dizzy, and we follow her. We leave the table. And in the cloakroom she makes her way up to Peder's dad and asks, 'Did you know my husband?' He clears his throat. 'I met him on just the one occasion. As I said before, he made a strong impression on me.' Mum is startled. 'Where did you meet him?' 'He came to my shop. He wanted to sell an unusual letter from Greenland.' Boletta sighs deeply – it's more a groan than anything else – and has to lean against the counter for support. The cloak-room attendant thinks for a moment she's going to faint and holds her up, but Boletta fights him off with an umbrella. 'Do you by any chance still have this letter?' she asks calmly. Peder's father shakes his head. 'No, it was immediately sold on abroad. A lot of interest in it.' Mum smiles. She tries to smile. 'Well, that was interesting,' she says. 'Thank you. Thank you all.'

We went home. Mum slept for two days. Boletta sat at the North Pole and cooled her wrath in beer. I lay in the bedroom and waited for Fred. And I thought of the amaz-ing chain of events that led to where I was lying now and thinking as I did. First of all I'd begun at dancing classes, had met Peder and Vivian there, and had got thrown out in the first lesson, but didn't dare tell Mum. Then Dad sold the letter with the stamp from Greenland in com-plete secrecy to Peder's dad and died after getting a discus in the head. And the very same day he'd been buried, he'd been found out – it was he who'd pinched the letter, our letter, and sold it. One thing carries the other in its wake and it's impossible to say where the first begins – it's a case of one thing after another – a shadow that spreads, slowly but surely. A pool round my shoes that grows into an ocean in the crematorium; a mirror you can lean over when you're tying your laces to see a caterpillar wriggling away. It was Dad's fault. That was the way my mind was working when Boletta came in. She'd been at the North Pole thinking of us, and our thoughts had been running along the same lines; now she sat down by the bedside. She smelled of beer. 'You two must forgive me,' she whispered. 'For thinking you'd taken the letter.' 'It doesn't matter,' I whispered back. She put her hand on my brow as if she imagined I had a temperature. 'How are you?' she asked all at once. I began laughing. It sounded so funny. Boletta laughed herself. 'My condolences,' I said. Boletta kept on laugh-ing but then suddenly stopped, as if the laughter had been cut off. 'I mean it, Barnum,' she said. 'How are you?' I actually didn't know how I was; I tried all I could to find something genuine inside me. 'I'm angry,' I breathed. 'And I'm just as angry as you are, Barnum.' 'And I'm afraid, Boletta.' 'We're all of us afraid, Barnum.' 'But I'm relieved too,' I said, my voice as quiet as it could be. 'And you're allowed to be relieved,' Boletta said. I was on the verge of crying. I hid my face in the pillow. 'I'm everything at the same time,' I sobbed. Boletta sat down again. 'Then you're lucky, Barnum. To have so many feelings to choose between.' She didn't move and she scratched my back. She knew there was nothing I loved more, even though I'd long since grown too old for it. 'D'you want to be with me tonight?' she asked. 'No, but thank you very much all the same,' I murmured. Boletta stole over to the door. And just as quietly she went out. Later Fred came in. He closed the door soundlessly behind him and lay down fully clothed, saying nothing. It had already begun to grow light. I wondered if I'd been asleep after all and had just dreamed all I'd thought and heard, but someone had at least scratched my back. 'It wasn't you who took the letter,' I whispered. Fred took a deep breath and turned a fraction. 'Thanks for telling me, Barnum. Because for a while there I thought it was me.' He was quiet for a time. His fists were restless. 'Have you become a complete thick-head just because your father died, huh?' 'It was him,' I said. 'It was Dad. Who sold the letter to Peder's father.' Fred smiled. 'Get the Bible,' he said. 'The Bible?' 'Come on, Barnum, you know what I mean.' I got up and went to get the *Medical Dictionary for Norwegian Homes* from our bookcase. It was there between the atlas and *Who, What, Where*. 'Look up under burial,' Fred said. 'Please,' I begged. 'Just do as I say, Barnum.' I did as he said. I sat on the bed and looked up under B. *Burial* came after *Burglary*. I read to myself about *Burglary*, just to let the seconds tick by. Fred raised his hand. 'I'm going to get annoyed soon, Barnum.' I moved my eyes down the page. *Burial*. 'Found it,' I breathed. Fred gave a groan. 'Great. Now read it loudly and clearly. Then we can both go to sleep. Right?' So I read it. '*Burial*.

The lowering of a corpse into a tomb where it decomposes and returns to earth once more. Decomposition takes place through a particular bacterial action in the corpse effected by the surrounding area of earth. If this ground is sandy and porous the corpse will decompose in a few years; if it has a high clay content it may take twenty years or longer. If the ground's bacterial capability in this respect is too efficient the corpse will not decompose whatsoever, but rather be transformed into a fatty mass called corpse wax. I didn't read any further. The next word was *Burlesque.* I lay down once more. Fred kicked off his shoes. It would be getting light soon. 'Who was that girl?' Fred asked suddenly. 'Which girl?' 'Which one? Were there many girls at Arnold Nilsen's funeral, Barnum?' I closed my eyes. 'Vivian,' I whispered.

Two months later a letter arrived for Mum which considerably darkened her state of mind. It was from Coch's Hostel. It was a bill. It was the longest bill we'd ever seen. It was fourteen years long. Mum read it slowly. She drew her finger down the page and her forehead went white. She gave the letter to Boletta. 'Fourteen years!' she exclaimed. 'Has Arnold Nilsen had a room at Coch's Hostel for fourteen years?' 'He kept it after we got married,' Mum whispered, only understanding it all now for the first time. 'Good Lord.' 'He even kept it after he was dead, the rascal!' Boletta said. She got up, enraged, and her voice shrill. 'And we're going there this very minute! Perhaps he's hidden away the money for the letter there!' Boletta dragged Mum up from her chair and the two of them turned abruptly and saw me. I had been standing by the door taking in every word. 'Can I come?' I asked. 'No!' Mum snarled. But Boletta smiled. 'Oh, yes,' she said. 'It won't do you any harm to see what kind of man your father really was.'

And that was perhaps what they imagined, that we'd discover who Arnold Nilsen really was – the man who'd driven up Church Road in a Buick Roadmaster, with his leather gloves and his hair combed like a black lid over his broad head. Is this where we search for one another, in abandoned rooms and unpaid bills? Is this how we shed light on our dark deeds in order to be able to see, perhaps, in the end, a genuine face there?

At any rate, once Boletta had been to the Majorstuen bank to take out the rest of her pension from the Exchange, we went to Coch's Hostel at the bottom of Bogstad Road. When we got there Mum lost her nerve and wanted to go back home to Fred instead. But Boletta had made up her mind. She opened the door right away and shoved Mum inside; we had to go up a steep staircase to a place that passed for the reception. A woman with big eyelids was standing behind the counter. She raised one of them when she saw us. 'What can I help you with?' she asked. Boletta put her hands down on the counter. 'Well, I'll tell you, little lady. We're here to see Arnold Nilsen's room.' 'He's moved,' the woman replied. Boletta smiled. 'Yes, that's one way of putting it. But he didn't take his room with him, did he?' 'He's moved,' the woman repeated. 'He's dead,' Boletta said. Mum leant against the counter too. Her face was trembling. 'Did he stay here often?' she whispered. The woman's mouth grew weary and she just shrugged her shoulders. Mum's voice was quieter still now. 'Did he stay here with anyone else?' Some guests came up the stairs – a couple – neither of them all that sober. Mum covered her eyes with her hand. I heard their laughter disappearing out into the city. 'Can we see the room now?' Boletta demanded. The woman found her voice again. 'And why?' Then Boletta slammed down the fat letter in its envelope onto the counter so the woman jumped. 'This is a demand for payment for 4,982 days. We are a family that happens to like to settle our accounts! Give me the key!' And the woman got down the key for Room 502 from the board and handed it over. We went up three floors. At the bottom of the corridor was Room 502. 'Wait here,' Mum said. She went with Boletta past all the other rooms. But I sneaked after them. I wanted to see and hear every single thing. Boletta gave the key to Mum but she could barely bring herself to hold it and threw it back to Boletta who put it in the keyhole, drew in her breath, turned it, and slowly pushed open the door.

What had she expected to see? An overflowing grave? Arnold Nilsen caught in the act, *post mortem*? The room was tidy and bare. The bed was made. The curtains were drawn. The silent darkness was still. The place smelled of mould and long holidays. Boletta went in first. Mum followed in her wake. I remained where I was, on the threshold of Dad's room. Mum didn't quite know what to do. Boletta did. She pulled out the drawer of the bedside table. The only thing she found there was a worn Bible. She leafed through it as if she thought there might be something hidden behind the covers. 'He even rips pages out of the Bible,' she sighed. Mum looked at me but said nothing. Instead she tore open a cupboard – it was empty, but for a row of hangers that jangled on a metal rail and dust that rose and fell. I stood on the threshold and thought of forests; when we go into forests, I thought, we have to push branches and cobwebs and nettles out of the way so as to be able to see. I closed my eyes. 'D'you see anything?' Boletta asked. I opened my eyes again. Mum shook her head. Boletta lay down on all fours and crawled round on the floor looking. Then she lifted the mattress. She even got out a pair of nail scissors and poked the whole mattress with them, and put her hand inside to feel for something. Mum suddenly started laughing. She laughed loudly and uncontrollably and Boletta whirled round in anger. 'This is no laughing matter!' 'D'you really think Arnold hid money in the mattress?' Mum asked her. 'You can never be too sure of anything,' Boletta replied, the corners of her mouth taut. 'And for heaven's sake stop that awful cackling!' But Mum just went on laughing. I don't know what came over her. She had to sit down on the bed and Boletta managed to free her arm from the mattress; she sat down beside Mum and soon enough they were both laughing. Yes, that's what they did. I couldn't understand it. What sort of laughter was this?

They sat there laughing, quite helpless on that green bed; they had to support each other so as not to collapse with laughter. Perhaps they had no choice but to laugh or they'd have started crying instead. 'Shag mattress,' I said. I bit my tongue hard. It was so long since my mouth had last let slip like that. Mum and Boletta looked at me. But they just laughed. Everything was perhaps in my own head, deep inside me. Maybe I was just talking to myself, saying things that were the opposite to what I should say. 'Shag mattress!' I shouted, and took a heavy step inside and pointed to a small cupboard behind the door. 'You haven't looked there,' I told them. Silence fell; the laughter sank to small smiles, lines of thought in their faces. I pointed again. And in the end it was Mum who got up from the bed, went over to the cupboard behind the door, and opened it. A gust of warm darkness flooded out. There was a suitcase in the cupboard, a black suitcase with thick string round it. It couldn't have been particularly weighty because Mum lifted it like a feather and laid it down on the bed. Immediately the string broke. Boletta fiddled with the knot and it just fell to dust like a dry flower. The suitcase wasn't locked either. Mum pushed the lid open. It was empty. That was it – a ruined Bible, the thick dust and an empty suitcase. 'Well, well,' Boletta said. 'Was there really nothing else?' Mum let the lid drop. 'We'll have to leave it here,' she sighed. Then I took another step closer. 'I'd like to have it!' Mum turned to me and stood like that a long time, her hand on the lid and her fingers full of string and dust. Then she nodded and gave yet another sigh. 'All right. If you absolutely must.'

We went out. I carried the suitcase. Boletta locked the door behind us. 'Now we've shut this door for ever,' she said. And Mum never mentioned Room 502 at Coch's Hostel again. Not even when I asked her a long time later, in another time altogether, what she thought Dad used that room for, just a few blocks away, would she speak of it. She first put her fingers to her own lips and then to mine, and smiled. 'It's forgotten,' she breathed. 'Don't forget that, Barnum.' But I couldn't forget. I'm not one to remove things. I'm rather the one who adds. That's the way I am. I'd stay there one day myself. Many years in the future. I insist on getting Room 502. I lie there, on the point of unconsciousness, in that narrow bed, and try to imagine what Dad dreamed when he lay there staring at that same ceiling in Room 502 of Coch's Hostel. But I have no dreams. I call out for Fred. My only thought is this – here everyone's a liar.

And Esther leans out of her kiosk, greets Mum and Boletta, and looks at the case I'm carrying. 'You haven't thought of leaving us, have you, Barnum?' 'I'm going home,' I reply. And once I was there Fred asked exactly the same question as I shoved the case under the bed. 'You'll certainly have enough room in there,' he said, 'if you lie at an angle'. He started laughing. 'Then I can carry you.' I turned towards him. I said, 'Now Dad's dead.'

Dad had his nickname on his headstone too. Arnold 'the Wheel' Nilsen were the words inscribed on it. I haven't been to see it for a long time, and it's ages since I last went there.

Punishment

Fred got beaten up. He was beaten up so badly we could barely recognize him afterwards. He'd finally been down to Miil's Stamps to ask about the Greenland letter. Peder's dad said later that to begin with Fred wouldn't believe it had been sold on to a foreign customer; and that this individual, a German, had sold it on to another collector, also abroad, whose name Peder's father didn't know. Fred refused to believe that point blank. For long enough he'd been saving up to buy the letter back (I've no idea where he got hold of the money), though I have my suspicions. Now it was too late and he went wild. He shoved Peder's father out of the way, threatened to lock him up in the back premises, and proceeded to pull out every drawer, open each and every cupboard, and leaf through all the files in the entire place. 'I wasn't really frightened,' Peder's dad said. 'I recognized him from the funeral and Peder had told me a fair bit about him. I was more worried he'd damage something. But that wasn't what he was out to do.' Had that been his intention, Peder's father could have closed Miil's Stamps for good and opened a flea market instead. But Fred didn't so much as crease a stamp or crumple an envelope. All he wanted was to find the Greenland letter. He didn't, though. It wasn't there. In the end he realized that. Fred sat down on a chair and hid his face in his hands – embarrassed and angry at one and the same time, I imagine. Peder's dad offered him a free packet of stamps. Fred wasn't interested. He just sat there like that for several minutes. Then all of a sudden he got up. 'How much did you get for it?' he asked. 'I'm afraid I can't tell you,' Peder's dad said. 'Oh, well,' Fred said, and just stared at him. 'But it was less than you usually get for a Swedish shilling stamp, and more than for a Danish first day cover.' Fred kept on staring at Peder's father. 'For a shilling stamp you can maybe get 10,000 kroner. And a Danish first-day cover may be worth 8,000.' Fred was silent for a bit. 'I couldn't give a damn about the money,' he said at last. 'That's good,' Peder's dad told him. 'Money's not everything.' 'I couldn't give a damn about the money,' Fred repeated. 'I'd just like to know how much he screwed us for.' Peder's dad was taken aback. 'D'you want a Coke?' he asked. Fred raised his hand. 'And how much did you make on the letter?' Peder's dad shook his head. 'In all honesty it was not a good deal from my point of view. At the end of the day I made fifty kroner. And sixty had to go for tax. In other words, I lost ten kroner.' 'Why did you buy the letter then?' 'Because I don't give a damn about money.' Fred smiled. Peder's dad opened the door and as Fred was going out he said, 'Can I ask you something?' Fred stopped, having already turned away. 'Why are you so interested in this letter?' Fred shrugged. 'Because I liked it,' he replied. Peder's dad began to warm to Fred. 'Yes, I feel the same way. I'd love not to have to sell a single stamp. But there'd be no business then.' Fred was already out on the pavement. 'Say hi to your mum from me. And Barnum.' 'Doubt it,' Fred said. 'Bye.'

But Fred didn't go up to Solli Square to take the tram there for Majorstuen – that would have been the quickest way home. Instead he went down towards the railway tracks and the bridges. He went inwards. He went through the shadowy part of town whose boundaries are Munkedam Road to the south and Arbien Street to the east. I don't know why he did it. Perhaps he wanted to take a short cut to the harbour. Perhaps he was just confused and didn't know what he was doing. He should never have gone there. Because by the first of the bridges, where the netting over the rusted railways casts shadows like dappled water and a foul stench from the rubbish on the tracks comes up from below, was a gang of four, bored out of their skulls and with nothing more to do than get the last out of a cigarette end, reluctant to go home for a dinner of leftovers and a mouthful of abuse, and with the day too young for anything of importance to be happening. And then something happened after all. They see Fred coming, a thin Fred in his tight trousers, coming towards them like a gift – a stranger, an interloper, sent right into their arms. Fred sees them too; he slows his pace, just a fraction, so they don't notice. But he doesn't turn tail; he could have run away, got the hell out, but he goes on. There's four of them; they're all wearing dark clothes but their faces are pale – one of them, the smallest, has a black eye, a swelling. That's the one standing at the front and smiling. Two others stand slowly combing their hair; Fred sees all of it – the quick glint of metal shining harshly in the sunlight, a keyring perhaps, brass knuckles. A nerve in a neck twitches; there's a jerk at the corner of a mouth – and at the back the oldest of them waits. He seems uninterested, careless, aloof; but when Fred passes them he's the one who stretches out his arm, drops the cigarette end to the ground and says, 'Hell of a lot of rubbish on the road today.' Fred's forced to stop. They stand round him. The smallest blinks his damaged eye and a dark stain runs down his swollen cheek. 'Ow.' The two others laugh. In actual fact they're not threatening. And if anyone had seen them from a window close by, they might have imagined these were just five good friends standing there talking about the summer holidays, girls, jobs up for grabs at Akers Mek, training, games – five guys having a good time in the flickering, yellow afternoon shadows. But Fred knows it isn't like that. He stands between them and feels their quick, warm breath. He knows what they're going to do. He's in the wrong place. He went down the wrong street. It doesn't matter what he does. It doesn't matter what he says. He's on the other side. A train passes by beneath them. The bridge shudders. His shoes itch. Fred's already done his sums. The arithmetic's simple. But working it out doesn't make any difference. The one who spoke is the leader. But the smallest of them, the one with the damaged eye – he's the most dangerous. The two others are just there. They comb their hair. 'Hell of a lot of rubbish,' the smallest echoes; the most dangerous of the lot of them. 'I can see that,' Fred says. They shuffle closer. 'Talking to us?' Fred smiles and slowly turns round and counts. 'One, two, three, four. Four bits of rubbish.' There's quiet. It lasts only a moment. This silence isn't real. Fred feels a stab in the back, but he doesn't turn round. The one who's the leader puts his hand on Fred's shoulder. 'Shall we do some tidying?' he asks. Fred doesn't answer and it isn't a question anyway. And perhaps it's exactly what he wants, for them to take the money he's saved; perhaps he thinks it'll make it easier to bear that he got to Miil's Stamps too late and didn't manage to buy back the letter. But none of them realizes Fred has anything more valuable on him than a comb and a lighter. They take him down to the slope beside the railway line where a tall fence of planks hides them from the blocks of flats closest by, and where the drunks sit with their glinting bottles. They get up and go when they see who's coming. Fred waits. But no one does anything yet. All of them are waiting. Fred stands between them. Someone calls for their kids. A window bangs. Slowly they start to move round him. They're counting too. They're counting the seconds. They're counting and waiting, waiting for the next train. It's on time; a thunder approaching through the tunnel – goods wagons passing. And then the fists come – the youngest first – he hits wildly and without thinking and only gets in a few punches. *Fuck*, he shouts, but no one can hear what he's saying. He jumps instead and smashes his fist right in Fred's face, his mouth – as if he's banging in a nail – and at that moment the last goods wagon passes and the silence comes back in a chill shadow. And Fred stands there, hands against his side, the blood trickling from his lips. Blood and gravel – it feels like that – blood and gravel. His mouth has come loose and in the very heart of this mire he smiles, Fred stands there smiling. The smallest, the wild man among them, wipes his hands in the grass and groans. He's the one who groans. The leader weighs up Fred, for a moment taken aback, more taken aback than enraged – then he smiles too and the sun suddenly blinds them. A train comes from the other side – a locomotive through the heart, a locomotive through the blood that deadens the pain. And it's the two others who punch now; Fred sees the windows like a film rolling, and passengers looking out at them – they think they're dreaming. He hears the train whistle as a thin and shining streak of sound in the air. Fred stands there. Hands by his sides. He can't feel his own face, as if someone's put a mask on him. Soon he won't be able to see. He smiles with his broken mouth. It's that smile which makes the smallest of the gang madder still. He tears a plank from the fence, storms towards Fred, and smashes it against the back of his head. Fred staggers forward but keeps his feet. 'Ow,' he whispers and laughs. There's a wave at the back of his forehead, a black wave pitching within him. There's a nail in the plank – a bent, brown nail. The smallest one wants to hit him again. He can't bear this any longer. But the leader holds him back. They move away. They're the ones who get the hell out. They're the ones who're frightened. They see Fred stagger but keep his feet – they don't understand it, it's all wrong, it's unnatural. He should be on the ground, begging for mercy. And perhaps they'd have picked him up, made sure he was still alive – but Fred's on his feet, he's standing there laughing. The smallest guy sees there's blood on the plank he's holding and chucks it away. He climbs over the fence after the others. Fred slowly raises his hands.

And I can hear Montgomery screaming. And when Montgomery screams he wakes the entire city, whether we're sleeping or not. Montgomery screams like a possessed cockerel, and no longer knows the difference between the sun and the moon. He crawls along the

railway tracks in his long army jacket, weeping and
screaming, the old and broken soldier. He's still at war
because the war is still in him. He left his senses in
Normandy in 1944, and now there's just a front-line
trench in his soul and a bloody beach in his heart as far as
he can see. And every night Montgomery screams to
waken the dead. He lies down beside Fred who's sunk
into the frail brown grass now. And Montgomery carefully lifts his head and pours brandy into his mutilated
mouth. Montgomery cries; he screams and cries and
whispers. 'Don't be frightened, boy. The Allies are
coming soon.'

And I'm dancing with Mum. She's cleared the living
room and we have the floor to ourselves. We dance
together and Boletta's sitting on the divan following
every step. I have my arms round Mum and lead her as
well as I can from corner to corner and diagonally over the
floor and back again. Boletta's most disappointed. 'Did
you learn nothing at all at Svae's?' she asks. Mum laughs
and pushes me against the wall. 'He'll dance better with
Vivian,' she says, and gives me a quick kiss on the cheek.
Boletta comes and takes over. I dance with her. Mum sits
on the divan and lets out her breath. I dance with Boletta.
She leads. She shakes her head. 'Have you forgotten
everything I told you about who should lead?' she asks.
'Yes,' I say and push her away; I'm rough and firm, and
after a moment the ghost of a smile crosses her face. 'That
was better, Barnum! You're allowed to be a bit rough!'
And we dance like that for the rest of the evening. We sit
on the divan and let out our breath one after the other
until Mum and Boletta dance together, and they look like
two old wallflowers, full of mirth, whom no one wants to
dance with. And when there's no music left on the radio
we give up and go to bed.

It's far into the night when Fred comes back, it's almost
morning. The light's frail and shimmers in the room. I've
been sleeping and dreamt something weird. I dreamed I
was lying in the coffin that Fred brought home. And I'm

not alone. Vivian's holding me. It's cramped but that makes no difference. She takes her hand and strokes it down over my stomach. We're not dead yet, by the way. And she takes my hand and takes it where she wants it to go and I rub. Someone knocks on the lid. We pretend we don't hear. I remember wondering just who it could be knocking on the lid – Peder or someone else entirely? It's from this dream I wake suddenly to find Fred there. I see him. He's turned away. My stomach is all wet. He says nothing. I dry myself off on the quilt. 'Where have you been?' I ask. Fred doesn't reply. He's breathing heavily, as if he has a cold – it sounds like whining, the noise of a draught. It makes me think of Dad. I feel afraid. I sit up. There's something on the floor, something dark. There's something dripping from Fred's bed, dripping onto the floor. 'What was it Dad said before he died?' I whisper. 'Shut it,' Fred tells me. But there's something wrong with his voice. He can barely speak; he's like a radio that's not tuned right. There's a grating noise there. I grow still more afraid. I tiptoe over to him. I can't see his face. I light the lamp over his bed. I shut my eyes because what I've seen can't be right. I open them again. It is. Fred turns and stares up at me. He's unrecognizable. His face has been mashed. There's blood everywhere. His hair is full of it; his nose is smeared over his swollen cheeks, and his mouth is just a hole from which more blood trickles now and again. Everything is crooked and shattered in Fred's face. His eyes are barely visible between blue chunks of flesh. I don't know if he can see me. I feel like crying. 'Who's done this?' I breathe. He doesn't answer that either. He just lies there. 'You have to go to the doctor's, Fred.' 'Shut it,' he says again, almost inaudibly – it's more like a groan, and he takes my hand, holds it in a vice-like grip and won't let go. I have to sit down on the bed. I sit there for a good while. I don't quite know who's comforting whom. Finally he lets go of his hold. I get a cloth from the bathroom and wash his face as delicately as I can. 'Dry my eyes,' he whispers. 'What?' I ask him, because his speech is so unclear. 'I can't see, Barnum.' So I wash his eyes. Slowly his face comes to view, just a shattered mess, and he sees me now too, as if doing so for the first time. 'Thank you,' Fred says. 'Thank you.' 'Who did this to you?' I ask him again. 'Shut it,' is the only answer I get. After that he sleeps. At any rate I hear no more from him except his heavy breathing which somehow seems locked in his flattened nose. And I can't help thinking that it reminds me of Dad, and it seems so bizarre that Fred should be lying there making me remember Dad. I wipe the blood from the floor. I sit with Fred for the remainder of the night and once I'm absolutely sure he's asleep Mum and Boletta have already got up and I go out to join them in the kitchen. Boletta waves at me with a teaspoon and laughs craftily. 'I reckon you look tired, Barnum. Did we old ladies exhaust you completely yesterday evening?' I just shake my head and realize I'm not hungry. I've even forgotten what day it is, though most likely it's an ordinary day in the middle of the week, as far from one of the high days on the calendar as it's possible to be. 'Has Fred kept you awake?' Mum asks me out of the blue. I shake my head. And just as suddenly she gets up and makes for our room. 'Don't,' I tell her. She stops and looks at me surprised. 'Don't what, Barnum?' 'Don't go in to Fred,' I whisper. Mum stands still a few seconds, then shrugs her shoulders, annoyed, and quickly opens the door. I look at Boletta. Her brow is furrowed and she leans over the table. 'Has something happened, Barnum?' she asks. And at that moment Mum screams. She screams and immediately afterwards storms out and stares at me wild-eyed. 'What has happened to Fred?' 'He tripped,' I tell her. Boletta's got up too and she goes in to look. She shrieks at the sight of him herself. She's just even quieter when she comes back. 'He's tripped, Barnum?' 'Yes, when he came home during the night. Right on his face.' Mum takes hold of my arm. 'You're not telling lies? This isn't just something you've made up?' 'I swear! I had to dry up the blood too. Just look at the cloth!' Mum goes

back into the room and fetches the blood-soaked rag
which has somehow stiffened; it resembles one of those
marzipan roses you put on expensive cakes, except that
the cloth is a lot larger and not particularly appetizing.
But it does look as if Mum's holding a ruined artificial
rose in her hand and she just shakes her head. 'He won't
say a thing. I think he's been drinking. He stinks of
brandy!'

Boletta called the surgery. I took a taxi to school. That
was the way Mum was, until long after Dad's death – she
got me a taxi to school so I wouldn't get there late. But I
was late anyway. I asked the driver to go round Wester
Gravlund three times, slowly, and I could see that someone had been digging right down in the corner of the
dark-green graveyard. And anyway it didn't matter a jot
that I went into school late, nor was I made to give
answers to my homework, because my father had just
died. Since that day I had been shielded, but not as I'd
dreamt when I thought up accidents and suffering, and
that I aroused everyone's pity so I was crowned the all-
powerful ruler of world compassion. Now I imagined
instead I could see laughter behind each and every face, a
hidden laughter on everyone's lips, because a more hilar-
ious death than Arnold Nilsen's was impossible to imagine – a discus in the head in the middle of Bislet on a
Sunday morning. They laughed behind their faces and
behind my back, and I thought of the list I'd found in
Dad's pocket because this laughter should have been
included. I'd have called it shameful, the shameful laughter, which ought to fall backwards and stick in the throat,
and slowly but surely strangle the person who's dared to
emit it. That was fairly much my thinking as I sat by the
classroom window, shielded into loneliness and aban-
donment like a leper, covered with scabs of mockery and
grief. Right at that moment I wished that Peder and
Vivian were in my class; one thing I could have done
would have been to send a note to them with no more
than the words *the shameful laughter* on it, and right away

they'd have understood what I meant. But Peder went to
another school outside town and had to take the bus
there every morning or else go by car with his Dad if he
managed to get the Vauxhall started. And Vivian had private lessons – that's what she said at least, perhaps it was
her mother who tutored her. So we never did go to the
same school, and perhaps that was for the best, perhaps
that was what rendered us inseparable, the fact that we
longed, yes, longed for each other when we were separated. Perhaps the tyranny of break times would have
caused trouble; perhaps music, woodwork, gym and Norwegian periods would have made us enemies. Instead we
could meet beyond the playground, beyond the timetable,
in our own great free period – under the red tree in the
park, inside the cool cinemas. It was just the three of us –
Peder, Vivian and Barnum – we were outside, no, we were
inside; we had our *own* places, and it was all the others
who were outside. 'Aren't you feeling so good again,
Barnum?' Knuckles is the one asking the question, and
her voice is brittle, her words wrinkled. She's beginning
to grow tired of me and everything that has to do with
me. I turn round slowly and everything is still. But far off
I can hear Montgomery screaming. The war goes on.
Every day is D-Day. Knuckles stands with her hands
folded and behind her the board is completely black.
We're having Religious Education. 'Just a bit leprous,' I
tell her. And I get up and go. Knuckles tries to stop me,
for a moment impatient, indignant. She feels the time for
shielding me should be over soon (widows mourn for just
one year), but I won't let it go, this lonely freedom of
mine, even though I realize it can't last. I leave and don't
turn round. And the others in the class are envious of
broken-hearted Barnum; they'd like to have a dead father
too.

By the time I got home the doctor had been. Mum was
in the living room and I had to go in there. She was sitting there mournfully. Her eyes rolled emptily back and
forth. She even whistled. That was no good sign. She

wanted to talk to me but would say nothing. In the end I
was the one to speak. 'What is it, Mum? Is it something
to do with Fred?' She suddenly smiled and the whistling
stopped. 'Such an amusing doctor we had here,' she said.
'Really?' 'Yes, really. He said that if Fred had fallen and hit
the floor then the floor would have had to hit him at least
twenty times and finally jumped on him from behind.' I
looked down. Mum gave a sigh. 'Why do you lie to me,
Barnum?' 'I don't know,' I murmured. Mum pulled me
towards her. 'Don't you really know why you do?' I shook
my head quickly. 'I don't know what happened.' Mum
gave another deep sigh. 'Someone's attacked Fred, but
he'll say nothing, of course.' She leaned back on the divan
and for a moment looked like Boletta. The sighs came in
quick succession now. 'No, no one tells me anything. The
doctor said we should report the attack to the police, but
what can we report when Fred won't say a word?' Mum
hid her face in her hands. Everything was just too much
for her. And then she said something that always scared
me and which I wished she'd never say. There was something about the words, words she tended to use when she
was in a particular frame of mind, which left me feeling
so helpless. It was something about the way she stressed
the words, the matter-of-factness in the midst of the
horror, which could rob me of sleep for several weeks at a
stretch. It was the ultimate rejection, the final threat. She
said, as she breathed out, 'What am I to do with the two
of you, Barnum?' 'Don't say that,' I breathed. 'Please.'
She took my hand. 'Go in to your brother and see if you
can get him to admit it.' 'Admit it?' 'Well, he was the one
who was attacked.' She let me go and I was already on my
way to the room because I'd rather sit with Fred than
listen to Mum. But suddenly she got up and fanned herself with both hands. It was too much for her again.
Everything was too much for her. 'No!' she exclaimed. 'I
don't want to know! I don't want to know who beat up
my son! I don't want to know anything!' She kept on talking like that, to herself and with herself, that of all the

people in the world she was the one who knew least. She knew nothing; the world treated her like a fool, we were strangers to each other and she barely knew who she was herself except a lonely widow, still too young to go clad in black the rest of her days and already too old to start a new life. 'Poor Fred!' she suddenly cried out. 'Poor Fred!' Quietly I withdrew without her noticing and went in to sit with him. He was lying on his back looking like a mummy. It made me think of a photograph I'd seen in *Who, What, Where* of Lenin. Fred resembled Lenin as he lay there like that; a photographer had actually managed to take a photograph of Lenin's embalmed body in the mausoleum in Red Square. Very carefully I touched the great bandage round Fred's head. 'Now Mum's in a bad way,' I breathed. Beside Lenin was Stalin – he was also in the picture – they were like two old friends. Stalin was wearing his uniform; you can see the polished buttons, and thus they'll lie for eternity. I didn't like the picture but I couldn't take my eyes off it either, because it was as if the photographer had managed to take a picture of death itself – he'd developed death. There's a pale white glow to the faces which is perhaps because their brains have been removed; Soviet doctors drew them out of both Lenin and Stalin, through their noses using a sharp hook – just like the ancient Egyptians when a Pharaoh was to sleep for 3,000 years. I wrote an essay about it. 'Concussion,' Fred says. I bend closer. 'Who? Has Mum got concussion?' Fred sighs. 'No, me. Have you become completely thick again, or what?' 'Does it hurt?' He doesn't say anything for a time. 'Get a mirror, Barnum.' 'Why?' 'Just get one, damn it!' I steal out and get a mirror from the bathroom. Boletta's come home. She's sitting with Mum. That's the way things are. We're sitting with each other, each of us alone. I hurry back into the bedroom. 'Hold the mirror for me,' Fred mumbles. 'Where?' 'Over my face, Barnum. I want to see how I look.' And I hold it low over his face for him, and finally his heavy breaths cloud the mirror. 'You're alive,' I tell him. 'Or d'you want me to stick a hatpin in your heart? Boletta's bound to have one.' He just laughs. 'Put a glass of brandy on me instead,' he whispers. But when I take the mirror away I see that Fred has turned away and is crying.

Next morning there's not a move out of him and the amusing doctor has to return. He isn't amusing any more. He shines a light in Fred's eyes and changes the bandage. Afterwards he speaks to Mum, his voice low, and writes out a prescription. There's a taxi waiting down at the corner; Mum's got a taxi that day too – a taxi and a doctor – and Boletta tells me to hurry. I go down to the taxi while the doctor shines his light once more in Fred's eyes and feels his nose. I tell the driver just to go a couple of times round the graveyard; I'll get there late anyway. I sit inside at break times and can't be bothered changing when we have gym; but now I notice the impatience round me, the irritation. The laughter is starting to become visible; there's mockery in some of the looks. How long can Dad's death last? How long can I remain a fatherless son, in quarantine, so my sorrow doesn't infect the others? It might last perhaps until the summer holidays, and afterwards maybe everything would be changed and different. The school might have burned down; Preben, Hamster and Aslak drowned, and I could have gained the centimetres due me. The sun's so warm against the window I almost sweat. I can't take any more. I get up and go. Knuckles has just written something on the board and she turns round abruptly. I think we're doing geography. She points with the chalk and there's a cloud of white dust which never quite reaches the floor. 'Do you know what this means, Barnum?' I can't understand the symbols she's written; they look like letters that have fallen apart. I shake my head. Knuckles comes closer and hides the chalk. 'This is a language called Urdu, Barnum. And Urdu's a language spoken in a land far away called Pakistan. Remember that for next time. You never know, you may be tested on it.' Knuckles smiles. 'And how is your esteemed state of health?' she asks. 'Getting there,' I murmur. Knuckles claps her hands and stands there in a dry, white cloud. 'That isn't what I meant, Barnum. That's what I've written on the board. In Urdu. How is your esteemed state of health?' I flee before I hear the sound of laughter. But there's a guy I've never seen before standing over by the gates. He's dressed in black and he's slowly combing his hair, as if reflecting himself in the light round about. I go to the other exit instead, thinking I'll perhaps catch a tram. But when I get there he's there as well, and someone else with him. They're as like as peas in a pod and both of them follow me as I make my way towards the church. I begin to speed up. It's no good. I run. They catch me just the same and the first thing I notice is that they have cuts on their knuckles and the same hairstyles. 'Are you Fred's brother?' one of them asks. He resembles the other one so much it might equally well have been the second who spoke. I nod. I try to run again, round the church this time, but they catch hold of me and won't let me go. 'How is he?' 'He's alive,' I tell them. They glance at each other. 'Ask him to meet us in Sten Park tonight,' the first one says. 'Ten o'clock.' They let me go and chase off down the hill. I keep standing there till I can see them no longer. Then the bell rings in the playground. It's a long time until ten o'clock. *How's your health?* I don't want to go home. Montgomery's screaming. I trail the streets. And Peder's already standing waiting beside our tree. I run the last bit of the way, as always, because I'm so glad to see him. 'Guess what!' Peder shouts. 'Me first!' I call back, just as loudly, almost unable to speak. 'I got knocked down!' Peder stops. 'Knocked down? Who by?' We sit in the grass under the red tree and have to wait for the tram to pass before we can hear ourselves talking. 'Don't know,' I told him. 'The same ones who knocked down my brother.' 'They knocked him down?' 'You can say that again! And tonight they want to meet him again.' 'Why?' 'Perhaps they want to apologize,' I tell him. 'Or beat him up again,' Peder suggests. I have to draw breath.

'They were waiting for me outside school,' I tell him. Peder mulls this over. 'But they knocked you down too?' he finally asks. 'Not quite. Almost. They held me. Look!' I show him the arm they grabbed hold of. Peder looks. 'Bloody hell,' he says. I roll down my shirt again. Peder moves closer. 'But why did they knock down your brother?' 'Probably lots who'd like to,' I breathe. 'He looked like raw mince when he came home. Raw mince and gravy.' 'Bloody hell,' Peder says again. 'His nose was smashed.' 'Really?' 'Yeah. And his teeth were stuck in his tongue. I had to get them out.' 'Bad as that,' Peder says, and we're both quiet for a bit. Then I say, 'There's something I don't get.' Peder smiles. 'And what's that then?' 'That they managed to beat Fred up.' We lie there in the grass considering this, that anyone's able to give Fred a hiding in the first place. There had to have been a fair number of them. The grass tickles my neck. The skies flow over and are all but invisible above the spread branches of the beech. 'And you then?' I ask him. Peder sits up. 'You remember the guy Mum was drawing the first time you came to visit?' 'Just,' I tell him. 'The one who was in the living room?' 'Exactly. The guy who was naked in the living room.' 'Isn't your Mum finished drawing him yet?' Peder smiles in that sad way of his, lopsided. 'Mum's never finished,' he says, and lies down again, suddenly quiet, as if he's forgotten what he was going to say. I wait because I don't want to hurry him. 'What about the guy then?' I ask. And Peder rolls round and sits on me. He's pretty heavy. I let him sit like that nonetheless. Now it's his turn to be all but unable to speak. 'He knows someone who runs a film club where they show films that aren't normally shown!' Peder rocks above me. Soon I won't be able to breathe. 'So?' 'He said they can sneak us in tonight!' 'No?' 'Oh, yes!' 'What film is it?' Peder starts hammering on my chest as if I were a drum in a boy band. 'D'you remember the picture of the woman on the wall in Vivian's room?' 'Stop it!' I shout. But he won't stop. He keeps on hammering my chest.

Soon enough I'll be completely black and blue beneath Peder in all his fullness. 'Do you remember her or don't you remember her?' 'I do! But not what she was called!' Peder bends right down and his mouth smells of liquorice; his tongue is completely black. 'Lauren Bacall,' he says, slowly, each letter dragged out. 'Lauren Bacall.' Then we hear laughter behind us. It's Vivian. She's standing there laughing. Peder gets up quickly and pulls me up with him, and I only just manage to keep my balance. We brush the grass off ourselves. I put my hands in my pockets. Peder smacks his lips. Vivian doesn't stop laughing. The two of us go over to her. Peder clears his throat and folds his arms. 'D'you want to go to the cinema?' he asks. 'Film club,' I add quickly. 'Want to join us?'

It's three hours till then and none of us has any wish to go home in between. Instead we go over to the telephone box in Solli Square, scrape together some coins, and Peder calls his father to say he's having dinner with me, and I call Mum and say I'm having dinner with Peder. I can hear that Mum's voice is rather worn. 'Say hello,' she says. And I put the receiver down before she starts asking where I'm calling from and let Vivian have my place, but she can't be bothered phoning anyone. After that we find a table for ourselves at Samson's in Frogner Road, and order some tea and have just enough for one raisin bun between the three of us. The waitress dries her hands on her apron and stares at us long and hard. 'How many buns is that?' 'One,' Peder repeats. The waitress takes out a pad and writes very slowly. 'And that's a bun with raisins?' Peder nods. 'That's right. Raisins with buns are of no interest to us.' The waitress disappears and we have to hold our breath so as not to fall about laughing. 'What film are we going to see?' Vivian asks. Peder leans over the table once he's got himself together. 'I don't remember the exact title. But Lauren Bacall's in it.' 'The one you've got a picture of on your wall,' I quickly add. Vivian looks at me mildly. 'Don't you think I know what pictures I have on the wall?' 'Yes, of course,' I say. Peder calls the waitress. Perhaps she's gone home. There are no other customers there. Perhaps we've been locked into Samson's and will have to spend the night amid the clammy atmosphere of the pastries and melting glazes under the glass counter. 'Barnum was almost knocked down today,' Peder says. Vivian smiles for one reason or another. 'Were you?' 'They just cuffed me here and there,' I murmur. Peder leans over the table. 'But Barnum's brother was almost kicked to pieces.' Vivian looks at me even more intently, and I realize at that moment I suddenly don't want to talk about it, that I don't want to talk about Fred. 'Just got a smack on the face,' I mumble. And finally the waitress comes over. She's put the bun in the middle of an enormous plate and sets it down with great ceremony on the table. 'There we are,' she says. 'Here's your bun.' She probably had a sense of humour in a previous life. 'How many raisins are there in it?' Peder asks. 'How many?' 'Yes, how many raisins are there in the bun? I can't pay for it until I know how many raisins there are.' I'm the one who begins picking the raisins out and I get to seven before we're thrown out – probably the only ones to have been ejected from Samson's in Frogner Road. We rock along the tramlines, rock with laughter, and I suddenly think to myself – *where does this laughter belong on Dad's list? Is this the public's malicious laughter? Are we mocking the waitress? No, we're laughing at ourselves, because this is a liberating laughter, let loose and sovereign.* We laugh at all that will happen to us, at all that's ahead; we sit on a bench behind our tree and share out the raisins. That's two each and the last can go to Montgomery who walks past with a bottle like a red flower in his hand. 'You don't look much like him,' Vivian says all of a sudden. She's sitting between us, between Peder and me. I don't get what she means. 'Who? Montgomery?' Peder shrieks and Vivian laughs. 'Your brother, of course.' My mind goes blank. 'How d'you know that?' I whisper. She sticks a raisin in her mouth. 'Because I saw Fred at your father's funeral, you slowcoach.' And all I can think of is that she

remembers that while I don't. Peder gets up abruptly.
'And you can be bloody happy about that,' he says. I look
at him. 'Glad about what?' Peder pulls Vivian up from the
grass. 'Is Barnum a bit thicker than usual today, or is it
that we're just too smart?' 'It's Barnum who's thick,'
Vivian says. She takes my hands and holds me close and
Peder puts his paw on my shoulder and speaks quietly.
'You can be bloody glad you don't look like your brother.'

The title of the film is *The Big Sleep*. It's an over-18 and
we're allowed in. It hasn't begun yet. We sit in row 14 of
Rosenborg Cinema – seats 18, 19 and 20. As I carefully
put my arm around her, as the light starts to dim, I meet
Peder's hand, because he's done exactly the same thing –
put his arm around Vivian. She leans back in our arms
and that's how we sit. My polo neck is making my neck
itch, but I don't dare scratch myself now. The cinema's
only half-full and everyone's older than we are. A man in
a black jacket and wearing dark glasses stands in front of
the screen and says something to the effect that this isn't
just a classic film it's bloody well meatier than Ibsen's collected works, and that those who don't get who the mur-
derer is will have to pay double the membership fee the
coming autumn. Welcome to outer darkness. Low laughter in the cinema. We laugh low too because now is the
moment for low laughter. We laugh lowest of the lot.
'Cool,' Peder whispers. 'Cool,' I whisper. Someone turns
round and tells us to be quiet. We sink into our seats and
don't say another word for the next 110 minutes.

And how often have I seen *The Big Sleep* since? I've lost
count, but that was the first time and what can compare to
the first time? Nothing. Everything else is a repeat, a copy
– plagiarism. Afterwards it's just a continuation. Next
time it's just a shadow. But the first time is real. You are
present, you are suddenly there in your own life; you can
put your finger on the moment and feel the pulse of time.
And at the same time you know too that the moment has
passed, slipped away in the pulse's muddied wake. But not
yet, not yet, because this is the first that we see – the cig-

arettes in the ashtray, two cigarette ends left lying there, and the white letters against the all but grey screen: Humphrey Bogart and Lauren Bacall. Then we see a nameplate on a door – Sternwood – and a rather stubby finger, Bogart's wrinkled finger, ringing the bell. The door is opened by a formal servant and Bogart is admitted; when the servant is going to announce to the General that Marlowe has arrived, a lady in a short white skirt appears, who looks as if she could pick up a tennis-racket at any moment. At first I assume that this is Lauren Bacall, but it isn't – it's her little sister, Carmen Sternwood, played by Martha Vickers. And it's she who gives the line I can never forget; Martha Vickers looks at Bogart, who isn't exactly feeling at home there, in the cold atmosphere of a rich man's world. She weighs up this strange fellow and says, *You're not very tall, are you*? Bogart curls his lips like thin paper over his teeth and answers *I try to be*. This film is an over-18. I can hear the audience laugh – no, chuckle. No one laughs here, they chuckle; all the shoulders bob up and down. That's how one laughs at a black-and-white over-18 film. And the lady in the short skirt suddenly folds herself into Bogart's arms, and I think to myself in a flash (for my thoughts are flying in all directions now), that this is what the Chocolate Girl must have looked like, the Chocolate Girl at Circus Mundus that Dad told us about. Then the servant's standing there once more and Bogart has to push her gently away, and in the next scene he's in a greenhouse and the General's sitting in a wheelchair. *How do you like your brandy, sir*? he asks. *In a glass*, Bogart replies. There's another ripple of chuckling and more bobbing of shoulders, and it's now he's given his commission. My shirt's sticking to my skin; I drift away and stop following, but it doesn't matter – I feel instead the cold in the heat of the greenhouse. Bogart is sweating liquid ice – he could mix his drinks with it – and I try to work out how tall he is. He doesn't seem particularly tall – Martha Vickers was right – but perhaps he appears even smaller because he's hoisted up his trousers so much, almost to his chest. I don't have time to think about anything else, because on the way out Bogart's shown into another room by the servant. It must be a bedroom because there's a bed there, a four-poster, and over by the window there's a table covered with bottles. By that table a woman is standing pouring a glass to the brim, and when she's done she turns in Bogart's direction. It's Lauren Bacall. We see Lauren Bacall for the first time. Peder's fingers run over my hand. I turn to look at Vivian. She doesn't move. It's as if she's slowly breathing in, inhaling all the air there is. And Lauren Bacall looks at Bogart – she glows, glows in black and white, and her nostrils flare like an animal's, the nostrils of a lioness. And she laughs – Bacall's laughter – she mocks him, *You're a mess, aren't you?* And Bogart just answers, *I'm not very tall either. Next time I'll come on stilts.* And maybe it's impossible to describe that first time, which one always does afterwards, in another light, in another time. Perhaps the moment is just like a stamp which loses its jagged edges and which slowly but surely rises in value in your private collection, the collection you've insured for more than your children. You can't collect everything, the whole world; you have to choose – some things you reject or exchange. Perhaps this time in Rosenborg cinema – in row 14, seats 18, 19 and 20 – with the restless grey light over our faces, there where we're sitting none the wiser (both on the outside and the inside at one and the same time), perhaps it's just a scene onto which I put new subtitles. Or for which I make another voice-over – with *my* voice, the one that speaks to me throughout my life, my days, my years – so that the scene fits in with the rest of my story? But this I know is true – I saw it. I heard it. And I can't forget it. When I next look at Vivian I see she's crying.

Afterwards we walk though the warm streets, where fathers are washing their cars and mothers are standing in windows, leant against the sills, laughing at something. Perhaps they laugh at the dedication and vanity of their men who see their own reflections in shining bonnets and gleaming hubcaps. It's like a sort of interval and everything's in colour again. Kiddies with plasters on their knees and far too big handlebars turn and pedal back on their bikes when their mothers whistle to them. We are somewhere else. We go *alongside* everything. 'Not much of a film,' Peder says. 'No, not much at all,' I agree. 'Bloody hell.' 'Yes, bloody hell,' Peder says. 'Not at all.' Vivian says nothing; she's silent, soundless, moves quietly along. Peder and I walk her home. She says nothing there either, just disappears up the steps adjacent to the church, and I fancy there's a fluttering in the curtains on the second floor, a shadow that closes them the tighter. The lights go out. Nothing else happens. Then we go over Gimle Road and a woman laughs loudly in the restaurant at the Norum Hotel, and from a room we hear strange music disappearing behind us in the softly falling darkness. 'Vivian was crying,' I say, my voice low. Peder nods. 'I heard her. She was crying.' We go on a bit without saying any more. I feel troubled inside. 'Why was it she was crying?' I ask. Peder shrugs his shoulders. 'Maybe she thought the film was sad.' 'Maybe. Did you think it was?' 'I didn't understand a bloody thing,' Peder answers. 'Did you?' We stop outside his house. I shrug my shoulders. 'Lauren Bacall was pretty beautiful,' I breathe. Peder smiles. 'Lauren Bacall is pretty beautiful.' 'Yeah, bloody hell,' I say. 'Did you see those nostrils, huh?' Peder looks at me and starts to laugh. 'You didn't understand a bloody thing either. You didn't even get the title of the film.' We laugh a bit more. Then we stop. 'All right, what was she called?' I ask. 'She was called Vivian,' Peder says.

That's how I run home that bizarre night, with all those names on my lips. And as I run (because perhaps someone's behind me, coming to beat me up), I think about what Dad used to say, that *it's not what you see that counts but rather what you think you see*. And what did Dad think he was seeing when the discus came whistling right at him and Fred stood in the circle, rooted to the spot, following the same discus with his eyes? What was of

greatest importance then, what he saw or what he
thought he saw? Mum's already asleep. There's no sign of
Boletta. Fred's lying in bed. He hasn't moved. I sit down
beside him. 'There's people who want to talk to you,' I
tell him. Fred tilts his swollen, blue face on the pillow.
'Who?' he whispers. 'Two guys. They waited for me outside school.' Fred's quiet for a bit. 'What did they look
like?' he asks me slowly. 'They were identical,' I tell him.
Fred laughs and has to hold his hand over his mouth.
There's blood between his fingers. Then suddenly he puts
his hand on my shoulder instead. 'They didn't do anything to you, did they, Barnum?' And I'm so moved by
this depth of care for me when he's lying there beaten to
a pulp that I can barely utter a word. I just shake my head.
Fred takes his hand from my shoulder. 'What did they say,
Barnum?' 'They asked if you were alive,' I reply. Fred has
to hide his mouth again while he laughs, and he has tears
in his eyes. 'They asked that?' he breathes. 'Yes.' 'And
what did you say?' 'That you were alive, Fred. And then
they asked that you meet them in Sten Park. At ten.' Fred
doesn't move for a time. I wished he'd been asleep.
'What's the time now?' he asks me. 'Half past nine.
You're not going, are you?' 'Out of the way, Barnum.'

Fred gets up out of bed. I have to support him. He can
barely stand up. I have to dress him. He's blue and
swollen over his whole body. Fred laughs. I dress him. It's
my fault. I shouldn't have said they'd asked about him.
'Don't do it,' I whisper. 'The white shirt, Barnum.'
'Please, Fred.' 'I want the white shirt, Barnum.' I find his
white shirt in the cupboard, put it on him and button it
up, apart from the three top ones. 'I'll come with you,
Fred.' 'Fine.' He says no more than that. That's fine. But
neither of us is fine. We slip out. Mum's asleep. Boletta
hasn't come home. We go over to Sten Park. The city's
still. The darkness is soft. The lilac bushes are glowing.
We go up onto Blåsen. I have to push him the last part of
the way. We sit down on a bench there. Here we can see
just about everything, but few can see us. There's no one

to see. 'Have you heard about the Night Man?' I ask him. Fred doesn't reply. He's scouting. 'The Night Man buried horses here, Fred. Dead horses. But by day nobody could see him.' 'Shut it,' he whispers. 'It's true,' I tell him. 'You believe in crap like that?' And then they come. There are four of them; slowly they come up behind the church. They look about them, quickly, restlessly, urgently. They walk close together, in a huddle, almost indistinguishable from each other – except that I recognize two of them, the twins. I point. Fred shoves my arm away. He remains where he is. I have the urge to run. 'Wait,' he breathes. He smiles. 'Now we're the night men, Barnum.' Fred wipes away the smile and gets up, like a cripple. We go down the steps, to the fountain in the corner. We can see them. They can't see us. They stand over by the merry-go-round. 'What time's it?' he whispers. I show him. It's ten. Fred nods. He begins walking. But the gang up there have spotted him. One of them shouts his name. Fred stops. I stand right behind him. His white shirt is shining. I think I know why he wanted to wear that particular shirt. He stands utterly still. They weigh each other up, Fred and the gang by the merry-go-round. There are four of them. Fred and I make two. Well, one and a half. No one moves. We're statues in Sten Park. Who'll hold out longest? Who can bite this night into themselves? Who has the greatest stamina when it comes to waiting? It's Fred. The others start walking slowly down towards us. Fred has his hands on his back. His white shirt's shining. He doesn't move. They don't stop until they're a couple of metres away. They stare at him. I can believe Fred's smiling, smiling with his shattered mouth, but I can't see because I'm standing behind him. 'Oh, for fuck's sake,' one of them says; he has a black eye, perhaps given to him by Fred, and for a moment I imagine he's going to fly at him, but instead he steps backwards to stand between the twins. And the fourth one comes closer still. He puts his hand in his pocket. A tremor passes through Fred, from elbow to shoulders – an electric shock. Then the calm returns. The

other guy gets out a packet of Teddy, takes out two and
gives one to Fred. 'The name's Erling,' he says. 'But most
folk call me Tenner.' Fred gives an almost imperceptible
nod and takes the cigarette. Erling, who most people
know as Tenner, sees me in the shadows behind Fred.
'D'you want one too?' he asks. 'He doesn't smoke,' Fred
tells him. I say it to myself, *How do you like your brandy, sir?
In a glass*. Erling lights the cigarettes with a shining
lighter. They stand for a bit like this, smoking silently –
never before has it taken such a time to finish a cigarette.
The moon disappears and finally they drop their cigarette
ends down on the banking, use their shoes to put them
out so the sparks fly in all directions – it looks as if their
feet will catch fire. Then Fred puts his hands behind his
back again. Erling looks at him. 'Can you punch as well?'
he asks. He asks if Fred can punch. I see him unfolding
his hands behind his back. 'Maybe.' The guy looks at Fred
for a bit. Then he turns in the direction of the others.
'Come here, Tommy.' And the one with the blue eyes goes
over to Fred and stands right in front of him. Fred hesitates. Then he punches. But the one called Tommy makes
a quick feint with his upper body, like a swimming stroke,
and the punch just grazes his temple. 'Ow,' Tommy says,
and goes back to join the twins. Erling stares at Fred long
and hard, and takes out his cigarettes again. I haven't the
slightest idea what will happen next. Fred's thrown a
punch but missed. He turns to face me and I can see the
sudden bewilderment in his crooked face, because he
doesn't know what's going to happen now himself, what
the next move will be – and his bewilderment makes me
doubly afraid. Erling, Tenner, shakes out two more cigarettes. 'You're better at getting hit than hitting,' he says.
Then Fred punches again. It's just as if I feel the blow, feel
it hitting home; I tremble, am shaken by happiness and
fear. Erling folds up and lies on the ground as his cigarettes roll down the slope. And all at once I think to
myself – *Now we'll bury the dead horses*. Fred keeps standing, his hand bleeding. Tommy and the twins come a step

closer and Fred raises both hands; it's hard, for him to get them up. But they're not about to attack him. Instead they start counting. Slowly they count to nine and before they reach ten Erling gets up again, smiling. 'Not bad,' he says. 'But you've a lot to learn. Shall we take a pew?' Erling and Fred go over to the bench by the kindergarten and sit down there. The two of them talk together. I can't hear what they're saying. Tommy picks up the cigarettes. The twins comb their hair. I don't move. I've no idea what length of time this'll take. Fred and Erling haven't finished. It's mostly Erling who's doing the talking. Then they sit there silent for a moment and when they get up they shake hands, as if they've agreed on something. Erling, Tommy and the twins walk down past the toilets. Fred goes on round Blåsen. I run after him. 'Did you become friends?' I ask. Fred doesn't reply. 'But how did they know who I was?' Fred stops and looks at me. One of the wounds in his face has broken open. 'Huh?' 'How did they know I was your brother, Fred?' 'Everyone knows who you are, Barnum,' he says softly. 'How? How does everyone know who I am?' Fred wipes away the blood and thinks. 'Just forget it,' he whispers and walks on. But I can't forget it. Does everyone really know who I am – not just at school but across town, on the other side of the river, in the last dark alleyways of Vika and all the way down to the harbour? But Fred can't be bothered talking any more. And when we get home Mum's standing enraged in the hall, utterly distraught. 'Where have you been?' she shrieks. Fred goes straight past her and it's me she pins to the wall. 'We just went for a walk,' I tell her. Mum looms over me. 'A walk? In the middle of the night?' 'Fred had to get some air, Mum. He could barely breathe. Because of his nose.' Mum lets go of me and hugs her nightie round her instead. 'You're going to be the death of me,' she breathes. I try to put my arm round her. 'No, Mum,' I tell her. She stamps the floor. 'Yes, you are. Just keep going. Killing me. Disappearing in the middle of the night in a white shirt and with concussion!' She looks at me sharply. 'This has nothing to do with him being knocked down? Has it?' I shake my head and meet her gaze. 'Do you miss Dad?' I ask her. And I see how her face begins to crack that very moment, and the thought comes to me, before she leans against my shoulder, that we have so many different faces. We change them all the time; we carry them with us, as many faces as we can carry – faces and names. And she smiles and her breath is wet. 'Yes, I do indeed, my love. I miss your Dad.'

Three days later mail arrives for me. It was the first time I'd got a letter. My name was on the envelope, my name and address. It was like being discovered, coming into existence. Someone had found me. This letter had been carried through the city and put in the right mail box. I thought to myself, before wondering who it was from – *will the stamp be valuable one day*? We were sitting in the kitchen having dinner. It was at least thirty degrees. Just lifting the fork made you sweat. Fred was there too. He drank water and ate potatoes. His face had sort of begun to join up again in the wrong order. I had to look at him twice to make sure it was him. 'What are you gawping at?' he demanded. 'Nothing,' I said quickly. Fred put his finger on his nose and pushed it back and forth. It creaked. Boletta held her ears. And then Mum took out the envelope and passed it over the table. She was so happy for me; I'd got a letter in Oslo and maybe she'd read it already. 'There's a letter for you,' she said. I became very slow and silent. There it was written – Barnum Nilsen – in tall, narrow letters. Barnum Nilsen, my name, with the address underneath. Yes, I'd been dis-covered, found, I was a person, there was no doubt about it – I was accounted for. Then I ripped open the envelope with my knife and read the letter. It was from Peder's dad. My eyes grew heavy. Mum smiled. 'Read it to us then, Barnum!' And I read it to them as quietly as I could; the words that Oscar Miil, that cheerful and careful man had written. *Dear Barnum. Now that Peder and you have become such good friends, something we're delighted about, we'd like to invite you to our place on Ildjernet this summer, if this is all right with your mother.* I looked at Mum. 'Is it all right?' I asked her. She nodded many times. 'Of course! But aren't you going to read all of it?' 'I have,' I breathed. 'No, you haven't, Barnum.' 'Yes, I have,' I told her. But Mum took the letter from me and continued reading. *Your brother's most welcome too! Best wishes from Oscar Miil.* I looked down. Fred breathed quickly through his crooked nose and the sound was reminiscent of the noise Dad used to make when he was sleeping. I shuddered. 'Wouldn't that be nice, Fred?' Mum asked him. I could hear Fred smiling. 'Can't,' was all he said. 'You can't? And what are you so busy with this summer?' 'Training.' Mum slowly folded up the letter from Oscar Miil and even Boletta put down her knife and fork. 'Training? Training for what, may I ask?' 'I've joined the Central Boxing Club, if you really must know.' Fred helped himself to more potatoes and mashed them on his plate. There was quiet round the table. And I felt so relieved. Fred was going to train instead. First they'd knocked him down. Then they'd got him to join the Central Boxing Club, and now he couldn't come on holiday with Peder's family. That was the way of it. One thing always leads to another. I felt both happy and ashamed. 'You're not boxing in some boxing club,' Mum said, her face angry. Fred couldn't be bothered answering her. He ate his potatoes. 'Haven't you had enough of a beating? Look at yourself, Fred!' Fred just shrugged his shoulders. 'Boxing isn't the same as a beating,' he said. Mum leaned over the table. 'And was it the Central Boxing Club that beat you up, huh?' Fred laughed quietly. 'I wouldn't bother your head about that.' Mum was fizzing. Boletta put her hand on her shoulder. 'Where is Ildjernet, out of interest?' she inquired. Mum gave a deep sigh and unfolded the letter once more. That was the way things were. Good news never came on its own. And bad news could be good for others. Fred was going to box and I was going on holiday with my best friend and could avoid having Fred there too. And Peder's dad had drawn a map on the back of the sheet of paper. Ildjernet was an island in the Oslo fiord and to get there I'd have to take the Nesodden ferry along the whole length of that bit of land. Immediately I went into my room to pack. Fred came in soon afterwards. He lay down on his bed. I didn't dare look at him. I packed. 'Don't eat too much mackerel,' he said in the end. 'Why not?' I asked him. 'Don't you know why?' 'No.' 'Mackerel eat German corpses. Lying on the bottom of the Oslo fiord.' 'You're kidding?' 'So when you eat mackerel you're actually eating a German corpse.' I turned to look at him. 'You can come too,' I whispered. He just shut his eyes. It was as though a stranger had visited his face and wouldn't leave again. 'Be quiet,' he said. 'Don't lie.'

And the following Saturday, Midsummer Eve, I stood on the deck of the *Prince* and waved goodbye to Mum and Boletta, even though I'd told them they shouldn't come. Fortunately, before long I couldn't see them any more and the clock on the City Chambers grew small as a wristwatch and the town sank in the blue wind. I saw everything I was to leave disappear from sight. I wasn't seasick. I felt strong. I had only travelled alone once before, when Mum, Boletta and the school doctor discovered that I was too thin and sent me to a farm in the country to be fattened up. But I'd rather not talk about that – no, I'd prefer not to talk about it at all, it's forgotten for good. And this was something else. I was going to my friend's. After Flaskebekk the boat began to roll. I carried Dad's suitcase into the saloon and bought a small Coke from the kiosk. The passengers smiled at me. We were going on our summer holidays. I smiled at them. An old lady with fine hair and a wrinkled mouth leaned over a basket with a growling puppy. 'Are you going far?' she asked, and ran a dry hand though my curls. I decided to be polite. 'As far as the boat goes,' I replied. And on Ildjernet, the last quay before the fiord bends and widens out towards the open sea – where the Old One and Boletta and King Haakon came sailing in and saw Oslo for the first time – Peder and his father stood waiting. I carried my suitcase down the gangway. Peder came running towards me. He was quite brown already, and thinner. I almost didn't recognize him and nearly felt envious, but of what I didn't quite know. He stopped in front of me and stretched out his hand. 'You're a mess,' he said. 'Next time I'll come on stilts,' I said. Peder gave a sigh. 'Wrong, Bogart. You first say, I'm not very tall either.' 'I'm not very tall either,' I said. 'We'll take it from the start,' Peder said, and breathed in. 'Ready?' 'Ready as I'll ever be.' 'You're a mess, Mr Barnum Nilsen.' 'And you've got bloody brown,' I reply. Peder groaned and almost pushed me into the water. Then his dad came over to us; he had a pipe clamped between his jaws and sunglasses over his spectacles. He took my case. 'Why don't we get over there before the holiday's over, boys?' We followed him until he stopped by a small rope bridge connecting the mainland with the island where their summer house was. Peder's dad looked at me. 'Afraid of heights, Barnum?' 'Not yet,' I whispered. Peder laughed. 'Barnum's so small he doesn't know what it means to have a fear of heights,' he said. His dad had to take off both pairs of glasses for a moment. 'What was that you said, Peder?' 'Nothing,' Peder replied, and ran out onto the bridge; I followed and his dad came behind us. 'Don't look down!' he shouted. I looked down. The whole bridge swayed and the waves grew stronger still – the wind in my head, the waves in my mouth. I tried to cling tightly to the side, but it was just a rope looping away through my hands. I heard Peder who was still laughing, and suddenly I thought of Der Rote Teufel. I hung there between the mainland and Ildjernet and couldn't stop thinking of The Red Devil who died of laughter. 'Don't look down!' Peder's dad shouts again. Peder himself just keeps on laughing; he was probably born on the bridge. He turns and stretches out his arms as if to hug me. 'It's not dangerous,' he says. And it was a strange week, a strange week in my finest summer ever –

that first summer with Peder on Ildjernet. Because I can't
remember the order of all the things that happened; it's
like a film whose scenes have been put together ran-
domly, and maybe the last bit has ended up somewhere in
the middle of the action, like a riddle you only get the
hang of later or maybe never at all. When I came back,
brown from head to toe, and Fred stood at the quayside
waiting, and the City Chambers' clock became visible
once more with its mighty hands and golden figures – it
was just as if the Ildjernet days opened up into a bouquet
bending in every direction. And if you picked just one
single flower from this hour-glass, this blue vase, the rest
would wilt right away. But something did happen there
that summer; I don't quite know what it was – it just happened in a different way, gentle and slow. And this is how
my summer begins; I let go my hold of the rope, open my
eyes, and fall right into the arms of Peder's mum who's
sitting on the other side in her wheelchair. 'Hi there,
Barnum! Was your journey all right?' I breathe out. 'Oh,
yes. But the sea was rough at Faskebekk.' Peder swings
the wheelchair round and laughs. 'Now Barnum's got a
fear of heights,' he says. 'He'll have to sit with you going
the other way!' His dad slaps me on the back, and I
wonder how Peder's mum got there, because a wheelchair on a rope bridge is something I've never heard of
before. Peder wheels her into the shadows at the back of
the low, white house in the middle of the island, and
afterwards he shows me the room where we're staying.
There's a bed over by the window, a double bed, and
Peder collapses on it and lies there watching me unpack.
And I'm hardly travelling light, but it's better to have too
much with you when you go on holiday for a week with a
friend on an island. Part of the load includes pyjamas,
swimming shoes and two pairs of trunks (so I can put on
a dry pair straight after swimming and thus avoid getting
chilled), extra underwear, a tube of suntan lotion, a pen
and a piece of paper on which Mum's put our address and
telephone number, just for safety's sake; nor have I

forgotten insect repellent, my comb and deodorant, not to mention the old camera. 'Are you planning on staying for the rest of your life?' Peder inquires. And I turn towards the bed and take a picture of him – Peder lying with his hands behind his head; his smile, one eye closed as if he's making fun of me or has just told a rather bad joke, his bare torso, his tummy spreading over the belt of his shorts a bit, even though he's lying down, his toes extended; and a shadow divides the picture in two, from corner to corner. That's how I remember him – Peder on the bed, that first day of our summer together. Then he looks at me with both eyes. 'What side d'you want to lie on?' he asks. I keep standing. 'D'you know what's been in this suitcase, Peder?' 'Haven't a clue.' 'Applause.' He shuts one eye again as if it's me that's having him on now. 'Applause?' 'Yes. I inherited it from Dad.' Peder lay there thinking. 'But now there's no applause left in it?' he finally asks. I shake my head and carefully lie down beside him. The mattress is soft and there's a kind of deep hollow in the middle we both roll down into. Peder's skin is warm; it glows when I touch it. 'A suitcase of applause,' he whispers. 'Wonderful.' I find the Nivea, get the top off it, and dip my finger in the thick, white lotion and begin to cream him. He turns round. His shoulders are red and the skin on his back is flaking. I peel off the thin flakes of dead skin. And right between his shoulder blades he has a mosquito bite that I have to scratch for him. Afterwards I take off the clothes I've travelled in and put on swimming trunks instead, and Peder creams me all over and does a good job – he doesn't miss out a single spot where I could get sunburned. Then we lie there quite still. 'Did you wonder how Mum got over here?' Peder suddenly asks me. 'By boat?' 'Nope. She sailed in the wheelchair.' 'That's impossible!' 'I mean it. She just speeds up on the quayside and splashes right across. A bit like on skis.' 'No?' 'Really. Everyone comes to the quayside to see Mum when she's going to go over to the island. People look forward to it all year round.' And I can see it in my mind's eye, his mother on the fiord in her wheelchair; I close my eyes and see it all, the wheelchair in the waves. And then I hear someone calling us from far away, from the sun and the wind. We lie there a bit longer just the same. 'I'm glad you're here,' Peder whispers. 'Me too, Peder.' Then we run out onto the terrace where a table has been set under an umbrella; we sit down in soft chairs and pour golden juice into our glasses, and drink the sweet liquid as a wasp hums over the cloth – a wasp that's allowed to go on humming. Peder's dad appears in the wide door to the living room and stands between the thin curtains which all but enclose him. He's holding a dish in his hands and smiling. 'Hungry, boys?' 'Hungry as hell,' Peder says. His dad takes a step away from the curtains and puts the dish on his table. 'Don't swear on my island,' he says. Peder laughs. I have a peek into the dish. It's fish. Peder's dad rolls up a newspaper and tries to swat the wasp, but doesn't get it. Then he flicks up his sunglasses and looks down in the direction of the beach and the diving board. 'Maria!' he shouts. 'Food!' Soon enough I hear the sound of her chair, and maybe it could do with some oil; she rolls in from the shadows and Peder and his dad lift her into a normal chair. For a second I catch a glimpse of her thin body – her hips that are just skin and bone; the grey skin hanging from her joints. And she sees that I've seen and that I'm appalled and horrified – even though I look the other way, at the sailing boats out on the water, the heart of the fiord, the wasp that comes back and lands on the edge of my glass, the sun that glistens on the forks. And I think of everything we shouldn't see, that we could well avoid seeing. Once I saw Fred standing in front of the mirror in Mum's bedroom; he leant forward and kissed – no, licked – his own reflection. I didn't want to see it because everything you see you carry inside; every single image is mingled into one great picture, too heavy for our eyes. And I have to look again one more time all the same – I can't help it – at her thin legs where the blanket has slipped a bit to one side; she's almost blue, puckered, and she smiles as she pulls the blanket over her knees. 'After you, Barnum,' she says. Peder pushes the dish closer. It smells of vinegar. It's cold fish. Peder's dad opens two bottles of beer and gives one to his wife. They drink straight from the bottle. 'Mackerel!' he says, and turns to me. 'Mackerel?' I whisper. 'Fine, fat mackerel, Barnum. They came early this year. But they didn't fool me!' Peder yawns and turns the umbrella. The shadow slides over the cloth as if someone has spilled a full glass over it. I put the smallest piece I can find on my plate. Peder's mother laughs. 'There's no need to be polite, Barnum!' Fortunately Peder takes the dish from me and isn't particularly polite. 'If you don't have at least three mackerel Dad'll be dead offended,' Peder says. I try to laugh. Peder's dad puts down his bottle of beer. 'Mackerel's more than just tasty, boys. It's healthy too. Just see how much fat there is in its fur!' 'Mackerel doesn't have fur, Dad,' Peder says. I laugh loudly. But his dad just takes his finger over the shining skin with a sigh. I bow my head. Mackerel on the plate. German soldiers. On the bottom of the fiord. A German corpse on my plate. This is the war that goes on. It's now I become seasick. I mustn't get seasick. I mustn't be sick. Because perhaps Peder's mother will think that it's she who's made me sick, that I can't bear the sight of her paralysed body under the blanket, her skin and bone. That mustn't happen. I swallow. The slippery flesh, the slippery flesh from the bottom of the sea slides down and I get up, go round the house without looking back and there I kneel down and vomit in the grass. 'What is it, Barnum?' I dry my mouth with the back of my hand and it tastes of suntan lotion and vinegar. Peder's standing behind me. 'Can't stand mackerel,' I whisper. And Peder hunkers down beside me. 'D'you have to be sick before you have the courage to tell us that?'

Now Fred's training. He's running up the kitchen steps, twelve times – because no one's to see him running. Now he's doing thirty press-ups in our room and next time it's forty. In the middle of the night he can wake up, restless and uneasy, and lie down on the floor and do forty more press-ups before running up to the loft again. Now he's going in the door of the Central Boxing Club in Stor Street and everyone turns to look. Fred hears the punches dying away, he sees the sandbags still swinging, he sees the smiles in the sweaty faces. Now the guy who's best in town's going to get a right good hiding. They can't wait.

Peder followed me back to the table on the terrace. 'Barnum believes that mackerel are German soldiers in disguise,' he said. The ghost of a smile flickered over his Mum's lips and she stroked her finger quickly over my arm. 'Better now?' I nodded. But his father opened his eyes wide and all but knocked over his bottle of beer. 'What was that you said, Peder?' 'Barnum's brother said that mackerel eat German soldiers.' His father slowly turned in my direction, as if his thoughts needed time to follow his body round. 'Did your brother really say that?' 'Yes,' I breathed. 'But he was probably just kidding.' Now his dad stuck his whole arm down into the dish and pulled out the biggest fish he could find and held it up. 'Tell me! Is this a Nazi fish? Huh? Does it have a moustache, for instance?' 'It's got fur,' Peder said. 'Maybe it's a Russian mackerel then,' his dad said. 'Let's see.' With that he ate it; he shoved the whole fish into his mouth, chewed a good while and looked about him. His cheeks turned rather pale and he had to take off his sunglasses. '*Wer ist Blücher, mein Schiff? Ich muss nach Oslo fahren!*' 'You're drunk!' Peder's mother screeched. And we laughed and had to sit down on the ground so as not to fall off our chairs. Peder's dad had still more beer and let his mackerel swim. 'I think it's going to be sausages this evening, boys.' For the rest of the day we collected wood for the fire, and when the sun had just sunk over the fiord in a weak shadow and it was still mild, cool and mild – Peder's dad lit the planks and sticks we'd made into a pyramid there beside the edge of the beach. And soon we could see the other bonfires glowing – restless points in every direction, and we could hear the music coming from the jetties closest by. The flames and the voices became clearer with every passing second that evening, as though it was time that amplified everything and not the dark. We ate up the last sausages, put on jumpers and sat closer in to one another. Peder counted the bonfires and got to twenty-eight – three more than the year before. I couldn't remember feeling such a sense of peace – perhaps I never *had* felt it and was only realizing now it could exist at all – my deep, never before experienced, peace.

When Peder's mother was asleep Peder wheeled her up the path to the house. I sat on where I was with his dad. The fire slowly burned away, just as the others did, like lamps in the night. 'Couldn't your brother come with you?' Peder's dad asked. 'He's training,' I told him. 'Training for what?' 'Boxing.' He laughed a bit and lit his pipe. 'Ah, boxing. The noble art of self-defence,' he said in English. 'Perhaps the mackerel had eaten a British soldier,' I said. He laughed and put his arm round my shoulder. 'Is he any use at boxing, your brother?' 'Well, he's good at getting punched, that's for sure.' He knocked the ash from his pipe and it floated away over the water. 'Well, well. That's an art too, Barnum. And some are better at it than others.'

Peder didn't come back. Silently we went up to the house. Suddenly, Peder's dad took my hand and held it a long time. When he finally let go of it again he trotted down to the black bonfire and just stood there. I could hear the sound of the wheelchair, somewhere or other, or perhaps it was just the noise of the rope bridge creaking in the wind. I ran into the room. Peder was already asleep. I got undressed and lay down on my side of the bed, carefully, so as not to waken him. Peder turned round and snored a couple of times, but then his breathing became calm and regular again. I don't remember if I dreamed anything. I think just sleeping was sufficient. I couldn't lose the calm I felt.

Early next morning we were wakened by Peder's mother. 'I'm going to paint the two of you!' she exclaimed. She'd come in her chair right into the room. I sat up straight away, so light was my sleep – I slept just as the Old One had taught me, with my eyes open. Peder just pulled the quilt over his head and gave a groan. 'Barnum has his camera with him. Take a picture instead. Saves time.' His mum reached forward in the wheelchair and pulled the quilt off him. Peder was naked. I'd never seen Peder blush before, nor have I seen him blush since. I felt myself going red too (though it was certainly not the last time). A glow spread though my cheeks – I burned slowly downwards. And for a second, his mother was embarrassed herself; at any rate she had to hold on hard to her wheels. Peder tore the quilt back over himself again. Then his mother's small mouth quickly transformed into a smile. 'Don't insult me, Peder. Come to the diving board in a quarter of an hour. Right, Barnum?' 'Of course,' I whispered. With that she went out once more and after a time Peder's head emerged and looked at me. 'Can't sleep with pyjamas,' he said.

All day we sit down on the rock ledge by the diving board, while Peder's mum, who's set her chair in the flickering shadows under the apple tree, paints us. She has a huge white hat on her head, and that's all we can see of her. There isn't a cloud in the skies; we turn brown and it's as if Peder's hair fades – it suits him, even though he looks pretty annoyed. I wonder to myself if Peder's mum can paint the changes in us before the picture's finished, the way we're no longer the same. But we don't get to see what she's painting. Peder's dad comes with orange juice whenever we get thirsty and every hour we have a swim. We jump together from the diving board and sink until our feet reach the slippery stones – once there we push away and swim up into the sun that's hanging by a thread of shining drops. 'I'll have got you soon!' Peder's mum shouts. And we sit in our places once more and are dry again in the blink of an eye. Peder's mum hums a familiar tune there under the apple tree, from underneath her broad, white hat and behind her easel. And whenever I hear that tune again I can feel the heat on the rock ledge; I had to close my eyes so as not to be blinded, and the scents of warm suntan lotion and tobacco filled me with a strange, trembling sense of sorrow I couldn't quite fathom. Because never had I been happier than now: the hot rock ledge, Ildjernet, that summer with Peder – and perhaps it's precisely this which is the hub on sorrow's wheel, spinning through our lives – that it's passed, that the moment's gone already. 'I'll have got you soon!' Peder's mum shouts again. And even Peder smiles; pulls in his tummy and tries to show off his muscles. His dad slips chunks of ice into our glasses – a clinking, chilly sound in contrast to the sun.

And now Fred's standing in the changing rooms at the Central Boxing Club. Tenner points to a locker and says, 'That's yours. You'll get the key later.' Fred goes over there and changes. Tommy and the twins stare silently at him. Fred turns in their direction. They look away. A man comes in. He stops behind Tenner who immediately moves off. He stands a long while looking at Fred. 'I'm Willy,' he says in the end. 'I'm the trainer here.' Fred says nothing but gives him a quick glance. He's wearing a worn, blue tracksuit and on his feet he's got something that resembles slippers. Willy's fifty-two, lives alone in a bedsit near the bus stop at Ankertorget, works at Akers Mek, and all he knows is welding and boxing, and that's all he needs. 'I hear you can take just about anything,' he says. 'D'you want to learn to punch too?' Fred shrugs his shoulders. Willy turns to Tenner. 'Can he speak?' 'He can speak,' Tenner assures him. Tommy laughs, but stops as quickly as he started. Willy looks at Fred again. 'Have you done any other sport?' Fred ties his laces. 'The discus,' he replies.

I've fallen asleep in the sun, my head against Peder's warm, smooth shoulder, and far away I hear his mother's voice. 'I don't need you any more, boys!' And as I open my eyes I see her moving out of the shadows under the apple tree, or perhaps it's the soft whining sounds of the wheel-chair that awaken me this time. 'Let's see!' Peder shouts and gets up. His mother just shakes her head and laughs. 'Not before I'm finished.' She takes the canvas down from the easel and turns in the direction of the house. She's finished with us, but not with the picture. Nor is she done with it that summer. There's always something that's missing – a stroke, a line, a point. It was only after her husband's funeral, when Peder didn't manage to get back in time from America, that I got to see the portrait of the two of us, and even then she wasn't quite satisfied with it. I was shocked when I saw it; I can't use any other word than that. But she'd given the painting a beautiful title – *friends on the rock ledge*. That's what she called it – quite simple, and the lack of the definite article in the title dis-connected the motif from us, in the same way that time had created a distance, as if I could never manage to stretch out my arm and touch this picture. 'You'll never be finished anyway!' Peder shouts. His mother stops and spins the chair round. 'Want a bet?' Peder laughs. 'You'll only lose.' 'Want a bet?' his mother says. 'No,' Peder says. 'But I'll photobloodygraph you instead!' And he gets out my camera which he's hidden under our towels; his mother shrieks and hides her face in her hands as Peder clicks away at least four times before she gets the wheel-chair turned and flees round the side of the house at a good speed. Suddenly Peder's dad's standing at our backs. 'What's going on here?' he demands. 'We're just doing some photobloodygraphing,' Peder says, and hands me the camera. I'm on the verge of laughing out loud, because the word is still quite new to me and it almost tickles in my mouth. But something in Peder's dad's expression stops me; I don't laugh, instead I try to hide the camera behind me. 'You know your mother doesn't like pictures being taken of her,' he says. 'So don't. Nor you, Barnum.'

I put the camera in my case and decided not to use it again that summer. Peder comes in after me and sits

down on the bed. 'Sometimes Mum can be a bit supersti-
tious,' he says. I stand with my back to him. 'How d'you
mean?' 'She believes her soul is stolen when her picture's
taken.' 'Her soul?' 'Yes. That's what she's got into her
head.' I turn to Peder. 'I won't develop the film,' I tell him.
Peder sighs. 'D'you believe it too? Huh?' I didn't quite
know what to say. 'If that's what she thinks,' I answer.
'Really?' Peder begins to grow impatient. 'So it doesn't
matter what we think.' Peder sits silent a moment. 'At
least develop the picture of me,' he says.

And now Fred's standing at the far end of the training
hall at the Central Boxing Club. Everyone's attention is
focused on him, and Fred's attention is focused on himself. 'Left foot forward!' Willy shouts. 'Or are you some
bloody southpaw from the West End!' Fred retracts his
right foot, punches at the mirror – his muscles frail, his
face crooked. 'Up on your toes!' Willy shouts. 'Or are you
some bloody flat-footed sod from the West End!' Fred
stretches up on his toes, gets his balance, and then Willy
comes from behind and pokes him in the back with one
finger, and Fred falls towards the mirror. 'A boxer whose
feet are knackered is finished, Fred. Because a boxer who
has tired feet has a tired heart.' Tommy hands a bottle to
Tenner and Tenner gives it to Willy who hands it on to
Fred. He drinks. It tastes sweet and heavy. He gives the
bottle back to Willy who chucks it over to Tommy. 'I've
been running on stairs,' Fred says. Willy looks at him.
'Hit me, Fred.' 'What?' 'Hit me, Fred.' Fred thinks a
moment. He punches. But Willy's somewhere else. 'Hit
me, Fred!' Fred punches. Willy's suddenly on the other
side. This fat, old man is dancing circles round Fred.
'Don't run on stairs,' Willy tells him. Fred sits down on
the bench along the wall. The hall's still. Willy takes a
seat beside him. 'Feet, hands, head,' Willy says. 'Head,
hands, feet. Tell me them, Fred.' Fred just looks at him.
'Feet, hands, head,' Willy says again. 'Head, hands, feet.
Can you say that much?' Fred looks down. 'Feet, hands,
head,' he whispers. 'Head, hands, feet.' Willy leans

against him. 'You've a lot to learn, Fred. D'you want to learn?' Fred nods. Willy turns to the other boys. They're already standing in line. Kalle, Jørgen, Salva, Junior, Talent, Arve – all the boys who dream of punching up, punching out, punching through the sound barrier, the pain threshold, to carry a belt with a golden buckle and wings. Tommy's jumping up and down; Tenner, the twins – they're standing queuing from here to Bjølsen. 'Talent,' Willy says. 'Get ready.' Talent, a thick, silent guy from Torshov, nods and goes quietly to the changing room. Willy gets a pair of gloves and puts them on Fred. 'Have you heard of the noble art of self-defence?' he asks. 'English,' Fred says. 'English crap,' Willy says. 'It's the kind of crap writers with moustaches put in their books. Boxing isn't about self-defence. Boxing's about attack. Punching when you mean it. Dancing when you have to.' Talent comes out of the changing room and climbs into the ring. 'Look me in the eyes,' Willy says. Fred looks him in the eyes. They sit like that a good while. 'How does it feel?' Willy asks him. Fred raises his gloves. 'Good,' he says. 'Good,' Willy tells him. 'I want to see you.' 'You are seeing me,' Fred says. 'I want to see you in the ring,' Willy tells him. Someone pushes a clammy protective helmet onto his head. Now Fred clambers over the ropes. Talent's waiting for him in the middle. He stands there with his gloves at his side – serious, silent. *Don't be afraid. I'm thinking of you now. I'm with you. I'm sitting in your corner.* And Fred goes right over to Talent and starts punching. He punches wildly, but the blows hit nothing more than thin air. Talent dances, Talent is everywhere and nowhere, and Fred hits out at him but feels instead heavy shocks against his body – his chest and shoulders – as if his own blows are returned with double ferocity. And Fred punches even harder and faster, but he misses, and that makes him lose his head, makes him mad. He punches and hits nothing; Talent is a shadow round him – yes, Talent shadows him, that's how it is. And Fred gets hit in the chest again; his breath explodes from him, and there's a groan. That groan, the stillness in the hall, and the impossible, quick steps in the ring make Fred lose his head completely. He hits out in all directions; he jumps on Talent, breaks through a storm of blows – he fights like a raging child. For this is worse than a beating, this is humiliation. He's reduced to mockery and he can suffer anything except that; Fred shoves Talent against the ropes and he feels someone freeing his arms from behind. It's Willy, and Willy pulls him away, out of the ring and into the changing room. He sits him down on a bench, loosens his gloves and takes off the protective helmet. 'Go and take a shower,' Willy tells him. 'Cold.'

And Peder points above us. 'Mackerel sky,' he says. The clouds slide slowly by, like paper streamers, coloured red by a light which comes from below, from the sun which is sinking now, down towards the crest of the hills on the other side of the fiord, where a sailing boat is becalmed in the windless dusk. Peder laughs. 'It can't be true that mackerel eat dead Germans. Because Germans soldiers don't go to heaven.' We lie in the grass between the terrace and the beach. And the clouds break up and disappear, or perhaps it's just the colours that change, because soon everything is blue – the whole landscape's like a staircase of high, blue steps. 'Are you there?' Peder asks. 'Sure,' I tell him. I'm lying right beside him. We move even closer together. We're bare-legged, our toes sprouting upwards with pale skin between them – it's never struck me before just how different toes could be. Peder counts to twenty, twenty toes. I can hear the grating sound of his mother's wheelchair over by the flagpole – perhaps she's searching for her soul. I'll give her the film. But when she paints us, what happens to our souls then? Do we get to keep them because a painting takes such a long time to complete? 'What are you best at, Barnum?' 'What?' 'What are you best at?' he asks again. I have to think. 'Best at?' 'Yes. Best at. There must be something you're better at than anything else.' 'I don't know.' 'Don't know? Of course you must!' I have to think about the question again. 'Dreaming,' I whisper. Peder brushes away a wasp. 'Dreaming? Everyone dreams.' 'I just dream during the day,' I tell him. 'I'm pretty good at it.' 'But what d'you dream, Barnum? That you'll get taller?' It's just as if I could stretch up my arm and touch the skies, move to one side a chink of blue. Even the grass we're lying in is blue. 'I dream that things happen to me.' 'Happen? What sort of things?' 'Accidents. Catastrophes. Things like that.' I close my eyes. Peder waits for me to go on. 'I dream that I get knocked down by a car and only just survive, but I'm left blind and dumb for the rest of my life. I dream that I'm lost from a plane that comes down over Africa and have to live with a tribe of natives, and that no one finds me for thirteen years.' I open my eyes. Peder's silent. It feels strange to have said it. I've never said a word about this to anyone before. I almost feel tired. 'Well,' Peder says, no more than that, and waits for me to go on. 'I've dreamed too that I go to the graveyard and put flowers on a grave, and when someone asks me who it is that's lying there I say that it's my mother and that she died of cancer.' Peder pulls on his vest. I don't find it cold. 'Why d'you do it?' he asks me. 'Dream like that?' 'So that people'll feel sorry for me.' 'You're as much of a nutter as that nutty brother of yours,' Peder says. I roll round, sit on top of him and start hitting him. I hit him as hard as I can. I hit him everywhere. Peder screams. His arms are locked in his vest. He tries to twist away but I grip his body tight between my legs and keep hitting; I thump my fists into his chest and his face. Peder howls and rips his vest to shreds; I just keep on hitting and hitting, and he punches me too, but I don't feel a thing. 'Don't say that!' I shriek. 'Don't say that!' There's blood pouring from Peder's nose and then someone lifts me up and throws me to one side – it's Peder's dad and he stands there between the two of us. 'What the hell are you doing?' he shouts. Peder gets up, shaking. 'Don't swear on my island,' he says. His father grabs him and pulls him to him. 'Don't try to be smart with me, young man! Are you

trying to kill each other?' Peder wipes away blood with
his ruined vest. 'No, Barnum's trying to kill me first.' His
dad turns to face me. 'Perhaps you can give me an explanation, Barnum!' I look down. I can't breathe. I can't say
a word. Peder stands beside me. 'We just argued,' he said.
'I told Barnum that he was small and Barnum said that I
was fat.' Peder's dad just looks at us for a long time. Then
he betrays the vaguest curl of a smile. 'That's not how
friends talk to each other, boys. We can leave that sort of
talk to our enemies.' We each look away. Peder's dad
gives him a handkerchief. 'Well, then. Shall we shake
hands?' The two of us hesitate. Then I stretch out my
hand. Peder stretches out his. We clasp each other's
hands. It's a strange moment. 'That's that then,' his dad
says, and pats both of us on the back.

  And now Fred comes out of the showers. He goes over
to his locker. He's freezing. Quickly he gets dressed.
There's no one else but Willy there. They can hear the
punches from the training hall – the breath, the steps, the
thundering – like goods wagons rolling past. 'You're too
angry, boy,' Willy tells him. Fred doesn't look at him. 'A
boxer shouldn't be angry, Fred. Angry people do stupid
things. A boxer should be cool and sensible and crafty.'
Fred slams the locker door shut. But the door just opens
again. 'Why are you so angry with yourself?' Willy asks.
Now Fred turns to face him and Willy takes a step backwards. Fred's forgotten to turn off the shower. It's dripping. Willy goes and turns it off and Fred hasn't moved a
muscle by the time he comes back. Willy scrabbles in the
pocket of his tracksuit and finds something, a small key,
and gives it to Fred. 'Are you not going to lock it?' Fred
smiles for a second and shuts his locker, number 9. Willy
lays a hand on his back. 'And now go home and go to bed.
And rest your anger, Fred.'

  I went to bed first that evening. I lay there waiting for
Peder. I thought to myself that it was the first time I'd
ever hit anyone, and that the first time I did it had been
my best and only friend I'd hit, Peder Miil. I sank under

the quilt. Now everyone was angry with me. Perhaps they'd chase me away over the rope bridge the following day. That's all I deserved. I deserved no better. I was so ashamed. Peder had even lied for me. Never had I felt it stronger, that feeling of shame, which is heavy and dry and tight. Because I'd let them down; I'd let all of them down – Mum and Boletta too. I'd let the whole world down, and that was the last thing I wanted, to disappoint anyone at all. I was filled to the brim with shame. Peder most likely hated me, even though he'd shaken hands with me afterwards. At last he came in. He sat on the bed with his back to me. He was all hunched over. I pretended to be asleep. 'Sorry,' he said. I lay completely still. 'It's me who should say sorry,' I whispered. 'No, it's me,' Peder said. 'I was the one who hit you,' I said. 'But it was me who started it, Barnum. I should never have said what I did about your brother.' 'And I should never have hit you. Never. Does it hurt?' 'No. Just a bit. And you?' 'Not so bad,' I said. I felt at peace again, more than ever. Peder remained sitting where he was. I ran my hand over the curve of his back. He was wearing pyjamas. 'Sh,' he whispered. I didn't move. We could hear his mother and father going to bed; the whining of the wheels of her chair ceased and he lifted her over into bed – there was laughter, whispering, then silence. The moon went behind a cloud. 'Guess what I have?' Peder said. 'No, what?' He straightened up, swung round and held a red bottle in front of me. 'A bottle,' I said. 'Campari,' he whispered. 'And how do you like your brandy, sir?' 'In a glass,' I answered. Peder got out our tooth glasses and filled them to the brim. He sat beside me. 'Cheers,' he said. 'Cheers,' I said. It was like shaking hands all over again. It was more than that. We drank together. Peder's face crumpled into one pinched, hard knot, as if his head had been put into cold water and rubbed with green soap and orange peel. 'Soh lah fuck me doh!' he gasped. I laughed and wanted some more. I just drank. This was something for me. Peder got better after glass number two. I was fine after the third. Now I realized why Boletta went to the North Pole to drink beer. It was something about forgetting, taking a step to one side where no one could hurt you. The shame had gone. The disappointment had gone. Everything had gone that I wanted gone. I didn't just have a light heart, my body became weightless too. I forgot my own body and blood, and when I closed my eyes I could just as well have been one metre seventy-eight tall, or one metre ninety for that matter. I knew it already. The effect meant escape. The effect was an escape you could fill with whatever you chose. Perhaps this was what really happened that summer, that I drank Campari from a tooth glass with Peder, in that double bed in the middle of the night. The fiord stroked the edges of the rocks. In several million years those rocks would be worn down to dust and would blow away in the wind, if something else didn't happen in the meantime. The birds were still. I wished so much that the rest of our lives could be like this moment, right now. Just that, other than the two of us in that great escape, and the stillness of the birds. 'Guess what I'm best at?' Peder said. I drank. I thought. But my mind was elsewhere and I was thinking my own thoughts. 'Dancing,' I said. Peder's Campari went down the wrong way and I had to massage his back for about a quarter of an hour. 'One more try,' he whispered. 'Counting,' I suggested. Peder sat up and nodded. 'Dead right. Counting. How in the world did you know that, Barnum?' 'Twenty guesses,' I told him. Peder smiled and closed his eyes. 'I can count everything. I can count until there are no numbers left. Once I counted all the noses in Bygdøy Alley.' 'All the noses? Did you really?' 'Yes, I did, bugger it. I'll never do it again either.' He looked at me once more. I laughed and he started counting my teeth as if I were a horse, and got to thirty-one. 'You've one tooth missing,' he told me. 'Cheers.' 'It's probably in the glass,' I said. 'Cheers, Peder.' We drank. I thought I heard a wasp in the room but a short time later I couldn't hear it any longer; it had most likely found its way through the slightly open window, or perhaps it was just a fuse in my head that was about to blow. 'But why do you count everything?' I asked him. Peder slid down in the bed. I did too. He whispered, ecstatic. 'It gives me such a sense of calm. When I count, everything falls into place. Numbers are the best thing I know, Barnum. Numbers that go up.' 'You're as nuts as me,' I said. Peder upset his glass and sat over me and held my arms tight. 'Maths and dreams. That's us, Barnum!' I could barely breathe. 'Yes,' I whispered. 'Think of all we can achieve!' He leant even closer, still holding me just as tightly. 'What? What, Peder?' 'Think about it!' he exclaimed. 'I can't breathe!' I told him, my voice as loud as his. But he wouldn't let me out of his grasp. 'You dream,' he said. 'And I can work out how much it'll cost! There's just one thing.' 'One thing what?' 'Are you drunk, Barnum?' Peder smelled my mouth. 'That's possible,' I whispered. Peder began gagging. The whole bed was swaying. The mattress was creaking. 'You have to change the sign for your dreams, Barnum.' 'Change the sign?' 'Minus, Barnum. You dream in minus. You have to dream in plus. Otherwise it won't work!' Peder sank down beside me and we lay like that for a fair while. A thin light came through the curtains; it oozed into the eyes and spread through the head like a burning fan. 'Maths and dreams,' Peder said slowly, and that was the last he said that night. 'That's us, Barnum.'

Now Fred's asleep. He sleeps for ten hours. Before breakfast he goes out to train. He doesn't run. He walks quickly, swings his arms hard and high, forwards and backwards. People look at him and smile. Fred doesn't care. Fred doesn't give a damn. He does exactly as Willy says. For the first time ever he does as someone tells him. It's raining. That suits him fine. He turns at Wester Gravlund, uses a tree to stretch against, then goes home as quickly as he got there. He's warm, not sweating. He showers, eats some porridge and drinks boiled water.

Mum and Boletta are silent. Nor does Fred throw away
any energy on conversation. He conserves his strength.
He stores it. He saves it for the long rounds. He takes the
tram down to the Central Boxing Club. Willy's waiting
there already. Fred changes. They're alone there. Willy
gives him a skipping rope. 'Jump,' Willy tells him. And
Fred does. 'Up on your toes!' Willy shouts. Fred skips.
Oh, wouldn't I have given anything to see that, Fred with
a skipping rope in front of the mirror at the Central
Boxing Club, going faster and faster until he collapses on
the floor, his legs swollen and sore, and Willy standing
over him smiling. 'Feet, hands, head,' he says again.
'Head, hands, feet,' Fred says, and gets up again. Willy
ties a pair of gloves onto his hands. 'Sack,' is all he says.
Fred goes over to the sack of sand hanging from a rope in
the ceiling and starts punching. Willy stands behind him,
guiding his arms, raising his elbows, turning his fists.
Willy lets him go. Fred punches. The thundering in that
empty hall. There's a smell that remains there, of camphor, it might be camphor – a chill gust of it, and of heavy
sweat and old cloth. 'What are you punching?' Willy
shouts. 'I'm punching a bloody sack!' Fred tells him. He
bends his neck, lifts his shoulders, keeps punching. 'It's
no bloody sack!' Willy shouts. 'You're hitting a body now!
You're knackering it!' And Fred punches; heavy body
blows that have their origins deep inside, right in your
heels – no, in your very thoughts and your dreams. It's a
movement that quivers through your whole life – a
muscle of time. 'Who are you punching?' Willy demands.
Fred laughs, he laughs and he punches. 'I'm punching a
bloody sack!' he shouts. Willy holds him. Fred lets his
own arms fall. 'Imagination, Fred, have you got that?'
Fred sinks down on the bench, knackered by his own
punches. 'It's not what you see that matters most but
rather what you think you see,' he says. 'Bullshit,' Willy
exclaims. 'Who told you that?' 'Everyone who said it's
dead,' Fred replies. Willy dries the sweat from him and
gives him something to drink – sweetened water.

'Shadow boxing,' Willy says. And Fred boxes alone in the ring; he dances, he punches, he's aware that it's more tiring to hit nothing than to hit something – a punch in the air hits the one who's punching. 'Who're you boxing?' Willy shouts. 'My shadow,' Fred says. 'Wrong, Fred. You have to imagine you're boxing someone.' 'Tommy,' Fred says, and punches. 'Forget Tommy,' Willy tells him. 'Tenner,' Fred says instead, and punches. 'Forget Tenner.' 'Talent,' Fred says, and gives a quick flurry of punches. 'Forget Talent, too.' Fred stops and turns to the corner where Willy's standing. 'Who am I boxing then?' he asks. 'No one,' Willy replies. 'No one?' 'Your opponent, Fred. He's nobody. He's no name. He's no address. He's no family. The only thing you know about him is that you'll hit him as hard as you can and beat him. And that's all you need to know. D'you understand?' Fred nods. Fred smiles. 'Yes,' he says. 'I got that from the beginning.' And Fred punches, he punches his shadow, and his only desire is to hit his shadow and see it sink forever at his feet.

I waken with the rain on the roof. I lie there listening to the rain – it's summer, it's early, it's wonderful. Then Peder turns to face me. There's a bad smell. 'Dream anything?' he whispers. 'Nothing,' I tell him. 'And you? Counted anything?' 'Nothing.' His expression clouds. 'But now I'm going to count how many times I have to be sick,' he says. He turns away and makes a series of unhappy noises, and the bad smell gets worse. 'One,' Peder says. Then I go out. I get dressed and go out and leave him in peace. One foot trails in a pool of Campari. I hear a further gulping sound from the bed. 'Two,' Peder says. I'm gone. No one else is up yet. It's just me. It's just me in the thin rain. I go round the island. It isn't big. Islands shouldn't be big. Islands should be small enough to go round on a morning of rain. The fiord's grey and has goose pimples. I sit on the steps by the diving board and dip my face in the water. That helps. I take the time I need. The steps are slippery and green. Everything is

strange and ordinary. I see the ferry turning and heading
for the city once more. Soon I'll go back to Peder. We'll
talk about maths and dreams. That's us. Then I notice
her. Or maybe she's the one to see me first. It's Vivian.
She's standing in the middle of the rope bridge with a
rucksack and an umbrella. Never will I forget the sight of
Vivian underneath a yellow umbrella on the swaying rope
bridge over to Ildjernet. Whoever takes an umbrella with
them on holiday? Vivian. I don't know what to think. I
wave. I don't know what it makes me feel. I don't know
what I want. I wave again. And Vivian walks the last part
of the way and stops once she's set foot on our island. 'Hi,
Tiny!' she shouts. I run over to her. 'You here?' I say. 'Yes.
Why not?' And she looks at me, her head on one side.
'What a sight you are,' she says. 'Really?' 'You look as if
you've been sleeping in water.' I smile at her. 'Peder and I
had a party last night,' I tell her. Vivian puts down her
yellow umbrella. It's still raining. 'A party?' she repeats.
'Yes. You bet!' She gives the umbrella a hard shake to dry
it. 'Who was at your party then?' 'Peder and me.' Vivian
looks at me again. 'It's raining,' she says. We go up
towards the house. Everything's quiet. The water's dripping from the blue umbrella onto the terrace. I carry the
umbrella for her. The grass is cold round my feet. 'Is no
one up?' Vivian asks me. 'Not Peder at any rate.' We slip
into the bedroom. Peder's lying with his head the wrong
way round. He isn't dead. He's made a moat of sick round
the bed. Airing the room isn't going to help much. Vivian
holds her nose. I open the umbrella, just for safety's sake.
'I dreamt something after all,' I said. Peder jumps in a
slow kind of way. His eyes move in his head like a crab's.
'What?' he groans. 'That Vivian came here.' Peder tumbles onto the floor and lands on his knees, as if he's pray-
ing. But he isn't. It looks more like he's getting electric
shocks in the mouth, and he's making some pretty horrible noises. 'Four and a half,' he whispers. He climbs back
onto the bed and notices Vivian. 'Hi, Fatty,' she says.
'You're really brown.' Peder smiles at her, but it's me he's

looking at. 'Good, Barnum. Now you're dreaming in plus.' I put down the umbrella. Vivian steps over the vomit and sits down on the bed. 'Is there room for me between the two of you?' Then I hear the wheelchair behind us. 'You'll have your own room, Vivian!' We turn to look at Peder's mother. Peder's given up already. He manages to hide the bottle, but not to wish away eight kilos of vomit. 'Hi, Mum, I think I've caught a bug. It's infectious.' Vivian goes off with Peder's mother. The rain's clearing. The sun's coming in the window at an angle; a bundle of light on the blue sill. Peder gets up from the bed. 'Thanks for the dream,' he says. 'Did you know she was coming?' I ask him. Peder shrugs his shoulders. 'Maybe. Maybe not. Shall we do some clearing up?' And when we next see Vivian she's wearing a bikini. I don't remember the colour of it. I almost don't dare look at her. But I can't take my eyes away all the same. She's thin – lean would be the right word to describe her. Her skin is smooth and firm over her whole body, particularly her tummy, which still goes in a slight curve down to the edge of her bikini. And there are no differences in the colour of her skin – her whole body is equally pale, but not grey, more a deep white that's reminiscent of the colour of old crockery. She's got sunglasses on. I can't see where she's looking. Her mouth seems larger than normal. She has her hair tied at her neck and has freed the thin band fastening it on her back. We lie together on the rock ledge. Peder creams her shoulders. Peder counts her ribs. She's got more than we have. She laughs. I stare down the slope. I can see her nonetheless. It's the hottest day of the summer. Suddenly Peder throws the suntan lotion over to me. He fights a wasp. The wasp is on the point of winning. Vivian sits up abruptly. I catch a glimpse of her breasts before she gets her bikini and her hands into place. Peder fights the wasp with a towel. But I saw her breasts. They aren't large. They're sufficient. If I put my hand on one of them it would fit perfectly. I don't. But I'd like to. I imagine doing it. Putting my hand

carefully on her breast and she sighing. Her eyes behind
the dark sunglasses. I don't see where she's looking. The
suntan lotion melts on my fingers, drips onto the ledge
and runs away down a deep crevice. Peder chucks a stone
at the wasp. 'I fancy swimming,' Vivian announces. She
goes onto the diving board and plunges in. There's barely
a splash when she lands, her arms like a spear – no, a
sword, a sabre that cuts the waves and soundlessly
pushes them apart. Peder looks at me. 'Not going to
swim?' he asks. 'Think I'll wait a bit,' I reply. 'Same here.
We can swim later.' 'Sure,' I agree. His mother sits by the
flagpole and waves. Vivian is almost invisible in the midst
of all the light that flickers round her like shifting mirrors.
'Think we have to get ourselves some sunglasses,
Barnum,' Peder says. Then Vivian comes up the steps.
Carefully we lie down on our tummies. She sits between
us. I see the water on her skin drying, drop by drop. Tiny,
fair hairs rise along the ridge of her back. I want to touch
them. There's a raw, warm smell from the rock ledge, the
hot stones, the hillside, which makes me a bit light-
headed. I dip my fingers in the suntan lotion again. 'You
mustn't get burnt,' I murmur. She lies down on her back.
She closes her eyes. Peder's borrowed the sunglasses.
They make him look quite tough. He sucks in his cheeks
and gives a lop-sided smile. I squat down beside Vivian. I
squirt a warm, white pool of Nivea onto her tummy. 'I
met your brother,' she says out of the blue. My hand
stops. 'What?' 'Your brother Fred. I met him.' Peder slips
the sunglasses up onto his brow and lets out his cheeks
again. 'Where?' I ask her. 'In Bygdøy Alley. He was running.' 'Running? Fred never runs.' 'Well, he was walking
mighty fast at any rate. And using his arms. Looked a bit
weird.' 'The difference between running and walking is
that when you run you only ever have one foot on the
ground,' Peder says. 'Doesn't have anything to do with
speed. So you can actually run much more slowly than
you can walk. Just so you know.' 'He's training,' I tell
them. Peder laughs. 'Training? In Bygdøy Alley? What's

he training for?' 'Boxing,' I breathe, as quietly as I can, and have to shade my eyes. Vivian sits up and rubs the lotion on herself. 'He's got a fight in September,' she says. Suddenly I get a pain in my head – it throbs, my mouth goes dry and a wave of sickness passes through me. Peder looks at me. It's as if he's got spare tyres on his forehead too. 'Everything all right, Barnum?' I nod and take deep breaths. But everything isn't all right. I don't know what's wrong with me. But the thought that Fred's spoken to Vivian and that she's spoken to him is unbearable. I feel sick and dizzy. Peder sits up. Vivian lies back down. 'Did you talk to him?' I breathe, and have almost no voice whatsoever. 'A bit.' 'A bit? Did he stop?' 'He had to do some stretching.' 'Stretching? He had to stretch?' 'Yes, against a tree.' 'Then he must have knocked it over,' Peder says. I'm still taking deep breaths. 'What did he say? When he was stretching, I mean?' Vivian sighed. 'You're not keeping up, Barnum. He said he would box in September. His first match. Didn't you know that?' I laugh. 'Of course I knew that,' I tell her loudly. 'Fred's the best in town. No one'll take the kind of beating he will. Bloody hell!' I look at Peder. I'm proud of my brother. That's what I want to be. Peder looks the other way. His Dad's standing on the terrace waving his hands. 'Food and drink!' he calls. Peder's already off. Vivian follows him. She turns and hesitates a moment. 'Not coming, Barnum?' 'Oh, yes, in a minute.' I go up to Peder's mum instead to help her up the path. 'Why don't you oil the wheels?' I ask her. 'So you'll hear me coming,' she replies. 'Just like squeaking shoes,' I tell her. She bends her head backwards and smiles, but her mouth is hanging the wrong way. 'You're not ill, Barnum?' 'Not in the least.' 'Because it wouldn't surprise me if you felt somewhat ill today. After a night like that.' 'I know,' I agree. She puts her hand on my arm. 'I'm glad you're here,' she says gently. 'You're a good boy.' 'No,' I tell her. 'I'm not that good.'

And now Fred's going home, through the city and the rain, beaten up – beaten up by no one but his shadow and himself. He walks slowly and stiffly, his bag over his shoulder, looking all about him in the deserted streets. Beside him walks Willy. Willy talks all the time. 'There are two voices in a boxer's head, Fred. One of them says *attack*! The other whispers *get out*. That's exactly one voice too many.' Fred nods. Willy takes hold of his arm. 'If you end up standing somewhere in between you're done for. Your mind has to be concentrated and focused. A boxer who starts doubting's down already.' Willy laughs. 'Basically, boxing's as easy as giving someone a good hiding.' They stop. 'Your fist first, Fred. That's all you have to remember. Your fist first!' Willy lets go of his arm. 'You owe me fifty kroner, Fred.' 'Do I?' 'I paid your subscription. Otherwise you couldn't have boxed in September.' 'Many thanks,' Fred says. Willy puts his hands in his pockets, for a moment embarrassed. 'I wasn't bloody well splashing out on you!' They stand together at the City Chambers Square. 'See you,' Fred says quietly. Willy holds him back. 'Have you heard of Bob Fitzsimmons?' Fred shakes his head. Willy smiles. ''Course you won't have. But Bob Fitzsimmons is the greatest, Fred. When he got beaten to pulp by Jack Johnson in 1907 every paper in the land said he was down and out. Two months later he beat Corbett. Knocked him out in the third.' 'Bloody hell,' Fred says. 'Yes, bloody hell. Don't believe what the papers say. There are people who say that boxers never come back. It's not true.' 'No,' Fred says. The clock on the tower strikes three. Willy has to hurry. 'See you tomorrow,' he says quickly, slapping Fred on the back and running in the direction of the Akers Mek gates; the heavy figure springs easily over the cobbles. 'D'you work there?' Fred shouts after him. Willy turns as he's running. 'Everyone works here!' He manages to make his shift, and Fred just stands there watching the backs disappearing through the shipyard gates, and the gate closing behind them. The rain slides over the city. And at a precise moment, eight minutes past three, the square's divided in two, between light and shadow, rain and sunlight. And

Fred stands in the middle, one arm in the rain, the other in the light. He stands like that for a moment in wonderment, blinded and wet, at the edge of the sunlight, before it covers him completely. And had he been able to see far enough, out to the fiord, along the steep green point of Nesoddlandet, to Ildjernet and the white summer house that stood there (and I'm glad Fred can't see that well), he'd first have seen Vivian drinking cola through a straw. Her mouth's a soft, wet tip and with two fingers she's carefully holding the yellow straw, and glancing over at Peder's dad who's trying to get up from his deckchair. But Peder's dad is too full and his deckchair is far too deep; he topples back down once more and we laugh at him – that grown man, the seller of postage stamps, Oscar Miil. 'Oh Lord, what a time we're having,' he says. 'Mum and I and Peder and Barnum and Vivian!' He looks round at each of us as if he can't quite believe it's all real, that his island is inhabited, that the sun's come out after all, that we're full of mirth and gratitude, that we're in such good company. He lets his gaze rest on Vivian. 'It was time you came,' he tells her. Vivian smiles and looks up from her glass. The melting chunks of ice clink. 'Thank you,' she murmurs. 'We need someone to look after the boys anyway, right?' We laugh once more; Peder's mother takes a swipe at a wasp with one of last year's papers and his dad turns to me. 'Isn't that right, Barnum?' 'Dead right,' I agree. 'You're not feeling rocky again, Barnum? There wasn't a single mackerel in that salad!' I shake my head carefully. 'Particularly Peder,' I say. 'Someone has to look after him.' 'Oh, would you listen to that!' Peder exclaims. 'It's Barnum who needs looking after. He's afraid of heights!' We all laugh even more and finally Peder's dad manages to get to his feet; he takes a look out over the fiord and nods, as if he's seen something that meets with his approval. Then he looks at his wife. 'Low tide,' he announces. 'Time for a Campari, Maria! Shall I bring one for you?' Peder's mother thinks for a minute. 'Why don't we try some Martini instead?' 'Martini at low tide! Oh, please, no!' Peder's dad goes concussed into the house. I look at Peder. Peder looks up at the sky and whistles. 'Peder,' his mother says. 'Yes, Mother,' he answers, and continues scrutinizing the skies. 'You have to sort this yourself, Peder.' Vivian looks at me. I just shrug my shoulders. I'm incapable of anything else. Then his father re-emerges. 'Have you seen the Campari, Maria?' 'Is it not in the fridge?' 'No, it's not.' Peder's mum looks at her son again. 'Find anything?' she enquires. 'Find anything?' 'In the skies? Is there anything written there, Peder?' His father starts losing his cool. 'The Campari, Maria. It'll soon be high tide!' Then Peder gets up. 'I have an announcement to make,' he says. His father turns to look at him. 'What are you on about?' 'I've an announcement to make, Dad.' 'Yes, I heard that. What's going on?' Peder bows his head. 'There's no Campari left, Dad. Neither in the fridge nor anywhere else on Ildjernet.' His dad turns towards Maria. 'What can our son mean by this?' She gives a sigh. 'I think what he means is that they've drunk your Campari.' Peder's dad turns again, this time to me. 'Well, now I know why you're looking a bit rough today, Barnum.' And I sense myself beginning to feel sick once more – getting queasy, because I see Fred in my mind's eye stretching against a tree, a chestnut tree in Bygdöy Alley, and Vivian stopping and talking to him. Fred and Vivian chat away and he tells her he'll be boxing in September; he's the one who tells her. I have to be sick. I can't be sick twice on the same island. Peder's father scratches his brow. His skin's peeling in the middle of his forehead; he scratches at it for a good long time. 'Well, well,' he says. 'At least you're alive. I'll just have to buy another bottle when I'm next in town.' He keeps standing there a while longer, reflecting, I imagine. 'Never heard the like,' he says. Then he strolls back inside. I look at Peder. He's watching his dad go. We'd got off pretty lightly. I make up my mind to treat Peder's dad to something nice in the future. Vivian gets up and goes over to Peder. 'You've a nice dad,' she says. And suddenly Peder gets mad. I can't understand it. He becomes totally beside himself with rage. 'Dad!' he screams. 'Dad!' His father looks out from the verandah door. 'Yes? I hope you're not going to ask me for a Martini, Peder. Because you're not getting one.' Peder shakes his head. He's completely red. 'D'you know why we drank your Campari?' he says. His father smiles. 'Yes, I have a suspicion.' 'Because you sold on Fred's letter!' His dad's smile sinks. His forehead is bleeding; a tiny thread of blood runs down towards the bridge of his nose. He wipes it away with the back of his hand and is about to say something, but stops and look at me instead. I don't understand; I don't understand what Peder's said and I just sit there silent and bewildered and feeling a little rough, afraid to say something wrong, something completely insane. Then Peder's dad disappears behind the curtains and I hear the whine of his mother's wheelchair, and when she speaks her voice is both angry and sorrowful. 'That was unnecessary, Peder. In fact it was just wicked.' I turn towards them. Peder looks down. He's lost all the colour in his face. Vivian goes over to the diving board. She stands right out at the end, bends her knees a little to make a tall thin *S* in the sunlight, and dives. I don't hear her landing. 'Sorry,' Peder says. 'Don't say sorry to me! Say sorry to your father!' Peder shrugs and goes into the living room. He's there for a while. Slowly I get up. 'Perhaps Peder's lost his soul,' I whisper. His mother looks up at me. 'What's that, Barnum?' 'I took a picture of him,' I tell her. She opens her mouth, as if to laugh, and then changes her mind. 'What matters is getting it back as quickly as possible.' 'How?' 'By doing the right things,' she replies. Finally Peder comes back. He has a glass with him that he gives to his mother. 'There you are, Mum,' he says, and gives a deep bow. 'Martini, low tide and lemon.' 'Where's Dad?' 'He's resting, Mum. On the sofa in the living room.' His mother holds her glass in both hands. 'D'you know what I think you should do, Peder?' 'Not entirely.' 'Mow the lawn.' Peder thinks about this. 'All right.' 'And when you've done that you can collect some seaweed from the beach.' 'Oh, no.' 'Oh, yes. And after that it would be tremendous if you could clean the diving board and the steps. I'm sure Barnum'll help you.' And for the rest of that day we work at recovering our souls. We mow the lawn at the back of the house. Each of us rakes the grass. We rub away the slime from the bathing steps. We clean the seagull shit from the diving board. It works. My soul is there. It'll soon be back in place. It's just the same as a coded padlock; when you finally think you remember the numbers correctly and feel it giving, there's a quiver through your hand – and then it tightens and one of the numbers is wrong after all. Fred's letter? Why had Peder called it Fred's letter? All that's left now is the beach. Vivian's sitting there and her eyes follow us. We collect seaweed. She has a red towel over her shoulders. She looks as if she's cold. The seaweed has a sour smell – of old rubbish, piss, something rotting slowly in the heat, carcasses. 'Is this your punishment?' Vivian shouts. Peder looks up. 'Punishment? Are you religious or what?' Vivian draws a circle in the sand round her. 'I think I believe in God,' she says. Peder smiles. 'Just because you live within spitting distance of Frogner church. I bet everyone in Bygdøy Alley thinks they believe in God.' 'Idiot,' Vivian exclaims, and hides in her towel. We put the seaweed in a huge bucket. Peder's sweating. 'Why did you say what you did about the letter?' I ask him. He shrugs his shoulders. 'Wanted to.' 'You shouldn't have.' 'Maybe. Maybe not.' Peder finds a bottle top he secretes in the tiny pocket of his trunks. 'But why did you say it was Fred's letter, Peder?' He turns towards me abruptly and unsure for a moment, he hesitates. 'That's enough,' he says simply, and gets up. 'There's more seaweed,' I tell him. Peder laughs. 'And there's more seaweed where that comes from, Barnum. You could end up collecting seaweed for the rest of your life and still not be finished!' 'You can't count seaweed,' I tell him. 'No, exactly! That's what's shit about seaweed. Can't count the stuff.' 'I'll keep going a bit longer,' I tell him. Peder chucks the bottle top out into the water again. 'Just as you like. I can't be bothered doing any more.' He goes over to Vivian and rips the towel away from her and she gets up with a shriek. Peder chases off in the direction of the house, whirling the towel about his head like a lasso; she runs after him and catches up with him right away, and I have no idea where they disappear to. I crouch down on the shore. The bladders in the wet seaweed burst. And the dry seaweed lies in the sand, crumbling into pieces at my touch. A jellyfish has been washed ashore. If a star was to tumble from the skies then perhaps this is how it would look. When I stick my finger in it I almost can't free it again. I have to scrape it free. I read once about a man who drowned in jellyfish; they trapped him down there – a whole roof of them. He couldn't get through and remained down there under the shadow of the jellyfish. But it would be better to get a discus in the head. I vomit into the bucket. I stick my finger down my throat and vomit even more. Someone puts a hand on my back. I turn and look right at Peder's dad. 'Well, well,' he says. 'If it's not mackerel it's Campari.' I sink down into the sand. He sits beside me. He lends me a handkerchief. 'It'll pass, Barnum. It'll pass. But your body will punish you in the meantime.' 'Punish?' 'Call it a kind of postal surcharge. You put too few stamps on the fun yesterday and today your body's paying what's owed.' Peder's dad suddenly laughs and pours sand out of his shoes. 'No, now I'm just talking nonsense,' he says. 'I thought it sounded fine,' I murmur. He's silent as he puts his shoes on again. He takes his time over it. The laces are thin and worn, on the point of breaking. 'I was sorry about the letter,' he said in the end. 'It was Dad who sold it.' 'Yes, it was. I didn't know who he was then. That he was your father.' 'It's strange that old things can become so valuable,' I say. Peder's dad chuckles. 'Not all old things, Barnum. My shoes, for instance. Doubt I'd get much for them.' 'No, and they squeak too.' 'They squeak and they leak. And I wouldn't sell them anyway. These hopeless old shoes are precious to me. Just me.' 'But if I were to write a letter to my mother now and she were to hide it for thirty years, would it be worth something then?' 'Depends,' he replies. 'On what?' 'If you become famous or not, Barnum.' I have to mull that one over a bit. I can't quite imagine it. Famous? Me famous? What would I be famous for? My height? My name? My dreams? My imagination won't stretch that far. 'It isn't right to read other people's letters anyway,' I say. Peder's dad nods. 'That was just what your brother said, too.' 'My brother?' 'He was in my shop, you know. He wanted the letter back. It must have meant a lot to you, Barnum.' I didn't say anything. Fred's everywhere. Fred's talked to everyone. Peder's dad puts his arm round me. 'He wanted the letter back for your sake, Barnum. That was precisely what he said.' 'Did he?' 'Oh, yes. It was.' And then I reckoned that Fred was a fine big brother. I no longer know what I should think. But somewhere inside I feel so happy. I want to believe it, believe what I think I'm hearing, what Peder's father's telling me, that Fred did something for my sake. 'I think Peder is almost a little envious of you,' he whispers. I stand up and start walking towards the house. But I go a different way so as to be alone with my thoughts. It's as if my head's eaten too much. I've got a stitch in my brain. The outside loo's unoccupied and I sit down inside. When I peer down into the hole I can't see the bottom. Nor can I even hear the shit landing. If I were to tumble down there I wouldn't be found again before the autumn. On the walls there are pictures of the royal family and the face of Van Gogh; there's a picture of a boy too, who must be Peder, but the photograph's old now. He's standing right out at the end of the diving board wearing a great lifebelt, and he looks pretty mad – maybe at that moment he loses his soul. That was before we got to know each other, before he knew who I was or I knew that he existed, in the very same city. It was before either of us knew that Vivian walked through the same streets too; maybe we'd taken the same tram together, or got off at the same station. And I get as far as thinking this, in the outside loo on Ildjernet, that strange summer that afterwards I came to call my first summer, that we don't actually know most things. We know so little that it barely exists in relation to what we don't know – it's like an ant on Mount Everest or a single drop in the Dead Sea. And the little we do know we mustn't forget, and what we think we know must be included too. And at last I can hear these thoughts getting through, because after a long time falling they become words in my mouth. 'I know less than I don't know,' I breathe. And once more I'm filled with a great feeling of tender-heartedness for Fred; I see him there before me, going round quietly doing all his good deeds in secret. I sit on there a bit yet. I don't quite know why but I feel like crying. Things are good. The paper's stiff, but when I rub it quickly between my fingers it becomes soft enough. Then I go outside. Peder's dad is pushing the wheelchair along the shore. Peder and Vivian are each sitting on the terrace reading weeklies. Peder sees me coming. 'You know what's great about keeping old magazines, Barnum?' 'No,' I reply. 'You can see the horoscopes weren't right.' 'Really?' Peder leafs through the pages till he finds what he's looking for. 'Now listen to what they wrote about you last year. *One of the best and most interesting weeks of the year. Lively contact is embarked upon with foreign friends or business contacts. You'll have plenty of opportunity to engage in some flirting and you'll maybe find it takes a serious turn.*' Peder chucks the magazine away and looks at me. 'Did any of that happen, Barnum?' 'Not that I remember,' I agree. 'Not even a little bit of flirting with foreign friends?' 'I couldn't honestly say so.' 'You see. It's just crap.' 'It's not a certainty they'll be right for every-one,' Vivian says. Peder turns to her. 'D'you think you believe in horoscopes then?' 'Sometimes.' 'That it's God Himself who writes the horoscopes for *Now*? In Norwegian?' Peder pretends to look amazed and shakes his head over and over. 'In the autumn it said I would

meet two interesting men,' Vivian says. 'And then I met
you two.' All at once she gives a loud laugh. 'Sheer
chance,' Peder says. 'If you make things up the whole
time a bit of truth'll slip in sometimes. By the law of aver-
ages.' Vivian closes her eyes. 'What do you believe in?'
she asks. 'Peder believes in figures,' I tell her. He smiles.
He leans close to Vivian and speaks in hushed tones. 'If
you come to our room tonight at thirteen minutes past
twelve, Barnum'll show you something.' Vivian opens her
eyes again. 'What?' 'That will be revealed,' Peder tells her.
And he says no more that evening. He just sits in his
deckchair counting boats on their way into the fiord, and
he records the number in a book with a whole lot of earlier calculations. When we've gone to bed we don't actually *go* to bed, but sit instead at the edge of it waiting for
Vivian. The house is utterly still. I'm the one who cracks.
'What is it we're going to show her?' I demand. 'Be quiet,'
Peder says. 'You stink of seaweed.' I pour some water
from a blue jug to wash my hands and face – it's lukewarm and no longer fresh. 'It was just something you
said, right? Right, Peder?' 'What? That you stink of seaweed?' 'That I'd show her something.' Peder leans backwards. I can see him in the dark window; a shifting,
blurred image in the reflection thrown by the low, red
lamp by the bedside. And all this is mixed with the light
of a lop-sided moon that looks as if it's hanging by a
single thread right down into the fiord. 'D'you think
she'll come, Barnum?' I turn towards him. 'No.' 'But I
think so.' He gets up again. 'No, I don't think so,' he says.
'I know so.' 'How can you know?' Peder smiles. 'Because
she's curious, of course. Wouldn't you have come if she
was going to show you something?' 'Yes.' 'You see, then.
She'll come. Just you wait.' I sit down on the bed beside
him. Peder smells my hands. 'That's better,' he says.
'Women don't like seaweed.' We rub some deodorant
under our arms too and don't say any more for a bit.
'What's the time?' Peder asks. 'Eight minutes to twelve.'
'We mustn't drift off, Barnum.' 'No, we'll keep each other

awake.' Peder washes his face in the same water. 'Wish I had a big brother,' he suddenly says. 'Do you?' He sits back down and borrows my towel. 'Mum couldn't have any more children after I was born.' I think about this for a bit. 'But then you'd have had a little brother anyway,' I tell him. 'If you'd had a brother after you were born.' Peder gave this some thought too. 'You're bloody well right, Barnum.' We're awake. 'D'you think she'll come?' I ask him. 'Just wait,' Peder says. 'Vivian'll come.'

And she did come. At thirteen minutes past twelve there was a cautious knock on the door. Peder opened up. Vivian sneaked in. Peder closed the door and listened – we all listened. The house was still. No one had heard us. The fiord glided past. 'What is it you wanted to show me, Barnum?' Vivian whispered. I looked at Peder. Peder just smiled. Vivian walked back in the direction of the door. 'If you two are just going to be smutty then I'm off!' Peder laughed quietly. 'Sh,' he said. But Vivian wasn't about to be shut up. 'If you two try anything, I'll scream!' She suddenly took a step towards me. 'I'll beat you up, Barnum! Just so you know!' She was on the point of going for me. Peder had to intervene and stand between us. 'Vivian, did it not say in your horoscope that we were two interesting men?' Vivian calmed down. Now she was just impatient. 'Tell me what it is then!' Peder pushed me round the side of the bed. Vivian followed us with her eyes. 'Barnum wants to show you his suitcase,' Peder told her. Vivian became suspicious again. 'I don't want to see Barnum's suitcase!' It looked as though the very thought made her ill and she hid her face in her hands. What did she think, that I'd pull my trousers down and reveal everything? Barnum's suitcase? Peder laughed. 'Just relax, Vivian. Barnum isn't a suitcase.' He glanced at me, blinked twice, then pulled out my old suitcase and laid it on the bed. 'This is Barnum's magic suitcase,' he whispered. Vivian let her hands drop and she stared at the case. 'What's inside it?' Peder opened it. Vivian backed away, even more suspicious. Then she came closer again. 'But it's empty,' she said. Peder turned to me. 'Explain, Barnum!' 'There was applause in it,' I tell her. Vivian sat down beside the suitcase and traced one finger carefully along the soft lining on the inside. 'Applause?' 'I inherited it from my dad. And he'd been given it by the circus ringmaster, Mundus.' 'The one who was at the funeral?' 'Yes. Dad was to look after it. It was in this they packed down all the applause. And my dad used to carry this suitcase.' Vivian looked at me. 'And where's all the applause now?' 'Perhaps it's used up. I don't know. Perhaps he lost it.' Peder stood by the window looking at us. He didn't say a thing. He just stood there and shook his head now and again. 'Was this what you wanted to show me, Barnum?' Vivian asked. 'Yes,' I told her. She just touched my hand. 'That was lovely,' she said. We were silent for a time. Suddenly we were drenched in a brief, white light – as if there had been a flash of lightning. We turned towards Peder, squinting. He put my camera down on the window sill. I thought of our souls, that to lose your soul is the same as dying, that being photographed is the equivalent of being executed – if it was right what Peder's mother said. But how many times can you lose your soul? 'Barnum's camera,' Peder breathed. Vivian looked up at me. She had dark shadows under her eyes. 'Sure there's no applause left in the suitcase?' she asked. 'Doesn't look like it.' 'Not a single clap? Perhaps your dad hid some for himself?' Peder got excited. 'Good thinking, Vivian. Of course he must have saved some. We'll have a look!' Peder got out a knife and sat down on the bed. He looked at us. 'Shall we?' he breathed. I nodded. And Peder cut into the lining, made an incision in the board inside the lid to see if there was some secret chamber there where Dad could have hidden the rest of the applause. There was nothing. It just smelled strongly of mould and mothballs. Peder put the knife back in its sheath. 'Did you really think we'd find anything?' He lay back on the bed and laughed. 'What was it your father used to say, Barnum?' he asked. I looked at Vivian. She was looking at the ripped and empty suitcase. 'It's not what you see that matters most but rather what you think you see,' I whispered. Peder sat up again. 'But I think it's the other way round,' he said. 'It's what you see that's most important. What do you reckon, Vivian?' Vivian didn't say anything. She just pointed at the edge of the lid. 'Look,' she said. Something was sticking out there, the corner of a sheet or a book – something. I worked it free. It was a card that Dad must have hidden there, or forgotten, an old postcard. And I can still remember the simultaneous feelings of joy and fear that came with the shock of finding it; the pride of having something to show them because my suitcase wasn't empty after all, but the equal sense of fear too at what this could be that lay concealed in the lid of the case I'd inherited. It was a picture of the world's tallest man, Paturson from Akureyri. I breathed a sigh of relief. His name appeared at the bottom, both printed and signed, and his height of 273 centimetres was recorded, as measured by the Copenhagen medical congress. Peder and Vivian peered over my shoulders. My hands shook with happiness, with wonder, with I don't know what – but my hands shook. The hand-coloured drawing of Paturson was faded; the colours were pale shadows. And the sight of it stirred me; I became sad and excited at one and the same time, and had to hold onto my own hands. Paturson's face was long and his mouth small, a thin bow above a broad chin. He had a very pronounced parting, almost right in the middle of his head, and the eyes that once had been blue resembled two holes in a mask. He was wearing a black suit. His shoes were white and without any laces. 'Two metres seventy-three,' Peder whispered. 'That's not possible.' 'That's what it says,' I told him. Peder looked more closely. 'His face would have had to have been at least a metre in length. That's impossible. It's a con.' 'D'you think the entire medical congress in Copenhagen would make something like that up, huh?' Peder sighed. 'Almost three metres tall? No bloody way.' I got annoyed. 'D'you think my father would make it up?'

Peder looked at me, was about to say something, and didn't get that far. It was Vivian who spoke. 'There's something on the back, too,' she said. I turned it over. There was a stamp on it. It was Icelandic. It had been franked. Akureyri. 10.5.1945. We could just make out the date which appeared obliquely over the green Icelandic stamp. 10 May 1945. The card was to Dad. Arnold Nilsen. Finding him had been no easy task. First it had been sent to Sirkus Mundus, Stockholm, Sweden. That address had been scored out and a new one written underneath – Coch's Hostel, Oslo, Norway. And in my mind's eye I could see the postmen with this card for Dad, having to take it from Iceland to Sweden, from Sweden to Norway, to the abandoned room in Coch's Hostel in Bogstad Road. But they hadn't found him there either. He'd moved. And once again the card was sent on, north now, back to the scattering of islands he'd escaped from – Røst. But no one there knew where Arnold Nilsen was, and the card must have lain there for several years as a scandalous reminder of the prodigal son who'd slipped away one night and fallen as far as any man could fall – to the big top of the circus. But so it was he found the card himself when he journeyed there with Mum to have me christened. 'Read it,' Vivian whispered. The writing was pretty indistinct and the words had lots of mistakes in them, and the lines were cramped to make sufficient room. I read it aloud. *Dear Arnold, my good friend.* I looked at Peder and Vivian. 'That's my father,' I said. 'Arnold.' I had to begin again. My own voice was unrecognizable. *Dear Arnold, my good friend. I'm writing to you now to share the good news of the end of the war and the wretched Germans' defeat. Now you can hold your tail in the air for good! Are you still with the circus? I'm banking on that. I myself have returned to Iceland. And can you remember the one we always called the Chocolate Girl? Sadly she's dead now. She got an illness that she couldn't get over. She was a good person. She always spoke of you with great affection. I hope our paths will cross one day. I wish you all the very best in life, Arnold. With good wishes from the world's tallest man,*

Paturson. We were silent a long while. I could have cried. I'd already made up my mind. This card would never be seen by anyone else. I put it in the pocket of my toilet bag. Peder looked at me and nodded, as if he understood what had gone though my head and agreed. 'Now you've got your own letter,' he said.

I didn't sleep that night. I lay awake excited, listening to Peder's easy breathing and the wind in the apple trees, the sounds in the grass, the moon in the fiord. And if I listened carefully I could hear Vivian slowly turning in her bed in her room. There was no longer space for everything inside me. I was overflowing – I had to get up. I had to breathe out. I sat in the chair by the window and thought to myself that it *was* possible to be happy, that it wasn't all that difficult after all – it was just so unfamiliar, and happiness was a bewildering bouquet to hold in one's hands. We got up and lay once more on the rock ledge and slept there instead, while Peder's dad sat in the shade reading a stamp catalogue and his mother worked on with her painting. The sun was hot and heavy on our backs. And then I experienced something strange. I woke up sharply, dizzy and frightened, with one single thought in my head – *an accident happened*. It was just as if I could feel someone else's pain. And right at that moment I was stung by a wasp. It got me in the throat. I began swelling immediately. I screamed. Peder and Vivian got up. 'I'm dying!' I shrieked. 'I'm being strangled!' My voice left me as I rolled around. My head exploded. I was dying. And the last thing I saw was Peder who thought I was just kidding. I tried to say something but it was too late. Soon I'd be on the other side. I gave up. I was filled with a deep sense of peace, veering on unconsciousness. My soul was slipping away. *Goodbye, dear friends*. But then Vivian bent down over me and put her lips on my throat, as if to kiss me for the first, or the final, time. She was pretty rough with me. She bit. She sucked. She spat. She sucked some more, sucked the poison out of me and saved me, for the first, but not the last, time.

And so suddenly the holiday was over, with a wasp sting and a kiss. I travelled back to the city again with Vivian. Peder stood in the middle of the rope bridge waving until he could see us no longer. My suitcase was heavier than when I'd come. We sat outside in the seats at the back of the boat. Then I caught sight of something, in the channel between the island and the mainland. 'Look!' I shouted. Vivian turned. 'What?' she said. 'Can't you see?' 'What?' 'Peder's mum!' And I saw the wheelchair rushing over the water at top speed; the wheels spun through the waves and the gulls were a shrieking white swarm about her. Vivian leant against my shoulder, closed her eyes and said nothing.

It was Fred who was waiting for me at Quay B when *Prince* docked. I felt frightened, almost sick. Where was Mum? Why was Fred there? I hoped Vivian wouldn't see him. He was thin, exhausted. He had on a jumper that was way too big for him. Vivian had already seen him. But Fred couldn't be bothered looking in her direction. It was me he stared at and came over to. 'Bye,' said Vivian loudly. She let go of my hand and slowly walked over to where her dad was waiting for her in a taxi beside the shop. I followed her with my eyes. I hoped she wouldn't turn round. She turned and waved. I raised my hand. She hesitated a moment, then sat down in the back seat and the door was closed. 'Got yourself a girlfriend now?' Fred asked. I shook my head. 'Where's Mum?' 'Mum's with Boletta, Barnum.' 'Why?' 'Boletta fell on the stairs this morning. When she was coming home from the North Pole.' 'Was she all right?' 'No.' 'How not?' 'She thought she was in Italy, Barnum.' Fred took my case and we went up to Ullevål Hospital. There was Mum. She'd been crying a lot. There were streaks down her face, tunnels. And when she saw me she cried all the more. 'You're brown,' she murmured. 'Did you have a good time?' 'I was stung by a wasp,' I told her. Fred grew impatient. 'Has she come to yet?' he demanded. Mum shook her head and let go of me. A doctor appeared from Boletta's room. We went in. She was so small there in the bed. She had a bandage round her head and was attached to a piece of equipment on which various lights and lines lit up and flashed like some gigantic radio. We had to whisper. Boletta was completely blue and her eyes were enormous, but empty all the same. She could have been dead. She'd come back from the North Pole and hadn't managed the last steps. She'd toppled backwards and fractured her cranium before rolling all the way down to the ground floor. It was there that Mum had found her, lying in a pool of blood. That was what I'd sensed, just before the wasp stung me – Boletta falling. 'Boletta,' I whispered. Mum caught my hand. 'She can't hear you, Barnum.' The doctor came back in. He said something to Mum. She became nervous and upset. Can we feel one another's pain? Yes, we can. I'd felt it, I'd felt Boletta falling. Fred stood silent against the wall, staring at the floor. What had I felt when he was hit? Is pain infectious? How much of each other's pain can we stand? 'It isn't certain she'll waken again,' the doctor said, his voice low. I turned and pointed at him. 'I'll photobloodygraph you!' I shouted. Mum buried her face in her hands. Fred looked up. The doctor left once more. 'What are you saying, Barnum?' 'Boletta's going to wake up,' I told her.

She did. But it took seven days. Mum sat with her the entire time. Fred trained harder than ever. Bang the caretaker had to wash the blood from behind the mailboxes. 'Terrible,' he breathed. 'How is she?' 'Unconscious,' I said, and walked past him. 'Perhaps she was fortunate all the same,' he whispered. 'You fall a lot more gently when you're under the influence.' I thought about the skull, a dome of skin and hair protecting the brain, and that when an infant sleeps its head goes backwards, while the skull of an old person falls forwards, down. The child is dreaming up against heaven, while the old person's thoughts are dragged down towards the ground.

I hid the card from Paturson to Dad in a tear in the wall-paper behind the bureau. And one evening Fred said something; he was lying in bed, knackered after training. 'Perhaps it's a punishment,' he breathed. 'Punishment?' I repeated, my voice as low as his. 'Yes, after everything that's happened.' 'Boletta hasn't done anything wrong, has she?' Fred had changed. I almost didn't know him any more. He talked differently. Punishment? Maybe it was the boxing that had done it. 'Are you religious or some-thing?' I said, and laughed. Fred got up and came towards me. He bent over my head and the muscles bunched under his skin like cables, electric flexes, and his eyes were darker than ever. He breathed heavily through his nose. 'Have you shagged Vivian, Barnum?' 'No,' I whis-pered. 'Did she enjoy it?' 'But I haven't, Fred.' 'Certain?' 'Yes, I've never shagged anyone.' 'Thought that was why you'd become so rough, Barnum.' He lay down on his bed once more. He stayed like that, silent and sullen. 'Do you have a boxing match in September?' I asked him. He didn't say anything. I waited, but he gave no answer. Only his heavy breathing filled the room. 'D'you think Bolet-ta'll come too?' he asked. 'Yes,' I whispered. 'Yes.' And I could sense her thin and brittle eyelashes fluttering over my face.

She woke that same night. Mum was sitting with her. She told us that first a shudder passed though Boletta, a shaking, as if she was freezing cold. Her eyelids closed and Mum thought that this was her way of dying, shut-ting her eyes deep inside in a different sleep. But Mum didn't have time to call the doctor, she didn't have so much as time to cry – for Boletta changed her mind, her time wasn't up yet and there was still something she didn't want to miss out on. So instead of giving up the ghost for good she opened her eyes wide and turned to look at Mum. 'Has Fred boxed yet?' she asked. Mum was almost angry. 'It's still June,' she told her. 'Just stay unconscious a while longer if you want!' 'Wonderful. Then we'll both make the match.'

And it's Fred who takes over now. He's the one who pushes the days to one side; he's the one who impels this remarkable summer to its conclusion. Boletta has to rest for a month; she can no longer tolerate beer and starts using a stick, something she employs more frequently to lash out with than to support herself. Peder remains on Ildjernet. He sends a card from Drøbak which he's visiting with his Dad. He writes that he intends dreaming up a number that no one has heard of before. And how are my dreams going? With best wishes from the world's fattest man. Vivian travels to a hospital in Switzerland where there are still some doctors who think they can reconstruct her mother's face. And I stand by the window and watch Fred going out early each and every morning – rain or shine; in the fine, clammy fog that sometimes seeps into the city at this time of year, and which then dissolves and blends with the light. I see Fred coming home up Church Road, stepping out hard – on summer evenings that smell of exhaust fumes and sunlight. He pays no attention to Esther who waves to him. He pays attention to nothing. He doesn't speak. He saves his energy. He cuts away anything and everything that's unnecessary. More and more he becomes like a wild animal. Mum washes his kit and I get to hang it out in the yard – his shorts, thick stockings and singlet. The caretaker stands by the bins and turns the singlet. 'Hope he doesn't kill anyone,' he says. 'Or get killed himself.' But I'm not allowed to join Fred when he goes to the Central Boxing Club. He wants to be alone. He doesn't want to be disturbed. One morning Mum stands there beside me. It's raining. She smiles. Fred's walking quickly through the rain. He barely gets wet at all. He dodges the rain's punches. 'Are you proud of your brother?' Mum asks me. And I know why she's asking; it's because she's proud of him herself – perhaps for the very first time she feels proud of him. Afraid for him too, but mainly just proud. 'Yes, Mum,' I murmur. And he turns round out there in the rain but doesn't see us. 'I'm so happy,' she says all of a sudden, but then checks herself and all but groans, as if immediately feeling guilty as soon as she'd uttered the words for allowing herself to be happy at all, and she hugs me close. We can't see Fred any more. The rain's running down the window. 'It's nice that Peder writes to you,' she says softly. 'Oh, yes. Should send my best wishes, by the way.' Mum waits a moment. We can hear the sound of Boletta's stick. She's thumping the wall. 'What do you dream about, Barnum?' Mum asks, and the words come out in a torrent. I'm about to say that I dream she won't read the cards which are addressed to me. But instead I reply, 'That Fred wins his match.'

School began again. Things were much as always, but something was new nonetheless – the rumours about Fred. I don't know who carried those rumours round through the countryside, the holiday villages, the beaches, the parks and the swimming pools – perhaps the rumours had gathered of their own accord, raised aloft like dust in the dry, deserted city and whispered with the raindrops on everyone's ears. I was no longer Barnum the midget, I was Fred's brother; and Fred was no longer the silent wanderer, he'd become the boxer, the one who endured everything and whom no one could beat. Fred was no longer a threat, he'd become Fagerborg's lithe, white hope. A miracle had taken place in the course of the summer – a boxer was born – and if there was anything this city needed it was a real boxer. And the rumours about Fred were unstoppable and became true: he ran twenty miles a morning, he did ninety press-ups with just one hand, he boxed without gloves, no one dared even spar with him – two people were already lying in a coma. Some even made him out to be so nasty he'd beaten up his own grandmother and she'd ended up in Ullevål Hospital. He was going to be greater than Otto von Porat, greater than Ingo, greater than them all. And I denied nothing when I was interrogated; I just shrugged my shoulders. 'He's a champion already,' I told them.

Three days before the match Fred was sitting waiting in the bedroom when I came home from school. He sat on his bed with his hands in his lap, just staring at me. I grew uneasy. 'Aren't you training?' I asked him. Fred took a deep breath; his shoulders shuddered beneath his jumper. 'Yes. I'm resting.' He rested a while longer. I didn't want to disturb him any more. Fred was resting. Rest was training's glue. Without rest he'd fall apart. I tried to do my homework. It was a composition. But I couldn't concentrate. Fred didn't take his gaze away. I could feel it. I turned to look at him. He passed his hand over his brow. 'I'm being interviewed tomorrow,' he told me. I put down my pen. 'Are you?' 'By *Aftensposten*.' 'Crikey. *Aftenposten*?' 'Yes, crikey. But I don't want to be.' That was all he would say. His hands were fidgety. The knuckles of his right hand were blue. 'You don't want to be?' I repeated. 'No, I don't want to talk to anyone about it.' 'So why are you doing it then?' I asked him. 'Because Willy says so.' 'And that means you have to?' 'That means I have to. Willy's the trainer.' Fred's silent once more. 'Maybe there'll be a picture of you,' I murmured. 'In the sports pages.' 'I don't want to be photobloodygraphed,' Fred said slowly, and looked up. There was a ghost of a smile on his lips. 'Can't you come with me, Barnum?' he asked. I had to lean closer. 'What did you say, Fred?' He became irritated and got that dark look back in his eyes again. 'You heard what I said, midge brain!' I held my breath and hardly dared look at him. 'Of course. But why?' Fred got up and stretched against the door frame. 'You'll make sure I don't say something stupid.' Fred pulled out a sheet of paper from his back pocket, unfolded it and handed it to me. It was a list that Willy, his trainer, had written out for him. Written on this was everything Fred mustn't say to the journalist. It was quite a long list. 'Why can't Willy go with you?' I asked. 'Doesn't read the papers,' Fred answered.

The journalist would have preferred to do the interview at home, but Fred said no point-blank to that. So it was

decided we'd meet instead at Samson's in Majorstuen at
three o'clock the following afternoon. Mum got completely carried away. She suggested that she and Boletta
could sit at a table at the very back, just to be on the safe
side. At this point Fred threatened to withdraw from the
fight altogether and Mum had to throw in the towel. And
at three o'clock the following day Fred and I – the boxer
and his brother – went into the brown coffee shop in
Majorstuen which smelled of old coffee, cigarettes and
the damp furs of all the elderly ladies who sat waiting for
their own funerals. Fred was wearing a long raincoat over
his tracksuit. I'd finally chosen to put on a polo neck, a
windproof jacket, and cords, and I had an umbrella with
me. The journalist was there already. We realized who he
was long before he'd spotted us. Generally you didn't find
men over thirty like him at Samson's. He was slowly
smoking a cigar as he ate a piece of cake with a spoon. We
went over to his table. He put the cigar down on his plate.
The piece of cake was about to catch fire. He wiped his
hands on his napkin. It was Fred he was looking at. 'And
you're Fred Nilsen?' Fred nodded and kept on his feet.
The journalist extended his hand. 'And my name's Ditlev.
From *Aftenposten*. Good you could make it, Fred.' We sat
down. Ditlev ordered some mineral water and more cake.
He was pretty fat in the face; there was sweat on his brow
and he yawned. Two pens lay beside a notebook in
between the ashtray and the plate which were covered in
light brown crumbs and ash. The third of the pens was
sticking out of the breast pocket of his crumpled blue
jacket with its shining buttons. 'Really good you could
make it, Fred,' he said a second time. 'Who's this you
have with you?' 'Barnum. My brother.' Ditlev scribbled in
his notebook and turned in my direction. 'Good you could
make it too, Barnum. Where did you get your name?'
'From my father,' I told him. 'He was Barnum, too?' 'No,
he was Arnold.' Fred kicked me under the table. I didn't
say any more. The waitress came with cake and mineral
water. The journalist looked at him again. 'Well, we'd

thought of doing a feature on you, Fred. Before the match. Are we ready to go?' Fred didn't say anything. He looked as if he were bored, but that wasn't what it was – he just felt uncomfortable. 'Fire away,' I said. Ditlev took a draw of the cigar and breathed life into it. 'Are you dreading it?' he asked. 'Fred never dreads things,' I answered. Ditlev coughed. 'I'm talking to Fred now. Is that all right? Maybe I can talk to you afterwards.' 'I never dread things,' Fred repeated. Ditlev scribbled. 'So you're looking forward to it, in other words?' Fred shook his head. 'I never look forward to things.' Ditlev put down his cigar. 'How long have you actually been boxing?' Fred hesitated. I whispered something in his ear. 'All my life,' Fred said finally. 'All your life,' Ditlev repeated. 'That's good. You look like a real boxer all right. Even before your first fight.' Ditlev pointed at Fred's crooked nose with his cigar. Fred looked away. 'Is it true you run twenty miles each morning?' Ditlev asked. 'I never run,' Fred said. Ditlev looked up from his notebook. 'No? Why not?' 'Only slaves run.' Ditlev chuckled and the pen was busy once more. 'This is going to be good, Fred.' Ditlev had some more cake and swapped pens. We waited. Fred was keen to go. The elderly ladies were looking at us and I suddenly heard the complete silence that had fallen in Samson's coffee shop. 'You're welcome to take off your coat, Fred,' Ditlev told him. 'No,' Fred said. Ditlev smiled and kept writing. He wrote for some time. I tried to see what it was he was writing but his arm was in the way. He surely didn't need such a long time to record just two letters – *no*. I took another piece of cake and brushed his hand. Ditlev looked up. 'Who's been your inspiration?' he asked. Fred turned quickly to me. I whispered in his ear again. 'Bang the caretaker,' Fred said. Ditlev's hand stopped writing. 'Bang the caretaker? When was he boxing?' Fred smiled. 'He was a triple jumper.' Ditlev looked impatient for a moment but checked himself. 'The triple jump's fine,' he said, 'but I was thinking more of boxers. Otto von Porat, for example.' Fred sat there in silence for a time. 'Bob

Fitzsimmons,' he said at last. 'Bob Fitzsimmons? All right. And why him?' 'He never gave up,' Fred said. 'He always came back.' 'So you admire those who never give up, Fred?' 'No,' Fred said. Ditlev scratched his forehead with his pen. 'But you just said so.' 'I like Bob Fitzsimmons. D'you not listen, or what?' Ditlev swapped pens again and attempted a laugh. 'Is he always like this, Barnum?' 'Almost,' I answered. Fred kicked me in the leg again. Ditlev laughed and had a mouthful of coffee. Sweat dripped onto his notebook. The cigar went out. 'You're obviously a tough nut, Fred,' he said. Fred said nothing. Ditlev sweated and turned his page. 'What's your greatest strength?' 'Not saying,' Fred told him. Ditlev scribbled. 'So you won't let on either what your greatest weakness is?' 'Nope.' Now it was Ditlev's turn to go quiet. He thought for a long while about something or other. 'You've been a member of the Central Boxing Club since June,' Ditlev finally said. Fred nodded. Ditlev leaned across the table. 'Who d'you fight for? The club, your trainer or yourself?' 'For my brother,' Fred said. 'Barnum.' Ditlev looked at me. I think I went red. At least I felt all warm in my head. 'What's it like having a big brother like Fred?' Ditlev asked. 'Just great,' I breathed. Ditlev wrote this down in his notebook – *just great* – and turned to Fred once more. 'How are you going to beat Asle Braten?' Fred took a deep breath. 'Who?' 'Asle Braten. That's who you're fighting in a couple of days.' Fred twisted round on his seat. 'Hard,' he said. 'Hard?' 'Yes, I'll beat him hard.' Ditlev laughed quietly as he wrote this down. 'You can say it, Fred. Perhaps you can tell me a bit about yourself.' 'I have to go and have a piss,' Fred said. He got up, fetched the key from the counter, and went over to the toilet at the back of the coffee shop. All the elderly ladies in their damp furs followed him with their gaze. Ditlev sighed. Fred was away a long time. 'We can talk a bit in the meantime, you and I,' Ditlev said. He turned over to a fresh page in his notebook. 'Do you do any sport, Barnum?' 'No, not really.' Ditlev nodded. 'You could well be a cox, you know.' 'A cox?' 'The person who steers in rowing. They need little guys like you.' Now I no longer cared for Ditlev. 'I'll mention you to the guys in the rowing club. There aren't so many of your height here in the city.' There was still no sign of Fred. Ditlev moved closer and lowered his voice. 'Be honest now, Barnum. D'you reckon Fred'll win?' 'He'll decide it in the third,' I told him. Ditlev scribbled and shook his head. 'All right, whatever you say. Is it right that you're just half brothers, by the way?' It hurt so much when he put it like that, *just half brothers*, as if we were divided in the middle, split. I liked Ditlev still less now. 'Yes,' I breathed. 'Is there any-thing else you can tell me about Fred?' I thought hard. 'He was born in a taxi,' I said. And at that very moment I saw he was standing there. He was behind us and could have been there long enough, for Fred was noiseless, an Indian in a raincoat at Samson's; and it was only when he let out his breath through his nose in that tiny whine, that draught through his head, that we noticed he was there at all. Ditlev dropped his pen on the floor and turned round quickly. 'Hi, there, Fred,' he says. 'I think I've probably got what I need now. If there isn't anything else you'd like to add?' 'Don't put in any crap,' Fred told him. Ditlev laughed a bit too loudly. 'We don't put crap into *Aftenposten*, Fred. You're welcome to read through what I've written first.' 'Barnum can read through it.' Ditlev gave me his notebook. 'On you go, Barnum.' I glanced at what he'd written. But it didn't make any sense. It was just single words and abbreviations, capitals and exclamation marks. The word *taxi. All his life. Odd-balls. Barnum. Half. Fitzsimmons.* I put the pad down on the table and glanced at Fred. 'Looks fine to me,' I said. Ditlev got up. 'Let's go and find the photographer then!' He was waiting for us in Frogner Park beside Sinnataggen.* He had a huge camera round his neck. Ditlev slapped his shoulder. 'I'd like both boys to be in the picture, Tormod.'

---

* Famous sculpture of an angry child

The photographer, whose name was Tormod, looked at us with tired eyes. 'Both of them?' 'Yes, both. That's what I said.' 'I'd thought the white hope could do a bit of sparring with Sinnataggen.' 'Good thinking, Tormod. But the white hope can do some sparring with Barnum instead.' 'Barnum?' Ditlev pointed at me. 'Pretend he's Sinnataggen,' he said. And this is what the picture of Fred and myself is like; we're standing on the bridge in the rain and the photographer uses flash – it's like lightning, illuminating our faces in a strange and unnatural way. Fred has his arm round me and I don't even reach up to his shoulder; I'm smaller than ever or maybe it's just that Fred's taller, leaner and darker. He's raising the other hand in a clenched fist, and while Fred stares straight ahead without any hesitation and without blinking, with wide open eyes – I've shut my own as if the very second the picture's taken I've seen something I can't bear to look at. The picture was in the sports pages of the following day's edition of *Aftenposten*. Fred was training.

Mum read the opening sentence aloud: *The wild boxer – I was born in a taxi and have boxed my whole life, says Fred Nilsen, Oslo's new hope in the ring*. And beneath the picture of the two of us was written: *Barnum's betting on victory in the third round*. Mum groaned, gave the newspaper to Boletta, and turned to me. 'Did you tell them Fred was born in a taxi, Barnum?' I looked down. Boletta began to read aloud for us instead: *When we met Fred at Samson's coffee shop he had with him his half brother who bears the rather original name of Barnum. Fred says he's fighting for his little half brother. Barnum for his part dreams of becoming a cox.* 'That's not true!' I exclaimed. 'What's not true?' Boletta demanded. 'That I dream of becoming a cox!' Mum was close to tears. 'Soon the whole of Norway's going to know Fred was born in a taxi,' she murmured. 'Oh, there aren't that many who read the afternoon edition of *Aftenposten*,' Boletta assured her. 'But why have you shut your eyes in the picture, Barnum?' 'So my soul wouldn't disappear,' I said quietly.

I lay awake waiting for Fred when he came home on the last night before the fight. He lay down with his training things on. I could hear that he wasn't sleeping either. 'Are you mad?' I asked him. 'Mad? Why?' 'With what Ditlev wrote.' 'Haven't read it,' Fred said. 'Won't read it either. And you keep your mouth shut.' I waited a bit. There was a piping sound from Fred's nose. 'But the picture was pretty good,' I whispered.

It was sunny the day of Fred's fight. He left before breakfast. He didn't say a thing. Mum had an appointment at the hairdresser's. She wanted to look good for the match. I stayed off school and kept Boletta company; either that or she kept me company. I was edgy. We were uptight and nervous the whole lot of us. My hands were shaking. I stood by the window and suddenly saw that autumn had come. The city had a different colour. The leaves were falling from the Church Road trees. Everything was burning down. It was beautiful, but I didn't like it. I heard the sound of Boletta's stick behind me. She took my hand. 'You don't need to be frightened, Barnum.' 'I'm not frightened.' 'Good. Because it won't do Fred the least bit of good if we are.' I turned to face her. She'll soon be as small as me. 'D'you think he's frightened?' I asked her. She smiled and let go of my hand. 'Who knows what's going on in that boy's head? No, I think he's angry.' 'Angry with who, though?' Boletta had to sit down on the divan. 'Fred's angry with everyone,' she said. 'Us. Himself. He inherited the Old One's rage.' 'Perhaps it's a punishment,' I breathed. Boletta gave the floor a hard thump with her stick. 'A punishment! And who's to punish us, Barnum?' 'No, I don't know,' I admitted. Boletta sighed. 'Perhaps the punishment's being a human being, when everything's said and done.' She raked her dry fingers through my curls, even though she knew I disliked it. 'It's a good thing you don't have your brother's rage, Barnum.' And it was then Mum came home. She smiled, almost shyly. Boletta got up from the divan. 'Yes, yes, today we'll all do our best for Fred's sake. But normally I consider boxing to be ridiculous, uncivilized, revolting and tedious.' She went out to the bathroom. I looked at Mum. She clung to her handbag as if it were a railing in front of a cliff. 'You look nice,' I told her. 'Thank you, Barnum.' 'I'm sure Fred'll like it too,' I said. 'Your hairdo, I mean.' 'You haven't heard from him, have you?' I shook my head. 'No, he's got more than enough on his mind,' she sighed. And so we circled each other for the remainder of the day and had no idea how to make the time go a bit faster. Neither could we be bothered eating. The only thing we could do was wait. I cut out the interview from the afternoon edition of *Aftenposten* and hid it in the tear in the wallpaper along with Paturson's card. And I realized that of all times it's time spent waiting that's most difficult to pass. And it struck me as strange. Strange that I should want time to speed up, to go as fast as possible, even though I dreaded what it was I was waiting for. I just wanted it to be over. And I no longer knew which it was I dreaded most – the fight itself or the thought that Vivian would be there.

We got a taxi at six. When the driver heard we were going to the Central Boxing Club he glanced at me and grinned. I was sitting in the front. 'Are you the brother of the guy who's going to beat up the boxer from up north?' 'Yes,' I breathed. He thumped his palms against the steering wheel enthusiastically. 'Saw the piece in the paper. Born in a taxi too – he can beat up whoever he likes!' Even Mum had to smile. And with that he switched off the meter. He refused to take any payment. It was an honour to drive us. And we could tell Fred the boxer, Fagerborg's white hope, who'd been born in a taxi – that he could drive free any time he liked. We thanked him and got off in Stor Street. There was a queue already. We were let through. Someone patted me on the back. Then we were in, inside the Central Boxing Club. A young lad lay on all fours drying the floor of the ring. An older fellow in a black suit and with almost white hair was checking the ropes. He looked like a vicar. There were chairs arranged round the ring. There was complete silence. The hall was soundless; there were just slow movements and heavy smells. Mum grew anxious again. 'I want to see Fred,' she said. Everyone heard her. The old gentleman in black turned round abruptly, climbed out of the ring and came down to where we were. He greeted Mum. 'I'm the referee for this evening,' he said. 'Come with me.' We followed him to the changing rooms. We had to wait there while he went in. It took some time. He emerged once more with the trainer, Willy. Willy whispered something. We bent closer. And Dad's funeral came to mind, the chapel where everyone had whispered too, as if they were afraid to waken the dead, or that there would be a curse on anyone who dared speak loudly. 'Fred can't be disturbed,' Willy whispered. 'Is he all right?' Mum whispered back. Willy smiled. 'Oh, he's all right. He says hello.' But before Willy closed the door I caught a glimpse of Fred inside the changing room. He was lying on a bench between the lockers, under a shining white light. He was staring up into it. He was laughing. I couldn't hear his laughter. Then I wasn't able to see him any more. The referee took us back to the ring and we sat down in the front row, nearest Fred's corner. 'Aren't you going to keep some room for Peder and Vivian?' Mum whispered. I put her gloves down on the seats beside me. We waited. I saw that the ring wasn't a ring at all but rather a square, as if the boxers wouldn't have been able to stand being confined in a circle, so that instead they'd fitted it with sharp corners, corners to rest in – for who can find rest in a circle? People started coming. Ditlev and the photographer and Esther from the kiosk; Aslak, Preben and Hamster – everyone wanted to see Fred box, whether he won or lost. Not least Bang the caretaker came – he'd had his name in the paper, in the afternoon edition of *Aftenposten* – the triple jumper with the limp who'd never made it to the podium, the role model. *Me and Fitzsimmons*, he said to those on duty, and got in for free that night. The air was crackling; there was a fever in everyone, and Fred would box it out of us, cool us with his inexorable blows. Then Atle Braten's supporters came in and sat down closest to his corner. They'd travelled far enough, all the way from a place called Melhus. Suddenly there were shouts from behind. 'Smell the silage!' came the cry. It was Tenner and his gang. Tommy shouted loudest. 'Smell the silage!' Asle Braten's supporters got up. Perhaps they were his brothers. They weighed at least ninety kilos each and had red hair. Stillness fell behind me. And finally Peder and Vivian came in. It was twenty-five past seven. They slipped in between the seats and sat down. Vivian gave my hand a quick squeeze. Mum saw and smiled. Peder just shook his head. 'Welcome to the Colosseum,' he said. 'The gladiators are prepared.' Now we were ready. I was knackered already. The referee climbed into the ring. He'd taken off his jacket. The shirt underneath must once have been white. Now it was all but yellow, stained as if the sweat from every fight he'd refereed had steeped into the stiff fabric. The crowd applauded and stamped their feet. The seats were shaking. Peder leaned closer to me. 'The lions are hungry, Barnum.' The referee raised both arms and quiet fell over the place. First Talent was to fight a pale southpaw from Lørenskog. They ran along the edge of the ropes and poked each other. Some whistling began. Talent, who'd lost his nerve over the course of the summer, narrowly won on points. It was a victory that was forgotten already. 'But that went really nicely,' Mum breathed, and seemed relieved. 'They didn't have the guts to box each other,' Boletta said loudly and thumped her stick on the floor. Then Asle Bråten came out with his trainer; Asle Bråten, the Trondheim county champ, undefeated in his last nine fights. Everyone in his corner got to their feet and roared. Asle Bråten himself was broad and heavy. He almost came across as shy. He looked down when the photographer from the afternoon edition of *Aftenposten* took a picture, and sat down on his stool in the corner, resting his arms on the ropes. The trainer massaged his shoulders. Fred was to go three rounds with him; the first two of three minutes each and the final round of four – with a sixty-second time out between each round. Queensberry's Rules applied. The referee had total charge of things. He could add a minute round if things weren't conclusive after normal time. Now the referee was looking at his watch. But there was no sign of Fred. We waited. The referee spoke to Asle Bråten's trainer. Asle Bråten got up and began warming up. We looked over in the direction of the changing rooms. Time was dragging. I thought to myself, not without a certain feeling of relief – yes, relief and triumph, that Fred had just gone off. Because that would have been just like him to go out the back and leave us in the lurch, let Asle Bråten from Melhus win without so much as throwing a single punch – to make the afternoon edition of *Aftenposten*, the Central Boxing Club, Willy, Tenner, Tommy, the twins and myself all look really silly. Then the door opened after all. Fred came out from the changing rooms. He was shining. It was as if the bright light I'd seen in there had fastened itself to him. Willy followed, carrying a towel, a box and a sponge. We cheered. We shouted. Vivian clapped and couldn't keep still. Fred went calmly forward to the ring, slipped through the ropes, and just stared at Asle Bråten. The referee inspected their gloves. The referee spoke into a microphone. A loudspeaker crackled behind us. He announced their names. Fred raised his arms and stared at Asle Bråten. Asle Bråten raised his arms and stared at Fred. They were like two mirrors, reflecting each other's dread and strength, the sweat that quickly poured from their skin, mingling with their muscles to create a single quivering surface. The one who stares the longest has won. He who flinches has lost. The first weakness is to be found in the eyes. A rattlesnake entraps its prey with its eyes. Fred tried to paralyse Asle Bråten before the fight started. But Asle Bråten didn't crumble. He just bowed. Then it was underway. 'Hit him!' Boletta shouted. But it was Asle Bråten who got there first. The punch came slowly, unfolding from the shoulder. Fred danced away. Asle Bråten missed, but his hook caused the very air between the ropes to tremble. A sigh went through the crowd. No one, except for Asle Bråten's brothers, would allow anyone to get in the way of the glove on his right hand. It was said that he delivered just one punch in each fight. That tended to be sufficient. But not this time. Fred was too quick. Asle Bråten threw his second punch. Fred wasn't there. Fred hit him in the ear. Asle Bråten just gave his head a shake, as if a fly was bothering him a moment. And then the two of them calmed down. They'd seen each other. They butted each other a bit. They circled round, their guard high and their chins low. And so the first round was over and each went back to his respective corner. Willy said a whole lot to Fred we couldn't hear. The second round continued in similar fashion. They waited. They scowled. They jabbed. The cigarette smoke built up beneath the ceiling. It clouded over in the Central Boxing Club. Boletta grew impatient. 'I'm going if nothing happens soon!' she exclaimed. Mum tried to tell her to be quiet but Boletta wasn't going to be muzzled. 'I've seen better boxing than this at the North Pole!' Fred punched. It came suddenly; his arm found a gap in Asle Bråten's visor. Glove against brow, the head tilted backwards, and Asle Bråten was shaken. Fred punched a second time – a left hook – which started somewhere down in his Achilles' tendon and hit Asle Bråten's broad chin that was like a drawer full of teeth. But Asle Bråten threw himself bodily on Fred and shoved him against the ropes and they were one bundle of flesh, glued together in an embrace that was both rough and utterly unloving, until the referee had to separate them at last and the second round was over and it was Fred's. We roared. We were captivated. We were carried away. Peder got up on his seat. Vivian was standing. Even Mum applauded and Boletta shouted as she hammered with her stick. 'Well done, Fred! Get him, Fred!' And Willy dried his face with the damp sponge as if he were carefully wiping away words on a blackboard. Then the last round had begun. Asle Bråten was on the offensive from the start. He launched heavy punches at Fred – at his chest, his stomach, his shoulders – he wanted to tire him out, physically exhaust him. But the punches didn't get through – Fred was a shadow – and we just heard the hiss of the glove as it sliced right past his ear. Asle Bråten was exhausting himself and amid this fog, Asle Bråten's fog, Fred got in a punch, a quick combination. No one saw it, at least not Asle Bråten – we only saw the result. His knees buckled, his body went to the floor in a thunder, and the referee bent down and began counting, his fingers spread wide, one number after the next. The silence after each – one, two, three, four – Fred went over towards his corner and Willy closed his eyes. Five, six – the referee counted – the only numbers there were in the world, and at eight Asle Bråten, the champion from Melhus, got to his feet. He stood up slowly, wobbled, but kept upright. The referee took a closer look at his eyes, exchanged some words with the trainer, and re-started the fight. There was quiet. Just thirty seconds remained. It was only a case of Fred keeping on his feet, keeping away from Asle Bråten, keeping going – because he'd won, he was half a minute from victory. And then I notice that Fred lets his arms drop – as if he's utterly exhausted or simply can't take any more – he lowers his guard, he leaves himself exposed. He stands there naked – for not more than a moment, but that's sufficient. Asle Bråten sees it too, but he hesitates as if he's equally surprised, finds it difficult to believe that Fred has lowered his gloves and is giving him an open road. His thoughts are slower than his body and Fred takes a step forwards, naked, exposed – and a gasp goes through the hall. Then Asle Bråten punches. It's a mighty, wild punch to the face and it sends up a cloud of sweat round Fred's head – a wet, shining powder like a shining halo. Fred is shaken but keeps his feet. Asle Bråten punches again. He hits equally hard, Fred's jaw this time, and there's a grating sound of something breaking. Mum buries her face in her hands and moans. Boletta cries out but has no voice. Vivian holds my hand. Peder just turns to look at me, sorrowful. And as for me I can't feel the pain now; I try to, but I'm outside Fred's pain. It isn't mine; he's alone right inside this pain, and all I can feel is shame, and I feel deeply ashamed of this shame. Fred sinks to his knees. The blood drips from his mouth and runs from his eyes. Willy leans against the ropes. The referee stops the fight. Asle Bråten's won. The referee raises his arms aloft. But it's no triumph. The defeat is greater than the victory. The defeat puts the victory in the shadows. And so I was right after all. Fred decided the fight in the third and final round.

Mum and Boletta went with Fred to the hospital where they fitted his nose and jaw back together. He was in such a bad state that he even got out of military service, though I don't know if it was just because of that. At any rate they didn't need a dyslexic, dizzy individual with tinnitus who roamed the streets, was poorly sighted in his left eye, had headaches and whose behaviour was unpredictable – they didn't need him in the Norwegian services. I went with Peder and Vivian. We walked slowly through the unfamiliar streets, but for one reason or another weren't scared; we'd been at the Central Boxing Club and it couldn't get any worse than that – we were invulnerable. 'Now I know where the impossible number is,' Peder said. 'Where?' 'Between nine and ten.' We managed to catch a tram at Stortorget and sat right at the back. The yellow light made our faces pale. The dark outside became a black flood that ran in the opposite direction, back into the hollow of the city. We jumped off at Frogner Place. We stood there for a bit and didn't quite know what to do with ourselves. 'I feel sorry for him,' Vivian whispered. Peder looked away. 'Who?' I asked. 'Fred, of course.'

He didn't come home until the following day. He came quietly. I hadn't heard him. And it was then I caught him unawares in front of the mirror in Mum's room. I was on my way out and stopped, held my breath; I didn't want to see him like this, but what had been seen had been seen. He leaned against the mirror, against his own lop-sided reflection; he grimaced and preened himself. And I thought perhaps he was searching for his own face (or else that's what I think now), that perhaps he could see all the masks in there, inside the dull glass, a long gallery that ended with his own real face. All of a sudden Fred laughed, pressed his lips against the mirror and licked. I didn't want to see. But I already had. It was too late. 'Why did you lose?' I asked. Fred turned round, for a moment embarrassed and furious. 'D'you hear that, Barnum?' he said. 'What?' He breathed deeply a couple of times and smiled. 'My nose. It's all right again.' He sat down on Mum's bed, leaned backwards. It still smelled of Malaga there. The air was heavy and sweet. I wanted to feel drunk. 'Why did you lose, Fred?' He got up again, surprised and almost sad. 'Lost? I won, Barnum. Don't you get anything?'

Many years would elapse before I developed the pictures from this summer, the summer I called my first. I had put off doing it. I couldn't forget Peder's mother, hiding her face and turning away her wheelchair, enraged and afraid of losing her wretched soul. I had promised not to develop those pictures. But there came a time when the dreams slipped away as soon as I tried to put them on paper; they dissolved into dust and disappeared. I needed instead some kind of handle; something to hold on to, to see before me – something from which to create. For that reason I took with me the old film that had lain undisturbed in my drawer all that time, down to the shop in Bogstad Road. I thought that maybe I could link all those memories into a story from which I could make a script. A week later I went to fetch the envelope of pictures. I went to Gamle Major and opened it there. The first picture had been taken by Mum in the May days of 1945; the Old One and Boletta are standing out on the balcony in Church Road and they're looking at the one taking their picture in astonishment, almost in fear. Boletta's about to say something and the Old One's fingers are spread out – perhaps she's afraid of losing her soul too at that moment. And the rest of the pictures belong to another time, as if a whole life has been missed out. Peder lying on the double bed in the summer house on Ildjernet, his upper body bare, one eye shut and his hand between his legs; and a shadow divides the room and the picture obliquely. It's my shadow. Vivian and I are sitting on the bed, the suitcase between us; Vivian bending towards me to kiss my thin shoulder. I don't remember Peder taking it. I don't remember the kiss, her touch. Peder's mother's swinging the wheelchair round, but it isn't the camera she's afraid of, she's just blinded by the sun – that's how I see it – the light that's falling full and sharp over the fiord in my first summer. And in the background, by the corner of the veranda, Peder's father's standing, half-hidden, as if he's been caught just as he's taking a step forwards, or backwards – he's the one who's putting the curse on her. I have another beer. It's started to rain. People come in and drape their ugly garments over the backs of their chairs and order half-bottles of red wine. The last picture's of Fred. It's not me who took it. He must have taken it himself, up in the drying loft, for I can just make out the attic window and the lines with their pegs. He must have held the camera in his extended arm and taken the picture that way. His face is almost unrecognizable, all twisted. His mouth is open and he's saying something, he's trying to talk. He's speaking to me, he's shouting from the drying loft, down through time – and I hear nothing, I can't hear him.

Hunger

One evening, Peder phoned and was pretty worked up. I was the one to get to the phone before anyone else reached it – actually I was the only one in the house. To say that Peder was worked up isn't exactly an exaggeration. It sounded as if he were on another planet screeching through a foghorn. 'Meet me under the tree!' he shouted. I held the receiver at arm's length so as not to suffer permanent deafness. Peder screamed even louder from out there in the universe. 'Are you there, Barnum?' I held the receiver as normal again. 'Yes, yes. What's up?' 'Wait and see!' 'Oh, come on! What's up?' Peder became impatient. 'Are you coming or are you not coming, you tiny toadstool?' 'I'm coming!' I roared. And I went. I slammed down the receiver, grabbed my jacket, chased down the kitchen stairs and all but knocked over Mum who was on her way up with the empty rubbish basket. And I was on the point of setting a personal record, because when Peder called me a tiny toadstool it was serious, then there was no excuse. Had he just called me a toad then I could have dawdled; if he'd said sandal then I'd perhaps have stayed at home, and if he'd only called me a mitten I wouldn't have bothered answering at all. But tiny toadstool, that was beyond being serious – at the very least it meant a forest fire in Frogner Park. 'Haven't time!' I called to Boletta who was eighteen steps behind Mum, before either of them managed to say a word. I ran out across the yard, ducked under the drying lines, trampled over the caretaker's withered flowers and went on down Jacob Aall Street. I got no further than Vestkanttorget because somebody called my name, and it was Fred calling me; Fred whom nobody had seen for five days. I wished it wasn't him, that I'd gone a different way. Slowly I went over to him. He was sitting on the only bench left there. It was already October and there were almost no benches in the city left to sit on except for this one. He didn't look good. He had begun to look like himself again after the Asle Bråten fight – he was just even thinner, his muscles were somehow thinned out as if they'd lain a long time in water and had been hung up afterwards to dry in the sun. He was smoking a cigarette and dropped it on the gravel between his crooked toes. 'Sit down, Barnum,' Fred said. I sat down. Now Peder would be waiting. Perhaps he wouldn't bother waiting any longer. 'Where've you been?' I asked. 'Why d'you ask that?' 'Just did.' 'Is Mum annoyed?' 'Don't think so.' 'Sure?' 'She hasn't said anything at any rate.' Fred lit a cigarette end and had a drag of it. 'Maybe I've been at Willy's,' he said. 'The trainer? Are you going to box again?' Fred shook his head. 'Willy's given up as a trainer.' 'Has he?' Fred looked at me. 'In a hurry, Barnum?' 'I'm meeting Peder,' I murmured. Fred shrugged his shoulders. 'On you go then.' I stayed where I was. 'What have you been doing at Willy's, Fred?' 'Haven't you arranged to meet Peder, huh?' 'Yes, shortly.' 'Is Vivian coming too?' I didn't like him saying her name. I suddenly wanted to call her something different. I could call her Lauren. I made up my mind that that was what she was called. Lauren. Lauren and Barnum. It had a ring to it – made us sound like a famous couple – and it meant Fred could use the name Vivian as much as he liked because he'd have no idea I called her Lauren instead. 'Don't know,' I muttered. I got up and remained on my feet. 'What are you and your best friend off to do then, Barnum?' 'Don't know,' I said a second time. 'Don't you know that either? Something you won't tell me, Barnum?' 'I don't know, Fred. I swear.' 'You swear, now that's good.' 'I'd better be off, Fred.' 'Turn round,' he said. I closed my eyes and turned round. 'What is it?' I asked him. 'Just wanted to see if you had your fingers crossed. ''Cos then it wouldn't count.' 'What wouldn't, Fred?' 'Your promise, Barnum. Say hi to Peder.' 'Sure,' I told him. 'I'll do that.' Fred smiled. 'And say hi to

Vivian from me. If she comes too.' I began walking over the square towards the street lights; more than anything I wanted to run, but I didn't dare. Fred suddenly got up. 'Don't do anything you'll regret,' he called. I stopped for a second. 'What d'you mean?' Fred smiled. 'What do I mean? You know fine.' 'No, Fred, I don't.' Fred sat down again, as if all of a sudden he was frightfully bored and couldn't be bothered so much as opening his mouth to talk to me any more. 'Then you'll find out yourself, Barnum.' I didn't run before I'd got as far as the fountain – turned off now since it was autumn and the frost could come at any time. I ran all the way to Solli Square and there was Peder standing under our tree in the Hydro Park, unable to keep still. I stopped, completely out of breath, and it was Peder who ran the last part of the way through the huge leaves coming in clouds from the branches. 'You're bloody late!' 'Came as fast as I could!' 'As fast as you could? Could have been faster!' We gave each other a long bear hug. We were up to our knees in leaves – blood-red and wet flakes that were never still – a sea of leaves. 'But what is it?' I demanded. 'They're filming in Solli Street, damn it!' 'Now?' 'Yes! They're filming right at this moment! D'you think I'm kidding, or what?' No, I didn't think Peder Miil was kidding; he could do a fair amount of that, he kidded about almost everything – but he wasn't kidding about this, that they were filming in Solli Street on an ordinary evening in October. 'But where's Vivian?' I asked him. Peder looked at his watch and his brow was drenched in sweat. 'She's about as late as you,' he moaned. We waited a bit longer. But Vivian didn't appear. Perhaps she hadn't been allowed out. Perhaps she'd got sick in the interim. Had to be something. There had to be some reason for her not coming, and I was struck by a savage thought; it came like a blow but because I didn't think it to completion, it slipped away. We couldn't wait any longer. We went down to Solli Street. They were there. Peder hadn't been kidding. Something was being filmed. It was another world. And we went slowly into it. The tarmac was covered in earth. The red pillar box had been removed. The cars that were usually parked there had been taken away. Beside the doorway to Number 2, a constable was standing in old-fashioned dress with a flat cap and enormous shining buttons. He raised his hand in salute to a coachman trundling past with his horse-drawn cab. Even the curtains in the ground-floor windows had been changed, and for some reason or another it was this that made the greatest impression on me. Perhaps they'd refurbished the flats that lay behind the curtains too: re-papered the walls, brought in different chairs and sofas, exchanged the books on the shelves, hung paintings on the walls, pulled out the showers, hidden washing machines and fridges, and sent the people who really lived there off to the country. Because I had this strange thought that not even I could quite understand or ever explain to anyone – how far do you have to go to suspend the disbelief of those who will see this film one day? How much has to be covered? How far is it necessary to go behind the façades, the buildings, the people and their lives to make us believe that all of this is true? And I could hear Dad's laughter and his voice – *It's not what you see that matters most, but rather what you think you see*. I took Peder's hand. 'Look,' I whispered. 'The curtains have been changed!' But then something happened down at the bottom of the street. We were blinded by a powerful light and a man with a megaphone rose from the shadows. 'Get those idiots out of the way!' he shouted. The constable came running and chased us almost right up to Solli Square again, and we crouched there behind a rubbish bin. 'Bloody hell,' Peder breathed. 'Yeah, bloody hell. That was close.' The constable hurried back to his doorway and took up position there. We edged forwards and now things started happening. A lady with a fur coat and hat appeared and began walking down the pavement. A camera followed, right behind her. Our backs were cold. This wasn't a film. This was real. We were on the inside, in a double reality. She came towards us, she and the cameraman, and it looked as if she were freezing herself; she had her hands buried in a thick muff on her middle. And she kept turning round the whole time as if she were frightened someone was following her, someone she was scared of. Maybe she was going home alone and someone was going to assault her – but it was just the cameraman who was there and he posed no threat. And so she stopped outside the entrance where the constable was standing doffing his cap; she hesitated for a moment, her face completely white, and she had to turn once more before disappearing into the darkness. The director got up from a chair and applauded. The lady in the fur coat reappeared from the entryway, smiling now, and was given a peck on the cheek by the director as, with a quivering sound, the lights dimmed. 'Lauren Bacall's better,' Peder whispered. When he said that I missed Vivian and I'm sure Peder missed her too. She should have been here. We should have been seeing this together. 'What sort of film d'you think it is?' I hissed. 'An over-40,' Peder replied. And we kept crouching there behind that stinking bin. It smelled of summers past. Time went by. A dog trotted past with something in its mouth. Perhaps they were done filming. The constable lit a cigarette. We waited. Everyone waited. That was the way it was. This was a time for waiting. The director sat in his chair and slowly leafed through a thick bundle of sheets. And suddenly there came a gust of wind, the sort that can come up Munkedam's Road from the bottom of town, like a puff of storm though the streets. A single sheet of paper was blown from the director's lap; it flew over a fence and I got up. Peder tried to hold me back but I chased after it; I got hold of it and as I ran back equally fast to the director (who'd got up and seemed pretty mad), I managed to read what was at the top of the page. And I remember it; I remember it as if it were yesterday, as if it were today or right this minute – because this was the first script I ever held in my hands: Page 48, *EXT. AFTERNOON. STREET*

IV. A few pedestrians and a cab. PONTUS sees a little dog running home in the gutter with a bone in its mouth. These were the words which would become film: Pontus, a dog, the gutter. They would be lifted from that sheet, torn loose from the paper to become movements, pictures and sound. And it was as I read those ordinary words in that ordinary sentence, so low-key and yet of such power, that I decided, there and then I made a decision without thinking – I just made it and knew it was right – that I would write down my dreams. And I could sense a deep and lasting joy over having made that decision. I gave Page 48 to the director and bowed. He tore it out of my hands. 'There you are,' I said. He didn't so much as say thanks. He just waved me away. I ran back to Peder behind the litterbin. And now things started happening again. A tall, thin man in worn clothes and with round glasses and a gaunt, unshaven face went walking down the same street. But now the camera was in front; he was walking towards it, and suddenly he halted and polished his glasses, and it looked as if he was talking and arguing with himself. 'That must be Pontus,' I whispered. 'Who?' 'Pontus. It was in the script.' And the one who had to be Pontus kept walking, coming closer and closer to the camera – it was as if he'd thought of assaulting it. Then the director clapped his hands, shouted something, and the thin man, Pontus, had to do it all again – walk towards the camera, stop, polish his spectacles, talk to himself –and I couldn't notice any difference, but he had to do it twice before the director was satisfied. Then the lights were dimmed for good, the equipment was packed away and they all drove off in a van. Peder and I got up. People appeared at their windows. A caretaker began sweeping the earth off the cobbles. The pillar box was brought out again. The horses went up towards the Palace. Everything was put back and slowly but surely the street returned to normal. It had almost been like a dream. We walked along Bygdøy Alley and I couldn't wait to tell Peder that my life had taken a sudden and unexpected course when I stood there with Page 48 in my hands and read those tranquil words concerning Pontus and the dog, written in Danish. But I said nothing at that point to Peder – not yet – because I first wanted to go home and write something I could show him. 'Wonder what happened to Vivian,' I said. We stopped outside her stairs and looked up at her window. It was dark. Peder chucked a conker and hit the glass. But it wasn't Vivian who gave the curtains a twitch, it was her mother; she glanced down at us for a second before retreating once more. Peder looked at me and shuddered. 'Glad my Mum's just in a wheelchair,' he said. And at that moment Vivian appeared; she was approaching from the other side of the church and we ran towards her. 'Where were you?' Peder exclaimed. 'Just went for a walk,' she said. 'Then I had to help my mother.' 'Help your mother?' Vivian shrugged her shoulders. 'I usually read to her. When she can't get to sleep.' Peder didn't say any more. 'Bloody hell, just think what you've been missing then!' Vivian looked at me but not for any length of time; she looked down instead and suddenly came across as unhappy and fearful – but who wouldn't have been, with a mother who had no face you had to read to. 'No, what?' she asked. 'They were making a film in Solli Street! With a camera and floodlights and everything!' 'I know,' Vivian said. 'Know? You know?' 'Yes, it was in the paper. It's called *Hunger*.' '*Hunger*? Not a bad title.' 'It's actually a book by Knut Hamsun. That's what I'm reading to Mum.' Vivian went over to the stairs. She turned. 'They'll most likely be filming tomorrow too. Can't we try to catch up with them, then?' We nodded. Of course we'd find them. That couldn't be so difficult, to find a film being made in a city like ours. Vivian laughed and began to be more like herself, as if she'd been in a film too and had at last taken off her costume. 'We can meet at twelve,' she said. 'If you two have the nerve to skip school.'

Peder was equally silent on the way home, and I was too, because I had my own thoughts going through my head – I was going to write – and the thought was of such immensity that there was barely room for anything else. But when we went our separate ways Peder said something after all. 'I think we really have to look after Vivian,' he said. 'We always look after Vivian,' I retorted. All at once Peder gave me a hug. 'Good-night then, Barnum. Tomorrow we're going to bloody well bunk off school.' And I walked the last part of the way alone up Church Road. It was a strange evening. I stopped at Marienlyst and looked about me. All this was mine. This was my world. The streets I walked in, the wood behind the town, the skies above the roofs. This was what I'd write about. It was here my characters would live – Esther from the kiosk, the Old One, Fred, Mum, Peder and Vivian, Dad (even though he was dead) – every one of them would have their place here, both the living and the dead. Then Fred appeared. He came across the grass, walked right through the little city where once upon a time we learned the Green Cross Code – through the small streets, the small pedestrian precincts no larger than the lines on the tarmac, over the pavements and between the tiny houses which were supposed to resemble real ones. And when I saw him walking like this an idea came to me, my very first idea. Fred stopped in front of me. 'You look a bit sad, Barnum.' 'I was just thinking,' I told him. 'Thinking? About what? Something sad?' I had to tell him. 'I was thinking about everything I'm going to write.' Fred bent closer. 'Write?' 'I've made up my mind, Fred. I'm going to write.' 'Write what?' 'Film scripts,' I told him. Fred looked in the opposite direction, as if he were afraid someone was following him. But we were the only ones at Marienlyst that evening. 'I'm tired,' he said, and laid his hand on my shoulder, and we walked like that the rest of the way home. Mum came rampaging out of the living room when she saw that Fred had finally appeared, but he just went on into the bedroom without so much as saying good-morning. 'Where have you been?' she demanded. 'Just went for a walk,' Fred said, and banged the door behind him. 'For five days!' she shouted after him and

then looked at me instead. 'Just went for a walk,' I
repeated. And Mum smiled nevertheless; she was glad
Fred had come home, despite the fact it had taken five
days. And that was what we'd go on saying, time after
time, when he began disappearing and finally had vanished for so long that he was declared dead – *Fred's just
gone for a walk.* And it came to me that it was Vivian who'd
first spoken the words earlier that evening, she'd said
she'd just gone for a walk. 'Shall I make you some
supper?' Mum asked, and then I realized she really was in
a good mood. 'No, thanks,' I said, 'but do you know if we
have a book called *Hunger*?' Her smile became one of
wonderment, and she turned towards Boletta who'd
already got up from the divan and was making her way
slowly towards us. 'Unfortunately, we burned that particular novel,' Boletta said. 'Burned?' 'The author was a
troublemaker during the war, Barnum. His books were no
longer fit for our shelves. So we dumped his collected
works right here in the stove.' Boletta had to support herself against my shoulder. Soon we'd be as small as each
other. She gave a deep sigh. 'But now I regret having done
it. Even troublemakers can be good writers.'

I thought about that when I went to bed, and it served
to strengthen my resolve. *Even troublemakers can be good
writers.* Then I could manage it too – I, Barnum, the height
of my own pen. I got up again, sat down at the table,
switched on the lamp, got out a pen and pad and wrote:
*A boy is walking slowly down a street. He's bigger than the
houses. He's taller than the traffic lights. He stops at a corner.
He's all alone.* That was as far as I got because I'd forgotten that Fred was there. 'What are you calling the thing
you're writing?' he asked me. '*The Little City*,' I told him.
'Fine title, Barnum.' I was so happy. I put out the lamp.
'Won't you write any more?' 'I'll wait until tomorrow.'
'But why?' 'I don't know how it's going to continue.'
'You're the only one who can know that,' Fred said. I
curled under the quilt. It was a long time since we'd
talked together like this. I'd keep this conversation safe.

I closed my eyes. I'd smile myself slowly to sleep. Then I heard Fred coming and sitting down on my bed. He could ruin everything now. But he didn't. What he said made our conversation all the more significant, and I knew I'd never forget it. I grew afraid all the same. 'I've been doing some thinking myself,' he said, his voice low. 'Thinking about what?' He was silent a good while. 'That I'm going to find the letter the late Arnold Nilsen sold.' That was how he expressed it – the late Arnold Nilsen. I opened my eyes. Fred leaned right over me, very close to my face. 'Don't tell anyone, Barnum.' 'No,' I said. 'Don't tell a soul.' I held up my hands so he could see my fingers. He gave a laugh, got up and stood there looking down at my pad which was just visible in the golden glow of the street light that shone in through the curtains in a narrow, shimmering beam. And he began to read aloud; he read carefully and clearly. *'A boy is walking slowly down a street. He's bigger than the houses. He's taller than the traffic lights. He stops at a corner. He's all alone.'* Fred read the first thing I'd written without making a single mistake – not one syllable did he get wrong. I didn't dare say anything. I might begin to cry. That mustn't happen. Whatever happened it mustn't be that. Fred closed my notebook and lay down once more. We lay there in the dark with a line of chalk on the floor between us. 'He's all alone,' he breathed.

Fred was sleeping when I got up the following morning, or at least he appeared to be. Mum padded round the flat, her voice low, hushing us at the slightest noise lest Fred be wakened. I didn't go to school. I went to Sten Park and sat up at the top of Blåsen. I got out my notebook, pen and packed lunch and hid my schoolbag under a bush. It was a fine day. The air was clear and cool, but not cold. It was as if everything was brought closer – Ekeberg Hill on the far side, the grey buildings, the church towers. The city became smaller and smaller. I started writing. *He is all alone. The light changes. But there are no cars there. He goes over the pedestrian crossing. The yellow lines are smaller*

*than his shoes. He goes into a shop and has to stoop right down
to get in. It's a flower shop. He's all alone there, too. He calls out,
'Is there anyone here?' But no one answers. He starts picking
flowers from vases and they stick up just over his fingers. He
leaves some money on the counter and goes out. And in the same
moment he leaves, all hunched up, he's blinded by a dazzling
light and has to shield his eyes. A voice shouts out, 'You're under
arrest!'* I felt hungry after all this and had a slice of bread
with sausage and cheese, and as I sat up there like this on
Blåsen, on a hilltop of dead horses, right in the middle of
my story, I noticed something happening over on St Hans
Hill, the other point of elevation in the vicinity, and soon
enough I saw what it was. It was the group making the
film. They were back in business. Here I was sitting writing and there they were making the film, each of us atop
our respective hills. I packed up my stuff, climbed down
the steep path and ran over in their direction. By the time
I got there they'd already stopped for a break. I recognized Pontus. He was sitting on a bench, resting against
his shiny trouser knees, agitatedly smoking a cigarette.
He looked just as knackered as he had the day before. The
director sat in his own chair eating sandwiches while he
leafed through the script. The same constable was in evidence too. Surely walking there wouldn't be banned? I
went along the path through the trees and lessened my
pace when I got close to Pontus. He glanced up and drew
a thin finger behind his glasses to scratch his eye. All at
once he threw away his cigarette and said something.
'Would you be so gracious as to tell me what time it is?' I
halted, quite taken aback, and just managed to roll up the
sleeve of my jacket. 'It's ten o'clock,' I said. Pontus shook
his head. 'No, it is not! It's two!' I had to take a second
look. My watch said ten. 'It's ten o'clock,' I repeated.
Pontus got up and became quite infuriated. 'You are
completely mistaken. It is two o'clock. Correct your
watch accordingly, my good man!' I heard the sound of
laughter from up by the camera. 'Would you like a
sausage sandwich, Pontus?' I asked him. Pontus was

momentarily staggered, taken off guard – you could have knocked him over with a feather. He sat down once more. 'And what's your name?' he asked. 'Barnum,' I replied. He nodded and didn't take his eyes off me. 'Pontus and Barnum. Sounds like an old pair from the silent films. Is your name really Barnum?' 'Yes, I was christened Barnum by the vicar on Røst.' 'But I'm afraid I'm not actually called Pontus. My name's Per Oscarsson.' He stretched out his hand. I took it. It was more or less like shaking a bunch of bones. 'Thank you, Barnum. I'd love to have a sausage sandwich. But I'm afraid it's not possible. I'm playing a hungry madman in this film, so that means I have to be hungry.' 'I see that,' I said. He let go of my hand and pointed down at his shoes. They were equally thin. 'I've walked bare-legged from Stockholm to Oslo,' he said. 'Do you know how many miles that is?' I shook my head. 'Nor do I. But it's a lot.' Pontus leaned back on the bench. 'I'm hungry,' he sighed. 'I barely know where I am.' 'You're on St Hans Hill in Oslo,' I told him. Pontus nodded slowly. 'Thank you, Barnum. That means we're off to Palace Park later today.' He gave a deep sigh. 'Next time I want to play a fat king.' A lady in expansive trousers came down to where we were. She had with her a case containing various tubes and something that resembled a shaving-brush. 'The maestro's waiting,' she hissed. Then she began bringing out Pontus' features – she darkened his stubble, made his hair thinner and his eyes even wilder-looking than they already were. While she was doing this the maestro got up and shouted, 'Would all intruders leave the set at once!' The maestro was the director. Intruders meant me. 'What's the time?' I asked quickly. Pontus took out his pocket watch, smiled, and with great ceremony opened it. There was nothing inside at all – it was like a silver shell with the flesh scraped out. Pontus smiled. 'The time is precisely five minutes to twelve.'

I ran down to Solli Square, but at the last corner I slowed down and sauntered the final bit of the way. Peder and Vivian were under the tree already. I was in good time. I snatched up a couple of leaves and studied their fine patterning; veins on a green sheet. Peder and Vivian came over. 'Barnum's in plenty of time today,' Peder exclaimed. I dropped the leaves carefully down onto the ground again. 'They're in Palace Park,' I announced. 'And how d'you know that?' I shrugged my shoulders. 'I was talking to Pontus.' Vivian put her head on one side. She tended to do that when there was something she didn't get, as if somehow that would help, having her head at an angle. The corner of her eyes were red; thin sores she'd tried to brush away. Perhaps she hadn't slept the night before? Perhaps she'd sat up reading the rest of the novel to her mother? 'Pontus?' she asked quietly. 'The main character in the film. I met him on St Hans Hill.' Peder took a step closer. 'D'you mean it?' 'Of course I do!' Peder began whirling his arms. 'So what was he like then?' I thought about it a long while. Peder was bursting with curiosity. 'Pontus was hungry,' I said. Together we went down to Palace Park. Nothing was happening there. Only King Olav was at home. Perhaps he'd been told to keep away from the windows. I couldn't get these thoughts out of my head. *What does it take for us to believe in the things we see? Did Pontus speak Swedish because we were still part of Sweden? How much can we really see? And if a plane crossed the city, would everything have to be done from scratch? This was my thought – how much do you have to lie before someone believes it's actually the truth?* 'I'm hungry, too,' Peder said. Slowly he started down towards the kiosk by the National Theatre. He'd grown fatter again in the wake of the summer. We could hear his laboured breathing all the way to where we were standing. There was a faint smile on Vivian's lips and she was about to say something, but then didn't in the end. We sat down in the leaves behind the largest of the trees so the guardsmen wouldn't see us. Vivian was silent. When I looked at her for any length of time she almost became transparent, as if her skin was water I could have leaned right into. I suddenly remembered what she'd said, that she'd been born in an accident. 'What is it?' she asked. 'Nothing,' I whispered. I wanted to move closer to her but she leaned away and instead brought out a book from her shoulder bag. She then gave it to me. The book was *Hunger* by Knut Hamsun, the troublemaker. 'You can have it,' Vivian said. 'Have you finished it?' She nodded. 'Many thanks,' I said. I leafed through it a bit. I didn't find Pontus anywhere. 'How does it end?' I asked her. 'The main character leaves town,' Vivian told me. 'Does he come back?' Vivian looked down. 'That I can't tell you. It's not mentioned.' 'It sounds like a pretty sad ending,' I said. Vivian looked at me again. 'You think so?' But I couldn't say any more because at that moment Peder was coming back and had bought enough food for a fortnight – he had half the Freia chocolate factory with him and hadn't forgotten to get himself real gingerbread and peppermint drops (Vivian's absolute favourite, even though her slender figure was none the worse for them). 'The probability of one of two events occurring is equal to the sum total of each of the events' probability,' Peder said, and let three packets of chocolate twirls tumble into the leaves. 'In other words, are we going to choose chocolate or hunger?' We started with chocolate. And someone must have taken a picture of us there without our noticing, because several years later I came across a photograph in *Who What Where*, and I gradually started to recognize the three blurred figures who sat there all hunched over scrabbling in the leaves. It was ourselves – Peder, Vivian and myself – and we had a kind of sly look as if something nefarious was on the go, rather than just the eating of a few twirls in the autumn leaves. And under the picture was this caption: *The first young people to seek out the drug scene in Palace Park, in protest against what they called the dance of death round the plastic god and the golden calf*. And it was then I understood, once and for all, abashed and perhaps amused too, and yet with a degree of sorrow, that it's the eye that decides what it wants to see. The eye twists the world, and everything you see now and will see in the future has revisionist power.

They came just before dusk – Pontus, the maestro and the whole crew. They came in that half-light which rises shimmering and somehow won't let the day depart, in the month before the fog from the fiord sweeps through the streets and rubs away distances and corners. The sun was a red shadow between the trees. There was a glimmer in the leaves that trembled along the banks. They rigged everything up behind the guardsmen's sheds. We went a bit closer. Everything seemed rather chaotic. Everyone was running round in circles. Perhaps they were short of time. The pale lady with her furs had her face made-up and became paler still. Pontus sat down on a bench that had been brought there for him. It looked like the bench from St Hans Hill. Lights came on. A machine blew leaves in Pontus' direction. I hoped the whole script might blow away so that I could pick it up page by page and bring it back to the director in the correct order. I tried to wave to Pontus but he didn't see me. He wrote something on a scrap of paper and was in a world of his own. I knew there and then that I'd like to be him. Peder took hold of my arm. 'Tell him your grandmother was a famous actress,' he hissed. 'Who, Pontus?' 'No, the direc- tor, of course! He's the one who makes the decisions.' 'Decisions about what?' 'Everything, Barnum.' The direc- tor waved his arms about and looked like a conductor who couldn't get his orchestra to play in tune. Finally he sat down in his chair and folded his arms. I thought about the Old One who never came to be in any films at the end of the day. 'My great-grandmother,' I whispered. 'It was my great-grandmother who was the actress.' 'Same thing. Just tell him.' Peder gave me a nudge in the back. I think Vivian nudged me too, more carefully. I took a deep breath and slowly made my way over to the director. He seemed pretty annoyed when I stood there in front of

him. 'Can't we ever get rid of these kids?' he exclaimed. I
gave a deep bow. 'My great grandmother was a famous
actress,' I told him. The director looked at me with a
single eye. 'Really. Your great-grandmother was a famous
actress in Denmark? And what was her name?' I told him.
He shook his head. 'Not familiar with the name, I'm
afraid. It was way before my time.' The director looked
down at the script again. I stayed standing where I was,
mostly because I didn't quite *know* what to do, and
because the leaves were so heavy to walk through. I stood
like this for a fair time. The director looked up from his
bundle of sheets and took off his glasses. 'How many are
there of you?' 'Three,' I answered. The director flung
wide his arms. 'All right. Since I can't get rid of you I'll use
you instead.' He got up and went over to two women, one
of whom was the make-up artist, and spoke to them. And
what happened now I really have to relate as quietly as I
can, because the following year when we sat in the Saga
cinema for the première, our disappointment was so
great. Yes, we felt downright cheated, and that deep sense
of disappointment was mingled with something still
worse – namely shame. For that reason I'll relate this *sotto
voce*, I'll just whisper – we were to be extras. We were
dressed up in old-fashioned clothes, expansive trousers
that scratched our thighs, overlarge shoes and jackets
with more buttons than we had fingers. 'You have such
fine curls,' the make-up lady whispered, and combed
them a bit too much. Vivian was given a long rustling
dress, high boots and a heavy mantle. We were quite a
trio. The year was 1890. The city was called Kristiania.
We were on our way home through Palace Park, having
been to visit an aunt and uncle in Wergeland Road.
'You're siblings,' the director told us. 'Isn't that a bit
odd?' Peder objected. 'Odd? What d'you mean?' Peder
took up position beside me and pulled Vivian in closer.
'Do we really look like siblings?' The director sighed
heavily. 'In past centuries siblings looked as you do. You
can just walk completely naturally. And don't turn round!

Got that?' We nodded. 'Should we think of anything in particular?' I enquired. The director gave me a hard stare. 'Think?' 'Yes, what should we be thinking about?' Pontus was there himself now. 'Have we become colleagues then, Barnum?' 'Looks like it,' I said. Pontus laughed with yellow teeth and hollow cheeks. 'I'll tell you what you can think about. You can think about all the sandwiches you'll eat when you get home. Turkey. Ham. Beef. Sausage. With rich mayonnaise. And chocolate with cream.' The director broke in. 'That's enough, Oscarsson. You've given them plenty to think about now.' Shortly afterwards things were underway. We walked down towards the shadowed pond where a few ducks were swimming as the filming began at our backs. We didn't turn round. We didn't say a word. I don't know what Peder and Vivian thought about, but I worked out in my mind how I'd write this. To start with we wouldn't have been siblings. Rather three friends on our way home from a party or a ball – yes, a ball, and Peder and I are both in love with Vivian, and that's the catalyst for a showdown between the two of us – it's either him or me. But then Vivian falls in the pond at the point where the water's deepest; she can't swim, the water's freezing at this time of year and she's on the point of drowning. And Peder and I have to join forces to save her; we throw ourselves into the water and get her to the bank. But it's too late. She doesn't manage to survive the ordeal and dies in our helpless arms. 'Think we've gone far enough now,' Peder murmured. We'd all but crossed Park Road. And when we did finally turn, the director was standing in a shadow in front of the floodlight, waving. We ran back. 'Perfect,' he said. 'Shall we do it again?' I asked. 'No need. That was perfect.' We got changed once more and were given a fiver each. We got paid. We went the same way down towards the pond and we'd been paid for being in a film – five kroner each, fifteen kroner altogether. 'We have to celebrate this!' Peder exclaimed. 'We'll get drunk!' The ducks rose up from the water with heavy, dripping wings. 'Yes!'

I shouted. And we did get pretty drunk, particularly Peder, and most likely me too. 'Barnum gets drunk quickest because he's small,' Peder used to say. And then I'd say that Peder took the longest to get drunk because he was so fat. Then we'd drink still more. We went to Miil's Stamps – Bought and Sold, and we emptied the fridge in the back premises. There was a bottle of champagne there, in the event of a really exceptional deal being struck – and maybe Dad and Oscar Miil had drunk champagne the day great grandfather's letter was sold and bought. We drank it at any rate. We opened it with a pop and drank the foaming, tickling juice right from the bottle, because wasn't this an exceptional occasion, too? We'd been in a film, we'd acted in *Hunger*. And we sat there for the remainder of the evening, in that cramped back room, with the heavy smell of old letters, toasting each other with champagne and Campari and cola. Peder used to say that Vivian didn't get drunk because she was so beautiful. But I felt it again, that giddiness I'd first experienced on Ildjernet, and which I'd first sensed in Mum's bedroom when I drank in lungfuls of air and got the sweet, dark taste of Malaga on my tongue. Together we sat there and drank. I took off, slowly at first, and then it was just as though a switch was flicked, and the strange thing was that most of me was plunged into darkness, but at the same time a light came on in another room. It was a room I hadn't known existed, and in this room I was king, for as long as the light lasted. There I could lay out Barnum's ruler; the shadows I cast were long and lithe – the ideas came so easily, they queued up and I was king. I got out my notebook and wrote on a blank page – *Fattening*. That was the word I wrote. *Fattening*. That was my new idea, even though many years would pass before I finished writing the piece and won the new scripts competition at Norwegian Film for it. I'd started. 'What d'you have there?' Peder asked me. I flicked back through my notebook to *The Little City*. 'Just something I've written,' I told him. 'Written? Have you written something?' I got up. I wasn't standing completely steadily; I floated over the floor in the same way my thoughts floated through me. 'Yes,' I said loudly. 'I've started writing!' Peder clapped his hands. 'Read your work to us, Barnum!' And I did read, the start of the first things I'd written, apart from my school compositions which didn't count. When I was done Vivian smiled while Peder fell silent and opened another bottle of beer. 'Great,' Vivian said, and gave me a quick hug. I tried to hold onto her but couldn't manage to. It isn't true that she didn't get drunk because she was so beautiful. She didn't get drunk because she didn't drink. That was maybe why she was so beautiful. 'You're so beautiful,' I said, and sank down on the sofa. 'Don't be silly,' she said. I looked at her and suddenly saw she'd kept her wig and that her face was covered in make-up. 'Yes, you are! I'll write about you one day!' Peder grew impatient. 'But what happens after that? You can't just finish it like that?' I thought about it. My mind was working. Things were rolling now. I was a wheel. 'He's put in prison!' I shouted. 'And everything there's much bigger, just as everything was tiny in the Little City. So he who'd been the world's biggest person becomes its smallest. The only thing he has to remind him of the Little City are the flowers he has hidden away.' I said no more and for a time there was quiet. 'I liked that bit with the flowers,' Vivian whispered. Peder got up. 'But what does it mean?' Vivian laughed. 'You can always count how many words there are,' she told him. I laughed too. 'Yes! Count up the number of words I've written! Then you can see if you understand it!' Peder came closer. 'But d'you understand it yourself, Barnum?' I shook my head and really shouldn't have. 'Not a clue,' I admitted. It was Peder who got me home. When I came to once more I was sitting in front of the clock in the hall. It stood still. There were no coins in the drawer. Time was penniless. Mum was standing in front of me too. But she didn't stand still. The whole of her was moving about; it was as if she was trying to keep her balance with just her fingers. Behind her, behind the dead clock, was Boletta – leaning against her stick, and I thought I could hear Fred laughing in our room. Someone was laughing. It was only me. Mum was crying. 'The headmaster phoned.' 'Did he? What did he say?' Mum stopped crying and grabbed my schoolbag. 'You have just one chance, Barnum! To tell the truth!' 'The truth?' 'Yes, what is it you've been doing today? Because you certainly haven't been at school!' I turned it over in my mind. I wasn't floating any more. I was sinking. I wasn't a wheel. I was a lop-sided, unusable wheel rolling down a hillside covered in hedgehogs. 'I've been writing,' I whispered. 'Writing?' 'Yes, and afterwards filming. Don't you believe me, or what?' Now Mum got angry instead. She opened my bag and scrabbled about inside it with feverish hands. 'The headmaster's fed up with you skipping school!' she shouted as she went on scrabbling. 'You won't pass your exams if you go on like this!' I shrugged my shoulders. They were heavy to lift. 'All the same to me,' I said. Mum leant towards me, her mouth trembling. 'Don't try to imitate Fred, Barnum! Because you'd never manage to do it anyway!' But my mouth was trembling as much as hers. 'It's true!' I told her. She took a step backwards. She stood with *Hunger* in one hand and my notebook in the other. She melted for a moment. But she froze again just as quickly and bent down once more. 'Have you been drinking too, Barnum?' I nodded. I shouldn't have done. I slid down from the chair into the clock's shadow. I didn't have much to say for myself. And I can't say all that much now either. I just slid down from the chair and what I say now has been related about me by others. I am the story, the one that's told – there I lie like dead time at Mum's feet. But this much I know – Boletta's cure was administered, something that she in her time had inherited from the Old One and given to Mum. It was Chinese wine minus the Malaga, and the next time I woke up I was mercifully lying in my own bed, and I'd heard right after all – Fred was laughing. Fred lay in his bed and his laughter was deep and low. 'What are you laughing at?' I murmured.

'Guess,' he said. 'Me?' 'Wrong. I'm not laughing at my little brother.' 'Thanks, Fred. Thank you.' 'Have you written anything today?' 'Yes, half a page of the notebook.' 'Good, Barnum.' Fred held his laughter inside him for a time. There was a humming in my heart, as if the speed had been increased so that time went faster inside me; perhaps I'd aged by several years in the course of that one night, perhaps I'd died, or maybe I'd awoken old and wise. 'Were you drunk?' Fred asked. 'I reckon so,' I whispered. 'Did you like it?' he asked. I tried to remember. 'For the time that it lasted.' And I felt frightened then, because I couldn't remember how I got home, from the time we shut the door of Miil's Stamps to when I sat there in front of the clock. It was as if a sheet of my life had been ripped from top to bottom; it was my first black hole and it certainly wouldn't be my last. Fred let out his laughter once more. 'Now it's Barnum who's the naughty boy,' he said. 'It is me you're laughing at then,' I said. Fred stopped. 'I'm laughing at Arnesen.' 'Arnesen? Why him?' 'Just wait,' Fred said. 'D'you not hear how quiet it is?' I listened. Yes. There was stillness. It was a long while since it had been so quiet in the yard. Mrs Arnesen wasn't playing the piano. 'Good night, Barnum.' I dreamed nothing and the following morning Fred had already got up and gone. Mum was sitting on the edge of the bed stroking her hand through my hair and smiling. 'You really got to act in *Hunger*,' she said when she was sure I was awake. I felt old all right, but not particularly wise. 'Yes, as extras. Peder and Vivian and me.' 'If only the Old One had known,' Mum sighed. 'Just imagine.' 'Yes, just imagine. We walked through Palace Park and were filmed.' Mum stayed her hand, let it rest in my curls. 'But promise me never to get drunk again. You're far too young.' 'Yes, Mum.' 'Drink turns the heart nasty, Barnum.' 'Has Boletta's heart become nasty?' I asked. She pulled my hair quite hard. 'By rights I should be furious with you, Barnum. You should be grounded for at least a month!' 'All right,' I breathed. 'But first you can tell me

how you got hold of the alcohol.' 'We borrowed a bottle
of champagne belonging to Peder's dad. 'Borrowed?'
Mum's face loomed nearer mine. 'Have you a sore head?'
I wanted to be honest. 'Yes,' I said. Mum smiled. 'That's
the idea. That you should have a sore head.' 'Yes, it's
what's called postal surcharge,' I told her. Mum stared at
me for a long while and her eyes weren't quite right. Then
she went to fetch the *Medical Dictionary for Norwegian
Homes*, for heaven's sake, and she sat down once more on
the edge of the bed. 'Pay close attention now, Barnum.'
And she read to me, slowly and clearly, so I wouldn't miss
a single word: *Alcoholism. Under the slight influence of alcohol
self-esteem is increased, while control over speech and thinking is
impaired. If the effect is greater then control both of sense and
sensibility will be weakened or effectively lost altogether, mastery
of muscle activity restricted, and ultimately only a mass of flesh,
bone and blood will remain, under the authority of chance or
other people. The most powerful intoxication will, through poi-
soning of the system, lead to full unconsciousness and paralysis.
The result of intoxication is indisposition – a foul taste in the
mouth, bad breath, ill temper, depression – as a consequence this
will, for many, necessitate a renewal of the effect of intoxication.
This often leads to a state of chronic alcoholism. The body is
weakened and the hands shake. The face takes on a blue-red
colouring and the nose in particular swells. Bit by bit all mental
faculties will be lost; all that remains will be the unbroken torment of a desire for alcohol which in the end will not itself be tol-
erable, making death for the remaining shell of a body an
inevitability*. Mum shut Greve's *Medical Dictionary* with a
thump and turned towards Boletta who was standing by
the door. 'Don't terrify the life out of the boy,' Boletta
said. Mum got up and put the book back in its place on
the shelf. 'Barnum needs to know what he's doing when
he gets himself drunk.' 'Yes, yes, and Dr Greve thinks my
death should have been an inevitability years ago!' 'Don't
talk like that, mother!' 'I'll talk just as I please and
say here and now that Greve was a killjoy and has more
lives on his conscience than champagne!' 'Barnum's still

under age,' Mum breathed. 'I don't want him to ruin his life.' Boletta laughed. 'Oh, it'll take more than that to ruin his life. Wouldn't you have had some champagne too if you'd just become a film star?' That's how they conversed, as if they thought I was already dead and couldn't hear a thing. But I lay there; I looked at my hands and couldn't detect any shaking; I tested the smell of my breath, and I felt my nose to see if it had grown any bigger. I thought if I was hungry and decided I wasn't – I was thirsty, though, and in my heart of hearts (and it both tempted me and scared the living daylights out of me), I'd have loved a bit more champagne. Just one gulp to pick me up, to take me somewhere else. I was already just the shell of a body. 'Per Oscarsson walked bare-legged from Stockholm to Oslo,' I said in a loud voice. Mum and Boletta turned towards the bed. 'I had to tell the headmaster you had flu,' Mum murmured. 'You'll have to stay at home for two more days. And that's the very last time I'll tell a lie on your behalf! Do you understand me?' 'Yes, Mum.' She came closer once more and her eyes overflowed with a sudden, unexpected gentleness. 'Fred has promised to pull himself together, Barnum. And you can manage that, too.' 'Pull himself together? How?' 'He's going to get himself a job. And don't you see a change in here?' I couldn't see any noticeable difference, except that Fred had made his bed. Mum pointed to the floor and smiled. 'The line has gone at last,' she said. Now I saw it. Fred's line had been rubbed out. The room was no longer divided in two and this, which should have made me happy, caused me anxiety instead, almost terror. Because I didn't know what it meant, and Boletta must have felt the same because she looked away and closed her eyes. But for Mum it was a good sign that Fred had removed the white line between us. How wrong can you be? We read signs according to our likes; we make them what we want them to be, and slowly but surely those signs turn their wrath upon us. Mum smiled. 'What you wrote was great, Barnum. About the little city.' I sat up in bed. 'Have you read it?' 'We couldn't stop once we began,' Mum breathed, almost shamefully. 'But you must finish it.' Boletta thumped her stick against the door frame, as if it was her way of applauding. 'And see it has a happy ending, Barnum. There are far too many sad stories in this world. And when we tell sad stories we begin to resemble them ourselves.' I still didn't know how the story was going to end – my story. 'I'll try,' I promise. Mum put my notebook down on the quilt and flicked over to the last page. 'But what does it say here?' she asked me. I could barely read my own letters. Perhaps that was how Fred experienced words, like small, black creatures crawling over the page, pulling the wool over his eyes all the time. 'Fattening,' I said in the end. Mum was startled. 'That's certainly something you won't write about.' I looked up at her and made-up my mind that nobody would ever read anything I'd written before I myself had authorized it. 'What's the business with Arnesen?' I enquired. Mum went over towards the door. 'Arnesen? What d'you mean?'

Yet there was something. For the second time, two strange men came with catastrophic news to Mrs Arnesen. But now there was no mistake about it. Now it wasn't a case of having found a business card by chance in the anorak pocket of a corpse on Nordmarka. Now they had evidence. They parked in Jacob Aall Street and right away aroused a good deal of attention. Faces behind curtains. Doors left ajar. Me at the window. There was a light rain falling. A hush over Fagerborg and everyone knows everything at the same time. They ring the bell up on the second floor. Mrs Arnesen opens the door. She takes in the two men and smiles. Does she think they're there to sell something? Does she maybe imagine they're from the Jehovah's Witnesses and want to convert her? There were a couple of missionaries in the district earlier in the year; they always come in pairs and are so alike they could be twins. These two men are also like one another, but they aren't smiling. Does she really not know, or is she aware of what's going to happen and still attempting to keep the mask intact with as much dignity as possible for a person who's about to go into free fall? The men don't introduce themselves. They just ask if her husband is at home. He is. He's sitting in the innermost room, waiting. He's been waiting for them. He knew this had to happen. She calls him and he gets up, tightens his tie and thinks over the fact that this is the last normal moment of his life. When he appears, he's wearing his outdoor clothes. He's ready. He gives his wife a quick kiss on the cheek. The two men look down, embarrassed. She tries to hold him back. 'What is it?' she asks. She actually doesn't know. That's to her advantage. But it doesn't help her. 'It's all over,' is all he says. 'Over? What do you mean?' She finds out soon enough. Perhaps she understands even as she sees them get into the car, the black car, that speeds out of sight. He has been an unfaithful servant. He'd dug too deep in the drawers beneath the clocks; he'd grown greedy, he'd taken time before he should, and eaten up his clients' life insurances until he couldn't stop. It would have been better had he been an unfaithful husband. That could be hushed up. But it would have been best if he'd been dead, if he'd been the one lying in the melting snow between Mylla and Kikut, a pile of bones and poles and skis – dead long before the temptation to put coins in his own pocket (that special hidden inner pocket), became too great. Then Mrs Arnesen could have looked everyone in the face, because sorrow elevates and tragedy ennobles. But shame eats away at you and debases you – it consumes your eyes, it drinks your blood and it bends your back. 'What's going on?' Mum asked. She stood behind me and put her hands on my shoulders, and was the only one who didn't know. 'Arnesen's been done for embezzlement,' I whispered. 'What are you talking about?' 'They came for him just now.' Mum ran in to Boletta's. 'Arnesen's been arrested!' she exclaimed. Boletta thumped all round her with the stick. 'I've always said that man was made of the wrong stuff. He had too many pockets!' Mum pulled out the drawer from under the clock. 'But it's sad for Mrs Arnesen,' she whispered. Boletta gave a snort. 'And when did they last feel sorry for anyone? Other than themselves!' 'Be quiet,' Mum told her. 'Stop telling me to be quiet! You know as well as I do that they moved into that flat before anyone had the slightest inkling that Rakel was dead!' Mum leaned against the clock. 'That was all a long time ago,' she said softly. 'And what's that got to do with it?' Boletta demanded. Then the doorbell rang. It was Peder and Vivian. Mum wiped the tears away and attempted a smile instead. 'Here we have the other actors,' she said. Peder and Vivian shook hands and were polite to a fault, but they looked away the whole time as if each had double sties. I got them fairly smartly into my room and Vivian sat on Fred's bed, and all at once I hoped they'd go before he came back. Peder wasn't in particularly good form either. He looked like a crumpled rucksack and resembled the Sun King on a bad day. But at least his hands weren't shaking. 'Thanks for yesterday,' he said. 'Yeah, crikey,' I said. 'What a night.' 'You got pretty drunk,' Peder said. 'You too,' I told him. He smiled. 'But you got drunk quickest because you're so small.' I chucked an eraser at his ear. 'And you have to drink twice as much because you're so fat.' We both turned to Vivian. She didn't need to drink at all, even though she had been born in an accident. I wished she was sitting somewhere else and not on Fred's bed. 'You could do with some make-up, Barnum,' she said. And perhaps it was at that moment, as she spoke the words, that she decided that's what she'd be – a make-up artist – when she saw my grey and blotchy face the day after the night before. Or perhaps she'd known it all along, from the time when she saw her own mother's shattered visage. Peder laughed and thumped me so hard on the back I all but banged my forehead on the floor. 'That was great what you read to us,' he said. 'Bloody great.' 'Thank you,' I spluttered. 'You're welcome. Nothing to be thanked for.' 'I mean to both of you for getting me home.' Peder fell silent and glanced at Vivian. 'You took the tram,' she said in a low voice. 'Don't you remember?' Now it was my turn to laugh. ''Course I remember! D'you think I'm stupid, or what?' But I still couldn't remember taking the tram from Solli Square, buying my ticket, getting off at Majorstuen, making my way along the rest of Church Road, unlocking the door and sitting down in the chair in front of the stopped clock. I'd lost all that for good. 'Is your Mum furious?' Peder asked me. We turned towards the door, where she was standing with some food and three huge glasses of milk. 'Unfortunately I don't have champagne,' she said. I looked down and my face became the way Dr Greve described, blue-red and swollen. But Peder just got up and bowed. 'Thanks, but we had enough champagne yesterday.' Mum had to laugh and she put the plate down on the desk and courteously withdrew once more. Peder was hungry so we didn't need to worry about him; he ate all the sandwiches and drank the milk – his appetite was pretty much insatiable. Vivian moved over to my bed; she leaned back and put her head on my pillow – I reckoned I'd never be able to sleep there again without thinking of her. 'Your Mum's nice,' she said. 'Oh, yes. When she is nice.' Vivian looked at me. 'Is it true she was in an accident herself?' I heard what she was saying. But I didn't understand. 'What do you mean?' I asked, and my voice was porous and unstable. Peder coughed so mightily that his mouth was ringed by white crumbs. 'What I was going to say,' he all but shouted, 'was that we have to replace those bottles for my dad. Otherwise he might get a bit grumpy.' We pooled our earnings – fifteen kroner – that was barely enough for some tonic water and a stamp, but Peder was pleased. 'I'll borrow the rest from Dad,' he said. They went before Fred came home. Vivian had to go to the loo first. Peder and I waited in the hall. Mum and Boletta sat smiling in the living room. We smiled to them. 'Vivian's in love with you,' Peder whispered. I assumed an air of nonchalance. 'Really?' 'Yes, she is. Why's your clock stopped?'

'Because the man who winds it's been arrested for embezzlement.' 'Cool.' 'How d'you know?' 'Know what, Barnum?' 'That she's in love with me?' I was speaking even more quietly. The words in my mouth were impossible. 'I've counted all the times she's looked at you.' 'Have you?' 'Sixty-eight times, Barnum.' I considered this. 'She's taking a long time in there,' I commented, and must have said it rather loudly because Mum suddenly stared at me and Peder smiled all the more. 'Thanks for your hospitality!' he called out. 'It was great!' I heard Vivian flushing. 'Girls take a long time in the loo,' Peder said. 'Particularly Vivian.' Now she was washing her hands. Those hands had been places. I sighed. 'Hasn't she looked at you, though?' I murmured. 'Only forty-two times. You're in the lead, Barnum.' Then she emerged. The two of them went. Most people go before Fred comes home. After that I lay in bed, my cheek where Vivian had been lying – her hair, her fair skin, her eyelashes that were so long and curved, and which I'd have given anything to have touched. But I wasn't dreaming. I lay quite still, bewildered and afraid. Could anyone be in love with me, the midget from Fagerborg, the littlest midge in the whole neighbourhood – the mitten, the dwarf? Or had she looked at me sixty-eight times because she'd never seen anything so ridiculous before? That was more probable – yes, that had to be the truth of it. No one fell in love with me. I aroused no deeper emotions than kindheartedness, amazement and laughter – rather like the well-groomed poodles on the exercise ground for dogs in Frogner Park. These poodles with their bottoms like bright red dents under their stiff tails; these curly creatures that the old ladies bent down to make such a fuss of and to talk in tongues to. I was a poodle. I never aroused so much as alarm. And why had Vivian asked if Mum had been in an accident? It was intolerable. Wasn't there a single feeling that was pure and unsullied? I tried to read the novel I'd been given by Vivian, *Hunger*, but I couldn't get further than the title page where she'd written *To*

Barnum from Vivian. I studied the letters; was there any deeper meaning behind those four words? Could there be some secret message here, some clue? The B of my name was pretty big, and her V was like a giant vase – was this also a sign? I looked up instead under H in Greve's bible to see what he had on *Hunger*. *The feeling of hunger resides in the heart*, was what I read. *Adult humans can, with adequate supplies of drinking water, starve for several months – as so-called fasting professionals*. That's what I'd become – a fasting professional – with the world's most starved heart. Fred came in once I'd gone to sleep. I dreamed that Vivian measured me with the reverse side of Dad's tape and discovered I was over one metre ninety tall, and afterwards she licked every single one of my golden centimetres. 'Who was sitting on my bed?' Fred asked. I woke up. 'Peder,' I said. Fred turned round. 'Peder? The fat guy?' I nodded. 'Don't believe it,' Fred said. 'The mattress would have shattered.' 'Maybe Vivian then,' I whispered. 'She was here too.' Fred lay down and looked up at the ceiling for a bit. Then he switched off the light. 'It doesn't matter, Barnum. Just good to know who's been on your bed, you know.' 'Of course,' I said. I thought I'd ask him about the line on the floor that was gone now. But my courage failed me. 'Have you got a job?' I asked instead. Fred put the light on again, tore off the shade and stuck his face right in under the bulb. 'Look at me,' he said. I didn't want to. I did all the same. I looked at him. I shut my eyes. 'D'you think anyone'll have me? Huh? D'you think they will?' He was almost shouting. 'Don't know,' I whispered. It was dark. 'Have you done any writing today?' he asked me. 'Not really.' 'Not really? And how much is that?' 'Nothing, Fred.' 'Damn it to hell, Barnum! Half stories are nothing but crap!' Then we heard it, the last chord of Mrs Arnesen's piano – Mozart – and nobody opened their windows to shout for quiet because Mrs Arnesen should be allowed to bring her twenty year concert to a close in peace. And a dark sound hung on in the blackness and slowly died out, between the rubbish bins and the drying lines. 'Did you know?' I asked him. 'Know what, Barnum?' 'That Arnesen had been done?' Fred didn't answer. He lay there smiling for a while. 'What you don't know won't hurt you,' was all he said. 'You reckon?' 'Yes,' he said. 'I'm sure of it.' All at once he sat up in bed. 'When's the première of your film, by the way?' 'Which film?' Fred laughed. 'Have you been in many films recently? *Ben Hur*, for instance?' 'I don't know,' I murmured. 'I don't know when the première will be.' 'Looking forward to it?' 'Yes, Fred.' And so began that which I call my in between time, my first one – and there would be many. Those sections, which some immediately want to scrub, to cut out; dramaturges see red when these long, quiet scenes materialize, and producers chuck the script in the nearest waste-paper basket. Directors ask you to put in a strange man with a rifle or an unhappy childhood, and disappear to the bathroom while you compose a new draft. They'd rather have murder and loud music and toning down to black; they'd rather have adverts, they'd rather have anything but this, because what scares them most of all is getting bored. But they still haven't got the hang of the fact that it's in these corners of the story that the turning point may lie – the anticipated unrest – rising slowly from the bottom and spreading its rings from below. And the image I carry of that in between time – my dark image – is of Mrs Arnesen's empty flat. They can't afford to keep it now and we stand on the opposite pavement watching the removal men carrying out furniture, carpets, vases, lamps, paintings. We nod, silent and comprehending; we all think the same, absolutely, that it was coming. We knew that, that something wasn't right, and we see someone taking down the curtains; we see the bare windows and the sills with their flowers gone. Finally they take out the piano; two men carried it up twenty years before but four men are needed to take it out – black, shining, its lid shut. And a sigh goes through us – some are on the point of applauding. We wait for Mrs Arnesen; we keep warm under the wet and glistening trees – and I'm one of the women in the street now, until Mum comes and drags me away like some urchin. She grabs me by the scruff of the neck and I wonder if I've ever seen her so fierce and enraged. Once we're home she keeps a hold of me and she shakes her fist against my Adam's apple, and says, with her mouth shoved right up at my face, 'Mrs Arnesen has done nothing wrong! And you stand there like an old housewife making fun of her!' 'I wasn't making fun of her,' I whispered. 'Yes, you were! You made fun of her simply by standing there gloating! Go to your room!' She shoves me away; I nearly tumble and I close the door, shaking all over. Because something had broken in Mum that day; I hear her crying out there and then there's utter stillness. Later that same evening she comes into the room, all beautifully dressed up and wearing a coat she'd otherwise only put on on Sundays. She's almost herself again and she takes my hand. 'Forgive me, Barnum,' she says. I look down. 'I shouldn't have stood there like that,' I breathe. She takes out a comb and runs it through my hair. 'Go and get your jacket.' I look up at her. 'Where are we going?' 'We're going to say goodbye to Mrs Arnesen, Barnum.'

We cross the yard and take the kitchen steps. On the second floor the door's ajar. The plate that bore their name has been unscrewed, and we can see that another plate has hung there at one time; the holes for the screws are there, smaller than those for the Arnesens'. Mum rings the bell. More than anything I want to get away, but she keeps a hold of me. She attempts a smile. Her breath is held inside her like a heavy wave. No one comes to the door. Mum rings the bell again and then we realize it isn't working. The stillness only intensifies. Mum pushes the door open. I follow her in. She stops and looks about her with wondering, shining eyes. The walls are bare and covered with splotches. The stove has been removed. There's a border of soot and grease along the upper edge. And behind everything we can see other marks, marks that can't be hidden, signs of people who lived here before the

Arnesens. And then we see her, Mrs Arnesen herself, standing in the empty living room under the light in the ceiling – the only light that encircles her in one yellow, unsteady pool of illumination. She turns towards us. Mum lets go of my arm and goes closer. I'm the one who sees them, these two women, wounded and proud. They've given birth in the same maternity ward, they've lived in the same building, and in the course of all these years have barely exchanged a word. They've lived their own lives; yet in that moment, here, in this deserted flat – my unfurnished memory – there's nothing between them. 'You knew the people who lived here before us, didn't you?' Mrs Arnesen says. Mum just nods, and smiles again. 'She was my best friend. Her name was Rakel.' 'Where is she now?' 'She and her family were sent to Ravensbrück.' Mum stretches out her hand. 'She gave me this ring,' she says. 'I was to look after it for her.' Mrs Arnesen extends her hand too. They shake hands. 'We just wanted to say goodbye,' Mum tells her. 'Thank you. That was nice of you.' 'Where are you moving to?' 'To my parents' house. Outside town. A long way from here.' Mrs Arnesen drops Mum's hand. 'I'll miss your playing,' Mum tells her. 'Most people will be glad to be rid of it.' Suddenly she turns in my direction, as if she's only now realized I'm there. 'Are you here, too?' she says. I bow and hear a sound from somewhere else, that of running water being turned off. 'A shame we didn't get to talk more,' Mum says. Mrs Arnesen looks at her again. 'Yes, and now it's too late.' Mum looks awkward for a moment and I feel the desire to go. 'Is it?' Suddenly Mrs Arnesen laughs. 'D'you remember how Fred kept everyone in the ward awake? How that boy shrieked!' Mum laughs herself. 'Mercifully, he stopped all that once we got home.' They're silent for a bit. I take a step backwards. There are others in the flat. There's someone else here. 'How are things doing with your son?' Mum finally asks. Mrs Arnesen holds her hands in a knot in front of her. 'Fortunately he got leave from military service. So he could help me. With the removal.' And Aslak materializes from the bathroom – Aslak, my tormentor, our tormentor. He's wearing a dark-green outfit and his hands are dripping. He doesn't give us so much as a glance and just wants to get past. But his mother stops him. 'Don't you remember Barnum?' she says. Aslak turns slowly in my direction. 'Oh, yes. He hasn't changed in the least.' Aslak extends his dripping hand and I have no choice but to take it. 'My condolences,' I breathe. Mum flushes in horror and a tremor passes through Aslak's arm. 'Yes, that's right,' he says. 'My father's dead, too.' And when we're standing down in the yard once more, Mum lets out her breath. 'I know you didn't mean it, Barnum. But you have to watch what you say.' It has cleared up. The darkness is close and clear. The heavens are a shining, black square above our heads. 'I'll stay here a bit,' I murmur. Mum hesitates. Finally she goes. And I sit down on the steps by the bins. The windows darken round me one by one until only the stars are visible. I listen. I hear. Because just as Fred said once in the graveyard, it's true that you can listen to the building, that there are stories all around that never fall silent, that never stop. But none of them can tell who Fred's father was, who it was that destroyed Mum; not the drying lines in the loft, nor even the dusty light in the angled attic window. The stories have their secrets too, secrets they won't reveal, and when you get too close they begin to tell another story instead. They tell, for instance, that Arnesen's flat lies vacant a long time after his wife has gone home to her parents' house where no one plays the piano. But in the new year a third nameplate goes onto the front door – bigger still this time and of polished, shining copper: Ole Arvid Bang. It's the caretaker who's moving up from his gloomy bedsit by the gate to four rooms, a balcony and early morning sunlight on the second floor. This is his reward for long and faithful service; it's his final triple jump, his longest leap yet – a personal record. At last he's got to the top of the tree, but it's said he feels so lonely there that when he sits in the kitchen in the morning talking to himself he doesn't get an answer till he's gone to bed. And many years later, once Arnesen had been released for quite some time, he returned to his old flat, saw the new nameplate and rang the bell. Bang just stared at him through the peep-hole he'd fitted in the door; he saw Arnesen's pale face like a moon, stole back to the kitchen and drew the curtains. Bang had been promoted to loneliness and Arnesen had been released, but the latter gained admission nowhere – for he bore an infection with him, a shadow of shame. And there are those who say that thereafter he slept in a box on Krankaia, shaved beside the hydrant on Bispekaia, and earned eight kroner a day buying brandy at the 'pole' in the City Chambers Square for the tramps who couldn't keep sober once the clouds of frost from the fiord caused their tongues to wilt in their parched mouths.

I go upstairs and lie down. This is my in between time. I dream and I invent. One morning I wake up and it's my birthday. Mum stands by my bed singing while Boletta keeps time with her stick. Fred leans against the door frame where I stopped growing a long time ago. The first parcel I open is from Mum. It's a tie. The other parcel's Boletta's. It's a tie-pin. The third parcel is a joint present from Mum and Boletta. It's heavy. It's Knut Hamsun's collected works. The flakes of ash from the stove have been washed and put together, side by side, and bound, volume by volume – eighteen spines raised from the flames. 'Thank you,' I breathe. And then it's Fred's turn. He bends down and pulls out something he's kept hidden under his bed. I've never had a present from Fred before. Mum opens her mouth in astonishment. Boletta straightens her hunched back. Fred places a great angular parcel on the quilt. 'Many happy returns,' he says. I almost don't dare open it. I'd rather wait. I'd like to hold on to this moment while I'm still in ignorance of what's inside; it could be anything whatsoever or exactly what I want it to be. Fred has bought me a present. *To Branum from Fred.* I make out I haven't seen that. I don't see it. Branum is my name. The line on the floor is gone. I feel the parcel. It's hard. There's a jarring noise when I shake it. Mum starts growing impatient. Fred gives a laugh. 'It's not grenades,' he says. And I tear off the wrapping paper. It's a type-writer. I have to close my eyes and open them again. It's still a typewriter – a Diplomat – with a carrying case and three different line settings. Boletta thumps her stick against the wall. Mum's face is dark and worried, but the delight inside her is greater, and she claps her hands because this moment mustn't be spoiled. 'Now the only thing you need is something to write on,' she murmurs, almost moved. Fred points to the table. There's already a stack of white paper there. 'Now the only thing he needs is something to write,' he says. I get up. I take his hand. 'Next time you'll get the finest thing I have,' I tell him. Fred looks at me in surprise. 'What?' he says. But that I don't yet know. 'Many thanks,' I say, that's all. Fred's smiling now. 'Good, Barnum.' And he drops my hand and disappears.

I put my tie and the pin in my drawer, and Hamsun's collected works on the bookshelf between the *Medical Dictionary for Norwegian Homes* and *The World in Pictures*. I begin writing that same evening. I type out *The Little City* on the machine. I copy it out from my notebook. I begin. It isn't easy. I have to start again several times. Now it's no longer the sound of Mrs Arnesen's piano that's to be heard across the yard, but rather that of my typewriter. There's something wrong with two of the letters. The k is all but invisible and the e is fairly worn too. It makes no odds. Perhaps Fred got it cheap. But it looks a bit strange when, for instance, I type the word *kindness*. What ends up there is *indness*. That isn't a word. But it doesn't matter. I don't write the word all that often anyway. And afterwards I correct all the mistakes with my pen. By the time I'm finished it's one and a half pages altogether. Two pages really. This is mine. This is no one else's. This is something only I could have done. I've never thought of it like that before. What I've written on those two pages isn't to be found anywhere else in the world, the entire universe – just here. And it's from my head, my very own head; my hand wrote it and now it's there – *The Little City* by Barnum Nilsen – forty-eight lines the world has never seen before. I have to lie down for a bit. I'm intoxicated. I'm all trembling there where I lie. Then Peder comes in. And Peder isn't exactly the type to knock and wait for an answer. He just storms in and Mum's standing there with a cake and the requisite number of candles in the cream on top. 'Happy Birthday!' Peder exclaims. Then he stops a moment and goes straight over to the gleaming type-writer and gives it a long look. 'Got that from my brother,' I tell him with pride. 'Oh, bloody hell,' Peder murmurs. At once he whirls round to face Mum. 'Please excuse my language. I only wanted to express my enthusiasm for the best present I've ever seen.' Mum smiles. 'Would you like a little cake?' 'A little? Peder Miil has never said no to a lot of cake.' And this is my birthday. I blow out the candles. I manage it at the third attempt. Mum leaves us in peace. We have some cake, but I'm not especially hungry and Peder beats me by five slices. 'Have you tried it?' he asks. And I show him the pages I've produced. Peder studies them carefully himself, smiles and nods. Then he finally remembers he's brought a present with him too. He pulls a square parcel from his pocket. I open it. It's a square, red metal box. 'What is it?' I ask him. Peder points. 'Press the button, idiot.' It starts laughing. To begin with it's just a low chuckling. It chuckles. Then it grows stronger. The chuckling becomes a spluttering and the spluttering becomes laughter. And Peder and I laugh too; it's infec-tious – the mechanical laughter is infectious. We have to hold onto each other and we laugh like that, we laugh at the laughter, and it lasts two minutes before the box falls silent once more. And we breathe out, dry our tears, and can hardly manage to talk properly. 'Closest I could get,' Peder breathes. 'Closest you could get to what?' Peder has to massage his stomach. 'After we didn't find any applause in your suitcase.' My head grows dark for a time. 'Couldn't Vivian come?' I ask, and look the other way. Peder puts the machine on again. It laughs. And when there's no more laughter left in it, Mum's standing in the doorway with her hands over her ears. 'Help us all. What are you laughing at?' Peder gets up. 'Barnum laughed at me, and I laughed at him.' Mum just shakes her head, laughs herself, and takes out the empty cake plate and the candles. Peder stays on his feet. 'Now I know,' he says. 'You'll write my essays for me and I'll do your maths.' 'Couldn't Vivian come?' I ask him again. 'She had to look after her mother,' Peder murmurs. 'Bloody hell.' 'Yes, bloody hell,' I agree. And when I'm on the point of putting the typewriter in its carrying case I find something else, another present, that Fred must have put there for me. It's a dozen Durex – gossamer. Peder looks at me, long and hard. 'Can I borrow one?' he asks. 'What for?' Peder groans. 'You don't need the whole dozen!' So he gets one and the remainder are secreted in Oscar Mathisen's left shoe, right in as far as possible in the cupboard. And I fold up *The Little City* and put it in my right shoe. But I try one of the condoms that same night; it stings and I think certain thoughts, and afterwards I don't know where to hide it. I chuck it out of the window. The lights come on in the caretaker's by the gate. Now the building has something else to talk about, but my mouth is shut. I write Peder's essays and he does my maths. We both get As. I read *Hunger*. Fred comes home. He undresses. I see his long, thin body in the dark by the bed. He has his back to me. If I were to run my hand over his shoulder, past his neck and along his cheek that's blue and almost swollen – what would he say? I don't know. I can't sleep. That which we do is only a shadow of all we could have done. 'Why did you never say that Vivian was born in a car too?' he suddenly asked.

One day, when I come home from school, there's another letter waiting for me. Mum is so impatient she can barely wait, and I'm certain she's held it up to the light to try to read it. But that hasn't worked because the envelope is fat and impossible to see through. Boletta's pretty excited herself. She's probably tried to slip it open with Malaga steam. 'But aren't you going to open it?' Mum exclaims. I turn away and slowly tear it open. Boletta thumps her stick on the floor. Mum leans over my shoulder. 'What does it say, Barnum?' 'I've won,' I tell her, amazed and bewildered. Mum puts her arms round me. 'I knew it!' And so it comes to light that she has submitted *The Little City* to the School of Oslo's major creative writing contest, and I don't know whether to be happy or angry, proud or put out – because Mum has, in other words, unearthed my typescript in Oscar Mathisen's right shoe, and gone behind my back. And that means she must have found the condoms in my left shoe too. Mum tears the letter out of my hands and reads it aloud. *'Dear Barnum Nilsen, It is a joy to inform you that you have won the School of Oslo's creative writing contest for your age group with your story* The Little City. *The prize will be awarded in the City Chambers on Friday the 12th and we would be delighted if you would be present to receive this.'* Mum gives me a kiss on the brow and is suddenly all flustered. 'Good Lord, Barnum, it's only four days away!' Boletta's already poured two glasses of Malaga. I have to go into my room to get my breath back. Soon I'll be famous. I don't quite know why but I start crying; I sit in at the windowsill and cry for joy, and I'm glad Fred can't see me now. But when I turn round he's standing in the doorway after all. I hide my face. Fred throws himself down on the bed. 'Not long now,' he says. 'To what, Fred?' He just looks at me and gives me that crooked smile; his lips slide over his teeth. 'You remember what you promised, Barnum, huh?' 'Of course.' 'That you won't say anything?' 'I won't say a thing, Fred.' 'Brothers don't grass on each other, do they?' 'Of course not.' Suddenly he gets up. 'I'm forgetting to congratulate you! Well done, Barnum! I'm proud of you!' I look down. 'Had it not been for the typewriter,' I murmur. 'Don't put yourself down, Barnum.'

That evening I go to Vivian's. The stairs are chilly. I ring the bell. The seconds pass. I hear steps inside. I peer through the keyhole. Her mother's called the Veil. In the wake of the accident she's always worn a veil to cover her face. She is the eternal widow. She lost her beauty in the bend above Holmenkollen. She is hideous and forsaken. There are those who scare their children with her name. *If you aren't good the Veil will come and get you,* they say. *If you don't eat your food. If you don't do your homework and wash your hands.* And it is not this which scares us the most – that which we don't see, but rather what we imagine and believe to be there – under the bed, round the corner, in the dark, behind the veil. The misgivings we allow grow arms and legs. There's no limit to people's fantasies about what she must look like. They invent something they themselves have never seen – a face without features, a face that's one open hole, inhuman and unrecognizable. But once we've beheld that face, seen it with our own eyes – there's nothing to be afraid of any more. It's Vivian who opens the door. 'Guess what!' I exclaim. She has a think while she looks at me with a side-on, uncommitted expression. 'You've grown eight centimetres,' she says. I shake my head. 'Does it really look like it, huh?' 'Has Peder lost three kilos?' she suggests. I shake my head again. 'I've become a writer!' I shout. Finally she lets me in and we sit in her bedroom, under the photograph on the wall. And it wasn't until many years later that Vivian told me it wasn't Lauren Bacall's picture that was hanging there, but her mother's – as she was when she was young, before the accident, unblemished and beautiful. I tell her what's transpired. I can hardly manage to get the words out right. That Mum silently and secretly smuggled in my script to the School of Oslo's creative writing contest, that I've won the prize for my age group, and that this is on a par with the Nobel Prize for Literature. I'll receive my award in the City Chambers – maybe a world cruise for two, a painting by Munch or free travel on the trams for a year, presented by the council chairman. And if Vivian wants to be there then it's bound to be possible to reserve seats. I bury my face in her lap. 'Have you spoken to Fred?' I ask her. Vivian strokes my neck with her hand. 'Why d'you ask me that?' I make no reply. I stay where I am with my head in her lap, and she keeps stroking my neck. I open the top button of her trousers, and then a second; I can see the edge of her knickers and there's a strong, almost dizzying smell. She twists a little and her hand doesn't move at all; I hold my breath and lick her skin and get one more button undone. Then she gets up abruptly and I tumble onto the floor and can't bring myself to look at her and haven't the faintest idea how I'll get up again – maybe I'll have to stay where I am for the rest of my days. 'Will you say hello to Mum?' Vivian asks me. She takes my arm and hoists me up. 'Forgive me,' I whisper. Vivian closes her eyes and kisses my mouth. Her lips are soft and they move – it's as though she laughs in the middle of her kiss. And I follow her out through the flat, the one room darker than the next – I don't want to but I go with her all the same; I have no choice. Finally we reach her mother's bedroom and Vivian knocks and opens the door – she lets me go in first. I don't see her mother immediately. Then I find I can discern her. She's sitting in a chair in the shadows by the window, a window hidden by long, thick curtains. I stop. Still she hasn't moved a muscle. The air's heavy. Vivian's standing beside me. I hear the door slide shut behind us. And I get a strong sense that all this means more than I can fathom, that Vivian wants to test me, to see if I can cope with this. I decide I will cope with it. 'Here is Barnum,' Vivian says. I take a step forward and bow. Her mother slowly moves towards me. 'Well, well. So you're Barnum?' Her voice is childish and light; it's as if it's a little girl who's sitting talking there. 'Yes,' I murmur. 'It's me.' Vivian's mother suddenly raises her veil, but I can't see her face – it's as if it isn't there at all and I feel glad, I'm glad and yet would like to have seen it nonetheless, seen what isn't there. 'Barnum's won first prize in the School of Oslo's creative writing contest,'

Vivian tells her. She leans forward in her chair. 'Congratulations, Barnum,' she says. I give an even deeper bow.
That way I can avoid looking at her. 'Thank you very
much,' I whisper. She lays her hand on my arm. I'm trembling. She senses it, for she holds me even tighter. 'You're
obviously a clever boy, Barnum.' I hear her delicate, twin-
kling voice – it's as if it's the only undamaged thing about
her, the only thing that hasn't been changed since the
accident. All that remains of the beautiful young girl in
the Chevrolet is her voice, and it speaks still in that
ruined body. She doesn't let me go. I remain where I am.
'You've fine curls,' she says. She can see me but I can't see
her. All I can see is the veil that falls back down over the
remains of her face. She retracts her arm; the visit is over
and I have been initiated. And I wonder just how many
have been here before me – if I'm the first, if I've passed
the test – and Vivian pulls me out. Now her father's come
home too; he's sitting asleep in the living room, but I
reckon he's just pretending – this man who'll one day be
my father-in-law – for one eye remains all but open and
secretly watching me, and it looks as though the eye
doesn't like what it sees. Even I get the message that it's
time to leave. 'That was what I wanted to ask you,' I
murmur. Vivian furrows her brow. 'What?' 'My curls. I
wouldn't mind losing them for the prize-giving.' Vivian
gives my hair a pull and lets it go again. 'Either you can
get the whole lot cut,' she says. 'Or else?' I ask, my voice
quieter still. Vivian smiles a long while. And I get to
borrow her hairnet and hairgrips, and have them for three
nights. When I get up on the fourth day my head feels flat
and different, as though someone's taken a plane to it. I
tear off the net, take out the hairgrips, and chase to the
bathroom. I see someone else in the mirror. To begin with
I'm in seventh heaven. This is the day I'll receive my prize
at the City Chambers and I've become someone else. I no
longer look like myself. I'll probably have to pay an adult
fare on the tram and no old ladies'll put their hands on my
head any more. My hair's all smooth and flat against my

skull; not so much as one solitary strand is standing upright. But soon enough I'm not as pleased as I was. Something isn't right. It takes a while before I know what it is, what's wrong; I think I'm going to faint, and then Mum's at my back, looking at me with worry. 'You're not ill, Barnum?' 'No, no,' I murmur, and scrabble about for the toothbrush. Mum pulls me round. 'Yes,' she says. 'There is something.' 'I've just got butterflies, Mum.' She takes a step back again. 'Have you shrunk, Barnum?' 'Yes,' I sob. Now Boletta's there in the bathroom too. 'He's lost his beautiful curls,' she sighs. And Mum all but shrieks. 'He's lost his curls!' I look at least eight centimetres shorter and resemble a tortoise. 'I want my curls back!' I cry. And for the remainder of the morning Mum winds them up again, one after another – it's a laborious task, but as soon as she lets go of them my locks unravel as though my hair's rubber tapped from brain bark, and vulcanized at about 170 degrees, and she has to begin all over again. When I do finally stand in the great hall of the City Chambers in my blazer, and with my blue tie and tie-pin in place, and wearing my narrow shoes that contain neither scripts nor condoms, just my fat and clammy feet, my hair's back to normal. And in the celebrated picture that was taken of me (by the photographer from the afternoon edition of *Aftenposten*), of that moment when I'm presented with my shining certificate bearing the city's emblem and a cheque for fifty kroner by the council chairman, I resemble a rather worn mini-version of Einstein. And underneath this picture, which Mum had framed and which she hung above the stove in the living room, was the caption – *Barnum Nilsen, the little genius*. And after the chairman's sweated his way through the line of nervous prizewinners, and the mothers have done their weeping, and Peder and Vivian have got to their feet and shouted my name and done some stamping – none other than Ditlev himself makes his way over, notebook in hand, and we go out into the courtyard to find some quiet. 'Well, well,' Ditlev says. 'You've not brought your brother with you? Or is he still out for the count?' But before I can say anything, Peder's materialized and is shaking hands with Ditlev. 'Peder Miil,' says Peder. 'Barnum Nilsen will only speak to the press when I'm present.' Ditlev sighs heavily and lights a cigarette. 'Well, well,' he says again. 'What was the point behind this strange story of yours then?' I give the question some thought. Vivian's standing waving with Mum and Boletta over by the ornamental porch. I wave back. Water is running everywhere – dripping and pouring – the last snow's in the process of melting and the sun's shining in pools where the light's reflected, so the whole city looks as if glass has been scattered over it. Easter's over. 'That everyone's sufficiently big,' Peder says. Ditlev gets irritated and turns to Peder. 'Is it Barnum Nilsen or you who won today?' Peder points to me. 'That everyone's sufficiently big. If they just acknowledge it.' Ditlev scribbles on his pad and flicks over to a fresh sheet of paper. 'Have you any literary models, Barnum?' 'One would have to be Hamsun,' I reply. 'What d'you admire in particular about Hamsun then?' I consider this for a bit. 'He was a troublemaker who wrote well,' I reply. Ditlev goes on writing furiously. 'Good, Barnum. This'll be great. Hamsun's a troublemaker.' Peder rolls his eyes. 'Barnum's also been inspired by his great-grandfather,' he says. Ditlev raises his pen to his mouth. 'Your great-grandfather? Was he a writer too?' 'He wrote letters,' I tell him. 'But unfortunately I can't say any more than that.' 'No? Why's that, Barnum?' 'Because he wrote that we shouldn't talk to gossip columnists.' Peder intervenes at once. 'I'd also like to mention that Barnum Nilsen's had a small part in the forthcoming film, *Hunger*.' Ditlev sticks his pen in his breast pocket and bangs his notebook shut. 'The gossip columnist is most grateful for the information.' It's obvious that the interview's over. And then we go off to the Grand – that's Mum's decision – because it's where Ibsen went in his time, and we sit at the same table as before, on that day when Dad had died and been buried – Mum and Boletta,

Peder and Vivian and me. We have prawn sandwiches with thick mayonnaise on a bed of lettuce leaves, while outside, people pass revealing brown faces above light-blue shirts and white blouses. We're waiting for Fred. 'He said he'd be coming to the City Chambers,' Mum says, and her voice betrays a momentary shadow. I look away. 'It doesn't matter.' I try to appear disappointed – heroic and disappointed – a brother with an award. I'm actually relieved. Mum places the whole of her hand on my own and I try to push it away. 'He'll come all right, just you see.' Boletta raises her beer glass (even though she's given up drinking because her system won't tolerate it, but today's an exception, today's a day without rival or rules), and she drinks my health. The ice rattles in Vivian's cola. All at once Peder and I have to exit to the loo. We chase down to the gents and find a stall, but neither of us needs a pee. Peder has something in both the pockets of the tweed jacket he can only just manage to button up at the middle. Two rum miniatures. We unscrew the tops of our respective bottles. We drink. We cough. Our heads burn. 'I'm proud of you, Barnum!' 'Oh, don't,' I say. Peder puts his arms round me. 'I mean it! I'm bloody well proud of you, Barnum!' He has one miniature left and we share it between the two of us, and it's in there, in a stall in the Grand's gents, that I lay the foundation for my prodigious use of miniatures – the playthings of the minibar. They're somehow in line with my smallness,   and   it's   possible to secrete them in the tiniest pockets and folds and gloves – yes, I've even hidden them in shoes. 'I've seen her,' I whisper to Peder. 'Seen who?' 'Vivian's mother.' 'Did you see her?' 'Not really. It was pretty dark in the bedroom. But I *heard* her at any rate.' Peder shakes his head. 'What did I tell you? Vivian's in love with you.' 'You think so?' 'Think? I know, Barnum. It's a simple case of mathematics.' Then we emerged and washed our mouths out with soap, and the venerable gentlemen who probably *lived* here in the toilets in between engagements, turned up their noses at us – their porous, burgundy noses that spread over their blotchy faces and looked as if they were completely falling apart. By the time we got back to our window table once more Fred still hadn't shown up. I had to look extra specially at Vivian, and she smiled back in her own way – a smile without anything behind it. Because everything about Vivian was so tranquil – at least on the outside. And twice or more Mum gave Peder and myself particularly hard stares; then we got coffee and meringues and went home through the mild evening – but when we got there Fred wasn't there either. Mum became even more agitated. The special atmosphere had disappeared. Boletta got a headache and lamented her own distress. 'You shouldn't have had beer!' Mum told her. 'Oh, leave it out!' Boletta shouted. 'Have you forgotten I worked at the Exchange? I get a sore head just seeing a telephone wire between two posts!' Mum refused to carry on a debate with her, sat down in the living room instead, and started waiting. Mum started to wait and Fred's absence from us began. The following day I had to read *The Little City* aloud in the school hall to all the pupils, and I don't think there were many who understood a thing about it, because at breaktime no one said anything to me – quite the opposite, they kept their distance and left me on my own by the fountain. So my isolation in the playground grew yet more obvious, sharp and short as a shadow. I didn't give a damn. It felt so good not to give a damn. I had Peder. I had Vivian. I had the typewriter! That was sufficient. That was all I needed. And that was the day the interview with me appeared in the afternoon edition of *Aftenposten*, that and the wild picture of me which Mum ordered a copy of from the paper and got framed, and which hangs above the stove to this very day. *The little genius. Prizewinner Barnum Nilsen speaks out*. But Fred still hadn't shown up. And when this dragged into over a week – the first time he'd disappeared for such a stretch at one time – Mum came into my room while I was sitting composing the opening lines of what would become my story, *Fattening*. She came in without knocking and proceeded to go through his drawers, look in the wardrobe and peer under the bed. All she found was that nothing was missing – everything lay where it should lie, nor had he taken anything with him. Then she sat down beside me. I took the sheet of paper out of the machine and put it in my drawer. 'Barnum,' she said. 'We don't need to keep secrets from each other, do we?' I didn't answer that. I reckoned it was a trap, and that keeping quiet would be my strongest card. Mum's face was pale and sleepless. 'You can't keep secrets,' she said, when she realized an answer was there in hiding. 'D'you really think I didn't find the condoms?' That was certainly something I couldn't respond to, and for a time the two of us were silent. Then Mum gave a laugh. 'Barnum, Barnum,' she said. It was Fred who'd got them. My mouth was under lock and key. I realized I'd do pretty well under interrogation. Mum sighed and ran her hand through my curls that had sprouted once more, higher than ever. 'Has Fred said anything to you?' she murmured. 'About where he is?' And I remembered what I'd promised him, and that brothers didn't grass on each other. 'I don't know,' I told her, my voice as quiet as possible, as though our conversation was being bugged. 'Look me in the eyes, Barnum! You're not lying to your own mother?' I looked her in the eyes. It was not a pretty sight. It was as if her eyes were hanging by two thin threads above shadows of skin. I couldn't tell her there was a chance Fred had gone to search for the Greenland letter. 'Perhaps he's at Willy's,' I said instead. Mum's eyes narrowed. 'Willy? That idiot of a trainer?' I nodded. 'He's been there before.' Mum found him in the telephone book and went over there in a taxi, to the other side of town, that same evening. She didn't want to phone and give Fred the chance to slip away once more – if indeed he was there at all. Boletta and I sat at home in the living room waiting. Her headache had passed but it was as if she were absent, and was disappearing gram by gram.

Perhaps that was what it was like to die, that you dried up like a juicy piece of fruit that's been in the sun too long. I wondered if I might use some of this for my fattening story. Boletta looked round at me and smiled. 'You look thoughtful,' she said. 'Or are you just sad?' 'What d'you think's happened?' I asked her. 'I'm too old to believe anything at all, Barnum. So I believe nothing before I know for sure.' Boletta was drinking tea and she slowly stirred the spoon round her cup. 'But then you don't think,' I said. 'You know.' Boletta sighed. 'I only know that Fred is restless. He wanders.' I moved closer. I liked the aroma of the sweet tea. I liked having Boletta all to myself. 'Wanders? In the streets round about? But then I'd have seen him.' 'Oh, no. He wanders a lot further afield now. Much further. And there's no one who can stop him.' 'Can't we?' Boletta shook her head. 'Fred's a night man, Barnum.' She drank up the last of her tea and there was a clump of brown sugar left at the bottom of the cup which she ate with her spoon. 'And I'm not?' I asked, my voice quiet. 'No, Barnum. You're no night man.' I went into the bedroom. I was no night man. I was the one who stayed. I'd travel in different ways. I had a laughter machine, a typewriter, and a measuring tape with two different sides. I managed. And I remember something, something I was told by someone, and I mention it now and pass it on. And it isn't a story but rather a picture, a picture that floats up from a story rather like a photograph from developing fluid. A mother in Siberia stands beside a golden beach looking out over the sea day after day eating sunflower seeds she has in her hand. A stranger asks her what it is she's looking for. 'My son,' she replies. 'He hasn't come back yet.' 'Has he been away long?' the stranger asks in ignorance. 'Eighteen years,' the mother replies, and chews her sunflower seeds as she stares out over the sea.

Mum came back late that evening. I ran out into the living room. She'd already sat down on the sofa. There was something about her that was different. I'd never seen her like this before. She hadn't taken off her coat and she clutched her handbag on her lap with both hands as if it was the only thing that kept her from falling. And yet there was the ghost of a smile on her lips, and it was this smile that somehow didn't fit in with the rest of her. Boletta grew impatient but kept quiet and didn't bang about with her stick, for she'd seen that there was something about Mum that evening too. And I could see that Boletta's dry eyes were huge with wonder and not a little angst. At last Mum said something. 'Fred's gone to sea,' she said. Boletta sat down on the sofa. 'To sea? Are you sure?' Mum whispered now. 'Willy told me. Willy Halvorsen, I mean.' Boletta let out her breath. 'Is he to be relied upon?' she asked. 'A simple boxing trainer?' Mum nodded. 'He helped Fred get hired.' Mum looked at me but said nothing. Boletta helped her off with her coat and still refused to be convinced. 'How can you be so sure? That Willy Halvorsen couldn't even teach Fred to box properly!' Mum got up. 'I phoned the office, the ship owner's office. Fred's gone to sea.' We looked at each other. Boletta shrugged her small shoulders. 'Well, well. It isn't the worst thing that's ever happened. But he could have said goodbye before he left.' It was only now Mum started crying. She had to sit down again. She shook. Boletta tried to hold her but it didn't help. And it came home to me that Mum was suddenly thinking she'd never see Fred again. And yet he did come back, but each time he left again it was like a small death, a small death that grew bigger all the time and became a memorial service in Majorstuen church – a funeral with no body, just a huge sense of loss – and it was myself, as I've mentioned before, who gave the eulogy. Boletta let Mum cry till she had no more tears, and yet it wasn't the tears that ran out but rather her own strength. And I had the same thought, that Fred had left us for good, for a moment later Boletta asked, 'What sort of ship has he got himself mixed up with?' 'The *Polar Bear*,' Mum breathed. 'Yes, but where's it bound for?' Mum looked at neither Boletta nor me but just down, down. 'Greenland,' she said. And she looked up as she spoke the word, worried and all twisted, and she spoke the words we'd repeat so often when we tried to comfort ourselves. 'And he didn't even take a jumper with him.'

I went to the bedroom again, the bedroom which perhaps was mine now – perhaps that evening I'd got my own room – as Fred went on his way to Greenland aboard the *Polar Bear*. And if they passed Rost at that moment, before heading north towards the blue horizon and the sinking, green sun – I hoped that Skomvaer would light up for them, the final lighthouse, Fresnell's crystal flash, to burn their image into the wind. *A warm greeting I send all of you at home from the land of the midnight sun in the land of ice and snow*. Perhaps Fred would find a musk ox. Perhaps he'd have to eat seal meat. Was that Fred's thinking, that he had to follow in the same footsteps, sail in the wake of the SS *Antarctic* that went there to the northern seas sixty-six years before? Did he have to do that in order to find the letter? Did he have to see the same sun that great-grandfather had seen – feel the cold and hear the shifting of the ice – before he started searching? Perhaps he'd find him, frozen in a glacier, a coat round a skeleton, and in the pocket of that coat a stub of a pencil that once had scribed the letter. I was happy, yes, happy that Fred had gone. But it gave me no joy. I put away the Diplomat – it was too late to compose any more, enough had been done already – and I lay in bed with the laughter machine instead. I put it on. It laughed away under the quilt. I listened to that mechanical laughter. It was heartless and evil. If snakes could have laughed they'd have laughed like that. The laughter I'd thought so generous when I listened to it with Peder, so generous and infectious, filled me now with great, restless blackness. And it came home to me that laughter doesn't work when you're alone. I had to write this down so I wouldn't forget

it. Perhaps I could make use of such a revelation. That
laughter yearns company. But I was asleep before I got
that far, and the batteries in the mechanism went flat, and
the laughter got slower and deeper and deeper. Finally it
died out altogether with a tiny click and only a low and
distant hissing remained, like the wind in a long-
abandoned house, I could imagine. Then the hissing died
out too, and left in its wake fine thread spun with nothing my dreams could hang to dry on. Mum woke me.
'We're going to the Exchange,' she told me. 'And there's
no need for you to sleep in Fred's bed yet!' I got up at
once, shameful and sleepy, for I'd barely slept at all. 'Can
I come with you?' I did go with them. Boletta had on her
finest garb, but right outside the heavy door in Tolbu
Street her nerve failed her and she grew reluctant and
demanded we should go back. She'd got her headache –
the Morse – but Mum shoved her decisively inside, and
there we stood, in the great hall in which Boletta hadn't
set foot since she resigned the day King Haakon and the
Old One died nine years previously. It was no longer
silent here, as in a church. Now the hall was more reminiscent of a repository, a repository for conversations and
telegrams. There was humming everywhere, as if a giant
swarm of bees was moving from corner to corner at a furious pace. Shoes chased over the stone floor. The clock on
the wall jerked time forwards with firm clicks. Mum gave
Boletta a tug. 'Don't just stand there gawping!' But
Boletta did just stand there gawping. 'Changed,' she
whispered. 'What are you on about?' Mum demanded.
'Ships' names can be written as one word,' Boletta said.
'As long as they don't come to more than fifteen letters.'
'The *Polar Bear*,' Mum said, and quickly worked it out
with her fingers. 'That's just twelve letters. Let's get it
sent.' And we climbed the broad stairs to the first floor.
Boletta greeted some of the women, but they no longer
had any idea who she was, and just hurried past. And
each time Boletta went unrecognized she became more
stooped – yes, she grew smaller and smaller with every

step. Not even Director Egede stopped – that poor wreck of humanity – he just halted on the landing below and looked at us, as if something dawned on him at the sight of Boletta, and she met his gaze stubbornly and expectantly. But it was to me the wretched creature spoke. 'The little genius,' he said, and laughed. And Miss Stang, the manageress, the virgin of the relays – she'd been pensioned off long ago and sat at home in her dark, two-roomed flat in Uranienborg with a damp cloth over her brow to ease her stinging headache. And she'd seen the black, Bakelite telephones exchanged for grey and white contraptions – low and discreet – which for a short period in the 1970s were replaced by impractical and ridiculous things in the most lurid colours – red, yellow and orange – colours that have nothing whatsoever to do with telephones. These phones actually stood on their own dial plates, and for that reason were called homophones by some quick-witted individuals – because you dialled the number from behind. And later the Exchange itself was shut down as there was one great explosion of verbal diarrhoea in the 1990s; the whole industry was privatized and thrown to the four winds. It was impossible to get away from cordless conversation – the most intimate of things were shouted out at restaurant tables, secrets were spilled in supermarket queues and at bus stops. You were forced to listen to other people's arguments, threats and billing and cooing – in short, society became one big bedroom where everyone talked to everyone else but mostly to themselves, and no one had anything to say.

And so we came to the long-distance message section. There was a queue. It was from here the most urgent communications were sent, those that were a matter of life and death and which couldn't be calculated. Because the voice is an imprecise instrument; the voice is full of misunderstandings, changes of emphasis, slips of the tongue and exaggerations. But the telegram is unmistakable, silent and clear – the telegram is reserved for catastrophe and for affairs of the heart. Eight women were sitting here, each at individual desks. None of them knew Boletta either. We said nothing. The telephone is wearing on the nerves and on one's hearing, and telephone operators shouldn't work for any more than four hours at one stretch. The sending of telegraphs primarily affects the hand and the fingers, and can lead to cramping and arthritis. Mum had scribbled down her message on a scrap of paper, and she handed this to the operator once her turn came, and the operator found the right codes and keyed in the scant but significant words. And I saw in my mind's eye that at that very moment, the Wireless Operator onboard the *Polar Bear* could interpret the message, translate the various dots to letters, and go up and deliver it to the new boy, who wasn't so much as green about the gills on this his first passage, and who'd seemingly been a promising boxer given a drubbing by a fairly mediocre opponent from Melhus. 'Hi, Nilsen! Mummy's missing you!' And the rest of the crew, all those there with him in the mess, would snigger and cackle, and Fred, I imagine, would simply crumple up the message and stuff it in his pocket, fed up and embarrassed. And later, when he was on watch, he'd dig it out again, read Mum's scattering of words and chuck the bit of paper into the sea, where already the icebergs were drifting past like dirty crusts, thudding against the hull and keeping him awake when he should be sleeping.

He didn't send Mum any reply. Every day she waited for a telegram from the *Polar Bear* – just a word, some sign of life, a ray of hope. It didn't come. She rushed to the door whenever anyone rang the bell, only to discover it was some salesman or other wanting to palm off Tupperware, or else a rag-and-bone man or Jehovah's Witness. She chased the lot of them back down the stairs. She turned grey in the course of that time. Boletta and I walked on eggshells; the least thing could make her blow her top – and yes, for a time we really feared for her sanity. Boletta whispered to me that waiting was an art, one that took time to learn – few master it, and time itself is the teacher. And after a certain period had gone by without any sound, a single letter or message in Morse from Fred, she calmed down again. It was as if she accepted her fate and submitted to it – a quiescent rage – and one evening, just before the summer holidays, the bell rang once more and Mum didn't leap for the door. We knew then that she'd entered that quiet time of waiting when one does nothing more than wait – just as the Old One had, before her, made an art of waiting, made it an element of the soul. It was me who went out to open the door. It was Peder. And right behind him was Vivian peering over his shoulder smiling. It was a while since I'd last seen them. I was delighted. I had friends round to visit. 'Would it be here that the great, but rather small, writer lives?' Peder asked. I gave a deep bow and let them both in, and we sat down in our room, the room I still didn't call my own, and Vivian wanted to listen to the laughter machine but I'd forgotten to change the batteries. Instead she asked, 'Has Fred gone away?' 'He's in the army,' I replied. And I'd no idea why I said exactly that, but that was my answer all the same, that he was in the army. Peder gave a long, loud whistle. 'Well, the country's in safe hands. Now we can all sleep peacefully in our beds at night.' Vivian looked at me. 'Where?' she asked. I had to think. The lie had started growing already. Like a worm it quite simply divided in the middle to become two lies, and in that way it would go on – it was pure science. 'That's secret.' Vivian lowered her gaze. 'Secret?' Peder began to whistle again and the liar had to find something else to talk about. I thumped Peder on the shoulder. 'Couldn't the model get us in to that film club again?' I said, rather louder than necessary. Peder stopped whistling abruptly. 'Mum's finished with him.' 'Finished? Is she completely finished with the painting?' Peder suddenly got annoyed and stood up. 'Did you hear what I said, or not?' I'd heard what he'd said all right, but I didn't understand what he meant. Vivian looked away so there was no salvation there. If only I'd remembered to buy batteries for the laughter machine everything would have been different.

I hurried to find the essay I owed Peder. He was still standing facing away. He just snatched the piece of paper out of my hands. I'd chosen, *Describe a job you've done.* Peder looked at the title. 'I said you should choose, *The advantages and drawbacks of modern technology.* Bugger!' 'I've really managed to cover both topics in the same essay,' I told him cautiously. Peder started reading. 'You've written about when we were extras in *Hunger,* you idiot!' 'Yes, and so I've written about the development of the film camera.' 'Crikey,' Peder said. Vivian wanted to see it too and read aloud. *'It's beyond all doubt that the lighter and smaller the camera becomes, the better it is for filming, because the director can follow the actors, or that which he might otherwise be filming, in a simpler way. But the camera's size mustn't affect its ability to film in breadth as well as in depth. This was one of the things I came to realize when I, along with my two best friends, acted as an extra in the new film* Hunger, *which unfortunately has not yet had its première.'* Peder turned slowly and smiled. 'Good, Barnum. This is good. I get the distinct whiff of an A here.' But Vivian just sat facing even more deliberately away. Peder and I looked at each other and there followed a conversation I've pondered over a long while. And I really wish a telegraph operator had been present to punch everything out in Morse, so that a ribbon with those symbols could tick out one night when I understood more, a night when I was the great wireless operator who could see behind the signs and beneath the words. 'What is it?' Peder asked. Vivian said nothing. 'What is it?' I asked. Vivian glanced over her shoulder. 'Am I just your best friend, Barnum?' I was confused. Just? And it struck me that a lie is more comforting than being bewildered – bewilderment had nothing in it to dull the pain, whereas a lie was total narcosis. Perhaps Dad had been right that time when he said it was only possible to understand about two per cent of a woman, and that it would take your whole life to do so. 'Yes, you and Peder,' I whispered. 'Aren't we?' And now Peder said something even stranger, to Vivian, something

I'd really have liked in writing. 'This is my essay, right. Not Barnum's. He's just written it for me.' We were silent for a time after that until Peder clapped his hands and clambered up onto a chair. 'And anyway, I know when the première's to be!' Vivian got up too and my hand slid quickly down her light blue jumper that lay in folds along the sharp ridge of her back. 'When then, you plonker!' I shouted. Peder looked down at me. 'It's exactly 84 days away. And tomorrow it'll be just 83.'

They left before Mum had finished making supper. I ran out to the kitchen. She was still cutting wafers of goat's cheese. Waiting had made her meticulous and slow. 'The première's on 19 August!' I told her. She was just as sluggish turning round. 'Have they gone already?' 'Yes, and the première of *Hunger* will be on 19 August!' Mum gave a sigh. 'Perhaps Fred'll have come home by then.' At that moment the bell went again and I saw a tremor pass through her, and she dropped the cheese slicer on the floor. I ran to get the door. It was Peder again. 'I forgot something,' he breathed. He brought out an envelope and pushed it towards me. 'Don't exactly think your brother's in the army,' he muttered, his voice even quieter. I stared at the envelope. *Branum Nilsen, Miil's stamps, Oslo, Norway*. One corner was plastered in Danish stamps. Fred had sent it to Peder's dad. Now Peder was giving it to me. I said nothing. I just stared at the envelope. 'Well, well,' Peder murmured. 'Everything has a meaning.' He turned and retreated down the stairs. I sneaked back into the bedroom, the letter secreted under my shirt. Once there I hid it under the mattress. Suddenly Mum was behind me. 'Was that Peder again?' she asked me. I nodded. 'What did he want?' I swallowed and sat down on the bed. 'He was just giving me some maths questions he'd forgotten.' 'Didn't he want any supper?' I shook my head. 'He didn't have time.' Mum smiled. 'If he didn't have time for supper then he really is in a hurry.' 'Yes, you're right.' 'Are you going to bed already?' I gave a long yawn. 'I'm pretty tired,' I said. Mum sat down beside me. She was searching for the right words. Under the mattress was the letter from Fred. 'It'll be fun with the film,' she said. 'To think we've got a second actor in the family.' She laughed a little. 'An extra,' I reminded her. 'Well, it's almost the same.' Mum was silent for a time. I wished she'd go. I yawned again and stretched out my arms in the air, and it struck me, as I opened my mouth, yawned loudly, and lifted my arms – that everything I did was exaggerated, each and every action was larger than life, as if that would render me more genuine, as though the exaggeration was twice as real. 'I can't sleep,' she said. 'I can't sleep as long as he's away.' 'I'm sure Fred's fine,' I breathed. 'He's a night man.' A tremor passed through her once more, as if my words had given her an electric shock. She took my hand and clasped it, whether in anger or sorrow I don't know – perhaps in love, too. I don't believe she slept that night either. But when things were sufficiently still I brought out the envelope and opened it carefully. Inside there was a postcard. It was a picture of a musk ox. It was standing on a barren slope, head bent, and it looked pretty shabby and lost. And on the back Fred had written in his clumsy handwriting – *Don't say anything. Fred.* That was all. *Don't say anything. Fred.* I've no idea how long I sat staring at those words. And I made up my mind. I'd say nothing. Yes, I could have done, I had a choice – isn't it always about that, a choice one has to make, and for which there's no excuse? I could have done otherwise. I could have broken my promise to Fred, gone in to Mum and shown her the card. I didn't. I kept my promise and let her lie there sleepless. I cried a little. 'Satan fanny shit!' I shouted and bashed my own mouth. I listened. Everything was just as still as before. Then I put the card back in the envelope once more and hid the envelope somewhere I knew Mum would never find it. And so began the lie that lasted so long.

And each and every day that passed was a continuation of that lie. I said nothing, so I lied. I kept my word and I lied at the same time. I have two tongues and one face, or rather, I have many faces and one tongue. Mum lies sleepless each night. She visits Willy sporadically to get any news of the *Polar Bear*. When she comes back she's more silent then ever and Boletta sits in the living room and shakes her head. I compose the first draft of *Fattening* but am dissatisfied with it and discard it as soon as I'm finished. I have to change the typewriter ribbon. We wait. Time is slow and reluctant. Fred does not come back. A summer fades. Peder starts at Katta that autumn and is elected treasurer of the college club. Vivian sits at home reading, studying one subject at a time, and I go through the Fagerborg gates to begin yet another first day of school, the sun at my back. I see the whole crowd of them turning away as one and weighing me up with their eyes, and I decide to set a new record in skipping school. I manage that fine.

Three days later, *Hunger* has its première. We warm up at the Stortorget Inn, but don't get the beer we order, just tea. That's of no consequence. For Peder has got hold of a bottle of champagne and has it hidden under the table, and Peder's the only one ever to have taken the cork out of a bottle of champagne at Stortorget Inn without getting caught red-handed. A bit of a damp lap is all he suffers. We gulp our tea as fast as we can and slosh champagne into our cups. We're sitting at the table furthest in. There's a strange scent coming from Vivian. After two cups of champagne I get a wildness in my head and twist my face down into the hollow of her throat. Vivian shoves me away, but I only come back. 'Barnum!' she bursts out. 'You're biting me!' She disappears to the loo and Peder stretches over the cloth on the table and laughs. The other customers turn in our direction; dark faces in the golden light of the pints they raise with both hands. The waiter's expression becomes rather stony and he comes to empty the ashtray. Our teacups are bubbling. 'I trust you're not consuming alcohol you've brought onto the premises?' 'Musk ox,' Peder replies. The waiter shakes his head, walks round the table and slowly goes back to the counter. I lean towards Peder. 'Musk ox?' I murmur. Peder manages to get more champagne into our glasses. 'Vivian's perfume, Barnum. Tapped from the balls of musk ox.' 'Musk ox balls?' 'Makes you really horny.' 'Horny? Who?' 'You.' Then Vivian comes back from the loo. The scent's gone. Perhaps she's washed her throat. I say nothing. I can't think straight. There's too much to consider and my thoughts just don't fit together. Peder looks at his watch and raises his cup. 'Time to hit Saga,' he says. We drink up and head over to the cinema, arm in arm, for our very first première. It's the evening performance. There's a queue outside. And I'm the one who has to produce my identity card to prove my age. Peder puts his hand on the ticket collector's blue arm. 'Let me inform you that we are in this evening's film,' Peder explains to him. 'And you surely aren't going to refuse actors admission?' 'Extras,' I put in. 'Shut up,' Peder says. 'If he's old enough he's old enough,' the ticket collector says. Peder gives a loud sigh. 'If he's old enough to have a part in the film then he's got to be old enough to see it.' Vivian laughs and we get in. And everyone's there. I see them the moment we take our seats, down in the front row – Mum and Boletta, Esther from the kiosk, Peder's parents (his mother is in her chair at the bottom of the steps), and yes, Vivian's father is there, and behind him is Ditlev from the afternoon edition of *Aftenposten*. He can't see a great deal and is moving about in his seat and gets told to be quiet. They're all there because the news has missed no one that we – Peder, Vivian and myself – are in the film; we've even written about it in essays and spoken about it in interviews. I spy Bang the caretaker, Knuckles, the Goat, Aslak, Hamster and Preben – distant faces in the sloping cinema. I see Tenner, the twins, Talent and Tommy – the boys from the boxing club, with their crooked noses and slightly longer hair. I see the parents of T, pale and thin and closest to the emergency exit; and I think to myself as the curtain slides to one side and the lights are dimmed, that almost everyone who's played a part in my life is here. Some have just passed by in the background while others have loomed large, and as the darkness and the silence fall together I think to myself that there are perhaps more here than would be at my own funeral, were I to die now. And just before Vivian takes my hand and Pontus comes into view on the screen with his back to us, leaning against the railing on a bridge over the Aker river, as he writes furiously on a scrap of paper which he then puts in his mouth and eats, I see that someone's sitting in the shadows beside Mum and that someone is Willy.

We're not in it. We're not in Palace Park. We're invisible. We've been cut out. We're on a roll of film that's been chucked in a bin somewhere in Denmark – surplus to requirements, rejected. And so it's a kind of funeral after all. It's Barnum's ruler again. Barnum's ruler's too short. There's always one centimetre missing. We leave before the credits have finished. 'At least you got to keep your souls,' Peder's mother whispers as we hurry past her. We're already outside. The streets are wet. Autumn's arrived. Peder and I have to pee behind a bin. We chuck away our tickets and pee on them. 'Shit film!' Peder exclaims. And that's all that's said before we get to Solli Square. Our tree is red and shining in the dark. Then Peder says, 'If he was so bloody hungry, why didn't he just go up to Nordmarka and pick a few berries? Huh?' 'Maybe it was another sort of hunger he was feeling,' I whispered. 'Oh, really? He bloody well went on about sausages the whole way through the film! All he had to do was make a hook, use his shoelaces as line and haul in a couple of cod, you know! Bloody nutter!' 'At least he could have eaten the chocolate twirls,' Vivian puts in. We look at her. 'Twirls?' Peder repeats. 'Didn't you notice? There were a couple of carabloodymels and a liquorice twist left in the leaves in Palace Park.' Peder looked at me. I looked at Peder. 'Really?' Vivian nods. 'Absolutely.'

Peder's on the point of shaking the tree down he's laughing so much. 'We ruined the film! Chocolate twirls in 1890!' I laugh too, but something makes me so sad all the same – everything that comes to nothing, that's cut and thrown away – as if scissors were my own emblem. 'See you!' Peder suddenly says, and he starts walking away over Bygdøy Alley, between the chestnuts. 'Hang on!' Vivian calls after him. But Peder doesn't wait. He keeps on going. I let go of Vivian's hand and chase after him. 'What's up with you?' Peder leans against the fence and smiles. 'Is there something up with me?' I lay my hand on his shoulder. 'You don't need to go home yet, surely?' 'Maybe I'm hungry.' And his smile, his laughter, has a softness to it, a fragility – as if his mouth might start crying at any given moment. 'It's you two now,' he says. 'It's the three of us,' I tell him. Peder shakes his head. 'No, I'm one too many. I'll see you.' And he keeps on going over the crossroads. He doesn't turn round. I just stand there. I don't know what to do. I want to run after Peder. And I want to go back to Vivian. It's she who comes over to me.

That evening something else happens. We go together to Frogner Park. It's beginning to get dark. It's still raining. Up by the white summer house Vivian sits down in the grass. I sit down beside her. It isn't particularly comfortable. It's wet. I lend her my jacket. And it's now it happens. Vivian sits on top of me instead. I can't move. She's gripping me tight. I twist my head from side to side and feel the soaking grass in my hair and neck. She starts doing something. She pulls down her knickers and whips them over her feet. Then she opens my fly. I don't dare move a muscle. She fits a condom and guides me in. She just sinks down, heavy and hard. She's utterly still. I am too. I can sense it again – the scent of musk ox – heedless and raging, that's to be my gateway that evening, musk ox and scissors. I've come. It's over already. Vivian gets up, her back to me, pulls on her knickers and straightens her skirt. I lie there. I'm freezing. I shut my eyes. I don't dare

open them. There's a stinging. I feel ashamed. I hear her
moving away. By the time I get to my feet she's gone. I
tear off the condom, scream, and throw it after her. I take
my jacket, stagger my way to the fence and clamber over
it. I rip my trousers, fall down in the bushes on the other
side, and crawl out onto the pavement. A tram goes past.
There's a whine as it tilts at the sharp bend. I hold my
ears. I could go to Peder's. But I don't. I've nothing to say.
And how would I say it? I run up Church Road. I'm glad
it's raining. I run till I can't be bothered running any
more. Now I am, I tell myself. I say it again. Now I am.
Now I've done it. I'm relieved. I'm not happy, but I am
relieved. It's not so bad. It was really me who got *her*. Of
course it was me. It was my fault. It was me who took her
with me to Frogner Park, to the summer house, to the
shadows by the summer house. As if no one realizes what
that means. I went so far as to put my jacket in the grass
for her to lie on, in the wet grass, if that was how she
wanted it. It's not so bad. I've done it. Done it with
Vivian. It was me. It's my fault. I stop. I can't remember.
If I finished. If I finished completely. If I did it. If I came.
I search about for a bit in the grass among the bushes
below the summer house. A black dog comes over to me.
I shoo it away. It won't go. It comes right up to me again.
I kick out at it. But it's to no avail. Then I find what
I'm looking for. I pick up the condom. The dog whines.
It's impossible to see. It's raining. The twisted yellow
condom's dripping. I can see nothing at the tip of it. Just
water, rain and mud. I throw it away. The dog's there at
once and catches it in its jaws. Someone whistles a long
way off, perhaps from the bridge, and the dog vanishes.

I go back home. Boletta's sitting in the living room. 'At
last you're back!' she says. I stand there, in the shadows
behind the stove, beside the picture of the little genius. I
say nothing. Boletta stretches forward in her chair.
'You're not disappointed, Barnum?' I just shake my head.
'Because you really shouldn't be. You're not the first to
have been cut out. The Old One's almost world famous

for all the films she was cut from!' Boletta laughs. 'And I'll tell you this – even though it's long enough since I was last at the cinema, and that was back when they were using the Cinema Palace as a potato store during the war – I thought it was an extremely strange film. To think that a beautiful woman like that would touch such an unkempt daddy-long-legs of a man!' 'It was just a dream,' I told her. Boletta falls silent for a moment and stretches out her arms. Slowly I go forward between them. It's only now she sees just what a sight I am. I'm a mess. I'm stinking. 'Have you been fighting?' she asks. I look down. Boletta holds my soaking jacket, takes a quick deep breath, and looks up at me in surprise. 'No, you obviously haven't, Barnum.' She smiles. 'Where's Mum?' I ask her. Boletta lets me go. 'She's with Willy. Willy Halvorsen.' 'What's she doing there?' Boletta sighs. 'Your mother needs friends too, Barnum.' And just then she returns home. We can hear even now, before she's properly closed the door, that something's up, everything's far from well. All at once she's there in the living room. 'The ship's come to grief,' she breathes. Boletta gets up. 'What are you talking about?' 'The *Polar Bear*. In the ice. Oh, God.' Mum sits down. She brings something from her handbag. Her hands are trembling. It's a cutting from a Danish newspaper that she's been given by Willy, Willy Halvorsen. Boletta puts on one of the lamps. It's a photograph, an aerial shot, of a ship trapped in the ice. It's the *Polar Bear*. The crew, ten men in all, have gone over the side of the ship and are standing in a huddle on the floe, midway between two fissures in the ice. Mum reads the accompanying text, and her voice trembles every bit as much as her hands. '*On the passage back from Myggbukten at the end of July, the whaler the* Polar Bear *was trapped in an ice floe south of Greenland. The vessel took in water, deck planks snapped like matchwood, and the ship had to be evacuated. The crew on the ice are awaiting an American helicopter to bring them to safety. All those on board were rescued.*' Mum stops abruptly and searches for a handkerchief. 'But then things

are pretty much all right,' Boletta sighs. 'If they were all
rescued!' Mum shakes her head and all but tears the
handkerchief in two. 'But he isn't there! Fred isn't there!'
Boletta holds Vera's hands in her own. 'Are you sure?' I
pull the lamp closer and take off the shade while Boletta
goes for a magnifying glass. And despite the fact that the
far-off men in the photo resemble small, black marks on
the ice, it's not impossible to see that Fred isn't among
them. Fred is not there. Suddenly Mum glares at me in
the sharp light, for a moment back in this world. 'What a
mess you're in! Go and get yourself cleaned up!' I get up
and go before Mum bursts into tears again. I go into my
room. I call it my room now. But as I shut the door I hear
a whisper. 'Quiet, Tiny.' I turn on my heel towards the
other bed. It's Fred. Fred's lying there with one finger on
his lips. He's changed. There's something in his face
that's different, some characteristic that wasn't there
before. Maybe it's just because he's tanned – his face is
quite dark and his hair's shorter. I could have lain down
beside him. I don't, though. Perhaps my lie's over. That's
all I can think of, that now my lie's over. Fred's come
back. He removes the finger from his mouth. He's lost a
tooth. 'When did you come in?' I hiss. 'While you were at
the cinema. Was it good then?' 'Yes, quite.' 'Quite? Was
it good or wasn't it?' 'It was pretty average. But I liked the
ending.' 'How did it finish?' 'The main character leaves
the city.' Fred looks at me. I know I mustn't start crying.
I don't. He reaches out his hand and smiles. 'Been fighting, Barnum?' 'No, shagging.' Mum's in tears in the living
room. Boletta's comforting her. It's raining. 'Good,' Fred
murmurs. 'And who were you shagging?' I turn in the
direction of the door. 'Why weren't you there when the
Polar Bear went down?' Fred sits up. He's smiling. 'I quit
in Godthap. I'd seen enough.' Stillness has fallen once
more. 'Go in and see Mum,' I whisper. Fred runs his hand
through his cropped hair. His smile evaporates, as if his
lips are sucked in through the dark gap between his teeth.
'What'll I say, Barnum?' 'Just say you're getting a jumper.'

I open the door. Fred hesitates a moment; then he goes in to where they are in the living room. I'm the one who stands there watching it all. I see Mum getting up and Boletta with her hands over her eyes. I see Mum growing mad and almost ugly with joy, fury, helplessness. She doesn't throw her arms about him. She doesn't kiss him. She hits him. This is how I'd express it – Mum hits him in wicked joy and splendid terror. And he doesn't put up any fight. He lets her hit him. In the end Boletta has to make her stop, and it's only then she becomes different. She takes Fred's hand, and I don't hear him speaking the words but I'm sure he does: 'Just getting a jumper, Mum.'

They've sat at the kitchen table all evening. Finally Fred comes in and lies down himself. Mum stands there between us. She'll keep this moment. She is a squirrel. She'll hide her happiness and spread it through her forest, as if she knows too in her heart of hearts that Fred'll soon be gone again. Her voice is almost as it was before. 'Good night then, boys.' We are kids; the clock with the money in it has started again, but it's going the other way, it's going backwards. The coins are clattering down, and each coin is a memory that Mum can polish and with which she can buy time. She kisses Fred on the brow. 'Tomorrow you're going to the dentist!' she tells him. She leans over me and whispers, 'The film would have been a whole lot better if you'd been in it.' After that we hear the washing machine, its quick whirring; we lie awake in the dark and listen to Mum washing Fred's clothes. Now and again she sings to herself, it's the middle of the night and she washes Fred's clothes and sings. 'Evalet,' Fred says slowly, letter by letter. 'Washing machine,' I say, equally slowly. We laugh together there in the dark. 'I bet your Dad nicked it,' Fred whispers. Stillness falls. Mum hangs up the clothes to dry on a line suspended over the bath. 'What was it you'd seen enough of?' I ask. 'The same as great-granddad saw. Ice and snow.' 'Wasn't there anything else?' 'I saw a glacier calving.' 'Calving?' 'All at once half the mountain slid down into the sea. Right in front of us. You should have heard the noise.' 'What d'you mean?' 'Did you think ice was quiet? Ice makes one hell of a noise, Barnum. The whole time. When you're going through ice in a ship no one can sleep.' 'Didn't you see any musk oxen?' Fred scrabbles about for something. I hear several clicks. He swears. 'Did you get the card?' he asks. 'Yes, Peder came with it.' Fred bursts out laughing, and his laughter is low and deep. 'Why did you send Mum straight to Willy, Barnum?' 'I didn't send Mum straight to Willy.' 'Yes, you did. You said I'd been at his place. And Mum went to Willy's. D'you really think Mum's likely to take up boxing, Barnum?' 'Mum was frightened. She wasn't sleeping.' 'But next time I'll not go to Willy's first.' Finally Fred gets a light; a flicker spreads over his dark, rough skin; he lights the cigarette and locks the flame in the shining Zippo lighter. 'I don't think it's the letter you're looking for,' I breathe. 'And what do you think I'm looking for then, Barnum the wise?' 'Your father,' I answer, very quietly, as if I almost hadn't spoken the words at all. Fred sucks the glowing cigarette end down to nothing. The glow of it is all I can see. 'Who was it you shagged?' he asks. I close my eyes. 'D'you remember what you said when I started dancing classes? That I should see what everyone else was doing and then do the exact opposite?' Fred doesn't reply. I open my eyes. The glow hovers still in the air. I wait. 'So?' he says in the end. 'What if you did the opposite of what you yourself want?' 'It'd be a bloody mess, Barnum.' Fred gets up, opens the window, and flicks out the cigarette end. It's like a tiny firework extinguishing in the dark rain. Then he turns round and comes closer. 'Don't you have the guts to say who it was you shagged?' I look up at him. 'Lauren Bacall,' I breathe.

One day she stood waiting for me outside school. She'd changed, grown older in a way – or maybe it was just the huge duffel coat she was wearing, the blue scarf she'd wound at least eight times round her neck, and the hat she had pulled right down as far as her eyes. 'Hi,' she said. 'Crikey,' I responded. We stood there and gave each other a hug. It was a while since we'd seen each other, and the last time had been outside the summer house in Frogner Park. 'School all right?' I shrugged. 'Specially when I get expelled.' She laughed quietly and hid her mouth behind her hand. Her breath made a ring of rime on her thick, green mitten. 'Seen anything of Peder?' she suddenly asked. 'Have you?' 'His Mum's got worse.' 'Worse? What d'you mean?' 'She'll soon not be able to move her arms either.' I felt a sort of melancholy, a shock; there was something we put behind us without fully understanding it, something that had passed. And I was struck by a picture in my mind – I have no idea where it came from – of being reflected in the hub of a passing car. We couldn't just stand there any longer. It was too cold. I was freezing. I couldn't take any more. 'What about going to the cinema?' I suggested. 'The cinema? There won't be any open at the moment.' 'Oh, yes,' I said. We went down to Rosenborg. I knocked on the glass door, and it rattled and shook. I knocked again and finally the old projectionist appeared, opened the door with a couple of keys and admitted us to the foyer. 'Well, well, is it you?' I couldn't deny it. 'Would you show us a film?' I asked. He shook his head a long time. 'You want to see a film in the middle of the blinking afternoon?' I laughed. 'That's right! In the middle of the blinking afternoon.' He considered things, buttoned up his burgundy uniform and locked the door again with both keys. 'Well, well, we'll see what we have.' We went with him up to the projection room, that cramped space where projectors were ranged like cannons in front of embrasures, ready to bombard the screen with light when it was dark enough. There was a packet of sandwiches on the seat; the paper that wrapped them had been partially removed and one cheese sandwich had been half-eaten. The projectionist searched through some rolls of film that were piled in a corner behind his desk. He gave a sudden groan and pulled out one of them – a flat, shining box – a wheel. 'Good Lord,' he groaned. 'This one here should have been sent back.' 'That's the one we'd like to see,' I told him. The projectionist straightened up. 'You can't.' 'Why not?' 'It's an over-18.' Vivian laughed. 'Barnum's over eighteen,' she said. 'Anyway, there's no one to see us,' I put in. He opened the lid and took out the rolls of film. 'All right then, hurry up so we're done before the evening performance!' And we went down the stairs to the main part of the cinema which seemed much bigger without people coughing, whispering, stamping, taking off chocolate wrappers, blowing their noses and crunching. We ran down between the rows, Vivian and me and no one else, entranced, searching for seats – at least now I wouldn't have to end up behind somebody who was two metres tall with an Afro and ears sticking out. 'Where d'you want to sit?' I called out. But Vivian couldn't make up her mind and neither could I. We had 600 tickets between the two of us and didn't know which to choose. The projectionist shouted something from his room and finally we sat down in row 14, seats 18 and 19 – naturally enough. I put my hand in her lap. She took off her mitten and carefully laid her hand on mine. The lights dimmed – not softly and slowly as with a sunset, like we were used to; no blue and gradual twilight in which we could get ready for the darkness and the trailers – but abruptly, and all we heard was the heavy curtain sliding to one side and then the film began. And it was as if time threw a noose about me and pulled it tight. It was *Days of Wine and Roses*. I remembered the title, the posters in the rain, the projectionist who carried them in, the steps I counted, someone following me and Fred coming out of the round toilet by the church. Was this also a mark on Barnum's ruler; time which catches up with you again? And how long does such a moment last, a moment that doesn't set its mark in the door frame with a knife but which cuts free a point in time in your memory? I only know that *Days of Wine and Roses* lasts one hour and fifty-seven minutes, and I'll never forget the

scene when Jack Lemmon's on his way into the Union
Square Bar and stops abruptly when he glimpses his own
reflection in the window. And he thinks, for just a split
second before it's passed, that it's a stranger standing
there instead – a tramp, a ruined and pathetic drunk –
until he realizes it's none other than himself.

Afterwards we went to Krølle's. We sat right in at the
furthest away section. 'One hell of a film,' I said. Vivian
unwound her scarf. 'A shit film,' she said. I found a cigarette in my pocket. 'Shit? Why d'you say that?' Vivian's
face was pale with the cold; her mouth was small and
slow. 'I don't like films with sad endings.' The waiter had
stopped at our table. 'A pint,' I said quickly. He bent right
down to my level. 'Very funny.' It was now I should have
responded with a reply from another film entirely, our
film – *What's wrong with you*? 'Tea,' said Vivian. 'Same for
me,' I whispered. The waiter drew himself up. 'And what
will you have to eat?' 'Nothing,' I told him. 'We don't
serve drinks only here, littl'un.' He really was starting to
get on my nerves. 'Then I'll have some lemon in my tea,'
I said. The waiter looked down. 'So you've a sense of
humour too. Perhaps you'd like to eat your packed lunch
outside?' 'Some apple cake,' Vivian said. 'I'll have the
same,' I breathed. 'With cream.' The waiter went over to
the hatch through to the kitchens and turned twice in the
course of the short walk. 'Waiter wanker.' I held my hand
over my mouth. Vivian was thawing; a warmth was rising
from her throat and her lips became soft. I didn't say any
more before the waiter returned with our order. We had
to pay there and then. I treated her. I gave the waiter a
fistful of coins I'd found in the drawer under the dead
clock. It took about a quarter of an hour for them to be
counted. When he'd finally gone I leant over the table.
'Why don't you like films with sad endings?' I asked.
'Because it makes me think of my parents,' she replied. I
ate cream with my fingers and considered my response
intently. 'There's a difference between film and reality,' I
explained. Vivian started laughing. 'My, you're clever,

Barnum.' I blushed and went to the loo. Someone had hidden a hip flask behind the toilet bowl. It wasn't empty. I locked the door and drank what was left. My head burned quickly and quietly. I looked at myself in the mirror above the basin, pulled my curls down over my brow and went back to join Vivian. 'Happy endings are a load of crap,' I said. 'Why d'you think that, Barnum?' 'Because there's no such bloody thing as a happy ending! We'll all die anyway, won't we?' Vivian smiled. 'Perhaps it would have been best if they'd died in the accident,' she said. 'Who?' 'My parents.' I drained my cup. The flames in my head were going down and down. Soon there'd just be ash left on my tongue. 'You don't mean that,' I whispered. Now it was Vivian's turn to lean over the table. 'They don't think about anything else but the accident, Barnum.' 'It's maybe no surprise,' I said. Vivian looked at me a long time. 'They're self-obsessed and selfish sods,' she breathed. 'And the accident lets them be like that. They worship that accident. They love it.' I no longer knew what to say. I'd never seen such anger in her; even though she was whispering her voice shook as if any moment it might crack and become a scream. 'D'you want more tea?' I asked. Vivian shook her head. 'Let me tell you something, Barnum. Mum got rid of every mirror in the flat. From the bathroom, the living room, the hall – she threw away every pocket mirror and wouldn't use silver dishes because she could see her face in them too. Dad went down to the yard and got rid of them there – not even he could bring himself to look at her. And one day the doorbell rang. It was Mum who went to see who it was and outside there were some kids holding out a mirror – a beautiful, framed oval mirror that used to hang in the hall. They thought it had been thrown away by accident and wanted to do her a favour. But Mum saw her reflection in it, smashed the mirror with her fist, and chased those kids down the steps and terrified the living daylights out of them.' Vivian pushed her empty cup towards the side of the table, the very edge. The waiter was keeping a weather eye on us. 'She thought they'd done it out of sheer devilment,' I said. Vivian looked at me. 'What's so special about the face? It's just a mask, isn't it? Does it really matter if it's beautiful or ugly?' I took her hand before the cup went tumbling to the floor. 'If they'd been killed we wouldn't be sitting here,' I murmured. Vivian smiled. 'No, only you. Shall we go to Peder's?'

We went to Peder's. He wasn't at home. But his mother refused to let us go. She could only just manage to push the wheels of her chair. I helped her into the living room. The place was swimming in brushes, tubes of paint, frames and canvases. I noticed that the wheels of her chair weren't whining now, they'd been oiled. And in the midst of this chaos stood her model; he'd been standing there all those years – just as naked, but he was no longer Greek. He'd begun to get fat and to sag; he was sliding away and becoming a shadow of himself. Vivian stared at him. I stared at Vivian. Peder's mother whistled. The model picked up a white towel and disappeared. 'Long time no see,' she said to us. We felt a bit embarrassed. It struck me that almost everything was a long while back and that we'd let time pass, on both sides, in this little city. 'How are you doing?' I asked. 'As long as I can finish my pictures before my arms are completely gone, I'll be happy.' She laughed. 'But don't let's talk about me! How are you two?' 'Trying to write a bit,' I told her. 'What do you write about, Barnum?' 'Things I've seen.' Peder's mother brought her chair nearer, soundlessly. 'Have you seen anything that no one else has seen?' 'Yes,' I told her. She looked right at me. 'Don't say what it is, because then you won't be able to write about it.' She turned to Vivian. 'And what about you then?' 'I've got into a school in Switzerland for next year,' Vivian answered. I felt a great lift plummet through me. There weren't all that many floors, but it didn't stop at any of them. 'What sort of school?' Peder's mum asked her. Vivian looked down. 'A school for make-up artists,' she said. At that moment the bell rang. I ran out to answer it, glad to get away. Was that why she'd waited for me outside school, to tell me she'd be going to Switzerland to become a make-up artist? The bell rang again. It was Peder. He always forgot his key. Peder remembered just about everything else, but never his key. He stood in the light on the steps with ear muffs and a bag under his arm; he shaded his eyes, blinking. 'Is Peder in?' Peder asked. 'Peder's not home yet,' I replied. 'Well, say that Barnum was here,' Peder said. 'Goodbye then, Barnum,' I told him, and made to shut the door. 'Goodbye, Barnum,' Peder said, and flung his arms round me and we tumbled into the hall and rolled round there and clasped each other tight in an avalanche of boots and shoes and slippers. We laughed, the same laughter as always, but all at once he pushed me away and got to his feet. It was Vivian. She stood leaning against the wall, her arms folded, taking us in with a smile, and I got up myself. 'A full house,' Peder said. And when we sat together in his room I saw that we three, who were always to be together, had lost our equilibrium. Peder babbled on for about three quarters of an hour about the shortfall in his college club funds, and explained in meticulous detail how he would raise new capital, namely by demanding advertising revenue from the bakery in Ulleval Road – if they refused he'd get the students to find somewhere else to eat their buns. There was quiet for a time. We heard his dad park in the garage. A stack of logs tumbled to the ground, or maybe it was just thunder, thunder in November. Vivian turned to me. 'What is it you've seen?' she asked. 'Nothing,' I said, my voice low. Peder looked at us and smiled, but lost his smile equally fast. Again there was silence. The number and the dream didn't add up. We had a shortfall too. And then it was Peder who brought him up, as though we needed someone else to talk about. 'Has that nutter of a brother of yours settled down yet?' he asked.

I thought about precisely that as I went home that evening – whether Fred had settled down or not. I wanted him to stay. And I wanted him to leave. My thoughts were in halves too. He was lying on the bed, with his clothes on and his back to me. I undressed, quietly and quickly, and as I stood there naked in the scanty light from the window, he turned round and I could see that he was crying.

He'd been silent for twenty-two months and Cliff Richard had got him to talk. He'd sailed to Greenland with the whaler the *Polar Bear*, left the ship in Godthåb, peeled potatoes onboard *Bremen* and lost a tooth in a storm round Cape Farewell. But he hadn't settled down. Soon enough he'd set out on his third journey, his last and his longest, the one that would take all of twenty-eight years.

It was a Monday at the beginning of December. I stood at the kitchen window watching the snow falling in thick flakes, and Bang the caretaker trying to sweep them away. But he never managed and in the end gave up, sat down on the steps instead and just let it snow – he was snowed in. If he sat there long enough he'd disappear completely. I didn't have school to go to. I'd been expelled again. It was quite a good arrangement. I stayed off. Then I got expelled. It was almost like getting a reward. But I didn't see any more films at Rosenborg Cinema; the projectionist had either died or retired. I had begun going out with Vivian that winter. I heard Fred coming in and standing right behind me. 'I'll be off then,' he said. 'Where to?' I asked. 'That's what I'm going to find out,' he replied. And maybe I imagined he'd be back in a couple of days' time, or at least before Christmas; that he'd just go off wandering for a bit to begin with. There were nights I lay awake, many years later, after we'd held a memorial service for him, and I believed he'd checked in to Coch's Hostel – Room 502, Dad's old room – and that now he stood in the window laughing at us. 'D'you mind telling Mum?' he whispered. 'Sure. What'll I say?' 'That I've gone.' I turned round. 'Gone? Where?' Fred shook his head. He was wearing his suede jacket and his black suitcase was standing by the door – Dad's old suitcase – empty of applause. 'Can I borrow it?' Fred asked. 'Sure,' I replied. He raised his hand and touched my cheek, gently. I should have known then that he didn't intend coming back.

And when Fred had been away over a month and Christmas had passed, Mum took a taxi to the other side of town, to Willy, the welder who'd tried to teach Fred to punch. But he didn't know where Fred was and hadn't heard a thing from him. Mum wasn't worth approaching for several weeks after that. Later, once a full six months had elapsed and we were still waiting for Fred, she and Boletta went to the police and reported his disappearance. I went to the cinema, with Peder or Vivian, but preferably alone. In the end, when Mum couldn't take much more, the Salvation Army's missing person's team was brought into the hunt.

And this was the last thing Fred said to me before he left, 'Hope you get something written while I'm away, Barnum.'

I turn slowly and all that's twenty-eight years ago. I'm sitting at the desk, between the window and the wall. The room's dark. The curtains are drawn. Only the computer screen's bright, a blue hum against my face. In the top corner is the film title – *The Night Man*. I click on *home*. The text jumps, as if nothing is there behind the screen, as if the writing is just an illusion, a thin film – and I'm overcome yet again, as the words slide into blue emptiness, by this eternal fear of losing them, of deleting. On occasion, I get out the old Diplomat, but I can no longer type with it. And so the beginning comes into view; I'm equally relieved each time it does, and I print out the first two scenes. I hear the dragging of the printer – the ink has to fill the electronic points – it's a mouth that speaks slowly. I haven't slept. I've stopped sleeping. I take pills to keep me awake. A sheet sweeps down onto the floor. I can't be bothered picking it up. I sit down on the stool and read.

Scene 1. ext. city. early morning (dream)

A BOY, pale and thin, eight years old, is running through the streets. No one else about. Only him. He runs for all he's worth. He has a dogged expression, full of anticipation. Fog swirls round the boy and all but hides him for a moment. He runs on. The fog grows thicker still. He comes round a corner and arrives at . . .

Scene 2. ext. harbour. early morning (dream)

The harbour. The boy stops. Out of breath. Smiling. The boy's POV: The wharves are empty. No boats. Hawsers hang down into the still, dark water. The fog slides in from the fiord. Close to the boy's face. His eyes. The disappointment. He's on the verge of tears. He takes a few steps. Stops again. Looks about him. Quickly wipes a tear away with the back of his hand. Then he hears the ringing of a SHIP'S BELL, far away. The boy listens. He hears the breaking of waves somewhere through the fog. He runs forward right to the edge of the quayside. The shadows of the ship can be glimpsed right at the heart of the driving fog. The boy shouts something, but without our being able to hear the words. And a sailing vessel appears out of the fog, made ready for the ice. The ship's name is ANTARCTIC. Right at the head of the prow stands a MAN in a white uniform keeping watch. The boy calls again. Now the man hears him.

THE BOY: Father!

The man on the ship turns for a moment in the direction of the quayside. He raises his hand and smiles as he slowly shakes his head. The boy stands with his arm raised aloft. He lowers his arm. He calls out a final time. Soundlessly. And he sees the ship disappearing into the fog once more. The fog that's close to the boy's face. He shuts his eyes. THE BOY'S POV: The inside of his eyelashes – thin, almost transparent skin, veins, and a sharp light that's coming closer.

I pick up the sheet, cross out the word *dream* in both scene directions, and do the same with the on-screen text. Isn't film one long dream anyway? Can dream be separated from dream, like water in a wave, like wind in a storm? I cross out that thought too. There's hardly a producer who could be bothered reading a script that begins with a dream, and most likely that producer doesn't have the money to make films. And if he has any money at all it's just too little to buy an option on the script (something he'd much prefer avoiding anyway), but he has enough to buy you a drink in the bar. And after five drinks (which you yourself have paid for), he suggests you write something else, at lightning speed, before anyone nicks the idea. What idea, you ask, tired but happy, and he leans against your ear and pitches some idea of less merit than the current chat-up lines trotted out to the girls, as he puts his tongue into your ear and fills your brain with spit and bad breath. The phone rings. I don't answer it. I leave the machine on; it's like in childhood days – I don't dare turn out the light. It's winter, early in February. I'm white, too. I've been white for a long time now and cross off the days in the almanac, a line for each white day – like a prisoner marking time to the date of his release, or his execution. I am a white lie. I don't go from café to café, I go the rounds of the antique shops. I start off in the best of them, down in the city centre, where first editions and leather-bound collected works are arrayed in locked glass cases, where you have to hand over your bag at the counter when you go in and where smoking isn't permitted – *libri rare*. And I end up in the dun-coloured second-hand bookshops with their pocket series where they don't take credit cards. And it's in one of those, the last one – Volvat Antiquarian Books – in among the empty premises along Sørkedal Road, that it happens – as the owner asks in a tired and impatient voice, after I've been trawling the shelves for at least an hour: 'Is there something in particular you're looking for before we close?' 'Good ideas no one realizes I'm stealing,' I reply. 'Stealing? No one steals anything here. I'll have to ask you to leave now.' 'I pay good money for everything I steal,' I say. It's then my eye falls on it, in the section devoted to rare volumes – a script, 200 yellowed, type-written sheets with a cover, and a sticky label like the ones put onto old-fashioned jam jars. And in small, red letters are written the words – *scenario, Aug.* And it's there and then, twenty-eight years later, at that moment, that the images mingle as they tumble together into a form that appears clear and incomprehensible to me – scissors plus musk ox equals hunger. From all of my life that's been cut away there rises a smell – a hot, strong smell. Barnum's ruler's burning. It's the script I once saved from being blown away in the streets of Oslo. I give the shop owner what change I have and hurry home – to what I call home – the one room and balcony in Bolteløkka where Vivian and I spent our first years. I take the stairs at a run and unlock the door. I have to get changed first. I go out onto the balcony and see the red sun going down over the fiord and the clouds of frost piling over the city like moving mountains. Then I sit down at my desk. I open the script. *Knut Hamsun's* Hunger – *Henning Carlsen's scenario from the script of Peter Seeburg.* On the following page is a full cast list, from Pontus to Inspector Brand, and under Inspector Brand's name two columns of extras: a cyclist, a street sweeper, a sick man, a maid, six ghosts – over fifty extras in all. And I realize I can barely recall them – they're faces that are gone now. Vivian could have been *little girl (with response).* Peder and I could have been *children in Vaterland.* Two of us could have been *a pair of lovers.* I light a cigarette. There are twice as many external scenes as internal ones. YLAJALIS STREET. That was where we were. That's the trick, to find the right place. There's a draught from the balcony door. I shut it. I catch a glimpse of a hearse moving behind the thin trees and I think to myself – *it has to be empty, it's after hours, the graveyards are all closed.* I keep standing for a moment, dizzy, and have to support myself against the table. This is the scriptwriter's credo – the nerves that connect the eye to the brain are twenty-three times bigger than those connecting the ear to the brain. Write pictures, not sounds. I sit down in the tall chair. I begin reading and I understand now. It's the camera that's the main protagonist. I'm quite simply reading a three-sided story between Pontus, the city and the camera. But the camera is the main character – intrusive and threatening. The camera should have appeared at the top of the cast list. All of a sudden I shout out loud, 'God's eye! It's God's eye, damn it!' I put my hand over my mouth. I'm a sad single occupant with over-loud thoughts. When God's eye shuts we cease to exist. I've pulled out the phone. I'm playing. I'm retrieving things and I'm adding. I'm writing us in. We're running through Palace Park, the camera at our backs. I'm making us visible once more. I find the sheet I carried back to the director; that simple scene which made me decide to become a screenwriter. A gust of wind in a street was all that it took. *PONTUS sees – a little dog running home in the gutter, a bone in its mouth.* Then I hear the postman on the stairs. It's morning already. That means I didn't sleep last night either. The snow's lying like thick quilts on the balcony. I cross off a day on the almanac – yet another white day – and go down to get my mail. There are two letters for me. I take them up with me. The fattest of the envelopes is from Peder. It's my tickets to Berlin: Oslo Fornebu – Berlin. I'm travelling that night. Peder's gone ahead to arrange our appointments. My reservation for the Kempinski Hotel's enclosed too. That's costing a fortune. About the equivalent of four options plus script development funding. Peder says it's worth it. The Kempinski Hotel's halfway to a contract. If you've a suite at the Kempinski and a card at the bar then all you need's the small talk. Peder's still an optimist. He goes on thinking he'll manage to lose weight and he trusts me. I open the other envelope. There's a button there. That's all. I recognize it. It's the button that lay hidden in the Old One's jewellery box. It's almost weightless. There's a note there, too. The letters are sloping, comprise just two words – *Dad's button*. I look at the envelope again. It's blank, has neither my name nor my address. He must have left it there himself. No. It's not possible. It can't be right. I go over to the window. The snow's lying like thick quilts on the balcony. A red bird flies up from the railing. I quickly pull the curtains once more. Barnum's ruler's burning now. I know it. It doesn't help. Ninety per cent of our knowledge comes to us via the eye, five per cent from our hearing, the remainder from touch and scent. I crumple up the sheet and put it in my mouth – chew and chew and then swallow it. I chuck the button in the loo and pull the chain. And with the pressing of just one finger, lighter than a butterfly, I could delete it all – cut myself out and empty the screen to leave a smooth and shining silence. I go into the kitchenette instead, climb onto a stool, open the air vent and stick my hand in to bring out what I'm looking for, something I've hidden there myself, but not well enough for the white liar – a bottle of vodka. The juice is in the fridge.

FATTENING

A filmscript by Barnum Nilsen

1. INT. EVENING. CINEMA.

A boy, BARNUM, *is sitting in a cinema. He's twelve years old and extremely small. He can't see anything. A lady with a great deal of hair is blocking his view. He moves to another seat and ends up sitting behind a man with a hat. He moves yet again, but to no avail. Everyone's taller than he is. He stretches from one side to the other. He can barely see the screen.*

Adverts are shown. For Coca-Cola. Ajax. Chocolate. Finally Barnum gets up and stands on his seat so he can see. The audience laughs at him. A furious USHER *swears his way between the rows and drags him out with him. The audience laughs and applauds.*

Darkness falls.

There's quiet, broken only by the rustle of sweet wrappers.

We see the film title appear on the screen: FATTENING.

The film begins.

A boy appears – PHILIP *– twelve years of age and also extremely small. He's standing against the door frame in his room measuring his height. He's wearing only his underpants. And high-heeled shoes on his feet. He stretches up to become taller. We can see a whole series of marks on the door frame with different years and individual dates recorded beside them.*

Someone shouts from the cinema:

MAN: Take off your shoes, you dwarf!

*Some people in the audience laugh. Others tell them to be quiet.
Philip turns round quickly and gets rid of his shoes as fast as he
can, but doesn't manage it before his FATHER appears. He's a
small but extremely fat man – almost square. He bends down and
picks up the high-heeled shoes. He then proceeds to box his son's
ears.*

2. INT. DAY. THE SCHOOL DOCTOR'S ROOM

*Philip's standing getting measured in his underpants. The
SCHOOL DOCTOR – a strict, tall man in a white coat – looks
closely at his height measure. Then he glances down at Philip's
feet. The boy hasn't taken off his stockings.*

SCHOOL DOCTOR: Take off your stockings too.

Philip reluctantly removes them and gives them to the nurse.

*The school doctor pushes the top of the measure down onto his
head and looks at the measure once more.*

SCHOOL DOCTOR: Have you done something wrong,
Philip?

Philip shakes his head.

SCHOOL DOCTOR: Oh, yes, you have. Otherwise you
wouldn't be so small.

3. INT. EVENING. AT HOME.

*Philip's eating dinner with his parents. His MOTHER is quiet and
nervy. His father's eating a vast amount. Philip stares at him
and stops eating. The fat shines on his father's bloated face and
trickles down his double chin. He looks at his son and talks with
his mouth full.*

FATHER: You're getting more and more like me, Philip.

*Philip doesn't reply. He just stares at his father who keeps eating
and eating.*

MOTHER: You have to eat up now, Philip.

His mother gives him another helping of food. Philip doesn't touch it. He just stares in terror at his father.

PHILIP'S VOICE: I don't want to be like Dad.

His father looks up at him sharply.

FATHER: What did you say?
PHILIP: Nothing.
FATHER: Nothing? I'm sure I heard you say something.
PHILIP: Thanks for dinner.
MOTHER: You have to eat up before you're finished.

His father gets up. He appears even smaller now, and fatter too. He's been sitting on a large cushion which he takes with him to the divan over in the corner. Suddenly he stops and gives a large fart. His mother looks down in shame.

MOTHER: Dad, please.
PHILIP'S VOICE: It was at that moment I made up my mind to stop eating. Because if I stopped eating then perhaps I'd start growing instead.

His father lies down on the living-room divan with a newspaper over his face – the death notices.

PHILIP'S VOICE: At least I had nothing to lose.

4. INT. FORENOON. SCHOOL CANTEEN.

Philip's sitting at a long table with other pupils. There's milk, carrots and biscuits with caviar. Philip appears to eat but doesn't actually swallow a thing.

5. INT. FORENOON. SCHOOL LOOS.

Philip stands bent over a toilet bowl and vomits. Someone KNOCKS hard on the door several times. Philip straightens up and opens the door. Outside are the biggest boys in the school waiting for him. They drag him over to the urinal which is blocked with toilet paper and overflowing.

BOY: D'you think he can swim, boys?

All of them laugh. They get hold of his neck and shove him nearer all the piss. Finally he's sucked down through the mass of toilet paper.

6. INT. SEWER.

Philip is floating in a dark underground channel. He tries to keep afloat in a sea of excrement, paper, rubbish and rats.

7. EXT. AFTERNOON. STREET.

In a deserted street a manhole cover is lifted to one side. Philip climbs up – wet, filthy and exhausted. He manages to get to his feet, just, and totters off along the street.

8. INT. EVENING. BATH.

Philip's lying naked in the bath, underwater. There's knocking at the door. He doesn't hear it.

MOTHER: Philip? Aren't you finished yet? What are you up to, Philip? You're not doing something bad, are you?

Philip gets out, pads over the floor and bends down to the key-hole. He puts his mouth to it and blows for all he's worth. There's a shrill shriek from outside.

9. INT. EVENING. LIVING ROOM.

The family are sitting round the dinner table. One of Philip's mother's eyes is red and infected, and it's running, as if she's crying from just the one eye. His father is sitting on his cushion stuffing his face. Philip hides his food in his pockets.

His FATHER always talks with his mouth full.

FATHER: How's it going at school, Philip?
PHILIP'S VOICE: It's Dad's fault I'm so small. I wish he would die.

His father looks at him and wipes his mouth with his napkin.

FATHER: What was that you said?
PHILIP: Nothing.

His father puts a huge piece of meat into his mouth. Suddenly his face goes red. He starts gasping for breath. He gets up. Philip and his mother just look at him in amazement. He sinks to the floor. In the distance church bells can be heard.

10. INT. FORENOON. CHAPEL.

The church bells keep on ringing. Philip and his mother are sitting in the front pew. They are the only ones in the chapel.

The coffin, extremely short and broad, sinks down through a hole in the floor.

The VICAR comes down to shake hands with Philip's mother.

Philip goes forward to the hole. He empties his pockets without anyone seeing him doing so: pieces of meat, sausages, cakes and potatoes. He throws all of it down where the coffin's gone before. He bends over the hole and peers into the crematorium's fire. And he's sucked down into the flames, just as he disappeared into the urinal.

11. INT. CREMATORIUM.

Philip struggles through the flames. A dark form stands before him, untouched by the conflagration. Philip stops. It's his father.

FATHER: Have you got what you wanted now, son?

The flames engulf Philip.

12. INT. EVENING. BEDROOM.

Philip stands against the door frame to measure his height. His mother is weeping in the next room. Philip checks the new measurement. He's grown a centimetre. He shouts for joy.

His mother comes to him in her mourning clothes, choked with grief.

MOTHER: How dare you rejoice on this day of all days?

13. INT. FORENOON. CLASSROOM.

The teacher, Miss KNUCKLES, is standing by the blackboard looking round at her pupils. She focuses her attention on Philip. He's sitting at the front desk. He's grown very thin and pale; he's short, and nothing more than skin and bones.

KNUCKLES: And what is the fourth commandment, Philip? Can you tell me?

Philip gets up, but immediately sinks to the floor in a faint.

14. INT. FORENOON. SCHOOL DOCTOR'S ROOM

Philip's lying on a mattress. The school doctor's examining him. Knuckles and the school nurse are standing close by.

KNUCKLES: His father has just died. It's all been too much for little Philip.
SCHOOL DOCTOR: The boy's undernourished. That's what's wrong with him.

The school doctor rouses Philip.

SCHOOL DOCTOR: Don't you get enough food at home, Philip?

Philip looks at him.

PHILIP: Yes.
SCHOOL DOCTOR: You're lying, Philip.

The school doctor signals to the nurse, who goes over to the telephone.

15. EXT. DAY. STREET.

Philip's mother hurries down the street. But then she has to stop. In front of her on the pavement, men in white, bloodied overalls are carrying pig carcasses from a lorry into the abattoir. Finally she has to fight her way between them.

16. INT. AFTERNOON. CORRIDOR.

Philip's standing alone in the corridor outside the door to the school doctor's. He bends down and peers through the keyhole. Philip sees his mother sitting inside listening to the doctor. She's clinging to the handbag on her lap.

Suddenly he sees that the room is filling up with water. It's like an aquarium. His mother and the school doctor leave their chairs and float round in the green water, bubbles coming out of their mouths.

Then everything goes dark.

Immediately afterwards he sees the nurse's face. She puts her lips over the keyhole as if she's kissing his eye.

The door is opened and Philip comes tumbling in.

SCHOOL DOCTOR'S VOICE: The boy must be put at once on Weir Mitchel's Remedy!

17. EXT. MORNING. EAST END STATION.

Philip's standing on the platform. He's holding a heavy suitcase. His mother pulls the zip of his jacket right up to his throat.

SCHOOL DOCTOR'S VOICE: Or fattening, a remedy availed of by the undernourished, the nervous, the anaemic, the emaciated and convalescents, to get them back on their feet again.

Philip's mother hugs him. She's sobbing. The sound of the train whistle is shrill and close by. She lets him go. Philip climbs aboard the train.

His mother is left standing on the platform. The train starts moving out of the station. She lifts her hand and waves.

SCHOOL DOCTOR'S VOICE: The remedy consists of a twelve-day diet, as prescribed by Professor Burkart.

18. EXT. DAY. RAILWAY STATION.

Philip tumbles off the train and onto the platform, suitcase in hand. He's immediately swept up by a man, the FARMER, *who's wearing his local costume.*

FARMER: Oh, yes, here we have a city kid in need of some feeding!

The farmer takes his case from him and leads him over to a lorry. He throws the case into the back and lifts Philip into the cab.

19. INT. DAY. LORRY.

Philip sits beside the farmer as he drives. The farmer whistles contentedly and now and again looks at Philip, a smile on his face. The lorry rattles and bounces along the uneven road surface. Philip clings to the door and can only just see over the dashboard.

The farmer hits the brakes. A flock of all sorts of creatures – sheep, cows, steers, pigs and hens – is crossing the road ahead of them. The farmer slaps Philip on the back and points.

FARMER: You'll eat these, Philip. The whole lot.

The farmer puts down his foot and drives straight through the menagerie.

20. EXT. DAY. LORRY.

We see, from above, the lorry driving along a narrow road between two fields, where the corn ripples gold in the wind and sunlight. Norwegian flags fly from flagpoles on all the farms. Beautiful people, full of health, wave at them.

The suitcase is lying in the back of the lorry.

A boys' choir sings NOW OUR LAND IS LIVING.

Soon we're so high that we can barely see the vehicle in the farmland. We disappear into the clouds and everything is transformed into swirling mist and utter silence. A hand parts the mist. We're blinded by a mighty light.

SCHOOL DOCTOR'S VOICE: You will love your food as yourself.

21. EXT. DAY. FARM.

The lorry drives into the yard where the WIFE, *a large woman, also wearing local costume, is waiting. Philip clambers down from the cab. The farmer fetches his case from the back of the lorry and carries it inside. Philip goes over to the farmer's wife to greet her. She pumps his whole arm.*

WIFE: Welcome to the farm, Philip. Now you're going to get fat.

She follows him inside. In a window on the first floor two FAT BOYS *stand looking down at him.*

SCHOOL DOCTOR'S VOICE : Day one. At six-thirty – a pint of milk to be drunk slowly over three quarters of an hour.

22. INT. MORNING. FARM.

An assortment of boys are sitting at a long table in a dining-room drinking warm, lumpy milk. Some are as thin as Philip, others have put on weight. They've been put in a kind of order – the thinnest at the bottom, the fattest at the top. Philip's right at the bottom. All attention is focused on him as the new boy.

The farmer's wife goes slowly round the table inspecting them all.

No one says anything. All we hear is the sound of cutlery. Philip looks at the over-heaped and unsavoury plate of food in front of him. He lifts his spoon but can't swallow. The food swells in his mouth.

SCHOOL DOCTOR'S VOICE : At twelve o'clock – soup with egg, fifty grams of meat and potatoes. Two wholemeal biscuits and plum compôte.

The two boys we saw in the window, PREBEN *and* ASLAK, *who are sitting at the top and have grown really fat, start thumping the table. They begin softly, but gradually the thumping becomes harder and harder. In the end everyone's hammering the table. Philip's sweating. The tears run from his eyes. He's on the point of exploding. The hammering reaches a crescendo. Philip hunches over his plate and gulps down the lot.*

Complete silence reigns once more.

The farmer's wife stands behind Philip. She puts her hands on his shoulders.

WIFE: You must eat up, Philip. Otherwise God'll be angry with you.

Philip sticks his spoon in the vomit as the farmer's wife pats his head.

23. INT. NIGHT. FARM. DORMITORY.

All the boys are lying in bed in a cramped dormitory. The farmer goes past all the beds to make sure everything is as it should be. The boys are all pretending to be asleep. The farmer puts out the light, goes out and locks the door.

The moon shines through the window and is reflected in the lake outside.

Philip's eyes are open and afraid. He hears steps coming towards his bed. He shuts his eyes.

Preben and Aslak take up position on each side of his bed. They're dressed in just their underpants. They're fat and pale.

PREBEN (*in a whisper*): Philip?
ASLAK (*in a whisper*): Philip? Come on, come here.

Philip opens his eyes once more, still more frightened now. They drag him out of bed and take him with them over to the wall. There they push him to the floor. Philip kneels there shivering.

PREBEN: Look.

Philip doesn't understand. He doesn't dare say anything. Aslak points to a hole in the floorboards.

ASLAK (*in a whisper*): Look, down there!

Philip puts his eye to the little hole. He sees on the floor below, in the kitchen, the farmer's wife bending over the stove and the farmer taking her roughly from behind.

24. EXT. DAY. FIELD.

All the boys are bent double in the field lifting potatoes. Philip's there between Preben and Aslak.

SCHOOL DOCTOR'S VOICE: Day two. A massage, wheat bread with butter and mashed potatoes.

Philip digs in the ground with his hands. Preben and Aslak hurl potatoes at him. The farmer comes racing over. He boxes their ears, and they obediently bend down to the potatoes once more. The farmer puts his arm round Philip.

FARMER: I reckon you've put on weight already, you know, Philip.

Aslak and Preben scowl at Philip.

25. INT. EVENING. FARM. DINING-ROOM.

Philip's sitting alone at the long table eating. He can't manage any more. He lets his knife and fork fall onto his plate. At once the farmer's wife is there and she hits him on the back of the head. Philip keeps on stuffing himself with food.

The farmer's wife smiles and puts her hands on his shoulders and massages him as he eats.

26. PHILIP'S DREAM

Philip's lying naked in the lake. The moonlight's shining on his face. He's sleeping. Everything is utterly still. Then the water round him goes red and he's slowly pulled down. Philip panics.

He opens his mouth to shout aloud, but his voice is utterly silent and he just sinks down into the murky, red water.

27. INT. DORMITORY.

Philip sits bolt upright in bed, gasping for breath. He's looking right at Aslak and Preben. They bend down over him. They whisper.

PREBEN: D'you know what the farmer and his wife are?

Philip shakes his head.

PREBEN: They're angel-makers.
PHILIP: Angel-makers?
PREBEN: They put unwanted children out into the woods to die.
ASLAK: That's why you're here.
PREBEN: Will you tell?

Philip shakes his head.

ASLAK: Will you tell, fanny boy?

Philip stares at them in terror. They drag him out of bed and back over to the hole in the floor. They press his face down to the ground. Philip sees the farmer bending over the stove, naked; his wife taking him from behind.

28. INT. MORNING. DINING-ROOM.

The boys are standing at their places singing in chorus. The farmer is conducting them. They sing NOW OUR LAND IS LIVING. *Philip stands pale and silent between Aslak and Preben, who are both singing lustily.*

The farmer stops the singing abruptly and looks at Philip.

FARMER: Aren't you singing?

Philip doesn't reply. The farmer goes up to him.

FARMER: Won't you sing with us? Are you better than us, is that it? Are you better than us?

29. EXT. DAY. FIELD.

Philip stands alone in the field digging. We see him from above – a little figure on the bare, grey landscape.

SCHOOL DOCTOR'S VOICE: The quantity of food for dinner is increased. Eighty grams of meat, grilled potatoes and butter, kidneys and boiled testicles.

Philip looks up at the sky. It starts raining. He throws the spade away and runs for all he's worth towards the woods.

30. EXT. AFTERNOON. FOREST.

Philip stops out of breath among the trees, and leans against one of the trunks. There's utter stillness. He turns round. No one's following him. Then he carries on.

And then he sees that the wood is full of boys. They're sitting on the ground, half-naked and blue with cold. Some are already dead. The others are simply waiting to die.

Philip turns round once more. The farmer and his wife are standing hand in hand at the edge of the wood, dressed in their finest garb, smiling at him.

31. INT. EVENING. FARM.

Philip's standing naked in the communal shower, washing mud and earth from himself. He's the only one there. He stares at the filthy water swirling into the drain. He feels the rolls of fat round his belly.

Then he hears the strains of NOW OUR LAND IS LIVING. *Philip turns the shower off at once and hears the song more clearly now. It's coming closer and closer. Philip reaches for his towel, which is hanging on a hook. But he doesn't get it in time. Preben and Aslak are standing in front of him. They're singing and looking at him. Then there's quiet.*

Preben takes the towel from the hook.

ASLAK: Are you better than us, huh?
PHILIP (*in a whisper*): No.
PREBEN: D'you need the towel?
PHILIP: Yes, please.

Preben stretches out the towel, but snatches it back again. Philip remains standing where he is. He tries to cover himself with his hands.

ASLAK: Are you sure you aren't better than us?
PHILIP: I don't want to get fat. I just want to be taller.

Preben and Aslak look at each other and laugh. Then they drag Philip with them into the dormitory and over to the hole in the floor. They force him onto his knees and press his face to the floor. Philip sees an empty kitchen. A kettle of water's on the stove, and it's beginning to boil.

Philip screams. The scream's muffled. Preben secures the towel tightly over his mouth. Aslak kneels behind him.

SCHOOL DOCTOR'S VOICE: He who does not follow Weir Mitchel's Remedy will go to thin hell.

Philip's face is twisted in agony and fear.

32. INT. EXT. MORNING. DORMITORY.

Philip's standing by the window looking down over the yard. Aslak and Preben appear, smartly dressed, each with case in hand, fat and polite, in the company of the farmer's wife. They stand there, beside the flagpole, the flag waving from it.

Then the truck comes into the yard and stops. The farmer's wife says a tearful goodbye to Aslak and Preben. They clamber onto the back of the lorry and sit there with their luggage.

From the cab there appears an extremely thin and stunted boy with a cardboard case in his hand. It's Barnum, whom we recognize from the cinema as the boy who was thrown out. He's frightened and bewildered. The farmer's wife gives him a hearty welcome.

The farmer drives off with Aslak and Preben.

33. EXT. MORNING. FARMYARD.

At last Barnum frees himself from the arms of the farmer's wife. She bends down towards his face.

WIFE: Now you're going to get good and fat, Barnum.

She takes Barnum by the hand and drags him towards the farmhouse. He looks up at the windows. He sees Philip. He sees his fat face up on the top storey staring down at him.

The choirboys sing: GOD IS GOD THOUGH EVERY MAN WERE DEAD.

Barnum struggles and tries to pull himself away. The farmer's wife drags him on.

34. INT. EVENING. CINEMA.

The USHER drags Barnum out of the cinema towards the foyer. We hear the sound of the film in the background – the boys singing GOD IS GOD. Barnum tears himself loose and rushes up some stairs. The usher pursues him for all he's worth, but trips on the stairs. Barnum pushes open a door and enters a dark, cramped corridor.

Barnum stops and looks about him. He sees a pillar of light slanting across the darkness. He carries on towards it. He fumbles forward towards the light.

35. INT. MORNING. FARM. DINING-ROOM.

Philip sits at the head of the table. Now he's the heaviest of the lot of them. His face is bulging with fat. He's stuffing himself with food. Fat dribbles from his lips.

The farmer stands behind Philip and pats him on the shoulder.

Barnum comes in and sits at the bottom of the table, thin as a rake and petrified.

SCHOOL DOCTOR'S VOICE: Day one. At six-thirty, a pint of milk, to be drunk slowly over three quarters of an hour.

Barnum looks down at the mug of grey, impure milk, swimming with globules of fat.

36. INT. EVENING. CINEMA.

Barnum's standing right in the beam of light. He doesn't have much time. He's in a panic. He tries to push the light away. He whirls his arms about in the air.

From the cinema there's booing and catcalls and the shouting of insults.

We see Barnum's moving shadow all but obliterating the screen.

37. INT. EVENING. FARM. DORMITORY.

Philip's standing beside Barnum's bed. Philip is naked and fat. Barnum's awake and terrified.

Philip drags him over to the wall and pushes his face down to the floor.

38. INT. CINEMA. EVENING.

Barnum opens a low door. The PROJECTIONIST *– an elderly, friendly man – is standing inside a cramped, low room that's little more than a cupboard. The man is keeping his eye on the running of the film.*

Barnum goes into the projection room.

BARNUM: I don't want to see any more.
PROJECTIONIST: What's that?
BARNUM: I don't want to see it any more.

PROJECTIONIST: I thought you wanted to see it.
BARNUM: Not any more.

The projectionist looks at him sorrowfully.

PROJECTIONIST: I can't stop the film before it's finished. You know that well enough.

39. INT. NIGHT. KITCHEN. FARM.

Barnum's eye is visible in the hole in the ceiling. It presses down into the hole, a wide-open eye. And then it tumbles, the eye tumbles down into the boiling pan of water on the stove.

40. INT. EVENING. CINEMA.

BARNUM has sat down now. The PROJECTIONIST is standing beside the rolls of film he has to change.

BARNUM: I thought it was you who decided.
PROJECTIONIST: You have to see the rest, Barnum.
BARNUM: But I don't want to.
PROJECTIONIST: You don't have any choice.
BARNUM: I thought you were God.
PROJECTIONIST: Yes, unfortunately I am God. But I don't have any choice either.

The projectionist turns towards Barnum.

PROJECTIONIST: There's something familiar about you. Haven't I seen you before?
BARNUM: Haven't you seen everyone?
PROJECTIONIST: But I've a bad memory, you see. I'm starting to get old.

The projectionist peers through his little window once more.

PROJECTIONIST: Come here. Hurry!

Barnum goes over and looks through the window.

Barnum sees the screen down below, a long way off. The beautiful field and the boys working there – happy and industrious in the glorious weather. Birdsong. And Barnum, a black patch over one eye, appears with the farmer at his back, and is put to work beside Philip.

In the background the wood's visible like a tall, dense shadow.

PROJECTIONIST: Now I know who you are.

The projectionist glances quickly at Barnum and smiles.
PROJECTIONIST: It's not what you see that matters most, but rather what you think you see.

Barnum lifts a box in which rolls of film have been stored and hits the projectionist's head with it for all he's worth. The projectionist sinks to the floor.

Barnum tears the film from the projector.

From the cinema comes the noise of catcalls and shouting.

41. INT. EVENING. CINEMA.

The screen is black and the cinema lies in empty darkness. There's no one there. Only the audience's things are left behind – their jackets, sweet wrappers, umbrellas, gloves, shoes and scarves. There isn't a sound to be heard.

And then a crackling strip of light appears on the screen.

A faded black and white picture is finally shown – of the door frame in the original bedroom. Different marks and dates. The last of them – 4/9/1962.

THE END

THE ELECTRIC THEATRE

The Nameplate

We got married at the platemaker's in Pilestredet. We'd chosen a copper plate with large letters – VIVIAN AND BARNUM. I'd have preferred it to be WIE AND NILSEN. That had a better ring to it. But I let Vivian have her way. The shop assistant wrapped it in brown paper and put in four screws. I paid for it and we went home and screwed the plate onto our door. VIVIAN AND BARNUM. On the letter box down at the front door I'd just glued up a bit of paper on which I'd written our surnames – Nilsen and Wie. That was our engagement ring. Now it was for real. VIVIAN AND BARNUM was etched in copper on the first-floor door in Boltelökka, a small red-brick block of flats entered from Johannes Brun Street. It was Vivian's father who'd got us the place – one room, a sleeping recess and a veranda. We sat down there. It was early autumn, a Saturday, and the air was clear and sharp, the sun still warm. Right behind the dwellings to the west I could see the spire of Sten Park – Blåsen; I was in my landscape, I was there where my story belonged. To the south we could see the fiord; it lay clear and still and colourless, as if it had frozen over already. I opened the first bottle of champagne and filled our two glasses. A neighbour stood below on the small lawn; she waved up to us, earth on her fingers. I drank. Vivian closed her eyes and leaned back. The light became gold on her face. I sensed a happiness I hadn't known before – the ease of alcohol and the peace of the moment – the dizziness and the occasion fused to become as one. 'How long d'you have to be missing before you're presumed dead?' I asked. 'Your whole life perhaps.' Vivian didn't open her eyes. I sloshed more drink into my glass. I drank. I laughed. 'Your whole life? That means people who're missing have eternal life. They never die. They just keep on living.' Vivian turned towards me. All of a sudden there was a tiredness in her eyes. She held the tall, thin stem of her glass in both hands. 'D'you miss Fred?' she whispered. I could have asked her the same question. I didn't reply. I went in for a new bottle instead. I drank a first glass. When I came out once more, Vivian had put on sunglasses. I sat down beside her. Half the veranda had fallen into shadow. Soon it would get colder. 'I want to have kids,' Vivian said. I drained my glass. 'Then we will,' I said. I took the bottle in with me; Vivian pulled out the sofa and made up the bed, and we lay down together. It didn't take long. We were – how shall I put it? – to the point and single-minded in bed. After that bit of madness in Frogner Park by the summer house all those years ago, an event we never talked about again and didn't so much as allude to, we'd become scared and shy, except when I'd had a drink. It was as if we opened up to a kind of darkness when we made love, and for that reason didn't dare look each other in the eye. We just wanted to get it over and done with. But I could still get a faint hint of musk ox. I filled our glasses again. 'Did I reach?' I asked. 'Oh, stop it,' Vivian said. 'Did I reach my public?' Vivian laughed too. I made her laugh, for the time being. I bent down to her stomach and listened. 'D'you think there's a child there now?' I breathed. 'Perhaps, perhaps not,' Vivian said. I sat up. I was cold. There was still a bit left in the bottle. Vivian held my hand. 'Aren't you drinking a bit too much?' she said. 'A bit too much?' 'Yes, a bit too much. You've all but managed two bottles all on your own.' 'Are you count-ing?' 'Not all that difficult, Barnum. One and one's two.' 'You're as good as Peder,' I said. Vivian let go of my hand. I lay down once more. 'I drink because I'm happy,' I whis-pered. She got up and went out into the bathroom, where there was room for just one person at a time – one and a half when things were desperate. I heard her turning on the shower. I drank up what was left. Vivian tended to take a long time in the bathroom. When she came back I got up. 'Can we go to bed early tonight?' she sighed. 'I have to write,' I told her. She turned away. She just had her red towel round her. Her wet hair lay fanned out on the white pillow and made a dark shadow that grew and grew. 'You mustn't get cold, Vivian.' 'I'm warm. Are you cold?' 'No, fine. Shall I put out the light?' 'Sure you can, Barnum.' I turned-out the bracket lamps above the bed and sat down at the narrow work table we had just enough room for in front of the window, between the veranda door and the bookshelves. But when I put on the lamp there it lit up the rest of the room too, even when I bent down as close to the paper as possible. Vivian pulled the quilt over her head. That was how small the place was. We had two pictures on the wall – the photograph of Lauren Bacall and the poster of *Hunger*. All at once I thought of the Little City. Now I was grown up at last and lived in the little flat. I was, if not old, then at least over the first threshold – that which follows innocence's meridian, and where laughter changes colour. All the same there were still lots of people who didn't think I was twenty yet, and must therefore still be something of a threadbare teenager. From time to time I'd be refused admission to an over-18 film and had to show my identity card. I stopped going to see them. The last time I got stopped it was for *The Shining* and Peder laughed his head off. After that I had to produce some form of identity in bars instead. That came to an end too. But those who came close enough and had a really good look, who didn't let themselves be fooled by my curls and my small stature (which in better moments I called my quiet length), could see by my facial features what the reality was, and those features were unmistakable. Vivian was already asleep. I often envied her that sleep. I got myself ready. This is an inventory of my tools: 400 sheets of Andvord paper, my ruler, a pencil, three pens, M. S. Greve's *Medical Dictionary for Norwegian Homes*, an eraser, correction fluid, and my typewriter from Fred. I went out into the little kitchen and had a drink from the little bottle. And had a little thought – *The Little City*, part two (or part one and a half) – a dwarf who lives in the world's smallest bedsit begins a relationship with the world's tallest woman. I drank a second bottle, made some coffee and sat down at the desk again. I got out my notebook. These were my ideas. 1. *Laughter and tears, Barnum's account of the human condition*. 2. *The swimming pool*. 3. *Close encounters with the famous – The Beatles, Per Oscarsson, Sean Connery, etc*. 4. *Fattening*. 5. *The triple jump*. 6. *The Night Man*. These were just some of my titles – my working titles – each listed precisely and with a detailed breakdown of direction and dialogue, and a character list. This was my finest hour, when I brought the paper down between the rollers or raised my pencil instead, so as not to waken Vivian. Then I reigned supreme. Then I was my own master and master of time too. Darkness hugged the window. The lights down in the city centre were never still. It was raining. Someone was playing the Sex Pistols at full blast. The Boteløkka cats were yowling. Then, all at once, there was silence. I heard nothing more than Vivian's easy breathing. She was our engine. This was my time. I would make my stories tall – not small and slow – no, I'd lift them higher than the marks on the door frame, higher than myself. Was this too great an expectation? And it's at that moment, when the hand holding the pencil nears the page, when the finger falls towards a letter on the buckled, worn keyboard, that I'm in my element. From this moment on anything can happen. I am the little god. Now I'm heavier than my own weight, bigger than my own thoughts, wider than my own authority – in this in-between place, in this hesitation of a second, like a drop of water under a leaky tap or a nose, and this drop has the power to become an ocean. Vivian turned over and moaned softly. Perhaps she'd dreamt something. Perhaps a person was growing inside her now – that was the way my mind began working – my cell and her egg, no less; the characteristics already lying embryonic in there in the warmth – a boy's wrinkles, a girl's dimples, a child's heart. In M. S. Greve's *Medical Dictionary* this was the definition: *Fertilization, the process through which the fertile egg cell is readied in order to develop a new independent individual.* And my pencil landed on the *Night Man.* I wrote the first scene. *A BOY, eight years old, thin and pale, runs through the streets.* When I shut my eyes I could see him running through the empty streets in a deserted city in the early morning. His clothes are old-fashioned; I can hear his breathing, his laboured breathing. I can hear music too, because this scene has to have music – something soft, slow and symphonic. Where is the boy going? What is it he has to reach, given that he's running so fast? I put down my pencil. It became too much for me. I wasn't ready for this story yet – my cornerstone, my major work – this story that would centre around absence. I wrote the word in the margin and underlined it. Absence. I knew the things I wanted to write, but not the order in which I wanted to write them. This is what the narrative is: the order of things, the course of events, what comes next – that lop-sided logic which isn't composed of cause and effect but with another sort of humanity, the poetic chronology. I still wasn't tall enough for this task. I had to grow with it, stretch out beyond my mandate to become my own superman. I would fill the absence and so cancel it out – Fred, who'd been gone for ten years, our great-grandfather, Wilhelm, who'd disappeared in the ice, Boletta's unknown husband, Dad's shadowy journey, from the time when he carried his suitcase of applause round the corner of the road, to the day he came driving up Church Road in a shining gold Buick. And I couldn't forget Peder either – Peder who'd studied economics at the University of Los Angeles. Perhaps it's these very people the boy's running to meet? Vivian slept. I went to get myself a beer and tiptoed out onto the veranda. I

could see the shadow of Blåsen. That's where the Old One
used to sit and where Mum would go to find her. I had yet
another idea and hurried inside so as not to forget it – that
was my great fear already, forgetting things, and it's for
this reason I went and recorded it. I wrote: *Places. Stories
about people's attachment to individual, set places. For instance,
the Old One to Blåsen. Boletta to the North Pole. Esther's kiosk.
The backyard. A place is not a place before a person has been
there. A person isn't a person before they have a place in which to
be.* And is it in these places that our memory lies? Where's
my place? I don't know. But can't time be a place too? I
would have my place in time. I wrote at the bottom in
large letters: *Graveyards. Whose are they?* Then I leafed back
to an old and trusty idea – *the Triple Jump.* I would make the
triple jump my poetics. The various stages of the triple
jump are inescapable and definitive – the fast run-up, the
springy take-off and equally springy contact with the
ground. The hop, the stride, then every atom of strength
gathered for the last mighty leap towards the sandpit, as
the legs stretch forward in descent – an almost impossible
and yet more beautiful movement. I imagine an account
of the triple jump's history, how the technique has been
refined over the years without disturbing the quintessen-
tial properties of the discipline itself – the hop, stride and
leap – the very trinity of the triple jump. In particular I'm
interested in the run-up; it's here the foundation is laid,
for a bad jump may be detected as early as the run-up. I'd
imagine there's a whole series of stock shots from various
sports' tournaments and championships, both from home
and abroad, which can shed light on the triple jump's
composition and significance. I have, after a lot of to-ing
and fro-ing, made up my mind to have Bang the caretaker
as the main protagonist – the lame hero of the triple jump.
This is what I imagine – the old caretaker has brought in
sand to the backyard and dug a pit for it. Everyone has
now gathered to see him jump. It's springtime, a Saturday
afternoon; we're leaning out of the windows and crowd-
ing the steps; we've positioned ourselves along the length

of the run-up, the narrow path strewn with gravel. We cheer, and now Bang the caretaker makes his appearance, clad in his worn shorts and yellow singlet, to the sound of great jubilation and much applause. Determined and limping as he runs, he hits the wooden platform and leaps upwards with a groan, and it's right there I freeze him – I let Bang the caretaker hang like that in mid-air, and from that point I go backwards in time to the morning of the jump. Who was the first in the world to devise the triple jump?

I went to bed when Vivian got up. She put on her training gear and slipped out. I heard her quick steps going down the stairs. She was away a half hour and still I hadn't slept. Then the phone rang, or was it the church bells? It was Vivian's father. 'Can I talk to Vivian, please?' he asked. 'She's out jogging,' I told him. There was silence for a time. 'I just wanted to remind her about dinner later today.' His voice seemed far away, almost as if he'd put down the receiver and gone into another room. 'Hallo?' I breathed. 'Seven o'clock,' he said, his voice sounding closer now. 'Seven o'clock,' I repeated. 'Good, that's settled then.' 'Yes, indeed,' I said. His tone changed, was suddenly more confiding. 'Don't you jog, too?' 'Vivian likes running on her own,' I tell him. He was still there. I could hear Vivian on the stairs, her breathing. 'How are the two of you?' he asked suddenly, in a gentle voice that sounded so strange, like a man trying to find a friend for himself. 'We bought a nameplate for the door yesterday,' I said. He hung up. Vivian turned to me, wet – she was dripping. 'Is it raining?' I asked. 'I'm sweating,' she said. 'Shall we make another baby?' 'I have to do some stretching.' She grasped the door frame and hung from it. Her thin fingers held her up. There was something unnatural about this image, as with that of Bang the caretaker whom I left hanging in the air – a sort of suspended animation, I thought, like the purgatory of waiting in which Fred had left us. I slept, and my sleep was heavy and short and meaningless. When I woke up,

Vivian was sitting in the kitchen having breakfast. I caught the smells of coffee, toast and marmalade. I remained where I was, looking at her. This was no purgatory. This was the everyday, that which we take for granted and therefore forget. This was the kind of moment of which most of our time was composed – the still and uneventful moments, the Sunday moments – and this was how I wanted it to be. Then it came to me that it wasn't all that commonplace after all. This was our first morning. I brought out the little parcel I'd hidden under the pillow and went through to where she was. 'Is there room for me, too?' I asked. Vivian looked up. 'Yes, I'm finished.' I sat down just the same. She poured out coffee for us both. 'Did you get anything written?' she asked. 'I can't make up my mind,' I told her. 'Make up your mind? How d'you mean?' 'I have too many ideas, Vivian.' 'Is that such a problem?' 'Yes, I can't get any further. I start something new the whole time. I don't know what I want.' Vivian pushed the breadbasket towards me. 'I think you'll write about Fred just the same,' she said. I didn't like her saying that. She was right. I put the little parcel in front of her. She looked at me thunderstruck. 'What is it?' 'It's a morning present,' I told her. Vivian shook her head. 'I had no idea you could be so thoughtful.' She smiled. I nodded. 'You mean bourgeois?' 'No, I mean thoughtful, Barnum.' 'Open it then!' I shrieked. Vivian opened the box. It was a ring, simple and gold. Carefully she took it out. 'Mum wanted you to have it,' I told her. As I watched Vivian push that thin ring onto her finger a new idea came to me; I suddenly saw a leap, a triple jump – the ring that Rakel gave to Mum and which I was now passing on to Vivian. And inside this small circle, the circumference of the ring, I glimpsed a story that was bigger than itself, which burst those barriers. And I saw in my mind's eye the mountain of jewels that the Nazis stole from the Jews before they sent them to the gas chambers – this ring should have ended up there, but somehow Rakel managed to take it off in time. And I saw too a room full of shoes, gentlemen's and ladies' shoes, moving in time to Mum's words – *it's these steps I hear going out of my life*. I had to write this down. I made to get up. 'Thank you,' Vivian murmured. I remained where I was. I laid my hand on hers. Everything I touched turned to ideas.

Later that Sunday we went for a walk. We were arm in arm. The trees were shaking themselves free of their leaves. There was barely anyone about except for a dog owner with an ugly chihuahua and some panting joggers. Even they turned round to look at us. We were a topsy-turvy couple. I'd put my platform shoes away in the cupboard. Now I just wore platforms. Autumn had come during the night. People were at home putting away their summer things. I felt the atmosphere was strange. It was the ring's fault. I shouldn't have given it to her. I was regretting it already. I could have bought a different one, or an ear stud. We could have made do with the name-plate on the door – VIVIAN AND BARNUM. That was more than sufficient. Now I'd gone too far. This ring was too heavy on her hand. For a moment, she leaned her head against my shoulder. 'Thank you,' she said again. 'You suit it,' I breathed.

We went up Blåsen and sat down there. A flock of doves took off from the roofs, flew to the four winds. 'What's your place?' I asked her. 'What d'you mean?' 'Everyone has a place. This is the Old One's place.' 'I don't have any place,' Vivian said. I laughed. 'Of course you do.' Suddenly she lost her temper completely. 'Perhaps I don't want any place!' she raged. 'Fine,' I said. I lit a match. Vivian blew out the flame. 'Shall I tell you where my place is, Barnum? It's at the bend where Dad drove off the road and I was born.' I put the cigarette in my pocket again. I didn't like that place. I wanted to find somewhere else for her that wasn't the scene of something so terrible. 'Have you forgotten that we're going to dinner at 1900 hours?' I asked her. Vivian hid her face in her hands. She didn't move for at least ten minutes. It began to get dark. 'I'm not going,' she said. But we went all the same, to what Vivian later called the seven o'clock performance at Dracula's. We nipped into Krölle's on the way and even Vivian had a beer. I ordered two more. I got served here without having to produce any kind of identification. 'What's your place?' she asked me. 'Guess,' I said. She didn't waste any time. 'The tree in Solli Square.' 'That's not *mine*,' I said, 'it's *ours*.' A shadow crossed Vivian's face – maybe it came from me, maybe I cast it over her. It was called Peder. 'Rosenborg Cinema,' she whispered. 'You're getting close,' I told her. She leant close. 'I know, Barnum. The Little City.' I raised my glass, said cheers. 'Your answer is quite correct.' Vivian raised her own glass. 'What do we really want with places anyway? Can you tell me that?' I put down my glass on the soft beer mat. 'They make us whole,' I said quietly. Vivian was silent for a time. Voices were raised round us; things were getting ugly. Someone thumped a table with their fist. I lit the cigarette. 'That's what I'm writing about,' I whispered. 'The places that make us whole.' I took her hand and felt the edge of the ring against her skin. Vivian gave me a sudden look. 'Where's Fred's place?' I shrugged my shoulders. 'Perhaps that's what he's looking for.' I let go of her hand and swallowed some more beer. 'D'you miss Peder?' I asked her. She could have asked me the same thing. She went to the loo. I caught the waiter and grabbed a pint from his tray. The Little City. That was my place. It was where I'd been chosen, by a constable with big gloves, and stopped growing. It was where I got my first idea and wrote it. The Little City was both time and place; impossible to get away from. All at once a leaflet landed in front of me. *No to the sale of Norway. Torch-lit procession from Young's Market – 20 October*. I glanced up. I met the gaze of a rather severe-looking man looming over me. 'Norway's a place too,' I told him. 'Are you a student?' he asked. 'No, I'm a shopkeeper.' He grew suspicious. 'A shopkeeper?' 'That's right.' 'What d'you sell?' 'I don't sell things,' I said. 'I keep things.' 'What d'you keep then?' 'I keep chocolate, juice, hot dogs, weeklies and sweets.' The fellow thumped the table, impatient and contemptuous. 'Bloody capitalist!' he exclaimed. 'But exploited nonetheless,' I said. He retracted his hand, confused for a moment. 'An exploited shopkeeper? Don't make me laugh.' I got up. I reached as high as his ribs, even in my platform shoes. He didn't laugh. And as I stood like that, something occurred to me. 'It's four years since the referendum,' I said. The guy grew annoyed again. 'So? What the hell has that got to do with it?' He stuffed the leaflet in his pocket and made his way out between the waiters. And when I took my seat again, Vivian had finally come back. 'You have to send them in,' she said. 'Send them in?' I was in the dark. She leaned forward over the cloth. 'Send in your scripts! You have to show them to someone!' 'I'm not ready yet,' I told her. Vivian put in front of me an advertisement she'd torn out of a paper. Norwegian Film Limited were announcing a script contest. Both complete scripts and synopses could be submitted. But that was what scared me. I was frightened someone would reject me, reject everything I wrote and bin it. At the moment I could still dream, be my own master along the full length of Barnum's ruler. I closed my eyes. The deadline for submissions was 1 March. 'What's today's date?' I asked. 'The 20th of September,' Vivian said. And I thought to myself that if we were to run like hell we'd perhaps make the torchlit procession at Young's Market four years before. I opened my eyes. 'I'll show them to you first,' I said. 'You were a long way away just then,' Vivian breathed. I laughed. 'Just outside having a pee.' She laughed herself. 'D'you mean it? Will you show them to me?' 'Who else?' Vivian had a swig of my beer and I liked her when she drank like that, in a kind of reckless way – she could laugh spontaneously then, we were somehow working in tandem – not like two clocks showing different times in hotel receptions, Vivian being Tokyo and me Buenos Aires. Now we drank and laughed at one and the same time, but all the greater was the stillness when her father opened the door and we followed him down – I say down – into the dark apartment. Vivian left us as soon as we were in the hall and went in to her mother in the bedroom, and I sank into the deep uphol- stery in the library while Vivian's father poured Scotch into two glasses, dropped ice into them with a crash and drew up his own chair. 'It's time we got to know each other,' he said. 'Yes,' I murmured. Even though there was barely any light in the room, I noticed that he was staring at me and that his eyes were hard and sharp. 'After the accident Vivian's mother threw away all the mirrors we possessed. But one day the doorbell rang. She went to see who it was and there were some kids standing there. They were holding a mirror up in front of her. Can you believe children could be so wicked?' I just shook my head. Vivian's father raised his glass to his lips. 'As some- one who does a bit of writing, what do you think of a story like that?' I looked down. 'It's a good story,' I said. The ice clinked. 'Good? Are you sentimental, Barnum?' 'I doubt it.' 'Then you should realize there's no such thing as a good story. Just ones that are true and ones that aren't.' He drank more of his whisky and sighed heavily. 'What has Vivian said about the accident?' 'Said?' Her father poured more Scotch into his glass, impatient, but not into mine – despite the fact that it too was empty. 'She told you how it happened?' I glanced in the direction of the door which was slightly ajar. There was no Vivian. She wouldn't join us until this conversation was concluded. 'She wasn't even born then,' I said, and regretted the words as soon as I'd uttered them. He leant forward towards me and I could just make out a dour smile. 'Everyone has their own version, Barnum. Things they've heard. Things they've dreamed. You know that, don't you?' I sank down in my seat. 'She told me you lost con- trol of the car at a bend and drove into the ditch.' He sighed. 'No one loses control of a Chevrolet Deluxe, Barnum.' He raised his hands as if he was holding a steer- ing wheel between them. 'Another car came towards us at the bend,' he whispered. 'An open-topped Buick. It was going far too fast. It swung over to my side of the road and I had to get the Chevrolet out of the way.' Vivian's father spun his hands round and stamped his foot on the floor. Then he let his hands fall into his lap again. 'That's how it happened,' he said. 'I avoided an accident and destroyed my family.' Slowly he lifted his glass. Did we know each other any better now? Did I know who he was now? 'Didn't the other car stop?' I asked him. He shook his head and suddenly his voice was unrecognizable, the words were twisted and something inside him broke. 'The dammed swine just kept driving!' And at that moment the bell rang. I felt a dent, a tear in the heart, the kind that hurts so badly it feels good. Maybe it was Peder. I listened. I heard someone opening the door – it had to be Vivian – perhaps Vivian and Peder were hugging at that very moment, and I wanted to be with them in that embrace, that moment. Vivian's father remained where he was. He put his hand on my knee. I wished he'd remove it. 'Now you know,' he said, and his voice was as before, toneless, a deep line in his mouth. 'What?' I breathed. 'Now you know the truth, Barnum.' And it was as if I could hear Peder, somewhere far away, very distant and yet quite close just the same – *Perhaps. Perhaps not.* Vivian's father got up. 'We'll never talk about this,' he said. 'Never.' Someone knocked cautiously on the door and opened it. An elderly, grey-haired lady with a white apron and a black shirt peered in. She curtsied. 'Your guest has arrived, Mr Wie.' She vanished again into the darkness as quickly as she'd appeared. I followed Vivian's father to the living room. There was the guest. It was Mum. She'd done herself up. She looked lost. Vivian's father took her hand in both his own. 'Is no one looking after you? I'm so sorry. But Barnum and I were talking about life and forgot ourselves completely.' 'Oh, it doesn't matter,' Mum breathed. 'Thank you for coming at such short notice.' Mum smiled. 'I'm the one who should be

thanking you.' Vivian's father let her hand drop. 'Now I'll
go for my girls,' he said. He quickly went out into the hall.
I turned to Mum. 'Why didn't you phone? We could have
come together?' 'Because I was invited ten minutes ago.
And by then you'd left.' 'Didn't they ask Boletta?'
'Boletta's tired. Have you been drinking, Barnum?' The
elderly lady, the maid, suddenly appeared with a tray and
I managed to gulp a dry Martini before she vanished once
more. 'No,' I said. Mum sighed and looked about her.
'How can they bear to have the place so dark?' 'I know,' I
said. 'They can't stand daylight.' 'Be quiet, Barnum.' And
I thought about what Vivian's father had said about the
accident – what he called the truth. Was that why he'd
invited us, to reveal the guilty party? Mum mustn't say a
word about the Buick. I had drunk too much and I realized, for the first time, that it was far too little. 'What the
hell do they want?' I hissed. 'They just want to be nice,
Barnum. We're almost family now.' I laughed. 'Almost
family?' Mum nipped my arm. 'Pull yourself together,
Barnum.' Vivian's father came back. He had his daughter
with him. She was both happy and anxious when she saw
Mum there. She kissed her on the cheek. 'Thank you,
Vera.' Mum lifted her hand and touched the ring. 'It suits
you.' Vivian's father looked at me, his mouth still sullen
as he brushed his finger over his lips. I was suspicious of
him. Then at last he looked back at Vivian again. 'Are you
finished with Annie?' he asked. Vivian nodded. He
smiled. 'Good. We'll go and eat then.' He pushed open
the white doors into the dining-room. She was sitting at
the bottom of the table, in the shadows behind the can-
delabra, staring right at us. Vivian had done a fine job.
Her face was smooth, her features perfect and clear – she
resembled a photograph framed by darkness. But when I
had to sit down beside her I could see that beneath the
make-up, under all this beautiful putty, was the former
visage that time had frozen the moment it shattered
against the windscreen of the Chevrolet Deluxe. The rest
was a mask and she wore it with a kind of dignity, and

maybe defiance. The elderly lady served us. I don't remember what we ate. It was game of some kind. I wasn't hungry. Vivian was holding her knife and fork in a strange way, with clenched fists, like some badly brought up child. I'd never noticed before. The ring looked too tight on her finger. I just saw our hands, our ten hands and fifty fingers, none of them alike. And my own hand, lifting the glass to my lips, each mouthful of red wine a gust through my head. And I realize that these hands have to be a motif in Barnum's account of humanity; I'm possessed by this thought of the severed, unconnected hands – but I've nothing to write on and I haven't the nerve to leave the table either because perhaps something frightful will happen in my absence. Vivian's father lays down his knife and fork and drinks Mum's health. 'I always have this feeling we've seen each other before,' he says. Mum smiles. 'But we have. At the première of *Hunger*.' 'No, longer ago than that.' Vivian's father puts down his glass. It's as if there's a kind of membrane over us, a skin, that could break at any moment. 'And where would that have been?' I say loudly and laugh. But no one hears me. My glass is empty. Vivian's father looks over the table. 'Annie, where have we seen Barnum's mother before?' She turns slowly to Vivian and her words are as drawn-out as her movement. 'Haven't you two thought of getting married properly?' Vivian takes a deep breath. 'Properly? What d'you mean?' 'You know fine what I mean, Vivian. In church, of course.' Vivian looks at me. 'Barnum and I have come to the conclusion that God doesn't exist. That's why we let the platemaker marry us instead.' Her mother smiles. She looks at me, too. The make-up cracks. 'I always thought it should be Peder and Vivian,' she says. Vivian pushes back her chair. 'Why did you think that, Mother?' 'Because you were so well suited.' Vivian's father suddenly leans over towards Mum; it's as if he's found a trail he doesn't want to lose, the pieces of a dream after a heavy night. 'What was it your husband did?' he asks. Mum hesitates for a moment.

'He was a clown and a shopkeeper,' she says. It's quiet for a time after that; just the sound of our cutlery, the food in our mouths. Then Vivian's father asks something else. 'Didn't you have another son? Who disappeared?' Vivian looks down and whispers something I can't hear. Mum straightens up. 'He didn't disappear,' she responds peacefully. 'He's just roaming.' And it strikes me that this dialogue only points backwards, nothing that's said moves our stories onward – this conversation is water that stands still. Here, in this place, in this dining-room, is nothing but the past, and not even that is something we can put into words. But suddenly Vivian's mother puts her hand on her daughter's arm in a not quite sober gesture. The make-up slides from her mouth, and the scar – a bulging diagonal line across her face – comes into view, as if her visage is made up of different segments that don't quite fit together. 'Have the two of you thought of having children?' she asks. Vivian draws back her arm. Her mother's hand is left twitching on the table between the plates and the glasses and the cutlery. It's just as if it's breathing; then it disappears too, abruptly, and only a crease is left in the cloth, a shadow over the whiteness. 'No,' Vivian answers. 'I wouldn't want to put someone through that.' 'Put someone through what?' her mother breathes. 'Being a child, mother.' And Vivian gets up from the table and walks out of the dining-room. She leaves a heavy silence behind her. Mum kicks my leg. I go after Vivian. She's sitting on her bed in her old room, where everything's just as it was except for the picture of Lauren Bacall, which isn't hanging there now – all that's in its place is a dark square on the wallpaper, like a negative. I lay my head in Vivian's lap. 'Couldn't you just have said yes?' I ask her. 'Why?' 'Yes is just as short as no.' 'Wrong, Barnum. No is always shorter than yes. You should know that.' I kiss her. 'Shall we go back in or shall we go home?' 'What do you think?' 'I don't like leaving them,' I tell her. Vivian gets up. 'Shall we play happy?' she asks. 'Aren't you? Happy, I mean.' Vivian smiles. 'Not here.'

As it happens, that was the last time we had dinner at her parents'. Mum went home by taxi to Boletta. Vivian wanted to walk. We stopped at Peder's house. Light shone from the ground floor but there was no sign of life inside. 'Did you think it would be Peder and you, too?' I asked her. Vivian didn't answer immediately. 'No, I thought it would be you and Peder,' she said. We continued up Tiedemann Street and I see us passing through the seasons in one single stretch – it's autumn when we turn the corner and the lights go out in Peder's house; at the Vestkanttonget we go into winter; spring approaches as we arrive at Bislet, and at Boltelokka summer's come already – yet another summer. I open the windows to air the place; I get a cloth while the neighbour goes out with the rubbish, and in the hallway I polish our nameplate till it's shining bright – VIVIAN AND BARNUM. I hear her right behind me. She hasn't made a sound on the stairs. Now she puts her hands over my eyes. I laugh. 'I've been at the doctor's,' she whispers. 'The doctor's? There's nothing wrong?' 'I'm fine, Barnum. You'll have to get checked, too.' She takes her hands away. I stand there still with my back to her. 'Are you sure you want to have a child with me, Vivian?'

The Half Dark

'Many thanks!' the polite little boy says when I give him his fifty øre change. His fingers close round the shiny coin and in the other hand he clutches a red carton of juice. 'You don't need to say many thanks,' I tell him. I give him a pat on the head. He twists free. 'Huh?' he murmurs. 'Whose money is this?' I ask him. 'Whose money?' 'Yes, who does this fifty öre belong to?' He clenches his fist even tighter round the coin. 'It's mine!' 'Exactly,' I agree. 'So there's no need to say many thanks.' The boy chases over the road. 'Cuckoo!' he shouts. I'm standing on an empty lemonade crate leaning against the kiosk window. It's pretty good to see the world from here, from the inside of Esther's kiosk. I'm the one who's running it now, together with Mum. Just before summer Esther took a turn that made her forget the price of sugar candy, how many öre there are to a krone, and when to turn off the stove. On the other hand she can remember every single thing that happened between 1945 and 1972 – the weather, international elections, Holmenkollen competitions, the moon landing, and the most frequent choices on the requests programme. She shares a room at the Prince August Memorial in Storgata, no longer remembers her own name but has an entire almanac in her head. Autumn's arrived. I've hung the latest weeklies by clips from a little line in the window. The juice cartons are stored in the freezer and the bottles of cola are in the fridge. What I like least are the sausages. They're just a nuisance. They lie there in the tepid water till they turn grey and wrinkly and are of no use whatsoever except as dog food. I'm going to stop doing sausages. I'll have a kiosk with dry goods: colour supplements, cigarettes and sweets. But Mum doesn't want any changes, she'd like to continue just where Esther left off. They've started doing prawn salad and fried onions at the stall in Sørkedal's Road, but I've no intention of trying to compete – they're welcome to go on serving their muck. I've a fine view over to the Little City too. A class is there to learn the Green Cross Code from a constable. They're standing to the left and to the right, most likely listening to him going on about cycle lights and Cats eyes, because the dark nights aren't far away now and being visible's what counts then. And when I see them like this, these kids, with their serious expressions and their incomplete features, it's as if I can put my finger on time and see it passing. I note this down in my jotter. *Time. How can time be shown passing in a new way? If it were possible you could, for instance, put someone in front of a camera for fifty years and film the changes in their face. Possible title – Echo.* Then the lesson's over and the kids rush across the road as the constable is left standing sorrowfully in the little pedestrian crossing, able to confirm that they haven't learned a thing, or that they've forgotten anything they did learn already. None of them looks to see if it's safe to cross, they just chase out over the road to be first at Barnum's kiosk. Soon enough there's a long queue in front of the little window. I lean out and peer down at them, and they look up at me. They can't know I'm standing on a crate in there. 'What's it to be then?' I ask. And the boy at the front, a chubby fellow with his hair down over his eyes, puts five kroner on the ledge. 'Sausage and sauce,' he says. I put paper round a pale sausage, smear on some ketchup and mustard, and put the carcasses in his hand. He gets four kroner back – this dead meat is worth no more than that – and the overweight boy thinks I've given him the wrong change, too much; he doesn't much thank me but hurries off down the pavement as he stuffs the sausage into his mouth. 'You could say thank you,' I shout after him. But he doesn't hear a thing and the next in the queue is a slender girl with a much too large schoolbag; she's on the verge of toppling backwards with it. 'What can I get for twenty-five øre?' she asks. I have a think. 'For twenty-five øre you can get sugar candy,' I tell her. 'What's sugar candy?' 'It's good,' I assure her. I give her a big chunk in a twist of paper and drop the small coin in her hand once more. 'I almost forgot that sugar candy's free if you share it with someone else.' She looks up at me in astonishment and walks off alone towards Majorstuen. And at the end of the queue are two boys on a mission that's troubling them. They look all round and don't risk saying a word until the coast's clear for at least a mile in every direction. I know what they're after all right. I just let them sweat a bit. Then one of them strains towards the little window. '*Cocktail*,' he says, suddenly and speedily; he all but swallows the word before he's spoken it. 'What was that?' I ask. The other one kicks his friend in the leg and the poor soul has to go through the whole thing again. '*Cocktail*,' he repeats, more clearly this time; the sweat's running from the smooth, as yet untroubled, brow. 'Do you mean the men's magazine *Cocktail*?' Both of them nod their heads off, impatient and glancing this way and that, as if mum at any moment could appear on the scene and catch them in the act. And who would have thought that this type of reading would be in among all the stuff that Esther left to me? Oh yes, a whole pile of *Cocktail* magazines from the 1960s were still lying in a box under the chocolate. I'd long wondered who it was who bought *Cocktail* from Esther's kiosk – it certainly wasn't me – and I'd come to the conclusion that it probably had to be Bang the caretaker. I took my time opening the box as the hearts of the boys outside went like dynamos. I chose Number 13 from 1967, that had the lady with the hair-do squatting on a rug at the foot of a tree. It'll be a good start for these two young gents. They've already put a tenner through the window. I give it back, pat them both on the head and ruffle their hair a bit. 'You don't need to pay for old ladies,' I tell them. Then I roll up the magazine, put a band round it and hand it over like a relay baton to these wild lads who set a new record for running the last part of Church Road that autumn. That's enough for today. I close the window, pull down the little blinds, and finally get myself into the camp-chair I've inherited from Esther. I can sit here and write a bit and have a beer in peace and quiet. Ought not the kiosk itself to be the starting point for a script? It could be a way of showing time too – time as seen from the window of Esther's kiosk at the beginning of Church Road: the changing customers, the hairstyles, the wares, the passing cars, the money, the street lights. Time and place; time seen from the place, and, not least, the place seen through time. Possible title – *Barnum's kiosk*. I sense this warmth in the shoulders, a sort of good fever, the joy of being in the proximity of something. But that day I don't have the calm to develop my thoughts all the same. In my pocket I have a letter I still haven't opened. I can't wait any longer. Vivian'll ask me soon and I ought to be able to give her an answer. The letter's from a Dr Lund. *Barnum Nilsen. Please come to Lab III at the Royal Infirmary on Thursday 12 September at 1.00 p.m. Please bring with you a sample of sperm which should be no more than three hours old; at least five days should have passed since intercourse or your last ejaculation*. Inside the voluminous envelope was a transparent container with a lid. Tomorrow is Thursday and the last time we made love was on Midsummer night. It was raining that evening and the bonfires would hardly burn. I drain my bottle of beer, chew some salt sweets and nip up to visit Mum. I haven't seen her for a while. She's pleased to see me and puts her arms round me. Boletta's sleeping on the living-room divan. 'How is she?' 'Dreaming,' Mum whispers. We go into the kitchen. I stop for a moment by our room. Fred's bed is still made-up ready. It's been like that a long time. Mum changes the sheets twice a month. 'D'you want a coffee?' she asks. 'You wouldn't have a beer?' She sighs, her back to me. 'It's not more than three in the afternoon, Barnum.' I sit down at the kitchen table. 'Would you like some good news, Mum?' She turns abruptly. Her voice barely reaches over her lips. 'Fred? Have you heard from Fred?' There was such a great stillness in my head. I smile. 'No. But Vivian and I are going to have a baby.' Mum looks at me for a long time. It's as if she has to set her face to a different speed. 'Oh, Barnum,' she says at last, and pulls at my curls a bit and kisses my brow. I bend away. She laughs. 'Beer I can't give you. But champagne I can.' And at the back of the fridge she finds a green bottle, and I carefully uncork it so as not to waken Boletta. There's a fine crackling in our tall glasses. We drink each other's health. We sit there at the kitchen table on a Wednesday in September drinking champagne. Mum takes my hand. 'When?' she asks me. 'When?' 'Yes, when are you having the baby?' 'As soon as possible,' I answer. 'As soon as possible?' 'We've only *decided* to have a baby, Mum.' She pulls back her arm and pushes the bottle away. 'Why do you say things like that?' 'Like what?' 'That you're having a baby. D'you do it just to get a drink?' I don't quite know what comes over me, but I'm consumed with a sudden rage. 'Our child'll at least have a father,' I all but scream. Mum doesn't look away from me. It's me who looks down as soon as I've uttered the words and drink my champagne. 'That wasn't necessary,' she breathes. I shake my head and want to try to make it look like righteous indignation. But I can't. 'Forgive me,' I say. I look up. Mum's eyes are black. And I see, perhaps for the first time, because it's so clearly etched in her face, her expression – how like Fred she is. She takes my hand once more. 'It's of no consequence, Barnum.' 'But it is, and I'd like to talk about it.' 'Talk about what?' 'D'you remember the time Fred and I went to get Boletta from the North Pole?' Mum smiles. I pour some more into our glasses. 'Who could forget? We thought you were dead.' 'Was it your father she was drinking with there?' I ask her. Mum clammed up and grew restive. 'I said I didn't want to talk about it,' she says in the end. I get up and go over with the bottle to the window. The flower beds beside the bins are almost overgrown. There are weeds round the stairs. The creeper's begun to turn red against the bricks like veins. I shrug my shoulders. 'Fine then. Don't talk about it.' Mum gets up herself. 'Boletta wanted it that way,' she says, her voice low. 'Why?' 'Because it was me she wanted, Barnum.' I understand what Mum's saying, but I can't comprehend it. 'What do you mean?' 'She didn't just want a man who disappeared.' 'In the same way as with the Old One? Did Boletta find a sailor too?' 'I don't know, Barnum. And I don't want to know either.' 'I always imagined that grand-dad was a tram driver,' I tell her. 'That he looked after me every time I took the tram from Majorstuen.' 'Stop it, Barnum.' 'I liked to think that, Mum. That he kept an eye on us as he was driving the tram.' Then something hits me, slowly but surely, and I start laughing, laughing out loud. 'What is it now?' Mum asks me crossly. 'Fleming Brant,' I murmur. 'What about him?' 'Maybe he was Boletta's husband?' 'Don't be silly, Barnum.' 'I mean it! The man who cut the films is your father! That's it!' Mum boxes my ears. Then she lays her hand on my shoulder. 'I was back at the police station yesterday. To ask about Fred.' I close my eyes. 'Anything new?' 'They said that being missing was no crime,' she goes on. Then I notice three men in shiny suits emerging from the entrance by the gate. They're accompanied by Bang the caretaker who's wearing a suit himself, the same one he used to come to funerals in. They stop on the stairs. Bang points with a stick and the whole group looks up at the roof. 'What's going on?' I ask. Mum glances over my shoulder. 'There seems to be talk of converting the drying lofts into flats.' 'Who the hell would want to live up there?' Mum takes the bottle from me and puts it back in the fridge. 'You and Vivian perhaps. And the child,' she adds. 'Or Fred,' I breathe.

I go back to the kiosk before Boletta wakes up. She's become a creature of the night. She just sleeps by day. I settled myself in the camp-chair, opened a beer, and kept the curtains closed. I added a section in my notebook under *places – the drying loft. What becomes of a place when it's no longer to be found, when it's obliterated and levelled to*

*the ground? Does that place become nothing more than a mark on
some old and useless map?* But I couldn't manage to carry the
thought any further, I stopped in mid-jump; I wasn't just
lacking height, I lacked length too. I chewed a sweet and
instead got out some faded editions of *Cocktail* from the
Middle Ages. I quickly flicked through the pictures of
these women who'd turned pale and shy-looking in the
course of the years. They almost looked as if they were
about to fall asleep or burst out crying there where they
sat crouching in baths with foam between their breasts.
And to think I'd gone all the way to Frogner Road just to
buy *Cocktail*. But I was struck by another idea as I flicked
through this forbidden archive – maybe I could write a
story for the magazine to make a few kroner. If I took out
this and that and did a bit of expanding, I could maybe
use the experience in Frogner Park when Vivian had her
way with me. For instance it could be on a warm summer
night instead of in the middle of a wet autumn – a soft,
still glow in the trees. I could imagine that Vivian was a
lonely upper-class lady close on thirty out on a horse ride,
and that I was a poor but good-hearted gardener cutting
the grass outside the summer house. And she'd set upon
me with the same wild fever, she'd get me down on the
ground and take me in the mouth, greedily and decisively.
Or maybe I could write a pornographic comedy? I'd never
heard of such a thing before. But when I thought about it
I quickly realized that wasn't such a surprise. Because
aren't laughter and pornography incompatible? Romance
is amusing, but pornography is nothing more than silence
and action, and who gets randy seeing a funny man? I
noted this down too. Then someone knocked on the little
door at the back of the kiosk. I didn't have time to get up.
They came in, three of them, and took up position round
the deckchair. One of them got out a bottle of Coke from
the cupboard and hit me right on the front of the head
with it. 'Are you touching up my brother?' he demanded.
I'd never seen them before. I only knew they belonged to
the bullying fraternity. There's forever a bully who can

pass on the gift. Here they were again. I felt an arm round
my throat. I was pulled backwards and the one who'd
spoken kicked me in the groin. 'Are you touching up my
brother?' he screeched. I heard a scrunching, like that of
something breaking – the sound came first and the pain
followed, and in that white no-man's-land between the
sound of something breaking and the heavy, nauseating
pain, I could sink as deep as I wanted. Was he meaning
the boys I'd given *Cocktail* and had patted on the head? I
tried to say something but my voice was gone. I only
remember suddenly lying on the floor and somebody
standing on my neck. The same voice shouted, 'Bloody
poof! Sitting here wanking!' I couldn't breathe. I just
waited. It had to pass. Was that how they spoke of me, as
that poof of a midget in the kiosk who gave away free
sweets and couldn't keep his hands to himself – was that
what rumour had made me? I could have shouted for the
constable in The Little City. I could have called on Fred.
But the constable had gone home and no one knew where
Fred was. I managed to get as far as thinking that I'd
never felt so lonely. There was the glint of a knife. They
hacked off my belt, pulled it off me and whipped me in the
face with it. The buckle got caught like a hook in my
eyelid, and the blood ran down into my mouth. Perhaps it
was all the blood that scared them. At any rate they
scarpered, after smashing the box I used as a stool and
washing my face in the water for the sausages. After that
things became dark and silent. When I came to I could
only see out of one eye. I managed to get up onto my feet.
I had an extra shirt hanging by the door for when I spilled
mustard or ketchup. I changed. I tidied up a bit. I threw
out the copies of *Cocktail* and put the sausages in the bin
in the entryway. Then I went down to the beauty salon in
Jacob Aall Street where Vivian worked. I tended to put my
head round the door at the end of the day. I liked seeing
her like that as she restored those tired ladies from
Majorstuen and Fagerborg – hid their wrinkles and lifted
their faces to a temporary triumph – this quiet hubris

broken only by small bits of conversation, perhaps about some presenter or other's new hairstylist or the latest night cream from Paris which could waken the dead. Her clients always came back. They became dependent on her. She was a magician. Now she was working on the neck of an elderly lady, putting shadow on the limp skin – and I thought to myself, with a certain amount of sorrow, that all beauty at the end of the day is just a mirage. Then Vivian caught sight of me in the mirror. She put down what she had in her hands and came over to the chair where I was sitting. 'Good God, what a state you're in,' she breathed. 'I got broken into.' Vivian bent down closer. 'You have to go to the doctor's, Barnum.' 'You can put me together again,' I told her. 'Wait in at the back,' she hissed. 'Am I scaring your client?' 'Yes,' she said. I went through to the back premises. The smell of make-up and creams was quite overpowering. I fell asleep. Vivian woke me up. It was my turn. The salon was closed and at last I could sit in the soft chair in front of the mirror. I couldn't recognize my own face. I was a stranger. Vivian wiped away the blood with a bit of cotton wool. 'Were you really broken into?' 'They didn't get much.' 'But you'll have to report it?' 'It was just some kids, Vivian. I don't want to ruin their lives.' Vivian sighed. 'You're just too kind,' she said. I laughed. 'I'm just a rotten shopkeeper.' I liked her fixing me up like this. I liked the softness of her hands, and yet their confidence too. 'Guess what,' I told her. 'What?' 'The drying lofts at Mum's are going to be converted. We could get a flat there.' 'Is that what you want?' 'You haven't actually considered staying in just one room when we have kids?' Vivian looked at me in the mirror. 'D'you think we'll manage to make a baby?' 'I'm going to the Royal tomorrow.' 'Good, Barnum.' She went on putting my face back together. She cleaned the cuts and put some cream on my eyelid. 'A bit of rouge too, please,' I asked politely. And that's how I came to have the eye I did, the eye that both puzzled and annoyed people. The nerves in my left eyelid were ruined – I couldn't actually feel it – and as a result the lid often drooped down of its own accord and it was impossible to raise it again. It could appear to people that I was blinking deceptively or that I was already drunk, in the process of nodding off or else quite simply being impertinent and arrogant. My face took on a crooked look, a furtive appearance, one open and one closed side. The ring muscle of my eye no longer functioned, and I'm described as having a halfway face.

Barnum's Divine Comedy

It was raining. I'd never seen rain like it before. A wall of water, papered over with leaves, coming down at an angle from low and heavy skies. I drew the curtains and went back to bed. The little transparent container they'd sent from the Royal Infirmary was a pathetic invention. I had to lie on my side and aim, extremely uncomfortably, at the same time as fighting to get an erection; they were two contradictory movements that short-circuited my thinking, blanked out my concentration and left me soft between the legs. My balls hurt. When I held them it felt as if they were bags of shattered glass. Vivian emerged from the bathroom. 'Can't you manage?' she asked me. 'I'm trying,' I answered. 'Shall I help you?' 'Thanks for the offer.' What else could I say? I was helpless. She lay behind me, stroked her hand over my stomach and took hold of my cock. But she was too aggressive. Did she think it was a tap she was turning on? My dead eyelid came down and shut me half in, and a horrid thought struck me – a sudden image – which made each and every hint of arousal flee my mind. *The eyelid's the foreskin of the eye.* 'Be careful,' I whispered. 'Does it hurt?' 'A bit.' Vivian let go, lay on the other side and took me in her mouth instead. It was then I realized just how important this was to her, the filling of this container with sticky, grey, alkaline liquid. She'd never taken me in her mouth before, nor had I ever asked her to. I was so surprised that I got a hard-on straight away; I became firm and tight between Vivian's thin lips and now it was just a question of time. The rain kept on. The sound of rain surrounded us; it was as if we lived on an island in the middle of a roaring river. 'Yes,' I breathed. She moved away. I twisted round over the container and filled it as well as I was able.

Vivian already had a paper towel at the ready. She wiped up what hadn't gone inside and put on the lid. Then she went out to the bathroom and I heard her being sick. In three hours the container had to be delivered to the lab at the Royal Infirmary so my sperm could be approved for the long journey in to Vivian's egg, or washed down the nearest basin. I looked at the clock. It was ten. Vivian sat down beside me again. 'Shall I come with you?' she asked. I took her hand. 'You don't need to. But thanks anyway.' 'Take care of the goods then.' That's the way we talked. We used the word goods. A coldness had come into our conversation. We measured the relationship in temperatures. We counted the days between each period and crossed them off on the calendar. And I delivered the goods. But it was a long while since I'd delivered them to her shop. That's how we talked. 'I'll take a taxi straight to the lab,' I said. She gave me a quick kiss on the brow, fetched an umbrella and went off to the beauty salon. I lay where I was. I heard her feet on the stairs. I heard the rain and the wind. The container lay at my side, a grey mass on the bottom – my goods – which could be half a person, a complete matrix. I showered, put on fresh clothes, had a cigarette and called the central taxi service. There was no reply. In the end the dialling tone cut out too. I tried the one at St Hans Hill. The line was busy. I phoned the one at Majorstuen instead. That number was engaged too. I called the central depot again. After somewhere in the region of twelve minutes I was connected to an automatic answering service. *Demand is extremely high at present. Please try one of our sixty local depots*. I'd tried to. I gave one other one a try – Bislet. That number was engaged, too. It got to ten-thirty. I began to get a bit worked up. I grabbed my raincoat, secreted the container in the inner pocket and ran over to St Hans Hill. There wasn't so much as one solitary taxi there. The phone just rang and rang in the green booth. The rain was coming from every direction. I was about to continue down Ullevål Road, past the kiosk. Then I heard someone calling my name. I

stopped and looked about me. He was sitting on the
bench beside the pond. 'Barnum!' he called again, and
waved. I went over to him. I didn't have much desire to,
but I went all the same. It was my old enemy, Hamster. I'd
heard a few rumours about him and realized they were
true. Now he was the one to suffer and I felt no compassion. He looked like Dustin Hoffmann in *Midnight
Cowboy*, after he was dead. He'd got that dry look. And for
a moment it came to me that I could be the one sitting
there, that one day I might end up there myself – alone in
the rain in a park. The difference between us was just that
I chose a slow and laboured alcoholic road while he had
gone for the chemistry set and the blood – the sharpened
bombs. Clumps of veins showed in his face. He put on a
pair of sunglasses. 'It's you, Barnum?' I nodded. 'You
remember me, don't you, Barnum?' 'No,' I told him.
Hamster laughed heavily. 'Don't bullshit me, huh? I was
a mate of your brother's.' 'Were you?' 'Hell, Barnum, yes.
Of course I was friends with that crazy brother of yours.'
I thought to myself – time and addiction make it easy to
lie – no, not easy, necessary. 'Now I remember you,' I told
him. Hamster raised his hand and spread his yellow fingers. 'That's what I'm telling you. We're mates, right?'
'Was that why you used to beat me up?' I asked him.
Hamster lit a cigarette stub. The flame died away long
before he could get it going. 'That wasn't me. It was Aslak
and Preben who beat you up. Don't you remember?' I
didn't say anything. That was my response. 'Come on,
don't be so mean, Barnum. I was the one who tried to
stop them.' I couldn't endure any more of this. 'Nice to
see you, Hamster,' I said. But he wouldn't let me go. He
held me back. There was strength in him yet – thin and
sinewy – or maybe panic's muscles were at work. I heard
the container sloshing about in my pocket. 'Let me go,
damn it!' I shrieked. Hamster let me go. 'Have you any
spare change, Barnum?' he murmured. I gave him a fiver.
He looked sullenly at the money and stuffed it in his
pocket. And it was as if he had no more to lose; he didn't

need to wheedle any more since there was only a fiver to be got out of me – finally he could be really nasty and honest again. 'Think you're something special, do you, Tiny?' he yelled. I just went. I heard Hamster's laughter at my back and suddenly I couldn't stand it any more; I couldn't take that laughter any longer. I'd settle things with him once and for all. Now Hamster was the small one and the time was past when he could treat me like a dog. He'd find that out shortly. He was going to be finished off. The time for revenge had come, after all the years that had passed since they emptied my bag in Holte Street and pulled off my trousers in Riddervold Square. Now the sleepless nights would be made up for. I had him under my feet. I stopped right in front of Hamster. He couldn't even be bothered looking up. I could have smashed his sunglasses to smithereens. If I'd had a mirror I could have let him see just what had become of him. I stood like that for a time. And then I dropped a fifty kroner note into his filthy lap and left him, without uttering a word. Good luck to him. That fifty kroner note would singe his soul. A cab swung into the taxi rank. I chased over. But when I got there I realized I was broke. Hamster had got the last of my money. I looked over at the bench. All there was to see was a flat, blue tobacco pouch and a pair of bent sunglasses in the rain. He wasn't there. Hamster had already gone and I never saw him again. An elderly lady, her hands laden with bags from the 'pole', scrabbled into the back seat of the taxi and off it drove. She turned round and waved, smiled from behind the wet back window; she looked like the corpse in a hearse rising up to wave goodbye, and I recognized the white face of Knuckles. Miss Knuckles waved to her old pupil left behind in the miserable morning, before she too was gone, into the traffic lights and the falling rain. I rushed down to the bank in Waldemar Thrane Street to take out some money. From the clock above the door I could see it was half past ten. I filled in a form and handed it over the counter together with some identification. The cashier, a young woman perhaps the same age as myself, took a terrifically long time to complete the transaction. Now and again she glanced at me; her mouth was small and red. My eyelid slid down. She quickly looked the other way. The clock marched on towards eleven. And I felt the deep and stressful discomfort of standing still, of being stuck, as in a feverish dream. 'I'm in a bit of a hurry,' I breathed. The young cashier shook her head as she returned my identification. 'Unfortunately your account's empty,' she said, and spoke the words loudly, as if she thought I was hard of hearing or retarded – her pink mouth became a megaphone when she opened it. 'Well, I suppose we'd better hurry off and earn some more,' I said equally loudly. But behind me in the queue was Vivian's father, blocking the way – Aleksander Wie himself whom I hadn't seen since that last dinner at their house. He must have been standing there a fair time because he didn't come across as particularly surprised. He just looked at me and said, 'Now we can go and have a cup of coffee'. The hand of the clock jerked forwards to quarter past eleven. I held my hand over the inner pocket of my jacket and looked up at him. 'I'm actually in a real, real hurry,' I breathed. There was the ghost of a smile on Aleksander Wie's lips. 'So let's go right away!' He let the others in the queue pass him and we went out together. It was still raining. I had to join him under his black umbrella. I'd happily have avoided that. We went to The Ugly Duckling and sat over by the window. He ordered coffee and Danish pastries for the two of us, and polished his glasses as we sat waiting. It was uncomfortably warm in there. The sweat poured down my neck. I wondered if my goods could be damaged by a temperature change like this. Aleksander Wie studied me suddenly. 'Have you heart pain?' 'No, why?' 'You have your hand there the whole time.' I put my hand down on the table instead. Finally the waiter came back. In the middle of the round pastry laid in front of me was a lake of warm, grey syrup. I shut both eyes. I couldn't eat. I drank my coffee instead.

My balls hurt. This had to end soon. 'I apologize for the way things were that evening you came to dinner with us,' Aleksander Wie said. 'It's all right,' I replied. 'We'd really looked forward to it, you know.' 'Yes, of course.' The sweat was pouring from me now. How polite is it possible for a human being to be? Can you actually die of politeness, or is it rather shyness, submissiveness or weakness that's actually the issue – a lack of determination which enslaves you and renders you a victim of chance? Aleksander Wie leaned over the tablecloth and I saw that he was changed. A sort of dark peace had descended on him, a deep resignation; he'd become someone who took things for granted and had let them go. Everything turned out as it did just the same. 'It takes so little for something to go wrong,' he whispered. 'I know,' I said. He smiled again, but his smile was not one of revelation and openness – it was a smile of resignation which is just as much a sigh, a facial shrug, at the weight of this world's folly. It was both a beautiful and disquieting smile. I grew more nervous still. '*Do* you know?' he asked. 'I really must go,' I said. 'You haven't eaten your pastry.' I attacked it. The smooth, soft, syrupy sugar trickled over my lips. I tried to swallow as quickly as I could, but the top stuck to my tongue. I gulped down the rest of my coffee. Aleksander Wie handed me a serviette. 'Thanks,' I murmured. He leant even further over. 'One word follows the next,' he said. 'Soon enough what you've said can't be taken back.' I dried my mouth with the stiff paper. 'All right,' I said. But it wasn't me he wanted to hear, it was his own words he listened to. 'It's like in some trial where a witness says so much they end up being accused of the crime themselves.' 'I don't quite understand,' I said. Aleksander Wie raised his coffee cup but then slowly set it down once more. The coffee became cold before it reached the table. 'When my wife was destroyed in the accident I wanted to leave her,' he said. I couldn't face hearing all this. I had no wish to learn any more. 'But you didn't!' I all but shouted. Aleksander Wie shook his head. 'No, I remained with Annie out of compassion.' 'That's not the worst of reasons,' I told him. He gave a laugh, low and rumbling. 'Compassion is just a nicer form of contempt, Barnum.' I took a deep breath. 'You had a daughter, too,' I said. Aleksander Wie looked down, for a moment shamefaced. So his resignation wasn't complete yet. There was a crack in his dark calm through which the light just got in. He wanted to talk about something else. 'Do you believe in coincidence?' he asked. 'Well, I did meet you in the bank today,' I said. 'That's not all that remarkable. I was going in to pay your rent.' 'What?' 'I thought more about what your mother told me. That your father once owned a Buick.' 'Dad was a good driver,' I told him. Aleksander Wie smiled. 'I'm sure. Do you think it's possible to make things right again? To right what's wrong?' 'I don't believe in coincidence,' I said. Aleksander Wie sat there silent for a time. 'Isn't it strange that humans won't let themselves be mended,' he whispered. Then he produced his wallet and put 200 kroner on the table between us. 'Buy something nice for Vivian on your way home, Barnum.' I didn't want to take the money. 'It really isn't necessary,' I told him. 'I'd like you to buy something nice for Vivian.' 'It really isn't necessary,' I said again. But Aleksander Wie wasn't about to take no for an answer. It was as if no one could hear what I was saying. He shoved the money into my raincoat. I had to clutch the little container. 'Many thanks,' I said. 'Tell her we miss her,' he murmured. 'Yes,' I said. I got up and went out. It hadn't stopped raining. There were no taxis waiting at the rank. The phone just went on and on ringing. In time the rain itself would lift the receiver and answer. I ran down Ullevål Road. It was a quarter to twelve. But as I passed the black fence that bordered Our Saviour's, I saw a helpless figure there I recognized. I stopped. I was caught in confusion. Should I go in or should I turn a blind eye and fulfil the duty of the day, namely the delivery of my goods to the Royal Infirmary before one o'clock? It was Esther who was standing there among the graves. She was hitting out with a stick on every side as if she was either trying to beat up the bad weather or put up an inside-out umbrella. I had no choice. I found the gate and went in. Was this compassion, Aleksander Wie's nicer form of contempt? No, because the opposite, to go past, would have been cynicism itself – indifference for everything that has to do with health and personal hygiene – and that punishes too. I have a kind heart. I stopped a few steps away from her so I wouldn't get hit by the stick. 'Hi, Esther,' I said. Slowly she stopped going round in the rain. Her eyes were empty. 'It's me,' I told her. She stood completely still. I went closer and stretched out my hand. She retreated. 'Don't you recognize me, Esther?' She quickly shook her head. Perhaps she didn't understand what I was saying either; perhaps language had simply run out of her. I saw that under her coat she was just wearing a yellow nightie. And on her feet she was wearing misshapen, brown slippers. 'It's Barnum,' I whispered. 'Who served in your kiosk.' But words had no effect on her any longer. 'Sugar candy,' I suggested. It was to no avail. Esther's face only grew the emptier. How could I get through to her? I brought out the container from my inner pocket and showed it to her, waved it about a bit so the liquid ran from side to side – all at once it reminded me of these glass balls in which it snows when you turn them upside down. And it was as if she suddenly became aware of everything again – a reverse stroke, a force that ordered her senses once more. She was embarrassed, shy; she looked down at herself – at her nightie and slippers – she even turned crimson, as if she'd been caught in the act of being human. 'I think I've got lost, Barnum,' she whispered. 'Yes, you're not coming to the graveyard yet,' I said. She came closer and was on the verge of tears. 'I haven't done anything wrong,' she sobbed. 'Of course not, Esther. We haven't done anything wrong.' And so I took her hand and went with her to Prince August Memorial in Stor Street. There was a great hubbub there.

Esther had been gone since the previous evening. The police had been contacted hours before and several of the nurses were out looking for her at the Ankertorget and along the Aker River. She was taken care of right away and I had to explain where I'd found her and in what condition she'd been. I said that she'd sought out her old kiosk, the one I now looked after, and that everything was all right. I got to wait in the room she shared while they washed her and got her tidied. The other lady lay in her bed in the room, so small and thin she'd barely have been able to cast a shadow. She turned round beneath her quilt. 'Has Esther come back?' she whispered. 'Esther's here,' I told her. And disappointment swelled in her bright eyes; it was as if I'd told her that the Indian in *One Flew Over the Cuckoo's Nest* had changed his mind, crawled back through the shattered window and demanded chewing gum and electric shock treatment. 'Well, well,' was all she said, and turned away to face the pale green wall. A couple of nurses came and put Esther in the other bed. It was now ten past twelve. I suspect they'd fed her some pills because her hands were heavy as saucepans. I sat with her for a bit. I reckoned her mind had gone walka-bout again, yet when she suddenly spoke it was with a tired clarity, in the same way that a moment of real clear-sightedness can be imparted just before sleep comes – a flame that makes the dark visible. 'Your father was a no-good man,' she said. I let go of her hand. 'What d'you mean?' But the flame diminished and spread a great shadow through her. 'Even though he had nylon stock-ings with him,' she breathed. Then Esther fell asleep and that was the last time I got a sensible word out of her. And when I stood once more in the rain in Stor Street, my eyes searching for a taxi because now I really had to get to the Royal Infirmary with the container (it was almost ten to one), someone tooted loudly several times and a wreck of a car screamed to a halt in front of me, sending a wave of mud over my shoes. It was a Vauxhall. And it was Oscar Miil who wound down the window. 'D'you want a lift,

Barnum?' I climbed in. He patted my shoulder. 'Where can I take you?' he asked. 'The Royal Infirmary,' I told him. 'Quickly!' The smile vanished. 'You're not sick?' he asked. 'I just have to deliver some goods there,' I said. Oscar Miil tore at the gear lever, kicked the pedals, and the car backfired and leapt out into Stor Street so I had to clutch hold of the little container with both hands. Only one of the windscreen wipers was working. Mercifully it was the one on his side. He had a small window through the rain and he swung up towards the Central Cinema. 'Are you working as a delivery man?' Oscar Miil looked at me and I wished he'd keep his eyes on the road instead. 'A delivery man?' 'I thought you were going to deliver some goods there?' I laughed. 'A sperm sample,' I told him. 'I have it here in my inside pocket.' He hunched over the wheel. 'It was good that you and Vivian found each other,' he said. 'Thank you. It came to be as it came to be.' 'You two'll have a wonderful child, I bet.' He tried to wind up the window but it was obviously stuck fast. We were driving in a Vauxhall full of rain. 'D'you hear anything from Peder?' Oscar Miil asked. 'No,' I told him. 'Do you?' 'He's called a few times. But he will phone in the middle of the night.' Oscar Miil didn't say any more before he'd crashed to a halt outside the Royal. It was five to one. 'Everything's fine,' he said. 'With Peder?' Oscar Miil turned to face me once more. Rain was streaming into the car. 'With all of us,' he said. And then he pointed at my face. 'You ought to do something about that eye of yours, too,' he said. I felt my weighty eyelid tickling. 'And you ought to do something about that window,' I told him. He put his arms round me and hugged me. 'We're all fine,' he said again. 'Yes,' I said. 'Of course. Things are fine.' And I wasn't sure who was comforting whom. Finally he let go of his hold; I crawled out and Oscar Miil went on his way in the cramped Vauxhall, tooted the horn three times and vanished round a corner. I waved even though I couldn't see him any more but only the rain that trickled down my good eye. Then it was as if I suddenly remembered why I was there. I'd made it. I entered this worn, sick city where no one can escape the smell of rubbish and soap. The sound of sirens disappeared into the distance and came closer all the time. Doctors moving from one department to another ran beneath black umbrellas. It was like some tragic musical. I had to ask a caretaker the way. He pointed in the direction of a particular entryway and I found the correct lab in the backyard there. I took the lift down to the basement, the service lift. The arrow in the little glass display on the side had stopped at H; it no longer worked, H was the last letter in the lift's alphabet. But it kept descending nonetheless; I lost count and when it landed my ears were plugged. I pushed the gate to one side and shuffled out into a green corridor. I saw a thin man in a white coat disappearing into a room. I hurried after him. Dr Lund's name was on the door. I'd got there. I'd made it. I knocked. The thin man, Dr Lund, opened the door himself. 'Barnum Nilsen,' I said, and handed over the container. He held it up to the light. 'Wait out-side,' he told me. I found an unoccupied seat further down the corridor. I sat down. There were two men wait-ing there already. They were both older than me, perhaps getting on for forty. But we were of average age all the same. Because here everyone was ageless. We were all the same. We were equals. We glanced at one another – embarrassed, maybe even shamefaced – before looking away somewhere else, to some mark on the linoleum, an empty hook on the wall, a light that flickered and finally went out altogether. None of us said anything. There was nothing more to be said. We had delivered our seed. Somewhere else our women were waiting. They were waiting for an answer. Could one of these cells penetrate an egg, merge with the nucleus and begin the laborious building up of a new life? In short, were we men who were fit for it? I fall asleep. I dream I am in a boat head-ing for a steep, green coastline. A black bird rises up in front of the bow, spreads its wings and smothers the sun. I get up, lift an oar and hit out at this sleek, black bird. I fall down. I lie in the bottom of the boat with the sail over me. I scrabble about for a knife with which to cut myself free. I'm wakened by a nurse. 'You can come now,' she murmured. I followed her into the lab. The two other men have gone. The doctor was standing with his back to me, bent over a microscope. The room was white. The shelves along the walls were full of test tubes and thin glass containers. Then he spun round abruptly to look at me. 'Are you a lorry driver, Barnum Nilsen?' he demanded. 'A lorry driver? I haven't even passed my test.' 'D'you often wear tight trousers?' 'No, I tend to prefer loose trousers as a matter of fact.' 'Have you any siblings?' 'Yes, one brother. Half brother.' The doctor pushed a pair of thin glasses into place over his stiff nose and leafed through some papers. 'Is there any history of madness in the family?' 'Madness? Not that I know of.' 'So you don't know then?' 'No one's mad in my family.' 'Have you ever had gonorrhoea?' 'What?' 'Syphilis?' 'Syphilis? Never.' 'Are you a hypochondriac?' 'No.' 'Hysterical?' 'No!' I exclaimed. 'Do you drink a lot?' I had to find the wall for support. 'Only when I do drink,' I breathed. 'And how often is that?' 'Special occasions.' 'Don't develop bad habits, Barnum Nilsen.' 'No, doctor.' He came closer. 'Because in alcoholism all mental faculties will be lost, and all that will remain will be the unbroken torment of a ceaseless desire for alcohol, whereupon death for the remaining shell of a body will be an inevitability. Do you understand, Barnum Nilsen?' 'Yes,' I breathed. 'What do you do for a living?' 'I write.' 'And then you're seated, of course?' 'Seated?' 'You sit down when you're writing?' 'Yes, I always sit when I'm writing.' The doctor whips off his glasses. 'We can see that,' he said. 'What can we see?' I murmured. 'Look here,' said Dr Lund. He pointed to the microscope. I went over and put my good eye to the lens. I'm not sure if I shrieked or not. It was my own sperm I was seeing, magnified a thousand times. And this was my first thought – *a midge in mustard*. Yes, like a midge in mustard. And the midge wasn't moving. I heard the doctor

talking – far, far away. 'The testicles are a precious bag,
Barnum Nilsen. And yours is empty.' I straightened up.
'Not a hope?' I asked him. He shook his head. 'You can
have a good life without children too. Just don't allow
cynicism to get the upper hand.' And then I noticed that
he wasn't called Dr Lund after all. On a shining nameplate attached to his white coat were the words – M. S.
GREVE. DIRECTOR OF THE ROYAL INFIRMARY. He shook
hands with me and the nurse disposed of the container in
a special bin. I found my way to the lift. It brought me up
through the various levels. I pushed the gate to one side
and ran out onto the pavement. The clouds piled over the
roofs and spires, carrying their rain with them, leaving
the heavens high and clear like a blue dome over the city.
The light made the streets glimmer like rivers. People
stood on the banks looking up with surprise and gratitude at the sun. I had to shield my eyes, blinded and
naked. I remembered the dread I'd experienced down in
the basement. Now I knew what it meant – the cormorant
shits on the rocks so it can find its way back. I went up to
St Hans Hill. I stood in the middle of the crossroads. I
had 200 kroner in my pocket. I thought to myself – flowers or beer? I had a pint at Schröder's and with the rest
bought some roses – twelve roses with long stalks. Then
I go on home to Vivian. She's waiting for me. I see an
impatience in her. There's a fever in her eyes. She gets up
as soon as I come in. I hide the bouquet behind my raincoat. And before I can say anything she beats me to it.
'There's a letter for you, Barnum.' She holds out the
envelope. It might be from Peder. No, because then it
wouldn't have been for me but rather the two of us. It
must be from Fred. 'Who's it from?' I ask her. 'Norwegian
Film,' Vivian says. 'Norwegian Film? Why should they be
writing to me?' Vivian shrugs her shoulders and grows
more impatient still. 'Aren't you going to open it?' I take
the envelope. Norwegian Film is written in the corner
together with the oval logo which must represent an eye
with winding film in it. I pull out the sheet inside and

read it. I can't fathom it. The words don't register with me. Is this how Fred's blindness was with words, when the letters suddenly stop functioning as they should? I give the letter to Vivian. 'You read it,' I breathe. And Vivian reads it aloud. '*Dear Barnum Nilsen, It's a pleasure to inform you that* Fattening *has won first prize in Norwegian Film's filmscript competition. The jury has remarked that your script possesses an originality, a* joie de vivre *in terms of its narration, and a personal expression which gives free rein to the author's bizarre fantasies that may be interpreted as a representation of a perverse, gluttonous and oppressive society. The prize will be awarded at the premises of Norwegian Film at Jar on 1 October at 1 p.m.*' Vivian lets the letter fall to the floor and looks at me, her head on one side and a smile on her lips. I can barely speak. 'Did you send in my script?' She nods. 'You're not annoyed?' I laugh aloud. 'Of course I'm not annoyed. I'm thrilled!' She comes closer. 'Are you crying, Barnum?' I shake my head. I've started crying. I can't help it. And Vivian puts her arms round me and I stand there crying. 'I'm so proud of you,' she says. 'Me too,' I whisper. And Vivian puts her lips to my ear. 'How did it go today, my beloved boy?' And I don't want to destroy this moment. I don't want to bring down the good news with bad. We have an equilibrium. Never have we been so vulnerable. We mustn't be thrown now. 'Fine,' I tell her. 'Fine?' 'Everything's all right. The goods have been approved.' Vivian's lips are moist against my face. 'I knew it when you came home with flowers!' We pull out the bed, tear each other's clothes off and make love with a wildness we've never known before, not even on that evening in Frogner Park. There's no awkwardness. We gamble everything on one card. All at once I become afraid of injuring her, but she only wants me the more. This is both panic and exuberance – their fusing in a higher sense. Afterwards there's stillness. I light a cigarette and read the letter from Norwegian Film, to check one more time that it's true. It is true. I can see it with one eye. I've won. I lie down beside Vivian again. 'What did Dr Lund say?' she asked me. 'That my sperm are queuing up to visit your egg.' Vivian acts as if she's angry. 'Tell me properly what he said!' 'He said that the testicles are a precious bag!' I give her a quick kiss and her mouth is soft as a jellyfish. Vivian laughs and suddenly takes hold of my balls. I moan. 'Have you any more then in your precious bag?' she murmurs. 'Per Oscarsson can play the farmer,' I tell her. 'Or the school doctor.' 'This child will have a good life,' Vivian says. 'And Ingrid Vardund can be the mother,' I go on. Vivian strokes her hand over her tummy. 'This child will have a good life,' she says again. 'Of course.' 'Not the kind of childhood we had,' she continues. I get up. 'What d'you mean?' Vivian looks up. 'Better than we had, Barnum,' she whispers. 'Better than ours.' I lie there quiet for a moment. 'I had a fine time as a child,' I say. Vivian smiles. 'Who'll play you?' she asks. I fetch the flowers and put them in water, and go out onto the stairs to throw the wet paper in the rubbish chute. I take with me M. S. Greve's *Medical Dictionary for Norwegian Homes* and throw it away too. The last word in the book is *Oysters. Oysters can become poisonous when the water about them is stagnant and impure.* When I come back I see for a moment the remains of the sun before it vanishes behind the oval, blue shadows between the trees and fills the room with a warm, red hue as if the flowers themselves have illuminated the floor and ceiling. Vivian lies with her legs along the length of the wall so my juices can run all the swifter through her system. I sit down on the edge of the bed. I put the bouquet down on the pillow. She takes my hand in her own. And just before the room sinks into darkness, I think to myself that the fragrance of these flowers is so powerful that just one single drop from their petals could perfume the sea, turn it ethereal as rose oil.

Yet Another Empty Table

We took a taxi to Norwegian Film at Jar. This was the day I was to receive my prize. Mum, Boletta and Vivian were with me. They sat in the back, full of pride. I felt equally proud. The driver swung through the wide gates in Wedel Jarlberg Road. Mum paid the driver. I got out. This was Norwegian Film. This was where the studios were. This was my place. From now on this would be my place. I could wander about, follow what was happening on the set, pen a few new scenes, polish odd bits of dialogue, sign contracts and have lunch with the actors. There wasn't a soul to be seen. Leaves fluttered from the tall trees. It was clouding over again. Vivian took my hand. 'Are you nervous?' I shook my head and kissed her. 'Just wish Peder was here,' I said. We found the reception area close by. A young girl behind the counter was chatting away on the phone, smoking constantly. I let her finish. She put down the receiver and looked at me. I extended my hand. 'I'm Barnum Nilsen,' I told her. 'Who?' 'Barnum Nilsen,' I repeated. She leafed through some sheets, but that wasn't to much avail either. 'What did you say your name was?' 'It's me who won the competition,' I breathed. Finally she got who I was. 'The director would like to have a word with you first,' she said. 'Wait here.' We seated ourselves in a rather cramped sofa. We waited. Time passed. Boletta went to sleep. Mum stared at Vivian. 'Are you all right?' she asked. Vivian looked at me and smiled instead. 'Of course,' she replied. A paper from the day before was lying on the table. I had a read of it. A fine day was forecast. It started raining. 'It isn't the wrong day?' Mum inquired. 'It's the paper that's old,' I said. 'Are you sure?' 'Be quiet,' I told her. And we waited. This was the start of my long time of waiting; the great wait that is the destiny of the scriptwriter. Soon it got to

one o'clock. I saw people disappearing into the building
on the other side. One of them looked like Arne Skouen.
My tie felt tight at my throat. I leant close to Vivian. 'Arne
Skouen's here,' I murmured. Finally the girl behind the
counter got up. 'The director's waiting for you,' she said.
I was tempted to point out that it was *me* who was waiting for *him*, but let it pass. 'Thank you,' I said. His office
was up on the first floor. I went up some stairs. There was
a forest of posters on the walls. *Guest Bardsen. Found. We
Die Alone*. I was in the very heart of Norwegian Film. Now
I myself was a part of Norwegian Film. One day my poster
would hang here too, on the stair wall that led to the
director's office – *Fattening*. I got to the right door,
combed my hair, took a deep breath, and knocked. I heard
a groan. I waited a bit. Then I went in. The director sat
behind a table covered with scripts; they were lying in
great heaps, on the floor too – everywhere in that
cramped room was so stuffed with scripts there was
barely room for anything else. The director was sitting
reading one of them. I closed the door carefully behind
me. I didn't want to interrupt. I just stood there. The
director gave another groan. He was wearing a worn
tweed jacket with leather elbow patches. He smoked a
pipe and had large, square glasses. I leant against a bookcase. I shouldn't even have contemplated it. It was most
likely from Ikea. It toppled over towards me and a whole
avalanche of scripts came with it. The director got up and
took the pipe from his mouth. 'I'm sorry,' I whispered.
'They're going out anyway,' he said. He cleared a chair for
me. We sat down. He stared hard at me as he got his pipe
lit again. 'So this is Barnum Nilsen himself,' he said. I
nodded. One o'clock had come and gone a good while
back. I should be receiving my prize now. 'Have I got the
time wrong?' I asked. The director shook his head. 'It'll
only do them good to wait a bit,' he said. I liked that
thought, liked it very much – that there were others who
were waiting for me. Everything should be turned to my
advantage. Time was on my side. I lit a cigarette. 'Tell me

a bit about yourself, Barnum.' 'There's not a great deal to tell,' I said. The director became a tad impatient; his teeth clicked in his mouth. 'A synopsis, Barnum. Not a whole script.' I mulled it over. And I remembered what Dad had once said, that it was necessary to sow doubt, because the whole truth was dull and made people lazy and forgetful, whereas doubt never loses its hold. 'Born and brought up in Oslo,' I said. 'A single child. My father died before I was born.' The director shrugged his shoulders. 'Is Barnum your real name?' 'I use it as a pseudonym,' I replied. The director smiled. 'Do you have a sore eye, Barnum?' I tried to blink. 'No, no. It's been like this from birth. I'm blind in that eye.' The director bent forward over the table. 'What I really wanted to know was if you'd written any more?' 'I have a book full of ideas,' I told him. The director sank in his chair. 'We're glad to have you here, Barnum. Really glad.' 'Oh, and one other thing,' I said. 'On you go, Barnum. This is your day.' 'My wife's a make-up artist. I'd like her to do the make-up for the film.' The director stared at me a long while. 'The film?' he repeated. I was confused for a moment. 'Yes, the film. *Fattening*. Have you decided who the director'll be yet?' The director got up, stood behind me and placed both hands on my shoulders. 'Barnum, Barnum,' he said. 'It isn't ever going to be a film.' It was as if I didn't hear what he said or else heard something else entirely. The subtitles in the room were all wrong. 'Won't it be a film?' 'Never,' the director said. 'Why did I win then?' I asked him. He raised his hands again and gave a sigh. 'Let's go down and become famous instead, Barnum.'

I went to the loo first. I stood in front of the mirror. *You're the one who's won*, I told myself. My eyelid slid down again, a wrinkled fold of skin that covered half my face. I pulled off my tie, put it in my pocket and got out the cognac I'd thought of saving till later. I took a gulp. When I'd drunk one I drank a second. The first was for the best script and the second was for the film that would never be. Then we hurried through the rain to the wooden

building on the other side, Norwegian Film's canteen.
That was where I was to become famous. It was there the
prize was to be awarded.

There weren't many there. Vivian, Mum and Boletta
were already sitting at a table eating halves of rolls. Two
journalists with cameras round their necks were standing
by the wine. They each took pictures. I managed to recognize one of them from before. It was Ditlev from the
afternoon edition of *Aftenposten*. He hadn't changed his
suit. He was time that had passed. I couldn't see Arne
Skouen. The director pulled me over to a sharp-looking
woman in big, brown clothes. She reminded me of Miss
Knuckles – yes, for a moment, I almost thought it *was* her
and could catch the dry whiff of chalk. 'This is our dramaturge,' the director said. I greeted her. 'You'll have to
change the beginning,' she barked. 'Thank you,' I murmured. She let my hand drop as if she'd got a wasp under
the nails. I wanted more to drink. Someone went past and
slapped me on the back. 'Good,' they said. 'Good.' I was
glad I'd taken off my tie. The director sat himself on a
stool. 'Friends! Welcome. We're starting a frantically busy
season here. The projects are lining up, a new generation
of film-makers is in the process of making their mark, and
I can certainly say that we out here at Norwegian Film
aren't letting the grass grow under our feet.' Everyone,
barring Boletta, laughed. The director clapped his hands.
'And so the time has come to reveal the winner of Norwegian Film's major script competition.' The director
handed over to the dramaturge at this point. She stood up
beside his stool and produced a sheet of paper that must
have been folded at least nine times. 'We received sixty-
three entries and finally chose the script entitled *Fattening*
as the winner. This tells the strange story of a boy who
stops eating because he wants to get taller, and who's
finally sent to a farm to be – yes, precisely – fattened up.
Here he's the victim of serious assault. He's abused sex-
ually by the other boys. The narrative can be read as a
didactic and imaginative attack on a perverse society.' She

turned the page. Mum was on the point of getting to her feet, but mercifully remained in her seat. 'And the winner is Barnum Nilsen.' Everyone, barring Mum, applauded. Both the journalists took pictures. I was given a glass of champagne and a cheque by the director. 'Would you like to say a few words?' he asked me. Utter quiet fell. Mum didn't take her eyes off me and kept on shaking her head. I drank my champagne. And all of a sudden my mouth ran amuck again. I couldn't remember the last time it had done so. I considered that time well and truly passed. 'To hell with you,' I said. The quiet only intensified. Vivian went crimson and looked down. Mum couldn't have been any more shocked than she already was. The dramaturge had to sit down. It was Boletta who saved the day. 'Bravo!' she exclaimed. 'Bravo!' And the whole lot of them began applauding once more, almost out of sheer panic, while the director filled everyone's glasses with champagne. 'Barnum Nilsen will now be available for press interviews,' he said very loudly. 'If they have the courage!' he laughed in a rather raucous manner. Ditlev was the first on the scene. 'Well, well,' he said. 'It's been a while now.' 'Yes, time flies,' I said, and looked down at his worn shoes. He got out his notebook, then changed his mind and put it back in his pocket. 'I was talking to your Mum for a bit just now,' he said. 'Oh? And what was she saying?' Ditlev smiled. 'She's very proud of you.' 'Thank you.' 'Could you expand on your rather original thank you speech, by the way, Barnum?' It was then the other journalist began to grow impatient. She tugged at Ditlev's jacket and turned on the charm. 'You're not intending hogging Barnum Nilsen for the rest of the day, are you?' Ditlev looked sheepish, shrank into the background, found his umbrella and went out into the rain. He'd gone soft. He'd shuffle down to the broom cupboard at the paper and write his last article. 'Shall we sit down?' The other journalist found a table. I found a bottle. Her name was Bente Synt, the woman we'd later call the Elk. She was one metre eighty in height and never took any notes.

'So you're the guy who's going to save Norwegian Film,' she said. 'Well, I'll certainly do my best,' I told her. She smiled. 'Is this autobiographical, this story of yours that's won?' And I added Peder's words to Dad's idea about spreading rumour and sowing doubt. 'Perhaps. Perhaps not,' I replied. She sat there looking at me. I drank champagne. Then she stole Ditlev's question. 'Could you expand on your rather original thank you speech, Barnum?' 'No comment,' I said. Bente Synt laughed a moment. 'Isn't it a little early in your career to be so precious?' The director came past. 'Everything going all right?' he inquired. Bente Synt looked up. 'I'm just trying to get Barnum Nilsen to say something about his little speech. To hell with you.' The director laid his hand on her shoulder and became all sphinx-like. 'It's the prerogative of the young to call us names when they get the chance, right, Bente?' He continued on his way. 'Exactly,' I said. Bente Synt got out a cigarette which she didn't light. 'What's your favourite film?' '*Hunger*,' I told her. She smiled, pleased with the answer. 'So your script is a kind of response to Hamsun?' 'You could well say that,' I agreed. 'And your description of this farm, which is almost synonymous with a penal colony, is a kind of revolt against Hamsun's fascism?' I mulled that one over. 'Perhaps. Perhaps not,' I said. Bente Synt wasn't pleased at all with this response. 'Have you got any new projects on the go?' she inquired. 'I'm working on a modern version of Dante's *Divine Comedy*.' 'Really.' 'I'm imagining the big city as hell and Beatrice as a guide in a travel agency.' 'Interesting.' Bente Synt put her cigarette back in the packet and got up. ' I really think I've got plenty,' she said. I was left sitting in her shadow long after she'd gone. Suddenly I sensed someone at my back. I turned round. For a moment I thought it was Fleming Brant, the cutter; it was as though I saw him going slowly through the room with a rusty rake in his hands – this illusion that would come back and back so many times. It was Arne Skouen. He leaned closer. 'Never talk about things you haven't written yet,' he whispered. 'Because then they'll never come to be.' And I remembered I'd heard something similar before – it was Peder's mum who'd said it ages ago. *Don't say it aloud, because then you'll never be able to write it down.* I went off to the loo and had some cognac. When I re-emerged the dramturge was waiting for me. 'The narrative structure has to go,' she said. 'The whole thing?' 'It's old news, Barnum Nilsen. Get rid of it.' She knocked back her champagne in great gulps. She didn't get drunk. Alcohol had rather the opposite effect on her. It made her more and more sober, or perhaps it was just me who was getting drunker. 'But the narrative structure's the whole point,' I tell her. 'The point?' 'I'm trying to show that life itself is like a kind of film. And that God is the projectionist.' 'Why isn't God the director?' 'I think it's better having him as the projectionist.' The dramaturge stared at me in the same way one looks down on helpless, foolish children. 'You ought to think rather of who the enemy is in the story,' she said. 'The enemy?' 'Is it the school doctor, the farmer or the other boys. You have to be clear about these things, Barnum.' I had no answer for her. 'I can certainly get rid of the narrative structure,' I murmured. I poured more into my glass. She smiled. 'Besides, isn't it a bit high and mighty using your own name?' 'Does that really matter when the film isn't even going to be made?' I retorted. Now it was my turn to hope she might be stuck for an answer. She wasn't. 'We still want the script to be as good as it possibly can be all the same,' she said.

I sat in the back seat when we took a taxi home again and they were no longer as proud of me as they had been. Vivian was silent and Mum was still uneasy. 'How could you write something like that?' she hissed. 'What d'you mean?' She almost couldn't bring herself to say what she meant aloud. 'That things like that happened on the farm, Barnum.' Boletta came to in the front seat. 'Let the boy write what he wants to,' she said. But Mum wouldn't leave it. 'He can't write something that isn't true!' She turned to me. 'You had a good enough time on that farm, didn't you, Barnum?' All at once I felt so very tired. For the second time that day I saw Fleming Brant, standing on a corner, leaning on his rake and looking at us as we passed. 'It doesn't matter anyway,' I said. 'There isn't going to be any film.' Vivian took my hand. 'Won't there be?' 'Never. The director said it would never be made into a film.' Mum grasped my other hand. 'Thank heavens for that.'

I put the cheque into the bank at Majorstuen and beside the bank was the 'pole'. Afterwards we walked slowly home. The rain had stopped. The air was thin and cold. 'Are you down?' Vivian asked me. I stopped at the telephone box at the Valkyrie. I had a few coins on me. I looked up the Theatre Café in the book and called their number. I booked a table for eight o'clock. I left a couple of coins in the slot. Perhaps some kids would find them and have enough for juice and sweets from Barnum's kiosk. I put my arm round Vivian. 'No,' I answered. 'Good, Barnum. It's just a case of writing more, isn't it?' And she kissed me until we all but dropped our 'pole' bags.

But I couldn't write. I wanted to begin on my divine comedy, but the words died as soon as they reached the page. Perhaps it was true, that when you talk about something it's impossible to write it thereafter, for you take the power of the story and dilute it in everyone's hearing. You've betrayed yourself. I wrote at the very top of the blank sheet – *professional discretion*. Then I leafed through my notebook instead. I felt like throwing it away. I felt suddenly that my ideas were pathetic. The notebook was weightless. If I chucked it in the rubbish chute it would never land. I could see the ideas before me, weightless, and the writing being rubbed out by rotting leftovers, grease, nappies, the dregs of coffee, cigarette ends, vomit, blood and other body fluids. Finally I got out *Fattening*. I put a line through the opening scene and changed my name to Pontus. But what difference did it make? That evening I drank faster than I thought.

The first time the phone rang it was six-thirty. Vivian came out from the bathroom and hesitated before answering it. I could hear the voice all the way over to where I was. It was the director of Norwegian Film Ltd. Vivian handed me the receiver. 'Perhaps he's changed his mind,' she hissed. From the word go he started talking in an equally loud voice. 'You're a fox, Barnum.' 'Am I?' 'Barnum's no pseudonym, nor are you an only child.' I didn't say a thing for a bit. 'Are you still there?' he enquired. 'Where else would I be?' The director laughed. Quickly he became serious too. 'Listen, Barnum, and listen carefully. I want this story. And only you can write it.' I grew quite bewildered. And underneath this bewilderment was an equally powerful disgust, a sense of nausea. 'What story?' 'The story of your missing brother,' the director said. Vivian sat on the bed drying her hair. She looked up sharply. 'How d'you know about that?' I asked him. He laughed again. 'Haven't you read the afternoon edition of the paper yet?' I put down the receiver. I rushed out to the stairs and pinched the copy belonging to the neighbour who always forgot to close the rubbish chute. Ditlev's last article was there on the last page. Now I knew what he'd been talking to Mum about. There was a picture of Fred, from the fight at the Central Boxing Club, taken just as he receives the deciding blow and his face twists, as if his skin is detached and being pushed round the side of his head. Underneath they had a much smaller picture of me being given my cheque by the director, and the cognac in my inner pocket's visible – the protruding cork of it. The heading read – *The winner and the loser*. I went back to Vivian and sat down on the bed. I gave her the paper. 'Read it,' I breathed. And she did: '*Barnum Nilsen was today awarded first prize in Norwegian Film's script competition. For readers with good memories, the name of Barnum Nilsen will not be entirely unfamiliar. Back in 1966 he was in Oslo City Chambers to receive his award for winning a junior writing contest for his story* The Little City. *What lies behind his new tale,* Fattening, *is something the author's reluctant to reveal, but it's possible his brother's story's more dramatic still. Fred Nilsen, our one-time hope in the ring, vanished twelve years ago. Vera Nilsen, the boy's mother, relates that she's sought the assistance both of the police and the Salvation Army, without success.'* I tore the paper from Vivian, crumpled it up and chucked it out onto the veranda. I couldn't even escape Fred's shadow. 'Come here,' Vivian whispered. I went over and lay down with her. 'Who's the winner and who's the loser?' I asked her. 'Now you're being stupid,' Vivian said. I turned away. 'Fine.' 'Don't be angry with your mother,' she told me. I tried to laugh. 'That's rich coming from you.' 'She just wants Fred back, right? Perhaps somebody reading the paper will have seen him in one place or another.' 'I'm not angry,' I said. Vivian unfastened my belt and pulled up my shirt. 'Have you told her we're going to have a child?' I lay there and for a moment froze completely. I had to defrost my voice. 'Are you pregnant, Vivian?' she laughed. 'Not yet, Barnum.' But she kept staring at my stomach. I could feel that she was naked. She sat over me. And while we were at it the phone rang for the second time. We didn't answer it. Her hair came down over my face and was still wet. She lay down beside me and put her legs along the side of the wall. 'What was it the director was actually wanting?' she asked. 'A script about Fred.' Vivian rubbed her hands over her stomach. 'D'you want to write it?' I waited a moment before answering. 'Maybe I've already begun on it.' 'Really?' 'Yes,' I told her. Vivian swung down her legs and turned to me. 'What's it called?' 'I think I'll call it *The Night Man*.' 'Can I read it?' 'Not yet, Vivian.' It was already seven. I showered, had a drink and got dressed. Vivian had put on a dress I hadn't seen her in before – it was blue with black stripes. It suited her. We looked at ourselves in the mirror. We didn't look too bad. We were off to the Theatre Café. Then the phone rang for the third time that evening. I answered it. It was Peder's mother. 'Congratulations,' she said. 'I see you've won a prize.' 'Yes, blimey,' I said. 'Many thanks!' 'I'm proud of you, Barnum.' And yet there was a strangeness about her voice. It was slow and joyless. 'I have to tell you something,' she breathed. I sat down on the bed. I was stone-cold sober once more. 'Yes?' 'Peder's father died last night.' 'Died? But how?' Vivian turned round and dropped her ear stud on the floor. Peder's mother was quiet a long while. I just heard her breathing. 'He took his own life, Barnum.' 'Oh, no,' I murmured. Vivian came a step closer – pale, shaky. 'I'd so much like it if you could both be at the funeral,' Peder's mother said. She put down the phone. I looked up. 'What is it?' Vivian whispered. I pulled her down to me and told her. And I sensed a tremor pass through her – a quick breath of relief, just as I sensed it in myself – for it isn't Peder that's dead. And this relief becomes at once shame and sorrow. We're dressed in our finest clothes. We stay at home. And I see before me the empty table at the Theatre Café with my reservation there – *Barnum Nilsen, 8 p.m.* – the only table no one sits at. And this is an echo too, an echo of time, the shadow of a discus spinning through blinding sunlight. I put my arms round Vivian. 'Now Peder must come home,' I whisper, and start to cry.

The Last Picture

But Peder didn't come. Vivian and I waited out at Fornebu. It was early in the morning on the day of his father's committal. We stood at the huge window through which we could see the plane landing, slowly, as if its wheels would never touch the ground. The runways shone after the night's rain. We rushed down to the arrivals area on the ground floor. We weren't alone. We could barely get through. I sat down. Perhaps I wouldn't recognize him. Perhaps it was he who would have to recognize us. But Peder wasn't on the plane from London. Peder didn't come. In the end only Vivian and I remained there, together with a dark-skinned cleaning lady sweeping away flowers, cigarettes, flags, and a child's shoe with her great wide brush.

We took a taxi back to his mother's. She was sitting ready in the wheelchair – tiny and all in black. 'The flight was cancelled,' I told her. Vivian nodded and looked the other way. Peder's mother put her withered hands on the wheels. She wanted to be pushed up to the crematorium. There was time enough. Perhaps this was her way of preparing herself and building up courage, by taking a roundabout way – because who wants to hurry where one doesn't want to go? We went slowly through Frogner Park, behind the Monolith, and came into Wester Gravlund where the Old One and Dad were buried. I saw T's grave too. The grass was tall and golden round the low stone. I had to stop for a moment and take a deep breath. We are forgotten. Peder's dad had closed the garage door, got into the car, and put on the engine. In the morning he was dead. It was the paper boy who found him. He was still holding the steering wheel and they had to break his fingers free.

The crematorium bells rang out. We walked the last part of the way, lifted the wheelchair up the steps, and wheeled her into the darkness nearest the white coffin. The place was already full. Only Peder was missing. There were wreaths from the family, fellow philatelists and friends all down the aisle. Vivian and I joined Mum and Boletta. The organist began playing. And I thought to myself that if we'd gone to see them that time we were coming back from Vivian's parents, and hadn't just stood there at the corner looking at the lights on the ground floor, then maybe everything might be different. If I hadn't complained about the broken window in the car and asked him to get it repaired, perhaps he'd be alive now. Is that all it takes? And I thought to myself, *how little does it take to save a person?* There was utter stillness – neither a cough nor a sob – as if this death had frightened us into muteness. We waited. Peder's mother laid a rose on the coffin. Then she turned the wheelchair and smiled to all those who'd come. She was transparent and beautiful. Her voice was clear and slow. 'Oscar didn't want there to be any vicar. He didn't believe in any life beyond this one. We often talked about death. But never that it would happen in this way.' She closed her eyes and the silence became more profound still. The seconds thudded past. Then she went on with her speech for her dead husband. 'I loved Oscar exceptionally deeply. He was patient with me. I love him just as much now, and I always will love him. I will remember his laughter and his forgetfulness and all the joy we shared. This is my only comfort today. That sorrow does not have retrospective effect. That the sorrow of today cannot erase all of yesterday's colours.' She had to stop a second time. And she said something as she bowed her head, quietly, and maybe I was the only one who heard her, and those words were branded into me – she whispered, she moaned, 'Oh, God. Oh, God, I didn't know him!' Then she straightened up again. 'Peder should have been with me now, but he's been prevented from doing so. My thanks to all those who are here.' She turned back once more to face the coffin.

Formality fizzled out at the graveside. And it was there I understood that the suicide of Oscar Miil hadn't frightened us into muteness, but instead had rendered us embarrassed and therefore dumb. That old word *condolences* didn't work. This was a shameful sorrow. Some people slipped quickly away, to the parking place or the station, and just left a visiting card in the basket at the exit. Peder's mother sat there, a green rug over her legs, accepting this silent compassion. I noticed that she could no longer manage to raise her hand. When it was my turn I bent down and kissed her cheek, not to try to be any better than the others but to hide the fact that I was crying. 'Come home with me too, both of you,' she whispered. And we pushed her the same way back. It was even further now. We helped her into the hall. 'Peder!' she suddenly shouted. But Peder gave no answer. Peder still hadn't come. She didn't want us to go. She wanted us to stay. There was already a bottle of wine on the table. We sat in the living room and drank in silence. We each said cheers. She could barely manage to hold her glass. She'd cleared away all her canvases and frames. I could see the garage through the window. The door had been brought down, but only halfway. Maybe it needed airing. And the only question I wanted to ask was *why*? But it was an impossible question. 'Did you ever finish your pictures?' I asked instead. She looked at me abruptly, and I realized there and then the question was indelicate in this brittle and fragile moment, that it was in danger of breaking it. With huge strength she raised both hands. 'Perhaps. Perhaps not,' she murmured. 'As Peder would have put it,' I said. Her arms fell into her lap once more. Vivian poured us more wine. I got up to go for a pee. I stopped in the hall and leaned against the wall. The door to the bedroom was open. Peder's dad's pyjamas were still lying there. On the bedside table were two clocks. The one showed a quarter past five. The other was set at American time, so they could always follow Peder's day. The door to his room was locked. I went for a pee and then returned to them. Vivian had got up. We ought to go. 'D'you need any help?' I asked. Peder's mum wheeled herself out into the hall. 'Oscar used to carry me to bed.' 'I can do that,' I told her. She smiled. 'I'd rather sleep down here tonight.' And she suddenly held me and I felt the grasp of her thin and wrinkled fingers already failing. 'D'you think things can ever be the way they were before, Barnum?' she murmured. I didn't know what to say and I couldn't lie to her. 'No,' I said, my voice as quiet as hers.

When I came out we saw that Peder's mother was putting out the lights and slowly the house fell into darkness. I don't know why but I wanted to go into the garage. Vivian held me back. 'Don't,' she told me. I went anyway. She came after me. She was livid and afraid. 'What are you doing here?' I didn't answer her. I didn't know myself. She let me go and went the other way. I bent under the garage door. I found a switch and a yellow light went on in the corner right at the back. The car was gone. Maybe the police had taken it away. This was no longer a place, it was the scene of a crime. I thought I could smell something dry and pungent. Peder's mother had displayed her paintings there. They were all along the wall. I glanced at some of them; most were unfinished. Then I caught sight of another painting – the one she must have begun work on that summer we went to Ildjernet and Vivian tried to suck the poison from me. I couldn't stand any longer. I went down on my knees. She'd written the title on the frame – *friends on the rock ledge*. It's evening beside the fiord and almost everything is blue, but the two boys in the foreground are standing in their own light – it shines round their young brown forms. I recognize us. The fat one and the small one. We are naked. We have our arms round each other. Our lips meet in a kiss and our eyes are closed.

Parasol in Snow

Mum's knitted a pair of mittens for me with just half fingers, similar to the things Louis Armstrong wore when he played the trumpet at Bislet. It means I can keep my hands warm at the same time as being able to get out goodies and count change. She says I'm wasting my time. She says I ought to find something better to do. But I like it fine here in the unsteady deckchair, and the mittens are grand to write with now that it's getting chillier, particularly in the mornings. Soon enough the snow'll be here, and the little blower I have by the door isn't much of a help because of all the draught. I've closed the little window and pulled down the curtains. There are neither customers nor bullies about. Not even after winning Norwegian Film's competition has custom increased. I thought there might be a queue in front of Barnum's kiosk when it became common knowledge that I'd won, but alas no. It doesn't really bother me. Sausages are ancient history now, but the weeklies come each Tuesday. Some of the brands of chocolate, particularly those designed for the cheering of the spirit, are beginning to grow hard and grey – I reckon they've been here since the middle of the 1960s.

I get out my notebook and try to make some headway with *The Night Man*. I have this picture of the boy, the skinny boy, running through deserted streets towards the harbour. It's become fixed in my mind, this image, and I can't dislodge it – and I see a ship sailing through the fog, so close the boy could just stretch out his hand and touch the hull made ready for the ice. *Antarctic*. But I have nothing more than those few fragments – the boy, the city and the ship – little points in a story bigger than myself (not that that takes a great deal). I'm stuck in the run-up. It's Fred I'm seeing. He's the one stretching out his arm to

halt the ship. Since Ditlev wrote about him in the paper
Mum's received letters every other day from people who
believe they've seen Fred some place or other. I think the
whole lot of them have screws loose; they're just individuals who want a bit of limelight either for themselves or
someone else. But they maintain all the same that they've
seen him – in Times Square in New York, at the market in
Montevideo, at Stroget and in Karl Johan, and on the ferry
between Moskenes and Røst. And these rumours, as
unreliable as they are cocky, have given Mum new hope –
the most hopeless thing of all. It's her duty, twenty-four
hours a day – to wait and hope, to hope and wait – for this
is the curse that's put on the one who waits by the one for
whom they wait. 'But someone has to be mistaken,' I
often say. 'What d'you mean?' she demands. 'Well, he
can't be in each and every place at the same time, can he?'
Then Mum just accuses me of being a killjoy and opens
yet another letter in which someone writes that they've
almost certainly seen Fred Nilsen on Mallorca or in
Arvika – they can recall that crooked nose and his lean
features. Mum gives all the letters to the Salvation
Army's missing persons' bureau so they can sort out all
the leads. I write in my margin – *To follow a letter. How far
backwards can one go*? I see before me a forest and there I
decide on one tree, this tree's the one that's felled. But
who cuts it down; who lops off the branches and chops it
up? Am I to trace them too? Instead I go quickly to the
river, to the timber that's floating there – the raft of tree
trunks like some colossal stick race – and the people there
who're freeing them. I take the tree into the factory just
beside the waterfall – or perhaps I'll make this paper by
hand in a family firm, in Italy for instance, in Bellagio, I
imagine. And so I'll follow the finished clear sheet of
paper all the way to the shop where it's bought by a young
man. Here I have to make a leap – my first leap – to a
deserted, frozen landscape, but before I do that I have to
find the springboard and I have to be sure of hitting it.
The springboard's the young man embracing his beloved,

a proud and beautiful girl, and going onboard the ship that will take him to the land of ice and snow. I see him there sitting in his cabin writing to his beloved – the tree becomes thoughts, thoughts become words, and these words will become pictures. I will have the hand that writes. I will have the pocket in which the letter is placed, and the coat that he doesn't put on, that's left hanging on a hook in the cramped cabin when he leaves on his final journey and disappears in a fissure or freezes in the ice which presses him into an everlasting grave. This is good. This is the beginning of a leap, a triple jump. I gulp down a mouthful of brandy. It's well deserved. The dark spirit sets me alight. And then I'm interrupted, right in the middle of my new run-up. Somebody taps on the window. I decide not to open it. Today Barnum's kiosk is closed. But the knocking comes again, and harder this time. I don't let myself be interrupted. I'm just getting into my stride. But when the person thunders on the window for the third time and all but brings down the kiosk, I've no choice but to unfasten the curtain and take a look at this nuisance. An oval face, which is far too brown and half enveloped by sunglasses, is all but filling the window. 'Sausage in a roll, please.' 'We don't serve sausages,' I tell him. 'Then I'll have a carton of juice instead.' 'I'm afraid they're all frozen.' 'Well, you can surely manage a packet of unfiltered Teddy, can't you, Tiny?' 'You're an ungrateful customer,' I tell him. 'And you're a diabolical shopkeeper, Barnum Nilsen!' It's Peder. It's none other than Peder Miil. He grabs hold of my jacket, hauls me through the kiosk window and we roll over on the pavement. We embrace each other, almost as in the old days, and a wild joy floods my heart. At last Peder's come back. We get up and brush the dust from ourselves. 'You've put on weight,' I remark. Peder gives his usual bellow of a laugh. 'And you've grown even smaller!' We stand there silent a moment, there in Church Road on a Sunday at the end of November, and we try to find that harmony – we search for it and know that nothing is the same any more. We see

that we've both changed. Peder's wearing a thin blue shirt
and a blazer. I lay my hand on his arm. 'Just hellish, the
whole thing with your Dad.' He takes off his sunglasses
and looks at me. 'What have you done to your eye?' he
asks. I don't mention his father again, not before he himself does. 'Now we'll go home to Vivian,' I say instead. I
put my mittens in the till and close the kiosk for the day.
We're silent right until we stand together outside the
door in Bolteløkka. Peder looks at the plate, the shining
bronze plate bearing our names – VIVIAN AND BARNUM.
'What was it I said?' he mused. 'What was it you said?'
'That it would be you two, right?' I unlock the door.
Vivian's standing by the window, facing away. We sneak
in and stand still. 'Is that you home already?' she asks. We
talk like some old married couple. We've nicked the dialogue from a film with Jean Gabin. 'Very quiet,' I answer.
'And you're sober too?' Peder looks at me again. I change
my repertoire. 'Guess who's coming to dinner?' I ask her
quickly. Vivian's changed too. It's something to do with
her posture. She's round-shouldered, her neck is all
hunched – it's as though she's lost something and is
having to bend over to look for it. I've often thought that
it's being with me that's made her that way; she's trying
to sink down to my level – perhaps that's also a kind of
love. And I think to myself that it should really be the
other way round, it should be a case of me stretching up
to her height. 'Fred,' she says all at once. I stand there
frozen. 'What?' 'Is it Fred who's coming to dinner?' I
laugh loudly. Peder takes off his sunglasses. 'Hallo, my
accident,' he says. Vivian turns round and her back
straightens, she lets her shoulders sink and she lifts her
neck – and in the moment she realizes that it's Peder she
becomes herself again. The years in between are rubbed
away and time is joined up. I can see it and it makes me
happy and bewildered. 'Hi, Fatty,' she says. Peder laughs
and pulls out his handkerchief to polish his sunglasses.
'Fine nameplate you have there, Vivian.' She takes him in,
meticulously, as if to assure herself it really is him, Peder

Miil, the fat one. 'When did you come?' she asks. 'A week ago.' 'Have you been here a whole week?' I roar. Peder doesn't take his eyes off Vivian. 'There were a couple of things I had to sort out,' he says. Then finally Vivian rushes over to him and they hug each other long and hard, and one of them's crying. It's Vivian. Peder once said that we were together with her, both of us. Now we are again. I go out to the kitchen to get some beer.

When we woke up Vivian had gone. There was a bottle on the bedside table. I had a drink from it and passed it to Peder. 'Lauren Bacall's still looking down at us,' he said. He pointed to the picture on the wall. It was hanging crooked that day. 'I thought it was Vivian's mother,' I said. 'Me too,' Peder laughed. He put the bottle down on the floor. 'Are you being good to Vivian?' he asked out of the blue. 'What d'you mean?' 'You know fine what I mean, Barnum.' 'No, I don't.' And I felt the angst growing inside, the heavy engine that drives you down to the depths – the submarine inside your soul. Peder went quiet. I noticed it had started snowing. I'd forgotten to take in the parasol from the verandah. And the sight of that blue parasol, amid the thick flakes of snow falling to make a slushy rim on the railing, still casts a shadow of sorrow and – bizarrely enough – joy, too, when the seconds shine too bright and blind me. 'Did I do anything yesterday?' I murmured. 'Nothing much other than drink and laugh.' I let out my breath. 'Why d'you ask then?' 'I saw the blackness in her eyes,' Peder said. Perhaps it took someone else to see it, someone who'd been away long enough. 'I can't make a baby,' I told him. Peder lay there silent a time. He didn't say any more about it. Instead he lay over me. 'D'you still dream, Barnum?' 'I dream the whole time, you thick-head!' But Peder wasn't satisfied. 'D'you dream in plus, though?' He laughed and pulled my arms backwards. I tried to break free of his grasp. 'Did you become commercial in America?' I shouted at him. Peder suddenly let me go. 'I'm going to show you something,' he told me.

We finished up the bottle, I went to get my scripts, and we went out. There were already ridges of snow left by the plough, and still the flakes kept falling. I must remember to take that parasol in. It couldn't stay out on the balcony. Peder looked like an immigrant worker in his thin blue shirt, open at the neck – the type that hasn't the foggiest what real cold is and needs a whole winter to learn what shivering means. We got a taxi in Therese Street and took it down to Solli Square. Our tree had white branches, as if it had become an albino since we saw it last. But it wasn't the tree Peder had wanted to show me. It was his father's shop. Above the door was no longer – MIIL'S STAMPS – BOUGHT AND SOLD. Now there were new words etched in sharp-edged plastic – MIIL AND BARNUM. I wanted to ask what the meaning of all this really was, but Peder unlocked the door and shoved me inside. There wasn't a stamp to be seen. The drawers and cupboards were empty. Everything was gone, even the unmistakable odour of paper and gum. Instead there was new furniture, a desk, a filing cabinet, a sofa and an office chair. 'What d'you reckon then?' Peder asked me. I turned to him. 'What's happened to everything?' 'Sold, of course.' 'You just came home and sold everything your father had here?' Peder lifted his hand, brushed it over his lips – self-conscious for a moment. There was a tremor in his voice. 'Have you grown sentimental, Barnum?' 'No,' I said. I saw the smile beginning on his lips. Nothing with Peder lasted for any length of time. 'Did you think I was going to count perforated edges the rest of my days?' I sat down on the office chair. It had a headrest, padding, wheels, and could swivel round. It made me think of Tati, *Playtime* – doors that are soundless when you slam them behind you. 'What's my name doing on that sign out there?' I asked. Peder sighed. 'Have you forgotten everything we talked about?' I got up and grabbed hold of his shirt. I think I tore off one of his buttons. 'I haven't forgotten there wasn't so much as a word out of you,' I hissed. Peder shoved me down again. 'That's your chair,

Barnum,' he said. I looked up. 'What?' And Peder whirled me round at lightning speed – I had to clutch hold of the armrests and became quite dizzy. I screeched and Peder roared with laughter, and finally the chair came to a standstill – it was a bit like spinning a bottle, me being the bottle. Peder bent down. 'Dreams and mathematics, Barnum. You're the dreamer and I'm going to work out how much they cost.' I closed my eyes and shook my head. Peder put his hands on my shoulders. 'We're going to make films, Barnum. You'll do the writing. I'll sell them.' 'And Vivian'll do the make-up!' I shouted. Peder went to get a cutting from the papers in the filing cabinet. It was Bente Synt's article. '*New fare in Norwegian film,*' he read aloud. He looked at me, and that smile, which was Peder's and Peder's alone, finally lit up his face. 'I'm so proud of you, Barnum,' he said. 'Thank you,' I breathed, and had to have a spin on the chair. 'D'you know what I almost did when I read this on the plane coming over?' 'Tell me, Peder, tell me.' 'I almost went through to the cockpit to shout to them that Barnum Nilsen was my best friend!' I laughed. 'You should have hijacked the whole plane!' I exclaimed. Peder went on reading. '*And Barnum Nilsen's vote of thanks will go down in history as the briefest and oddest we've ever heard.*' Peder looked up again. 'It just slipped out,' I told him. But Peder shook his head. 'To hell with you. Just perfect, Barnum. Now they'll never forget you.' He folded up the cutting and put it back in the cabinet. I didn't quite know if I liked what he'd said. I'd rather people forget it. But I couldn't be bothered arguing. I was thirsty and got up. 'Have you sold the fridge too?' I asked him. Peder flicked through a wad of notes and counted them. 'Did you bring the script?' I put *Fattening* down on the table. Peder gave me three notes. 'You go off to the "pole" while I read this,' he said. I stood there, for a moment amazed, almost annoyed, with Peder's money in my hand. What was he thinking? He sat down on the sofa and began going through the script. I went out into the snow to the 'pole' in Drammen Road. I wanted red wine and had to show identification. I always have it on me. There are age restrictions all over the place. The shop assistant looked at it long and hard, held it up to the light, and got out colleagues to hear what they had to say about the worn and tattered document, with a picture of me taken at the passport booth at the West End Station where the seat's highest. It's as if I no longer correspond with myself; a transition has taken place – I create uncertainty, but not the kind Dad meant, rather a *real* uncertainty that makes people believe everything. My doubt is impure, a clamp about the foot. They began to laugh behind the counter. I should have gone, turned round and gone and slammed the door behind me. I waited. I was thirsty. Finally I got my card back together with my bag of bottles. The assistant hesitated one final moment when he saw my eyelid droop. I hurried out. I was on the point of kicking the door but checked myself and held it open instead for one of the neighbourhood's old dears coming in with all her empties rolled up in newspaper. I closed the door quietly after her, because I'd more than likely return here many times in the future. I had a beer in Le Coq d'or. Peder was a slow reader. I left my identification lying on the counter. The bartender made a joke of it. 'I see you're afraid you'll forget who you are,' he said. 'I'm afraid of not getting any beer,' I said. I had another and went back to the shop. I stood outside looking at the new sign. MIIL & BARNUM. There was something wrong, something that grated – it reminded me of an advert for honey or some bad poem. 'You're still dreaming in minus,' he said. I opened a bottle of red wine. 'Didn't you like it?' I asked him. Peder got up and began a long drawn-out speech, all the while lifting his chubby hands as if he were pumping out the words. I managed to drink almost a whole bottle. And this is the gist of what he said. 'Did I like it? Sure I liked it. I don't just like it, I love it. But has that got anything to do with it? Has it? Answer, no. What *has* is that there's nobody who could be bothered to go and see it at the cinema. Fattening indeed!

There's nothing but minus here. Every single person in the story's in the red. All they do, each and every action, only increases their debt. The mother, the school doctor, the farmer and his wife and even the projectionist himself – you put the whole lot out of business. You have to make a profit, Barnum. That's what the public wants. When they go out of that cinema they want to take something away with them! They want to be full, not empty! Right?' Peder stopped, drew breath, and looked at me. 'Now I know what's wrong,' I told him. 'Good!' he exclaimed. 'My name should come first.' Peder was bewildered for a minute. 'What are you on about?' 'Barnum & Miil,' I said. 'Sounds much better.' Peder let his hands drop and grinned. 'That can be fixed.' He made a call, talked briefly to someone or other, put down the receiver and turned back to me. 'It's as good as done,' he said. He sat down. I've no idea whom he phoned, but I was impressed. 'Have you more?' he asked. I sloshed some more drink into his glass. Peder laughed. 'I mean *material*, Barnum.' I shut my eyes. Was I destroying my ideas now and using them up? How little should I reveal and how much should I keep to myself? And it struck me that I was halfway in regard to almost everything – my face, my height, my thoughts – I was a half person. The only thing that was whole was my halfness. 'The swimming pool.' Peder leaned closer. 'The swimming pool?' 'That's the title. The swimming pool.' Peder lifted his mug and set it down again. 'Miil wants more,' he said. I gave him more. I gave away my story. This is how I did it. 'I imagine two labourers who build swimming pools in the gardens of the rich. They dig, they build, they lay tiles – in short, they work around the clock to finish these luxurious swimming pools for the capitalists. And as they work parties go on in the gardens – the men in dinner jackets and the women in long dresses – they walk along the poolsides with drinks and canapés. But no water ever goes into the swimming pools. When autumn comes round, they're just as empty, full of leaves and rain. Like great tombs.' I had some more to drink and glanced at Peder. He had a rather lost expression on his face. His brow was furrowed. 'Is that all that happens?' he asked. 'D'you think there should be more?' 'Yes, I do, Barnum. Nothing really happens. Except for the building of the swimming pools.' 'The pool's a metaphor,' I explained. 'It never has water.' Peder sighed. 'That's what I mean. They never have water.' 'But that's the whole idea,' I went on. 'The idea?' 'The metaphor. That they build swimming pools without water.' 'Do the labourers do it deliberately, or is it a kind of sabotage?' 'I haven't considered that.' Peder grew impatient. 'Then you have to explain the whole thing to me in more detail. Take your time.' 'There's nothing to explain.' 'There's a great deal to explain, Barnum.' 'Life is an empty swimming pool.' Peder's sigh was more profound than before. 'Is it my fault or yours that I feel a right idiot at this moment?' 'What d'you mean?' 'D'you want your audience to feel like fools, Barnum?' 'Absolutely not.' 'We could send it to the television drama department.' A van stopped outside. Two men in overalls with reflectors round their legs put up a ladder against the window. Peder got up, opened the door and gave some instructions. Then he came back. I opened a new bottle and filled our mugs. Peder said cheers. 'D'you remember what Dad used to call a hangover?' he suddenly asked. 'Postal surcharge,' I said. Peder gave a laugh. 'Too few stamps on the celebration,' he said. And I saw the tremor in his eyes. He had to look down. 'Thank you both for being there for Mum,' he murmured. 'That was the least we could do, Peder.' 'I feel so ashamed, Barnum.' 'Why?' 'I couldn't manage to come back for the funeral. I'm a coward.' He looked up. 'I was so bloody angry when she told me what he'd done.' 'Angry?' 'I don't understand it. Him taking his own life. And I hate everything I don't understand.' Peder bent forward once more. 'To hell with him,' he breathed. 'To hell with him.' I had the urge to tell Peder about *The Night Man*, of the first scenes in *The Night Man* and my great plans. But he got in before me. 'There's another thing too,' he said. He had a swig of his drink and looked at me. 'I haven't done a single exam.' 'What have you done then?' 'Been on the beach.' 'Well, you've certainly got extremely brown,' I told him. Peder got up abruptly. 'Aren't you listening to what I'm saying? I'm nothing. Absolutely nothing.' 'Don't boast,' I said. Peder stood there, silent and bewildered – his shirt hanging out of his trousers, his brow drenched in sweat, his hands twitching. 'Now you know what kind of person you're dealing with,' he murmured. 'How many letters are there in our names?' I breathed. 'Ten,' Peder replied, tired. I got up too and took hold of his hand. 'That'll do,' I tell him. And he leaned his head against my shoulder.

Then one of the men knocked on the window. They were done and drove off with the ladder on the roof of the van. We went out. They'd changed the sign. 'I'll make your ideas visible,' Peder said. He ran in again. It was still snowing. Then something happened. The letters flickered, as if they were about to come loose from the wall. Peder came peacefully out, smiling, and stood beside me in the snow. Soon enough the letters stilled and our names were lit bright red above the door: BARNUM & MIIL. I put my arm round Peder. And that's the beginning of what I call (borrowing an expression from the silent film era), our electric theatre – that would take me to Room 502 in Coch's Hostel, and later to Røst where I dried up in the salty wind.

Row 14, Seats 18, 19 and 20

The silent film got its expressions from photography and the world of mime, from the brothels and the music halls, from ports, taverns, circuses and graveyards. The face never lies. The face's story is primitive and clear, just as the Old One's features were delineated by loss, but also by the joy of bearing the Lost One's daughter, Boletta. We are double. We are half. The face's story is both tragic and comic. The script wasn't there yet. The plot was a movement, a raised eyebrow, a tear, a smile. Words were only there in the form of explanatory text between scenes – flickering white letters on a black background, and the sole function of these words was to convey the fact that time had passed. *'Later.' 'Next morning.' 'The same afternoon.'* But after a while these simple pieces of information, these time indicators, became too brief. It was as though a great vanity infiltrated the words, and soon you could read things on the screen like – *'Long and terrible days drag by, filled with the hopelessness of doubt.' 'Imperceptibly the brutal morning slipped by.'* The language began to go wrong. In the end time stood still in the words. Not even the music could compensate. The pianist gave up. The actors began whispering to each other, gripped by the same panic the audience was experiencing. The plot had to develop. Speech forced its way through and with speech came the script. There are moments when I experience the same thing – time has stopped. The pages lie there. I can't get finished. I'm standing in the back premises. I drink as slowly as I can. Intoxication is also time, and at the heart of intoxication time runs amuck – a clock that explodes in sleep. I look out on the guests. I don't hear them. Peder's invited half the city. The place is heaving. I recognize faces from Norwegian Film; the director's there, the patches on his elbows have come undone. The dramaturge drops her cigarette and treads it into the carpet when she thinks no one's looking – but I am. There are a few journalists; Bente Synt's taking notes – she's the evening's bard, and in her pocket she has a camera. There are musicians in scruffy denims, bad-tempered directors (in particular the famous couple, one of them draped in furs), vociferous actors, tragic underground poets, child-minders, close relatives and other pale-faced inhabitants who weren't invited but who've sniffed out a party with the efficiency of trained bloodhounds. I'm impressed. Peder and Vivian go round smiling to everyone. They're host and hostess. They're elegant. My eye follows them. They're the finest fish in the aquarium. I'm standing on the other side, in a void. I like it there. Vivian turns and suddenly catches my eye – it's overwhelming and lasts no more than a second. Not even that, less, just a glance that's past, fleeting, a movement that doesn't stop. I smile and raise my glass, too late, and realize that she's no longer mine, and that perhaps she never was. I'm an incapable man. And at the same moment that thought gets through to me I feel closer to her than ever. Peder gets up on a chair and makes a speech. I see mouths collapsing in laughter and applauding hands. Then the voices suddenly impact on me, a wave of sound floods through to me and I can hear Peder calling. He wants me to say a few words. I go over to them. I clamber up onto the same chair. There's a certain expectation. I look at Vivian. She waits there peacefully. 'Come on, Barnum!' Bente Synt exclaims. Peder's sweating like a pig. One of the earliest films to be made in England was called *The Cheese Middens or the Lilliputians at the Restaurant*. The director, Robert W. Paul, well known for his stunts and particularly his dolly shots, filmed a scene as normal and then dressed his characters in black, rolled the camera thirty feet back, put in another lens and filmed over the original scene. In this way he could get both full-sized people and small, fantasy apparitions in one and the same picture. This is the most famous scene – a sailor's incredulity and utter astonishment when he sees a whole trail of dwarves crawling out of a cheese he's about to eat. I'd like to say something about this. I want to say that I'm a midden myself; I'll pop up everywhere – you'll find me when you pull out a drawer, leaf through a book, put your hand in your pocket, go to the loo, open the glove compartment and your spectacle case and the fridge – I'll be there when you fall asleep and not least when you wake up. I am a midden. I have to say something. But I don't say that. 'The night's still young,' I say instead. I climb back down. There's ragged applause. Others just look at each other. Bente Synt slips past. 'Have you become a good boy since we saw you last?' she asks. I nod. 'How boring,' she murmurs. She puts her head on one side. 'What do you really want with Peder Miil?' she inquires. I whisk away her camera and loom in towards her long face, her red snout. 'I'll photobloodygraph you!' I screech. I do it. I steal her soul. Bente Synt laughs. It's a great evening. The director stops right behind me. 'Have you thought about my suggestion?' he asks. 'No,' I reply. He gives me a pat on the shoulder. It's still a great evening.

Soon everyone's gone. The detritus is left behind – the cigarette ends, the coppers, the glasses, and particularly the crumpled, mucky serviettes which I suddenly see as damaged birds. I lift out one of them and smooth the wings that are soiled with lipstick and ash. No surprise they can't fly. We sit round the table and polish off the last bottle between us. Vivian, Peder and myself. 'We're on the road,' Peder says. 'We're on the road,' I repeat. Vivian's tired and happy. She raises her glass. 'Here's to Miil and Barnum,' she says. 'Barnum and Miil,' I correct her. Peder laughs. 'Here's to Vivian!' We toast each other. The evening's no longer young. It's night now and the sign above the door, still lit, is colouring the snow red. A Christmas tree with a star is lying in the middle of the street. Perhaps someone's thrown it out of a window or from a veranda. We're pensive and silent as we finish off that last bottle. 'A comedy,' Vivian says out of the blue.

We both look at her. Vivian's stopped smoking and lights up a cigarette. 'About mothers. Inspired by *Paul's Hens*.' Peder and I don't quite follow. We sing *Paul's Hens* and understand what she's on about when we get to the last line in the chorus. *Now I don't dare to come home, mother dear*. I kiss Vivian on the cheek. That night I'm in love. Peder thumps the table. 'Lauren Bacall!' he exclaims. I turn towards him. 'What about her?' 'If we can get Lauren Bacall involved in one of our projects it's in the bag, right?' 'Lauren Bacall? Are you exceptionally pissed, Peder?' 'Hell, are we to make do with the old crew in Dröbak, huh? Nothing's impossible!' That's how we talk and lift one another. Things are almost as they were before. But there's something different about our voices. We're talking too loudly. We're talking too quickly. 'The garage burned down,' Peder says quickly. 'It burned down?' I take his hand. He nods over and over again. 'The whole bloody thing burned down. Fair enough, eh?' Vivian and I go home. Peder wants to stay behind and clear up. I can't get that chorus out of my head. *Now I don't dare to come home, mother dear*. The cold makes me wide awake. I can't get to sleep. Vivian's back is naked. Carefully I put my hand on her hip. She pushes it away in her sleep. I get up. I sit down at the table. *The Night Man* is lying in a drawer. The drawers are full. I set a new piece of paper in the typewriter and hammer out – *Finally winter casts off her white cape and reveals her pale green dress*.

I look out. Vivian's sitting under the parasol on the balcony. On the little round table there's a red drink. She leans back her head and smiles, but not to me. In 1911 Will Barker made *Hamlet* in the course of just one day and the film lasted fifteen minutes. That's a record. Vivian's gone to the salon. The phone rings. It's Peder. Peder screams into the receiver as if he's standing in a telephone box away back in childhood and has a whole lot to say and only one coin. 'Something we have to talk about, Barnum!' 'Haven't time,' I tell him. 'Lunch then at Valka's.'

I put on my sunglasses and went out, and before I reached Marienlyst the summer was almost over. There was a crackling in the trees; that particular dry sound of leaves burning and falling – the great wheel. But it was the cranes I heard; they stood like mechanical predators in the street beyond our yard, and the entire roof was covered in green tarpaulin which billowed in the wind – it looked like some enormous balloon, and beneath it the yard hung by a thin thread. They had started building the attic flats already. And I thought to myself – *Now they're pulling down Mum's story*. I went down to Valka's. Peder was sitting by the window. I ordered a hair of the dog. Peder was drinking cola; he'd already eaten some cake. I looked round at the slow diners. 'Is this how I'm going to end up too?' I hissed. A silent waiter came to the table with my order. First I had my drink. 'Well, you're certainly well on the way,' Peder said. 'Was that what you wanted to talk about?' Peder shook his head. This was the corner for sullen men. Time stood still here, and on the rare occasions when it did pass (when someone needed a pee) it went backwards. Right in at the corner the director got up. He wasn't the director any more. The helicopters had taken over. It was just a case of looking out of the grey windows. The new men and women hurried past in their weightless capes, armed with credit cards and stiletto heels. American hamburger joints had opened up on each and every corner. Even the drunks on the Majorstuen steps had ironed trousers. It wasn't just our block, it was the whole city – ready to take off like another of André's flights, and who would come looking for *us*? The only thing that was immutable was the Salvation Army quartet. That was the one guy rope that held a shred of real life secure. They stood beside the tram stop with their frail guitars and sang the same old songs. And I thought to myself that these were the ones who were searching for Fred. In every city in every land they stand there singing and watching, singing and watching and saving. 'Have you heard of Arthur Burns?' I asked. Peder hadn't. No one ever has. I related Arthur Burns' story. He died the previous year. He was ninety-four years of age. One of the pioneers of film. He was a young and gifted dramatist who moved from New York to Hollywood and began writing filmscripts right back when Mary Pickford was at the height of her career. He kept on writing. He was writing scripts when Douglas Fairbanks was the great god; he wrote for James Cagney, Edward G. Robinson and John Wayne. He was writing when James Dean and Marlon Brando came with their melancholy to the screen; he wrote when Clint Eastwood got out his magnum, and didn't stop even when Sylvester Stallone entered stage right, his torso bare. Arthur Burns was one of Hollywood's most respected scriptwriters. No one had been at it longer than him. He was a living legend. He survived all the great screen heroes and Warner Brothers paid for his funeral. There was just one tiny flaw in Arthur Burns' magnificent career. Nothing came of it. Not one single script was filmed – not a scene, not a scrap of dialogue, not so much as a voice-over was used. Arthur Burns wrote in water. I ordered another drink. Peder yawned. 'And what is it you're trying to say?' 'I have a drawer full of scripts that no one wants either,' I told him. Peder leant over the table. 'Adaptations,' he said. I retracted my arm in a hurry. 'Adaptations?' 'You heard me correctly. We're going to talk adaptations.' 'Don't insult me, Peder.' 'Go to the library and find yourself some books with a good story to them. That's all I'm asking you.' 'I'd prefer to use my own ideas,' I told him. Peder folded his hands. 'But if your own ideas are waiting in the wings right now then you could always be inspired by other people's in the meantime, huh?' 'D'you know what Scott Fitzgerald says about adaptations?' 'No, Barnum. But I'm sure you do.' I nodded. 'Get a good friend to read the book, ask him to relate what he remembers of it, write that down and there you have your film.' 'Marvellous,' Peder said. At that moment the former director returned from the loo. He stopped beside our table and looked

down at me, as Peder paid. 'Are you writing?' he enquired.
'Yes,' I told him. 'But are you writing about your brother,
Barnum?' I don't quite know why but I got so mad. I
stood up and shoved him away. I'm convinced I didn't
push him all that hard, but push him I did. There must
have been something wrong with his balance. He toppled
backwards and lay there between the chairs. I was thrown
out of Valka's for good. It wasn't two o'clock yet and
Bente Synt was on her way in; I had time to catch her
smile – she was my bad omen, since each and every time
she appeared on the scene something awful happened.
Peder got hold of my arm and dragged me over to one
side of the street before I could do any more mischief. The
Salvation Army was singing. 'Are you writing about
Fred?' he asked. I pushed Peder away too, but he didn't
fall over – Peder was too heavy. 'No!' I shouted. We went
into Deichman's in Bogstad Road and borrowed twenty
novels – among them Hamsun's shortest, *The Swarms,
Little Lord Fauntleroy, Dracula*, the sagas, and the last one
by a young, long-haired writer by the name of Ingvar
Ambjörnsen. We took a taxi down to the office. One of
the letters over the door had gone out. We were Barum
and Miil. We were like a hotel with the loo in the hall.
Peder let us in and there sat Vivian. She got up straight
away. 'Haven't you heard?' she said. I went all cold. I'm
not sure what was in my head, but I expected the worst.
'What haven't we heard?' I breathed. 'They're pulling
down Rosenborg cinema,' she said. Peder dropped all the
books on the floor and we got a taxi and went there right
away. It was true. They were demolishing Rosenborg
cinema to put a fitness centre there. They were carrying
out everything to a huge skip blocking the entire road.
Now yet another place had gone. But they couldn't throw
away the images. They couldn't pack up the light in bags
and dispose of that. Something remained which could
never be lost. That was a comfort. Peder negotiated with
the foreman for approximately an hour. Then he wrote
out a rather weighty cheque and we were allowed to

clamber into the skip. In the end we found our seats – row 14, seats 18, 19 and 20. We lugged them (the best seats in the cinema) over to Bolteløkka and set them down on the balcony. 'I want to sit on the outside,' Vivian said. I protested. 'You have to be in the middle,' I told her. But she sits on the outside nonetheless – it doesn't matter what we say – in seat 18 in the fourteenth row, and I have to sit in the middle. Of course Peder has a bar of milk chocolate which he breaks into three equal pieces. The Sten Park trees still have their magnificent, trembling leaves. But the great wheel is creaking. The sun is going down. The Night Man is going over Blåsen and everything is coming closer. 'Can you see all right?' I ask. 'Quiet,' Peder and Vivian hiss.

Suede

Where the loft window once was there's now a great wide window with a view to the darkness and the skies. I wonder to myself if the glass would hold if the snow were to fall really heavily over a long period. The wall housing the chimney and the coke shaft has been whitewashed. The floor has been sanded; it's as if the planks are springy when I walk across them, and they've been given a beautiful, pale lacquer which has the effect of making the place feel bigger than I remember it. But maybe that's because it's still empty, for no one's moved in yet – this still hasn't *become* somewhere. There's an open kitchen area and the two storerooms to the side have been converted into a bedroom and a bathroom respectively. I know already I could never live here.

Then I hear someone coming up the stairs. I turn round. Mum stops and stands there under the drying lines. That's how I see her. I mingle these pictures that time develops at one and the same time; Mum has stopped under the drying lines that hang in slack loops in the light, attached to the walls by rusty hooks. And if she stretches just a bit she can reach the clothes pegs and bring down a garment that's been forgotten there – a flowery frock – as a dove sits cooing up on one of the beams. I almost say something, but at the last moment don't. There's something about her, something else – a calm that chills me. 'It's over,' Mum says. 'Over? What d'you mean?' 'Fred,' she murmurs. Rain patters on the angled window. I could never manage to sleep in these rooms. I go nearer her. It amazes me that I feel neither joy nor sorrow – I'm not even afraid. It's as if Mum's dark tranquillity has become my own. But when I speak, my voice suddenly breaks. 'Have they found him?' I ask. Mum shakes her head. 'They've found some of his clothes.' 'His clothes?' 'D'you remember his old suede jacket?' I nod. I once got to borrow it when he made me go with him to the graveyard, and it was far too big for me. 'They found it in Copenhagen. In Nyhavn. It was hanging over the railings on one of the bridges.' Mum smiles. 'Wasn't it a good thing I sewed those nametags on your clothes.' she says. 'Yes, Mum.' And I realize, after she's uttered those words, that she's given up. That's the way of it. She can't endure the waiting any longer. She can't hope any more. She wants to rest. We won't call him missing now, we'll give him a new name – dead. It's as though she's actually relieved. 'They've dragged the canals, but they haven't found him,' she breathes. 'The current's probably taken him miles away.' She comes another step closer. The floor trembles. I try to meet her gaze but can't. 'It could have been someone else who was wearing his jacket,' I point out. Mum smiles again and hands me a sheet of paper on which something's written. It's the last paragraph from the Greenland letter and for a moment there's a flicker of victory – he found the letter in the end, his journey wasn't in vain. But then I recognize Fred's own handwriting and his twisted letters. He'd just learned the words off by heart in the same way I had, in his own distorted way. But the very last sentence was missing. 'It was in his pocket,' Mum says. We stand there silent for a moment, as if we've reached a kind of consensus. Up here, in the place that once was the drying loft and where everything began, Mum now says that it's over. She takes back the sheet of paper from me. 'I want you to give the eulogy, Barnum.' I have to meet her gaze now. Her eyes are clear and dark. I don't like what I see there. 'Eulogy? Where?' 'At the memorial service for Fred,' she says.

    Later I go back to Bolteløkka. All the shelves, drawers and cupboards are empty. The wastepaper baskets are ranged along the sides of the walls. The photograph of the woman we thought was Lauren Bacall has left behind a pale, faded square on the wallpaper. I try to work on *The*

Night Man, but the images are frozen. Where is Fred's jacket now? That was something I forgot to ask Mum. Instead I drink until Vivian comes back home. I don't know where she's been. Nor do I ask her. She lies down beside me in the darkness. I can hear that she isn't sleeping. It's at that moment she says it. 'I'm going to have a baby,' she whispers. And I can sense that we're each in our own lie, the one bigger than the other and catching the other as with some soundless clockwork device. It's infuriating and it's shameful, and I have no idea what I will do with all this loneliness. I turn round slowly to Vivian and cautiously place my hand on her stomach, afraid to damage anything. A tremor passes through the thin and almost luminous skin, as if something is already alive inside. She sits over me. I can't see her face. I cry. She bends down, almost to my mouth, and takes her hand through my hair, over and over again as she softly rocks from side to side. 'Don't cry,' she whispers. 'Don't cry now, Barnum.' And this consolation (the only honest thing that night) is in danger of upsetting the equilibrium of our clockwork lies and giving our game away. 'Fred's dead,' I tell her. Vivian slides off me, pushes me forcibly away and pulls me close in one single, trembling movement. Her voice barely makes any sound whatsoever. 'Dead? Is Fred dead?' 'They found his jacket in Copenhagen. They reckoned he drowned in one of the canals.' 'But they haven't found him?' 'No,' I breathe. Vivian lets go of her hold of me. I put on the light. She hides her face in her hands. The room is white, it's a room that's in the process of being abandoned. It's like us. I close my eyes. I don't want to see this. 'I want him,' Vivian suddenly says, and there's something resolute, almost fierce, about her voice, as if I had contradicted her. At first I don't know what she means. My one eyelid hangs there like a thin, sticky bandage. Then I get the message. 'Him? You know it's going to be a boy?' Vivian turns away. 'I'm three months pregnant,' she whispers. I put on a shirt and sit outside on the balcony, in seat 18, at the end. I see nothing. Everything's one. It amazes me that the city's so still, as if we're the only ones there that night, paralysed. Is doubt a kind of lie too? I drink what's left over. I always do. What was Fred doing in Copenhagen, if he was actually there at all? Was he on his way home? Was he going to Koge or did he just want to see the musk oxen in the zoo? And I try to imagine him in my mind, the way he now must look, so many years older – soon middle-aged. But I can't; I can't imagine him any other way than as I remember him on that last morning in the Church Road kitchen, when he left for good, barely twenty years of age. That's the only way I can picture him – the thin, young Fred I once knew, tossing his old suede jacket on a Nyhavn bridge and going over to the darkness on the other side. 'D'you think he's dead?' Vivian stands by the door and the living-room light frames her in silver. I believe I can see a slight curve over her stomach, or maybe it's just something I imagine now that I know she's having the child I couldn't give her. We protect each other with lies. She's cold and puts her hands on her shoulders. Her arms form a cross. She asks the question a second time and her lips tremble around the words. 'Do you think Fred is dead, Barnum?' 'Mum wants to hold a memorial service for him,' I tell her. Vivian looks at me; it's as though she's standing in a shining hole in the darkness, at the bottom of a well of light. 'Get her to leave it be,' she whispers.

But Mum's mind wasn't going to be changed. I tried for long enough to dissuade her, but nothing would do it. She'd made up her mind, once and for all. Waiting had drained her and at last she had something she could focus on. And she did so with a zeal and a pride – almost an enthusiasm – I could barely remember having seen in her before, and it scared the life out of me. She told the Salvation Army's missing persons' bureau it was no longer necessary to go on looking for Fred. The search was over. She ordered flowers and wreaths. She put an announcement in *Aftenposten*. She had the hymns we'd sing printed. And she cleared away his things from our room. I stood leaning against the door frame and it was a weird sight. My half of the room had been empty long enough – only the bed frame remained. Now Fred's half went too, so that in a way the room became whole again – equally stripped, equally empty. Mum put away everything in the cupboard and turned to me, smiling, her face shining – almost young again, and beautiful. She'd rid herself of the suffocating mask that belongs to the one who waits, and she was free. It was like an intoxication, an even more powerful intoxication, and I was counting down to the moment of complete collapse. This couldn't last. I went in to Boletta and roused her. 'Can't you make Mum stop all this?' I murmured. Boletta shook her head, almost imperceptibly. 'Maybe she feels she owes him this,' she said. 'Owes him? What d'you mean?' Boletta got up from the divan. 'Fred wasn't planned, Barnum.' Mum was calling from the hall, impatiently and emphatically. 'Are you coming?' Quickly I took hold of Boletta's hand. 'D'you think he's dead?' Boletta looked up. 'Fred's roamed long enough now,' she said. Mum called again and I had to join her. 'Where are we going?' I asked. But she didn't have time to reply and when we got out onto the pavement we met Peder and Vivian. Mum put her arms round Vivian and kissed her on both cheeks. Vivian whispered something to her I couldn't hear. I looked at Peder. I couldn't see any difference. 'Vivian's going to show me the loft conversion,' he said. He turned quickly towards Mum. 'What can I say?' he murmured. 'My condolences.' Mum kissed him too. 'Thank you, Peder. You know all about losing someone.' It was only then he became self-conscious and fumbled a good deal with the umbrella he mainly used as a stick. 'Yes,' he said quietly. 'I do know.' Mum sighed. 'It's good it's over.' Then we stood there in silence for a bit, at the corner of Church Road and Gørbitz Street, in the frail cold rain that often falls in Oslo late in September. A number of fine, shining drops ran down Vivian's brow and she let them fall, down onto her eyebrows and eventually to her mouth – then she licked them away, and when I met her gaze it was as though she was standing on the other side of the rain, behind a trellis of water. I couldn't reach her. Finally Peder opened his black umbrella and it was sufficiently large to cover all four of us. 'Are you coming too?' he asked. Mum hadn't time to answer that either. Vivian and Peder went into the yard and we continued on our way towards Majorstuen. I could only just manage to keep up with Mum. She turned round. 'Is Vivian ill, Barnum?' 'Ill, no. What do you mean?' But she didn't answer. She'd already forgotten her own question. We passed the kiosk that was shut up now; several bits of wood had been pulled away and someone had scrawled on the little window in red letters – *occupied!* Mum didn't pay the slightest heed to it. She only walked the faster. We were going to Majorstuen police station.

We had to wait for three quarters of an hour. It became apparent that Mum had handed in the sheet that was in Fred's jacket pocket to an officer for his opinion, and perhaps it would be possible to obtain fingerprints too – whatever their use was now. I began to feel tired. Mum was even more alert than before. Then we were shown into an office. An older uniformed man with thin grey hair pressed down flat on his head by his hat, and with a groove-like ring round his head that was also a result of the hat, was sitting behind a desk. In front of him was a cake with a single candle on it. Mum shook hands with him and we sat down. The officer appeared rather lost in his own world. He inadvertently licked the cream from his finger, and went pink when he realized what he'd just done. 'Have you had a chance to have a look at it?' Mum asked him. The officer drew his finger through his thin beard, pulled out a drawer and took out a plastic folder containing the sheet. 'Are these his own words or ones he could have read somewhere else?' he asked. 'It's the last part of a letter sent from Greenland by my grandfather to my grandmother,' she told him. But she didn't make mention of the fact that the last sentence was missing. Perhaps she'd forgotten. Perhaps Fred had too. I could remember it, though. 'It's obviously a quote from an old Inuit,' I said. 'The shaman Odark.' The officer pushed the cake over the desk. 'Would you both like a piece?' We each took a bit. He smiled and picked up the sheet of paper. 'I'm retiring today,' he explained. 'This is my last case.' He went over to the wall and took down a certificate in a glass frame and put it in a box that was already full. We ate our cake in silence. Mum was finished long before me. 'But what d'you make of it?' she asked him. The officer came back and put the sheet back in the plastic folder. 'It isn't easy to know what to make of it,' he admitted. Mum grew impatient. What was it she wanted to know? What did she think these words, clumsily written from memory on a small sheet of paper, could reveal? She leant closer. 'You can read?' she said. The officer looked at her. 'Yes, I can read. But I don't necessarily read it in the same way you do.' Mum appeared dissatisfied with this response. 'What are you trying to say?' 'Tell me rather how you read it,' the officer said. Mum began crying. 'These are my son's parting words,' she murmured. 'That's what they are!' and I realized that Mum didn't want to know the truth at all. She didn't want to descend any further than she had. She wanted to believe what she'd made up her mind was the truth. Her time of waiting was over. I took the sheet of paper and had to support her as we went over towards the door. The officer got up. 'By the way, did your grandfather return from Greenland?' he enquired. Mum stopped. 'No,' she said. 'He was lost too.' And it was at that moment the old officer recognized something, a thread running through his life, a connection he'd been hunting for, some kind of meaning on this his final day. 'Vera Jebsen?' he suddenly said. Mum looked at him in amazement. 'That's my maiden name.' The officer had to sit down. 'Then it was your grandmother who came here just after the war to report a crime,' he said. Mum was silent and he stood up again. 'The case was never solved, as far as I remember. I was young and inexperienced in those days.' Mum staggered; it was as though she was standing dizzily on the edge of a cliff – it lasted only a second (she didn't fall yet), but blew the hair from her brow, smiling. 'Are you any the wiser now?' she asked him. The officer straightened his uniform and looked down – at the cake crumbs, the empty desk, the clock. In a few minutes he'd have done his duty and could go home for good. 'No,' he whispered.

The rain had stopped by the time we went out. Mum took my hand and looked up at the skies. She stood like that a long while and shut her eyes, blinded by the sun which broke obliquely through the clouds. 'I hope it'll be beautiful tomorrow,' she whispered. And she turned towards me. 'You won't say anything inappropriate about Fred in your speech, Barnum.' 'How would I do that?' I asked. Mum sighed. 'You know fine, Barnum.' And I tried yet again to dissuade her. 'Are you really sure this is what you want, Mum?' She smiled. 'Vivian asked me the very same question.' 'And what did you tell her?' 'That I was completely sure.'

Mum was certain. She'd never been so sure of anything. She was going to hold this memorial service – a committal without a coffin – death *in absentia*. She was even going to have the service in Majorstuen church, where the vicar in his time had refused to baptize both Fred and myself. There was something so gutsy about it all I couldn't but marvel at it – a living stubbornness. We went up Church Road once more. Mum had never let go of my hand. 'Don't drink tomorrow,' she said. I suddenly regretted not having reported the business at the kiosk while we were down at the station. 'No, Mum.' 'I want you to be sober, Barnum.' 'Yes, Mum.' 'D'you promise, my little one? For your brother's sake?'

Dregs

I woke up alone the following morning. I keep my promise to Mum, for my brother's sake. On the bedside table there's a note. Vivian's left a message saying she's gone for a check-up and that we can meet outside the church. It's a quarter past ten. The memorial service begins at one. I see that it's sunny; low, autumn light in the thin trees. Rain would have been better. I get up and have a shower. Vivian's cleared the bathroom cupboard as well. Only the absolute essentials are there – shampoo, some perfume, a nail file, skin cream, make-up, musk, a hairbrush, a half bottle of vodka and some toothpaste – in the main my own things. I close the cupboard. It's ages since I looked at myself in the mirror. I do so now. The mist clears, as if a veil's been drawn from my face. Have I remained the same in Fred's eyes as he did in mine? Did my time stop too that morning in Church Road, when he left the imprint of his hand on me and went? Is that how he's remembered me subsequently, as Barnum, the *little* little brother – sixteen years of age and kicked out of school? And as I think this I feel his absence so deeply and profoundly I have to lean my brow against the mirror and fight for breath. I wish so much I could say to him – *I managed all right, Fred. And you?* I open the cupboard again and see the bottle. It remains unopened. This is a promise that still hasn't been broken. Today I'll please Mum. But I don't find my old suit, Dad's suit. I open the boxes from the removal. It isn't there either. I go down to the basement. Our storage area is right at the back, behind the laundry room. The door isn't even locked. From time to time tramps from the park sleep in the warmth by the airing cupboard. There's nothing to steal here anyway, only things Vivian's decided to throw out or give to a flea market – a pair of chipped skis, clothes that

went out of fashion years ago, platform shoes, a standing
lamp with a check shade, empty bottles. The suit's hanging in a see-through plastic covering. I haven't used it in
ages. I get it down from the hook on the wall and it's
then my eye alights on something else – the suitcase. It's
the old suitcase Dad carried round for the ringmaster
Mundus, and which I inherited from Dad and subsequently lent to Fred when he disappeared. Now I've got it
back. I lift it up. It isn't light. It's just even more worn.
The strap on the lid has broken. I hold the suitcase, as if
it's my turn to leave. I open it. There's no applause. It's
empty. The lining has come loose and hangs in crumpled
folds. The journey's been a long one. I can't fathom it. I
chuck the suitcase into our storage cupboard and run up
the stairs. I've locked myself out. I stand there staring at
the door. The nameplate is covered in a pale, discoloured
film, as though our names are etched in fog and almost
invisible. I know it. He's been here. Perhaps he's slept
down there. He's seen my face. He's watched our time
pass. He's seen us. Why did he not show himself? Didn't
he dare? And another suspicion suddenly grips me, and I
can't bring myself to think the thought to its conclusion –
yet it's impossible to stop it, it's a locomotive in my
head. When was he here, on his secret visits? I hear
someone. It's the neighbour. 'You're the one who steals
my papers,' she says. I take off my clothes. She hurries
inside again. I put on the suit and dispose of my other garments in the rubbish chute. I'm on my way to Majorstuen
church. I go round by Blasen. I stop at the top. The cold
light draws everything closer. I think to myself – *Is this the
final scene in* The Night Man? I light a cigarette and am
sick. When I get to the church Mum and Peder are sitting
on the bench under the clock and the red creeper. They
get up the minute they see me. Mum is impatient and
nervous. She kisses my cheek, but I presume it's because
she wants to ascertain whether I've been drinking or not.
Peder puts his arm round my shoulder. 'The loft conversion's brilliant,' he says. We're able to go inside. A couple

from the Salvation Army are sitting right at the back. I
notice Bang the caretaker and recognize a few faces from
school; the chief inspector's sitting right at the far side
and Bente Synt's there too, my bad omen. But this day
couldn't be any worse than it already is. 'It'll go fine,'
Mum breathes. I sit between Vivian and Boletta in the
front pew. The doors are closed. Boletta lays her delicate,
blotchy hand in my lap. 'Thank heavens there's no vicar
here,' she says. Mum tells her to be quiet. The organist
begins to play. I don't know the words of the hymn.
Vivian stares straight ahead. Her mouth is shut. Her
cheeks are hollow. Where the coffin should be there's a
chair and round it are wreaths and flowers. On one of the
silk ribbons are the words *Thank you, Vivian and Barnum*.
Mum gets up and makes a small speech. I don't quite
follow what she's saying. I have this locomotive in my
head and it won't stop. I lean close to Vivian. 'This is the
next best thing,' I murmur. She grows edgy. 'Next best?
What d'you mean?' 'The best thing would have been is
they'd found him dead, right?' Mum looks at me. She
smiles. She's beautiful today, in the black dress she hasn't
worn since Dad died. It's my turn. I'm to make a speech
for Fred. I stand in front of the flowers and the empty
chair, my back to the congregation; I have no notion of
how long I stand there like that but when I do turn round
I see that the church is completely packed, there isn't a
single empty seat. And all at once it reminds me of the
première of *Hunger*. Now it's Fred who's been cut out.
Mum has sat down next to Vivian. Peder's behind her. I
can hear music; the locomotive's brought with it the song
by Morricone from *Once Upon a Time in America*. I begin to
speak. 'I've always dreamed Fred would come back, just
as Robert de Niro does at the railway station in New York.
But when we ask him what he's done all these years he's
been away, he'll not answer – *Gone to bed early*. Instead
he'll say – *I've seen all of you*.' I wait a bit. Peder's smiling;
he understands and he leans forward against Vivian, his
breath on her neck. Mum's still expectant; she bends

forward as if at any moment prepared to stop me.
Boletta's holding her arm. And as I stand there by the
empty chair in front of all these pale and silent faces, I
become a dreamer once more – Barnum the dreamer. I
imagine myself missing, presumed dead; I've drowned in
one of the canals and my body's floating there, circling
slowly towards the bottom. Finally I manage to dream of
my own funeral; it's me they've come to remember, here
in Majorstuen church, and I can take a last look at those
I'm going to leave behind, and I know they'll have forgotten me as soon as they go out of the door into Fagerborg's Indian summer. This image is so powerful my eyes
spill over and I have to wipe away a tear. My crying is
infectious. It's my crying I'm there to share. When they
see me moved to tears, they begin crying too – everyone
except Vivian and Peder. I think Boletta has gone to sleep,
bless her, but Mum has her hankie in her hand and nods
to me several times, pleased and grateful. I've kept my
promise, for my brother's sake. 'One night Fred came
home with a coffin,' I say aloud. Mum's on her guard
again and Boletta wakes up. It's my turn to close my eyes.
I'm the dreamer who dreams backwards. 'Perhaps he
knew what was to come. Perhaps it was a flashforward as
it's called in my line of work. Because here today we have
no coffin, we only have a memory, and that memory is
nothing but a picture multiplied by time.' Peder raises his
thumb. Mum's anxious. I have the desire to sit down, to
sit on Fred's chair, but I don't. And yet again I imagine I
see Fleming Brant, standing now by the font, his hands
dripping with water; he shakes his head and walks down
the aisle, his rake over his shoulder, so slowly he never
disappears. 'But my first memory of Fred is of the two of
us hiding under the living-room table listening to our
great-grandmother reading from our great-grandfather's
letter. I still know the words off by heart. *While we were in
the ice we often hunted for seal and shot a great number. They
should be shot whilst they lie sunning themselves on the ice
because once they are in the water they are difficult to get hold*

of.' I have to stop again. I look down. I'm standing amid flowers and wreaths. I could finish now. I don't. I say instead, *'When the hunter finds a trail he doesn't follow it. He turns and follows the trail back to where the animal came from.'* Mum's on the point of getting to her feet. Boletta holds her back. Vivian looks away. Peder doesn't take his eyes off me. There's utter stillness in Majorstuen church. I'm the one with the rake now, raking the sand along the way we've taken. I raise my voice. 'And Fred's last words were also taken from this letter, the letter that is the story of our family, of where we come from and return to always – the land between ice and snow.' I put my hand on my cheek and wait. And I have time to consider that life itself is mostly composed of waiting, that's what our days are made up of – waiting, waiting for something, for something else. We are here to bring to a close this time of waiting. I read aloud the words that were in Fred's pocket. *'You ask, yet of death I know nothing because all I know is life. All I can say is what I believe – that either death is the end of life or but the bridge to another way of living. Whichever it may be, there is nothing to fear.'* I turn towards Mum. She's folded her hands. And in a quiet voice I speak the final sentence which Fred had perhaps forgotten. Maybe no one hears it, but I think it's the finest line in the letter, composed of these words of the shaman Odark – opinionated and full of love and courage. Words that the young Wilhelm made his own when he put them into the letter to his beloved and didn't know they would form the end of his story. And it's now I make these words everyone's. *'Therefore it would be with great reluctance I would die now, so wonderful I think it is to be alive!'* Mum gets to her feet. She hangs Fred's jacket over the chair, his suede jacket; it's as if he's just been sitting here in a normal school period and has been sent out to the corridor or has gone for a pee. And I realize at the same moment that waiting has eaten away at Mum's sanity – and how is she to bear this empty missing with a jacket that no longer fits? She wants me to come back with her to the pew now.

'That's enough, Barnum,' she breathes. 'You've done well.' But I remain where I am, beside Fred's chair; I'm not done yet, and this stillness, which is within me, grows even greater and deeper. Never has Fred seemed more alive to me than right at that moment. 'Time plays games with us,' I say loudly – it's possible I even shout the words. Then I lower my voice. Mum has stopped. 'Time has many rooms,' I whisper. 'And everything happens at one and the same time in all those rooms at this moment.' I sit down on Fred's chair. 'Fred taught me never to say many thanks. But today I make an exception to that rule. Today I say many thanks. Because Vivian's to have a child at last.' Peder straightens up and opens his mouth, but instead of saying anything he laughs; I hear Peder's astonished laughter filling Majorstuen church. And I go down to where Vivian's sitting and kiss her, and she can do nothing to stop me. After that we stand by the church porch. The last ones greet us in silence on their way out. Vivian looks at me wrathfully, yet she's relieved too, for she won't be able to hide the fact that she's pregnant much longer anyway. 'We must celebrate this,' Mum says, on the verge of tears. Oh yes, now we can celebrate and mourn; one room is papered black and the other's full of sunlight, but we don't know which of them is for rejoicing all the same. 'I just have to get something,' I murmur. And I hurry over Church Road to the kiosk. In the little lemonade cabinet I've secreted two bottles; the dark brandy's for forgetting, the clear spirit to remember why you drink. I don't go back to the others. They can wait there until the cows come home. I pop the bottles in my pocket, climb over the fence and come out on the other side. I go down to Coch's Hostel. They have a free room; number 502 on the top floor – Dad's old room. I'm handed the key and I chase up the stairs. The curtains are drawn. The bulb crackles when I put on the main light. 'Fred!' I shout. 'Fred! I know you're here!' There's utter silence, barring that crackling sound, as if the light's on the verge of giving up the ghost. I shout his name again.

'Fred! Come on out, you coward! I know you're here!' I overturn a chair. I open a cupboard and hear the jangling of clothes hangers as they spill out over me. I shriek. 'You bastard! You can run but you can't bloody well hide!' Someone out in the corridor asks me to keep my voice down. I lock the door and begin drinking.

The Viking

It's the love of your life. Get a little and you want more.
When you've had more you have to have a lot. And then
you have to have the rest. There's no halfway house. It's
all or nothing. You have mistresses all over town – in left
luggage containers at the East End station, in a suitcase
in the basement storage room, in an office drawer, behind
Hamsun's collected works, in the cistern and the ventila-
tion shaft, in the rubbish chute, the bread bin and the
gutter, under the bed, in the dormant kiosk, the letter box
and your inner pocket – they are yours. And this great
romance begins so beautifully, with a kiss – no, not even
a kiss, just an encounter that doesn't need to be more
than the scent or the touch of her. And you remember
falling in love for the first time in childhood – the sweet
scent of Malaga – which you breathed deep and with
which you loaded your dreams. Because this is all that's
required – this is the beginning and in the beginning God
said *Let there be dark*. You find yourself a glass (because of
course that's what you'll use – you want to show you've
some style and the best of intentions). You'll have a
drink; no, not a drink, just a small one, a nip, as some
tend to say, or a straightforward glass – the neutral name –
a glass (so simple and easy). You'll enjoy having one glass
and so you've gone and found yourself a glass. It's self-
evident. And as you unscrew the top of the bottle and the
rank smell of vodka, gin or whisky hits you (whichever
drink does the trick), and unfolds like some shining bouquet – you're almost happy. You stand on the edge of happiness, the bouquet in your hand; and this is perhaps the
finest moment, for you can still wrap these flowers up
again. But you're only going to have that one nip, that
stalk – or call it a rose from your lover – a silent invitation.
And you carefully pour a measure into your glass, quickly

put the top back on the bottle and replace it in the cupboard or up on the top shelf, as far away as possible.
Because you aren't having any more, you only need the
one nip – and you believe in yourself when you take that
glass with you into another room or out onto a balcony to
sit down. You hold the bouquet in your hands. You still
haven't drunk a drop. But then you aren't going to drink
a drop. You're just going to nip. Every drop will be cher-
ished. You're going to make this last. You're just going to
get its scent. And slowly you lift the flower towards your
mouth, your dry mouth, and it's this flower that's going
to water you.

Two days later you wake somewhere else. You think
you've dreamed it all, but it happened. The flowers have
withered. You're thirstier than ever. You want to be loved
but you've been abandoned. You are the empty vase. You
raise your arm. Your hand is full of blood. You don't know
which bed you're in. The room round you's black. You try
to think. You can't manage. That makes no odds. The
darkness looms nearer. If you don't move, then you can
put off this angst. But it'll soon be there, because this
angst is the one thing you can depend on now – you have
your freedom for just a few more seconds. Then you hear
something. It's the sound of a windmill, spinning – a
wheel close to your face going faster and faster. You hear
an accident close by, a scream – a braking and a great
silence. And you know then – it's me who's lying there,
in Room 502 of Coch's Hostel. Someone's talking outside
the door. The door's locked. Someone opens it. 'Fred?' I
whisper. 'Is that you?' Someone closes the door and
opens the curtains. Peder looks down at me. 'My God,' he
says. Hastily he closes the curtains again and chucks the
empties and the shards of glass in the bin. He undresses
me and he washes me. I have a cut in the thumb of my
right hand. He cleans the wound and puts a plaster on it.
He has fresh clothes with him too. The fat one takes care
of the little one. He opens the window to air the place.
There's snow on the sill. I'm shivering. Then he sloshes

some cola and cough mixture into a beaker, crushes up a pill, and gives the whole thing a stir with his finger. I drink it. 'I'm one of the night men,' I breathe. Peder's standing facing away. 'Night men?' 'The family's full of them, Peder. Men who disappear.' 'You're not completely gone yet, Barnum. As far as I can see.' 'I'm well on the way,' I reply. 'Where to?' Peder wanted to know. 'Down. Away. Out. It's one and the same thing.' Peder turns round. 'And what if I were to tell you that there's someone who wants you to stay?' I look down. 'How did you find me?' I ask, my voice low. Peder sits down on the bed. 'I always find you, Barnum. Haven't you got that into your head yet?' I rest my forehead against his shoulder. 'Perhaps I don't want to be found,' I breathe. 'I'll find you just the same,' he says. 'I'm your friend. That's the way it is.' We sit there like that for a bit in silence. I want to cry but can't. I try to laugh instead. 'Don't I have any choice?' I breathe. Peder shakes his head, as grave as he was before. 'Vivian's worried,' he says. I look up at him. 'Are you the father?' I ask him. It happens so very quickly. Peder hits me right in the face. I tumble backwards on the bed. He sits over me and thumps me. 'Didn't you hear what I told you?' he shrieks. 'I'm your friend, you bloody drunk!' I have to hold him. I don't feel the blows. He thrashes his arms about him like a child with a tantrum. At last I manage to laugh. Peder falls still once more. 'You're welcome to hit me again,' I groan. 'Shut up,' he says. I take his hand. It's shaking. We lie on our backs in that worn, sloping double bed, staring up at the ceiling. There's a huge hook in the middle of it, and the paint round about is peeling and hanging in great flakes. 'Dad used to stay in this room,' I tell him. 'Was he a night man too?' 'Dad was the worst night man of the lot of us,' I murmur. Peder's silent a while longer. He's the one holding my hand now. 'Maybe the doctor who examined you made some mistake, Barnum?' 'Dr Greve never makes mistakes,' I reply. 'And you still haven't told Vivian?' I shut my eyes. It's the lies that keep rolling – these black wheels that are impossible to stop. 'D'you have anything to drink?' I ask him. 'You're cutting away your life and alcohol's the scissors,' Peder says. 'Could you please stop talking like me?' Peder finally smiles, lets go of my hand and gets up. 'Come on,' he says. 'Where are we going?' 'Out, Barnum.'

We go down to the reception area. Peder pays for two nights' accommodation, cleaning costs and complaints, but it's me the woman with the keys looks at the entire time – her mouth's a tight-drawn ring. 'I don't want you here again,' she says. Peder chucks an extra fifty kroner note on the counter, leans forward and whispers, 'He's not coming back'. And we run out over the crossroads where the Old One was knocked down and killed on 21 September 1957; we run through the snow which is starting to fall across our faces. And the moment is unchanged, for it's here the picture was taken; when I turn round I see Fred sitting restless in the gutter, comb in hand, as if to brush back time. The Old One's lying on the cobbles in a pool of blood; the driver clambers from his truck and people stream forward with silent screams before the snow covers everything once more. We've already sat down in the innermost section of Lorry's, and the waiter appears at our table. Peder orders two hamburgers with fried eggs, coffee, milk and biscuits. I ask for a pint and a Fernet Branca. Peder looks at me once the waiter's gone. He looks at me a long time. 'We're underway with the repairs,' he finally says. 'Is something broken?' I ask him. 'You are,' Peder says. The waiter comes back with my drinks. I lift the pint glass with both hands. This isn't a lover, it's an old whore who cackles at you as you pick off the petals on the only flower in the bouquet – *she loves you, she loves you not, she loves you . . .* The smaller glass just has medicine in it. 'You remember what I promised Miss Coch?' Peder says. I light a cigarette. 'Miss Coch?' 'That you'd never go back there, Barnum.' 'I hope you manage to keep your promise,' I tell him. The waiter sets the food on the table. I'm not

hungry. But I eat. I have to go to the toilet to get rid of it
again. Peder waits. He's put a stack of papers and books
beside his empty plate. I sit down. 'Ready now?' he asks.
I nod. 'Ready for what?' Peder smiles and leans towards
me. 'The Americans invented the Western, the Japanese
made the samurai films – Easterns, right – and the Italians
gave us Spaghetti. What's left for us, huh?' Peder answers
his own question before I can open my mouth. 'The
Northern, Barnum.' 'The Northern?' The waiter comes
and clears the plates away. He puts down a pint for me
without my having ordered it. Peder pushes the pile of
books in my direction. 'I did as you asked me,' he says.
'What did I ask you? For a pint?' 'I've done my reading,
Barnum. I've read the sagas. Everything we need we can
pinch from them. They're just lying there waiting to be
used. Action, drama, strong characters, love, death – you
name it. D'you need any more?' 'I don't do adaptations,'
I reply. Peder looks at me as I drink. 'You can use Odark's
words as voice-over,' he says. I keep my mouth shut.
Peder grows impatient. He lays his hand on my shoulder.
'This is our big chance,' he breathes. 'If you don't make a
mess of it, Barnum.' I shake free of his hand. 'And what
have you thought of calling this thing?' I ask. 'I'm selling
it under the title of *The Viking, A Northern*.' It's my turn to
look at him for a long while. 'Selling?' 'What I can say is
that there's incredible interest being shown in the project
by officialdom and the business community. There are
partnership companies queuing up.' I feel incensed and
thump the table. 'You could maybe have talked to me
first,' I tell him loudly. 'Before you went off to scrabble for
mammon.' People at other tables begin turning their
heads. Peder sighs. 'You haven't exactly been available
recently, Barnum.' He fishes an envelope from his pocket
and lays it down between us. 'What's that?' I enquire.
'The one who opens it will see,' Peder replies. I slowly
drink my beer. Then I open the envelope. There's a
cheque inside. There are several noughts after the
number. I can hear Peder smiling. 'Are you onboard then,

Barnum?' 'Perhaps. Perhaps not,' I reply. I raise my arm and order a bottle of red. There's weariness in Peder's expression. His eyes have a troubled look. 'Off again?' he asks. 'Call it research,' I reply. Peder gets to his feet. 'You've twelve hours to make up your mind, Barnum. And this time I won't find you.' The waiter puts the wine in front of me. 'Look after Vivian in the meantime,' I tell him. Peder bends down. 'You're pathetic,' he breathes. 'I can't be bothered playing games with you any more.' And he goes without once turning round. I hide in the red bouquet. Then I notice Peder's left behind some of his books. There's Njal's Saga, Egil's Saga, and the Saga of Ramnkjell Frøysgode and the King's Mirror. I leaf through the last of these. And I come to the chapter where the sun asks the father about Greenland. And the wise father answers, *Greenland lies to the north, on the world's edge, and it's my belief that there's no other land beyond, but that all that rings it is the mighty ocean. When conditions are bad there, it's often with greater intensity than anywhere else – the wind sharper, the frost and snow more severe. For the glaciers are such that they send out a terrible cold. And there can be great rends in the glaciers of that land. Those who have been on Greenland bear witness to the fact that the cold has an intense power. And both land and sea bear witness themselves to the omnipotence of frost and cold, for the ice remains in summer and winter – both land and sea are covered in ice.* The waiter's standing beside my chair. He's clearing the tables. I show him the cheque and tell him I'll pay the following day. He nods and lets me out. The snow's glimmering. There are barely any tracks in it. I walk down to the office. Another letter has died a death. We are Brum & Miil. Peder's sitting in the back premises. I reckon he's asleep. His face is all folded up like an accordion. In one hand he has a napkin for a hot dog, and there's mustard on his white shirt. I get out the bottle I have hidden in the bottom drawer and pour us a glass each. 'I'll play with you,' I tell him. Peder comes to in his slow and laboured way, one eye at a time, while the double chins and the furrows slide into place. 'I thought you were dead,' he breathes. 'Only skin-dead, damn it.' I sit down on the sofa and balance the glass on my chest. My heart's beating. Peder just smiles. 'What d'you want to play?' he asks. 'Viking. I'm onboard.' I drain my glass. I'm alive. Peder chucks the serviette in the wastepaper basket and changes his shirt. Just buttoning it up leaves him out of breath. He's got himself a new toy too – a fax machine. Paper slides out of it. Peder tears out the sheet that appears. It's as though he's standing there with the Dead Sea scrolls. He gives the table a thump. 'Black Ridge in Hollywood are interested already.' 'Good stuff,' I tell him. A deep furrow appears at the top of his brow. 'And we need a treatment ready by Christmas, Barnum. Can you manage that?' 'To hell with a treatment,' I tell him. 'I'll begin on the script.' Peder smiles from ear to ear. 'What persuaded you?' 'What does it matter,' I say. Peder shrugs. 'I'm just curious, Barnum.' 'I liked the father telling the son what the world's like,' I answer quietly. Peder comes over to where I'm sitting. He draws his hand over my cheek. It's a long time since he did anything like that. 'Go home to Vivian now,' he murmurs. 'All right,' I reply. 'Make her laugh again, Barnum.' I look at him. 'How?' 'Maybe by telling her the truth?' he says. 'The truth?' I repeat. Peder turns away. 'That you can't have children.'

By the time I get home Vivian's up. I hear her in the shower. She's humming something, a hymn I can't recall. I knock on the door. 'There's something I have to tell you,' I say loudly. There's silence from within. I sit down on the bed and wait. Her black dress is hanging over the last seat, number 18 – my seat. The light outside is wet and heavy. Vivian stands in front of me. She's dripping. She's naked. 'Why did you say what you did in church?' she asks me. 'That I was pregnant?' I look down. 'I wanted to make Mum happy,' I whisper. Quickly she runs her hand through my curls and tugs at them gently. 'I've been worried about you, Barnum.' And those words, this action – her hand through my hair – leave me submissive and bewildered; it's as if everything comes together in that single moment, in one drop, heavy as a cliff, that soon will break and fall away. But she doesn't ask where I've been. It's like a kind of pact between us; we don't want to know any more about each other. Perhaps Peder's already phoned to say he found me in Room 502 of Coch's Hostel. I kiss her hips. Her skin is sharp and soft against my lips; there's another scent there, strange and exciting. She tears herself away, goes over to the window and holds the black dress in front of her. 'The removal firm are picking up everything else today,' she says. I look past her. 'Have you sorted out the stuff in the basement?' 'It can all go,' Vivian replies. 'Everything? Are you sure?' 'Is there anything you want down there?' she asks. I shrug my shoulders. 'Perhaps I'll go back to my platform shoes,' I tell her. Vivian laughs. I did it. I got Vivian to laugh after all. 'Give them to the props department at Norwegian Film,' she suggests. 'Peder and I have something big cooking,' I tell her. 'Really big.' Vivian smiles cautiously. 'And what's that?' she inquires. 'A Viking film, Vivian. We're going to go berserk.' I show her the cheque and point to all the noughts. 'What was it you wanted to say to me?' she asks. And when she stands like that, in the heavy light from the window, I see that her body changes – I see it, from one second to the next, that she's someone else all the time and never the same. I get up. 'I just wanted to say that I'm not moving.' Vivian comes a step closer and stops there, right between the window and the bed. She doesn't protest; she doesn't get down on her knees and beg. There's rather a sad relief in her eyes, and perhaps she sees something comparable in my own expression, a tired melancholy. 'Have you thought of living here?' she murmurs. 'If that's all right with you?' Vivian nods. 'Sure, Barnum.' She gets dressed. It's a completely ordinary morning. I go out onto the balcony and light a cigarette. I'm both awake and tired at one and the same time. If I were to lie down now I could sleep for seven years. If I managed to stay on my feet, I need never sleep again. I have a swig of the hip flask, whose contents have got nice and cold in the snow in the window box, and go back in to find Vivian. 'What'll we do with the plate?' I ask her. At first she doesn't get what I mean. That wounds me. I take a step towards her – maybe I stamp hard on the floor – and she backs off. 'Please, Barnum.' Her voice is suddenly quiet and fearful. I stop, utterly taken aback. I start laughing. 'Our nameplate, Vivian. On the door. What'll we do with it?' She turns away. 'Can't it just stay there,' she murmurs. 'Stay there? Vivian and Barnum? It's a lie, isn't it? Or have you considered coming back, perhaps?' She looks at me, no longer afraid now but just impatient – no one stays afraid of me for any length of time. 'Do whatever you want with it,' she says. 'Yes, I'll hack the thing in two,' I shout. Then the bell rings. It's the removal men – a young guy who starts lifting the first thing he claps eyes on, and an older man who slowly goes through the room measuring its dimensions. He has a sad, cold look about him, as if he's seen this all too often in the past. Vivian shows him what can be taken. The bed, the desk and the chair are left where they are. The fridge and stove are fixed units in the kitchen. The flowers out on the balcony have frozen solid. And I think to myself as they carry the final boxes down to the van, that it was the signmaker in Pilestredet who married us and the removal firm from Adamstuen who separated us. Vivian takes my hand. 'I'm leaving the ring behind,' she says. I have to hold my breath. 'That was a gift.' 'I know.' 'Don't offend me any more than you have.' Vivian drops my hand. 'We can sort the rest out later,' she breathes. I nod. 'Yes, of course. We can sort the rest out later.' And her parting words, before she hurries off after the removal men to Church Road, are odd. 'It's not just your fault, Barnum,' she says. I stand there listening to her steps on the stairs. Soon I can't hear them any longer. The accident and the small one are living apart. But there are still times I wake up and think she'll come back. I find a knife in the kitchen drawer and break off the copper nameplate – the black letters of VIVIAN AND BARNUM. It's well and truly fixed in place and the door is left with some ugly marks. My neighbour's standing right behind me. I get the smell of her rubbish. 'Has she left you then?' she says. I turn round. She's beginning to take on the appearance of the rubbish she always has in a plastic bag; one day she'll maybe get mixed-up and squeeze herself into the chute and descend into the stinking darkness. 'She's just gone on holiday,' I say. The woman smiles and a wave of bad breath flows from her; it's as though her mouth is full of fish guts and old chicken wings. She whispers now, as if she's frightened of revealing a secret. 'She's taken her name from the mailbox too.' I have to take a step backwards. She's more hideous than Miss Donkey Head, proclaimed the world's ugliest woman in Connecticut in 1911. She could have entered a new competition and won hands down. Mundus lost out on a real winner. She laughs at me, right in my face. And all of a sudden I do something she never expected. I begin crying. She puts her hand on my shoulder, bewildered, and suddenly becomes humane and almost beautiful in all her ghastliness – and she says exactly what Vivian said, mysteriously and quietly, as a comfort perhaps, even though it sounds more like a threat: 'It's not just your fault.' I shove her aside, fling the nameplate into the rubbish chute and slam the bare door behind me. No one lives here and there's enough room. I go and get all the bottles I've hidden away and place them on the table, pull the curtains and put a sheet of paper into the machine. The first word that comes to me is this – *revenge*. I devise a plot – my bloody triple jump – an idyllic state, death and resurrection. A son comes back to avenge his family. One morning the phone rings. It's Mum. She first wants to know how I am. 'Busy,' I tell her. 'But not too busy to have Sunday dinner with us?' she asks. It's Sunday. I can hear that by the church bells. I put down the receiver and unplug the phone. I've come to the first turning point, the plank. I'm going at a good speed. The avenger has found his foe. The avenger is waiting for the right moment. I write – *the one eye doesn't see the other*. I've sixty pages left. I take a bottle of vodka with me into the shower. Then I find myself a white shirt in the clothes-basket. It blinds me, as the snow does too, when I walk over to Church Road. I need a pair of sunglasses. Mum's gone even greyer. We sit down at the table. Boletta's sullen and seething; smouldering with an inner rage. She can barely bring herself to pour me a glass of wine and she puts the bottle as far from me as possible. The table's set for four. 'Someone else coming?' I enquire. 'Vivian wasn't feeling well,' Mum replies. She passes me the serving dish. I've no appetite. I go over in my mind the scene I'm going to write; the enraged mother who humiliates her coward of a son by serving him raw meat on the day his brother is killed. I drink my wine instead. 'It'll be an awful burden for her, living up there,' I murmur. Boletta takes the bottle from me. 'Especially when there's no man in the house,' she says. Then Vivian shows up just the same. She's wearing an expansive, faded tracksuit. The hair that falls from her brow's thin and greasy. She has no appetite either. And it's as though I can hear an echo deep down; it's the oval clock in the hall that's begun to go again and the coins clink in the drawer, when I see them thus – Mum, Boletta and the pregnant Vivian round the living-room table – and now I'm the one visiting the house with only women within its walls. Silence has gone in a circle and made a black scarf of time. I have to search for something to say. 'What's happening about the kiosk?' I ask. Mum puts more meat on my plate. 'It isn't worth running a kiosk like that any longer,' she replies. 'Why not?' She attempts a smile. 'Well, it's only an entryway, Barnum.' I push my food to one side and reach out for the bottle. But Boletta pours the last of the wine into her own glass. I light a cigarette. 'I thought it was somewhat more than just a doorway.' Mum shakes her head. 'Even the beauty salon's shut down. Right, Vivian?' Vivian nods. Her facial skin is all shiny and greasy. 'There's a hairdresser for dogs there instead,' she says. 'Four paws instead of two.' I'm tempted to laugh but don't dare; it would be like dirtying the tablecloth, deliberately spilling laughter over the white cloth. 'Coffee,' I say loudly. Mum sighs. 'Coffee? But you haven't eaten anything, Barnum.' Now I can laugh. Now there's a place for laughter. 'I mean coffee in the kiosk, Mum. To sell coffee there, in a cup with a lid and a straw and everything.' Boletta gets up and leaves the table without a word. She shuts the door behind her with a bang. 'What's up with her?' I ask quietly. 'Perhaps she doesn't like your smoking,' Mum says. Vivian looks at me. 'Or your drinking.' I should never have broken that silence. I push back my chair and flick the cigarette end into the stove. The photograph's still up on the wall – the electric Barnum, the little genius – taken in the City Chambers that day I got my prize for *The Little City*. I turn to look at Mum. 'There's one thing I think's strange,' I say. 'What's that, Barnum?' 'That Fred's worn that jacket all those years.' Mum becomes awkward – her voice is cramped, cut short – there's barely room for all the words in it. 'You know he was fond of that suede jacket,' she murmurs. Vivian's got to her feet. 'Will you come up with me to see the place?' she asks. I excuse myself and go after her. She has to rest on each landing. She's carrying a heavy burden. And I see Mum in my mind's eye when she carried the clothes-basket from the basement right up to the drying loft; that woven basket full of wet clothes, her fingers numb, the ache in her hips spreading over her back, the net full of wooden pegs. Perhaps she had to rest herself as she silently counted the number of steps that were left and dreamed of something else entirely. Vivian turns round; she breathes through her mouth and her lips are swollen and dry. 'They'll be building a lift, of course, on the outside of the building,' she says. 'From the yard.' At last we're there. VIVIAN WIE – the name's on the door – a simple, grey plate with black lettering, and she lets me in. I stop under the angled ceiling window. The snow melts as soon as it touches the glass. The light runs off and pulls the darkness with it. And then I see, in the corner by the whitewashed chimney breast – the old pram, the playpen, a pile of baby clothes that Fred and I had, and the worn cradle that's been got out too and made ready – all these old things waiting now for a new person. I look over towards the kitchen instead; she's forgotten to put the milk in the fridge. 'What d'you think?' Vivian asks. I walk away from the window. 'D'you feel it swaying?' 'What was that?' 'It's swaying,' I say again. She stands there with a worried look, perfectly still, holding her hands over her stomach. 'It's not swaying, Barnum.' 'You'll notice it soon,' I assure her. All of a sudden she becomes exasperated. 'It isn't swaying!' she exclaims. I go nearer her. 'That's why the clothes became so fine and dry up here, Vivian.' She's almost in tears. 'Why?' 'Because of the swaying.' She goes off into the bathroom. I put the milk in the fridge and find myself a beer. The old baby clothes feel soft to the touch – a pair of pyjamas, leggings, a vest – in those days I still took normal sizes and wore Fred's old things. I never knew Mum had kept all this. And when I bend down over the pram where the leather pouch is lying with its thick, white lining, I suddenly feel a touch of cold along the edge of my mouth – just like when Mum used to put camphor oil on my lips. Yet the realization doesn't affect me; I'm detached – and it's perhaps this which frightens me most of all, that I feel nothing, I'm dead. Vivian's baby'll be born in the winter too, in the coldest month of the year, with the beautiful clouds of frost billowing in from the fiord. I hear her breathing. She must have stood there a good while looking at me, from the doorway to what will be the baby's room. I look away, for a moment dizzy and embarrassed all the same. 'How's it going with the Viking?' she asks. 'I think I've hit the plank.' Vivian smiles. 'Peder says it's going to be fine.' I turn slowly towards her. 'What about you? Didn't you get a job in the dog shop?' She wipes the smile away with the back of her hand. 'I've got a job in make-up at NRK from the new year.' 'Who'll look after the kid?' 'Vera and Boletta,' Vivian replies. And at that moment we're blinded by a bright flash; at first I imagine it must have been lightning, but the flash comes from somewhere else rather than the ceiling window. It's Mum. She's standing there in the entrance holding the old camera, and she blinds us a second time as we each look our separate ways. I don't have time to stop her. 'D'you remember this camera, Barnum?' I shake my head. Mum laughs. 'Once upon a time I dreamed of becoming a photographer,' she says. 'Why didn't you then?' I ask, and at once regret the question. Mum looks up at the window. 'So much else got in the way.' 'But it isn't too late,' I say. She raises the camera again. I have to hold onto her and I only barely manage to. She shakes and suddenly begins crying. And shouldn't I have realized that there was something Mum couldn't bear, something more, a weight that was greater than I was able to perceive and which she could no longer carry on her own? I was detached. Is this what I call the slow shutter of memory? Mum takes hold of both my hands. 'I so much regret not having taken pictures in the church, Barnum.' 'We'll remember it just the same,' I tell her. I look at Vivian. 'Would you take the pram down for me?' she asks. I do so willingly. Mum stays with Vivian. Vivian stays with Mum. And as I go past the flat Boletta comes out with her fur round her and her stick. 'I need some air,' she says. I stand the pram under the mailboxes and Boletta, who walks in front of me, doesn't say any more before she's at the top of Blåsen. Then she says, 'I can't be bothered going any further with you, you fool.' I brush the snow from the bench and we sit down. We just remain there like that a good while, not knowing what to say. The dusk makes everything flow into one; a rusty darkness framed by snow. 'Why aren't you living with Vivian?' Boletta asks. I dry my hands on my trousers. 'It's best that way,' I reply. Boletta searches for something in her coat. She finds it. She hands me a flat hip flask and when I unscrew the awkward top I get the powerful whiff of my first love, the one I was only able to smell and run my lips around – Malaga. And my whole childhood enfolds me like the snow – I'm no longer detached and I'm moved. I have a gulp of it and give the hip flask back to Boletta who takes a careful sip. 'This is the last Malaga in the city,' she whispers. 'Thank you, Boletta.' 'And you don't waste stuff like that.' 'Not Malaga,' I say. Boletta hides the hip flask in her coat again and leans on her stick. 'What the devil is it that's wrong with us?' she sighs. All at once I think of Fleming Brant when I see the windows going dark, the city sinking into another night under the snow and the skies. I want to say something about him, the cutter in the sand, but can't get the sentence together – the words are ranged against me and soon I'll be broken beyond repair. 'I can't have children,' I say. Boletta doesn't turn round. 'And so?' she demands. 'I can't have children,' I say again. 'And still you leave her?' 'It's she who's left me,' I murmur. Boletta gets up and thumps her stick into the snow. 'You're being petty.' I look up and can't get over it. Her face is just as in the days when she was afflicted and had to go to the North Pole to cool down. 'What was that you said, Boletta?' She points at me with the stick. 'I've never felt enraged at you, Barnum. But now I've more rage in me than's good for me.' I tried to smile. 'You were mad at me when I skipped dancing classes,' I remind her. Boletta sits down again, tired and resigned. 'Being mad isn't the same as being enraged, Barnum. Anger is nothing but a little dot in comparison to rage.' 'Then I'm enraged too,' I whisper. Boletta places her feeble hand on my own. 'And you shouldn't be,' she says. 'You should love Vivian and your child instead.' I look down. 'I can't.' Boletta withdraws her hand. 'Then you're only half a man, Barnum.' I feel enraged and that rage is real enough now; it's as if all the fury I've stored up since the constable picked me out in the Little City gathers in one great, trembling muscle. 'Do you dare repeat that, Boletta?' I demand. 'You won't be any the more whole if I do!' she says. I tear the stick from her grasp, break it in two and crash away down through the snow. 'I never want to see you again!' I shout. 'D'you hear me, you old bat!' and when I turn for the last time by the empty fountain, she's still sitting there on the bench at the top of Blåsen – a thin, hunched shadow in the ever thicker snow, and like that she's swallowed from sight.

I can't write that night. I plug in the telephone again. There's a further disquiet within me I can do nothing to prevent; a nerve of unhappiness. I drink up what's left and tidy my papers. I read through what I've written.

SEQUENCE 1. SEA. EVENING.

A ship with a dragon's head prow. There's no wind. The crew must row. The only sound that can be heard is the steady command before each new pull on the oars. The ship is like a shadow gliding past.

SEQUENCE 2. GRAN FARM. MORNING.

Vår, a pretty girl of nine, is amusing herself by making tracks in the snow. She's on her own. She moves further and further from the settlement towards the edge of the forest.

She drops something in the snow and stops to retrieve it; it's part of a necklace, one half of a star-shaped amulet. As she bends down she discovers something else – other footprints in the new snow. They're much bigger than her own. They disappear into the forest beside her.

Vår remains crouched there, looking towards the settlement and looking towards the forest. Carefully she puts the amulet round her neck.

Her mother appears from the main building and waves to her daughter.

Vår doesn't dare wave back. Her mother stands there looking at her. She waves again. Vår hears a sound from the edge of the forest. The breaking of a twig. A sword being drawn.

The stillness is violently broken – a dozen armed men ride out of the forest.

SEQUENCE 3. EXT. SHIP. MORNING.

The ship is nearing land. The sails are hoisted now. Everyone is working feverishly to ready the cargo, except for one man. He's lying at the back of the vessel sleeping. His face is hidden by a hood. But round his neck we can see one half of a star-shaped amulet, the same as Vår was wearing.

Three men put down a cage full of birds close by. They look at the sleeping man, then at one another, and nod. One of them pads over, bends down and cautiously reaches out for the adornment to try to work it free. Then an arm seizes his own in a vice-like grip. The 'sleeping' man holds him thus in this agonizingly strong grasp. The thief sinks to his knees. Now we see the man's face. He's twenty-five years of age, haggard. His name is Ulf.

Ulf lets the thief go, gets up and looks out towards the land.

VOICE-OVER: Seven winters have passed since he first set sail, from the forests to the seas, from the land to the wind. That first winter he was missed. The second passed without any word of his whereabouts. In the course of the fourth he was seen in three countries at the same time. By the seventh winter he was forgotten. He came home like a refugee and he came too late.

The phone rings. I haven't the guts to pick it up. I have to get finished first. That's what it all comes down to – getting finished. The ringing doesn't stop. I unplug the phone yet again. The paper boy races down the steps. I can hear my neighbour quickly retrieving her copy of *Aftenposten* from the doormat. And an even greater and more profound anxiety gnaws at me. Maybe Boletta wasn't able to stand the cold. I go over to Blåsen. My tracks are uneven in the snow. The bench is empty.

There's no one there. I'm done with this place. I have to get all of these places out of my system if I'm to move on; I have to find somewhere else, somewhere that's my own, and I still don't know where that is. I go off to the 'pole'. The guy serving looks at me long and hard but doesn't demand identification. I take a taxi home with what I've bought and go on writing *The Viking*. The run-up's done. I'm onto the jump. And I can't get Fred's suede jacket out of my head. It disturbs me. I have to free my mind of it too. I'm a tailor with a typewriter who re-works this garment to a blue leather hood – and this I give to my hero. I secrete it in what he's carrying and by the mid-point of the tale I have him clad in this shimmering hood which, from far away, shines like some dark flame. And later I let him pass the hood on to a treacherous serf who, because of a misunderstanding, loses his life – and as a result causes the enemy to believe that the hero, the son who's come home, is dead. One morning (or evening perhaps; I've been asleep at any rate and it's dark outside), I can see that Christmas trees are being lit over in Sten Park beside the kindergarten. I can just make out the sound of children singing. The good old songs. I sit down at the desk and read through the last of what I've written. And it's only then I realize I'm finished. A gentle voice-over rounds it off as a ship sets sail once more and the wind of an eighth winter begins to blow. I feel a kind of gladness, and it amazes me that a few words I've stolen and re-ordered into a triple jump could make me so happy. Or maybe it's the children singing at the foot of Blåsen. It hurts and I feel happy.

Later on I walk through the Christmas streets to find Peder. He's mended the sign. All our letters are shining again. He's sitting between two phones and turns round a quarter of an hour after I come in. He shades his eyes. 'You look absolutely hellish,' he tells me. 'You're an awfully superficial individual, Peder.' He just shakes his head at me. 'Can I tell you something, Barnum?' 'Be my guest.' 'I couldn't give a damn if you drink yourself to death as long as you finish *The Viking* before you do.' 'Thank you for your thoughtfulness, Peder. You're too kind.' 'Nothing to thank me for. But can you just tell me one small thing?' 'What's that, Peder?' 'Are you absolutely sure you're not dead? And I don't mean skin-dead. I mean really dead, as in coffin and candles dead?' 'I'm not dead, Peder.' He picks up a handkerchief and holds it under his nose. 'Are you aware just how long the moment of death can last? Whole weeks, Barnum. Years.' 'I'm alive,' I murmur. 'And how the hell can you be so sure?' he demands. 'Because I'm thirsty,' I reply. One of the phones starts ringing and an American voice immediately begins speaking on the answering machine – the voice speaks quickly, loudly and briefly. I just catch some of the words – Christmas Day, New Year, Vikings and dollars. Peder looks at me, his face tired and sinking into its double chins. 'That was our man in LA, Barnum. He wants to know how things are going. But how can I know how things are going when you don't tell me how things are going?' Peder gets up heavily, opens the cupboard and changes his shirt. 'What d'you want for Christmas?' I ask him. Peder's quiet for a moment. Then he sits down again. 'I'd like a script and a good friend,' he says softly. I take the parcel from my jacket and put it down in front of him. Peder gives the fat envelope I've secured with a red band a long, hard stare. *To Peder from Barnum*. 'What the hell is this? A letter bomb? Your will?' 'The one who opens it will see,' I tell him. He's suspicious and grumpy. 'You're not playing games with me, are you?' 'Barnum never plays games,' I reply. And finally Peder pulls out 102 pages comprising *The Viking, A Northern* – an original filmscript by Barnum Nilsen. 'Now I've everything I wanted in one,' he breathes. 'Yes, a good script and a bad friend.' Peder gets up and puts his arms round me. 'I love you, Barnum.' 'Don't get all American,' I tell him. 'Deep inside we're all American,' he laughs, and kisses me on the brow. And we stand like that holding each other and holding the moment, until his fresh shirt is wet too.

'What now?' I enquire. Peder lets go of me. 'Now you're going to go home and rest a bit, Barnum. And I can do some work.' 'And that means?' 'It means I'll read, translate and fax the script to Black Ridge in Los Angeles,' Peder says. He sits down by the phone once more. I keep standing where I am looking at him. Peder's into his stride now. It's good to see him like this. We're on our way. After a bit he becomes anxious. He looks up. 'Did you say you were thirsty?' he asks. 'I meant happy,' I tell him. And so I leave him and start off home. But I go a really roundabout way. I just want to be rid of all the other places too. I have to tidy up. I give the tree in Solli Square a last pat, and the hard bark scratches my palms; I hear the music from the dancing school's record player go quiet in the dust in the innermost grooves of childhood, and the steps on the parquet floor fly to the four winds. I sit at the corner of Palace Park and Wergeland Road and hold a one-minute silence for the Old One, and when I close my eyes I can see the shadow of Fred finally rising from the gutter, putting the shining comb in his back pocket and going on with her to the Palace. I put the place behind me. I go on over to the summer house in Frogner Park. It isn't white any longer. The frail walls are all daubed with graffiti. Someone has written *I was here*. That's always true. The person who writes *I am here* is right only for the time it takes to write the words. I spit in the snow and hurry on. I get the last bottle from the kiosk; I've hidden it away under the loose floorboard, and this place is now forgotten just as it fled Esther's memory long ago to become a dream composed of sugar candy and loose change. Then I run over to the Little City which is nothing more than a small ruin lying in grey and heavy sleet. The Little City's gone already and I bury it for good. I wipe it off the globe. Then I go up to Vivian's. I ring the bell. It's Mum who opens the door. She lets a bag fall to the floor and looks at me in amazement, just as I look at her with equal surprise. 'Vivian's at the hospital,' she says. I try to appear calm. I'm quite composed and there's nothing to get worked up about. 'Already?' 'They just want to be on the safe side.' 'The safe side? There's nothing wrong?' Mum lets me in. She fills the bag with toiletries and puts in some of Vivian's clothes. I go after her. 'There's nothing wrong?' I repeat. 'Vivian's so slender,' Mum breathes. That's all she says. *Vivian's so slender*. And those words fill me with a sense of great and supple strength that make me think of a ladybird crawling along a gently bending stalk of grass. I put my hand on Mum's shoulder. 'It'll all be fine?' Mum zips up the bag and straightens up. 'You can come with me, Barnum.' I turn away and don't say anything. Mum stands there like that for a bit. 'Have you fallen out with Boletta?' she asks all at once. 'No, has she said so?' 'She hasn't said anything at all, Barnum. She just lies on the divan moping.' Mum takes the bag and goes over to the door. Her voice is brittle. 'I don't know what's happened between Vivian and you, nor do I want to know, Barnum.' I take a step towards her and raise my hand. 'No, you'd rather not know anything, wouldn't you?' I shout. She looks at me sharply and a shadow crosses her eyes. 'What d'you mean by that?' My hand falls, hangs from my fallen arm. 'Tell Vivian I'm here,' I murmur.

I push a chair under the ceiling window and sit down. The door slides shut. I count Mum's steps going down the steep staircase till I can hear them no longer, and then I open the bottle. I was right. It still sways. The brandy rocks from side to side like an interior wave. When I look up the dark window becomes a mirror in which my face trembles and dances. The snow falls and slides away without a sound. I drink slowly. It takes time to be rid of this place and I take the time required. This is my memorial service. I rehearse my forgetting and I'm the only one present. Three floors below Boletta lies moping on the divan. Somewhere else, close by, Mum's looking after Vivian. I forget the coffin Fred carried up here. I forget the war, the drying lines and the dead pigeon. Once or twice I hear church bells. And it's then I remember the fact (so simple and obvious) that there's just one thing here that's mine – the ring, the ring I bought and never got to give away but hid in the coke shaft: T for Tale, T for tongue-tied, T for time. I find a knife in the kitchen and begin working away at the whitewashed wall. I hack, I hit, I jab and I dig – I'll find that bloody ring. But it's impossible to get into the aperture; I hammer and I poke about and I get nowhere – there's just a shower of paint and dust, and it isn't the church bells I hear now, it's suddenly the telephone. I don't know where it is. It's in the bedroom and when finally I get to it the person's hung up. There's just a single bed there with the cradle in the corner. The place is swaying. I have to sit down and the moment I do the phone begins ringing again. Slowly I lift the receiver and as I do so I think to myself that now Boletta's at the switchboard in the Exchange connecting all the calls, and that it's me she's discovered amid the electric darkness of the lines. It's Mum. 'Vivian's had a boy,' she says.

His name's to be Thomas.

The ring remains in the wall, invisible to everyone but myself. Then I go home. There's a bottle of champagne on the table and a bouquet of twelve roses. On a card Peder's written *To the great little genius. Congratulations*. He's sitting out on the balcony, leafing through a script and smoking a cigar. When he sees me there he gets up, brushes the snow from his shirt and comes in. 'Did you break the door down?' I ask him. Peder smiles. 'I got the keys from Vivian.' I look down. 'Have you been at the hospital?' 'Fine boy,' Peder says. 'Screamed his head off.' We're both silent for a moment. Peder puts his hand on my shoulder. 'The Americans are over the moon, Barnum. They just love you.' I take the script from him. It's the American translation. Peder's suddenly all self-conscious and opens the champagne, fills the glasses. It's the last one I'll have for at least seven years. 'Who the hell is Bruce Grant?' I ask him. Peder shrugs his shoulders. 'Who are you on about?' I stab my finger at the front page. 'It says here *revision by Bruce Grant*,' I tell him. 'Oh, right, Bruce Grant,'

Peder says. 'He's the script doctor at Black Ridge. He's just embroidered this and that.' 'Embroidered?' 'Don't get bogged down by technicalities, Barnum.' I start reading. But Bruce Grant, the script doctor, hasn't just embroidered here and there. He's operated on my voice and my words. He's amputated my imagery. Peder pads back and forth restlessly. 'Pacino's almost a cert,' he says. 'Not impossible Bacall will come onboard herself. And Bente Synt wants an interview.' 'But this is abuse,' I exclaim. Peder lays a hand on my shoulder. 'Don't start putting on airs now, Barnum.' 'Putting on airs? Bruce Grant's ruined the entire thing. He's a bloody quack! The patient's dead!' I shake off Peder's hand. 'You know how it is,' he says. 'A writer for film ought not to be too good.' I take a step towards him. 'Was that an insult or a compliment?' 'I'm just trying to say that you're too good. The Americans need to be a bit more straight to the point. If you get my drift?' 'Straight to the point? Vikings shagging on fur rugs and crying in alternate scenes!' 'Feelings, Barnum.' 'One eye doesn't see the other!' I shout. 'He's even ripped that out as well!' 'You're too good,' Peder says again. I chuck the script at him and collapse on the sofa. 'Whose side are you on, Peder Miil?' He gives a deep sigh. 'I'm on our side, damn it!' I look up at him. 'Now I finally know who it is I'm dealing with,' I tell him. Peder puts the keys on the table between the flowers and the champagne. 'Maybe you should go and visit Vivian too,' he says. I can barely speak. 'Nothing's mine any more,' I whisper. 'Nothing.'

Later I go down to the basement again. This is the last place I have to get rid of. I have a torch with me and I watch the frail beam weakly circling the walls. There's a pile of stinking, wet clothes by the dryer and an empty bottle rolls over the floor. I kick it for all I'm worth and hear the shattering of glass in the darkness. The silent suitcase is right at the back in the corner. It's then I become aware of people, swift shadows; and before I can turn round I'm pinned up against the door as the torch drops from my hand and a warm queasiness fills my head and blood runs into my mouth. Then I'm dragged round and a far stronger light blinds my eyes. One of the officers searches my pockets. 'Looking for somewhere to sleep tonight?' he demands. 'I live here,' I whisper. 'Witty little midget,' the other one says. I go mad, break something, and feel only a profound sense of resignation when they pull me out to their car and drive off with me. The neighbour's on the stairs, her hands full of rubbish. And the stars are shining in every window except my own. It is Christmas after all. I start laughing. I fall down. They get me back onto my feet and take me down a corridor. Behind a metal grill I catch sight of Fleming Brant; I thought he was dead, yet it's like him all right. He stretches out one thin hand and holds a pair of gleaming scissors in his fingers, and it's the last time I ever see him – the cutter. 'Happy Birthday, my friend,' he whispers. I try to tear myself free. Resignation is replaced by fear. They remove my belt, my shoelaces, my watch and my comb. And the door slams with a boom that throws my head backwards. I sit in the corner of the padded cell, beside the hole in the floor, and like that disappear before my own eyes.

The Cormorant

An island appears like a full stop on the very edge of the ocean. I sit out on deck, wrapped in a blanket. I've been here before. This was where I got my name. But when I go ashore on Røst there's not a soul who knows who I am. I have my typewriter and an almanac with me. For a moment I stop and take a deep breath, but I feel nothing except the raw wind. I go up to the Fishermen's Mission. They have a room vacant. A dark girl at the reception asks how long I'll be staying. 'Long enough,' I tell her. She smiles and wants to know my name as well. 'Bruce Grant,' I say. 'Bruce Grant,' she repeats slowly, and looks up quickly before recording both name and date in a book. Finally I'm given my key. The room's up on the first floor. The bed's over by a window discoloured by salt. I don't sleep. I cross off yet another white day. The following evening I do the same. On the morning of the third day there's a knock at the door. It's the dark girl from down at the reception. She's brought me some breakfast – eggs, bread and jam. I ask her to get me a roll of adhesive tape. She brings me one that evening. She takes the tray and sees I haven't eaten a thing. I write *The Night Man*, Sequence 1, and tape the sheet to the wall.

I try to sleep.

I hear the birds in the darkness.

One wet day I go out. The rain comes straight at me, as if the skies have slipped sideways. I bend my head forwards and follow the road across the flat island between the fish-drying frames that resemble great fish gardens. But I can't smell them – there's nothing; my senses have fallen away, just as the wind rubs these outcrops with its great sheets of sandpaper until their dust sinks into the sea and is gone. I open the door to the graveyard and can't manage to close it again. A flagpole stands there like a hoop amid the squalls of rain. I have to crawl along in the lee of the stonewall, and finally I discover their names on a tall, black column surrounded by white sand from the sea – EVERT AND AURORA. The letters are all but buried under guano. I'm about to wipe it off but at the last minute leave it be. I suddenly remember what the vicar said at Dad's funeral, that the cormorant shits on the rocks to find its way home.

When I turn round the wind's just as strong, a salt storm full in my face. It's not shyness and modesty that makes everyone look down, it's just the wind. I come past a shed, a lop-sided boathouse, and all at once recognize something – a car under a tarpaulin with a bit of the windscreen visible. I look around. There's no one about. I go in and pull back a bit more of the tarpaulin. It's the Buick, Dad's old car – worn, rusty and filled with rain. I shut my eyes. Then I see someone there after all. A stooped man, with a high, white brow above a dark face, is leaning across a broken fridge, saying nothing as he brushes earth off his boiler suit. I let the tarpaulin fall back into place. 'Rare car in these parts,' I observe. 'A Roadmaster Cabriolet.' The man's still silent, but doesn't seem antagonistic. He just looks at me, in the same way that a good tailor measures someone with his eyes. 'How did you get hold of it?' I inquire. 'At one time there was a fellow who owed us brandy and a gravestone,' the man replies. I nod. 'But why don't you use it?' It's now he smiles. 'We do use it, when the Italians come here.'

I cross off more days on the almanac.

That's all I get written.

One evening I go down to the café, drink apple juice and look at some television along with a number of the other guests – permanent residents – who come here to have some cake or because of the dark girl. These are men who've come ashore and they look at me with gentle curiosity, friendly and silent, as I stare at the flickering, distorted images that have no accompanying sound. It's as if the aerial's in the middle of the waves, plugged in to the wind; and I think to myself that these familiar faces which flicker over the salty screen here in the Fishermen's Mission – the last hotel before the ocean – have just been given their make-up by Vivian. I get up quickly. 'What are you doing here, Bruce Grant?' the girl asks when I give her my glass and am on my way back up to my room once more. The others are listening, but not letting on that they are; their forks just pause for a second. 'I'm drying out,' I reply. 'I think you ought to eat a bit all the same,' she says. Soon I'll need a new almanac.

It's getting lighter.

One morning I take a different route than usual, not to the graveyard and round the stone wall, but over the knoll and along the shore to the small inlet behind the jetties. It's there I see the house. It isn't actually a house any longer, a dwelling place for human beings, but just ruins falling slowly to the ground and washing away like driftwood. The coffin door bangs in the wind. In the frail, golden grass there's the whitewashed skull of a sheep. It's then it happens. The wind suddenly takes hold of my jacket and billows it into a black sail that lifts me right off the ground. I struggle and do all I can to make myself heavy and unwieldy, but it's to no avail; I'm nothing more than a little midge in these gusts of wind that carry me through the air. I shout out and flail my arms wildly, until at last the wind sets me down gently once more beside the narrow path.

I go back straight away to the Mission, dazed and shaken. The dark girl's there behind the counter, a hint of amusement on her lips, and the same men look at each other as their expressive faces break into crooked smiles and one of them says, loudly, before the laughter erupts, 'Well, if it isn't the cormorant himself!'

I spread the dust of stories and let it flower in everyone's mouths as bouquets of the most beautiful lies.

One morning there's a knock at the door again. It's the dark girl. She glances quickly all round at the walls that'll soon be covered in sheets of paper. 'I'm not hungry,' I

assure her. She smiles. 'But there's a letter for you.' I can't
fathom this. She hands me an envelope. I recognize
Peder's writing. And the letter's travelled far – address
after address has been scored out. 'Thank you,' I murmur.
The girl doesn't move. 'Shall I put the name Barnum
Nilsen in the visitors' book instead?' I go nearer her. Her
eyes are brown. 'How did you know it was me?' 'It wasn't
all that hard.' 'Do I look like my name?' She laughs now.
'My Dad said there weren't all that many who could recognize a Buick like that under a tarpaulin.'

I put the letter on my bedside table and can't face reading it. I dream for the first time in a long while. I dream
about the suitcase. Someone's carrying it, but I can't
make out who. In the dream I can see only the person's
shoes and legs, and the hand holding it – the suitcase is
heavy.

The sun wakes me up suddenly. It's filling the entire
room. I get up. The letter's on the bedside table. I open it.
Peder's written: *My friend, I don't know where you are, but
perhaps you'll get this letter. D'you remember the card we found
from the world's tallest man that summer on Ildjernet? I have to
tell you that nothing came of* The Viking *after all. A new boss
started at the film company. I met him in LA. He'd been living at
Venice Beach since 1969 and the only thing he could say was –*
What about Vikings in outer space? *Something for you perhaps, Barnum?* I had to sit down on the bed until my laughter had subsided. I couldn't remember the last time I'd
laughed. Then I hear noise from outside – voices, shouts
and music. I go over to the window and it's only now I see
that someone's washed it – everything's clear and seems
suddenly close. I'm blinded by the world. It's the ferry
that's come in. Just about everyone from the islands must
have congregated here today. And it's as if I've seen it all
before and yet am witnessing it for the first time too. It's
the Italians, as purchasers, who're coming to harvest
Röst's dry gardens, its coastal grapevines. They're accompanied down the gangway and the yellow Buick materializes from the other direction, all sleek and shining and

with the hood down – it bumps silently along like a polished, wheeled carriage. The driver's wearing a uniform and has on a bright cap that covers his high, white brow. He stops the car at the gangway; the guests take their seats and slowly he drives off between wind and people.

Peder's closed the letter thus: *PS Greetings from Vivian. Thomas has spoken his first word. Guess what it was!*

Later that day I take a wander over to the lop-sided shack. The Buick's parked outside. The driver's down on his knees polishing the hubcaps so they'll shine once more like four mirrors. 'D'you know where my dad set up the windmill?' I ask him. He wipes the sweat from his brow, for a moment embarrassed. 'We shelled out for the party after the baptism, and we had to bring the gravestone all the way from Bodø,' he murmurs. I put my hand on the warm bonnet. 'Then you deserved this beast.' He looks at me smiling. 'Come with me,' he says.

We row across the sound to the resolute pile of rock. We sit side by side on the thwart. The oar slides about in my hands. The driver laughs. 'You're sculling backwards like Arnold did.' We get the boat on an even keel. 'What do you know about my father?' I ask him. He just keeps rowing for a time and doesn't say anything. I have to pull hard to match his rhythm, and soon enough have almost no strength left. 'Arnold chopped off one of his fingers when he was a boy,' he says. We near land, a narrow bay with a rough shore. 'Was he a good man?' I breathe. The driver, the ferryman, the only son of Elendius – leans sorrowfully on his oar. 'When Arnold returned to christen you his whole hand was gone,' he says softly. Finally we're there. He helps me ashore. 'Shall I come up with you to the top?' I shake my head. 'I can manage myself.' But he won't let me go yet and he places two heavy rocks in my jacket pockets. 'You mustn't blow away again,' he says. And so I climb up the same path that Dad descended as a wheel. I've no idea how long it takes. The light hangs still in a shimmer of white birds. When I reach the last bit of the climb and the grass levels out in an oval curve, I see

Dad's windmill. It resembles a crashed plane or a broken cross. I sit down. The sun is lying on the horizon and I can see that that sun is green. I roll my stones back down the steep slope and the rank stench of guano hits me. The wind tears at the remains of the construction so they emit a beautiful keening sound – a rusty song. And I know now – this is my place.

Next morning I head south. I take the ferry to Bodø, the plane to Oslo, and a taxi back to Bolteløkka. I have to air the place for three whole days. It's like after an extended summer holiday. New folk have moved into the neighbour's flat, a young couple. I don't meet Vivian. I still haven't seen Thomas. But Peder and I keep up our electric theatre. I wait behind the scenes in the shadows counting white days, working on *The Night Man* and submitting synopses and treatments, right until the day I'm sent a button in the post with two words – *Dad's button* – the same day we leave for the film festival in Berlin.

Tempelhof

It's Peder who's breathing down my neck. He it is who follows me into Tempelhof, this architectural structure fashioned by the Nazis; it's still early morning and I'm suffused with a heavy calm. I'm going home. I'm going home to Fred, because Fred's come back. I haven't seen him for twenty-eight years and sixty days. But he's possibly seen me. Perhaps he's seen us the whole time. Peder takes my hand. He's changed bookings, cancelled meetings, paid bills, taken phone calls and apologized to the vast majority of those I've been in the vicinity of. 'Sure you don't want me to come with you?' he asks. 'You're more needed here,' I tell him. He bustles round in front of me so I'm forced to stop. 'You knew he'd come back one day, didn't you?' 'What d'you mean?' Peder looks away. 'You knew he wasn't dead, Barnum.' We stand there in the empty hall. There's a smell of soap. The walls are swaying and about to fall. I have to hold onto something. I sit down on my suitcase. 'Perhaps. Perhaps not,' I breathe. An armed guard suddenly rushes out from the toilet area, his gun in its black holster, a baton in his tightly fastened belt. He pushes his cap into place as he momentarily scans the place, and his eye lingers a little longer on me. His hands are dripping. Then he proceeds over to the luggage carousel where someone's forgotten a blue umbrella bearing the festival logo. There's a smell of soap here. 'D'you think it's possible to be forgiven for something you haven't done yet?' I ask. Peder bends down closer, even more worried. 'You aren't planning something crazy, are you?' I start laughing. 'It's no laughing matter,' he says. 'I'm not laughing.' 'D'you need some pills?' he whispers. I shake my head. 'I've been thinking about the fact that nothing's ever come of it all, Peder.' He doesn't follow what I'm on about. 'Nothing's ever come of what?' 'Of everything we've worked on. Not one film. Not a single image. Not a solitary frame.' Peder shrugs. 'That's not how I see it,' is all he says. I get up from my suitcase. 'D'you think everything would be different if we'd have made it with our films?' Peder smiles. 'At least we'd have been met in a limo.' 'I mean it, Peder. Would anything have been different?' Peder turns to look at the screen. The Oslo flight's on time. 'It would appear the world's done fine without us,' he says. 'But aren't we the world too?' 'Yes, we are, Barnum. And isn't it great that no one knows how good we really are?' 'I'm not sure,' I murmur. Peder's silent for a moment. The umbrella keeps going round and round on the carousel. 'Would it be untimely to inquire about the script you mentioned last night?' he finally says. I have it in my case. I open the script, cross out *The Night Man* and replace it with *The Night Men*. Peder slaps me on the back and can't wait to look at it. 'Good title, Barnum.' And Peder looks first at the final page. Peder's best at reading numbers. He's on the verge of being stunned into silence. 'Four and a half hours?' he breathes. I shut my case. 'So?' Peder sighs. 'That's long, Barnum.' 'And not so much as a comma's to be moved,' I tell him. We go over to the check-in desk. My suitcase slides down a hole and disappears. I get my boarding card. My flight's called. And Peder, the tired optimist, smiles once more. 'You'll manage all right?' 'I'll manage.' 'I'm going to buy something really special for Thomas,' he says. I close my eyes. 'You do that, Peder.' We hug each other there in the Tempelhof hall, just as we've done so often before. We hug each other – Peder and Barnum, the fat one and the small one. And how could I know that that would be the last time we'd hold each other thus? I couldn't, I don't. 'I'll be back tomorrow,' Peder says. He gives me a quick kiss on the cheek. 'And say hello from me to that bloody brother of yours!' And Peder laughs, that laughter I know so well; he nicks the umbrella from the carousel and hurries out to where the taxis are, the script under his arm. But he didn't come home the following day. There was an accident on the way to the Kempinski Hotel. I'm stopped in the security area. The armed guard takes me to one side into a cubicle. He draws a thin curtain. I have to empty all my pockets. I put my pen, my lighter, my comb, my keys and my mirror in a box. There's still bleeping when he moves his electronic baton up and down. I take off my belt. That doesn't help either. Finally he asks me to remove my shoes. I have to do as he says. He's wearing rubber gloves now. He feels inside my shoes. He turns them over and starts tapping the soles instead. Then he breaks off the high heels on both shoes. I turn away. Another guard comes and studies my mutilated footwear intently. It takes two armed men in uniform to declare my shoes safe – my trick shoes. I can get dressed again. They smile, tight-lipped. I've shrunk four centimetres. It doesn't matter any more. Finally I'm allowed through and I hear the laughter at my back. I go onboard the bus that takes us out to the small plane. It's raining. I run up the steep steps. From here the arrival hall looks like an oval temple with its pillars and arches – a dirty temple for travellers. It's me they're waiting for. Someone nods and I act as if I don't recognize them. I have the seat right at the back. I fasten my seatbelt and ask for a glass of water. The aircraft taxis out onto the runway. And as we take off from that airport in the heart of Berlin, as we rise between the houses, I can see the people inside, in the rooms of their flats, starting their new day – pulling the curtains, putting the lights on, watering plants, sitting down to breakfast, drinking coffee, opening the paper, feeding their children. It's just as in a film, I think to myself – the stories of people from window to window – their movements and their beautiful, everyday routines. This is my film, and in the last window I see an old couple sitting by the bedside kissing, before the plane breaks into the clouds and I get my glass of water.

Epilogue

It's Boletta who's waiting for me at Fornebu airport. We haven't seen each other since that day I went off and left her on the top of Blåsen. She's older now than the Old One was; it's as if life is going backwards in her. She's growing downwards and is smaller than I am – a hunched little wrinkle – and she smells like dried fruit. Her hand is still strong and steady when she takes my arm and guides me out to the taxis, where right away she jumps the queue and incurs immediate wrath for doing so. There's a light snow falling, flakes that melt before they've landed. We get into the back seat. Boletta lays her cheek against my shoulder. 'You're whole now, Barnum,' she says. 'What d'you mean?' But she doesn't answer me, and I think to myself as we drive up the gentle inclines around Gaustad that I don't want to be whole – I don't want that – and I clench Boletta's hand so hard she rattles. The red brick building appears between the bare, black trees – it resembles a castle, a fairy-tale castle with its towers and windows, not an asylum. 'Why is he here?' I ask her. Boletta pays the driver. 'It's your mother who's here,' she says softly. She turns abruptly, as if remembering now, too late. 'Didn't you have any luggage, Barnum?' I shake my head. 'It was lost.' 'Lost?' 'It doesn't matter,' I murmur. 'It was just an old suitcase.' Then we go inside to find them. The first person I see in a kind of day room is a little boy in grey trousers and a blue jumper. And it's the first time he sees me. He's sitting on a chair that's too high for him. He doesn't move. It's Thomas. I stop in front of him. His eyes are fearful and curious at one and the same time, as if he's watching everything and everyone. I don't know him, but I recognize myself in him. I only know that I'd go through fire and flood for those dark and vulnerable eyes. Helplessly and clumsily I put my hand on his head, but the frightened boy just twists away, exactly as I'd have done. Vivian looks at us and when I meet her gaze she suddenly blushes. She still has the ring on her finger. It's as though we both have to take deep breaths, concentrate our thoughts, so as not to sink beneath the weight of this silence. Boletta lifts Thomas and holds him. 'Fred's with Vera,' Vivian murmurs. I go down a corridor. A nurse is waiting outside. He opens the door. Mum's lying in bed. It looks as if she's sleeping, but as soon as I come in she smiles. A thin man's standing by the window, his back to us. Mum tries to say something, but her mouth is soundless and she starts crying instead. The thin, old man turns round. It's my brother. His eyes are still. 'Why have you come back?' I ask him. And I don't know if it's me or Mum Fred is looking at when he says, 'To tell you all this.'